TOR BOOKS BY JACQUELINE CAREY

KUSHIEL'S DART

JACQUELINE CAREY

TOR®
fantasy

A TOM DOHERTY ASSOCIATES BOOK
NEW YORK

This is a work of fiction. All of the characters, organizations, and events portrayed in this novel are either products of the author's imagination or are used fictitiously.

KUSHIEL'S DART

Copyright © 2001 by Jacqueline Carey

All rights reserved.

Edited by Claire Eddy

A Tor Book
Published by Tom Doherty Associates
120 Broadway
New York, NY 10271

www.tor-forge.com

Tor® is a registered trademark of Macmillan Publishing Group, LLC.

ISBN 978-1-250-75951-1

Our books may be purchased in bulk for promotional, educational, or business use. Please contact your local bookseller or the Macmillan Corporate and Premium Sales Department at 1-800-221-7945, extension 5442, or by email at MacmillanSpecialMarkets@macmillan.com.

First Edition: 2001
Second Mass Market Edition: 2020

Printed in the United States of America

10 9 8 7 6 5 4 3

Acknowledgments

Thank you to my parents, Marty and Rob, for a lifetime of love and encouragement, and to Julie, whose belief never wavered. To my great-aunt Harriett, a very special mahalo for all her stalwart support.

Dramatis Personae

Delaunay's Household

Anafiel Delaunay—noble
Alcuin nó Delaunay—Delaunay's pupil
Phèdre nó Delaunay—Delaunay's pupil; *anguissette*
Guy—Delaunay's man
Joscelin Verreuil—Cassiline Brother (Siovale)

Members of the Royal Family: Terre d'Ange

Ganelon de la Courcel—King of Terre d'Ange
Genevieve de la Courcel—Queen of Terre d'Ange
  (*deceased*)
Isabel L'Envers de la Courcel—wife of Rolande;
  Princess-Consort (*deceased*)
Rolande de la Courcel—son of Ganelon and Genevieve;
  Dauphin (*deceased*)
Ysandre de la Courcel—daughter of Rolande and
  Isabel; Dauphine
Barquiel L'Envers—brother of Isabel; Duc L'Envers
  (Namarre)
Baudoin de Trevalion—son of Lyonette and Marc;
  Prince of the Blood
Bernadette de Trevalion—daughter of Lyonette and
  Marc; Princess of the Blood

Lyonette de Trevalion—sister of Ganelon; Princess of the Blood; Lioness of Azzalle

Marc de Trevalion—Duc of Trevalion (Azzalle)

MEMBERS OF THE ROYAL FAMILY: LA SERENISSIMA

Benedicte de la Courcel—brother of Ganelon; Prince of the Blood

Maria Stregazza de la Courcel—wife of Benedicte

Dominic Stregazza—husband of Thérèse; cousin of the Doge of La Serenissima

Marie-Celeste de la Courcel Stregazza—daughter of Benedicte and Maria; Princess of the Blood; wed to Doge of La Serenissima's son

Thérèse de la Courcel Stregazza—daughter of Benedicte and Maria; Princess of the Blood

D'ANGELINE PEERAGE

Isidore d'Aiglemort—son of Maslin; Duc d'Aiglemort (Camlach)

Maslin d'Aiglemort—Duc d'Aiglemort (Camlach)

Marquise Solaine Belfours—noble; secretary of the Privy Seal

Rogier Clavel—noble; member of L'Envers entourage

Childric d'Essoms—noble; member of Court of Chancery

Cecilie Laveau-Perrin—wife of Chevalier Perrin (*deceased*); former adept of Cereus House; tutor to Phèdre and Alcuin

Roxanne de Mereliot—Lady of Marsilikos (Eisande)

Quincel de Morhban—Duc de Morhban (Kusheth)
Lord Rinforte—Prefect of the Cassiline Brotherhood
Edmée de Rocaille—betrothed of Rolande (*deceased*)
Melisande Shahrizai—noble (Kusheth)
Tabor, Sacriphant, Persia, Marmion, Fanchone—
  members of House Shahrizai; Melisande's kin)
Ghislain de Somerville—son of Percy
Percy de Somerville—Comte de Somerville
  (L'Agnace); Prince of the Blood; Royal Commander
Tibault de Toluard—Comte de Toluard (Siovale)
Gaspar Trevalion—Comte de Forcay (Azzalle) cousin
  to Marc
Luc and Mahieu Verreuil—sons of Millard; Joscelin's
  brothers
Millard Verreuil—Chevalier Verreuil; Joscelin's father
  (Siovale)

Night Court

Liliane de Souverain—adept of Jasmine House; mother
  of Phèdre
Miriam Bouscevre—Dowayne of Cereus House
Juliette, Ellyn, Etienne, Calantia, Jacinthe, Donatien—
  apprentices of Cereus House
Brother Louvel—priest of Elua
Jareth Moran—Second of Cereus House
Suriah—adept of Cereus House
Didier Vascon—Second of Valerian House

Skaldia

Ailsa—woman in Gunter's steading
Gunter Arnlaugson—head of steading

Evrard the Sharp-tongued—thane in Gunter's steading
Gerde—woman in Selig's steading
Harald the Beardless—thane in Gunter's steading
Hedwig—woman in Gunter's steading
Kolbjorn of the Manni—one of Selig's warleaders
Knud—thane in Gunter's steading
Lodur the One-Eyed—priest of Odhinn
Waldemar Selig—head of steading; warlord
Trygve—member of the White Brethren
White Brethren—Selig's thanes

TSINGANI

Abhirati—grandmother of Anasztaizia
Anasztaizia—mother of Hyacinthe
Csavin—nephew of Manoj
Gisella—wife of Neci
Hyacinthe—friend to Phèdre; "Prince of Travellers"
Manoj—father of Anasztaizia; King of the Tsingani
Neci—headman of a kumpania

ALBA AND EIRE

Breidaia—eldest daughter of Necthana
Brennan—son of Grainne
Cruarch of Alba—King of the Picti
Drustan mab Necthana—son of Necthana; Prince of the Picti
Eamonn mac Conor—Lord of the Dalriada
Foclaidha—wife of the Cruarch
Grainne mac Conor—sister of Eamonn; Lady of the Dalriada
Maelcon—son of the Cruarch and Foclaidha

Moiread—youngest daughter of Necthana
Necthana—sister of the Cruarch
Sibeal—middle daughter of Necthana

THREE SISTERS

Gildas—servant of the Master of the Straits
Master of the Straits—controls the seas between Alba
  and Terre d'Ange
Tilian—servant of the Master of the Straits

OTHERS

Vitale Bouvarre—merchant; Stregazza ally
Pierre Cantrel—merchant; father of Phèdre
Camilo—apprentice of Gonzago de Escabares
Danele—wife of Taavi; dyer
Emile—member of Hyacinthe's crew
Maestro Gonzago de Escabares—Aragonian historian;
  former teacher to Delaunay
Fortun—sailor; one of Phèdre's Boys
Gavin Friote—seneschal of Perrinwolde
Heloise Friote—wife of Gavin
Purnelle Friote—son of Gavin
Richeline Friote—wife of Purnelle
Aelric Leithe—sailor
Jean Marchand—second-in-command to Rousse
Thelesis de Mornay—King's Poet
Mierette nó Orchis—former adept of Orchis House
Remy—sailor; one of Phèdre's Boys
Quintilius Rousse—Royal Admiral
Taavi—Yeshuite weaver
Maia and Rena—daughters of Taavi and Danele)

Master Robert Tielhard—marquist
Ti-Philippe—sailor; one of Phèdre's Boys
Lelahiah Valais—chirurgeon (Eisande)
Japheth nó Eglantine-Vardennes—playwright
Seth ben Yavin—Yeshuite scholar

ONE

Lest anyone should suppose that I am a cuckoo's child, got on the wrong side of the blanket by lusty peasant stock and sold into indenture in a shortfallen season, I may say that I am House-born and reared in the Night Court proper, for all the good it did me.

It is hard for me to resent my parents, although I envy them their naïveté. No one even told them, when I was born, that they gifted me with an ill-luck name. Phèdre, they called me, neither one knowing that it is a Hellene name, and cursed.

When I was born, I daresay they still had reason for hope. My eyes, scarce open, were yet of indeterminate color, and the appearance of a newborn babe is a fluid thing, changing from week to week. Blonde wisps may give way to curls of jet, the pallor of birth deepen to a richness like amber, and so on. But when my series of amniotic sea-changes were done, the thing was obvious.

I was flawed.

It is not, of course, that I lacked beauty, even as a babe. I am a D'Angeline, after all, and ever since Blessed Elua set foot on the soil of our fair nation and called it home, the world has known what it means to be D'Angeline. My soft features echoed my mother's, carved in miniature perfection. My skin, too fair for the canon of Jasmine House, was nonetheless a perfectly acceptable shade of ivory. My hair, which grew to curl in charming profusion, was the color of sable-in-shadows, reckoned a coup in some of the Houses. My limbs were straight and supple, my bones a marvel of delicate strength.

No, the problem was elsewhere.

To be sure, it was my eyes; and not even the pair of them, but merely the one.

Such a small thing on which to hinge such a fate. Nothing more than a mote, a fleck, a mere speck of color. If it had been any other hue, perhaps, it would have been a different story. My eyes, when they settled, were that color the poets call bistre, a deep and lustrous darkness, like a forest pool under the shade of ancient oaks. Outside Terre d'Ange, perhaps, one might call it brown, but the language spoke outside our nation's bounds is a pitiful thing when it comes to describing beauty. Bistre, then, rich and liquid-dark; save for the left eye, where in the iris that ringed the black pupil, a fleck of color shone.

And it shone red, and indeed, red is a poor word for the color it shone. Scarlet, call it, or crimson; redder than a rooster's wattles or the glazed apple in a pig's mouth.

Thus did I enter the world, with an ill-luck name and a pinprick of blood emblazoned in my gaze.

My mother was Liliane de Souverain, an adept of Jasmine House, and her line was ancient in the service of Naamah. My father was another matter, for he was the third son of a merchant prince and, alas, the acumen that raised his father to emeritus status in the City of Elua was spent in the seed that produced his elder brothers. For all three of us would have been better served had his passions led him to the door of another House; Bryony, perhaps, whose adepts are trained in financial cunning.

But Pierre Cantrel had a weak head and strong passions, so when coin swelled the purse at his belt and seed filled to bursting the purse between his legs, it was to Jasmine House, indolent and sensual, that he hied himself.

And there, of course, betwixt the ebb tide in his wits and the rising tide in his loins, he lost his heart in the bargain.

On the outside, it may not look it, but there are intricate laws and regulations governing the Court of Night-Blooming Flowers, which only rustics from the provinces call anything but the Night Court. So it must be, for we—odd, that I say it still—serve not only Naamah herself, but the great Houses of Parliament, the scions of Elua and his Companions, and sometimes, even, the House Royal itself. Indeed, more often than Royal cares to admit, we have served its sons and daughters.

Outsiders say adepts are bred like livestock, to produce children who fall within the House canon. Not so; or at least, no more so than any other marriage is arranged, for reason of politics or finance. We wed for aesthetics, true; but no one ever within my recollection was forced into a union distasteful to him or her. It would have violated the precepts of Blessed Elua to do so.

Still, it is true that my parents were an ill match, and when my father bid for her hand, the Dowayne of Jasmine House was moved to decline. No wonder, for my mother was cast true to the mold of her House, honey-skinned and ebon-haired, with great dark eyes like black pearls. My father, alas, was of a paler cast, with flaxen hair and eyes of murky blue. Who could say what the commingling of their seed would produce?

Me, of course; proving the Dowayne in the right. I have never denied it.

Since he could not have her by decree of the Night Court, my father eloped with my mother. She was free to do so, having made her marque by the age of nineteen. On the strength of his jingling purse and his father's grace, and the dowry my mother had made above her marque, they eloped.

I am sure, though I have never seen them to ask since I was but four, that both believed my mother would throw true, a perfect child, a House treasure, and the Dowayne would take me in open-armed. I would be reared and cherished, taught to love Blessed Elua and serve Naamah, and once I had made my marque, the House would tithe a portion to my parents. This I am sure they believed.

Doubtless it was a pleasant dream.

The Night Court is not unduly cruel, and during my mother's lying-in, Jasmine House had welcomed her back. There would be no support from its coffers for her unsanctioned husband, but the marriage was acknowledged and tolerated, having been executed with due process before a rural priest of Elua. In the normal course of events, if my appearance and budding nature fell within the canon of the House, I would have been reared wholly therein. If I met the canon of some other House—as I nearly did—its Dowayne would pay surety for my rearing until ten, when I would be formally adopted into my new household. Either way, did she choose, my mother would have been given over to the training of adepts and granted a pension against my marque. As my father's purse, however ardent, was not deep, this would have been the course they chose.

Alas, when it grew obvious that the scarlet mote in my eye was a permanent fixture, the Dowayne drew the line. I was flawed. Among all the Thirteen Houses, there was not one whose canon allowed for flawed goods of this kind. Jasmine House would not pay for my upkeep, and if my mother wished to remain, she must support us both in service, not training.

If he had little else, my father had his passions, and

pride was one of them. He had taken my mother to wife, and her service was only for him and no longer to be laid at Naamah's altar. He begged of his father stewardship of a caravan en route to trade in Caerdicca Unitas, taking my mother and my two-year-old self with him, seeking our fortune.

It will come as no surprise, I think, that after a long and arduous journey in which he treated with brigands and mercenaries alike—and little enough difference between the two, since Tiberium fell and the surety of the highways was lost—that he traded at a loss. The Caerdicci no longer rule an empire, but they are shrewd traders.

So it was that fate found us two years later, travel-weary and nigh unto penniless. I remember little of it, of course. What I remember best is the road, the smells and colors of it, and a member of the mercenaries who took it upon himself to guard my small person. He was a Skaldi tribesman, a northerner, bigger than an ox and uglier than sin. I liked to pull his mustaches, which hung on either side of his mouth; it made him smile, and I would laugh. He made me to understand, with langue d'oc and eloquent gestures, that he had a wife and a daughter my age, whom he missed. When the mercenaries and the caravan parted ways, I missed him, and for many months after.

Of my parents, I remember only that they were much together and much in love, with little time or regard for me. On the road, my father had his hands full, protecting the virtue of his bride. Once it was seen that my mother bore the marque of Naamah, the offers came daily, some made at the point of a blade. But he protected her virtue, from all save himself. When we returned to the City, her belly was beginning to swell.

My father, undaunted, had the temerity to beg of his

father another chance, claiming the journey too long, the caravan ill-equipped, and himself naive in the ways of trade. This time, he vowed, it would be different. And this time, my grandfather, the merchant prince, drew his own line. He would allot a second chance to my parents, but they must guarantee the trade with a purse of their own.

What else were they to do? Nothing, I suppose. Aside from my mother's skills, which my father would not let her sell, I was their only commodity. To be fair, they would have shrunk in horror at the thought of selling me into indenture on the open market. It would come to that end, no matter, but I doubt either of them capable of looking so far down the line. No, instead my mother, whom after all, I must bless for it, took her courage in both hands and begged an audience with the Dowayne of Cereus House.

Of the Thirteen Houses, Night-Blooming Cereus is and has always been First. It was founded by Enediel Vintesoir some six hundred years past, and from it has grown the Night Court proper. Since the time of Vintesoir, it has been customary for the Dowayne of Cereus House to represent the Night Court with a seat on the City Judiciary; it is said, too, that many a Dowayne of that House has had privilege of the King's ear.

Mayhap it is true; from what I have learned, it is certainly possible. In its founder's time, Cereus House served only Naamah and the scions of Elua. Since then, trade has prospered, and while the court has thrived, it has grown notably more bourgeois in clientele: to wit, my father. But by any accounting, the Dowayne of Cereus House remained a formidable figure.

As everyone knows, beauty is at its most poignant when the cold hand of Death holds poised to wither it imminently. Upon such fragile transience was the fame of Cereus House founded. One could see, still, in the Dowayne, the ghostly echo of the beauty that had blossomed in her heyday, as a pressed flower retains its form, brittle and frail, its essence fled. In the general course of things, when beauty passes, the flower bows its head upon the stem and fails. Sometimes, though, when the petals droop, a framework of tempered steel is revealed within.

Such a one was Miriam Bouscevre, the Dowayne of Cereus House. Thin and fine as parchment was her skin, and her hair white with age, but her eyes, ah! She sat fixed in her chair, upright as a girl of seventeen, and her eyes were like gimlets, grey as steel.

I remember standing in the courtyard upon marble flagstones, holding my mother's hand as she stammered forth her plight. The advent of true love, the elopement, her own Dowayne's decree, the failure of the caravan and my grandfather's bargain. I remember how she spoke of my father still with love and admiration, sure that the next purse, the next sojourn, would make his fortune. I remember how she cited, voice bold and trembling, her years of service, the exhortation of Blessed Elua: *Love as thou wilt*. And I remember, at last, how the fountain of her voice ran dry, and the Dowayne moved one hand. Not lifted, not quite; a pair of fingers, perhaps, laden with rings.

"Bring the child here."

So we approached her chair, my mother trembling and I oddly fearless, as children are wont to be at the least apt of times. The Dowayne lifted my chin with one ring-laden finger and took survey of my features.

Did a flicker of something, some uncertainty, cross her mien when her gaze fell on the scarlet mote in my left eye? Even now, I am not sure; and if it did, it passed swiftly. She withdrew her hand and returned her gaze to my mother, stern and abiding.

"Jehan spoke truly," she said. "The child is unfit to serve the Thirteen Houses. Yet she is comely, and being raised to the Court, may fetch a considerable bond price. In recognition of your years of service, I will make you this offer."

The Dowayne named a figure, and I could feel a flutter of excitement set my mother atremble beside me. It was a charm of hers, this trembling. "Blessed lady—" my mother began.

Watching hawk-like, the ancient Dowayne cut her off with a gesture. "These are the terms," she said, voice remorseless. "You will tell no one. When you take up residence, it will be outside the City. For the world's concern, the child you spawn four months hence shall be the first. We will not have it said that Cereus House gives succor to a whore's unwanted get."

At that I heard my mother's soft indrawn breath of shock, and witnessed the old woman's eyes narrow in satisfaction. So that is what I am, then, my child-self thought; a whore's unwanted get.

"It is not—" My mother's voice trembled.

"It is my offer." The ancient voice was pitiless. *She will sell me to this cruel old woman,* I thought, and experienced a thrill of terror. Even then, unknowing, I knew it as such. "We will raise the child as one of our own, until she is ten. Any ability she has, we will foster. Her bond-price will command respect. That much, I offer you, Liliane. Can you offer her as much?"

My mother stood with my hand in hers and gazed down at my upturned face. It is my last memory of her, those great, dark, lambent eyes searching, searching my own, coming at last to rest upon the left. Through our joined hands, I felt the shudder she repressed.

"Take her, then." Letting go my hand, she shoved me violently. I stumbled forward, falling against the Dowayne's chair. She moved only to tug gently upon the silken cord of a bell-pull. A sound like silver chimes rang in the distance, and an adept glided unobtrusive from behind a discreet screen, gathering me effortlessly, drawing me away by one hand. I turned my head at the last for one final glimpse of my mother, but her face was averted, shoulders shaking with soundless tears. The sun that filtered through the high windows and cast a green-tinged shade through the flowers shone with blue highlights on the ebony river of her hair.

"Come," the adept said soothingly, and her voice was as cool and liquid as flowing water. Led away, I looked up in trust. She was a child of Cereus House, pale and exquisite. I had entered a different world.

Is it any wonder, then, that I became what I did? Delaunay maintains that it was ever my destiny, and perhaps he is right, but this I know is true: When Love cast me out, it was Cruelty who took pity upon me.

Two

I remember the moment when I discovered pain.

Life in Cereus House settled quickly into its own rhythm, unchanging and ceaseless. There were several of us younger children; four others, all told, and myself. I shared a room with two girls, both of them fragile and soft-spoken, with manners like exquisite china. The elder, Juliette, had hair darkening to a brassy gold in her seventh year, and it was reckoned that Dahlia House would buy her marque. With her reserve and solemn air, she was suited to its service.

The younger, Ellyn, was for Cereus House and no mistake. She had the frail bloom and pallor, skin so fair the lids were bluish over her eyes when she closed them, lashes breaking like a wave on her tender cheek.

I had little in common with them.

Nor with the others, in truth—pretty Etienne, half-brother to Ellyn, with his cherub's curls of palest gold; nor with Calantia, despite her merry laugh. They were known quantities, their worth determined, their futures assured, born of sanctioned union and destined, if not for this House, then another.

It is not, understand, that I was bitter. Years passed in this manner, pleasant and undemanding, spent in the company of the others. The adepts were kind, and took shifts to teach us the rudiments of knowledge; poetry, song and playing, how to pour wine and prepare a bed-chamber and serve at the table as pretty adornments. This I was permitted to do, providing I kept my eyes cast always downward.

I was what I was: a whore's unwanted get. If this sounds harsh, understand too what I learned at Cereus House: Blessed Elua loved me nonetheless for it. After all, what was he if not a whore's unwanted get? My parents had never bothered with teaching me the basics of faith, caught up in the rhapsody of their mortal de-votions. At Cereus House, even the children received the benefit of a priest's instruction.

He came every week, Brother Louvel, to sit cross-legged among us in the nursery and share with us the teachings of Elua. I loved him because he was beautiful, with long, fair hair he bound in a silken braid and eyes the color of deep ocean. Indeed, he had been an adept of Gentian House until a patron bought his marque, free-ing him to follow his mystic's dreams. Ministering unto children was one of them. He would draw us upon his lap, one or two at a time, and spin us the old tales in his dreamer's voice.

This is how I came to learn, then, dandled on a former adept's knee, how Blessed Elua came to be; how when Yeshua ben Yosef hung dying upon the cross, a soldier of Tiberium pierced his side with the cruel steel of a spearhead. How when Yeshua was lowered, the women grieved, and the Magdelene most of all, letting down the ruddy gold torrent of her hair to clothe his still, naked figure. How the bitter salt tears of the Magdelene fell upon soil ensanguined and moist with the shed blood of the Messiah.

And from this union the grieving Earth engendered her most precious son; Blessed Elua, most cherished of angels.

I listened with a child's rapt fascination as Brother Louvel told us of the wandering of Elua. Abhorred by the Yeshuites as an abomination, reviled by the empire of Tiberium as the scion of its enemy, Elua wandered the earth, across vast deserts and wastelands. Scorned by the One God of whose son he was begotten, Elua trod with bare feet on the bosom of his mother Earth and wandered singing, and where he went, flowers bloomed in his footprints.

He was captured in Persis, and shook his head smiling when the King put him in chains, and vines grew to wreath his cell. The tale of his wandering had come to reach the ear of Heaven, and when he was imprisoned, there were those among the angelic hierarchy who answered. Choosing to flout the will of the One God, they came to earth in ancient Persis.

Of these it was Naamah, eldest sister, who went smiling to the King and offered herself with lowered eyelids, in exchange for the freedom of Elua. Besotted, the King of Persis accepted, and there is a story still told of the

King's Night of Pleasure. When the door to Elua's cell was opened, a great fragrance of flowers poured forth, and Elua emerged singing, crowned with vines.

This is why, Brother Louvel explained, we revere Naamah and enter her service as a sacred trust. Afterward, he said, the King betrayed Elua and those who followed, and gave them strong wine laced with valerian to drink. While they slept, he had them cast on a boat with no sails and put out to sea; but when he awoke, Elua sang and the creatures of the deep came to answer, guiding the boat across the sea.

The boat came to land in Bhodistan, and Naamah and the others who had come followed Elua, not knowing or caring if the Eye of the One God was upon them, and where they went they sang, and wound in their hair the flowers that sprang up in Elua's wake. In Bhodistan, they are an ancient people, and they feared to turn from their multitude of gods, who are by turns capricious and compassionate. Yet they saw the light in him and would allow no harm to Blessed Elua, nor would they follow him, so he wandered singing, and people made the sign of peace and turned away. When he went hungry, Naamah lay down with strangers in the marketplace for coin.

From there, Elua's course drifted to the north, and he wandered long through lands harsh and stony, and the angels and creatures of the earth attended upon him, or surely he would have perished. These stories I loved, such as the Eagle of Tiroc Pass, who flew over the crags and ice each morning to stoop low above the head of Blessed Elua and drop a berry into his mouth.

In the dark woods of the Skaldic hinterlands, the ravens and wolves were his friends, but the tribesmen gave him no heed, brandishing their terrible axes and calling upon their gods, who have a taste for blood and iron. So he wandered, and snowdrops poked their heads above the drifts where he went.

At last he came to Terre d'Ange, still unnamed, a rich and beautiful land where olives, grapes and melons grew, and lavender bloomed in fragrant clouds. And here the people welcomed him as he crossed the fields and answered him in song, opening their arms.

So Elua; so Terre d'Ange, land of my birth and my soul. For three-score years, Blessed Elua and those who followed him—Naamah, Anael, Azza, Shemhazai, Camael, Cassiel, Eisheth and Kushiel—made to dwell here. And each of them followed the Precept of Blessed Elua save Cassiel, that which my mother had quoted to the Dowayne: *Love as thou wilt*. So did Terre d'Ange come to be what it is, and the world to know of D'Angeline beauty, born in the bloodlines from the seed of Blessed Elua and those who followed him. Cassiel alone held steadfast to the commandment of the One God and abjured mortal love for the love of the divine; but his heart was moved by Elua, and he stayed always by his side like a brother.

During this time, Brother Louvel said, the mind of the One God was much preoccupied with the death of his son, Yeshua ben Yosef, and the course of his chosen people. The time of deities does not move like our own, and three generations may live and die in the space between one thought and another. When the songs of the D'Angelines reached his ears, he turned his eye to Terre d'Ange, to Elua and those who had fled Heaven to follow him. The One God sent his commander-in-chief to fetch them back and bring Elua to stand before the throne, but Elua met him smiling and gave him the kiss of peace, laying wreaths of flowers about his neck and filling his glass with sweet wines, and the leader of God's host returned ashamed and empty-handed.

It came then to the One God that his persuasion held no sway over Elua, in whose veins ran the red wine of his mother Earth, through the womb she gave him and the tears of the Magdelene. And yet through this he was mortal, and thus subject to mortality. The One God pondered long, and sent not the angel of death, but his archherald to Elua and those who followed him. "Do you stay here and love as you wilt, thy offspring shall overrun the earth," said the herald of the One God. "And this is a thing which may not be. Come now in peace to the right hand of your God and Lord, and all is forgiven."

Brother Louvel told the stories well; he had a melodic voice, and knew when to pause, leaving his listeners hanging on his next breath. How would Elua answer? We were in a fever to know.

And this he told us: Blessed Elua smiled at the archherald, and turned to his boon companion Cassiel, holding out his hand for his knife. Taking it, he drew the point across the palm of his hand, scoring it. Bright blood welled from his palm and fell in fat drops to the earth, and anemones bloomed. "My grandfather's Heaven is bloodless," Elua told the arch-herald, "And I am not. Let him offer me a better place, where we may love and sing and grow as we are wont, where our children and our children's children may join us, and I will go."

The arch-herald paused, awaiting the One God's response. "There is no such place," he answered.

At that, Brother Louvel told us, such a thing happened as had not happened in many years and never since: Our mother Earth spoke to her once-husband, the One God, and said, "We may create it, you and I."

So was created the true Terre d'Ange, the one that lies beyond mortal perception, whose gate we may enter only after passing through the dark gate that leads out of this

world. And so Blessed Elua and those who followed him
did leave this plane, passing not through the dark gate,
but straightways through the bright one, into the greater
land that lies beyond. But this land he loved first, and
so we call it after that one, and revere him and his memory, in pride and love.

On the day he finished telling us the Eluine Cycle,
Brother Louvel brought a gift; a spray of anemones, one
for each, to be fastened on our plackets with a long pin.
They were the deep, rich red which I thought betokened
true love, but he explained that these were a sign of
understanding, of the mortal blood of Elua shed for his
love of earth and the D'Angeline people.

It was my wont to wander the grounds of Cereus
House, soaking in the day's lesson. On that day, as I
remember it, I was in my seventh year, and proud as any
adept of the anemones fastened to the front of my gown.

In the antechamber to the Receiving Room, those
adepts summoned would gather to prepare for the view-
ing and selection by patrons. I liked to visit for the refined air of urgency, the subtle tensions that marked the
waiting adepts as they prepared to vie for patrons' fa-
vours. Not that overt competition was permitted; such a
display of untoward emotion would have been reckoned
unbecoming. But it was there nonetheless, and there
were always tales—a bottle of scent switched for cat
piss, frayed ribbons, slit stays, the heel of a slipper cut
to unevenness. I never witnessed such a thing, but the
potential always eddied in the air.

On this day, all was quiet, and only two adepts waited
quietly, having been requested already in particular. I
held my tongue and sat quiet by the little fountain in the
corner, and I tried to imagine being one of these adepts,
waiting with a tranquil spirit to lie down with a patron,
but a dreadful excitement gripped me instead at the

thought of giving myself to a stranger. According to Brother Louvel, Naamah was filled with a mystic purity of spirit when she went to the King of Persis, and when she lay down with strangers in the market.

But that is what they say at Gentian House, and not at Alyssum, where they say she trembled to lay aside her modesty, nor at Balm, where they say she came in compassion. I know, for I listened to the adepts talk. At Bryony, they say she made a good bargain of it, and at Camellia, that her perfection unveiled left him blind for a fortnight, which led him to betray her out of uncomprehending fear. Dahlia claims she bestowed herself like a queen, while Heliotrope says she basked in love as in the sun, which shines on middens and kings' chambers alike. Jasmine House, to which I would have been heir, holds that she did it for pleasure, and Orchis, for a lark. Eglantine maintains she charmed with the sweetness of her song. What Valerian claims I know not, for of the two Houses that cater to tastes with a sharper edge, we heard less; but I heard once that Mandrake holds Naamah chose her patrons like victims and whipped them to violent pleasures, leaving them sated and half-dead.

These things I heard, for the adepts used to guess among them, when they thought I was not listening, to which House I would be bound if I were not flawed. While I had many moods in turn, as any child might, I was not sufficiently modest nor merry nor dignified nor shrewd nor ardent nor any of the others to mark me as a House's own, and I had, it seemed, no great gift for poetry nor song. So they wondered, then, idly; that day, I think, left no question.

The spray of anemones with which Brother Louvel had gifted me had slipped into disarray, and I drew out the pin to fix them. It was a long, sharp pin, exceedingly shiny, with a round head of mother-of-pearl. I sat by the fountain and admired it, anemones forgotten. I thought of Brother Louvel and his beauty, and how I would give myself to him once I was a woman proper. I thought of Blessed Elua and his long wandering, his startling answer to the arch-herald of the One God. The blood he shed might—who knows?—run in my very own veins, I thought; and resolved to see. I turned my left hand palm-upward and took the pin in a firm grip in my right, pushing it into my flesh.

The point sank in with surprising ease. For a second it seemed almost of no note; and then the pain blossomed, like an anemone, from the point I had driven into my palm. My hand sang in agony, and my nerves thrilled with it. It was an unfamiliar feeling, at once bad and good, terribly good, like when I thought of Naamah lying with strangers, only better; *more*. I withdrew the pin and watched with fascination as my own red blood filled the tiny indentation, a scarlet pearl in my palm to match the mote in my eye.

I did not know, then, that one of the adepts had seen and gasped, sending a servant straightways for the Dowayne. Mesmerized by pain and the thin trickle of my blood, I noticed nothing until her shadow fell over me.

"So," she said, and fastened her old claw around my left wrist, wrenching my hand up to peer at my palm. The pin dropped from my fingers and my heart beat in excited terror. Her gimlet gaze pierced my own and saw the stricken pleasure there. "It would have been Valerian House for you, then, would it?" There was a grim satisfaction in her voice; a riddle solved. "Send a messenger to the Dowayne, tell him we have such a one who might benefit from instruction in accommodating pain." The grey-steel gaze roamed my face once more, came to rest on my left eye, and stopped. "No, wait." Something again flickered in her mien; an uncertainty, something half-remembered. She dropped my wrist and turned away. "Send for Anafiel Delaunay. Tell him we have something to see."

*T*HREE

*W*hy did I run, on the day before I was scheduled to meet with Anafiel Delaunay, sometime potentate of the court—the real one—and potential buyer of my bond?

In truth, I know not, except that there was always a drive in me that sought out danger; for its own sake, for the chill it gave me or for the possible repercussion—who can say? I was thick with one of the scullery maids, and she had shown me the pear tree in the garden behind the kitchens, how it grew along the wall so one might climb it and thus over the wall.

I knew that the thing was done, for the Dowayne had told me a day prior, that I might be forewarned of the preparations to come. Truly, the adepts murmured, I would be prepared as if for a prince; washed, combed and adorned.

No one would say, of course, who Anafiel Delaunay was, nor why I should be grateful that he would come to look at me. Indeed, if any of them knew the whole truth, I would be much surprised to learn it now. But his name was spoken with a certain hush by the Dowayne of Cereus House, and there was no adept but took his or her cue from her.

So, between awe and fear, I bolted.

With skirts tucked about my waist, the pear tree was easy enough to navigate, and I jumped down unharmed on the far side of the wall. Cereus House sits atop the crest of a hill above the City of Elua. The wall lends it discretion, and there is nothing save the perfume of its gardens to distinguish it from the other estates that sprawl below it, wending down to the centre. It is, as are the others, marked with a discreet insignia upon the gate that admits patrons into its domain. For three years, I had been within those walls; now, outside, I gaped to see the bowl of the City open before me, ringed by gentle hills. There, the river cleft it like a broadsword; there, surely, was the Palace, gleaming in the sun.

A carriage went past at a good clip. Its curtains were drawn, but the coachman cast me a quick, wondering glance. Surely, if I did not move, someone would stop; I was conspicuous enough, a small girl-child in a damask gown, with my dark curls caught up in ribbons. And if the next coach stopped, surely someone inside would hear, and in a moment, the Dowayne's guards would be out to usher me gently back inside.

Elua was born unwanted to the Magdelene, and what had he done? Wandered, wandered the earth; so then, I resolved, I would follow his footsteps. I set off down the hill.

The closer I got to the City, the farther away it seemed. The broad, gracious streets lined with trees and gated manses gave way slowly to narrower, winding streets. These were filled with all manner of people, of a poorer sort than I was accustomed to seeing. I did not know, then, that below Mont Nuit, where the Thirteen Houses were situated, was a lower sort of entertainment; cafes frequented by poets and gentlefolk of ill-repute, unpedigreed bawdy houses, artists' dens, dubious chemists and fortunetellers. It gave spice, I learned later, to nobles venturing into the Night Court.

It was morning, though late. I clung to the edge of the street, overwhelmed by the noise and bustle. Above me, a woman leaned over a balustrade and emptied a wash-basin into the street. Water splashed at my feet and I jumped back, watching it edge its way downhill, forming rivulets between the cobblestones. A gentleman rushing out of an unmarked establishment near to tripped over me and cursed.

"Watch yourself, child!" His voice was brusque. He hurried down the street, his pumps striking a rhythm on the stones. I noted that his hosen were rucked and twisted, as though he had donned them in a hurry, and the hood of his cassock was inside out. No patron but left Cereus House cool and collected, having enjoyed a glass of wine or cordial; but then, no patron of Cereus House would come for leisure clothed in fustian.

Around the next corner, a small square opened, pleasantly shaded with trees, a fountain in its centre; it was market day, and a clamour of vendors abounded. I had made my escape without provisions, and at the sight and smell of food, my stomach reminded me. I paused at the sweet-seller's stall, mulling over her comfits and marchepain; unthinking, I picked up an almond-paste sweet.

"Ye've touched it now, ye must be buying it!" The old woman's voice rang sharp in my ear. Startled, I dropped the sweet and looked up at her.

For a second she glowered, florid-faced, the sturdy country beauty of her bones hidden under the suet with which over-sampling her wares had given her. I stared back, trembling; and saw beneath her weighty dour a not-uncompassionate heart, and feared less.

And then she saw my eyes, and her face changed.

"Devil-spawn!" Her arm rose like a loaf of bread and one plump finger pointed at me. "Mark this child!"

No one had told me that the neighborhood below Mont Nuit was superstitious in the extreme. Vendors began to turn, hands reaching to catch hold of me. In an excess of terror, I bolted. Unfortunately, the first obstacle in my path was a stand of peaches, which I promptly upset. Stumbling on the vendor's wares, I measured my length beneath the market's awnings. Something squished unpleasantly under my left elbow, and the odor of bruised peaches surrounded me like a miasma. I heard the vendor roar with anger as he charged around the toppled stall toward me.

"Hsst!" From beneath another stand peered a small, swarthy face; a boy, near to my age. Grinning, his teeth white against his skin, he beckoned with one grimy hand.

I scrambled madly across the fruit-strewn ground, feeling a seam part as I tore loose from someone's grip on the back of my gown. My youthful savior wasted no time, shoving me past him, guiding me at a rapid crawl under an elaborate series of stalls. Excitement raced in my veins, and when we burst out of the market and gained our feet, taking to our heels ahead of the shouts, I thought my heart would burst with it.

A few of the younger men pursued us half-heartedly, giving up once we dodged into the labyrinth of streets. We pelted along anyway, not stopping until my savior judged it safe, ducking into a doorway and peering carefully behind us.

"We're safe," he pronounced with satisfaction. "They're too lazy to run more than a block, any road, unless you swipe somewhat big, like a ham." He turned back to look at me and whistled through his teeth. "You've a spot in your eye, like blood. Is that what the old hen was squawking about?"

After three years in pale, swooning Cereus House, he was positively exotic to my eyes. His skin was as brown as a Bhodistani's, his eyes black and merry, and his hair hung to his shoulders in curls of jet. "Yes," I said, and because I thought him beautiful, "What House are you from?"

He squatted on his heels. "I live on the Rue Coupole, near the temple."

The stoop was dirty, but my gown was dirtier. I gathered it around my knees and sat. "My mother was of Jasmine House. You have their coloring, yes?"

With one hand, he touched the ribbons twined in my hair. "These are nice. They'd fetch a few coppers, in the market." His eyes widened, showing the whites. "You're of the Night Court."

"Yes," I said, then; "No. I've the spot, in my eye. They want to sell me."

"Oh." He pondered it for a moment. "I'm Tsingani," he said presently, pride puffing his voice. "Or my mother is, at least. She tells fortunes in the square, except on market days, and takes in washing. My name's Hyacinthe."

"Phèdre," I told him.

"Where do you live?"

I pointed up the hill, or in the direction I thought the hill might lie; in the maze of streets, I had lost sense of home and City.

"Ah." He sucked in his breath, clicking tongue on teeth. He smelled, not unpleasantly, of unwashed boy. "Do you want me to take you home? I know all the streets."

In that moment, both of us heard the clatter of hooves, quick and purposeful, parting from the general noise of the City. Hyacinthe made as if to bolt, but they were on us already, drawing up the horses with a fine racket. Two of the Dowayne's Guard, they were, in the livery of Cereus House, a deep twilight blue bearing a subtle gold cereus blossom.

I was caught.

"There," one of them said, pointing at me, exasperation in his deep voice. His features were handsome and regular; members of the Cereus Guard were chosen for their looks as well as their skill at arms. "You've annoyed the Dowayne and upset the marketplace, girl." With one gloved hand, he reached down and plucked me into the air, gathering a wad of fabric at the nape of my neck into his grip. I dangled, helpless. "Enough."

With that, he sat me down on the saddle before him and turned his horse, glancing at his companion and jerking his head homeward. Hyacinthe scrambled into the street, dangerous beneath the horses' hooves, and the other guard cursed and flicked his crop at him.

"Out of my way, filthy Tsingano brat."

Hyacinthe avoided the lash with ease born of long-practiced dexterity and ran after the horses a few paces as we departed. "Phèdre!" he shouted. "Come back and see me! Remember, Rue Coupole!"

I craned my neck to see past the guard's blue-swathed chest, trying to catch a last sight of him, for I was sad to see him go. For a few minutes, he had been a friend, and I had never had one of those.

Upon our return to Cereus House, I found myself much in disgrace. I was denied the privilege of serving at the evening's entertainment and confined to my room without supper, although Ellyn, who was tenderhearted, concealed a morsel of biscuit in her napkin for me.

In the morning, the adept Suriah came for me. Tall and fair, she had been the one who had taken my hand that first day at Cereus House, and I fancied she harbored some little fondness for me. She brought me to the baths and unbraided my hair, sitting patient and watchful as I splashed about in the deep marble pools.

"Suriah," I said, presenting myself for inspection, "who is Anafiel Delaunay and why might he want me?"

"You've the odor of the common stews in your hair." She turned me gently, pouring soap with a sweet, elusive scent atop my head. "Messire Delaunay is known at the royal court." Her slim fingers coaxed a lather from the soap, marvelously soothing on my scalp. "And he is a poet. That is all I know."

"What sort of poetry?" Obedient to her gesture, I submerged myself, shaking my head underwater to dispel the soap. Her hands gathered my hair expertly as I rose, gently twisting the excess water from my locks.

"The kind that would make an adept of Eglantine House blush."

I smile now, to remember my outrage. Delaunay laughed aloud when I told him. "He writes *bawdy lyrics*? You mean I'm getting dressed out like a Carnival goose to be sold to some seed-stained scribbler with one hand in the inkwell and the other in his breeches?"

"Hush." Suriah gathered me in a towel, chafing my skin dry. "Where do you learn such language? No, truly, they say he is a great poet, or was. But he offended a lord, perhaps even a member of the House Royal, and now he no longer writes and his poems are banned. It is a bargain he made, Phèdre, and I do not know the story of it. It is whispered that once he was the paramour of someone very powerful, and his name is known at court still and there are those who fear him and that is enough. Will you behave?"

"Yes." I peered over her shoulder. Her gown was cut low enough in back that I could see her marque, intricate patterns of pale green vines and night-blue flowers twining up her spine, etched into her fair skin by the marquist's needle. It was nearly done. In another patron-gift or two, she would be able to complete it. With a last blossom to shape the finial at the nape of her neck, Suriah would have made her marque. After that, her debt to

Naamah and the Dowayne alike was reckoned paid and she was free to leave Cereus House, if she willed it, or remain and tithe a portion of her fees to the House. She was nineteen, my mother's age. "Suriah, what's a Tsingano?"

"One of the travellers, the Tsingani." Drawing a comb through my wet curls, she made a moue of distaste, the frown that leaves no unpleasant lines. "What have you to do with them?"

"Nothing." I fell silent, submitting to her care. If the Dowayne's guards had said nothing, neither would I, for the keeping of secrets from adults is oft the only power a child may hope to possess.

In due course, I was groomed and made ready to meet Delaunay. As a child, of course, I was not painted, but my clean skin was lightly powdered and my shining, fresh-washed hair dressed with ribbons. Jareth Moran himself, the Dowayne's Second, came to fetch me to the audience. Awed, I clutched his hand and trotted beside him. He smiled down at me, once or twice.

We met not in the courtyard, but in the Dowayne's receiving room, an inner chamber with gracious appointments, designed for conversation and comfort alike.

There was a kneeling cushion set before the two chairs. Jareth released my hand as we entered, moving smoothly to stand at his post behind the Dowayne's chair. I scarce had time to glance at the two figures before I took my position, kneeling *abeyante* before them. The Dowayne, I knew; of Anafiel Delaunay, I had only an impression of lean height and russet hues before I knelt with bowed head and clasped hands.

For a long moment, there was only silence. I sat on my heels, hands clasped before me, itching in every particle of my being to look up and not daring to do so.

"She is a comely child," I heard at length spoken in

a bored voice; a man's rich tenor, cultivated, but with the lack of modulation that only nobles can afford to display. I know this now, because Delaunay taught me to listen for such things. Then, I thought merely that he disliked me. "And the incident you describe intrigues. But I see nothing to intrigue me overmuch, Miriam. I've a pupil in hand these two years past; I'm not looking for another."

"Phèdre."

My head jerked up at the command in the old Dowayne's tone and I stared at her wide-eyed. She was looking at Delaunay and smiling faintly, so I transferred my gaze to him.

Anafiel Delaunay sat at his ease, canted languidly, elbow propped on the arm of the chair, contemplating me with his chin on his hand. He had very fine D'Angeline features, long and mobile, with long-lashed grey eyes flecked with topaz. His hair was a pleasing shade of ginger, and he wore a velvet doublet of deep brown. His only adornment was a fine chain of chased gold-work. His sleeves were russet, a hint of topaz silk gleaming in the slashes. He stretched his well-turned legs out lazily, clad in rich brown, the heel of one highly polished boot propped on the toe of the other.

And as he studied me, his booted heel dropped to the floor with a thud.

"Elua's Balls!" He gave a bark of laughter that startled me. I saw Jareth and the Dowayne exchange a quick glance. Delaunay unfolded himself from the chair in one smooth, elegant motion, lowering himself to one knee before me. He took my face in both hands. "Do you know what mark you bear, little Phèdre?"

His voice had turned caressing and his thumbs stroked my cheekbones, perilously close to my eyes. I quivered between his hands like a rabbit in a trap, longing . .

longing for him to do something, something terrible, fearful that he would, rigid with suppressing it.

"No," I breathed.

He took his hands away, touching my cheek briefly in reassurance, and stood. "Kushiel's Dart," he said, and laughed. "You've an *anguissette* on your hands, Miriam; a true *anguissette*. Look at the way she trembles, even now, caught between fear and desire."

"Kushiel's Dart." There was an echo of uncertainty in Jareth's voice. The Dowayne sat unmoving, her expression shrewd. Anafiel Delaunay crossed to the side table and poured himself a glass of cordial uninvited.

"You should keep better archives," he said, amused, then spoke in a deeper voice. " 'Mighty Kushiel, of rod and weal/Late of the brazen portals/With blood-tipp'd dart a wound unhealed/Pricks the eyen of chosen mortals.' " His voice returned to its conversational tone. "From the marginalia of the Leucenaux version of the Eluine Cycle, of course."

"Of course," the Dowayne murmured, composed. "Thank you so much, Anafiel. Jean-Baptiste Marais at Valerian House will be gratified to learn it."

Delaunay raised one eyebrow. "I do not say that the adepts of Valerian House are unskilled in the arts of algolagnia, Miriam, but how long has it been since they've had a true *anguissette* under their roof?"

"Too long."

Her tone was honey-sweet, but butter wouldn't melt in the old woman's mouth. I watched, fascinated and forgotten. I wanted desperately for Anafiel Delaunay to prevail. He had laid his poet's hands on me and changed my very nature, transformed the prick of my unworth to a pearl of great price. Only Melisande Shahrizai ever named what I was so surely and swiftly; but that was later, and a different matter. As I watched, Delaunay shrugged eloquently.

"Do it, and she'll go to waste; another whipping-toy for the ham-fisted sons of merchants. I can make of her such a rare instrument that princes and queens will be moved to play exquisite music upon her."

"Except, of course, that you already have a pupil."

"Indeed." He drank off his cordial at one draught, set down the glass and leaned against the wall, folded his arms across his chest, smiling. "I am willing, for the sake of Kushiel's Dart, to consider a second. Have you set a bond-price?"

The Dowayne licked her lips, and I rejoiced to see her tremble at bargaining with him, even as my mother had trembled before her. This time, when she named a price, there was no surety in her voice.

It was high, higher than any bond-price set in my years at Cereus House. I heard Jareth draw in his breath softly.

"Done," Anafiel Delaunay said promptly, straightening with a negligent air. "I'll have my steward draw up the papers in the morning. She'll foster here until the age of ten as customary, yes?"

"As you wish, Anafiel." The Dowayne bowed her head to him. I could see, from my kneeling perspective, how she bit her cheek in ire at having set the bond-price so low he didn't even deign to barter. "We shall send for you upon the tenth anniversary of her birth."

And with that, my future was decided.

FOUR

Life within the Night Court was ever a closed society, and I would have left it with Anafiel Delaunay the moment the bargain was struck, had he allowed it; but he did not want me, not yet. I was too young.

Since I was to go into the service of a friend of the royal court, I must reflect well upon Cereus House, and the Dowayne gave orders to ensure I received proper instruction. Reading and elocution were added to my curriculum, and in my eighth year I began to learn the rudiments of the Caerdicci tongue, the language of scholars.

No one expected to make a scholar of me, of course, but it was rumored that Delaunay had attended the University of Tiberium in his youth, and he had a name as an educated man. He must not find embarrassment in a child fostered at Cereus House.

Much to the surprise of my tutors, I enjoyed my studies, and would even spend spare hours in the archives, puzzling out the riddles of Caerdicci poetry. I was much taken by the works of Felice Dolophilus, who joyfully unmanned himself for love of his mistress, but when Jareth found me reading them, he made me stop. Delaunay, it seemed, had given orders that I was to be rendered unto him in as pure and untainted a state as it was possible to maintain for a child raised in the Night Court.

If he wished me ignorant, it was, of a surety, too late. By the time I was seven, there was little I did not know—in theory—of the ways of Naamah. Adepts gossiped; we listened. I knew of the royal jeweler whose work adorned the necks of the fairest ladies at court; for himself, he preferred only the prettiest of youths decked in naught but nature's array. I knew of the judiciary who was renowned for the sagacity of his advice, whose private vow was to pleasure more women in one night than Blessed Elua. I knew of one noblewoman who professed to be a Yeshuite and required a particularly handsome and virile bodyguard to attend her for fear of persecution, and I knew what other duties he performed at length; I knew of another noblewoman renowned far and wide as a gracious hostess, who contracted maidservants skilled in the arts of flower arranging and *languisement*.

These things I knew, and reckoned myself wise in the knowing, little dreaming how small the sum of my knowledge. Events turned outside the Night Court, wheels within wheels, politics shifting, while inside we spoke only of this patron's tastes or that, petty rivalries among the Houses. I was too young to remember when the Dauphin had been killed, slain in a battle on the Skaldic border, but I remember the passing of his widowed bride. A day of mourning was declared; we wore black ribbons and closed the gates of Cereus House.

Even this I might not recall, except that I grieved for the little princess, the Dauphine. She was my age and alone now, unparented, save only for her solemn old grandfather the King. One day, I thought, a handsome Duc would ride to her rescue, as one day—soon— Anafiel Delaunay would come to mine.

Such drivel was the nature of my thoughts, for no one spoke in terms of gain and loss and political position, the possibility of poison and whether or not the royal cupbearer had mysteriously disappeared or the steward wore a new silver chain and a secret smile. These things, like so much else, I learned from Delaunay. This knowledge was not meant for the Servants of Naamah to bear.

We were Night-Blooming Flowers that wilt beneath the weight of the sun, let alone politics.

So the adepts held; if the Dowaynes of the Thirteen Houses thought otherwise, they kept this knowledge to themselves and used it for what gain they might. Nothing spoils idle pleasure like too much awareness, and the Night Court was built upon idle pleasure.

What little knowledge I gained—beyond such gleanings as the fact that there are twenty-seven places on a man's body and forty-five on a woman's that provoke intense desire when appropriately stimulated—I learned from the lower echelons; the cooks, the scullions, the livery-servants and the stable-boys. Bond-sold or not, I had no status at Cereus House, and they tolerated me on the edges of their society.

And I had my one true friend: Hyacinthe.

For you may be sure, having tasted the sweetness of freedom and capture once, I sought it again.

Once, at least, in a season—and more often in the warm ones—I would find my way over the wall, unchaperoned, unnoticed. From the high demesnes of the Night Court, I would make my way to the tawdry apron of the City spread at the base of Mont Nuit, and there I could usually find Hyacinthe.

Along with filching goods from the market-sellers, which he did mainly out of high spirits and mischief, he did a good trade as a messenger-boy. There was always some intrigue brewing in Night's Doorstep (so they called their quarter); some lover's quarrel or poet's duel. For a copper centime, Hyacinthe would carry a message; for more, he would keep his eyes and ears open, and report back.

Despite the good-natured curses directed his way, he was considered lucky, for he had spoken truly, and his mother was the lone Tsingano fortuneteller in Night's

Doorstep. As dark as her son and more so, eyes sunk in weary hollows, she wore gold, always; coins dangling from her ears, and a chain jingling with gold ducats about her neck. Hyacinthe told me it was the way of the Tsingani, to carry their wealth so.

I learned much later what he did not tell me; that his mother was outcast from the Tsingani for having done homage to Naamah with a man not of her people—who do not, anyway, reverence Blessed Elua, although I have never understood fully what they do believe—and that Hyacinthe himself, far from being a prince of the Tsingani, was street-born and a cuckoo's child. Still, she kept the customs and I believe indeed she had the gift of *dromonde*, to part the veils of what-might-be. I watched once while a man, a painter coming into some fame, crossed her palm that she might read his. She told him he would die at his own hand, and he laughed; but the next time I escaped to Night's Doorstep, Hyacinthe told me that man had died of poisoning, from wetting the tip of his paintbrush with his tongue.

Thus was my secret life, out from beneath the eye of Cereus House. The Dowayne's Guard, of course, knew where to find me; if Hyacinthe's trail of mischief was not easily traced, they merely did as I had come to do, and asked about of the brothel-keepers and at the wine-shops. Someone, inevitably, knew where to find us. It came to be something of a game, to see how long I might remain at my freedom, before I was caught up by a gauntleted hand and slung ignominiously over the pommel of a saddle to be returned to Cereus House.

The Guard, I think, saw it as such, for life in the Night Court was dull for a swordsman. I at least offered a challenge, albeit a small one.

The Dowayne was another matter.

After my third such escapade, she was rightfully infuriated and ordered a chastening. Straight from the pommel, struggling and squirming, I was brought to the courtyard before her. I had never seen, before that, a whipping post used for its purpose.

Other occasions blur before that vivid memory. The Dowayne sat in her chair, looking above my head. The guardsman who had brought me hither forced me to my knees, grasping my wrists together in one hand. In a trice, my wrists were bound above me to the iron ring atop the post. The Dowayne looked away. Someone behind me caught the nape of my gown and tore it open, all down the back.

I remember the air was warm and scented with flowers, a touch moist from the fountains that played freely there. I felt it upon the bare skin of my back. The marble flagstones were hard beneath my knees.

It was not a hard whipping, as such things go. Mindful of the fact that I was a child, the Dowayne's chastiser used a soft deerskin flogger and a delicate touch, *pizzicato* style. But child I was, and my skin was tender, and the lash fell like a rain of fire between my naked shoulders.

The first touch was the most exquisite, the fine thongs laying rivulets of pain coursing across my skin, awakening a fiery shudder at the base of my spine. Once, twice, thrice; I might have thrilled for days at the ecstatic pain, nursing the memory of it. But the chastiser kept on, and the rivulets swelled to streams, rivers, a flood of pain, overwhelming and drowning me.

It was then that I began to beg.

I cannot recall, now, such things as I said. I know that I writhed, bound hands extended in a rigid plea, and wept, and pledged my remorse and promised never to defy her again—and still the lash fell, over and over, inflaming my poor back until I thought the whole of it was afire. Adepts of the House stood by and watched, faces schooled not to show pity. The Dowayne herself never looked; that fine, ancient profile all she would give me. I wept and pleaded and the blows fell like rain, until a warm languor suffused my body and I sagged against the post, humiliated and beaten.

Only then was I released and taken away, and my weals tended, whilst I felt fine and sore and drowsy in all of my parts, grievously punished.

"It's a sickness in your blood," Hyacinthe told me knowledgeably when next I escaped to Night's Doorstep. We sat on the stoop of his building in Rue Coupole, sharing a bunch of stolen grapes between us and spitting out the pips into the street. "That's what my mother says."

"Do you think it's true?" I had come, ever since the painter's death, to share the quarter's solemn awe of Hyacinthe's mother's prophetic gift.

"Maybe." He spat a pip in a meditative fashion.

"I don't feel sick."

"Not like that." Although he was only a year older than me, Hyacinthe liked to act as if he had the wisdom of the ages. His mother was teaching him something of the *dromonde*, her art of fortunetelling. "It's like the falling-sickness. It means a god's laid his hand on you."

"Oh." I was disappointed, for this was nothing more than Delaunay had said, only he had been more specific. I had hoped for something more distinctive from Hyacinthe's mother. "What does she say of my fortune?"

"My mother is a princess of the Tsingani," Hyacinthe said in a lofty tone. "The *dromonde* is not for children. Do you think we've time to meddle in the affairs of a fledgling palace whore?"

"No," I agreed glumly. "I suppose not."

I was too credulous, Delaunay would tell me later,

laughing. After all, Hyacinthe's mother took in washing and told fortunes for rabble far worse situated than any Servant of Naamah. It is true, I learned that in much, Hyacinthe was mistaken; indeed, had he but known, it was forbidden for Tsingani men to attempt to part the veils of the future. What his mother taught him was taboo, *vrajna*, among his people.

"Maybe when you're older," Hyacinthe consoled me. "When you've gold to add to her wealth."

"She tells the inn-keep's for silver," I said irritably, "and the fiddler's for copper. And you know well, any coin I get above my contract will go to pay the marquist. And anyway, I'll not formally serve 'til I've reached womanhood, it's in the guild-laws."

"Maybe you'll bloom early." Unconcerned with my fate, Hyacinthe popped a grape into his mouth. I hated him a little bit, then, for being free. "Besides, a coin well-spent may be returned three times over in wisdom gained." He looked at me out of the corner of his eye, grinning. I had heard him part many a patron from his purse with similar lines. I grinned back, then, and loved him for it.

𝒥IVE

The Midwinter Masque fell before my tenth birthday, for I was born in the spring, but the Dowayne elected that I should be allowed to attend. I was not, it seemed, to leave the Night Court without seeing it full, in all its splendour.

Every House has its own masque at some point throughout the year, and each, I am told, is a splendid affair with a worthy history—but the Midwinter Masque is something different. Its roots are older than the coming of Elua, for it celebrates the passing of the old year and the return of the sun. Blessed Elua was so charmed, it is said, by the peasants' simple ritual that he embraced it as well, as a rite that honored his mother Earth and her solar consort.

It has always been the role of Cereus House, the First, to host the Midwinter Masque. On the Longest Night, the doors to all the other Houses are closed, their walls emptied, for everyone comes to Cereus House. No patrons are welcomed save those who bear the token of Naamah, a gift given only at a Dowayne's discretion. Even now, when the night of the Thirteen Houses wanes under the light of profit, the tokens remain another matter, held only by those who lay claim to royal lineage and are deemed worthy of Naamah's embrace.

Days before the event, the house was shrouded in mystery and bustle. Mystery, for no one knew who would be chosen from among our ranks to play the key roles in the great masque; the Winter Queen was chosen, always, from among the adepts of Cereus House. The Sun Prince, of course, might be selected from any of the Thirteen Houses, and the competition was fierce. In Night's Doorstep, Hyacinthe told me, they lay odds on the choosing. It is said that the Sun Prince brings a year's luck to his House.

I know why, now; Delaunay told me. There is an old, old story, older than Elua, about the Sun Prince wedding the Winter Queen to claim lordship of the land. Such stories, he said, are always the oldest, for they are born of our first ancestors' dreams and the eternal turning of the seasons. Whether or not this is true, I do not know; but I know of a surety that Anafiel Delaunay was not the only one who knew the story that night.

But this was yet to come, and in the preceding days, the

mystery-shrouded confines of Cereus House abounded with activity. The doors to the Great Hall were thrown open, and it was given such a cleaning as was seldom seen. The walls were scrubbed, the colonnades polished, the floor waxed and buffed until it shined like mahogany satin. Every speck of ash was emptied from the massive fireplace, and rickety scaffolding was erected so teams of agile painters' apprentices could cleanse a year's accumulation of soot from the frescoed ceiling. Slowly, the Exploits of Naamah brightened, colors emerging fresh and new from beneath the accretion of grime.

When the empty and pristine hall was judged ready, it was decorated with fresh white candles, all unlit and smelling of sweet beeswax, and great boughs of evergreen. And then the long tables were covered with brilliant white cloths to receive the bountiful feast that was being prepared in the kitchens. Indeed, I was manifestly unwelcome in all my usual haunts, as everyone from the concierge on down to the lowest scullery maid was busy making ready for the Midwinter Masque. Say what you will of the Night Court, but no one entered its service without pride. Even the stables were off-limits, as the Master of Horse supervised through gritted teeth a thorough scouring of the entire premises. If Ganelon de la Courcel himself, King of Terre d'Ange, were to attend the Midwinter Masque (and such a thing had happened in other times) he would find his horses better tended than in the royal stables.

Of course, I had witnessed such preparations before, but this year it was different, since I was to attend. Of my erstwhile companions, only the frail beauty, Ellyn, would be in attendance, for Juliette's marque had been bought by Dahlia House, as all had guessed, and the merry Calantia had gone on to foster at Orchis when her

tenth birthday had arrived. Ellyn's pretty half-brother
Etienne was too young, and must pass the Longest Night
in the nursery.

There were two other new fosterlings, though, whom
I'd not met, for Cereus House bought the marques of
children from other Houses too; pale Jacinthe, whose
blue eyes were almost-but-not-quite too dark for the
canon of Cereus, and a boy, Donatien, who never spoke.
Like Ellyn, they were destined to be initiated into the
mysteries of Naamah, and I envied them their surety of
place.

On the Longest Night, though, there would be no contracts, no exchange of coin. Among the Servants of Naamah and their elect guests, only such liaisons as pleased
the fancy would be made; our role was to adorn the
festivities. It is tradition to drink *joie* on Longest Night,
that clear, heady liqueur distilled from the juice of a rare
white flower which grows in the mountains and blossoms amid the snowdrifts. We were to circulate among
the guests, offering tiny crystalline glasses of *joie*, which
we bore on silver trays.

Because it is the privilege of Cereus House to elect
the Winter Queen, it is the theme we maintain, in costumes of white and silver. I was hoping to see Suriah,
to show her mine. All four of us were adorned as winter
sprites. We wore sheer white tunics of gossamer to
mimic the effect of snow drifting in the wind, with dag-
ged sleeves beaded in glass that hung down like icicles
when we raised our trays in offering. Simple white dom-
inos edged in silver, suitable for children, masked our
faces, and we wore only a touch of carmine on the lips
for colour. An apprentice ribbonnaire bound our hair,
and did a very fine job, too, plaiting our locks with white
ribbons to evoke a tumbling fall of snow.

But Suriah did not come to see us, and it was another

adept who gave us instruction in the kitchen. He wore white brocade trimmed in ermine, and the mask of a snow fox rode his brow, snarling above his own eyes.

"Like this," he said impatiently, correcting the line of Donatien's arm as the boy lifted his tray. "No, no; smooth, elegant. You're not hoisting tankards in a tavern, boy! What do they teach you in Mandrake House?"

What indeed, I wondered. The Dowayne's chastiser had been a Mandrake adept. Donatien trembled, and the delicate glasses trembled like chimes on the tray, but he raised it gracefully.

"Better," the adept said grudgingly. "And the invocation?"

"Joy." It was more breath than utterance, and Donatien looked like he might faint from the effort of it. The adept gave a wry smile.

"Such a fragile bloom . . . perfect, sweetheart. They'll be marking their calendars until you come of age. All right, then; you'll see that guests are given first offer, and the Dowaynes second. After that it's catch as catch can."

He turned then to go, drawing down his mask.

"But . . ."

It was Jacinthe who had spoken. The adept turned, his face now a mystery behind the sly features of the snow fox, dark shadows behind the eyeholes on either side of the sharp, cunning muzzle. "How will we know?" she asked sensibly. "Everyone's in masque."

"You'll know," said the snow fox. "Or err."

And with this none-too-reassuring piece of advice, he left us to the harried direction of the culinary staff.

Beyond the doors, we heard the trumpets blow, announcing the arrival of the first party. The musicians struck up a processional tune. In the stifling air of the kitchen, the Master Chef bellowed orders and people rushed to do his bidding. We four exchanged glances, uncertain.

"For the love of Naamah!" The Second Assistant Sommelier took charge of us, handing us our trays and shoving us toward the door. "Cereus is making its entrance; go now, and take your positions along the wall, wait until all the Houses and the first of the guests have entered." He made a shooing motion. "Go, go! I don't want to see you back until every glass is empty!"

In the Great Hall, I saw that kneeling cushions had been placed along the wall. We took our positions to wait, and had a good view of the procession as it entered between the marble colonnades.

The tray was not light, laden with glasses as it was, but I had been trained for this, as we all had. Gazing at the entering celebrants, I soon forgot the strain in my arms and shoulders.

I knew the Dowayne in an instant, as she entered leaning on Jareth's arm. She was masked as a great snowy owl, wearing a vast white-feathered mask that covered the whole of her face. It was rumored, I knew, that this would be her last Midwinter Masque. Jareth wore an eagle's mask, white feathers flecked with umber. The adepts of Cereus House followed them, a white-and-silver fantasia of creatures and wintery spirits; I lost count, with the froths of silk and gossamer and silver piping, horned and hooded and masked.

And this was only the beginning.

All Thirteen Houses made their entrance. Even now, past its heyday, to those who have never seen the Night Court in all its splendour, I say: I weep for you. I have gone farther than I ever reckoned from my birthplace, and I have attended grand functions at the royal court, but nowhere else have I seen such exultation in beauty, and beauty alone. It is, as nothing else in this world is, quintessentially D'Angeline.

If I had been trained by Delaunay then, which I had not, I would have noted and could now recall exactly what the theme of each house was, but some of the highlights remain with me still. Dahlia challenged the sovereignty of Cereus with cloth-of-gold, and the adepts of Gentian came masked as seers, preceded by incensors of opium. Eglantine House, in its madcap genius, entered as a company of Tsingani, singing and playing and tumbling. The adepts of Alyssum, famed for their modesty, were robed and veiled as Yeshuite priests and priestesses, profanely provocative. Jasmine House flaunted, as ever, the exotica of faraway lands, and their Dowayne's young Second danced in naught but dusky skin, night-black hair and a cloud of veils.

This was ill-received by Valerian's Dowayne, who had chosen a *hareem* motif for his adepts, but such things are bound to happen. For my part, I was minded of my distantly remembered mother, and then only briefly, for the procession continued.

One might suppose, and logically so, that I would be most curious about the adepts of Valerian House. It was there, as the Dowayne had said, that I would have gone, had I not been flawed. And curious I was, sufficient that some things I had learned: *I yield*, was the motto of the House; its adepts were those who had a propensity to find pleasure in the extremity of pain and were trained in the receiving thereof. Logical enough; but the magnet is drawn to iron. I dismissed the Pasha's Dream that was Valerian House, and thrilled instead to the arrival of the adepts of Mandrake House, arrayed as the Court of Tartarus.

There, amid all the froth and gaiety of the other masquers (Orchis House, I am minded, had a stunning

aquatic theme with mermaids and fantastic sea-beasts)
they struck a deliciously sinister note. Black velvet, like
a moonless night, and silk like a black river under stars;
bronze masks, horned and beaked, at once beautiful and
grotesque. I felt a tremor run through me, and heard the
crystalline sound of glasses shivering together.

Not my tray; I looked, and it was Donatien, his face
pale.

I pitied his fear, and envied it.

Then, at last, the procession was ended and the trumpets sounded again, and the guests entered.

Royal or no, they were a motley assortment relative
to the splendour of the Night Court; wolves, bears and
harts, sprites and imps, heros and heroines out of legend,
though there was no theme to it. Still I could see, once
they had entered, that when all began to mingle, it would
make for a glorious array.

The trumpets sounded once more, and everyone—Dowaynes, royalty and adepts alike—drew back along the
colonnade, for this sounded the entrance of the Winter
Queen.

She entered alone, hobbling.

It is said that the mask of the Winter Queen was made
four hundred years ago by Olivier the Oblique, so sub-
lime a master of the craft that no one knew his true
features. Of a surety, it was old, wafer-thin layers of
leather soaked and molded into the likeness of an ancient
crone, painted and lacquered until it mocked not life,
but the preservation of it. An old grey mare's-tail wig
crowned her head, and she was shrouded in grey rags, a
dingy shawl wrapped around her shoulders.

This, then, was the Winter Queen.

Everyone bowed as she entered the Great Hall, and
those of us kneeling bowed our heads. She hobbled to
the head of the colonnade, leaning on an old blackthorn

staff, and turned to face the crowd. Straightening only slightly, she hoisted her staff aloft. Trumpets blared, people cheered and the musicians struck up a merry tune; the Midwinter Masque had begun.

As for the Sun Prince, he would come later; or was already here, most likely, but not revealed in his costume. Not until the horologers cried the moment would he emerge to waken the Winter Queen to youth.

So it was begun. I rose from my cushion, stiff from kneeling, and began to circulate. We had all of us taken heed of the costumes in the procession; as the snow fox had said, it was not so difficult after all. We might not know the players, but the teams were easily identified. "Joy," I murmured, lifting my tray, eyes downcast. Each time, a glass was plucked and drained, set down empty.

Out of the corner of my eye, I watched the other three, gauging the moment when all of the guests would have been served a single glass of *joie*. I had a mind to serve the Dowayne of Mandrake House, who wore a bronze crown above his mask, and carried a cat-o'-nine-tails in his right hand. My tray was emptied ere the guests were all served, however, and I had to return to the kitchen, where the anxious Second Assistant Sommelier refilled my tray with tiny glasses of clear elixir.

In the Great Hall, liveried servants had begun the process of carrying out platter after platter of sumptuous food, until the tables fair groaned; I'd had to dodge among them, with my tray of *joie*. In the center, several couples had begun a pavane, and I could see in a far corner that one of Eglantine House's tumblers was entertaining.

Before me was a portly guest who had unwisely chosen to costume himself as the Chevalier of the Rose. I caught a swirl of black velvet and a glimmer of bronze beyond him, and sought to move past, but a strange waistcoat blocked my view. It bore bronze brocade and buttons shaped like silver acorns, and I remembered that its owner was a guest costumed as Faunus. Hiding my annoyance, I murmured a ritual, "Joy," and offered my tray.

"Phèdre."

I knew the voice, a man's rich tenor, at once amused and bored, and looked up, startled. Behind the rustic mask, his eyes were grey flecked with topaz, and the long braid at his back was auburn.

"My lord Delaunay!"

"Indeed." Why did he sound so amused? "I did not think to see you here, Phèdre. You've not turned ten without telling me, have you?"

"No, my lord." I could feel the blush rising in my face. "The Dowayne thought I should be allowed to serve; to see the masque, once."

He brushed my ribboned hair with his fingertips, adjusting a lock with a critical gaze. "You'll attend as you choose, unless I miss my guess. Though you'll never be a success en masque, my sweet; not with those eyes. Kushiel's Dart shall give you away."

I could have stood there forever, while he fussed over my appearance; I don't know why. "Is that how you knew me, my lord?" I asked, to keep his attention.

"Not at all. You never looked up." He grinned then, unexpectedly; even masked, it made him look younger. He was only in his mid-thirties then, I think. I never knew for certain, even when I knew far more than I knew then. "Think on it, Phèdre, and I'll tell you why when next we meet. And keep those dart-stricken eyes open tonight, my sweet. There may be more to see here than paid flagellants with a fetish for black velvet." With that, he plucked a glass from my tray and drained it. "Joy," he said, setting it back empty, and turned away.

Balancing the tray on one hand, I picked up the glass from which he had drunk and raised it to my lips. With the tip of my tongue, I caught a tiny drop of pure *joie* remaining at the bottom. The flavor blazed on my palate, clean and spicy, at once icy and burning. Watching him wind through the crowd, I savored the taste of it and the secret sharing; then, quick and guilty, I replaced the glass and continued on my rounds.

It was on that night that I first began to discern the deeper patterns at work in Terre d'Ange, the swirls and eddies of power and politics that governed our unknowing lives. Despite this encounter, one can hardly say, I think, that it was all due to Delaunay's influence. Surely I would have taken heed, by the stir it created, of what happened later, warning or no.

It was yet an hour shy of midnight, by the horologists' calculations, when Prince Baudoin's party arrived. By this time, I had lost count of the number of times I had circulated with my silver tray and the number of times the Second Assistant Sommelier had provided me with fresh glasses. We had been granted reprieve in shifts, and given leave to fill our plates at the great tables. I secured for myself a whole capon smothered in grape sauce, a tender slice of venison dressed with currants and even a small sallet of greens, and was well content.

I had just resumed my duties when I heard the commotion; a new party arriving, loud and high-spirited. Pushing my way through the crowd, I came upon the forefront of the audience.

It was four young men, and from their attire and demeanor alone, I could tell they were of royal blood, true scions of Elua and his Companions. "Prince Baudoin!" someone said in a tone of hushed awe, and I surmised which was he; slender and raven-haired, with fair skin and sea-grey eyes, the stamp of House Trevalion. The others deferred to him, for all that he leaned, drunken, on the shoulder of a comrade.

He wore a mask of Azza which was surpassingly lovely, though askew on his pure D'Angeline features, and a large velvet hat with a drooping feather. Seeing the gathering crowd, he pushed himself off his companion's supporting arm and raised a goblet in his right hand. "Joy!" he shouted, his voice clear and carrying, even slurred with wine. "Joy to the Night Court, on this Longest Night!"

To my left, I heard the faint sound of trembling crystal; Donatien. He glanced once at me, terrified. Well then, I thought, so be it. Squirming past an antlered hart, I approached the Prince's party. I could feel the eyes of the Night Court upon me, and my heart pounded.

"Joy," I echoed softly, holding up the tray.

"What's this?" A grip like a pincer caught my upper arm, fingers digging into flesh, making me gasp. I looked up into the gaze of the Prince's companion. He wore a jaguarondi mask, but behind it his eyes shone dark and cruel, smiling. His hair fell straight about his shoulders, a gold so pale it glittered like silver in the candlelight. "Denys, taste it."

One of the others took a glass from the tray I offered and tossed it down. "Owwooo!" He shook his head, wolf-masked, and smacked his lips. "Pure *joie*, Isidore; have some!"

I stood trembling, while the scions of Elua snatched with greedy hands at my tray. Glass after glass was drained, and hurled to smash on the gleaming parquet floor. The Prince let loose a laugh, high and wild, like trumpets. His mask rode crooked on his white brow and I could see a hectic gleam in his eyes. "A kiss for luck, little joy-bearer!" he declared, sweeping me into his arms. My tray was crushed between us and fell clattering to the floor, more glasses crushed to shards. His lips brushed the corner of mine for one breathless instant, tasting of *joie*; and then I was cast aside, forgotten, and the Prince's party swept onward into the Great Hall. The man in the jaguarondi mask glanced once my way, and smiled his cruel smile.

I knelt on the floor, gathering shards of broken glass upon my tray, not heeding the tears in my eyes; why, I could not even have said, whether it was the kiss or the casting aside that seared my heart. But I was a child, and such things are quickly forgotten. In the kitchen, Jacinthe shot me hateful glances, and I remembered only pride that a Prince of the royal blood had named me joy-bearer and kissed me for luck.

Ironic, that; as Anafiel Delaunay could have told him, mine was an ill-luck name. If I'd luck to spare, I'd have shared it with him. I could not have known, then, that I would be there when his luck turned at last. Some would say he was a fool to have trusted Melisande, and perhaps he was; even so, he would not have seen the other betrayal coming, from one he'd known longer.

But that night, such plots had not even begun to be dreamt. As if the revelry hadn't been in full stride before, it swung into a faster pace. Stately pavanes gave way to the galliard and the antic hey, and the musicians played in a frenzy, faces shining with sweat. So great were the proportions of the masque, it swallowed even the Prince's party. I circulated with my tray, dizzy from the noise and heat. The evergreen boughs above the roaring fireplace loosed a piney fragrance, rising above the olfactory din of a hundred competing perfumes and heated flesh, punctuated by the pungent opium smoke of Gentian House's incensors.

We were running short of glasses. The style of the evening had been set, and I'd no way of counting how many guests and adepts downed their *joie* and shattered their glasses on the floor, shouting. There was naught any of the four of us could do; we carried on, our trays sparsely laden, while the liveried servants of Cereus House darted amid the crowd with brooms and dustpans.

Such were the profundities that occupied my mind when, beneath the merry skirl of music, the slow beat of the tocsin began. It was the Longest Night; we had almost forgotten, all of us. But the horologists had not—they forget nothing—and the Night's Crier struck the gong at a measured pace, cutting through the din and slowing the revelry. Dancers parted and the floor cleared, celebrants falling back. From behind a screen the Winter Queen reemerged, leaning on her blackthorn staff, hobbling to the head of the colonnade.

Someone cheered, and was silenced. Everyone looked toward the fast-shut doors to the Great Hall, awaiting the Sun Prince.

Once, twice, thrice; from the far side, a spear-butt rapped upon the doors, and they fell open at the third blow with a shivering sound from the musicians' timbales.

He stood in the doorway: The Sun Prince.

He was a vision in cloth-of-gold, gilding his doublet and hosen, even his boots. His cloak was cloth-of-gold, falling to sweep the parquet floor as he entered. The mask of a smiling youth, gleaming with gold leaf, hid his face, and its rays hid his head. I heard murmurs and speculation as he strode the length of the colonnade, gilded spear in hand.

At the head of it, he bowed; but as he rose, so did the head of his spear, sweeping up to touch the breast of the Winter Queen. Bowing her head, she let fall her blackthorn staff. It clattered in the silence. With both hands, she raised her mask and swept the wig from her head, shrugging free of her encumbering rags and shawl.

I gasped, for the Winter Queen was young and beautiful, and she was Suriah.

But the masque was not done.

The Sun Prince dropped to one knee, grasping the hand of the Winter Queen. In one swift motion, he drew forth a ring and thrust it upon her finger; harshly, for I saw her wince. He rose, then, grasping her hand, and turned to face the crowd. When he lifted his mask, we saw: It was Prince Baudoin.

After a brief, indrawn breath of surprise, the Night's Crier swung his baton and struck the gong a resounding blow, letting the tocsin give shuddering voice to the New Year, and the trumpets leapt into the void of silence with a brassy shout, proclaiming joy to all. And in that indrawn moment of surprise, the celebrants found their breath, shouting with the trumpets, hailing the derring of one drunken young Prince of the Blood. And then the exhausted musicians found a new surge of energy, and their maestro tapped his toe, and they swung into a lively tune.

Somehow, amidst it all, my gaze settled on Anafiel Delaunay. He was watching them; lovely and bewildered Suriah, her ringed hand held aloft by the Prince, with his wild, gleaming eyes; and behind the wise, rustic mask of Faunus, Delaunay's features were composed and thoughtful.

Such was my introduction to politics.

Six

After the Midwinter Masque, you may be sure, the weeks could not pass quickly enough for me until my tenth birthday. Now more than ever, I was without place in Cereus House; no longer fit for the nursery, but too young for the fosterlings and apprentices, among whom I was never to be numbered anyway.

The house was abuzz with the events of the masque, seeing in Prince Baudoin's audacity the portent of a return to days of yore, when the scions of Elua freely sought pleasure and counsel of the Servants of Naamah. This much I learned: Baudoin was nephew to the King, by way of his royal sister, the Princess Lyonette, who was wed to Marc, Duc de Trevalion. He was only nineteen, and had earned a name for wildness at the University of Tiberium, where he had been suspended for unnamed escapades.

Beyond this, I knew little. Hyacinthe told me that it was rumored in Night's Doorstep that there had been, unlikely as it seemed, two wagers placed on Baudoin de Trevalion to play the role of the Sun Prince, and no one—not even he—knew into whose pocket the considerable sums had been paid. Other than this, there had been much money lost, and the backers at the counting-houses had grown fat on this Longest Night.

When the chill of winter began to give grudging way to the moist warmth of spring and the faintest haze of pale green clung to the branches, I turned ten.

For children of the Night Court, this was a grand and solemn occasion. It is upon this day that one moves out of the nursery, and into the fosterlings' quarter to live side by side with those favored apprentices who have come of age and been initiated into the mysteries of Naamah, who it is said will whisper secrets in the small hours of the night of the training they have begun. One takes the name of one's household and there is a celebration, with watered wine, and the ceremonial breaking of a honey-cake, which is shared by the adepts of one's House.

I was accorded none of this.

Instead, as before, I was sent to attend in the Dowayne's receiving room, where I once again knelt *abeyante* upon the cushion. Anafiel Delaunay was there, and the Dowayne, and Jareth, her Second. She had grown older and querulous, and I noted from beneath my lashes how her hand shook as she held the papers to review.

"Everything is in order," Jareth said soothingly, patting her hand. He cast an impatient glance toward the doorway, where the Chancellor of the House lurked with the official guild seal. "You have but to sign, and Phèdre has leave to go with my lord Delaunay."

"Should have asked for more!" the Dowayne complained. Her voice was louder than she thought it, as happens with the elderly. Anafiel Delaunay laid a hand on my head, briefly stroking my curls. I dared an upward glance and saw him smiling reassuringly. The Dowayne signed with a shaky hand, the crabbed veins blue through her fine old skin, and the Chancellor of the House glided forward with his taper to stamp the official guild seal on the documents, certifying that all had been executed within the laws of the Guild of the Servants of Naamah.

"Done." Jareth bowed, palms together, touching his fingertips to his lips. There was a merriment to him these days that spilled out at the slightest provocation, born of the surety that the Dowayneship of Cereus House was nearly in his lap. "May Naamah bless your enterprise, my lord Delaunay. It has been a pleasure."

"The pleasure has been mine," Delaunay said smoothly, returning his bow, though not as to an equal. "Miriam," he said to the Dowayne, in a graver tone. "I wish you health."

"Bah." She dismissed him and beckoned to me. "Phèdre." I rose as I had been taught, and knelt at her chair, suddenly terrified that she would recant. But her crabbed hand rose to smooth my cheek and her eyes, no less steely behind the rheum that veiled them, searched my face. "Should have asked for more," she repeated, almost kindly.

They say that money is one of the few pleasures that endure, and I understood that, despite everything, this was a blessing of sorts. Of a sudden, I felt great tenderness for the old woman, who had taken me in when my own mother had cast me out, and I leaned into her caress.

"Phèdre," Delaunay said gently, and I remembered that I had a new master and rose obediently. He smiled pleasantly at Jareth. "Have her things brought to my coach."

Jareth bowed.

And so I took my leave of Cereus House, and the Night Court, unto which I was born.

I don't know what I expected, in Delaunay's coach; whatever I expected, it did not happen. His coach awaited in the forecourt, an elegant trap drawn by a matched foursome of blood-bays. An apprentice brought the small bundle that contained such things as I might call my own, which was little more than nothing, and which the coachman stowed in the back.

Delaunay preceded me, patting the velvet cushions to indicate I should sit. He waved out the window to the coachman and we set out at a good clip, whereupon he settled back into his seat and drew the curtain partially closed.

I sat on tenterhooks, waiting and wondering.

Nothing happened. Delaunay, for his part, ignored me, humming to himself and gazing out the half-curtained window. After a while, I tired of waiting for something to occur and scooted to the window on my side, twitching the curtain back.

When I was scarce more than a babe-in-arms, I had seen the world; but since I had been four years old, I'd not ventured past Night's Doorstep. Now I looked out the window, and saw the City of Elua roll past my view and rejoiced. The streets seemed clean and new, the parks ready to burst into spring, and the houses and temples all aspired upward in joyous defiance of the earth. We crossed the river, and the bright sails of trade-ships made my heart sing.

The coach took us to an elegant quarter of the City, near to the Palace, though on the outskirts. Through a narrow gate we went, and into a modest courtyard. The coachman drew up and came around to open the door; Delaunay descended, and I hesitated, uncertain, gazing past his shoulder at a simple, elegant townhouse.

The door opened, and a figure not much larger than myself emerged at a run, caught himself, and proceeded at a more decorous pace.

I stared from the coach at the most beautiful boy I had ever seen.

His hair was white; and for those who never knew Alcuin, I say this in earnest: it was white, whiter than a snow fox's pelt. It fell like silk over his shoulders, in a river of moonlight. An albino, one might suppose—and indeed, his skin was surpassingly fair, but his eyes were dark, as dark as pansies at midnight. I, raised amid pearls of beauty, gaped. On the far side of Delaunay, he fretted with impatience, a smile at once kind and eager lighting his dark eyes.

I had forgotten that Delaunay already had a pupil.

"Alcuin." I could hear the affection in Delaunay's voice. It churned my gut. He put his hand on the boy's shoulder and turned to me. "This is Phèdre. Make her welcome."

I exited the coach, stumbling; he took my hands in his, cool and smooth, and kissed me in greeting.

I could feel Delaunay's wry smile at a distance.

A liveried servant emerged from the house to pay the coachman and take my small bundle, and Delaunay steered us gently inward. The boy Alcuin kept hold of my hand, tugging lightly.

Inside, Delaunay's house was gracious and pleasant. Another servant in livery bowed, which I scarce noticed, and Alcuin dropped my hand to scamper ahead, glancing back with a quick, eager smile. Already I hated him for what he knew of our mutual master. We passed through several rooms into an inner sanctum, a gardened courtyard where a terrace of early-greening vines threw verdant shadows on the flagstones and a fountain played. There was a niche with a statue of Elua, and a table laid with iced melons and pale grapes.

Alcuin spun in a circle, flinging out his arms. "For you, Phèdre!" he cried, laughing. "Welcome!" He dropped onto one of the reclining couches set about in a conversational circle, wrapped his arms around himself and grinned.

An unobtrusive servant glided into the courtyard, pouring chilled wine for Delaunay, and cool water for Alcuin and myself.

"Welcome." Delaunay seconded the toast, smiling, gauging my reaction. "Eat. Drink. Sit."

I took a slice of melon and perched on the edge of a

couch, watching them both, patently uncomfortable with the undefined nature of my role here. Delaunay reclined at leisure, looking amused, and Alcuin followed his lead, looking merry with anticipation. I could not help but glance around, looking for a kneeling cushion. There was none.

"We do not stand—nor kneel—on ceremony in my household, Phèdre," Delaunay said kindly, reading my mind. "It is one thing to observe the courtesies of rank, and quite another to treat humans as chattel."

I looked up to meet his eyes. "You own my marque," I said bluntly.

"Yes." He gave me that gauging look. "But I do not own *you*. And when one day your marque is made, I would have you remember me as one who lifted you up, and not cast you down. Do you understand?"

I plucked at a button on the velvet cushioning of the couch. "You like people to owe you favors."

There was a pause, and then he gave the startling bark of laughter I'd heard before, Alcuin's higher laugh echoing above it. "Yes," Delaunay said thoughtfully. "You might say that. Although I like to think I am a humanist, too, in the tradition of Blessed Elua." He shrugged, dismissing the matter in his amused fashion. "I am told you have learned somewhat of the Caerdicci tongue."

"I have read all of Tellicus the Elder, and half the Younger!" I retorted, nettled by his attitude. I did not mention the poetry of Felice Dolophilus.

"Good." He was unperturbed. "You're none too far behind Alcuin, then; you can take your lessons together. Have you other languages? No? No matter. When you've settled in, I'll arrange for you to start lessons in Skaldic and Cruithne."

My head swam; I picked up my plate of melon, and set it back down. "My lord Delaunay," I said, choosing my words carefully. "Is it not your will that I shall be apprenticed unto the service of Naamah?"

"Oh, that." With a wave of his hand, he discarded the tenets of the Night Court. "You can sing, I'm told, and play a passable harp; the Dowayne says you've an ear for poetry. I'll hire a tutor to continue your teaching in such arts, until you come of age and may decide for yourself if you wish to serve Naamah. But there are other matters of more import."

I sat up straight on the couch. "The arts of the salon are of the utmost import, my lord!"

"No." His grey eyes glinted. "They have value, Phèdre, and that is all. But what I will teach you, you will like, I think. You will learn to look, to see, and to think, and there is merit in such lessons as will last a lifetime."

"You will teach me what already I know," I said, sullen.

"Will I indeed?" Delaunay leaned back on the couch and popped a grape into his mouth. "Tell me, then, about the coach in which we rode here, Phèdre. Describe it to me."

"It was a black coach." I glared at him. "A coach-and-four, with matched bays. With red velvet on the seats, gold braid on the curtains, and sateen stripes on the walls."

"Well done." He glanced at Alcuin. "And you . . . ?"

The boy sat up, cross-legged on the couch. "It was a coach-for-hire," he said promptly, "because there was no insignia on the door, and the driver wore plain clothes and not livery. A wealthy hostelry, most like, because the horses were well-bred and matched; nor were they lathered, so most like you leased them here in the City. The driver was between eighteen and twenty-two, and country-bred to judge from his hat, but he has been in

e City long enough to need no direction nor bite good
oin when paid him by a gentleman. He carried no other
assengers, and left straightaway, so I would gauge you
ere his only fare today, my lord. If I were to seek your
lentity and your business, my lord, I think it would not
e so hard to find the driver of this coach-and-four and
nake inquiries."

His dark eyes danced with the pleasure of having an-
wered well; there was no malice in it. Delaunay smiled
t him. "And better done," he said, then glanced at me.
Do you see?"

I muttered something; I don't know what.

"This is the training I will ask of you, Phèdre," he
aid, his voice sterner. "You will learn to look, to see,
nd to think on what you see. You asked me at Mid-
vinter if I knew you by your eyes, and I said no. I did
ot need to see the mote in your eye to know you were
ne who had been stricken by Kushiel's Dart. It was in
very line of your body, as you gazed after the domi-
atrices of Mandrake House. It is to the glory of Elua
nd his Companions, in whose veins your blood flows;
ven as a child, you bear the mark of it. In time, you
nay become it, do you choose. But understand, my
weet, that this is only a beginning. Now, do you see?"

His face acquired a particular beauty when he put on
hat expression, stern and serious, like the portraits of
ld provincial nobles who could trace their lineage
traight back to one of Elua's Companions in an unbro-
en line. "Yes, my lord," I said, adoring him for it. If
Anafiel Delaunay wanted me to lay down in the stews,
ike Naamah, I would do it, I was sure . . . and if he
villed me to be more than an instrument for Mandragian
iddle-players, I would learn to be it. I thought on his
vords to me that Longest Night, and a connection
ormed in my mind, as easily as a nursing babe finds the

nipple. "My lord," I asked him, "did you place a wage in Night's Doorstep that Baudoin de Trevalion woul play the Sun Prince?"

Once more I was rewarded with his unexpected sho of laughter, longer this time, unchecked. Alcuin grinne and hugged his knees with glee. At last, Delaunay wre tled his mirth under control, removing a kerchief fro his pocket and dabbing his eyes. "Ah, Phèdre," sighed. "Miriam was right. She should have asked f more."

$\mathcal{S}$EVEN

So began the years of my long apprenticeship with A afiel Delaunay, wherein I began to learn how to look an see and think. And lest anyone should suppose that m time was taken with nothing more taxing than watchin and heeding my surroundings, I may assure you, this wa the least of it, if not the least important.

As Delaunay had indicated, I studied languages; Caer dicci, until I could speak it in my dreams, and Cruithn (for which I saw no need) and Skaldic, recalling to m the long-ago tribesman who had appointed himself m guardian on the Trader's Road. Alcuin, it transpire spoke Skaldic with some long-imprinted skill, for it ha been his milk-tongue, spoken to him in the cradle by Skaldic wetnurse. In truth, it was she who had saved hi from an ambush by her own people and given him unt Delaunay's keeping, but this I learned later.

In addition to languages, we were made to study his tory, until my head ached with it. We traced civilizatio from the golden age of Hellas to the rise of Tiberiun and followed her fall, dealt two-fisted by twin claimants

The followers of Yeshua held that his coming was a prophecy, that Tiberium should fall and they should restore the throne of the One God; historians, Delaunay told us guardedly, held that the dispersal of Yeshuite financiers from the city of Tiberium had more to do with it. Strained coffers, he maintained, were what eventually caused the great empire of Tiberium to be divided into the loose-knit republic of nation-states that comprises Caerdicca Unitas.

The second blow, no less doughty, was struck against the once-mighty Tiberian armies on the green island of Alba, when there arose amid the warring factions a tribal king named Cinhil ap Domnall, known as Cinhil Ru, who succeeded in making a treaty with the Dalriada of Eire and uniting the tribes against the Emperor's armies. Thus did the island come once and for all under the rule of the Cruithne, whom scholars call the Picti. They are a wild, half-civilized folk, and I saw no need to learn their tongue.

Once the Tiberian soldiers were driven out of Alba, they began retreating and never stopped, driven out of the Skaldic hinterlands by berserkers and—legends claimed—the spirits of raven and wolf.

Through this bloodstained tapestry ran the history of Terre d'Ange, shining like a golden thread. A peaceful and content to fruit and flower beneath the blessed sun, we had no history, Delaunay said, before the coming of Elua. We gave way with grace before the armies of Tiberium, who ate our grapes and olives, wed our women and held our borders against the Skaldi. We carried out our small rituals unchanged, and kept our language and our songs, unchanging. When the armies of Tiberium retreated like a wave across our lands, into the waiting emptiness came the wandering steps of Elua, and the land welcomed him like a bridegroom.

Thus was born Terre d'Ange, and thus did we acquire history and pride. In the three-score Years of Elua, the Companions dispersed, placing their numinous stamp on the land and its people. Blessed Elua himself claimed no portion, but delighted to roam at will, a wandering bride-groom in love with all that he saw. When he tarried, it was in the City, which is why she is the queen of all cities, and beloved in the nation; but he tarried seldom.

All this I knew, and yet it was a different thing, to learn it from Delaunay: not stories, but histories. For this too I learned, that a storyteller's tale may end, but history goes on always. These events, so distant in legend, play a part in shaping the very events we witness about us each and every day. When I understood this, Delaunay said, I might begin to understand.

What I was to understand, it seemed, was everything. It was not until I began to study the labyrinthine maze of court politics that I truly despaired of my sheltered life in the Night Court. Alcuin had been learning such things for two years and more, and could effortlessly recite the lineage of each of the seven sovereign duchies, the royal family and its myriad entanglements, the duties of the Exchequer, the limits of judiciary powers, even the by-laws of the Guild of Spice-Trading.

For this, as for so much else, I despised him; and yet I admit freely that I loved him, too. It was impossible not to love Alcuin, who loved nigh the entire world. Unlikely as it seemed to one raised in the Night Court, he was unaware of his startling beauty, which only increased as he got older. He had a quicksilver mind and a prodigious memory, which I envied, and yet he took no pride in it save the pride of pleasing Delaunay.

When Delaunay entertained, which in those days was often, it was Alcuin who waited on his guests. In contrast to the revels and delights staged by Cereus House, these

vere civilized, erudite affairs. What Delaunay liked best
vas to invite a small number of friends, who would re-
cline on couches à la Hellene in the inner courtyard,
enjoying an elegant meal and spinning out the night in
convivial conversation.

Alcuin stood by to serve wine or cordial at these affairs, and while I was contemptuous of his lack of sophistication, I could not deny that he was a charming
sight, all untutored grace and gentle eagerness, the vine-
cast shadows throwing traceries of green on his moon-
white hair. When Alcuin proffered the wine-jug with his
grave smile, as like as not guests smiled back and raised
their glasses, whether they wished them refilled or no,
merely to see the pleasure of serving light his dark eyes.

This, of course, was Delaunay's intent, and I've no
doubt that many a tongue was loosened in that courtyard
by virtue of Alcuin's smile. I have never known a mind
more subtle than that of Anafiel Delaunay. Yet to those
who cite such things as proof that he used us without
regard, I say: It is a lie. Of a surety, we loved him, both
of us in our differing ways, and I have no doubt in my
mind that Delaunay loved us in turn. I would have proof
enough of that ere things were done, little though I welcomed it at the time.

As for the guests, they varied, and so widely it scarce
seemed possible that one man could have so many acquaintances from such far-flung quarters of the nation. He
chose his guests with great care, and never did I see a mix
that soured, unless it was at his will. Delaunay knew court
officials and judiciaries, lords and ladies, shippers and
traders, poets and painters and moneylenders. He knew
singers and warriors and goldsmiths, breeders of the finest
horseflesh, scholars and historians, silk merchants and
milliners. He knew scions of Blessed Elua and his Companions, and members of all the Great Houses.

I learned that Gaspar Trevalion, Comte de Fourcay and kinsman to Marc, Duc de Trevalion, was a great friend of his. A clever, cynical man with streaks of grey at his temples, Gaspar was adept at sniffing the political winds to see which way they blew. It was he, doubtless, who had told Delaunay how the Princess Lyonette whispered in her son Baudoin's ear about an ailing King and an empty throne, and the portent people might take from the symbolic wedding at the Midwinter Masque.

Such things surrounded me and were a part of my life on a daily basis, for what I did not observe, I later learned when Delaunay obtained Alcuin's recitation of a night's events. He was ever scrupulous in including me during these sessions, that I might increase the knowledge that already crammed my aching skull. For a long time, I resented his favoritism of Alcuin, when I was better-trained to serve; but even so, I listened.

I understood, later, why he held me back during those first long years. Those whom Delaunay would choose for his clientele would be chosen with care. They were among the elite and mistrustful of the nation, too deeply embroiled in money and power to be lured easily into spilling pillow-secrets. With Alcuin, Delaunay was wise enough to set the wheels of desire in motion long before the day would arrive. There were nobles who yearned for years, watching him grow with tantalizing slowness from a beautiful child to a breathtaking youth. When they spilled their secrets, there were years of pressure behind the force that burst the dam.

With me, it was different. The desire that I elicited— would elicit—burned hotter, and with a shorter fuse. Delaunay, who knew much of human nature, knew this, and chose in his wisdom to keep me a secret from his guests. Word spread, as was inevitable, that he had taken a sec-

nd pupil; when his guests pressed him to reveal my
ature, he smiled and demurred. Thus did my reputation
pread, while I toiled toward adolescence, immersed in
he labors of ink and parchment.

There was one exception: Melisande.

Genius requires an audience. For all his cleverness,
Delaunay was an artist and as vulnerable as any of his
ind to the desire to vaunt his brilliance. And there were
ew, very few, people capable of appreciating his art. I
lid not know, then, how deep-laid a game they played
vith each other, nor what part in it I was to play. All I
new was that she was the audience he chose.

I had been three years and a half in his household,
nd had been some time training with a tumbling-master
Delaunay had found Elua-knows-where. He believed,
Delaunay did, in a balanced approach to shaping one's
ature, and thus were Alcuin and I subjected to an end-
ess series of physical training to ensure that our well-
oned minds were esconced in vigorous bodies.

I had just finished my day's lesson, in which I had
earned to throw a standing somersault, and was towel-
ing off the sweat when Delaunay entered the gymna-
ium with her. The tumbling-master was packing his
hings, and seeing her, bid to make a hasty retreat, which
Delaunay ignored.

To describe Melisande Shahrizai is, as the poets say,
o paint a nightingale's song; it is a thing which cannot
e done. She was three-and-twenty years of age at that
ime, though time never seemed to touch her, either way
t flowed. If I say her skin was like alabaster, her hair a
lack so true it gleamed blue where the light touched it
nd her eyes a sapphire that gemstones might envy, I
speak only the truth; but she was a D'Angeline, and this
only hints at the beginning of beauty.

"Melisande," Delaunay said, pride and amusement in his voice. "This is Phèdre."

As I am D'Angeline and Night Court-born, you may be sure, I am not easily awed by beauty; but I am what I am, and there are other things that awe me. The Shahrizai are an ancient house of courtiers, and many, knowing little of the nomenclature of Terre d'Ange, suppose they are of Shemhazai's lineage. It is not so. The namesakes among the descendents of Elua's Companions are intertwined in such a way that only a D'Angeline scholar can comprehend them.

I, who had studied such things, had no need of history to tell me House Shahrizai's lineage. When I glanced up politely to meet the blue eyes of Melisande Shahrizai, her look went through me like a spear, my knees turned to water, and I knew that she was a scion of Kushiel.

"How charming." She crossed the gymnasium floor with careless grace, sweeping the train of her gown over one arm. Cool fingers stroked my cheek, lacquered nails trailing lightly over my skin. I shuddered. With a faint smile, she held my chin up, forcing me to look her in the face. "Anafiel," she said lightly, amused, turning to him, "You've found a genuine *anguissette*."

He laughed, coming to join us. "I thought you would approve."

"Mmm." She loosed me, and I nearly fell on the floor. "I've wondered what you were hiding, you magician, you. I know people who've wagered a considerable amount of money in speculation."

Delaunay wagged one finger back and forth at her. "We had an agreement, Melisande. Do you want Cousin Ogier to know why his son cancelled his wedding at the last moment?"

"Just . . . thinking aloud, sweet man." She gave him the same treatment, a trailing caress down the side of his face. Delaunay merely smiled. "You must think of me when you decide it's time for her to serve Naamah, Anafiel." She turned back to me, smiling sweetly. "You do wish to serve Naamah, don't you, child?"

Her smile made me tremble, and at last, I understood what Delaunay had meant. The memory of the Dowayne's chastiser and the adepts of Mandrake House paled beside the exquisite cruelty etched in that smile. I would like to say that I sensed, then, the long corridor of history stretching before us, the role I was to play, and the terrible lengths to which it would drive me, but it would be a lie. I thought nothing of the kind. I thought nothing at all. Instead, I forgot my manners, my long training in the Night Court, and wallowed in her blue gaze. "Yes," I whispered in answer. "My lady."

"Good." She turned away again, dismissing me, taking Delaunay's hand and steering him toward the door. "There is a small matter I wish to discuss with you. . . ."

Thus was my introduction to Melisande Shahrizai, who had a mind as subtle as Delaunay's, and a far colder heart.

Eight

"And here," Delaunay said, pointing, "is the stronghold of Comte Michel de Ferraut, who commands six hundred men, and holds the border at Longview Pass."

History, politics, geography . . . the lessons were unending.

In accordance with the Diaspora of the Companions, the land of Terre d'Ange is divided into seven provinces and the King—or betimes the Queen—rules from the City in reverent memory of Blessed Elua.

Gentle Eisheth went to the southern coastal lands, which hold dreamers and sailors, healers and traders, as well as the thousand birds and wild cavaliers of the salt marshes. Her province is called Eisande, and it is the smallest of the seven. There are Tsingani who dwell there, and live unmolested.

Also to the south went Shemhazai, westerly to the mountainous borders of Aragonia, with whom our long peace still stands. Siovale is the name of this province, and it is a prosperous one with a great tradition for learning, for Shemhazai ever treasured knowledge.

Inland to the north of Siovale is L'Agnace, the grape-rich province of Anael, who is betimes called the Star of Love. Alongside it on the rocky coast is the province of Kusheth, where Kushiel made his home, all the way up to the Pointe d'Oeste. It is a harsh land, like its namesake.

Further northward is Azzalle, which clings along the coast, close enough at one point to see the white cliffs of Alba. Were it not for the fact that the Master of the Straits controls the waters that lie between us, indeed, there might be danger of a powerful alliance between Azzalle and Alba. Of this I took note, for Trevalion is the ruling duchy of Azzalle, and my heart still beat faster to remember Baudoin de Trevalion's kiss.

Beneath the province of Azzalle is Namarre, where Naamah dwelt, and it is a place of many rivers, very beautiful and fruitful. There is a shrine where the River Naamah arises from beneath the earth, and all her servants make a pilgrimage there within their lifetimes.

To the east, bordering the Skaldic territories, lies the long, narrow province of Camlach, where martial Camael made his home and founded the first armies of those bright, fierce D'Angeline troops who have for so long defended the nation from invasion.

This, I learned from Delaunay, is the nature of my homeland and the division of power within it. Slowly I came to an understanding of these divisions, and the implications of power that each province held its own; each reflecting to some degree the nature of their angelic founders. Cassiel alone among Elua's Companions took no province for his own, but remained faithful at his wandering lord's side. He had but one namesake in the land; the Cassiline Brotherhood, an order of priests who swear allegiance to the Precepts of Cassiel. It is a service as rigorous as that of Naamah's, and far sterner, which is perhaps why it is no longer popular. Only the oldest of provincial nobles maintain the tradition, passed within the family from generation to generation, of pledging a younger son to the Cassiline Brotherhood. Like us, they become fosterlings at the age of ten, but it is a harsh and ascetic life of training at arms, celibacy and denial.

"You see, Phèdre, why Camlach has always held the greatest strategic importance." Delaunay's finger traced its borderline on a map. I glanced up into his questioning eyes and sighed.

"Yes, my lord."

"Good." His finger moved back up, hovering. He had beautiful hands, with long, tapering fingers. "Here, see, is where the fighting has been." He indicated a dense patch of mountainous terrain. "You marked what the iron-trader was saying last night? The Skaldi have been threatening the passes again, as they've not done since the Battle of Three Princes."

There was an undertone of sorrow in his voice. "When Prince Rolande was killed," I said, remembering. "The Dauphin was one of the Three Princes."

"Yes." Delaunay pushed the map away brusquely. "And the other two?"

"The King's brother, Benedicte, and . . ." I struggled to recall.

"Percy of L'Agnace, Comte de Somerville, cousin-germane to Prince Rolande," Alcuin's soft voice supplied. He pushed his white hair from his eyes and smiled. "Kinsman on his mother's side to Queen Genevieve, which made him a Prince of the Blood in accordance with matrimonial law, though he seldom claims the title."

I glowered at him. "I knew that."

He shrugged and gave his inarguable smile.

"Bide your peace." There was no jest in Delaunay's tone and his gaze was somber. "We paid dear for that victory, when it cost Rolande de la Courcel's life. He was born to rule, and would have held the throne with strength and grace upon his father's passing, and none would have dared take up arms against him. We have paid for the security of our borders with instability in the City itself, and now our gains stand threatened in the bargain."

Pushing himself away from the table, he rose to pace the library, standing at last to gaze silently out a window onto the streets below. Alcuin and I exchanged wordless glances. Delaunay was in many ways the gentlest of masters, reprimanding us with nothing harsher than an unkind word, and that only when we were truly deserving. But there was a darkness in him that surfaced only sometimes, and we who attended his moods closer than a farmer watches the weather knew well enough not to rouse it.

"Were you there, my lord?" I ventured at length.

He answered without turning around, and his voice was flat. "If I could have saved his life, I would have. We shouldn't have been mounted, that was the problem. The ground was too uncertain. But Rolande was always rash. It was his only flaw, as a leader. When he led the third charge, he got too far ahead; his standard-bearer's horse stumbled and went down, and we were held back in getting around him. Not long . . . but long enough for the Skaldi to cut him off." He turned back to us with that same somber look. "On such small things, empires may hang. For want of a sure-footed mount, half the scions of Elua have their gaze set on becoming Prince Consort and claiming the throne through marriage; and Princes of the Blood like Baudoin de Trevalion scheme to take it by force of acclaim. Remember it, my dears, and when you plan, plan well and thoroughly."

"You think Prince Baudoin wants the throne?" I asked, startled; after more than three years, I still found myself struggling to grasp the shape of these patterns Delaunay studied. Alcuin looked unsurprised.

"No. Not exactly." Delaunay smiled wryly. "But he is the King's nephew, and I think his mother, who is called for good reason the Lioness of Azzalle, would like to see her son seated upon it."

"Ahhh." I blinked, and at last this pattern—Baudoin's actions, Delaunay's presence at the Midwinter Masque—came clear to me. "My lord, what has that to do with Skaldic raiders on the eastern border?"

"Who knows?" He shrugged. "Nothing, perhaps. But there is no saying how events in one place may affect what happens elsewhere, for the tapestry of history is woven of many threads. We needs must study the whole warp and weft of it to predict the pattern on the loom."

"Will the Skaldi invade?" Alcuin asked softly, a distant glimmer of fear in his dark eyes. Delaunay smiled kindly and stroked his hair.

"No," he said with certainty. "They are as unorganized as the tribes of Alba before Cinhil Ru, and lords such as the Comte de Ferraut and Duc Maslin d'Aiglemort hold the passes well-defended. They have built their strength since the Battle of Three Princes, that such may never occur again. But it is something to note, my dears, and you know what we say about that."

"All knowledge is worth having." I knew it by rote; if Delaunay had a motto, that was surely it.

"Indeed." He turned his smile on me, and my heart leapt at his approval. "Go on and entertain yourselves, you've earned a respite," he added, dismissing us.

We went, obedient to his words, though reluctant, always, to be denied his presence. For those who never knew him, I can say only that there was a charm about Delaunay that compelled the affections of all who surrounded him; for good or for ill, I might add, for I knew later some who despised him. But those who hated him were the sort who envied excellence in others. No matter what he did, Anafiel Delaunay did it with a grace that eludes most people in this world. A panderer, his detractors called him, and later, the Whoremaster of Spies, but I knew him better than most, and never did he conduct himself with less than perfect nobility.

Which is part of what made him such a mystery.

"It's not his real name," Hyacinthe informed me.

"How do you know?"

He flashed me his white grin, vivid in the dim light. "I've been asking." He thumped his slender chest. "I wanted to know about the man who took you away from me!"

"I came back," I said mildly.

Delaunay, to my great annoyance, had been amused. My first escape had been planned with much forethought, executed while he was away at court by climbing out a second-story window disguised in boy's clothes purloined from Alcuin's wardrobe. I had studied a map of the City and made my way on foot, alone and unaided, all the way to Night's Doorstep.

It had been a tremendous reunion. We stole tarts from the pastry-vendor in the marketplace for old time's sake, running all the way to Tertius' Crossing to crouch under the bridge and eat them, still warm, juices dripping down our chins. Afterward, Hyacinthe had taken me to an inn where he was known to the travelling players who lodged there, strutting about and making himself important by knowing bits of gossip this one or that would pay to hear. Players are notorious for their intrigues, worse even than adepts of the Night Court.

Filled with the thrill of my adventure and the edge of anticipatory dread of its repercussions, I scarce noticed when a boy of some eight or nine years wormed his way through the throng to whisper in Hyacinthe's ear. For the first time, I saw my friend frown.

"He says a man in livery sent him," Hyacinthe said to me. "Brown and gold, with a sheaf of corn on the crest?"

"Delaunay!" I gasped. My chest contracted with fear. "Those are his colors."

Hyacinthe looked irritated. "Well, his man is outside, with a coach. He said to send Ardile when you're ready to go."

The boy nodded vigorously; and thus did I learn that Hyacinthe had begun to create his own small net of messengers and errand-runners in Night's Doorstep, and that Anafiel Delaunay not only knew that I had gone and where I had gone, but who Hyacinthe was and what he was doing.

Delaunay never ceased to amaze.

When I returned, he was waiting.

"I am not going to punish you," he said without preamble. I don't know what expression I bore, but it seemed to entertain him. He pointed to a chair across from him. "Come in, Phèdre. Sit." Once I had, he rose, pacing about the room. Lamplight gleamed on his russet hair, bound in the sleek braid that showed off the noble lines of his face. "Did you think I didn't know about your penchant for escape?" he asked, stopping in front of me. I shook my head. "It is my business to know things, and that most certainly includes things about members of my household. What the Dowayne preferred to conceal, my sweet, the members of her Guard did not."

"I'm sorry, my lord!" I cried, guilt-stricken. He glanced at me with amusement and sat back down.

"Only insofar as you enjoy being sorry, my dear, which, while it is a considerable amount, occurs only after the fact, thus making it a singularly ineffective deterrent, yes?"

Confused, I nodded.

Delaunay sighed and crossed his legs, his expression turning serious. "Phèdre, I don't object to your ambitious young friend. Indeed, you may well learn things in that quarter you'd not hear elsewhere. And," a flicker of amusement returned, "to a certain degree, I don't object to your penchant for escape and," leaning forward to pluck at the sleeve of Alcuin's tunic which I wore, "disguise. But there are dangers for a child alone in the City to which I cannot have you exposed. Henceforth if you wish, in your free time, to visit your friend, you will inform Guy."

I waited for more. "That's all?"

"That's all."

I thought it through. A man who spoke softly and seldom, Guy served Delaunay with intense loyalty and efficiency in a variety of unnamed capacities. "He'll follow me," I said finally. "Or have me followed."

Delaunay smiled. "Very good. You're welcome to try

to detect and evade him, with my blessing; if you can do that, Phèdre, I've no need to worry about you on your own. But you *will* inform him if you leave these grounds, for any reason."

His complacency was maddening. "And if I don't?" I asked, challenging him with a toss of my head.

The change that came over his face frightened me; truly frightened me, without a single tremor of excitement. His eyes turned cold, and the lines of his face set. "I am not of Kushiel's line, Phèdre. I do not play games of defiance and punishment, and as I care for you, I will not allow you to endanger yourself for a childish whim. I don't demand unquestioning obedience, but I demand obedience nonetheless. If you cannot give it, I will sell your marque."

With that ringing in my ears, you may be sure I paid heed. I saw his eyes; I had no doubt that he meant his words. Which meant, of course, that as I sat with Hyacinthe in his mother's kitchen, somewhere nearby, quiet and efficient, Guy kept watch.

"What is it, then?" I asked Hyacinthe now. "Who is he really?"

He shook his head, black ringlets swinging. "That, I don't know. But there is something I do know." He grinned, baiting me. "I know why his poetry was banned."

"Why?" I was impatient to know. In the corner where she muttered over the stove, Hyacinthe's mother turned and glanced uneasily at us.

"Do you know how Prince Rolande's first betrothed died?" he asked.

It had happened before we were born, but thanks to Delaunay's ceaseless teachings, I was well-versed in the history of the royal family. "She broke her neck in a fall," I said. "A hunting accident."

"So they say," he said. "But after Rolande wed Isabel L'Envers, a song came to be heard in the stews and wineshops about a noble lady who seduced a stableboy and bid him to cut the girth on her rival's saddle the day she went a-hunting with her love."

"*Delaunay* wrote it? Why?"

Hyacinthe shrugged. "Who knows? This is what I heard. The men-at-arms of the Princess Consort caught the troubador who was spreading the song. When she had him interrogated, he named Delaunay as the author of the lyrics. The troubador was banished to Eisande, and it is said that he died mysteriously en route. She brought Delaunay in for questioning, but he refused to confess to authorship. So he was not banished, but to appease his daughter-in-law, the King banned his poetry and had every extant copy of his work destroyed."

"Then he is an enemy of the Crown," I marvelled.

"No." Hyacinthe shook his head with certainty. "If he were, he would surely have been banished, confession or no. The Princess Consort willed it, but he is still welcome at court. Someone protected him in this matter."

"How did you learn this?"

"Oh, that." His grin flashed again. "There is a certain court poet who conceives a hopeless passion for the wife of a certain innkeeper, whom he addresses in his rhymes as the Angel of Night's Door. She pays me in coin to tell him to go away and bother her no more, and he pays me in tales to tell him how she looked when she said it. I will learn for you what I can, Phèdre."

"You will learn it to your despair."

The words were spoken darkly and, I thought, to Hyacinthe; but when I looked, I saw his mother's arm extended, pointing at me. A dire portent gleamed in her hollow-shadowed eyes, the dusky, weathered beauty of her face framed in dangling gold.

"I do not understand," I said, confused.

"You seek to unravel the mystery of your master." She jabbed her pointing finger at me. "You think it is for curiosity's sake, but I tell you this: You will rue the day all is made clear. Do not seek to hasten its coming."

With that, she turned back to her stove, ignoring us. I looked at Hyacinthe. The mischief had left his expression; he respected very little, but his mother's gift of *dromonde* was among those few things. When she told fortunes for the denizens of Night's Doorstep, she made shift to use an ancient, tattered pack of cards, but I knew from what he had told me that this was only for show. *Dromonde* came when bidden and sometimes when not, the second sight that parted the veils of time.

We considered her warning in silence. Delaunay's words came, unbidden, to mind.

"All knowledge is worth having," I said.

Nine

By the end of my fourth year of my service to Anafiel Delaunay, I had come of age.

In the Night Court, I would have been been initiated into the mysteries of Naamah and begun the training of my apprenticeship when I turned thirteen; Delaunay, infuriatingly, had chosen to wait. I thought I would die of impatience before he posed me the question, although I did not.

"You have grown from a child to a young woman, Phèdre," he said. "May the blessing of Naamah be upon you." He took my shoulders in his hands then and looked gravely at me. "I am going to ask you a question now, and I swear by Blessed Elua, I want you to answer it freely. Will you do it?"

"Yes, my lord."

His topaz-flecked eyes searched mine. "Is it your will to be dedicated unto the service of Naamah?"

I held off giving an answer, glad of a chance to gaze at such leisure at his beloved face, elegant and austere. His hands on my shoulders, ah! I wished he would touch me more often. "Yes, my lord," I said at last, making my voice sound firm and resolute. As if there were any question! But, of course, Delaunay had to satisfy his sense of honor. Because I adored him, I understood.

"Good." He squeezed my shoulders once and released me, smiling. Faint lines crinkled at the corners of his eyes. Like the rest of him, they were beautiful. "We'll buy a dove, in the marketplace, and take you to the temple to be dedicated."

If I had felt cheated of ceremony upon my tenth birthday, this day compensated for it. Clapping his hands, Delaunay called for the mistress of the household and gave orders for a feast to be prepared. Lessons were dismissed for the day, and Alcuin and I were sent away to dress in our best festival attire.

"I'm glad," Alcuin whispered to me, grasping my hand and giving me his secret smile. He had turned fourteen earlier that year and been dedicated to Naamah; still a child by Delaunay's reckoning, I had been excluded from the rites.

"So am I," I whispered back, leaning over to kiss his cheek. Alcuin blushed, the color rising becomingly beneath his fair skin.

"Come on," he said, pulling away. "He's waiting."

In the marketplace, we strolled among the temple-vendors while the carriage waited patiently and Delaunay made a show of allowing me to choose the exact right dove for my offering. They were much alike, as birds are wont to be, but I studied them carefully and selected at length a beautiful white bird, with coral feet and alert black eyes. Delaunay paid the vendor, purchasing the best cage; a charming pagoda with gilt bars. The dove struggled a little as the vendor transferred her, wings beating at the bars. A good sign, as it meant she was healthy.

In the Night Court, the dedication is performed in the House temple, but, under the patronage of a noble citizen, we went to the Great Temple. It is a small, lovely building of white marble, surrounded by gardens. Doves roosted in the trees, sacred and unharmed. An acolyte met us at the open doors. Taking one look at Delaunay, she bowed. "In the name of Naamah, you are welcome, my lord. How may we serve you?"

I stood beside him, clutching the carrying-handle of the birdcage. Delaunay laid his hand upon my head.

"She is here to be dedicated to the service of Naamah."

The acolyte smiled at me. She was young, no more than eighteen, with a look of spring about her; red-gold hair the color of apricots and green eyes that tilted upward at the corners like a cat's. Young as she was, she wore the flowing scarlet surplice of the Priesthood of Naamah with an ease born of long familiarity. By this, I would guess, she had been dedicated as an infant, by parents or a mother who could not afford to raise her; by her speech, I would guess she was City-born.

"So," the acolyte said softly. "Be welcome, sister." Stooping only slightly—she was little taller than I—she kissed me in greeting. Her lips were soft and she smelled of sun-warmed herbs. When she turned to kiss Alcuin, they were of a height. "Be welcome, brother." Stepping back, she gestured us through the door. "Come in and worship. I will bring the priest."

Inside, the temple was filled with sunlight, adorned only by flowers and a blaze of candles. There was an oculus at the top of the dome, open to the sky. We approached the altar with its magnificent statue of Naamah, who stood with arms open, welcoming all worshippers. I set down the birdcage, knelt and gazed at her face, which radiated compassion and desire. Delaunay knelt too, grave and respectful, while Alcuin's expression was rapt.

When the priest emerged, attended by four acolytes—ours among them—he was tall and slender, handsome in his age, with fine lines engraving his face and silver hair bound in a long braid. He indicated that we should stand.

"Is it your wish to be dedicated to the service of Naamah?" he asked me, his voice solemn.

"It is."

Beckoning me forward, he pushed back his scarlet sleeves. One acolyte held a basin of water, and the priest dipped an aspergillum into the bowl and sprinkled a few drops over me. "By Naamah's sacred river, I baptise you into her service." Taking a honey-cake from another, he broke it open and placed a portion on my tongue. "May your flesh be bound unto the sweetness of desire," he said. I chewed and swallowed, tasting honey. The green-eyed acolyte handed him a chalice, which he held to my lips. "May your blood rise to the headiness of passion." The last acolyte held up a measure of oil, and the priest dipped his fingers into it. Smearing chrism on my brow, he held my eyes. "May your soul ever find grace in the service of Naamah," he intoned softly.

I could feel his fingertip cool on my skin beneath the oil, and the power vested in him. Naamah's face, transcendent and sensuous, swam before my eyes. I closed them and felt the air of the temple beating about me, filled with light and wings and celestial magics. All the stories of Naamah I had heard, told in all the Thirteen Houses; all of them were true, and none. She was all of that and more.

"So mote it be," said the priest, and I opened my eyes. He and the acolytes had withdrawn. He nodded at me. "You may offer your service, my child."

Alcuin held the birdcage for me. I opened it carefully and caught the dove in both hands, removing her. Whiter than snow, she weighed almost nothing in my hands, but I could feel the warm life pulsing in her, the fast, frightened heartbeat. Her feathers were soft and, when she stirred, I feared the gentle pressure of my hands would break fragile bones. Turning back to the altar, I knelt once more and held the dove up to the statue of Naamah.

"Blessed Naamah, I beg you to accept my service," I said, whispering without knowing why. I opened my hands.

Startled into freedom, the dove launched itself into the air, pinions churning in the sunlight. Certain and unerring, she flew up to the apex of the dome, circling once, then spiraling in a flurry of sun-edged white feathers out the oculus, into flight and the open skies. The priest tracked her progress with a smile.

"Welcome," he said, bending to aid me to my feet and giving me the kiss of greeting. His eyes, tranquil with peace and the wisdom of a thousand trysts, looked kindly at me. "Welcome, Servant of Naamah."

Thus was I dedicated to the life unto which I was born.

In the following week, my training began.

Delaunay had held off on initiating Alcuin into the training proper to a Servant of Naamah; waiting so that we might begin together, being so close in age. Our training, it seemed, was to commence simultaneously.

"I have arranged for a Showing," he said evenly, having summoned us to attend him. "It is not proper that you should study the mysteries of Naamah without one. Edmonde Noualt, the Dowayne of Camellia House, has honored my request."

It was so like Delaunay, his subtle tact, to make arrangements with a House to which I had no ties, to avoid evoking memories of my childhood in the Night Court. I didn't bother to tell him I wouldn't have minded. It would have spoiled the gift of his kindness.

While there are a myriad variations of pairings and pleasures, the Showing staged for a newly dedicated Servant of Naamah is always the traditional pairing; one man, one woman. Guy drove us to Camellia House that evening. I was surprised to find it even more punctilious than Cereus, though I shouldn't have been; the canon of Camellia is perfection, and they adhere to it in strict detail.

We were met at the door by the Dowayne's Second, a stunning, tall woman with a long fall of black hair and skin the color of new ivory. She greeted us gracefully, and if there was envy or curiosity in the way her gaze lingered on Alcuin's unlikely beauty or the unexpected scarlet mote in my eye, it was well disguised.

"Come," she said, beckoning us. "As you have been dedicated to the service of Naamah, come witness her mysteries enacted."

The Showing Chamber was much like the one at Cereus House, a three-quarter round sunken stage strewn with cushions and encircled with tiers of well-padded benchs. There was a gauze curtain drawn about the stage, lit from within, and I could make out behind it the velvet hangings concealing the entrance.

It is a rule of all the Thirteen Houses that any ritual Showing be open to all adepts of the House, so I was not surprised when others entered. A private titillation is another matter, but the rites of Naamah are open to all her servants. I fell into habit without a trace of forethought, kneeling on the cushions in the prescribed position; *abeyante*, head bowed, hands clasped before me. It was strangely comforting, although I sensed Alcuin's sidelong glance as he attempted to mimic my pose.

Somewhere in the background, a flautist began to play.

On the commencement of the second musical passage, the velvet hangings rustled, and the Pair entered. He was tall and black-haired, a veritable twin—he was indeed her brother—to the Second of Camellia House. She stood a handsbreadth shorter than he, even paler of skin, with hair like an autumn tumbrel. There is no canon save perfection in this House. When they faced each other and reached out to perform the disrobement, it was evident, even through veils of gauze, that both amply met the standards of their canon.

Their joining was like a dance.

He touched her with reverence, fingertips resting at the sides of her waist, drawing them up in a delicate caress and lifting the glorious weight of her hair, letting it flow over his hands and fall back in a shining mass. His hands caressed her face, tracing the feathery arch of her brows, the perfect line of her lips. She cupped the angle of his jaw, drew a line down the muscular column of his throat and flattened her palm against the pale planes of his breast.

The gifts of Naamah are born in the blood and belong to all of us by right; but one need not be an artist to enjoy art. These were adepts of the Night Court, and this was their art. As the arousement proceeded, the gauze veils were drawn back slowly, one by one. I watched raptly, and my breath came quickly, when I did not hold it in suspense. They embraced and kissed; he held her face in his hands as if it were a precious object, and she swayed like a willow into his kiss.

This is how we pray, who are Servants of Naamah.

Breaking the kiss, she knelt before him and flung her hair forward so it cascaded about his loins, silken tendrils twining about his erect phallus. I could not see how her mouth moved as she performed the *languisement* upon him, but his face grew tranquil with pleasure and I could see the muscles grow taut in his buttocks. Reaching behind his head with both hands, he undid his braid and shook out his hair, which fell in a black river of silk over his shoulders.

There was no sound from those assembled, only a reverent silence drawn tight by the sweet notes of the flautist. He drew away to kneel opposite her, and she reclined slowly on the cushions, opening her legs to him to share her wealth. Now it was his hair that hid them from my sight, spread like a black curtain across her thighs as he parted her cleft with his tongue, seeking the pearl of Naamah hidden in her folds.

It must be that he found it, for she arched with pleasure, reaching up to draw him to her. He held himself above her, the tip of his phallus poised at her entrance. His hair spilled down around his bowed head and mingled with hers, black and russet. I had never seen anything so beautiful as their lovemaking. The flautist paused; someone cried out, and he entered her in one fluid surge, sheathing himself to the hilt. A soft, whispering drumbeat entered the song as he thrust, her body rising to receive him.

Still kneeling, hands clasped tight together, I found myself weeping at the beauty of it. They were like birds, who mate on the wing. It was a ritual, and no mere spectacle; I could taste the worship and desire of it, flooding my mouth like the priest's honey. He surged against her like waves breaking, and she met him like the rising tide. Their pace increased and the music rose to a crescendo, until she gasped, hands clenching against the working muscles of his back, her legs wrapped around him. He arched back then and held hard. I could feel the heat rising between my own thighs as they met their climax together.

And then, too soon, the gauze curtains began slowly to close, veiling their figures in the soft aftermath of desire. I saw him move to her side, and their hands clasped as they lay entwined upon the cushions. At my own side, Alcuin released a long-held breath and we looked soberly at one another.

Presently an adept came to lead us to a sitting room, where we were served a restorative cordial and attended by the Second of Camellia House, who graciously expressed her hopes that the Showing had been well received and that we would communicate our good impressions to our master Anafiel Delaunay, who still held the power to set trends in the royal court. If she resented or despised us for enjoying his patronage, I could not tell it.

TEN

With good reason, I supposed that after the Showing we would begin our formal training in the arts of Naamah. And so we were; but not at all as I had imagined.

Delaunay contracted an instructor, the finest instructor one could have in the arts, to be sure. What I hadn't reckoned on was the fact that she was well into her fifties, and all our learning took place in the classroom and not the bedchamber.

In her prime, Cecilie Laveau-Perrin had been an adept of Cereus House; indeed, she had trained under my old mistress, the Dowayne. She was one of the few who had attained the pinnacle of success for a member of the Night Court, attracting sufficient following among peers of the realm that she was able to set up her own household upon making her marque. For seven years, she was the toast of royalty. Peers and poets flocked to her gatherings, and she held her own court, bestowing the favor of her bedchamber at her own choosing; or not at all.

Ultimately, she chose to wed and retired from the haute demimonde. Her choice fell upon Antoine Perrin, Chevalier of the Order of the Swan, a calm and steadfast man who had left his country estates to serve as a military consultant to the King. They lived quietly, entertaining seldom and on a wholly intellectual level. After his untimely death, she maintained this lifestyle. Delaunay, it seemed, was one of few people who knew her from both worlds.

I knew all of this because I eavesdropped upon their meeting when she agreed to take on our instruction. It is not a noble undertaking, but I felt no guilt at it. It was what I was trained to do. Delaunay had taught us: garner knowledge, by any means possible. There was a storeroom off the courtyard where herbs from the garden were hung to dry. If one were small enough, there was space between a cabinet and an open window where one could crouch and overhear almost any conversation taking place in the courtyard. And when the pleasantries were done, Delaunay made his request.

Her voice had retained all its charm, even and mellifluous. I could still hear in it the faint cadences of Cereus

House—the attentive pauses, a merest hint of breathiness—but I doubt it would have been evident to an untrained ear. Years of reserve had tempered it.

"What you ask is impossible, Anafiel." I heard a rustle; she shook her head. "You know I have been long retired from the service of Naamah."

"Do you take your pledge so lightly?" His voice countered hers smoothly. "I do not ask you to offer carnal instruction, Cecilie; merely to teach. All the great texts . . . the *Ecstatica*, the *Journey of Naamah*, the *Trois Milles Joies* . . ."

"Would you have me teach the boy 'Antinous's Ode to His Beloved?' " Her voice was light, but I heard for the first time steel in it.

"No!" Delaunay's reply was explosive. When he spoke again, I could tell it was from a different location. He had risen, then, pacing. His voice was under control now and his tone was dry. "To speak that poem aloud is proscibed, Cecilie. You know better than that."

"Yes." She offered the word simply, with no apology. "Why are you doing this?"

"You have to ask, who was the greatest courtesan of our age?" He was too charming; it was not often I heard Delaunay being evasive.

She would have none of it. "That's not what I meant."

"Why. Why, why, why." His voice was moving, he was pacing again. "Why? I will tell you. Because there are places I cannot go and people I cannot reach, Cecilie. In the Court of Chancery, the Exchequer, secretaries with access to the Privy Seal . . . everywhere the actual business of governing the realm takes place, Isabel's allies bar their doors to me. They cannot be swayed, Cecilie, but they can be seduced. I know their vices, I know their desires. I know how to reach them."

"That much, I know." Her tone was gentle, moderating his. "I have known you for a long time. You've taken me into your confidence, and I know how you think. What I am asking you, Anafiel, is *why*. Why do you do this?"

There was a long pause, and my muscles began to ache with the strain of crouching in that cramped space. No wind was stirring, and the close air of the storeroom was sweet and pungent with the scents of rosemary and lavender.

"You know why."

It was all he said; I bit my tongue to keep from urging her to question him further. But whatever he meant by it, she understood. She had, as she said, known him a very long time.

"Still?" she asked, kindly; and then, "Ah, but you made a promise. All right, then. I will honor it too, Anafiel, for what it is worth. I will instruct your pupils in the great texts of love—those that are not proscribed—and I will lecture them on the arts of Naamah. If you swear to me that both have entered this service of their own desire, this much I will do."

"I swear it." There was relief in his voice.

"How much do they know?"

"Enough." He grew reserved. "Enough to know what they are about. Not enough to get them killed."

"Isabel L'Envers is dead, Anafiel." She spoke softly, the way one does to a child who fears the darkness. "Do you truly think her grudge lives beyond the grave?"

"It lives in those who obeyed her," he said grimly. "Isabel L'Envers de la Courcel was my enemy, but we knew where we stood with one another. We might even have become allies, when Rolande's daughter was old enough to take the throne. Now, all is changed."

"Mmm." I heard a faint clink as the lip of the wine-jug touched the rim of a glass. "Maslin d'Aiglemort's wound turned septic; he died two days ago, did you hear? Isidore will be sworn in as Duc d'Aiglemort in a fortnight, and he's petitioned the King for another five hundred retainers."

"He'll have his hands full holding the border."

"True." The undertones of Cereus House had given way to a pensive edge in her voice. "Nonetheless, he found time to visit Namarre, and pay tribute to Melisande Shahrizai at her country house there. Now Melisande is seen in the company of Prince Baudoin, and it is said the Lioness of Azzalle is displeased."

"Melisande Shahrizai collects hearts as the royal gardener collects seedlings," Delaunay said dismissively. "Gaspar says Marc will have a word with his son, if it becomes needful."

Another soft clink; a glass being replaced on one of the low tiled tables. I had learned to discern such distinctions, even with a crick in my neck. "Perhaps. But don't underestimate either of them, the Shahrizai or the Lioness. I do not think they make that mistake with each other. And after all, the failure to understand women has been your downfall, Anafiel." I heard the swishing sound of her garments as she rose. "I will come in the morning, and the children's education will commence. Good night, my dear."

I listened to the sounds of their leaving, then squirmed out of my confinement, racing upstairs to tell Alcuin what I had learned.

And, of course, to speculate on what it all meant.

By light of day, Cecilie Laveau-Perrin was tall and slender, with fine bones and pale blue eyes, the color of a new-opened lobelia. It is a funny thing, with adepts of Cereus House, how the underlying steel is revealed in those who do not wither and fade. In this, she reminded me of the Dowayne, but she was younger, and kinder.

Still, she was a harsh taskmistress, and set us to read and memorize the first of the great texts of which Delaunay had spoken.

For Alcuin, it was a revelation. I had not understood fully, when we witnessed the Showing, the depth of his naïveté. Astonishing though it seemed to me, he had no comprehension of the mechanics of the deeds by which one offers homage to Naamah. I, who had never entered the dance, nonetheless knew the steps by heart. Alcuin had only the instincts of his gentle heart and eager flesh, such as any peasant in the field might have.

Later, I understood that this was part of his charm, as Delaunay meant it to be. The unspoiled sweetness that was ever a part of Alcuin was part and parcel of his charm, and irresistably seductive to the oversophisticated palate. But then, I did not understand. I would watch him in the evenings when we studied together, reading with lips parted and wonder suffusing his features. "The caress of winnowed chaff," he would read, murmuring. "Place your hands on the waist of your beloved, drawing them upward slowly, gathering and lifting your beloved's hair so that it floats like chaff above the threshing floor, letting it fall like soft rain. Did you know that, Phèdre?"

"Yes." I gazed into his wide, dark eyes. "They did that at the Showing. Remember?" I had known these things since I was a child, had grown up learning them. It was slowly and surely driving me mad not to practice any of them.

"I remember. The caress of the summer wind." He read the directions aloud, shaking his head in amazement. "Does that really work?"

"I'll show you." If I knew no more than he in practice, I at least had seen these things done. I led him to the floor, where we knelt, facing each other. His features were grave and uncertain. I placed my fingertips lightly on the crown of his head, barely touching his milk-white hair, then drew them slowly down; down the silken fall of his hair, over his shoulders, down his slender arms. My heartbeat quickened as I did it and a strange certainty rose in my blood. I was scarce touching him, fingertips hovering above his pale skin, but where they passed, the fine hair rose on his arms like a wheatfield stirred by the summer wind. "See?"

"Oh!" Alcuin drew back, gazing in awe at his skin, shivered into gooseflesh with subtle pleasure. "You know so much!"

"You are better than I at the things which matter to Delaunay," I said shortly. It was true. As much as I had learned, I could not match the quicksilver facility with which Alcuin observed and recorded. He could remember whole conversations and relate them in their entirety, right down to the speakers' intonations. "Alcuin." I changed my own tone, putting on the murmurous, beguiling inflections of Cereus House that I heard underlying Cecilie's voice. "We could practice, if you like. It would help us both to learn."

Alcuin shook his head with a susurrus of moonlight-colored hair, wide eyes ingenuous. "Delaunay doesn't want us to, Phèdre. You know that."

It was true; Delaunay had made it explicit, and not even the lure of gathered knowledge was enough to tempt Alcuin to disobedience. With a sigh, I returned to my books.

But of course, there was nothing to prevent me from practicing on myself.

It began that night, in the darkness of my little room, which I had all to myself. We were studying the opening caresses of arousement. Throwing off my coverlet to lie naked on my bed, I whispered their names to myself, tracing their patterns on my skin, until my blood burned beneath the touch of my fingers.

And yet I refrained from seeking the release I knew was to be gained, adhering strictly to the lessons we were allotted. I cannot say why, save that it was a torment, and as such, was sweet to me.

Older and wiser than Delaunay in the service of Naamah, Cecilie Laveau-Perrin discerned my predicament. We were reciting Emmeline of Eisande's *Log of Seven Hundred Kisses* (most of which I was unable to practice by myself) when I felt her shrewd gaze resting upon me and faltered.

"You are impatient with these studies, no?" she asked me.

"No, my lady." Long trained to obedience, my reply was automatic. I raised my eyes to meet her gaze and swallowed. "My lady, I was raised in the Night Court. Had I been allowed to stay, my training would have begun a year gone by. Even now, I might be saving toward my marque; perhaps even paying the marquist to limn the base, if my virgin-price were high enough. Yes, I am impatient."

"So it is money that is the spur which goads you, hmm?" She stroked my hair, smiling a little.

"No." I admitted it softly, leaning into her touch.

"It is Kushiel's Dart which pricks you, then." She waited until I looked up again, nodding, not a little surprised. She had never spoken of it, and no one in Cereus House had known me for what I was. Cecilie laughed. "Anafiel Delaunay is not the only scholar in the world, my sweet, and I have done a fair amount of reading since I left the Court of Night-Blooming Flowers. Never fear, I'll keep Anafiel's secret until he's ready to reveal you. But until that time, there is naught you can do but suffer the torments of your own devising."

A flush of embarrassment suffused my skin.

"There is no fulfillment that is not made sweeter for the prolonging of desire." She patted my burning cheek. "If you wish to improve your skills, use a mirror and a candle, that you may see what you're about and study the lineaments of desire."

That night, I did. By candlelight, I traced the patterns of arousal upon my skin, watching it change and flush, and thought about the fact that Cecilie knew, and Alcuin, and wondered in a delicious frisson of guilt and shame if either had told Delaunay what I did in secret.

So did my education continue.

ELEVEN

In the two years that followed, we did nothing but study until I thought I should die of it.

And to make matters worse, Hyacinthe, my one true friend, was no help at all.

"I cannot touch you, Phèdre," he said with regret, shaking his black ringlets. We sat in the Cockerel, an inn which he had made his informal headquarters. "Not in that way. I am Tsingano, and you're an indentured servant. It is *vrajna*, forbidden, according to the laws of my people."

I opened my mouth to reply, but before I could speak, a giggling young noblewoman detached herself from a party of revelers occupying the long table at the center of the inn. It was the fashion among daring young lords and ladies to gallivant about Night's Doorstep in groups of seven or eight, hoisting tankards and rubbing elbows with poets, players and commoners.

Hyacinthe had become something of a fashion too.

"O Prince of Travellers," she began solemnly, then giggled and cast a glance at her laughing friends, getting the rest of the words out with difficulty. "O . . . O Prince of Travellers, if I cross your . . . your palm with gold, will you read the fortune writ in mine?"

At the gleam of a gold coin, Hyacinthe—who had never to my knowledge ventured past Night's Doorstep—put on his best Prince of Travellers manner, rising to give her a graceful bow, his dark eyes mirthful.

"Star of the Evening," he said, at once wheedling and portentious, "I am at your command. For one coin, one answer, as scribed by the Fates upon your fair palm. What would you know, gracious lady?"

Deliberately ignoring me, she arranged her skirts and sat, rather closer to Hyacinthe than was necessary. She gave him her hand with the air of someone bestowing great favor, then whispered, "I wish to know if Rene LaSoeur will take me to wife."

"Hmm." Hyacinthe gazed intently at her palm. She stared at his bowed head. I could see the rapid, shallow breaths she took heaving her bosom, upon which she sported a daringly low decolletage beneath a daringly costly filigree necklace. Across the inn, her friends clustered and watched. The young lords surrounded one of their number, jabbing him with pointed elbows and laughing. He bore it with crossed arms, and a hint of displeasure flared his nostrils. One of the young noblewomen smiled, secretive and self-possessed. It needed no touch of *dromonde* to answer her question; but Hyacinthe answered without looking, shaking his head. "Fair lady, the answer is no. Nuptials I see, not now, but three years hence, and a chateau with three towers standing, and one that crumbles."

"The Comte de Tour Perdue!" Snatching her hand back, she covered her mouth. Her eyes shone. "Oh, oh!"

She reached out then and laid her fingers on his lips. "Oh, my mother will be joyed to hear it. You must tell no one of this. Swear it!"

Quick and graceful, Hyacinthe grasped her silencing fingers in his own and kissed them. "Sovereign lady, I am more discreet than the dead. May you be joyous and prosper."

Fumbling in the purse that hung from her girdle, she passed him another coin. "Thank you, oh, thank you! Remember, not a word!"

He rose to bow again as she hurried back to join her friends, babbling some heady nonsense to disguise her sudden fortune. Hyacinthe sat back down and made her coins disappear, looking pleased with himself.

"Was it true?" I asked him.

"Who knows?" He shrugged. "I saw what I saw. There is more than one chateau with a broken tower. She believes as she wishes."

It was no concern of mine if Hyacinthe sold dreams and half-truths to preening peers, but something else did concern me. "You know, Delaunay has a scroll, by a scholar who travelled with a company of Tsingani and documented their customs. He says it is *vrajna* for a Tsingano man to attempt the *dromonde*, Hyacinthe; worse than anything, worse than mingling with a *gadje* servant. What your mother teaches you is forbidden. And you cannot be a true Tsingano anyway, not with pure D'Angeline blood on one side. Your mother was cast out of the company for that, wasn't she?"

I spoke recklessly, driven to it by my thwarted desires and the annoyance of watching him cater to simpering noblewomen. This time, perhaps, I had gone too far. His eyes flashed, proud and angry.

"You speak where you have no knowledge and no right! My mother is a Princess of the Tsingani, and the gift of *dromonde* is mine by right of blood! What would your Delaunay's *gadje* scholar know of that?"

"Enough to know that Tsingani princesses do not take in washing for a living!" I shot back.

Unexpectedly, Hyacinthe laughed. "If he thinks that, then truly, he learned little of the Tsingani. We have survived many centuries in any way we could. Anyway, I earn enough money now that she no longer need wash the clothes of others." He looked soberly at me, shrugging. "Maybe it is a little bit true, what you say. I do not know. When I am old enough, I will seek out my mother's people. But until then, I must trust her words. I know enough of her gift to know I dare not defy it."

"Or you're afraid of Delaunay," I grumbled.

"I am afraid of no one!" He looked so like the boy I had first known, puffing out his slender chest, that I too laughed, and our quarrel was forgotten.

"Hey, Tsingano!"

It was one of the young lordlings, drunk and arrogant. He swaggered up to our table, one hand hovering over the hilt of his rapier. He had cruel eyes, and fine clothes. With a negligent gesture, he tossed his purse on the table. It fell with a heavy clinking sound. "How much for a night with your sister?"

I don't know what either of us would have answered. I was accustomed to venturing into Night's Doorstep well-cloaked, and we sat always in one of the darker corners, away from the hearth; Hyacinthe was known and tolerated with no small affection, and the inn-keep and regular patrons permitted him the small mystery of my visits without prying into my presence.

All these things I thought at a flash, and on their heels came pleasure and pride that this lordling's gaze had penetrated the shadows and come to rest on me with desire. And hard upon that thought came a swell of excitement, at the very prospect of selling myself from under Delaunay's nose and going with this stranger, whose blade-ready hands and careless offer promised the kind of hard usage I craved.

In the space of a breath, I thought these things and saw Hyacinthe eyeing the heavy purse.

And then Delaunay's man Guy was there.

"You cannot afford her virgin-price, my friend." His seldom-used voice was as mild as ever, but the point of his poniard rested below the lordling's chin and I caught glimpse of a second dagger poised at belly level. I had not even seen him enter the inn. The lordling stood with upraised chin and glaring eyes, pricked by steel into humiliating attentiveness. "Go now, and rejoin your companions."

The calm voice and cold steel were more convincing than brawn and volume could ever have been. I watched the lordling swallow, all arrogance leaving him. He turned without a word and retraced his steps. Guy sheathed his dagger without comment.

"We will leave now," he said to me, pulling up the hood of my cloak and fastening it under my chin. I went obediently, able to spare only a quick wave of farewell in Hyacinthe's direction as Guy shepherded me out of the crowded inn. Hyacinthe, who was used from our earliest acquaintance to abrupt and forceful departures on my part, took it with aplomb.

For me, it was a long coach ride home. I huddled silent in my cloak, until finally Guy began to speak. "It is not always for us to choose." It was dark in the carriage, and I could not see his face, only hear his flat voice. "My parents gave me to be reared by the Cassiline Brotherhood when I was but a babe, Phèdre; and the Brotherhood cast me out when I was fourteen and broke my oath with a farmer's daughter. I made my way to the City and fell into a life of crime. Though I was good at it, I despised myself, and wished to die. One day when I thought I could fall no lower, I took a commission from an agent of someone very powerful to assassinate a nobleman on his way home from a party."

"*Delaunay?*" I gasped, astonished. Guy ignored the interruption.

"I resolved to succeed or die, but the nobleman disarmed me. I waited for the killing blow, but he asked me instead, 'My friend, you fight like one trained by the Cassiline Brotherhood; how is it then that you come to be engaged in this least fraternal of acts?' And upon his query, I began to weep."

I waited for more, but Guy fell silent a long while. There was no sound but the clopping hooves of the horses and the coachman's tuneless whistle.

"We do not choose our debts," he said at length. "But indebted we are, both of us, to Anafiel Delaunay. Do not seek to betray him. Your debt may be discharged one day, but mine is unto the death, Phèdre."

The night was chilly and his words struck cold into my bones. I shivered in my thick cloak and thought about what he had said, wondering at the power in Delaunay to reach even a heart hardened by crime and despair.

But if Guy was Delaunay's man unto death, he was not what I was: his pupil. The words of his speech—the most he'd ever spoken in my presence—fell into place in the vast puzzle in my mind, forming one important question.

"Who wanted Delaunay dead?"

In the darkness of the coach, I could feel him glance at me. "Isabel de la Courcel," came the flat reply. "The Princess Consort."

The incident remained in my mind for it was the first

of its kind, and the last, for that matter. In all the time I knew him, Guy never spoke again of his history nor our mutual debt to Delaunay. And yet his words had the effect he desired, for never did I attempt to betray my bond-debt.

Delaunay's past and his long-standing enmity with the Princess Consort remained the central enigma in my life. For all that she was some seven years in the grave, as I well knew, their feud lived on where it touched on the strands of intelligence Delaunay gathered. To what end, I knew not, and spent long hours in fruitless speculation with Hyacinthe and Alcuin alike; for Alcuin was as fascinated as I with the mystery of Anafiel Delaunay, if not more so.

Indeed, as Alcuin grew from boy to youth, steeped in the teaching of Cecilie Laveau-Perrin, I witnessed the nature of his regard for Delaunay change. The spontaneous affection that had been so charming in him as a child gave way to a different kind of adoration, at once tender and cunning.

I envied him the luxury of this slow epiphany, and knew alarm at Delaunay's response, a careful distancing that spoke volumes. I don't think even Delaunay himself was aware of it; but I was.

It was some few weeks prior to Alcuin's sixteenth birthday that the Allies of Camlach won a great victory over Skaldic raiders. Led by the young Duc Isidore d'Aiglemort, the peerage of Camlach joined forces and succeeded in pushing the Skaldi clear back from the mountains and well into their own territory.

And at their side rode Prince Baudoin de Trevalion and his Glory-Seekers.

The Duc d'Aiglemort, it seemed, had received intelligence that the Skaldi were prepared to launch a concerted attack on the three Great Passes of the Camaeline Range. No one denied his wisdom in calling Camlach to arms under his banner . . . but at Delaunay's gatherings and in the dark corners of Night's Doorstep, I heard whispers about the happy coincidence that had Baudoin de Trevalion and the wild brigade of his personal guard visiting Aiglemort at the time.

Still, it was a great victory, the greatest gain of territory since the Battle of the Three Princes, and the King would have been a fool to have denied Camlach a royal triumph . . . or to have failed to acknowledge Prince Baudoin's part in the battle. One thing Ganelon de la Courcel was not was a fool.

As it happened, the triumph fell upon the eve of Alcuin's birthday and the processional route fell along the way of Cecilie's townhouse. Taking the convergence for an omen, she threw a fête and threw her house open, almost as in days of old.

Only this time, we were all invited.

*T*WELVE

I have never known Delaunay to fuss over his appearance—though he always looked the height of elegance—but the day of the triumph, he stewed over his attire like an adept with a prospective lover, settling at length upon a doublet and hosen of sober black velvet against which his braided hair lay like a twist of auburn flame.

"Why is it so important, my lord?" I asked, adjusting the pomander that hung from his belt. Delaunay had his own valet, of course, but on special occasions he allowed me to oversee the details. One did not grow up in Cereus House without acquiring a keen eye and nimble fingers for such niceties.

"For Cecilie, of course." He gave me his broad grin, always unexpected and thrilling. "She's not held a gathering such as this since before Antoine died. I've no wish to embarrass her."

He had loved her, then; I'd suspected it had been so in the old days. Delaunay had had mistresses aplenty in the five years I'd been in his household, that was nothing new. Many a time I had heard them after the other guests had gone; Delaunay's low voice, and the thrill of a woman's laughter. I felt no threat from them. In the end, they left, while I stayed.

Alcuin was another matter, of course, but this . . . this touched me, in truth, his devotion to a mistress who had long ago been one of the brightest blossoms in the Court of Night-Blooming Flowers. My eyes pricked with moisture, and I inhaled of the pomander with its sweet-sharp scent of beeswax and cloves to hide it, pressing my cheek to his velveted knee.

"Phèdre." Delaunay's hands drew me to my feet and I blinked up at him. "You will be a credit to my house, as ever. But remember this is Alcuin's debut, and be gracious." He broke out his infectious smile. "Come, then; shall we summon him for inspection?"

"Yes, my lord," I murmured, doing my best to sound gracious.

I would have guessed, if asked, that Delaunay would have attired Alcuin like a prince. I would have been wrong. It was ever easy to underrate his subtlety. We were gathering to watch a royal triumph; Cecilie's guests would see nobles by the score, decked out in their finest trumpery. If Alcuin looked anything close to royalty, it was as the King's stableboy.

So I thought at first glance.

Upon second glance, I saw that his white shirt was not canvas but cambric, the linen spun so fine one could barely see the weave, and what I had taken for buckram hose were breeches of moleskin. His knee-high boots were black leather, shined until they gave back reflections.

His remarkable hair simply hung loose, brushed into a shining river of ivory. It spilled over his shoulders and down his back, accenting a face that had emerged from adolescence with all its grave, shy beauty intact, from which Alcuin viewed the world out of dark and solemn eyes. Delaunay was a genius. Somehow the rustic garb— or elegant replication of it—served to point up all the more Alcuin's otherworldly charm.

"Very nice," Delaunay said. I heard satisfaction and maybe something else in his voice.

Be gracious, I thought to myself; after all, he is allowing you to attend. "You look beautiful," I told Alcuin sincerely; he did.

"So do you!" He grasped my hands, smiling, not a trace of envy in him. "Oh, Phèdre . . ."

I drew back a little, returning his smile with a shake of my head. "It is your night tonight, Alcuin. Mine will come."

"Soon, or you'll drive us to distraction," Delaunay said humorously. "Come on, then. The coach is waiting."

The house of Cecilie Laveau-Perrin was larger than Delaunay's, and closer to the Palace. We were met at the door by a liveried footman, who escorted us up a broad, winding staircase. The whole of the third story was designed for entertaining; an open plan with high ceilings, containing a long table set with silver and white linen, a parlour that combined comfort and elegance, giving way to the parquet floor of the ballroom. Arched doors opened from the dance floor onto the balcony, which overlooked the route of the triumph. A quartet played a stately air on a dais in the corner, largely ignored. Despite the chill, for it was still winter, those guests who had already arrived were clustered on the balcony.

"Anafiel!" With the unerring instincts that had given renown to her hospitality, Cecilie marked the precise moment of our arrival and swept through the doors to greet us. "How good to see you."

For all the hours I had spent under her tutelage, it was only then that I discerned the magnitude of her allure. Not all adepts of the Night Court weather the passing of youth with grace; Cecilie had succeeded. If her golden hair was dimmed with grey, it but made more youthful hues seem garish, and the fine lines about her eyes were the marks of care and wisdom.

"You are a vision," Delaunay said fondly.

She laughed, free and charming. "You still lie like a poet, Anafiel. Come, Alcuin, let me see you." With a critical eye, she adjusted his collar, letting it fall open to reveal the tender hollow at the base of his throat. "There." She patted his cheek. "The triumph has just left the Palace, there's time yet to meet my guests. You know you've only to say, if you've no wish to go through with this?"

"I know." Alcuin gave her his most serene smile.

"Good, then. You need only whisper it to me, or shake your head." She turned to me. "Phèdre . . ." With a shake of her own head, she set her diamond earrings to trembling, scintillating in the light. "Beware of setting brush-fires, my dear."

I murmured some acquiesence, thinking it an odd comment, but fully half my attention was already on the balcony, where in moments I would meet, at last, men and women who might soon number among my own patrons. I might not shine as Alcuin did this day—Delaunay had chosen for my attire an exceedingly simple gown of dark-brown velvet with a caul of silk mesh that held my abundant locks in restraint—but I had no mind to be overlooked, either.

Our entrance created a small stir. The guests were hand-picked by Cecilie, who moved in circles that overlapped, but did not overlay, Delaunay's. Some of them, such as Gaspar Trevalion, Comte de Fourcay, were friends of his.

Others were not.

I watched their faces when we were announced and saw who smiled, whose gazes slid away to make contact with others, communicating silently. These were the ones, ultimately, to be sought. Anyone with sufficient coin could pay the contract fee and put money toward my marque, but money was never what Delaunay sought. We were an investment of a different kind.

It was not long before I saw why Delaunay had allowed me to come. Alcuin moved among the scions of Elua like a stableboy-prince, drawing stares, and where he went, I heard the whisper of rumor follow. ". . . Servant of Naamah . . ." and ". . . eve of his birthday . . ." Delaunay and Cecilie had something planned; of that I had no doubt, nor did the guests. But while Delaunay mingled, conversing smoothly, and Alcuin found himself at the center of attention covert and overt alike, I was able to remain quiet on the fringes, watching and listening.

"Anafiel Delaunay sets his traps with interesting bait."

The amused comment of a tall man with dark hair in a tight braid and the hooded eyes of a bird of prey caught my ear. Lord Childric d'Essoms, I remembered, of the Court of Chancery. He spoke to a slight man in dark blue, whose name I had not heard.

"You are intrigued?" His companion raised his eyebrows. D'Essoms laughed, shaking his sleek head.

"My taste is for spices, and not sweets. But it is interesting to note, no?"

Yes, I thought, filing the comment away in my memory as Delaunay had taught me. It is interesting to note your interest, my lord, and your tastes as well.

The two men parted and I followed the smaller, straining to overhear as a tall woman with an elaborate headdress greeted him by name, but just then the trumpets sounded and someone cried out that the triumph was approaching. Everyone crowded to the edge of the balcony. I had lost sight of Delaunay and Cecilie, and was trapped behind the press of bodies. For a moment it seemed that my view of the royal triumph would consist of the brocaded and silk-swathed backsides of Cecilie's guests; then a portly gentleman with a grey beard and a gentle smile took note, and made room for me at the parapet. Thanking him, I gripped the stone and leaned over to see.

Every terrace along the route was crowded with people, and there were crowds lining the street. The triumph approached at a distance, shining under the weak winter sun, announced by the brazen call of trumpets. A detachment of the Palace Guard rode ahead, pressing the spectators back against the buildings. Behind them came the standard-bearer, riding alone. We were near enough that I could make out faces, and his was young, stern and handsome. He gripped the haft firmly, and the standard snapped in the air below us, a golden lily on a field of rich green surrounded by seven golden stars: the sign of Blessed Elua and his Companions, emblem of Terre d'Ange.

After the standard-bearer came another row of guards, and then Ganelon de la Courcel, scion of Elua, King of Terre d'Ange.

I had known the King was elderly, but still it surprised

me to see it. Though his carriage in the saddle was straight and tall, his hair and beard were almost completely white and his fierce eyes were set in hollows, partially overhung by grizzled white brows. At his side rode Ysandre de la Courcel, his granddaughter, Dauphine and heir to the throne of Terre d'Ange.

If this were an allegory play, they might have represented the Old Winter and New Spring, for Ysandre de la Courcel was as fresh and beautiful as the first day of spring. She rode sidesaddle on her dappled courser, clad in a gown the color of the first shoots of the crocus to poke through the cold earth, with a cloak of royal purple over it. A simple gold fillet bound her flowing hair, which was of the palest blonde, and her face was youthful and fair.

On the street, D'Angelines hailed her with affectionate cries, but on the balcony, I detected a murmurous undertone. Ysandre de la Courcel was young, beloved and beautiful, heir to a kingdom; and notably unwed, neither betrothed nor promised. Though her face betrayed nothing, she had to be aware of the undertone, I thought, watching from above. Surely it must follow her everywhere she went. The emblem of de la Courcel, the House Royal, flew beside them; lower than the flag of Terre d'Ange, but preceeding all others, as was custom. A silver swan on a field of midnight blue, the small party gathered beneath it made it look somehow forlorn. Ganelon de la Courcel's line ended with Ysandre. His only son was dead, and his only brother, Prince Benedicte, had wed into the ruling Caerdicci family in La Serenissima to a woman who gave him only daughters.

All these things, of course, I knew; yet somehow seeing it made it so. On that balcony, surrounded by murmurs, I watched the elderly King and the young Dauphine—no older than I myself—and I felt around me the eddies of hunger centered on a precariously held throne.

And behind the King rode his sister and her husband, the Princess Lyonette and her Duc, Marc de Trevalion. The Lioness of Azzalle looked indulgently pleased; the Duc's face was unreadable. Three ships and the Navigators' Star flew on their standard, and under these arms too rode their impetuous son. I could hear the chant rising up from the street as they passed; "Bau-doin! Baudoin!"

He was little changed from the young lord who had stolen the role of the Sun Prince five years past. A little older, perhaps; in the prime of his youth, rather than entering the threshold, but the wild gleam in his sea-grey eyes was the same. A chosen cadre of Glory-Seekers, the personal guard to which he was entitled as a Prince of the Blood, surrounded him loosely. They took up the chant too, shouting his name, raising their swords to catch the light.

And at his side, composed and serene, rode Melisande Shahrizai, Baudoin's delight, and the single thorn in the side of the Lionesse of Azzalle. Her raven hair fell in ripples, gleaming like black water in moonlight, and her beauty made the young Dauphine who preceded them look pallid and unfinished. It was only the second time I had seen her, but even at a distance, I shuddered.

"Well, that's clear enough," murmured the portly gentleman who had made room for me. His voice held a faint accent. I wanted to turn to look at his face, but I was pressed too tight against the stone parapet to do it with any subtlety.

A lone rider followed the company of House Trevalion bearing the standard of the Province of Camlach, a blazing sword on a sable field. It had a sobering effect on the gathered crowds, reminding us all that battle was the cause of the day.

"If d'Aiglemort had asked them to ride under his banner," a woman's voice said softly somewhere near me, "they would have acknowledged his right."

"Do you say he's politic enough to be dangerous?" The man who answered her sounded amused. "The scions of Camael think with their swords."

"Give thanks to Blessed Elua that they do," someone else said sharply. "For I've no wish to become part of Skaldi tribal holdings."

The Allies of Camlach made an impressive array, and whatever rights he may have ceded, the young Duc d'Aiglemort rode square in their midst. I counted the banners, putting faces to the names Delaunay had made me memorize. Ferraut, Montchapetre, Valliers, Basilisque; all the great holdings of Camlach. Hardened warriors, most of them, lean and keen-eyed. Isidore d'Aiglemort stood out among them, glittering like the silver eagle on his standard. His eyes were dark and merciless, and as his gaze swept over the crowds, I remembered where I had seen them. He had been the man in the jaguarondi mask at the Midwinter fête.

"He would be interesting to put to the test," another woman mused languidly.

"So would a mountain lion," one of the men who had spoken before answered tartly, "but I don't recommend taking one to bed!" I ignored the ensuing laughter, watching the Allies of Camlach pass. Even represented by a symbolic few—the bulk of their forces remained in Camlach securing the regained border—they made for a powerful assemblage. Azzalle and Camlach bracketed the realm to the west and east. The popular acclaim accorded Baudoin de Trevalion in combination with the might represented by the Allies of Camlach sent a message that was, indeed, frightening in its lack of subtlety.

After the Camlach host came the train of spoils, loot seized in battle. Arms aplenty were displayed, and I shivered at the massive battle-axes. The Skaldi are mighty poets—I know, having studied their tongue long enough—but their songs are all of blood and iron. And those whom they defeat, they enslave. We D'Angelines are civilized. Even one sold into debt-bondage, as I was, has the eventual hope of purchasing freedom.

At length the baggage train too passed, and Cecilie's guests began to move back into the house. I turned about to see the smiling face of the bearded man behind me. His features were distinctly un-D'Angeline. Recalling the trace of an accent, I marked him as Aragonian.

"You are of the household of Anafiel Delaunay, I think. Did you enjoy the parade?" he asked me kindly.

"Yes, my lord." I had no idea of his status, but the response was automatic. He laughed.

"I am Gonzago de Escabares, and no lord, but a sometime historian. Come, give me your name, and let us go inside together."

"Phèdre," I told him.

"Ah." He clucked his tongue and held out his arm. "An unlucky name, child. I will be your friend, then, for the ancient Hellenes said a good friend may stand between a man and his *moira*. Do you know what that means?"

"Fate." I answered unthinking, for Delaunay had specified that neither Alcuin nor I were to betray the extent of our learning without his approval. But a connection had formed in my mind, the linkage surfacing. "You were one of his teachers, at the University in Tiberium."

"Indeed." He made me a courtly little bow, with a click of his heels. "I have since retired, and travel at leisure to see the places of which I so long have spoken.

But I had the privilege of teaching your . . . your Delaunay, he and his . . ."

"Maestro!" Delaunay's voice, ringing with unalloyed pleasure, interrupted us as we entered the ballroom. He crossed the floor in great strides, beaming, embracing the older man with great affection. "Cecilie didn't tell me you would be here."

Gonzago de Escabares wheezed at his embrace, thumping Delaunay's back. "Ah, Anafiel my boy, I am old, and allow myself one luxury. Where the crux of history turns, I may be there to watch it grind. If it turns in Terre d'Ange, so much the better, where I may surround my aging form with such beauty." He patted Delaunay on the cheek, smiling. "You have lost none of yours, young Antinous."

"You flatter me, Maestro." Delaunay took de Escabares' hands in his, but there was a reserved quality to his smile. "I must remind you, though . . ."

"Ah!" The Aragonian professor's expression changed, growing sharper and sadder. "Yes, of course, forgive me. But it is good to see you, Anafiel. Very good."

"It is." Delaunay smiled again, meaning it. "May we speak, later? There is someone I wish Phèdre to meet."

"Of course, of course." He patted my shoulder with the same indulgent affection. "Go, child, and enjoy yourself. This is no time to waste on aging pedants."

Delaunay laughed and shook his head, leading me away.

Silently, I cursed his timing, but aloud, I merely asked, "He taught you at the University?"

"The Tiberians collect scholars the way they used to amass empires," Delaunay said absently. "Maestro Gonzago was one of the best."

Yes, my lord, I thought, and he called you Anafiel, and Antinous, which is a name from the title of a poem which is proscribed, but he stumbled once over the name Delaunay, which Hyacinthe says is not truly yours, and he might have told me a great deal more had you not intervened, so while I do as you say, be mindful that I do also as you have taught.

But these things I kept silent, and followed obediently as he turned in a way that caused me to bump into a blonde woman with aquiline features, who turned about with a sharp exclamation.

"Phèdre!" Delaunay's voice held a chastising note. "Solaine, I am sorry. This is Phèdre's first such gathering. Phèdre, this is the Marquise Solaine Belfours, to whom you will apologize."

"You might let the girl speak for herself, Delaunay." Her voice held irritation; Solaine Belfours had no great love for Delaunay, and I marked it well, even as I cast an annoyed glance at him for placing me in this position. The collision was of his manufacturing; no child was trained in Cereus House without learning to move gracefully and unobtrusively through a crowd.

"The Marquise is a secretary of the Privy Seal," Delaunay remarked casually, placing a hand on my shoulder, letting me know the import of her position.

He wanted contrition from me, I knew; but while Delaunay may have known his targets and their weaknesses, he was not what I was. What I knew was born in the blood.

"Sorry," I muttered with ill grace, and glanced sullenly up at her, feeling the thrill of defiance deep in my bones. Her blue-green eyes grew cold and her mouth hardened.

"Your charge needs a lesson, Delaunay." She turned away abruptly, stalking across the ballroom. I looked at Delaunay to see his brows arched with uncertainty and surprise.

Beware of setting brushfires, Cecilie had said. Her comment made more sense to me now, although I did not of a necessity agree with it. I shrugged Delaunay's hand off my shoulder. "Tend to Alcuin, my lord. *I* am well enough on my own."

"Too well, perhaps." He laughed ruefully and shook his head. "Stay out of trouble, Phèdre. I've enough to deal with this night."

"Of course, my lord." I smiled impudently at him. With another despairing shake of his head, he left me.

Left to my own devices, I daresay I did well enough. Several of the guests had brought companions and we made acquaintance. There was a slight, dark youth from Eglantine House whose quick grin reminded me of Hyacinthe. He did a tumbling dance alone with hoops and ribbons, and everyone applauded him. His patron, Lord Chavaise, smiled with pride. And there was Mierette, from Orchis House, who had made her marque and kept her own salon now. Steeped in the gaiety for which her house was renowned, she brought laughter and a sense of sunlight with her, and where she went, I saw pleasure and merriment light people's faces.

Many of them, though, eyed Alcuin, who moved through the gathering oblivious to it all, serene and dark-eyed. I watched their faces and marked that among them all, one stood out. I knew him, for Vitale Bouvarre was an acquaintance of Delaunay's; not a friend, I think, but he had been a guest at Delaunay's house. He was a trader, of common stock—indeed, it was rumored there was Caerdicci blood in his lineage—but an excessively wealthy one, by virtue of an exclusive charter with the Stregazza family in La Serenissima.

His gaze followed Alcuin and his face was sick with desire.

When the last rays of sun had gone and darkness filled

the long windows around the balcony, Cecilie clapped her hands and summoned us to dine. No fewer than twenty-seven guests were arrayed about the long table, ushered to our seats by solicitous servants clad in spotless white attire. Dishes came in an unceasing stream, soups and terrines followed by pigeon en daube, a rack of lamb, sallets and greens and a dish of white turnips whipped to a froth which everyone pronounced a delight of rustic sophistication, and all the while rivers of wine poured from chilled jugs into glasses only half-empty.

"A toast!" Cecilie cried, when the last dish—a dessert of winter apples baked in muscat wine and spiced with cloves—had been cleared. She lifted her glass and waited for silence. She had the gift, still, of commanding attention; the table fell quiet. "To the safety of our borders," she said, letting the words fall in a soft voice. "To the safety and well-being of blessed Terre d'Ange."

A murmurous accord sounded the length of the table; this was one point on which each of us agreed. I drank with a willing heart, and saw no one who did not do the same.

"Thelesis," Cecilie said in the same soft voice.

Near the head of the table, a woman rose.

She was small and dark and not, I thought, a great beauty. Her features were unremarkable, and her best asset, luminous dark eyes, were offset by a low brow.

And then she spoke.

There are many kinds of beauty. We are D'Angeline.

"Beneath the golden balm," she said aloud, simply, and her voice filled every corner of the room, imbued with golden light. "Settling on the fields/Evening steals in calm/And farmers count their yields." So simple, her lyric; and yet I saw it, saw it all. She offered the words up unadorned, plain and lovely. "The bee is in the lavender/The honey fills the comb," and then her voice changed to something still and lonely. "But here a rain falls never-ending/And I am far from home."

Everyone knows the words to *The Exile's Lament*. It was written by Thelesis de Mornay when she was twenty-three years old and living in exile on the rain-swept coast of Alba. I myself had heard it a dozen times over, and recited it at more than one tutor's behest. Still, hearing it now, tears filled my eyes. We were D'Angeline, bred and bound to this land which Blessed Elua loved so well he shed his blood for it.

In the silence that followed, Thelesis de Mornay took her seat. Cecilie kept her glass raised.

"My lords and ladies," she said in her gentle voice, marked by the cadences of Cereus House. "Let it never be forgotten what we are." With a solemn air, she lifted her glass and tipped it, spilling a libation. "Elua have mercy on us." Her solemnity caught us all, and many followed suit. I did, and saw Delaunay and Alcuin did as well. Then Cecilie looked up again, a mischievous light in her eyes. "And now," she declared, "Let the games begin! Kottabos!"

Amid shouts of laughter, we retired to the parlour, united by love of our country and Cecilie's conviviality. Her servants had prudently removed the carpet, and in its place was a silver floorstand. Standing on tripodal legs, it pierced and held a broad silver crater, polished to mirror-brightness. Chased figures around the rim depicted a D'Angeline drinking party, à la Hellene. D'Angelines regard the Golden Era of Hellas as the last great civilization before the coming of Elua, which is why such things never go out of style.

Spiring out of the center of the crater, the stand rose to some four feet and terminated. Balanced atop its finial was the silver disk of the *plastinx*. Cecilie's servants circulated with wine-jugs and fresh cups; shallow silver wine-bowls with ornate handles.

To get to the lees, of course, one must drink what is poured, and although I had been prudent in my drinking, I felt it warm my blood as I emptied my cup. It is an art which must be practiced, twirling the handle about one's finger, flinging the last drops of wine in such a way that they strike the *plastinx*, knocking it into the crater so that it sounds like a cymbal.

When I took my turn, five or six others had gone before me, and while some had hit the *plastinx*, none had knocked it off the shaft. I did not even do so well as that, but Thelesis de Mornay smiled kindly at me. Cecilie succeeded to much applause, but the *plastinx* rattled against the edge before dropping into the bowl of the crater. Lord Childric d'Essoms spun his cup so fast that the dregs of his wine flew like a bolt from a crossbow, knocking the *plastinx* clear off the shaft and onto the floor. Everyone cheered and laughed, though it didn't count. Mierette of Orchis House rang the bowl, and Gaspar, Comte de Fourcay, and to everyone's surprise, Gonzago de Escabares, who smiled into his beard.

Alcuin, who shared a couch with a tall woman in a headdress, fared worse than I and only spattered wine about. His companion raised his fingers to her lips and sucked droplets of wine from them. Alcuin blushed. Vitale Bouvarre was sufficiently unsettled that he let go the handle of his cup and threw it with his wine. The *plastinx* dropped into the basin, but it was not counted a legal shot.

When Delaunay took his turn—and somehow it fell out that he went last—he looked calm and collected, austere in his black velvet attire. Reclining on one of the couches and leaning on one arm, he spun the cup and let fly his lees with an elegant motion.

His aim was unerring and the silver *plastinx* toppled neatly into the basin, which rang like a chime. Not everyone applauded, I noted, but those who did, did so loudly, proclaiming him the victor.

"A forfeit, a forfeit!" Mierette cried, flushed and gorgeous on her couch. "Messire Delaunay claims a forfeit from the hostess!"

Cecilie acknowledged it, laughing. "What will you have, Anafiel?" she asked teasingly.

Delaunay smiled and went over to her. Bending down, he claimed a kiss—a sweet one, I thought—and whispered in her ear. Cecilie laughed again, and Delaunay went back to his couch.

"I am minded to grant this claim," Cecilie said archly. "At the stroke of midnight, Alcuin nó Delaunay, who is dedicated to Naamah, will gain sixteen years of age. The holder of his marque asks that we hold an auction for his virgin-price. Is anyone here minded to object?"

You may be sure, no one objected, and as if on cue—indeed, I am sure they planned it, Delaunay and Cecilie—the distant voice of a horologist crying midnight in the square filtered through the balcony windows into the waiting silence. Cecilie raised her glass.

"Let it be so! I declare the bidding open!"

In one smooth, graceful motion, Alcuin rose from his couch and stood before us, holding his hands out open and turning slowly. I have seen a hundred adepts of the First of the Thirteen Houses on display, and I have never seen anyone who matched his dignity in it.

Childric d'Essoms, who claimed no interest in Delaunay's bait, was the first to bid. "Two hundred ducats!" he shouted. Because I had been watching him that night, I saw the hunter's gleam in his eye and knew that, for him, this was not about desire.

"You insult the boy," Alcuin's couchmate declared; I

recollected her name, which was Madame Dufreyne. "Two hundred fifty."

Vitale Bouvarre looked apoplectic. "Three hundred," he offered in a strangled voice. Alcuin smiled in his direction.

"Three hundred fifty," Solaine Belfours said evenly.

"Oh, my." Mierette of Orchis House drained her cup and set it down delicately. Toying with the golden cascade of her hair, she looked merrily at Cecilie. "Cecilie, you are too bad. How often does such a chance come to one such as us? I will bid four, if the boy will thank me for it."

"Four hundred fifty!" Vitale retorted angrily.

Someone else bid higher; I cannot remember who, for it was at this point that matters escalated. For some of the bidders, like Childric d'Essoms, it was merely a game, and I think he at least took the most pleasure in seeing the despair of others as the chase grew heated. For others, I was not so sure. Mierette nó Orchis bid higher than I would have guessed, and I never knew if it was desire that spurred her, or complicity with Cecilie's design. But for the rest, there was no question. It was Alcuin they desired, serene and beautiful and like no one else in the world, with his white hair falling like a curtain over his shoulders and his dark, secret eyes.

Throughout it all, Delaunay never moved, nor gave anything away. When the bidding passed a thousand ducats, he glanced once at Cecilie, and she beckoned for her chancellor, who came forward with a contract and pen at the ready.

In the end, it came down to Vitale Bouvarre, Madame Dufreyne and another man, the Chevalier Gideon Landres, who had holdings in L'Agnace and was a member of Parliament. We, who had seen how matters would fall out, watched and waited.

"Six thousand ducats!" Vitale Bouvarre threw down the offer as if it were a gauntlet. His face was red. Madame Dufreyne touched her fingers to her lips, counted silently to herself, and shook her head. The Chevalier merely crossed his arms and looked impassive.

So it was done, and Alcuin's virgin-price fetched six thousand ducats. I, who had grown up in the Night Court, had never heard of such a thing; though oddly enough, it was not that of which I thought in that moment, but Hyacinthe's mother, who wore her wealth upon her person and might never hope to carry so much as Alcuin fetched in a single night.

When the matter was concluded, Cecilie's chancellor drew up the contract swiftly, though I don't believe Vitale even glanced at what he was signing. The night was young still, but he would have no more of this gathering.

"Come," he said to Alcuin, his voice thick. "My carriage is waiting." He glanced once at Delaunay. "My driver will bring him on the morrow. Is that acceptable?"

Delaunay, who had spoken little, inclined his head. Alcuin looked at him but once; a grave, solemn look. Delaunay returned it unflinching. Vitale reached out his hand, and Alcuin took it.

I recall that upon their leaving, Cecilie clapped her hands together and the musicians struck up a merry tune; though in truth, my memory may be somewhat blurred by the wine. There was dancing, and I danced with Gonzago de Escabares, and the Chevalier Landres, stoic at his loss, and once with Lord Childric d'Essoms, who smiled and looked at me as the hawk eyes the sparrow. And then Lord Chavaise called for a stamping rhythm with timbales and finger drums, and I danced with his lover from Eglantine House, the agile youth who had tumbled for us, and I kept the rhythm and was grateful for the lessons Delaunay had foisted upon me.

Late in the night, I remember, Delaunay brought Thelesis de Mornay to be introduced, and she touched my face lightly with her slim, dark fingers and declaimed the lines about Kushiel's Dart from the Leucenaux text, and there was a little silence, then murmuring.

So everyone knew, then, what the scarlet mote in my eye betokened, and I would have gone with any one of them, were it not for Delaunay's grip at my elbow reminding me like an anchor where my duty lay.

THIRTEEN

Alcuin was quiet for the better part of a week afterward.

Whether he and Delaunay spoke of it, I do not know. There are certain things one does not ask, certain privacies we respected. But after several days of silence, I could stand it no longer. I asked Alcuin what it had been like.

We were studying together at the time, facing each other across the great table in Delaunay's library and reading by lamplight. Alcuin, poring over a speculative treatise on the Master of the Straits, marked his place with one finger and looked up at me.

"It was fine," he said quietly. "Messire Bouvarre was pleased. He wishes to see me again when he returns from La Serenissima."

Confounded by his reticence, I cast about for something to keep him talking. "Did he give you anything toward your marque?"

"No." A hint of cynicism, dark and adult, flickered in his eyes. "Not after paying six thousand ducats for the privilege of having me. But he has promised to bring me a string of glass beads upon his return. I understand they do beautiful glasswork in La Serenissima." Closing his book, he added, "I do not think it is Messire Bouvarre's best interest that I make my marque any time soon."

I had seen the desire like a sickness on Vitale Bouvarre's face; I understood. "Why him? Delaunay and Cecilie picked the guests; they knew who would go highest. What does Delaunay want of him?"

"Poison." It was spoken so softly I wasn't sure I'd heard him aright. Alcuin pushed his hair back, frowning slightly. "They are expert in its usage, as well as glasswork, in La Serenissima. The King's brother, Prince Benedicte, is wed to Maria Stregazza, whose family rules the city. And the Stregazza signed an exclusive trade charter with Vitale Bouvarre not four months after Isabel de la Courcel died of poisoning."

"There is no proof of that."

"No." Alcuin shook his head. "If there were proof, one would not suspect the Stregazza. But after Rolande was killed at the Battle of Three Princes, Isabel de la Courcel began positioning members of her own family to assume power, and there was talk of a betrothal between Ysandre and a L'Envers cousin. It ended with her death." He shrugged. "It may be that Prince Benedicte would not condone such a thing; so Delaunay believes. But the Stregazza would, and Benedicte is still second in line to the throne of Terre d'Ange."

"Did Bouvarre tell you anything?"

"He said one could buy anything, for a price, in La Serenissima; even life and death. Nothing more, yet." Alcuin was quiet again for a moment. "Sometimes when I am serving at a gathering and I am there to overhear what Delaunay cannot, I can take my mind away from what my hands are doing and concentrate all of it on listening and remembering. But it was not so easy with

Bouvarre to take my mind away as it is when pouring wine," he finished, murmuring.

"He didn't ill-treat you?" I couldn't imagine that it was so; it was not in Alcuin's contract, and Delaunay would have sued for breach if Bouvarre had injured him.

"No. I daresay he was gentle enough." There was distaste in the words. "Phèdre, Naamah lay down with strangers for love of Elua. I would do that and more for him."

I did not need to ask to know that he meant Delaunay, and I did not tell him that each of the Thirteen Houses of the Night Court claims a different cause for the prostitution of Naamah. Instead, I simply asked him, thinking I knew the answer, "Why?"

"You don't know?" Alcuin gave me a funny look. My history was an open book, I supposed, although I found later that he did not know how I had come to Cereus House. "I was born in Trefail, in the Camaelines. One of Prince Rolande's men got me on a village girl, when they were patrolling all that year along the border."

"No small wonder Baudoin managed to be in Camlach," I said, thinking aloud. Alcuin nodded.

"Like Rolande, no? Anyway, my mother's family turned her out. There was gossip; she came near to starving, and word of it reached Rolande. He had my father court-martialed, paid my mother's family a dowry-price and hired a wetnurse, as her milk had failed. There are a few Skaldi living on the edge of Camlach, tribal exiles who've no wish to return to their homeland. That was all he could get."

"Alcuin." It was fascinating, and infuriating. "What does it have to do with Delaunay?"

"I don't know." He shook his head, swinging the ivory curtain of his hair. "Except that he rode with Prince Rolande that year at the Battle of Three Princes, and six years later, when the Skaldi were overrunning the border again, he came back for me. I asked if he was my father, and he laughed, and said no. He said he kept his promises, and sometimes other people's as well. I've been with him ever since."

"You've no wish to see your mother?"

He shuddered. "Delaunay was half a step ahead of the Skaldi. We were four hundred yards out of town when we heard the screaming start. He carried me on his pommel and covered my ears. There was nothing he could do. We could see the smoke rise up behind us all the way down the mountains. I wept for my nurse, but I never knew my mother. And I will never go back there."

I pitied him; and envied him a little, in truth, for my own story was not half so romantic. Escaping down a mountain! It was certainly more exciting than being sold into indenture. "You should ask him again. You have a right to know."

"He has a right not to say." Alcuin got up to put away the book he had been reading, then turned and cocked his head at me. "I don't remember very much of my childhood," he said softly, "but I remember how my nurse would speak to me in Skaldic. She used to tell me that a mighty Prince descended from angels had promised that I would always be taken care of. Delaunay is keeping Rolande de la Courcel's promise."

We talked late into the evening—Delaunay was away at a party that night—and I learned that Alcuin's marque was not a matter of contract, as was mine. Delaunay had moved at whim for years in and out of the royal court and the demimonde, but it was Alcuin who chose to follow, pledging himself to the service of Naamah to discharge a debt that could never be paid. I thought of Guy's story, and the invisible ties that bound us all to Anafiel Delaunay. I thought of Alcuin's story, and wondered what invisible ties bound Delaunay to the long-slain Prince Rolande.

But it was Hyacinthe who came up with the theory.

"So what do we know about Prince Rolande's first betrothed?" he asked rhetorically, sitting in the Cockerel with his boots propped on the table and waving a drumstick. I had helped him arrange a liaison between a married noblewoman and a handsome player, and he had splurged on spitted capon and tankards of ale for the both of us. "Other than the fact that she broke her neck in a hunting accident. We know that Anafiel Delaunay was alleged to have written the lyrics to a song which suggested Isabel L'Envers was to blame. Although he never confessed to it, we know that his poetry was thereafter proscribed, which suggests that someone in the royal court believed it was true, with evidence sufficient to convince the King. And we know that Delaunay was not banished, which suggests that someone else protected him, and had the grounds to do so. Some years later, he makes a point of honoring the promise of Prince Rolande, which suggests there was a debt between them. Where does it begin? With the Prince's betrothed. So who was she?"

Sometimes I despaired of the fact that Hyacinthe was better at what I was trained to do than I myself.

"Edmée, Edmée de Rocaille, daughter of the Comte de Rocaille, who is lord of one of the largest holdings in Siovale. There is a small university there, where the Kindred of Shemhazai study the sciences." I shrugged and took a sip of ale. "He donated his library, which is famous."

Hyacinthe tore at the drumstick with his white teeth, smearing grease on his chin. "Did he have sons?"

"I don't know." I stared at him. "You think Delaunay is her *brother*?"

"Why not?" He gnawed his capon to the bone and quaffed ale. "If he wrote the lyric—and if he would not confess, I have never heard he denied it—he had a powerful interest in discrediting her murderess. And if he wasn't her brother, maybe he was something else."

"Like what?" I eyed him suspiciously over the rim of my tankard. He set down his own mug, lowered his feet and leaned forward, a conspiratorial gleam in his gaze.

"Her lover." Seeing me form an incredulous response, he raised a finger. "No, wait, Phèdre. Maybe he loved her, and lost her to the heir to the throne, but loved her nonetheless. And when she meets a tragic end, he goes to the City in search of justice and finds only conspiracy—and within a year, the Prince weds another. A gentle-born country lad with a quick tongue and an absolute ignorance of politics, he dares all and makes an enemy of the Princess Consort, but wins an advocate in the Prince, whose sense of honor leads him to protect the rash young poet. What do you think?"

"I think you spend too much time among players and dramatists," I said, but I had to wonder. The first threads of the tangle did appear to surface with the death of Prince Rolande's betrothed. "Anyway, Delaunay studied at the University in Tiberium. He didn't exactly come straight from the provinces."

"Ah, well." Hyacinthe drank again and wiped the foam from his lip. "Pedants and demagogues. What can one learn from them?"

At that, I had to laugh; as clever as he was, Hyacinthe retained the prejudices of the streets. "A lot. Tell me, though; have you looked with the *dromonde*?"

"You know I haven't." His look grew serious. "You remember what my mother said? I will guess for you, Phèdre, where you are too close to the matter to see it aright, but I will not use my gift to hasten the coming of that day."

"You would mince words with Fate," I grumbled.

"So?" He grinned. "I am Tsingani. But they are good theories, no?"

Reluctantly, I admitted that they were, and we talked then of other things until Guy's face shone pale outside the window of the Cockerel, calling in the marque of my debt and beckoning me homeward.

It was not long after this conversation that two occurrences of note took place, though to be sure, one was notable only to me. The first, which was of note to the realm at large, was that the Cruarch of Alba paid a visit to the D'Angeline court. That is how their leader is styled among the Cruithne; in common parlance, of course, we called him the Pictish King, as the Caerdicci scholars had named him. The event was worthy of discussion, for it was a rarity that the Master of the Straits would allow such a crossing to take place.

For as long as anyone can remember, the Master of the Straits has ruled the Three Sisters, those tiny islands that lie off the coast of Azzalle, and by Blessed Elua's truth, I swear it is true what they say: the winds and the waters obey his command. You may believe it or not as you choose, but I have since seen it for myself and know it is so. It has afforded us great protection from the longboats of the Skaldi, but it has also kept us from alliance or trade with the Cruithne, whose land is rich in lead and iron ore. Why the Master of the Straits had allowed this embassy to land, no one knew; but land it had, and there were Picts to be dealt with. It caused considerable stir in our household. There were very few D'Angelines to be found who spoke Cruithne, and Delaunay had been summoned to attend the royal audience as translator.

I am ashamed to say that I paid less heed to this event

than I should have done, for the other occurrence of note occupied my mind. Cecilie Laveau-Perrin had declared to Delaunay that she had no more to teach me. What I had left to learn, she said, was beyond her scope; it would be best taught me by an adept of Valerian House.

While Delaunay was skeptical, he was forced to admit that his knowledge of the arts of algolagnia were as purely academic as Cecilie's. An instructional visit was arranged for me with the Second of Valerian House. The King's summons to Delaunay came after the arrangements were made, and I think he would have cancelled them had his attention not been elsewhere. But his mind was wholly on the upcoming audience, and he did not.

So it fell out that Alcuin, who was nigh as fluent as Delaunay, was to accompany him and transcribe the conversation. The royal coach came for them both, while I would be escorted by Delaunay's driver to Valerian House. If I had known what would one day come to pass, I would have begged to attend, for I was as fluent as Alcuin and wrote a fairer hand. It would have been of no small merit to have met the Cruarch of Alba and his heir—his sister-son and not his son, as the Pictish rule of descent is matrilineal, a fact which would also affect my life in ways I could not imagine.

But we are not granted such foreknowledge, and I, who tired of the yearning in my blood that ever grew unassuaged, was glad enough with my end of the bargain. A barbarian king is a fascinating thing, to be sure, but I was an *anguissette* condemned to the dull torment of virginity. I went to Valerian House.

FOURTEEN

It is a matter of some irony that I, of all people, had so little knowledge of the House to which I would have belonged, had not fate pricked my left eye. The gate-keeper admitted Delaunay's coach readily and we traversed a long entrance well-guarded by trees. I was met in the courtyard by two apprentices, a boy and a girl. Alyssum House is prized for its modesty, but I have never seen any of the Night Court maintain a more trembling decorum than these two, who kept their gazes steadily downcast as they guided me inside.

The receiving room was opulent and unseasonably warm. A roaring fire was laid in the hearth and the lamps burned scented oil. As I waited, I glanced at the rich tapestries which smothered the walls. Scenes out of Hellene mythology, I thought at first, then looked closer. Stories of rape and torture emerged from their fine-woven threads; fleeing maidens; pleading youths and vengeful gods and goddesses at their pleasure.

I sat staring spellbound at the contorted features of a nymph being buggered by a grinning satyr when the Dowayne's Second entered the room.

"Phèdre nó Delaunay," he said in a soft voice, "be welcome. I am Didier Vascon, the Second of this House." He came forward to give me the kiss of greeting, somehow imparting a yielding quality to the simple courtesy; it stirred and repulsed me at once. "So you are the *anguissette*." He searched my features, gazing contemplatively at the red fleck of Kushiel's Dart. "We would have known, you know. They were fools, at Cereus House." His tone held a hint of spite. "It is pride that keeps them from admitting to their ignorance of the breadth of Naamah's arts. Have you ever seen a shrine of Kushiel?"

The last was asked in a neutral tone, and I blinked at the sudden change of demeanor and subject. "No, my lord."

His lashes flickered ever so slightly at the form of address; you think you are better than me, they said, but I am not fooled by it. Aloud, he merely said, "I thought not. We have one here, many of our patrons are dedicated to Kushiel. Would you like to see it?"

"Yes. Please."

He called for servants with torches and led me down a long hallway, then a winding stair descending into darkness. It was hard to see. I kept my eyes on his back, moving steadily ahead of me. The torchlight made transparent the filmy white stuff of his shirt and I could see weal marks curving around his ribs like a caress.

"Here." At the bottom, he threw open a door. The stone-walled room beyond was lit and heated by another fire, and light washed over a bronze sculpture of Kushiel. Elua's Companion stood raised on a dais behind an altar and offering-bowl, a stern look on his beautiful face, the flail and rod in his hands. I stood for a long time gazing at him. "Do you know why Kushiel abdicated his duties to join Elua?"

I shook my head. "No."

"He was one of the Punishers of God, chosen to deliver torments to the souls of sinners that they might repent at the end of days." Didier Vascon was a disembodied voice behind me. "So the Yeshuite legends claim. Alone among angels, Kushiel understood that the act of chastisement was an act of love; and the sinners in his charge too came to understand, and loved him for it. He gave them pain like balm, and they begged him for it, finding in it not redemption, but a love that transcended the divine. The One God was displeased, for He desires worship above all things, but Kushiel saw a spark he would follow in the spirit of Blessed Elua, who said unto us, 'Love as thou wilt.' "

The breath went out of me with a profound shudder. No one had told me this, this story that was mine by birthright. I wondered how different my life would be if I had been raised and trained in Valerian House, and turned to Didier. "Is that what it's like?"

He hesitated before answering. "No." When his answer came, his tone was flat with reluctant truth. "But it is how I get my pleasure. It is the service to which I was born and to which I trained. They say Kushiel's Dart marks his true victims. Perhaps you will find it."

I understood, then, that he was envious. "How is it that adepts are trained to this service?" I asked him, wishing to change the subject.

"Come." He beckoned the torch-bearers and ushered me through a door on the far side of the room, continued talking as we proceeded down the broad stone hall. "It begins with the lesson of the spiced candies, of course; you know this? No? We do it with children of six. An adept explains that the pleasure of the taste is due to the touch of pain the spice provokes. Those who understand, we keep; others will have their marques sold. After that, it is a simple matter of consistency and conditioning. Never is a fosterling or apprentice of Valerian House allowed to experience pleasure without pain, nor pain without pleasure." He stopped before another door and looked curiously at me. "You have never received such training?"

I shook my head. He shrugged.

"It is Delaunay's business, I suppose." He pushed the door open. "This is one of the pleasure-chambers. We endeavor to provide environments for all of our patrons' particular desires."

Servants moved about the room lighting the wall sconces and the brazier. I gazed about me and shuddered again. There were lush carpets in the center of the room, surrounded by aisles of flagstone. The walls were bare of decoration, but hardly unadorned; one held manacles and chains for the wrists and ankles, bolted into the stone, and another held a great wooden wheel, with clamps to hold one spread-eagled.

"We have a reciprocal agreement with Mandrake House," Didier Vascon said, watching me take in the accoutrements. "Sometimes we have patrons who take pleasure only in watching, so we might contract a flagellant and an assistant to perform the excruciation on one of our adepts. And of course sometimes Mandrake has clients who must needs observe an abasement performed to move them, for which we provide subjects."

His words echoed distantly in my ears. I moved to the center of the room, lightly touching a padded pommel horse and looking inquiringly at him.

"Here." He was dryly amused by my ignorance and, with a deft hand, pushed me down across its back. My cheek was pressed to the padded leather. "You would be lashed in place, of course. Some patrons have a particular fetish for the buttocks. The pommel horse provides good advantage for their indulgence."

I straightened, flushed, and snapped at him. "I'm not here to receive training at your hands!"

Didier raised his eyebrows and lifted his hands. "May your patrons have the joy of breaking you," he murmured. "I've no interest in it. But I've taken a fee to ensure you'll not go to them in complete ignorance. Come here." He beckoned me to a cabinet and began pointing out items. "We provide all manner of accessories, of course; collars, blinds, gags, belts, whatever the patron might wish. Rings, pleasure-balls, aides d'amour, pincers—"

"I was raised in Cereus House," I reminded him, wondering if he thought I was so green I'd never seen a shaft-ring or a carven phallus.

"—pincers," he said, resuming as if I hadn't interrupted. He picked up one of the spring-forced clamps and squeezed it open, raising his eyebrows again. "Often placed on the nipples or nether lips. Do they use these in Cereus House?"

"No." I tugged at another drawer, but it was locked. Didier took a key from a chain about his waist and opened it. A row of slim-hafted, razor-edged steel blades gleamed against a red velvet lining, like a chirurgeon's tools, only beautiful.

"Flechettes," he said. "We require a reference and a guarantee for their usage." He gave an involuntary tremor beside me and his voice changed. "I hate them."

I imagined an anonymous hand pressing the sharp point of one into my skin, tracing it slowly, a trickle of red following the bright blade. It would be very vivid against my skin. I came out of the reverie to find Didier watching me again.

"You are what the stories say, aren't you?" The envy was mingled with an obscure pity. "I hope Delaunay screens his clients well. Come on, I'll show you the upper levels."

My tour of Valerian House continued for some time, through a myriad of rooms; seraglio boudoirs, baths, a folly garden, royal chambers, a harem, a throne room, a room of swings and harnesses, even a child's nursery, although Didier hastened to add that they abided by Guild laws regarding the minimum age for adepts. In the flagellary, he lectured at length on the different types of whips and rods; crops, quirts, scourges, floggers and tawses, the cat-o'-nine-tails and the bullwhip, birches, canes, straps and paddles. Of course many patrons, he told me in his dry voice, preferred to bring their own implements.

I never saw a single patron throughout the tour. It is the policy of the Night Court to provide privacy, but there were always patrons at Cereus House who treated it as a salon, meeting with friends and acquaintances to enjoy each other's company as well as the services of Naamah. By contrast, Valerian House was marked by an air of hushed secrecy. Fêtes and galas were arranged with great care, Didier said, for very select guest lists.

When all was said and seen, I was glad that I had gone to Delaunay and not to Valerian House. Although there was nothing I saw that did not in some way intrigue me, it seemed a dull life without the spice of mystery and danger—and indeed, even the cursed intellectual rigor—that life as a Servant of Naamah in the household of Anafiel Delaunay promised. Any spark of disobedience or rebellion had been long conditioned from the adepts of Valerian House; and how not, when their motto was, *I yield*? Mighty Kushiel did not minister to the yielding, but to those who disobeyed and dared suffer the agonies of defeat. This I believed then, and I believe it still, though I daresay I might not have then, had I any inkling how long and difficult the path would be. At any rate, you may be sure that if I left Valerian House without the wisdom of experience to support my beliefs, I left it considerably wiser in the ways of my art.

I returned to Delaunay's house full of new-found knowledge, finding to my dismay that he had invited friends for a small dining-party, and talk was of nothing but the Cruarch of Alba. Still, if there was consolation, it was in the fact that Delaunay was in high spirits and called me to join him on his couch.

"Surely if you are old enough to enter the service of Naamah, this evening's conversation merits hearing," he said, patting the cushion beside him. He was still dressed for court, and fair glowed with elegance and the flush of good wine and talk. "You know the Comte de Fourcay, of course . . . Gaspar, make her a bow, she is nigh a lady now . . . and our poetess; Thelesis, I cower in your shadow . . . this is Quintilius Rousse of Eisande, who is the finest admiral ever to command a fleet, and my lord Percy of L'Agnace, Comte de Somerville, of whom you have heard tell."

I don't know what I stammered—something inept, no doubt—as I rose to make my curtsy. I was used to Gaspar Trevalion, who was almost like an uncle to me (insofar as my notion of kin extended); Thelesis de Mornay awed me, though I had met her. But these new additions . . . the commander of the fleet of Eisande was legend in three nations, and the Comte de Somerville was a Prince of the Blood, who had led the charge against the Skaldi with Prince Rolande and Prince Benedicte. It was rumored that if the King should ever need to appoint a warlord, it would be the Comte de Somerville.

Because he figured in a tale out of my childhood, I expected he would be old, like the King, but he was no more than fifty years of age, hale and fit, with grey dimming his golden hair. A faint odor of apples clung to him; I learned later that this was a mark of the Scions of Anael in general, and of the Somerville line in particular. He smiled pleasantly at me, so I would be less fearful of him.

"Delaunay's *anguissette*!" Quintilius Rousse shouted, beckoning me to his couch, which Alcuin shared. He seized my face in both hands and planted a kiss on it, releasing me with a grin. His weather-beaten face was dragged down on one side by a thick scar where he had been struck by a snapped cable, but his blue eyes glinted unabashedly. I could not decide if he were handsome or ugly. "Too bad I've no taste for pain, eh?" He patted Alcuin's knee; Alcuin smiled serenely at him. I could tell he liked the bluff admiral well enough. Alcuin enjoyed frankness. "You're the spider's pupil, why d'ye reckon Elder Brother let the Cruarch through?"

It took me a moment to realize that by spider he meant Delaunay, and to recall that Elder Brother was a sailor's term for the Master of the Straits, who ruled from the Three Sisters.

"If I could answer that, my lord," I said, sitting on Delaunay's couch and arranging my skirts, "I would not be pupil, but master."

Quintilius Rousse roared with laughter, and the others chuckled. Delaunay stroked my hair and smiled. "Quintilius, my friend," he said, "if you cannot answer that, none of us can. Unless it be our gracious muse . . . ?" He looked inquiringly at Thelesis, who shook her dark head.

"He let me pass for the price of a song," she said, her rich voice holding us all in thrall; of course, I remembered, she was in exile in Alba, and would thus have been summoned to attend. "Once thence, and once back. As best I can tell, he is governed by whim. To what whim did the Cruarch of Alba cater? That is the question."

Alcuin cleared his throat. It was a small sound, but everyone listened.

"They spoke of a vision." He glanced apologetically at Delaunay. "I was stationed close to the Alban delegation, but it is difficult to transcribe accurately and overhear, my lord. Still, I heard somewhat of a vision, of the King's sister; a black boar and a silver swan."

"The King's sister." Quintilius Rousse made a sour face. "Ye gods beyond, *Lyonette*? What's she up to now?"

"No, no." Alcuin shook his head. "The sister of the Cruarch, the Pictish King, mother of his heir."

"Lyonette has naught to do with her," Gaspar Trevalion observed, "but I note she took the Cruarch's wife under her wing, or paw, as it might happen. One almost wished to warn the poor thing that there are claws beneath those velvet pads."

"Lyonette de la Courcel de Trevalion would be well advised to guard herself against such prey," Thelesis murmured. "The Cruarch's wife, Foclaidha, is descended from the Brugantii, under the aegis of the red bull. The Lioness of Azzalle would do well to beware her horns."

"Her boys are strapping things," Quintilius Rousse observed, nonplussed. "Did'ye see the size o' the eldest lad? None too pleased to play second fiddle to a cripple, either."

"You refer to the Prince of the Picti?" The Comte de Somerville's tone might have sounded condescending, were it not for the obvious affection with which he addressed the naval commander. "A dusky little thing, but almost pretty beneath the blue. Pity about the leg. What was his name?"

"Drustan." Delaunay said it laughing. "Don't even think it, Percy!"

"I'd never." The Comte de Somerville's eyes glinted with amusement. "You know I'm too politic for that, old friend."

I sipped at a glass of wine, my head spinning at the level of conversation. "Are they truly painted blue?" I asked. The question sounded plaintively naive to my own ears.

"As truly as the Servants of Naamah earn her marque," Thelesis de Mornay answered me kindly. "Warriors of the Cruithne bear the symbols of their caste upon their faces and bodies, tattooed in blue woad by their own marquists' needles. Our fine lords may laugh, but young Drustan's markings bear witness to his lineage and attest that he has won his spurs in battle. Do not be misled by his twisted foot."

"But what," asked Gaspar Trevalion, "do they want?" Having asked the question, he glanced around the couches. No one ventured an answer. "Do they come seeking trade? Fulfillment of a vision? Protection from Skaldic longboats? It is rumored on the coast of Azzalle that the Skaldi have sought to cross the Northernmost Seas to raid Alba, but what can we do? Even Quintilius Rousse cannot sail a fleet up the strait."

The admiral coughed. "It is also. . . . rumored . . . that D'Angeline ships have sought a southwesterly route, and that the Cruithne and the Dalriada make for inhospitable landings. I do not think it is protection at sea they seek."

"Trade." Delaunay ran his finger absently around the rim of his glass. "Everyone desires trade. And it is a form of power, of freedom; the propagation of culture is the guarantor of immortality. How it must gall them, to look across the straits and see a world untouchable. And we, the jewel of the land, so close; so far. Do you never wonder why the Skaldi ever press our borders?" He looked up sharply, his wits in full stride. "No? We are marked, my friends, by the heritage of Blessed Elua and his Companions. We thrive, where other nations struggle. We live out our days in wine, song and abundance, nestled on the breast of this golden land, raising our sons and daughters to peerless beauty, and wonder, then, why we must defend our borders. We raise desire to an art form, and cry foul when it awakens its bloody echoes."

"We have raised more than desire to an art form," said the Comte de Somerville, and there was a grim reminder of steel in his voice. "We defend our borders."

"So we do," Quintilius Rousse agreed. "So we do."

There is a martial solemnity that follows this sort of proclamation; I heard it then, and I have heard it since. In its silence, Alcuin shook his head. "But the Master of the Straits has no interest in trade," he murmured. "So there is somewhat more to the matter."

I have said it before, that Alcuin's gift surpassed my own in the recollection of facts, the swift drawing of connections. I saw that night a faint surprise on Delaunay's face, in his parted lips; I understood, then, that in this one thing, this quicksilver intuition, the pupil indeed surpassed the master. But where Alcuin went deep, Delaunay went far—and always, he had knowledge he withheld from the rest of us. Some far-ranging conclusion was reached that night, for I watched his face as he came to it.

"No mind," he said then, and his voice was gay as he reached for his lyre, which he played as well as any gentleman and better than most. "Tonight the King dines with his blue-marqued peer and Ysandre de la Courcel, flower of the realm, shall teach a clubfoot barbarian Prince to dance the gavotte. Thelesis, my dear muse, will you give us the honor of a song?"

I think, of any of the guests, she knew best what he was about; still she obliged him, singing in her deep, thrilling voice. So passed my first night accepted as a nigh-adult member of Anafiel Delaunay's household. Gaspar Trevalion left sober, while Quintilius Rousse drank deep and slept it off in Delaunay's guest chambers.

As for Alcuin, he took heed of Delaunay's nod at the end of things, and left that night with the Comte de

Somerville. I do not think any contract was signed, but the Comte was gracious, and the next day an appointment was made with the marquist, to limn the base of Alcuin's marque where his spine melded into his delicate buttocks.

ꟻifteen

Delaunay went twice more to court during the visit of the Cruarch of Alba, and on these occasions he went alone, and there were no parties nor speculation afterward; if he learned anything further, he kept it to himself. The King of Terre d'Ange and the King of the Picts exchanged gifts and pleasantries, so far as anyone knew, and the Alban delegation rode back to the coast and sailed across the strait, accompanied by fair winds, sea birds and the apparent good will of the Master of the Straits.

Having renewed his fealty to House Courcel, the Comte de Somerville returned to his inland troops and his vast tracts of apple trees.

Quintilius Rousse, having depleted our larder and drunk half of last year's pressing, went jovially back to Eisande and his fleet, and somewhat later we heard that he had won a pitched battle at sea against the ships of the Khalif of Khebbel-im-Akkad, securing a trade route for spices and silks from the East.

News such as this made the visit of a barbarian chieftain from a tiny island pale in significance, so it is no surprise that the Picts faded quickly from memory.

Life, after all, goes on.

Of a surety, I was anxious that mine should do so, and soon. Alcuin's success as a courtesan of the first rank continued. Rumor of the auction and his virgin-price spread, and I believe Delaunay received inquiries on almost a daily basis. This was what he wished; to be able to choose, selectively, and say no when he desired. And I will say this at the outset: Never did he contract with a patron before first securing our approval.

Delaunay's choice for Alcuin's third assignation was a true stroke of genius. Remembering the auction, Cecilie Laveau-Perrin contracted Alcuin's services for the night of Mierette nó Orchis' birthday, bestowing him, adorned in scarlet ribbons and nothing else, upon her friend. Mierette's laughter, I am told, rang from the rafters.

Later people would claim it an act of brilliance because word then spread that Delaunay's protegé could inspire even an adept of the Night Court, and this is true; but I claim a different reason. From that assignation, Alcuin came home heavy-lidded and smiling. He may have been her gift, but Mierette nó Orchis possessed the secret of bestowing joy in the act of worshipping Naamah. That is the canon of Orchis House, and that secret she shared with Alcuin. I remember it well, for the tender smile Alcuin took care not to turn on Delaunay, and the conversation our lord and master had with me that day.

He bid me attend him in the inner courtyard, which is where he preferred to stage all events of significance. I sat demurely on one of the couches, waiting on his attention while he strolled about the colonnade, hands clasped behind his back.

"You know I have received inquiries, Phèdre," he said, not quite looking at me. "Inquiries about you."

"No, my lord." It was true; he had never breathed a word of it, nor had anyone else, although my own birthday has passed some weeks gone by. I wondered if Alcuin had known, and resolved to give him a good shaking if I found he had.

"Yes, indeed. Ever since Alcuin's debut." Now Delaunay looked at me sidelong. It was early evening, and the long rays of sun picked out the gleam of topaz flecking his grey eyes. I found it hard to concentrate on what he was saying. "It is in my mind that you would not take it amiss if I accepted one of these offers."

That got my attention.

"My lord!" I breathed, scarce daring to believe. I had begun to think my ripening body would wither untasted on the vine. "No, my lord, I would not . . . take it amiss."

"I thought not." This time there was amusement in his glance. "But there is somewhat we must make clear first. You need a *signale*."

The word landed on uncomprehending ears. "My lord?"

"Didier didn't tell you?" He sat down. "It is something they have devised at Valerian House; I spoke to their Dowayne at some length, to learn what was needful. Betimes a patron goes too far in the throes of transport. You know that protestation is part of the game, yes? The *signale* is beyond that. It is a word, if spoken, that halts all play. You must have one, Phèdre." His gaze grew serious. "If a patron fails to heed the *signale*, he or she is guilty of heresy. It is your safeguard against injury, against violating the precept of Blessed Elua. They say it is best to choose a word that cannot be mistaken for loveplay. Do you wish to think on it?"

I shook my head; the word came unbidden to my lips. "Hyacinthe."

It is the first time, and perhaps the only, I saw Delaunay taken aback.

"The *Tsingano*?" If he hadn't been sitting in front of me, I would still have known his surprise from his voice.

"*That's* the first thing you think of when you think of a safeguard?"

"He is my one friend." I held his gaze stubbornly. "Everyone else desires something of me; even you, my lord. If you wish me to choose another word, I will. But you have asked, and I have answered."

"No." After a moment, he shrugged. "Why not? It's a good enough choice; no one need know you mean a Tsingani soothsayer's by-blow when you speak it. I'll have it drawn into your contract, and be certain your patrons know of it."

My words had given him pause, I could tell; I wondered if he were a little jealous, even. I hoped so, but didn't dare press the matter. "Who are they?" I asked him instead. "And whose offer are you minded to take, my lord?"

"There have been several." Delaunay rose to pace again. "Most relayed indirectly, through third and fourth parties, as is often done when special . . . talents . . . like your own are involved. Except for one." A frown creased his brow. He glanced reluctantly at me. "Childric d'Essoms approached me himself to make an offer."

A name, and a face to go with it. I felt my body tighten, but all I said was, "Why would he do that? He hates you, and he knows your game, my lord. He only bid on Alcuin to bait the others."

"That's part of it. He likes the sight of pain." He sat down again. "D'Essoms is a hunter; he loves the game, and he's clever at it, clever enough to know you're meant as a lure. He thinks he can take the bait and evade the hook, and he wants me to know it. He's too arrogant to pass up a chance to claim a prize like you and deal me an insult in the process."

"What do you want of him?" A simple enough question, fraught with so much meaning. This, beyond the provision of pleasure and the sight of pain, was my purpose; this was why Delaunay had bought my marque. No matter that he would not tell us the greater why of it, Alcuin and I had long ago realized that he valued us most of all for what we could learn.

"Any information he might betray," Delaunay said grimly. "D'Essoms ranks high in the Court of Chancery; there is no grant, no treaty, no appointment that does not cross his desk at some point. He knows who has petitioned for what, and what has been ceded in exchange. He knows who will be appointed to what post, and why. And like as not, he knows who profited from the death of Isabel L'Envers."

"And Edmée de Rocaille?" I shivered inwardly as I named Prince Rolande's first betrothed. Delaunay looked sharply at me.

"Isabel L'Envers profited from the death of Edmée de Rocaille," he said softly, "and so did Childric d'Essoms, for he received his appointment not long after Isabel wed Rolande. You ask what I wish to know? I wish to know who pulls D'Essoms' strings now. Isabel is dead; so who does he serve and to what end? Find that out for me, Phèdre, and I will owe you much."

"As you wish, my lord." I would do it, I resolved, if it killed me. I was naive enough still, in those days, not to reckon how real a possibility it might be.

"Then you assent to his offer?"

I started to say yes, then paused. "How much is it?"

Delaunay smiled at my asking. "You're a true child of the Night Court, Phèdre. Four thousand and a half." Seeing my expression, he stopped smiling. "My dear, Alcuin's virgin-price would never have gone so high were it not for the auction, and I am afraid that the patrons you attract are not the sort to air their penchants in public. If you have been struck as truly by Kushiel's

Dart as I believe, then experience will do naught but hone your gift. Your asking-price will rise, and not diminish with time." He cupped my face, looking sincerely at me. "Alcuin must trade on the asset of his rarity, and to preserve it, he may contract but seldom. To set a high mark on his debut was necessary. But you, Phèdre. . . . Valerian House knows of no *anguissette* in living memory. Indeed, it has been so long since the world has seen your like that even Cereus, the First House, failed to recognize you. This I promise; while you live, you will be a rarity."

I might have been seven years old again, standing in the Dowayne's receiving room where, with four lines of verse, Delaunay turned me from an ill-favored bastard into the chosen of Elua's Companions. I wanted to cry, but Delaunay didn't care for tears. "Childric d'Essoms will be getting a bargain," I said instead.

"Lord d'Essoms will be getting more than he bargained for." He looked sternly at me. "I want you to be careful, Phèdre. Seek nothing, ask him nothing. Let him take the hook, think he has won this victory from me. If all goes well, he will ask for you a third time, a fourth; risk nothing until then. Do you understand?"

"Yes, my lord. And if it goes poorly?"

"If it goes poorly, I will put half the contract fee toward your marque, and you have never to see him again." Delaunay poked me in the arm, quite sharply. "Under any circumstances, Phèdre, you will *not* hesitate to use the *signale*. Is that clear?"

"Yes, my lord. Hyacinthe." I said it a second time on purpose, just to bother him. He ignored it.

"And the same rules apply. You are not to betray your learning. As far as d'Essoms knows, such skills as you have, you learned in the Night Court."

"Yes, my lord." I paused. "You took Alcuin to court to transcribe the Alban interview."

"Ah, that." Delaunay broke out in his unexpected grin. "I said he wrote a fair hand; I didn't tell anyone he spoke Cruithne. As far as anyone but the King himself knows, Alcuin understood only what I translated. And our fair scribe was seen by a number of intrigued potentates that day."

As interesting as that was, I was more fascinated by the fact that Delaunay was actually suggesting Ganelon de la Courcel, the King of Terre d'Ange, knew what he was up to. I wished I could say the same. But, "I will be circumspect, my lord," was all I said aloud.

"Good." He stood up, looking satisfied. "Then I will make the arrangements."

Sixteen

On the day of my first assignation, I swear it, I think Delaunay was more nervous than I. Even with Alcuin, he had not fussed so much.

Later, when I knew my art better, I understood Delaunay better as well. As sophisticated as his knowledge and tastes might be, there was a threshold his own desires did not cross. Like many people, he understood the spice a touch of dominance might add to loveplay, but no more than a touch. Yet so thorough was his study of the desires of others that one forgot it was a comprehension of the mind only. In the marrow of his bones, he did not know what it was to crave the touch of the lash like a kiss. Thus, his nervousness.

When I understood this, I loved him all the better for it; though, of course, I had already long since forgiven him. There was nothing I would not forgive Delaunay.

"There," he breathed, standing behind me in the great mirror, tucking in an errant lock of my hair. "You look beautiful."

He rested his hands upon my shoulders and I gazed into the mirror. My own eyes looked back at me, dark and lustrous as bistre smudged in by an artist's pencil, save for the single mote of scarlet. In my mirror-image, it flecked the right eye, vivid as a scrap of rose-petal floating on calm waters. Delaunay liked the look of my hair caught in the silk mesh of a caul, restrained in its abundance. It weighed heavily against the fine strands, straining to escape, accentuating the delicate shape of my face and the ivory pallor of my skin.

It is vulgar to color youth, so the only cosmetic he had allowed me was a touch of carmine on my lips. They stood out, like the mote in my eye, vivid as rose-petals. I did not recall seeing such a sensuous pout to my lower lip before.

For my garb, Delaunay had again elected for simplicity; but the gown this time was red velvet, a deep and luscious shade. The bodice clung to my figure, and I marked with pleasure the way my breasts swelled, white-skinned and tempting, above its neckline. There was a line of tiny jet buttons all down the back. I wondered if Childric d'Essoms would undo them, or rip them asunder. In the Night Court, he would be charged extra for ripping them, but I doubted Delaunay incorporated such trivialities into his contract. The bodice dropped low on my hips, to emphasize the smallness of my waist and the flatness of my stomach. I was pleased with the youthful allure of my body, and was happy to see it emphasized. From thence, it hugged the fullness of my hips and dropped in straight folds, unexpectedly demure, save for the color and the luxuriant nature of the fabric.

"You are pleased at what you see," Delaunay said, amused.

"Yes, my lord." I saw no reason to dissemble; my appearance was his investment. I turned, craning my neck, trying to imagine how I would appear from the rear when I had made my marque and the lines of the finial would rise where the fabric ended to adorn the top of my spinal knob.

"So am I. Let us hope Lord Childric feels the same." Delaunay removed his hands from my shoulders. "I have a gift for you," he said, moving to his closet. "Here." Returning, he laid a hooded cloak about my shoulders where his hands had rested. Velvet lined with silk, it was a far deeper red than my dress, a red so dark and saturated it was almost black, the color of blood spilled on a moonless night. "The color is called *sangoire*," he said, watching my face in the mirror as I received his gift. "Thelesis told me that in the seventh century after Elua, it was decreed that only *anguissettes* might wear it. I had to send to Firezia to find dye-makers who remembered how to make the formula for it."

It was beautiful; truly and deeply beautiful. I wept at the sight of it, and this time Delaunay did not revile me for it, but embraced me. We are D'Angelines; we know what it is to weep at the sight of beauty.

"Be safe, Phèdre," he murmured. His voice stirred the caught weight of my hair. "Childric d'Essoms waits for you. Remember your *signale*, and remember that Guy will be there, if anything goes awry. I would not send you into the household of my enemy without protection."

My blood raced at the feel of his arms around me, and I turned in them, seeking his face. "I know, my lord," I whispered. But Delaunay dropped his arms and stepped back.

"It is time," he said, his expression grown distant and reserved. "Go, and may the blessing of Naamah protect you."

Thus did I go forth to my first assignation.

It was dark already when the carriage set forth. Guy, immaculate in livery, sat opposite me on the cushions and said nothing, nor did I speak to him. D'Essoms' house was small, but in close proximity to the Palace; he had a suite of rooms in the Palace itself, I learned later, but preferred to maintain his own lodgings for dalliance of this nature.

The servant who opened the door seemed surprised to see me attended by Guy, which emotion he marked with a haughty sniff. "That way," he said to me, pointing, and then to Guy, "You'll abide in the servants' quarters, then."

As if he had not spoken, Guy moved forward and made me a bow, crisp and elegant; I hadn't known he was capable of such a courtly manner. "My lady Phèdre nó Delaunay," he announced in his inflectionless voice, catching the servant's eye and holding it. "She is expected by Lord d'Essoms."

"Yes, of course." Flustered, the servant put his arm out. "My lady—"

Guy stepped smartly between us. "You will take her cloak," he said softly. Whether it was Delaunay's manner which he had adopted or the vestiges of his training in the Cassiline Brotherhood, it quelled d'Essoms' servant as surely as it had the lordling in the bar long ago.

"Yes. Yes, of course." D'Essoms' servant snapped his fingers, beckoning urgently at the bewildered maid who answered. "Take my lady's cloak," he said sharply to her. I unfastened the clasp and shrugged it off my shoulders. The material slithered, rich and opulent, into his waiting hands.

Delaunay knew what he was about. D'Essoms' servant drew in his breath at the weight of the *sangoire* cloak, handing it to the maid, who covertly stroked the nap of the dense velvet as she folded it carefully over her arm. I held my head high, receiving their curious glances and returning them, letting them take in my crimson-marked eye. Gentry gossip, but so do servants. All first impressions matter.

"This way, my lady," D'Essoms' servant said again, but there was respect in his tone as he extended his arm. I took it graciously, permitting my fingertips to brush— just barely—his forearm. In this manner, he conducted me into the presence of Childric d'Essoms.

His lordship was waiting in his trophy room. That was what I came to call it, at any rate; what he called it, I never knew. There were frescoes of hunting scenes on two walls. A third was taken up with a hearth, in which a fire was laid and above which hung the d'Essoms coat of arms and a panoply of weapons.

Against the last wall was something else.

Childric d'Essoms had the same look I had noted at Cecilie's fête; tight-braided hair and the hooded eyes of a bird of prey. He wore a subdued brocade doublet and sateen hosen, and held aloft a glass of cordial.

"Leave her, Philipe," he said dismissively. His servant bowed and departed, closing the door behind him.

I was alone with my first patron.

With swift strides, Childric d'Essoms closed the distance between us. His right hand, unencumbered, rose almost casually until he dashed it across my face. I staggered sideways, tasting blood, remembering the deadly accuracy with which he'd hurled his lees in the game of kottabos. He still held the glass of cordial in his left hand and hadn't spilled a drop.

"You will kneel in my presence, whore," he said nonchalantly.

I sank down on my knees, *abeyante*, red velvet skirts pooling around me on the flagstones. They were cold, despite the fire. I watched his polished boots as he paced around me.

"Why does Anafiel Delaunay send an *anguissette* to tempt the likes of me?" he asked, circling behind me. I felt his hand dig into my enmeshed curls, wrenching my head backward, and stared up at his hooded, gleaming eyes. My throat felt vulnerable and exposed.

"I don't know, my lord," I whispered, my voice constricted with fear.

"I don't believe you." He pressed his thigh hard against the back of my head, sliding his hand down to encircle my throat. "Tell me, Phèdre nó Delaunay, what your lord wishes of me. Does he think me so easily ensnared, hm?" He punctuated his words with a jerk of his hand. "Does he suppose I'll spill my secrets in idle pillow talk with a rented whore?" Another spasm of his clutching fingers. He was applying pressure to the spot where my pulse beat in my throat, and spots of black danced in my vision. "I . . . don't . . . know . . ." I whispered the words again, a strange languor invading my body as consciousness began to ebb. With an effort, I turned my head, feeling the muscles of his thigh move beneath my cheek. My breath seemed to come hot and labored.

"Elua!" D'Essoms froze, exhaling the word. His hand loosened on my throat, rising to cup the back of my head. "You really *are*, aren't you?" I heard wonder, and amusement, in his voice; he hadn't been sure, I thought, and in some part of my mind took note of the fact that it had been worth over four thousand ducats to him to claim a victory over Delaunay anyway. "Prove it, then, little *anguissette*; as you are, on your knees. Please me."

So he said, but he hadn't needed to tell me. I was already turning as I knelt, grasping his boots with unclasped hands, sliding my palms up the slick leather. I knew what he wished, knew his desire as surely as the sea knows the tidal urges of the moon. The muscles of his thighs twitched beneath my gliding hands. With a curse, he hurled his glass aside. I heard it shatter somewhere as my fingertips grazed his erect phallus, straining against the fabric of his hosen. He dug both hands into my hair as I undid the buttons.

The art of *languisement* is an ancient and subtle one, and I am ashamed to say that I employed none of its niceties. Then again, that is not always the nature of my art. D'Essoms groaned as his phallus sprang free, the tip of it nudging my parted lips, and his hands clenched on my head, urging me to take his shaft into my mouth, deep into my throat. Ah, if only he had known! I accepted him eagerly, lips and tongue working frantically, putting into practice at last the knowledge of a thousand hours' of study and more. He groaned again as he climaxed, shoving me away and tearing the mesh net loose from my hair.

I fell back, sprawling, my hair tumbling in wild disarray about my shoulders. Childric d'Essoms advanced upon me. "Whore!" he shouted, back-handing me across the mouth. I licked my lips, tasting blood mixed with his seed. "Ill-gotten spawn of Naamah!" Another blow, glancing. I looked up through the hair spilled over my eyes and saw his phallus stirring to erection. D'Essoms gained control of himself with a shudder. "On your feet," he said, grinding out the words. "Take off your clothes."

Rising, I reached behind my back with trembling

fingers and began to undo the jet buttons, one by one. D'Essoms watched, his eyes hooded.

"There," he said harshly, pointing to a pallet of cushions. A swatch of white silk was spread across them. "I have in mind to make a new coat of arms, in honor of Anafiel Delaunay." When I let fall the red velvet gown, he shoved me so that I stumbled, naked, toward the pallet. "I have paid your virgin-price," d'Essoms said menacingly, advancing toward me. "Pray you have played your lord true, and award me with the badge of victory, Phèdre. On your back."

He moved like a stalking beast, shedding clothes, looming over me as I lay upon the pallet, forcing my legs over his shoulders.

I do not know what it is like, for other women. There was no arousement such as I had seen in the Showing at Camellia House; and yet for me, I was ready, as ready as ever an adept was for her first joining. With one smooth thrust, d'Essoms pierced me to the core, and even as I cried out at the pain of it, the face of Blessed Naamah swam in my vision, and I gasped with pleasure. Again and again he thrust himself into me, and I felt my body pliant in his hands, while waves of pain and pleasure beat at me like the wings of Naamah's doves in her temple.

He was Delaunay's enemy and I should have hated him.

I found my arms were wound tight about his neck and I cried out his name as he spent himself inside of me.

It may be that it sobered him in some part. I do not know. He drew away and breathed heavily alongside me, loosening his hair at last from the tight confinements of his braid. He looked more handsome with it falling about his shoulders.

"I have this, then, at least." He eased the swatch of white silk from beneath me, bearing the vivid red stain of my virgin blood. His predatory eyes were strangely calm. "You know what I desire, Phèdre?"

"Yes, my lord," I murmured. I rose obediently from his pallet to cross to the device on the fourth wall; the last wall. I did not need to be told. I stood spread-eagled against the X-shaped cross, his whipping-post. I could feel his breath against my skin as he fastened the thongs at my wrists and ankles. The rough wood of the cross chafed my hipbones.

"You are the most splendid thing I have ever seen," he murmured, jerking tight the ties binding my left wrist. My fingers splayed out in anguished protest. "Tell me what Delaunay desires."

"I don't know." I gasped as he wrenched my right ankle and lashed it to the cross.

"Truly?" He rose and his breath tickled my ear, and I felt the trailing ends of a flogger caress my lower back.

"I swear it!"

And then the lash began to fall.

I could not count the number of times. It was not like my childhood punishment at the hand of the Dowayne's chastiser, for there was no mediator, no quota of blows. I know only that I writhed and pleaded against the rough wood, and still the lash fell mercilessly, bearing out Childric d'Essoms hatred of my lord. Once I gave up and sagged against my bonds, offering no resistance; he came to me then and reached between my legs with his fingers, stirring me until I pleaded, humiliated, for a different release. Then the lash fell again.

At last his arm tired, and he came behind me once more. I felt his fingers spread my buttocks. "I paid Anafiel Delaunay a virgin-price," he whispered in my ear. I felt the blunt head of his phallus probe at my nether orifice and dug my fingertips into the rude wood of the cross, driving splinters beneath my nails. "And I will take it, to the last centime."

He did.

SEVENTEEN

Afterward Cecilie came to visit and took me on an excursion to a sanctuary of Naamah some miles outside the City, famed for its hot springs.

It was strange to treat with her as an almost-equal, after so many years as her pupil, but she was gracious as ever and any awkwardness soon passed between us. There was a chill to the spring air, but the sun was warm and bright, and it was good to see the pale green shoots of new growth emerging as we drove into the countryside. We were well-received by the priests and priestesses of Naamah at the temple, and though they were discreet, I daresay they recognized the name of Cecilie Laveau-Perrin.

"After all," she said in the bathhouse, shrugging gracefully into one of the robes they had given us, "we are Servants of Naamah, my dear. We may as well indulge ourselves in such amenities as that avails us."

The hot springs bubbled in rocky pools, releasing wisps of steam in the cool air. Only a few early flowers bloomed, intrepid and pale, but there was a warble of birdsong, giving promise of summer to come. I followed Cecilie as she walked carefully over the rocks, following suit as she slipped out of her robe and lowered her body into the warm, slightly acrid waters.

"Aahhh." She sighed with pleasure, settling her sub-

merged form on rocks long since worn smooth by water
and the luxuriating bodies of innumerable bathers. "They
say the waters have good healing qualities, you know.
Come, let me see." She examined the welts on my back
as I turned obediently. "Skin-deep. There'll be no trace
of them in a week. I've heard Childric d'Essoms makes
love as if he's hunting boar. Is it true?"

I thought of him wielding his phallus like a spear and
almost laughed. "It is true enough," I said. The warmth
of the waters was beginning to seep into my bones, filling my limbs with a feeling of lassitude and soothing
the minor pains d'Essoms had dealt my flesh into a
sweet, warm ache. "He has the passion of his fury, at
least."

"Is there aught for which your studies with me left
you unprepared?"

"No." I answered truthfully, shaking my head. "Lord
d'Essoms desired little in the manner of art."

"Others will," she assured me, adding, "Phèdre, if you
have questions, do not hesitate to ask me." With that,
she dropped the matter, and her eyes took on a glint I
remembered well from the boudoir gossip of Cereus
House. "Do you think he will ask for you again?"

Remembering d'Essoms' rage, the wild blows of the
flogger against my skin and his breath hot against my
neck, I smiled. "You may be sure of it," I murmured,
tilting my head back to submerge my hair. It fell, wa-
terlogged and silken, down the length of my back as I
straightened. "He will tell himself it is to beat Delaunay
at his game," I told her. "But that is only what he will
tell himself."

"Be careful." The admonishment in her voice was
stern enough that I took heed, glancing at her. "If
d'Essoms realizes you know what you're about, he will
be frightened; and that, my dear, will make him truly

dangerous." Cecilie sighed, looking of a sudden tired and aged through the wreathing steam. "Anafiel Delaunay does not reckon he does, equipping a child of your proclivities with that much knowledge and sending you into certain danger."

There were a hundred things I longed to ask her, but I knew well enough that she would not answer. "My lord Delaunay knows full well what he does," I said instead.

"Let us hope you are right." Cecilie spoke the words firmly, sitting straighter in the hot spring and looking once more like the prized blossom of Cereus House that she had been. "Come, we are not too late to join in the luncheon meal, and the Servants of Naamah lay a fine table at her sanctuary. If we do not dawdle overmuch, there will be time to soak again before we need return to the City."

We dined well that day, and made our return to the City before sundown. I made my report to Delaunay that night, and he seemed well enough at ease with it, praising me for doing naught but letting d'Essoms swallow the bait of our assignation, hook and all.

"Tell him nothing," he said, satisfaction in his voice, "and he will tell you something in time, Phèdre, in hopes of priming the pump. It is human nature, to give in hope of getting. Lord d'Essoms will give. It is inevitable." Going to his desk, he took out a small pouch and tossed it to me. I caught it by reflex, surprised. Delaunay grinned. "He sent it by courier this afternoon. A patron-gift, toward your marque. It is his will, I think, that the marquist limn his conquest of you upon your skin as a fair reminder to me. Do you wish to refuse?"

The pouch weighed heavy in my hand. It was the first coin of my own I had ever owned. I shook my head. "If it serve your will, my lord, so let it be. He was the first."

I might have wished for some sign of jealousy, were

I less of a realist. Delaunay gazed into some unknowable distance, nodding to himself. He was not displeased. "Then let it be. I will make an appointment with the marquist."

And thus began my career as a Servant of Naamah.

A week later to the day, I had my first meeting with the marquist. As Cecilie had predicted, the weals marring my back and sides had faded to nothingness in that time, leaving my skin a clean slate for the marquist's art. Kushiel's chosen heal swiftly; we have need of it.

Because Delaunay was Delaunay, nothing but the finest would do for his adepts; I went to the same man as Alcuin, a master of the trade. Robert Tielhard had been at his art for two-score years, and his services came dear. I had long known this would be the case, for Delaunay had paid dear in purchasing my marque.

I was not Alcuin, to remember to the last clause and by-law the regulations governing every guild in the nation, but I knew the rules of my own well enough. The Guild of the Servants of Naamah does not allow for outright slavery. Delaunay did not own my marque so much as he held it in trust for Naamah—but until such time as I made it, I was indentured into his service. All contract fees belonged to Delaunay; only patron-gifts freely given in homage to Naamah could go toward my marque.

I spent the first hour in the marquist's shop naked, lying flat on my stomach with my head pillowed on my arms while Master Robert Tielhard muttered around my backside with a pair of calipers, taking my measurements and transferring them to paper. When he was done, I sat up and donned my clothes, admiring the masterful sketch of a part of me I seldom saw. I particularly liked the curve of my lower back, widening like the base of a fiddle from my narrow waist.

" 'Tis not for your vanity I do this, missy!" Master Tielhard snapped, turning to his apprentice. "Run down the street, lad, and fetch Lord Delaunay from the wineshop." While I sat waiting on his limning-table, he ignored me, fetching out a rolled scroll from its cubbyhole and pinning it up on a cork wall next to my sketch.

I recognized Alcuin's marque from its base, which he already bore on his skin, but still I gasped to see the design in its entirety. It was surpassingly beautiful, and I understood why Robert Tielhard had earned the right to be called Master.

Each of the Thirteen Houses has its own marque-pattern, but it is a different matter for Servants of Naamah not attached to any House. Our marques—within certain strictures—are highly individualized.

Of course the designs are highly abstracted, but a trained eye can pick out the underlying forms, and I soon saw many in Alcuin's. Elegant scrolling at the base suggested a mountain stream, and the slim, supple trunk of a white birch rose upward, a fine pattern of birch-leaves twining about it and crowning it in a delicate spray at the finial. The lines were strong, but the colors subtle, soft greys and charcoals that would echo Alcuin's unusual coloring, with the merest hint of a pale green along the edges of the leaves.

What Master Robert Tielhard designed for me was different.

Delaunay entered the marquist's shop laughing, bringing with him a breeze of wine and good conversation, but he soon sobered to the task at hand, poring with Master Tielhard over bits of foolscap as sketch after sketch was drafted and refined or discarded. I grew impatient, but he would not let me see until they had a sketch which pleased them both.

"What do you think, Phèdre?" Delaunay turned to me grinning, holding out the rough design.

It was bold, far bolder than Alcuin's marque. With some effort, I recognized the underlying design, which was based on a very old pattern, the briar rose. Somehow Master Tielhard had kept the dramatic vigor of the archaic lines, yet infused them with a subtlety that spoke at once of the vine, the bond and the lash. The thorny lines were stark black, accented in only a few choice hollows with a teardrop of scarlet—a petal, a drop of blood, the mote in my eye.

Primitive, yet sophisticated. I adored it. No matter how many visits to the marquist's were required to execute the design in full, to restore it to pristine condition after my patrons' untender mercies, it was worth it.

"My lord, it is wonderful," I answered him honestly.

"I thought as much." Delaunay preened with satisfaction while Master Tielhard set about transferring the design to the master sketch of my measurements, muttering to himself. It was astonishing to see how the lineaments bloomed beneath the sure gestures of his crabbed hands. His apprentice crowded near, craning to see around Delaunay. "I'll be in the wineshop," Delaunay said to Master Tielhard. "You'll send the boy for me when she's done?"

The marquist answered with an affirmative grunt, deep in concentration. Dropping a kiss on my disheveled curls, Delaunay waved and departed.

I waited, and waited some more while Master Tielhard copied the design to his very exacting satisfaction. And when that was done, it was time to disrobe again, lying naked while he retraced the base of my marque yet again, checking his measurements with the calipers. The quill scratched my skin and the ink tickled. He slapped my buttock once when I wriggled, absentmindedly, as one might reprimand a restless child. After that I held myself motionless.

After a small eternity, the base was outlined. Chin propped on my elbows, I watched as Master Tielhard gathered the tools of his profession; the ink-trough and his tappers. His apprentice watched me out of the corner of his eye, nervous and excited. The boy was no more than fourteen, and I smiled to think of my effect on him. He blushed as he mixed the ink, and covered it by bustling about the brazier, heaping it with coal until the marquist's shop was as warm and toasty as a baker's oven. Master Tielhard snapped at him for it, and he blushed again. I didn't care; being naked, it felt good.

And at last it was time for the marquist to start limning. As is customary, he began at the base of my spine, at the very knob where it ends, below the dimples of the lower back. I could not see him choose a tapper and dip it in the trough, but I felt it against my skin, the prick of a dozen tight-clustered needles and the seeping wetness of the ink.

Then he struck the tapper with his mallet and a dozen needles pierced my skin, impregnating the flesh at the base of my spine with a dollop of ink-black. The pain of it was an exquisite shock. I made an involuntary sound, my hips moving of their own volition to thrust against the hard surface below me, grinding my pubis into the limning table. Master Tielhard swatted me again.

"Damned *anguissettes*," he growled, concentrating on his work. "Grandpère always said they was worse than criers or bleeders. Now I know why."

Ignoring his complaint, I held myself still with the greatest of efforts while he continued, tapping, tapping, tapping with the mallet, piercing the lines of my marque into my skin.

I savored every moment of it.

Eighteen

This marked the beginning of a period of time that in many ways was the finest of my life. All that Delaunay had prophesied for me so long ago came to pass. Word of Delaunay's *anguissette* spread like a slow fire, the kind that smolders and burns below the surface, impossible to extinguish. The offers continued to come, most of them discreet, a few direct.

It was during the first year that Delaunay's cunning in the matter of our exposure became evident to me. Alcuin's patrons were a select group, most of them hand-picked and targeted by Delaunay. Friends, acquaintances or cordial enemies, they had been to Delaunay's house, had watched Alcuin grow from a beautiful boy. Delaunay had cast out a net with his auction, but he had certain fish in mind. As he drew it in, he selected his catch with care.

With me, it was another matter.

Many patrons, like Childric d'Essoms, Delaunay had anticipated; but others, many others, he had not. If Alcuin was a net cast on known waters, I was a line thrown out at sea and not even Anafiel Delaunay knew for certain who would rise to the bait.

And lest it be thought that my assignation with Childric d'Essoms laid the pattern for all further patrons, I hasten to disabuse anyone of this notion. My second assignation, a member of the Exchequer who paid dearly for the privilege, could not have been more different. Slight and deferential, Pepin Lachet seemed to me at first glance the sort of patron far more likely to contract Alcuin than I. Indeed, in the bedchamber he did naught but remove his clothes, lie upon the bed and bid me in an uninterested voice to please him.

If Childric d'Essoms required little of my art, Pepin Lachet required all of it. Disrobing, I climbed onto the bed and knelt beside him, beginning with the caress of trailing willows. I loosed my hair and flung it over him, letting it spill over him like water, slowly drawing it down the length of his body.

He lay unmoving and unexcited.

Undeterred, I set about the arousement, beginning with confidence. In the hour that followed, I tried every technique Cecilie had taught us, working with fingers, lips and tongue on every part of Pepin Lachet's body from the tips of his ears to the ends of his toes. In the end, desperate, I resorted to a measure usually used by the cheapest of prostitutes, a crude manipulation called coaxing the turtle. Pepin Lachet's member responded, stirring to a half-hearted salute.

Fearing to lose even that, I bestrode him and began to move urgently, but instead of rising further, his phallus grew limp and slipped out of me. Near to tears, I met his cold gaze.

"You're not much good at this, are you?" he asked contemptuously, spilling me off him. "I'll show you how it's done."

"My lord, I am sorry . . ." I fell silent as he reached into the nightstand and brought out silk bonds, making no protest as he tied my wrists and ankles to the bedposts. When he brought out the pincers and his phallus began to rise untouched, engorged and swollen, I understood.

Where Childric d'Essoms had been brutal, Pepin Lachet was the epitome of delicacy. I suppose it takes an exacting soul to maintain the balance of the royal treasury. He worked on me for what seemed like hours.

When I cried out at the torment of it, he thrust a padded leather gag in my mouth, asking first if I wished to give the *signale*. I shook my head, feeling tears of shame trickle backward from the corners of my eyes. My entire body was ablaze with pain, and painful with desire. "If you wish to give the *signale*," he said formally, prying my mouth open and inserting the thick gag, "rap upon the bedpost and I will hear. Do you understand?" I nodded, unable now to speak. "Good."

And with that, he continued to work upon me until I nearly bit through the gag.

After each assignation, always, came the interview. I have no way of knowing how many nuggets of knowledge we laid at Delaunay's feet, how many pieces of the puzzle he set in place after our recitations. At that time, it must be understood, while we knew a juicy morsel of information when we heard it, neither Alcuin nor I grasped the ends toward which he strove.

Of information, there was always a steady trickle, for there was increasing unrest in the realm. The King suffered a mild seizure which left him with a palsy in his right hand. Ysandre de la Courcel remained unwed. Suitors and claimants circled the throne like wolves in early winter; still wary enough to remain at a distance, but with growing hunger.

Most ambitious of the pack was no wolf, but a lion, the Lioness of Azzalle. Though I never met Lyonette de la Courcel de Trevalion in all this time, I heard much of her and her constant intrigues.

One I even learnt of firsthand.

I had been contracted for a two-day assignation to the Marquise Solaine Belfours at her country estate. Delaunay had picked his target well in her. It was her pleasure to assign me tasks I had no hope of completing, and chastise me for the failure. On this occasion, she led me to her receiving room, where she had ordered the gardeners to deliver a burgeoning pile of cut flowers. They sprawled in a mound on the sideboard, a profusion of blossoms and tangled stems, dripping onto the wood and shedding dirt and leaves.

"I'm going for a ride," she informed me with her customary arrogance. "When I return, I wish to have a glass of cordial in this room, and I wish it to be in proper array and you in waiting attendance. Is that clear, Phèdre?"

I despise being forced to perform menial work, which Solaine Belfours had somehow discerned; women are cleverer than men at such things, on the whole. I dreaded these assignations, except for the fact that she was splendid in her anger. So it was that I cursed and swore through the better part of an hour, separating stems and pricking my fingers as I shoved roses, asters and zinnia into various vessels. Her servants brought buckets of water, and a dustpan and rags and wax for the sideboard, but would not aid me in any way, being forbidden to do so. I do not know if country servants gossip as they do in the city, but of a surety, these had no illusion about why I was there.

Of course it was not possible to complete the chore in the allotted time, and Solaine Belfours strode through the door, still in riding attire, while I was just beginning to brush dirt into the dustpan. I knelt quickly, but she was faster with her riding crop, catching me across the shoulders. "Wretched slattern! I told you to have this room ready for me. What do you call this?" Sweeping one hand through the mess of water and dirt on the sideboard, she peeled off her glove and struck me in the face with it. I tossed my hair back and glared at her, not needing to feign sullenness.

"You ask too much," I retorted.

Solaine Belfours had blue-green eyes, the color of aquamarines; when she was angry, they indeed turned as cold and hard as gemstones. It made my breath come quicker to watch it. "I ask only to be well served," she said coolly. She took her crop in her bare hand, tapping it against the gloved palm of the other. "And you presume too much. Take off your dress."

It was not my first time with her and I knew how the scene played out. It is a strange thing, this playing and not playing. That my role was scripted to meet her desires, I knew well and played it accordingly; but there was no artifice in it when the crop stung my bare flesh over and over and I pleaded with her to let me make amends. There is a certain victory in it when they surrender. Much as I despised her, I trembled as she allowed me to perform an act of contrition, undoing the buttons of her riding breeches, pressing my mouth against her heated flesh. I closed my eyes as her hands came to rest on my head, the now-idle crop held loosely, gently brushing my back and reminding me of its cruelties.

And it was at this moment that her steward intruded, entering with averted eyes to announce the arrival of a courier with an urgent message from Lyonette de Trevalion.

"Blessed Elua!" There was mingled annoyance and alarm in her voice. "What does she want now? Show him in." Stepping away from me, Solaine Belfours refastened her riding attire and smoothed her hair. I remained as I was, kneeling. She cast a glance at me, all annoyance now. "I am not finished with you. Put your clothes on, and attend."

Of a surety, I did not need to be told twice. I had learned in Cereus House how to be unobtrusive, and I had learned the value of it from Delaunay. I knelt *abey-*

ante, quiet and nigh-invisible, as the Lioness of Azzalle's courier entered.

I do not know what he looked like; Delaunay might chide me for it, but I dared not raise my eyes. It was to my good fortune that the Marquise, like many people, could not read without murmuring the words aloud to herself. I can, and so can Alcuin, but only because Delaunay made us learn to do so. Solaine Belfours could not, and thus did I learn of Lyonette de Trevalion's request. It was rumored that the Khalif of Khebbel-im-Akkad had proposed an alliance between our countries with a marriage between his heir and the Princess Ysandre. Lyonette de Trevalion proposed that Solaine draft orders to the Akkadian ambassador, stamped with the Privy Seal, to string along the Khalif with false promises until he ceded rights to the island of Cythera.

It goes without saying that it was Lyonette de Trevalion's plan that these orders be discovered, destroying all hope of an Akkadian alliance.

Solaine Belfours was a Secretary of the Privy Seal; she had access and could do it, though it was high treason to falsify royal orders. I felt the wind of her pacing, and her crop swishing as she struck it absentmindedly against her boot. "What does your mistress offer?" she asked the courier.

A deep voice answered. "A title in Azzalle, my lady. The county of Vicharde, with two hundred men-at-arms and an income of forty thousand ducats annual."

The crop swished again; I saw it, out of the corner of my eye. "Tell her I'll take it," Solaine Belfours said decisively. "But I want the title in hand before the orders go out, and safe passage guaranteed to Azzalle." Even at a distance, I could sense her cold smile. "Tell her I want no less an escort than Prince Baudoin and his Glory-Seekers. Let us see if she is in earnest."

From the rustle and creak, I knew the courier bowed. "As you wish, my lady. Title in hand, and Prince Baudoin as escort. I will relay your words."

"Good." Some time after the courier had left, I felt her gaze upon me. It lingered for a moment before I looked up. She was smiling, swinging her crop in great, looping circles. My skin shuddered involuntarily at the sight of it. "I'm of a mind to celebrate, Phèdre," she said with cheerful malice. "What a happy coincidence that you're here."

As matters fell out, Lyonette de Trevalion declined Solaine Belfours counteroffer, and as the Marquise had foreseen, the sticking-price was Prince Baudoin. Whatever the Lioness of Azzalle had planned, it was not worth risking her precious son. It soon transpired that the rumors of an alliance were no more than that; rumors. Ysandre de la Courcel would not wed the Khalif's son, and the island of Cythera remained firmly in Akkadian control.

Nonetheless, Delaunay prized the information, for it revealed to him where the lines of communication lay, and shed some light upon the dim shape of Lyonette de Trevalion's ambition.

Throughout it all, the name of Baudoin de Trevalion continued to resound from the lips of peers of the realm. While the Allies of Camlach disbanded, returning to their homes and posting lighter guards on the border, Baudoin and his Glory-Seekers rode the length of Camlach, armed with a special dispensation from the King. They put the fear of Elua into Skaldic raiders; and not a few D'Angeline mountain villages, who bore the cost of putting up his riotous crew, taken out in food stores and eligible maidens. At court, Baudoin continued to evade a plethora of matrimonial snares and, despite the disapproval of his parents, continued to be seen with Melisande Shahrizai.

It was rumored that Lyonette de Trevalion had threatened to disown him if they wed, and I think there must be some truth to this, if only because of what would later come to pass. The Lioness of Azzalle did not make idle threats, and Melisande was clever enough to know which opponents could not be defeated face-to-face.

Her, I had seen only once since I began my service to Naamah, and that at one of Delaunay's gatherings; although I had thought of her often, you may be sure. In the courtyard, she shone, no less for her beauty than her barbed wit. To me she was courteous and pleasant; but I encountered her in the hall, on my way back from an errand to the kitchen, and her smile made my knees weak.

"Turn around," she murmured.

I did it without even thinking.

Her fingers unbuttoned the back of my bodice as skillfully as an adept's; indeed, I could have sworn the fabric yearned open at her mere touch. I felt her nails against my skin, tracing the base of my marque, following it upward. Her body radiated behind me and I could smell the scent she used, subtle and spicy, mixed with the musk of her flesh.

"Your name is being spoken in certain circles, Phèdre." Only the tips of her fingers touched me, but she was close enough that her breath was warm on my neck. The amusement in her voice reminded me of Delaunay; nothing else did. "You've never given the *signale*, have you?"

"No." I breathed the word, unable to summon the strength to speak it.

"I thought not." Melisande Shahrizai laid her palm flat in the small of my back, where it burned like a brand, then drew it away and did up my buttons, quick and professional. I could hear her smile in the darkness. "Some day we will see which throws truer, Kushiel's line or Kushiel's Dart."

I daresay neither of us knew how true her words would prove, nor in what manner. Melisande knew full well what Delaunay was about with Alcuin and me; and knew, too, that I was bait for her interest. And she had every intention of taking it—in her own time. My patrons were not known for their gifts of forbearance. I had learned patience and intrigue at Delaunay's knee, and I am not ashamed to say that the thought of a patron who could match it quite undid me. When I thought of Baudoin de Trevalion now, it was with a measure of pity and envy.

The Skaldi threat, at least, seemed quelled for the time being, or so popular court wisdom had it. Where the border lords of Camlach were not, Baudoin and his Glory-Seekers were. Delaunay was not so sure. He entertained his old friend and teacher, Gonzago de Escabares, when he returned from an academic's pilgrimage to Tiberium. They spoke privately, no one but Alcuin and I in attendance.

"There are rumors, Antinous," the Aragonian historian said over the rim of his wineglass, looking like a wise satyr.

There was that name again. My marque extended a full third of the way up my back, and yet I knew no more than before of the mystery of Delaunay. This time, he ignored it.

"There are always rumors," he retorted, toying with the end of his braid. "Sometimes I think each city-state in the whole of Caerdicca Unitas has its own Parliament expressly for the purpose of disseminating rumors. Which are these, Maestro?"

Gonzago de Escabares reached for a canape of goose-liver and chives rolled in flatbread. "These are delightful. I must have your cook note the recipe for mine." He ate fastidiously, licking his fingers and wiping crumbs from his beard. "They say the Skaldic tribes have found a leader," he said when he was done. "A Cinhil Ru of their own."

After a moment of staring surpise, Delaunay gave his bark of laughter. "Surely you jest! The Skaldi have never been so quiet in our lives, Maestro."

"Precisely." The Aragonian devoured another canape and held out his glass for Alcuin to refill. "They have found a leader who thinks."

Delaunay was silent, thinking about the implications. The Skaldic tribes were numerous, more numerous than the tribes of Alba and Eire, who had united to defeat the Tiberian army, the greatest military force the continent of Europa had ever seen. Islanded, isolated and hemmed in for centuries by the Master of the Straits, the armies of the kingdom of Alba had never constituted a true threat to our borders.

A united Skaldic force would be another matter.

"What are they saying?" he asked at length.

Gonzago set down his wineglass. "Not much, yet. But you know there are always Skaldi among the mercenaries, travelling the trade routes, yes? It began among them; a whisper, not even a rumor, of great doings in the north. Slowly, traders began to notice that their numbers were changing steadily . . . not more Skaldi, but different ones, changing places, replacing their numbers. Skaldi went and Skaldi came. It is hard to tell the difference," he added, "for they are wild and ungroomed to a man, but I spoke with a leather-merchant in Milazza who was certain that he detected a growing cunning among the Skaldi he hired to protect his caravan."

I thought of the Skaldic tribesman who had taken me under his wing so long ago, a faded memory of a laughing, mustached giant. There had been no cunning in him, and much kindness. Alcuin sat wide-eyed on his couch. His memories of the Skaldi held only blood, iron and fire.

"He thought they were gathering information," Delaunay said, tugging his braid restlessly as the wheels of his mind turned and processed. "To what end?"

"That, I do not know." Gonzago shrugged and nibbled at a canape. "But there is a name which is spoken around the Skaldi campfires in hushed tones: Waldemar, or Waldemar Selig; Waldemar the Blessed who is proof against iron. And last summer, for a fortnight, there was nary a Skaldi to be found in Caerdicca Unitas, and it was rumored that Waldemar Selig summoned a high council of the tribes of Skaldia somewhere in the old Helvetican holdings. I do not know if it is true, but my friend the leather-merchant told me a friend of his who is close to the duchy in Milazza swore that the Duke received an offer of marriage for his eldest daughter from a King Waldemar of Skaldia." Gonzago shrugged again and spread his open hands in an Aragonian gesture. "What can one do with such rumors? My friend said the Duke of Milazza laughed and sent the Skaldi envoy home with seven cartloads of silk and fustian. But I tell you I mistrust this quiet on the Skaldi borders."

Delaunay tapped his front teeth with the nail of one forefinger. "And meanwhile Baudoin de Trevalion gambols about the fringes of Camlach, skewering starving brigands and garnering acclaim for protecting the realm. You are right, Maestro, this bears watching. If you learn aught in your travels, send me word."

"You know I will, my dear." Gonzago de Escabares' tone softened, and his brown eyes were kind in his homely face. "Do not think I am not ever mindful of your promise, Antinous."

I was still puzzling out this last convoluted sentence when Delaunay's sharp gaze fell upon Alcuin and myself. He clapped his hands briskly. "Phèdre, Alcuin; to bed with the both of you. The Maestro and I have much to discuss, and none of it needful for your ears."

It need not be said that we obeyed, but I will add that one of us, at least, went reluctantly.

Nineteen

Despite the concerns of Gonzago de Escabares, the only news of note that occurred outside our borders in the following months lay not within Skaldic territories, but in the kingdom of Alba. And the rumor that crossed the waters was this: The Cruarch of Alba was dead, slain, it was said, by his own son, who sought to overturn the old matrilineal rites of succession and seize rulership of Alba for himself.

The Cruarch's rightful heir, his club-footed nephew, had fled with his mother and three younger sisters to the western shores of Alba, where the Dalriada of Eire, who had a foothold there, gave them asylum.

No one had ever paid much heed to the regency of Alba before, but because this Cruarch had set foot on D'Angeline soil, it merited a passing interest. In a joint venture with the royal House of Aragon, Quintilius Rousse was ordered to bring his fleet through the southerly Cadishon Strait and scout the coastline; he reported that Elder Brother maintained his sovereignty over Alban waters. Thus Ganelon de la Courcel strengthened his alliance with the King of Aragon, and Quintilius Rousse found an excuse to leave a portion of his fleet on the coast of Kusheth. At Delaunay's, he boasted of his cunning, but I liked him well enough to forgive it. Delaunay was summoned twice to court, and afterward said nothing of it.

No word came from de Escabares, nor any rumor of Waldemar Selig. The borders of Camlach remained quiet; so quiet that Prince Baudoin grew bored of seeking glory in the mountains and began to divide his time between the royal court and his home in Azzalle. His father, the Duc de Trevalion, was quarreling with the King. Azzalle maintained a small but capable fleet of its own, and the Duc was put out that the King had called upon Quintilius Rousse to scout the coastline instead of him.

There was some merit to his grievance, for Azzalle lay almost in hailing distance of Alba, whereas Quintilius had needed to bring his fleet a fortnight's journey around Aragonia. That the joint venture strengthened ties with the House of Aragon, Duc Marc knew full well; but Quintilius Rousse was not of royal blood, and the slight stung.

I do not know if the King mistrusted the Duc de Trevalion, on this score. I do know that he mistrusted his sister and her all-too-obvious ambition for her son, and was too canny to pass up a means of undermining her power when there was political gain to be had in the process.

All of these things I heard and knew—indeed, Delaunay and Gaspar Trevalion had a falling-out over the quarrel between House Courcel and Trevalion—but during this time they registered lightly on my consciousness. I was young and beautiful, and I chose my patrons from among the scions of Elua. I would be lying if I said all of this did not go to my head. There is a power in being able to choose one's patrons, and I learned to wield it well. Three times running, I declined offers from Lord Childric d'Essoms, until even Delaunay debated the wisdom of my judgment, but in this, I was the master of my art. When I acceded to his fourth offer—his final, his servant warned—his stored fury was prodigious indeed.

That was the night he burned me with a red-hot poker.

It was also the night he let slip his patron's name.

Servants of Naamah are not the only ones with patrons, of course; in court society, nearly everyone is either a patron or patronized. It is only the services which differ. One of the reasons I loved Delaunay so well was that he was one of very few people I ever met who truly stood free of the system. I suppose it is one of the reasons d'Essoms hated him so.

The other reason came clear with the name he so carelessly uttered. Always, without exception, it pleased Childric d'Essoms to press me to reveal Delaunay's motives. Where Solaine Belfours sought a myriad of reasons to punish me, d'Essoms needed only the one: Delaunay.

When he used the poker, he knew he had gone too far. For my part, I sagged in my bonds, splayed against the X-shaped cross he so favored, fighting to remain conscious and thinking how Delaunay would berate me for failing to give the *signale*. In truth, I hadn't thought he would do it. But d'Essoms had laid the poker against the inside of my thigh, and the stench of my own scorched flesh surrounded me. The poker had stuck when he pulled it loose, tearing skin.

There was no pleasure in this, at least not in the way that anyone but an *anguissette* would understand it. Pain strung my body like a plucked harpstring, and behind closed eyes my vision was washed in red. I was in it and of it, at once the taut, quivering string and the high sustained note of it, a note of purest beauty uttered in the depths of torment. In a crimson haze, I heard as if from a great distance d'Essom's agitated voice and felt his hands patting my cheeks. Somewhere I could hear the echoes of a great clangor and knew he had thrown the poker from him in horror. "Phèdre, Phèdre, speak to me! Oh, for Blessed Elua's sake, speak to me, child!" There was anxiety in his tone, and caring; more than he ever would have confessed. I felt his hands patting me, chafing, rough tenderness, and heard his mutter. "Barquiel L'Envers will have my head for this if Delaunay makes a charge . . . Phèdre, child, wake up, tell me you're well, 'tis naught but a burn . . ."

Head hanging, I opened my eyes and the wash of red receded, fading from my right eye and dwindling to a mote in my left. Seeing my lashes lift, Childric d'Essoms gave a cry of relief, undoing my bonds and easing my limp body down as it slipped loose of the whipping cross. Cradling me in his arms in the middle of his trophy room, he shouted for his physician.

I knew then that he was mine.

As I had guessed, Delaunay was not so pleased, though he withheld comment upon my return. He ordered me confined to bed and brought in a Yeshuite doctor to attend me. Although they are shunned in many nations, they are made welcome in Terre d'Ange, for Blessed Elua was fathered by the blood of Yeshua, which we do not forget. The doctor cut a solemn figure with his grave face and the long, curling sidelocks of his people, but his touch was gentle and I rested more comfortably when he had applied a poultice to draw the poisons and re-bandaged my thigh. It discomforted him to touch me in so intimate a fashion, which made me smile. "I will come in two days to examine her," he said to

Delaunay in his formal, accented D'Angeline. "But I bid you inspect the wound on the morrow, and if there is an odor of mortification, send for me without delay."

Delaunay nodded and thanked him, waiting courteously until the doctor was ushered from my room. Then he turned his dry look on me and raised his eyebrows.

"I hope it was worth it," he said curtly.

I did not take offense, for I knew it was only that he cared for me. "You may be the judge, my lord." I squirmed in my bed, rearranging pillows to sit propped until Delaunay swore softly and aided me, his careful movements at odds with his tone.

"All right," he said, unable to prevent a gleam of amusement from lighting his eye at my dissembling. "There is a pile of love-gifts from Childric d'Essoms amassing in the hallway in atonement for this injury, and if he doesn't stop soon, next it will be a brace of oxen or a copy of the Lost Book of Raziel itself. Now what information do you have that is so valuable it is worth turning yourself into a braised rack of lamb?"

Content to have his full regard, free of judgment, I relaxed against my cushions and gave it straight out. "Childric d'Essoms answers to Barquiel L'Envers."

To watch Delaunay's face at such a time was like watching a storm cross the horizon. Duc Barquiel L'Envers was full brother to the long-dead Isabel.

"So d'Essoms is the conduit for House Envers' ambitions," he mused aloud. "I wondered who kept the torch alight. He must be behind L'Envers' posting to the Khalifate. You told him nothing?"

His glance was swift and cutting. "My lord!" I protested, sitting upright and wincing at the pain.

"Phèdre, I'm sorry." Delaunay's face changed as he knelt at my bedside and grasped my hand. "This information you give me is a pearl of great price, truly, but it is not worth the pain you have suffered for it. Promise me that next time you will give the *signale*."

"My lord, I am what I am, and it is for that you bought my marque," I said reasonably. "But I did not think he would use the poker, truly." Seeing him take ease from my words, I pressed the moment's advantage. "My lord, who was Isabel L'Envers to you, that her enmity should pursue you beyond the grave?"

If I thought to catch him in a weak moment, I was mistaken; his features took on their stern look, which I loved. "Phèdre, we have spoken of this, and it is best you do not know why I do as I do. Mark my words, if Childric d'Essoms truly thought you knew aught you were not telling, he would not be so gentle with you; and his gentleness leaves little to commend it."

And with that, he kissed my brow and took his leave, bidding me to sleep and be healed.

Happily, I have good-healing flesh, legacy of Kushiel's Dart. When the Yeshuite doctor returned, he pronounced the ugly burn clean of any trace of festering and gave Delaunay a salve to spread on it that would aid the growth of new skin and help to prevent scarring. I saw adepts in Valerian House whose skin was thick with welted scars, but that was never the case with me. Delaunay always kept in stock a supply of unguents and balms to spread on such weals as I received; though I may say that none ever worked so well as the Yeshuite's salve.

Since I could not practice my art, I spent time with Hyacinthe.

Even as my station had changed, so had his. He had at long last convinced his mother to part with some of her hard-won gold to augment his own, and they now owned the building on Rue Coupole. It was no less small and squalid than before, but it was theirs. They lived as they always had on the lower floor, and let rooms to an interminable stream of Tsingani families who passed through the City with every horse fair and circus that followed the trade routes.

His mother had grown older and dwindled in size, but the fierce glare of her deep-set eyes had not diminished. I marked how the itinerant Tsingani paid her respect; and I marked how they avoided Hyacinthe, though I never spoke of it to him. Among the Tsingani, he was half-D'Angeline and shunned, but among D'Angelines, he was the Prince of Travellers and the denizens of Mont Nuit continued to pay good coin to have him read their palms.

For his part, Hyacinthe had not given up his dream of finding his mother's people and claiming his birthright as her son; but these were not such Tsingani as passed the City's boundaries and came to dwell for a time within it. They had done so once and once only, he told me—for so his mother had told him—and lost their fairest daughter to the wiles of D'Angeline seduction. Now only the poorest of companies entered the City gates, while the flower of Tsingani nobility wandered the earth, following the *Lungo Drom*, the long road.

So Hyacinthe believed, and it was not for me to disabuse him of this notion; perhaps, indeed, it was true. For now he seemed well-enough satisfied to remain the undisputed Prince of Travellers in Mont Nuit, and I was glad of it, for he was my friend. I never told him, though, that I had chosen his name as my *signale*. I loved Hyacinthe dearly, but he would have crowed like a cock to hear it, and I could not abide that much of his vanity all of a piece.

"So Childric d'Essoms is in the L'Envers' pocket," he said when I told him my news, and whistled through his teeth. "That *is* news, Phèdre. What does your Delaunay make of it?"

"Nothing." I made a sour face. "He gets closer-lipped with age, and would feign protect us with ignorance. Though I think sometimes he tells Alcuin things he would not have me hear."

We sat at the kitchen table, and I had thrown off my *sangoire* cloak, which I wore everywhere those days, for the air was stifling and smelled of cooking cabbage. His mother poked and muttered at the stove, ignoring us. It was a reassuring constant in my life. Hyacinthe grinned at me and tossed a silver coin in the air, catching it in one hand and making it walk across his knuckles, then disappear. He had learned the trick from a street-corner illusionist in exchange for two weeks' lodging. "You are jealous."

"No," I said, then; "Yes, perhaps."

"Has he bedded the boy?"

"No!" I exclaimed, offended at both the notion and his use of the word "boy," when Alcuin was no younger than he himself. "Delaunay would not do that!"

Hyacinthe shrugged. "Still, you must consider the possibility. You would be quick enough to boast of it, if it were you."

"It's not me." The lack of promise in that outlook made me glum. "No, he is freer with Alcuin because he reckons Alcuin's patrons are not so dangerous as mine, or at least more subtle in the ways of violence. Anyway, they have been thick in politics since the day he took Alcuin to court to pose as his scribe. I do not see the logic in it, when the Cruarch was slain and another rules in his place."

Hyacinthe's mother muttered louder at the stove.

Once, he had ignored such ominous rumblings; now,

I noted, his expression grew sharp, like a hound on the trail of scent. "What is it, Mother?"

The words were repeated, unintelligible, then turning, she brandished a ladle at us. I remembered her pointing finger, which had struck a note of fear in my heart. "Pay heed," she said in a dire tone. "Do not discount the Cullach Gorrym."

I looked at Hyacinthe, who blinked. "I do not understand your words," he said carefully to his mother.

She trembled and lowered the ladle, passing her other hand before her eyes. Her face looked sunken and old. "I know not," she admitted in a thready voice.

"The black boar." I cleared my throat, feeling strangely apologetic. Both of them glanced at me. "It is Cruithne, madame; the words you spoke." I had been so long dissembling among patrons, I was awkward in vaunting my learning. "Do not discount the black boar."

"Well, then." Her expression cleared, resuming its usual dour mien. Her jaw jutted forward obstinately, defying me and my knowledge and my *sangoire* cloak to contradict her. "There you have it, missy. Do not discount the black boar."

It was my second such prophesy granted free of charge by the mother of the Prince of Travellers and my one true friend; and as clear as the first had been, the second was oblique. I looked once more at Hyacinthe, who raised both hands and spread them, shaking his head. Whatever the black boar might be, he knew no better than I.

When I returned home, I related the incident to Delaunay, who had spent the day being fitted for a new suit of clothing. As he misliked wasting overmuch time on tailors, he was in a foul mood and quick to dismiss the warning. "You of all people should know that Tsingani fortune-telling is mere foolery," he said sharply.

I stared at Delaunay. "She has the gift. I have seen it. My lord, she did not seek to lie in this, nor before when she told me I would rue the day I unraveled your mystery."

"She . . ." Delaunay stopped. "She said that?"

"Yes, my lord."

Alcuin brought the wine-jug over to refill Delaunay's glass. His hair fell forward as he bent to his task and Delaunay ran a shining strand of it through his fingers absentmindedly, gazing at the flame of an oil lamp. "My lord," Alcuin said softly, straightening. "You remember I told you of the whispers of the Alban delegation? The Cruarch's sister had a vision, of a silver swan and a black boar."

"But who is . . . ?" Delaunay's face changed. "Alcuin, send word on the morrow to Thelesis de Mornay. Tell her I would speak with her."

"As you wish, my lord."

TWENTY

What became of that conversation, I never learned; or at least not until much later, when it mattered no longer. I might have been put out at it, were it not for the fact that my own interests, for a time, outweighed Delaunay's intrigues.

Melisande Shahrizai was giving a birthday party for Prince Baudoin de Trevalion. She had engaged the whole of Cereus House for an entire night to do it, and we were invited; all three of us.

I had not forgotten the promise she had made me when last we met; I had not forgotten her words when first I met her. *You do wish to serve Naamah, don't you child?* No matter how many patrons I had had, none of them had ever turned my knees to water with a glance.

If I have not said it, Melisande was exceedingly wealthy. House Shahrizai is prosperous to start, and she had at her disposal as well the estates of two deceased husbands. Indeed, if not for the rumors that surrounded those deaths, it is conceivable that Lyonette de Trevalion would have found Melisande a suitable daughter-in-law, although I doubt it. From what I had heard, she did not strike me as a woman capable of tolerating rivalry among equals.

For my part, I do not believe Melisande Shahrizai killed either of her husbands. Both were very rich and very old, and I do not think she had need. Although she was only sixteen the first time, and nineteen at her second wedding, I would fain believe she was no less calculating then than when first I encountered her; and the woman I knew was far too clever to take an unnecessary risk for mere gold.

Although I didn't know, then, how skilled she was at using the hands of others to meet her own ends. I know it now.

Whatever the truth of the matter, it left her a very rich woman, and the City was fair buzzing with the news of Baudoin's birthday party. Invitations, written in gold ink on thick vellum and scented with fragrance, were delivered and jealously guarded. Rumors abounded regarding the list of invitees and the possible slights that lay behind omissions.

Melisande delivered the invitation herself, sweeping into the house in a cloud of the same subtle fragrance that impregnated the card. Delaunay opened it and raised his eyebrows.

"All of my household?" he inquired dryly. "You do realize, I trust, that my protégées are not included in the contract-fee for Cereus House, Melisande."

She tossed her chin and laughed, showing the lovely line of her throat. "I knew you would say that, Anafiel; that's why I came to make the invitation in person. Yes, of course. This is my party, after all, and your little pupils are more interesting than any three courtiers together."

"I thought it was Baudoin's party."

His jibe made no mark. She merely looked at him through her lashes and smiled. "It is for Baudoin, of course, but it is *my* party, Anafiel. Surely you know me well enough for that."

Delaunay returned her smile, running the ball of his thumb over the edge of the vellum. "If you think to win the son of the Lioness of Azzalle over to defying his mother, you may be overstepping your bounds, Melisande. She makes a fearsome enemy."

"Ah, my dear Delaunay, always fishing for knowledge," she said lightly, putting her hand over his and taking hold of the card of invitation. "If you do not wish to attend . . . ?"

"No." Shaking his head, he grinned and took a step back, retaining possession of the card. "We will be there, you may be sure of it."

"I am overjoyed to hear it." Melisande Shahrizai made him a mocking curtsy and turned to leave. Catching sight of me standing in the shadows, she blew me a kiss as she made her exit. Delaunay saw me and frowned. What expression I wore, I cannot imagine.

"Whatever happens," he said, "you are to keep your eyes and ears open, Phèdre; and warn Alcuin, too. Melisande Shahrizai does nothing without reason, and I cannot fathom her motive in this. It inclines me to suspicion." A shadow crossed his face. "I suppose this means I must send for the tailor again," he added, annoyed at the prospect.

Annoyed or no, Delaunay ensured that all of us would cut a good figure at Baudoin's party. With his exquisite taste, it was a marvel how he had no patience for the process of fine attire—but the end result, you may be sure, was no less splendid for it. When all was done, Alcuin was resplendent in midnight-blue velvet, a color that made him look like a vision dreamt by moonlight. Delaunay wore the deep umber that made him look like an autumn feast, with his russet hair and saffron slashes in his sleeves. And I was delighted to find that he had commissioned another bolt of *sangoire* to have a gown made for me. Although it did not dip so low as I might have wished in the back—it is vulgar for a Servant of Naamah to display an unfinished marque—it had a low decolletage, and I wore a ruby pendant given me by Childric d'Essoms that nestled in the hollow between my breasts.

I had not returned to Cereus House since the day I had left it in Delaunay's coach, and it was strange to return. The first time aside, every time I had approached this place, it had been slung ignominiously across the pommel of a guard's saddle. Behind the closed gates, I could see that the house was ablaze with light and merriment. I shuddered as we drew up to the entrance and Delaunay descended from the coach.

"Are you all right?" Alcuin whispered, leaning over to grasp my hand. There was nothing but sweet concern on his face, and I repented of the number of times I had been jealous of him.

"I'm fine." I squeezed his hand in reply, gathered my skirts, and followed Delaunay.

Prince Baudoin de Trevalion's natal festivities were already in full stride. It was summer, and nigh every door in the house was flung open. I, who had lived there six years, had never seen such a fête. Great vases of roses, heliotrope and lavender were set on every surface, spilling an abundance of blossom and scent. In every niche, musicians played, and it seemed lovers groped and sighed in every corner. A night's fee had been paid for every adept in Cereus House. No guest would be refused.

The thought of it staggered my mind and struck me with a wave of envious desire. To be in such a situation, bought for the night, available to anyone at the crook of a finger! I wished, almost, that I were an adept of Cereus House.

And then I remembered that I was a guest, and my mind reeled further to think on it.

We were conducted to the Great Hall, which was lit and adorned as I had only seen it for the Midwinter Masque. A throng of people in gorgeous plumage had already gathered, the sound of laughter and flirtation mingling with music and a hundred savory odors wafting in the air. Beautiful apprentices of both sexes carried trays of food and drink, offering them to all and sundry. The liveried footman called out our names and a handsome blond man in the colors of Cereus House extricated himself gracefully from the throng and came over to us.

"Phèdre," he said, giving me the kiss of greeting. "Welcome. Welcome back." It was Jareth Moran, a little older, but much the same. I blinked in surprise, seeing that he wore a Dowayne's chain about his neck, with the seal of Cereus House upon it. He turned smiling to Delaunay. "My lord Delaunay, it is good to see you. Be welcome. And you are Alcuin nó Delaunay." He grasped Alcuin's hand briefly, seeing a hint of reserve flicker in the dark eyes. I had forgotten the exquisite courtesies of the Night Court; or rather, I had never been on the receiving end of them. "Be welcome."

"The Dow—" I began to ask, then corrected myself. "The old Dowayne?"

Jareth looked grave, although I could tell it was put on. "She died some seven years ago, Phèdre. It was a peaceful death, she went in her sleep." He touched his chain. "I have been Dowayne since."

"I am sorry," I murmured, unaccountably grieved. As fierce as the old woman had been, she was a part of my childhood. "You have been an able successor, I am sure."

"I do my best." Jareth smiled gently. "You remember Suriah? She is my Second now."

"Come," Delaunay said to Alcuin, nodding toward the interior of the Great Hall. "Let us meet the revelers, my dear; I'm sure Phèdre and the Dowayne have much to discuss."

I watched them fade into the crowd. At the far end of the hall, a table was set on a dais for Prince Baudoin and a select few. Suriah was there; the Prince was feeding her tidbits by hand. Melisande Shahrizai looked amused. "She was the Winter Queen."

"It gave her a lot of status." Jareth's voice changed, turning pragmatic, adept to adept. "People still tell the story every Midwinter. I'd have been a fool to choose anyone else."

He had never been a fool. "No," I said, agreeing. "You made the right choice." Even from a distance, I could see that her pallid beauty had already peaked, and there was no evidence in her of the unexpected steel that lay beneath the delicate veneer of the few rare adepts who survived the loss of youth's tender bloom. I did not think Suriah would live to make Dowayne, and I felt sorry for her. "She was always kind to me."

"I hope you have fond memories of Cereus House, Phèdre."

Looking into Jareth's blue eyes, I realized it mattered to him; in certain circles, my word could damage the reputation of his House. "Yes," I answered honestly. "If I never belonged, nor was I shunned, and what ill-treatment I received, I well deserved and," I smiled wickedly at him, "quite enjoyed." He blushed; it is a mark of delicacy in Cereus to find the stronger passions immodest. "There is no finer training than that of Cereus House," I added. "It has stood me in good stead, and I can only speak well of my time here."

"I am pleased," he said, recovering his aplomb and making me a bow. "We are honored to have fostered you." Reaching into a pocket of his waistcoat, he drew forth a token of Cereus House. "Please, take this, and know you are always welcome here."

I took it and thanked him graciously. Jareth smiled.

"Enjoy the night," he said. "It's not often a Servant of Naamah has a chance to be a patron."

With that, he took his leave of me, moving smoothly on to greet newly arriving guests. Neither Delaunay nor Alcuin were in sight, but they would surely be making their way toward to the dais and I hurried to join them. It would be inappropriate for a member of Delaunay's household to be absent when he paid his respects to the Prince. I had not lost the trick of slipping gracefully through a crowd, and had to remind myself that there was no need to keep my gaze downcast; still, I felt an unwarranted thrill of boldness as I looked other patrons full in the face.

Strange indeed, to be here again.

A handful of people had gathered at the foot of the dais, waiting to wish the Prince a joyous birthday, and there I found Delaunay and Alcuin. As always, there was a stillness to Delaunay's presence, an observant calm that lent him a dignity surpassing that of those who surrounded him.

On the dais, anything but dignity reigned. Prince Baudoin, older than the wild boy whom I had first seen in this hall, had lost neither his good looks nor the hectic gleam of gaiety that lit his sea-grey eyes. As I had seen from the back of the hall, he held poor Suriah on his lap, keeping her captive with one arm.

Adepts of Cereus House are ill-suited to undignified treatment; if this was to be the nature of the fête, Melisande would have done better to reserve another House—Orchis, perhaps, or Jasmine. She sat at Baudoin's right hand, and I understood, then, that the adept's discomfort entertained her. Melisande's choice had been deliberate.

Two of Baudoin's guard, high-ranking nobles' sons, were privileged to share his table. One, following the Prince's lead, dandled a female adept on his lap. The other had a young boy standing attendant at his shoulder, refilling his wineglass.

"Well, well." Baudoin lounged in his chair and regarded Delaunay from behind the burden of Suriah as our turn came to mount the dais. "Messire Anafiel Delaunay! I hope you've repaired your quarrel with my kinsman, the Comte de Fourcay. He has so few friends, after all. Come, what have you brought me? A charming pair of bedservants?"

"My Prince will have his jest." Delaunay bowed smoothly, and behind him, Alcuin and I followed suit. "Alcuin and Phèdre nó Delaunay, of my household. Please accept our most sincere wishes for a joyous natality." He turned to Alcuin, who held up the Prince's gift; a filigree silver pomander containing a fragrant lump of amber. Delaunay took it from Alcuin and presented it to the Prince with another bow.

"Nice." Baudoin took the pomander and sniffed it, then shook it next to Suriah's ear. A hidden bell tinkled sweetly. "Very nice. You have leave to enjoy my party, Anafiel; you and your little playmates. I swear it, my mother spoke truly of you! Only you would bring whores to a pleasure-house, messire."

Delaunay's expression never altered, but Alcuin flushed, the rising tide of blood clearly visible beneath his fair skin. At that moment, one of the Prince's guards—the unencumbered one—exclaimed, "I know that one; look at the eyes on her! That's Delaunay's *anguissette*, the one as likes being hurt." Drawing the sword he carried for the Prince's protection, he lodged the tip of it under the skirts of my gown and began to raise them. "Come, then, let us have a look!" he said, laughing. Baudoin's interest was piqued; he pushed Suriah to one side and leaned forward to look.

I never even saw Delaunay move, it was that swift. There was the ringing of steel striking stone and the guard wrung his empty stinging hand, his blade trapped flat on the floor beneath Delaunay's boot. His face was dangerous as he locked eyes with Baudoin. "My lord, may I remind you that these members of my household are your guests, here by invitation of your lady."

"Phèdre?" Suriah whispered, coming around the table to take my face in her hands. "It *is* you. Blessed Naamah, but you've prospered, child!"

Still seated, Baudoin waved his hand negligently. "All right, all right, Delaunay, your point is made, give Martin back his sword. Lads, with all of Cereus House at your disposal, I hardly think we need trouble Messire Delaunay over his playmates." Despite his casual manner, he truly did have a measure of command; and he was, after all, a Prince of the Blood. Delaunay picked up the guard's sword and handed it over with a stiff bow, which Martin returned, sheathing his sword and sitting. Everyone remained silent as Baudoin raised his glass and drained it. Setting it down with a bang, he eyed me thoughtfully, his gaze taking in the scarlet fleck in my eye and wandering over my body, clad in close-fitting *sangoire* velvet as if offered for his delectation.

This time, I blushed.

"A true *anguissette*, hm?" he mused. Melisande Shahrizai leaned over and whispered in his ear. Listening, he raised his eyebrows, smiled, then lifted her hand and kissed it passionately, looking into her sapphire eyes with nigh-doting affection. "You are without peer," he murmured to her, and waved his hand again in our general direction. "If you would serve my will, go now, and make merry. Your Prince commands it."

"Yes, my lord," Delaunay said dryly, motioning us to precede him. His tone was wasted on Baudoin, but I caught a gleam of amusement on Melisande's face as she watched us go.

Unnerved by the encounter, I let myself become isolated in the crowd and accepted a glass of cordial from a pretty fosterling. I drank it at a gulp, setting the glass back on the tray. I had not eaten, and the cordial burned sweetly down my throat. The girl stood in obedient attendance, just as I had. She was perhaps thirteen, near to the age of taking her vows; fair-haired and delicate, a true night-blooming flower. I touched her cheek and felt her shudder. This was what it was to be a patron, to have that power. I was discomfited by it, and moved away, feeling her lifted gaze at my back, wondering.

Delaunay had ordered us to watch and listen, but I was hard-put to concentrate. I moved among the crowds, pausing to converse here or there, trying to discern the patterns beneath the merriment, but my veins were afire with the cordial I had drunk, and the music and candles and scent of flowers made my head swim. Prince Baudoin's friends and supporters abounded, declaring in carelessly loud tones that they should call for a public referendum, that the King should appoint Baudoin his successor, that Parliament should intervene. None of the talk was new and none seemed more urgent nor serious than it had a year ago.

Growing weary of circulating and wishing to avoid the advances of a certain persistent Chevalier who was plaguing me to dance with him, I slipped out of the Great Hall and made my way to a seldom-used pleasure niche on the first floor that had served as a refuge sometimes in my childhood.

A flicker of lamplight and a man's beseeching voice stopped me before entering. I drew back into the shadows.

"I have sent word to you *five times*! How can you be so cruel to refuse me?"

There was desperation in the tone and I knew the voice. It was Vitale Bouvarre.

Alcuin's voice, cool and distant. "Sir, I did not think to see you here. You are not known to be a friend of Prince Baudoin's."

"Nor am I known to be an enemy!" After the alarm in Vitale Bouvarre's voice, there was a pause. "The Lady Shahrizai pays for information on the Stregazza, and the Stregazza pay for talk of House Trevalion. Where is the harm in it? I am a trader, sweet boy." His tone turned wheedling. "Why will you not deign to ply your trade?"

I heard a rustle and a scraping sound; Alcuin had shaken off his touch. "I am a Servant of Naamah, not a galley-slave, sir. Seven times I have agreed to your contract, and seven times you have stinted your offering!"

Another pause. "I will make you a patron-gift." Bouvarre's voice trembled. "Any amount you name! Only say it."

Alcuin drew a deep breath and his voice turned ardent as he answered. "Enough to make my marque. And the answer to Delaunay's question. That is my price, sir."

At this, even I caught my breath sharply. There was a long silence, and then Bouvarre spoke again. "You ask too much," he said dully.

"It is my price." There was adamant in the words. I was astonished at the depth of feeling in him. I had known, from the beginning, that he had no love for this work; I had not known, until then, how much he despised it. And if he had hidden it from me, how much better had he hidden it from Delaunay? Well indeed, I think, for Delaunay would never have permitted Alcuin to continue in the service of Naamah had he known. Not only was it against his nature, but blasphemous as well.

"And if I pay it," Bouvarre was saying, the tremor back in his voice, "I will see you no more."

"If you pay it," Alcuin said softly, "you will see me once more, messire. If you do not, you will never see me again."

Another long silence, then once more, Bouvarre. "It is too much," he said, repeating himself. "I will think on it."

Alcuin made no reply. I heard the swish of cloth as Bouvarre turned to leave, and retreated further into the darkness, not wanting to be seen. There was not much risk of it, as he had the look of a man much distracted as he hurried past me. When Alcuin didn't emerge, I stole forward to steal a glance.

There was a small statue of Naamah in the niche, before which he knelt. Lamplight flickered on the ghostly white of his hair as he gazed up at her. "Forgive me, my lady goddess," I heard him murmur. "If I violate your precepts, it is only to obey those of our lord Elua. What I do, I do for love."

It was enough; I did not want him to know I had witnessed it. Adepts of Cereus House and pupils of Anafiel Delaunay alike are taught to move without sound when need requires. I crept away in silence.

Lovers clinched in the hallways and boudoirs, revelers danced and drank in the Great Hall, musicians played, apprentices served and adepts offered pleasure; in all the gaiety, only I seemed to feel solitary and alone. As a child, I could not have imagined one might aspire any higher. To be a courtesan of such note that I might attend a fête such as this—before I had even made my marque!—as the invited guest of a Prince's mistress . . . it was more than ever I had dreamed. But my pleasure was tempered by too much knowledge; knowledge of Delaunay's teaching, knowledge of Alcuin's despite for this world I knew so well.

This world in which I had no place, as patron or Servant.

I missed Hyacinthe and wished he were here.

I even wished the old Dowayne were here.

Driven by melancholy, I sought solace in one of the lesser gardens, thinking to be alone with my unaccustomed emotions and soothed by the moonlit play of water in the fountain. Even in this, I failed, for the shadowed torches were lit and several others had found the garden already. In one dim corner, a knot of people writhed to the sound of giggles and moans. I tried to count their number by limbs, and failed; three at least, but perhaps four. Under an ornamental apple tree, another couple lay entwined. Since I had no place else to go, I sat by the fountain anyway, trailing my fingers in

he rippling water and wondering if the Dowayne's ancient golden carp still lived.

I felt a touch on the back on my neck.

"Phèdre."

I knew her voice; it sent a shiver of cold fire down
my spine. I looked up to see Melisande Shahrizai smiling
down upon me.

"Why are you here alone?" she asked. "Surely you
would not disdain my hospitality."

I stood quickly, brushing off my skirts. "No, my
lady."

"Good." She was standing close enough that I could
feel her warmth. It was too dark to see the blue of her
eyes, but I could see the langorous sweep of her lashes.
"Do you know what they say in Kusheth about sinners
in Kushiel's charge?" she asked, running the tip of one
finger over my lower lip. I shook my head, dazed by her
nearness. "It is said that when offered the chance for
repentance, they refused it for love of their lord." With
the same hand, she undid my hair, letting it fall in a
cascade. "I believe I have found the perfect gift for
Prince Baudoin tonight," she said casually, twining her
hand in my hair. "You." Jerking her grip tight, she
brought me hard up against her and kissed me.

I gasped when she released me and sat down hard on
the rim of the fountain, unable to stand, the entire length
of my body throbbing from the sudden contact with hers.
She had bitten my lip, and I touched it with my tongue,
wondering if she had drawn blood. Melisande laughed,
the sound liquid in the moonlight.

"Unfortunately," she said lightly, "he is well occupied
this night, and I have promised to join him. But I will
speak with Delaunay on the morrow about making an
arrangement for the Prince. After all, I owe him a farewell gift." Turning, she beckoned to the darkness behind

her. A fair young man, cast in the canon of Cereus House, stepped forward in compliance. "Jean-Louis," Melisande said, laying her hand on his chest. "Phèdre is my guest. See that she is well pleased."

He bowed gracefully. "Yes, my lady."

She patted his arm and took her leave of the garden. "Be gentle with her," she said over her shoulder, amusement in her voice.

Much to my dismay, he was.

TWENTY-ONE

I do not know if either Alcuin or Delaunay availed themselves of Melisande's hospitality in the same fashion; I rather doubt it. Delaunay gave my disheveled appearance a sidelong glance in the carriage ride home, but offered no comment.

True to her word, Melisande Shahrizai sent a man around the next day, bearing an invitation to Delaunay to pay her a visit that evening. I busied myself throughout the day and engaged in my too-oft-neglected studies in the latter hours, setting myself the task of translating a slim collection of Skaldic war-chants compiled by the younger son of a Tiberian statesman who had travelled extensively in his youth. Delaunay had a friend, a Caerdicci composer, who claimed that one could understand any culture through its songs.

Thus I was still awake when Delaunay returned, finding me ensconced in the library, all diligence and ink-stains. He gave me that look that meant he saw through my subterfuge and sighed, settling in his favorite chair. "So you caught Baudoin's eye, did you? Melisande is minded to buy him a night with you."

I shrugged and corked the ink, wiping my quill on a bit of rag, "My lord, is it not advantageous? You know I am nothing if not circumspect."

"You are agreeable, then." He held out his hand for the draft of my translation. "Let me see what you've done."

I passed it to him, watching him read. "How could I be otherwise? He is a Prince of the Blood. And, my lord, Gaspar Trevalion is close-mouthed with you still, and Solaine Belfours has fallen out with the Princess Lyonette; we have no conduit to doings in Azzalle."

Delaunay looked shrewdly at me. "Baudoin de Trevalion is a lion's cub and dangerous, Phèdre, and Melisande Shahrizai standing in his shadow makes him thrice dangerous. If you would do this thing, I bid you keep your tongue sealed. A word from her, and he would have your head." He handed the translation back to me. "A nice job. Make a fair copy when you've finished, and I'll send it to the Maestro. He would be interested."

The praise made me glow, but I stuck to the matter at hand. "My lord, Melisande Shahrizai is your friend. Do you trust her so little that you think she would betray me?"

To think that I asked such a question.

He leaned forward, propping an elbow on one knee and resting his chin in his hand. The lamplight caught threads of silver in his auburn hair. "Melisande plays a subtle game, and I do not know the nature of it. If ever we found ourselves at cross-purposes, I would not look to our friendship for protection. Melisande knows too well how far I would go to—" He caught himself and fell silent, shaking his head. "It matters not. Heed me well when I counsel discretion, Phèdre."

"Was she your lover?" Ofttimes when someone makes a stand in one place, they will cede ground elsewhere.

Delaunay had taught me the trick of it, and I used it on him now.

"A long time ago." He grinned at me. It was of no moment, then, if he revealed it so lightly. "We are well-matched in many ways, but that was not one of them; unless it be that we were too well-matched. If neither will give way in love, it is not pleasing in the eyes of Naamah." Delaunay shrugged, rising to his feet. "Still, I do not think either of us gave the other cause for regret," he added. "Well and good, if it is your will to accede, then I shall have the contract drawn."

"It is, my lord."

The assignation excited me, which I did not deny. A date was set for some weeks hence, and time passed slowly. I busied myself as best I could, taking great pains with the fair copy of the book of Skaldic songs for Gonzago de Escabares. They were songs of battle, and I showed them to Alcuin, but he did not care for them, and I did not blame him for it.

No word came for him from Vitale Bouvarre, and I did not speak to him of what I had overheard. Nor did I tell Delaunay, but when I made an excursion to the sanctuary of Naamah with Cecilie Laveau-Perrin, I spoke of it to her, for it weighed upon my mind and I knew she would understand. She was of the Night Court.

"You are right not to interfere," she said to me. "Alcuin has pledged his service, and it is between him and Naamah. If his heart is true, she will forgive. Naamah is compassionate."

"His heart has always been true," I said, knowing it was so.

"Well, then." Cecilie smiled gently, and my mind was eased. Of all the people I have known, none were kinder and wiser than Cecilie. So I believed then, and so I still maintain.

Though it seemed it never would, at length the day of my assignation arrived, and with it came a gown, sent by Melisande's messenger, of cloth-of-gold. My wardrobe was quite fine by now, for Delaunay was generous in such matters, but I had never owned anything quite so exquisite as this. There was a matching caul of gold mesh, strung with seed pearls. I dressed with great care, admiring myself in the mirror. Alcuin sat on the edge of my bed, watching with his grave, dark eyes.

"Be careful, Phèdre," he said softly.

"I am always careful," I retorted, meeting his gaze in the mirror.

He smiled faintly. "You were not careful with Lord d'Essoms, and you will not be careful with Melisande. You could lose yourself in her, I have seen it. And she knows what we are."

I tucked a stray curl into the mesh. "I am for Prince Baudoin this night. You know that."

Alcuin shook his head. "She will be there. It is his pleasure to have her present, in the bedchamber. I have heard it. Melisande Shahrizai is the goad to Baudoin's desire."

The thought of it made my heart quicken, but I took care not to show it. "I will be careful," I promised. And then the coach arrived, and we spoke no more of it. Alcuin accompanied me downstairs, where I presented myself for Delaunay's inspection.

"Very nice," he murmured, settling my *sangoire* cloak on my shoulders and pinning it for me. "A member of the house of Delaunay with a Prince of the Blood. Who would have thought it?" He smiled, but there was a reserve to his tone I didn't understand. "I shall be proud of you." He kissed me on the brow. "Be well."

Safe in the assurance of his blessing, I went out to meet Melisande's coach, Guy trailing me like a shadow.

I do not know how many properties Melisande Shahrizai owned, but one of them was a house in the City. I had supposed it would be close to the Palace, but it was in a quiet section near the outskirts of town, a rich little gem of a house surrounded by trees. Later I learned that she had quarters in the Palace itself. This was where she went when she wished to entertain in private; for her own sake as well as Prince Baudoin's.

I was not sure what kind of reception to expect, but when her servants ushered us into her home, Melisande welcomed me like a guest.

"Phèdre," she said, giving me the kiss of greeting. "I am pleased you accepted. You know my lord Prince Baudoin de Trevalion?"

I looked past her and saw him, and made a curtsy. "I am honored, my prince."

He came forward and took my hands, raising me. I remembered how he had swept me into his arms at the Midwinter Masque. "It is my honor, to receive such a gift," he said, and looked past me to smile at Melisande. "One so touched by the hand of Elua's Companions."

Melisande returned his smile, laying a hand lightly on my shoulder. Caught between the two of them, I trembled. "Come," she said. "We would have you play for us while we dine. Is that acceptable?"

I made myself nod. "It would be my pleasure."

She turned to a servant. "Attend to Messire Delaunay's man, and see that he is well quartered. We will adjourn to the table."

Although I was trained to it, it had been some time since I had been asked to play for a patron's pleasure. I saw clearly enough what was intended as I accompanied them; the velvet hassock and the lap-harp made it plain. I sat and took up the harp, playing softly while they dined. It was strange, to be welcomed as a guest, then ignored in such a manner. Servants in the black-and-gold Shahrizai livery moved smoothly and silently, serving an array of savory dishes. Melisande and Baudoin ate and bantered in low tones as they dined, speaking as lovers will, of inconsequential things. I played, feeling very odd indeed.

When they had finished and the dishes were cleared, Melisande ordered a third glass of wine poured and dismissed the servants. "Phèdre, join us," she said, setting the glass at Baudoin's elbow. "Drink."

I set down the harp and rose obediently, coming to stand next to him. I tasted the wine, and it was very good; subtle and spicy, with an undertone of currants and rich earth.

"So you were raised at Cereus House," Baudoin mused, grey eyes beginning to gleam. His hands encircled my waist and he lifted me to his lap effortlessly, so smoothly my wine didn't even spill. He was a trained warrior, and strong as steel with it. "Will you squirm with discomfort, then, like the adepts of that House, to be so treated?"

"No, my prince." His hands were at my hips now, pressing down. Beneath layers of cloth-of-gold and his velvet breeches, I could feel his phallus stir against my buttocks. My breath caught in my throat.

"Phèdre is an *anguissette*, my prince." Across the table, Melisande's face shone by candlelight, fair and beautiful and heartless. "If she squirms, it is not with discomfort."

"It is hard to fathom." He ran a hand up my body to cup my breast, squeezing it. My nipple hardened against his palm. "But you speak the truth," Baudoin said to Melisande, pinching my nipple. I gasped at the bolt of pain, rocking back against him. "And you've attired her fit for a prince." He transferred his hand to my hair, digging his fingers into the gold mesh and drawing my head back. I felt his mouth at my bared throat, sucking at my flesh. "Shall I have her for dessert?" he asked, lifting his head and laughing.

Melisande shrugged, sipping her wine and watching, cool and lovely. "You have all night, my prince; this is not dessert, but only the first course. Have her here at the table if you wish."

"So I shall," he said, smiling at her. "For I've a wish to see if this desire is truly unfeigned."

And with that he rose, pushing me down across the table and lifting my skirts. With one hand at the back of my neck, he kept me effortlessly in place as he undid his breeches. My cheek was pressed hard against the white linen that covered the table; all I could see was my overturned goblet of wine, and the pale red stain of wine seeping across the tablecloth as he thrust himself into me.

Baudoin de Trevalion was no green lad, and he had had years of training at Melisande Shahrizai's hands. If I hoped he would spend himself quickly and hasten an end to my humiliation, I hoped in vain. I closed my eyes and whimpered as he moved inside me with long, slow strokes. "Truth again, my lady," I heard him say above me, laughter and astonishment in his voice. "She is hotter than Camael's forge inside, and wetter than Eisheth's tears."

A chair scraped and I heard Melisande rise, knew by the rustle of clothing that she had come around to stand behind him. I could hear her hands slide over the breast of his doublet and knew that she whispered at his ear. "Do it hard, my love," her rich voice breathed. "I want to watch you make her spend."

Tears trickled from beneath my closed lids as he

laughed, obeying her order, bringing me to the brink of pleasure with fierce, hard thrusts.

"Mmm." Melisande's voice, low with approval. "My love, you do well." She touched my cheek, grazing it with her fingertips, and gave the command coolly. "Now, Phèdre."

I obeyed without volition, shuddering at the force of my climax and crying out. Baudoin laughed again and thrust once more, twice, letting himself spend.

"Ah," he said, withdrawing from me. "We should have one of these, my lady. Shall we buy one at market, do you think?"

Relieved of his weight, I straightened slowly, turning to meet Melisande's amused eyes. "You will not find one such as Phèdre, my prince," she assured him. "And her service is pledged only to Naamah and Anafiel Delaunay. But come, you have tasted only the smallest part of what it is to have an adept kissed by Kushiel's Dart. If you would know the full of it, the night lies at our disposal. Unless you wish to give the *signale*?" she added wryly, addressing the last to me.

"My lady knows I do not," I said softly. I did not care how skilled a lover Baudoin de Trevalion was; he would never hear the *signale* spoken from my lips. Nor, while she served his pleasure, would Melisande Shahrizai. If she could wait, so could I. That much, I vowed to myself.

Melisande laughed. "Well, then," she said, going to the far doors and flinging them open. "We shall play."

Beyond the dining hall lay a pleasure-chamber. Through the door, I could see it bathed in firelight, cushion-strewn, with a complete flagellary and a wooden wheel with manacles, an exact replica of the one I had seen in the halls of Valerian House. Baudoin looked at Melisande and smiled.

I thought of Hyacinthe's name and bit my tongue.

But if it is true that no soul is free of the touch of Kushiel's fire, it also true that in most, it is a mere smolder. Baudoin de Trevalion did not burn with it, without Melisande to fan the spark in him. It was her I feared, and not him; I made no protest as I was ushered into the pleasure-chamber and gently stripped of my cloth-of-gold. Melisande's touch was cool as she guided me onto the wheel and fastened the manacles about my wrists and ankles. Baudoin examined the flagellary, picking up a tawse and fingering the slit in the center of the leather paddle.

"How is it done?" he asked, turning to Melisande and raising his eyebrows. "Do I give a Skaldic war cry and charge at her?" He hefted the tawse two-handed, holding it like an axe. "Waldemar Selig!" he shouted, then laughed.

On the wheel, I started with surprise. Melisande looked patiently at Baudoin. "There is no 'how' to it, my prince. You may do as you wish." Making certain that I was secured, she tugged the wheel.

It was well-crafted and beautifully maintained, turning smoothly and soundlessly. The pleasure-chamber, and Melisande and Baudoin in it, rotated in my vision. I hadn't reckoned how disorienting it would be, as the blood rushed to my head, then receded as I came rightside-up again. As the wheel inverted me once more, I saw Melisande select a scourge from the flagellary. "Like this, my love," she said to Baudoin. The world careened around me as Melisande snapped her wrist sharply, then vanished briefly in a haze of red as the weighted tips of the scourge bit at my skin. The sound like a harpstring rang in my head, and I saw Kushiel's face swimming in the distance, stern and bronze. Then it faded, and there was only the dizzying vision and the ebb-tide of blood in my head. Melisande replaced the scourge and nodded to Baudoin. "As you wish," she said softly.

After that, he stepped up to it, and my flesh knew the slap of the tawse, the flat wash of pain where it landed, with a thin sharp line from the slit in the middle that felt as if it split my skin every time it landed. The wheel turned, and I knew not where I was, nor where the next blow would fall; but the red haze never returned. When at last he wearied of it, he turned to Melisande, drawing her reverently over to the cushions. I was left hanging, partially inverted. Before the pressure of my own blood grew too much and consciousness left me, I saw him undo her gown and draw it off slowly, tracing its path with his lips, kneeling before her. Melisande saw me watching and smiled, and then I saw no more.

I do not know how long I hung there, nor who took me down; I woke in the morning in a strange bed, and was treated like a guest by the servants when I arose.

Melisande came into the dining hall as I broke my fast, looking fresh and composed. "The coach is ready, and Delaunay's man is waiting." She set a purse on the table near me. "The gown is yours to keep, of course, and this is in honor of Naamah." Her blue gaze rested on me, filled with amusement. "You are indeed a gift fit for a Prince, Phèdre."

"My thanks, my lady," I said automatically, taking the purse. My limbs moved stiffly today. The purse was heavy, and clinked of gold. I regarded her thoughtfully. "Fit for a farewell gift, my lady? Who is saying good-bye?"

The beautifully arched eyebrows rose a fraction, and Melisande inclined her head. "Delaunay's pupil, indeed," she said, and gave her liquid laugh. "I will answer, if you tell me what you know of Waldemar Selig."

I made no reply. Melisande laughed again, and stooped to kiss my cheek. "Give your lord Delaunay my regards," she said, straightening and caressing my hair affectionately. "We will meet again, my *anguissette.* And perhaps the next time there will be no Prince between us."

And with that, she left.

TWENTY-TWO

You may be sure I related the exchange to Delaunay. It was never my practice to tell him everything that occurred in an assignation; there were things, I had learned by then, best left unsaid. He saw the marks, and knew enough. Of the things which left no marks, I did not speak. But I never failed to disclose any piece of information or careless conversation which might be of interest to him.

In this, I was not mistaken. He frowned and paced, pondering what I had told him.

"Baudoin thought it was a Skaldi war cry?" he asked. I nodded. "Did he give any sign that the words Waldemar Selig meant aught else to him?"

"No." I shook my head, sure of it. "He spoke in jest, and meant nothing by it. But it meant somewhat to Melisande."

"And he gave no sign of knowing that you were a . . . what did she call it? A farewell gift?"

I shook my head again. "No, my lord. There was no hint of it in his manner, and Melisande was careful to speak of it only when we were alone." I gazed at him, and thought of how he had brought her to see me, when Delaunay's *anguissette* was no more than a well-kept secret. "Every artist craves an audience, my lord, and she has chosen you. Whatever is to occur, it is her desire that you know she is its architect."

Delaunay gave me one of his deep, thoughtful looks. "You may have the right of it," he said. "But the question remains: What is to occur?"

We found out in less than a week's time.

It was Gaspar Trevalion who brought the news, stunned into dismissing any thoughts of a quarrel between himself and Delaunay.

The clatter of many hooves rang on the paved courtyard with unmistakeable urgency. I had known the Comte de Fourcay since my earliest days in Delaunay's household and, even during their disagreements, I had never heard him so much as raise his voice. This day, it echoed off the courtyard walls. "Delaunay!"

If anyone doubted that the household of Anafiel Delaunay was capable of moving quickly, they would have been hard put to prove it that day. Delaunay was out the door in a trice, pausing only to snatch up his seldom-used sword where it hung in his study. Guy appeared from nowhere, twin daggers in hand, shouldering two liveried servants out the door ahead of him, and Alcuin and I were but a few steps behind.

Surrounded by ten men-at-arms, Gaspar Trevalion sat his black horse, oblivious to our presence and the sword in Delaunay's hand. His mount, lathered and blown, snorted and shifted its weight; Gaspar tightened the reins and gazed down at Delaunay, a terrible look on his face.

"Isidore d'Aiglemort has just accused House Trevalion of high treason," he said grimly.

Delaunay stared and lowered his sword. "You're joking."

"No." Gaspar shook his head, his dreadful expression

unchanged. "He has proof: letters, addressed to Lyonette from Foclaidha of Alba."

"What?" Delaunay was still staring. "How?"

"Messenger birds." The black horse danced under him; Gaspar quieted it. "They've been corresponding since the Cruarch's visit. Delaunay, my friend, what do I do? I am innocent in this matter, but I have a home and a family to think of in Fourcay. The King has already sent his fastest riders to the Comte de Somerville. He is mustering the royal army."

Behind Delaunay's face, the wheels of thought began turning. "You swear you knew nothing of it?"

Gaspar's spine stiffened in the saddle. "My friend, you know me," he said softly. "I am as loyal as you to House Courcel."

"There will be a trial. There will have to be a trial." Delaunay rested the tip of his sword on the paving stones and leaned on it. "Send your three best men to Fourcay," he said decisively. "Tell them to turn out the guard, and admit no one unless they bear orders in the King's own hand. We'll draft a letter to Percy de Somerville. There's time to intercept him before he can make the border of Azzalle. He knows you, he won't move against Fourcay without orders from the King. It's Lyonette who's at the bottom of this, and not House Trevalion. The King won't take after your whole line."

Some of the stricken quality eased in Gaspar's expression, but not all. "Baudoin has been implicated."

I drew in my breath sharply at his words, and Alcuin's fingers closed on my elbow. I glanced at him and he shook his head, cautioning silence. Delaunay, frowning to himself, gave no sign that he had heard it.

"You'd best come in," he said to Gaspar, "and tell me what you know. Get your men en route to Fourcay. We'll devise a letter to de Somerville, and you'll petition the King for an audience. Ganelon de la Courcel is no fool. He will hear you."

After a moment, Gaspar nodded curtly, and gave the orders to his men, tossing them a purse for the journey. We heard the sound of their mounts' hoofbeats recede through the streets of the City. In the distance there was shouting as the news began to break like a wave through the D'Angeline populace.

"Come in," Delaunay repeated, holding out his hand. Gaspar Trevalion grasped it wordlessly and dismounted.

Once in the house, Delaunay ordered food and wine to be brought. I thought him mad to entertain at such a time, but once Gaspar had eaten a bite of bread and cheese and taken a long gulp of wine, he sighed and seemed to grow calmer. Since then, I have seen it is true, that people are reassured by the act of taking sustenance in time of great trauma. Alcuin and I hovered in the background, endeavoring to make ourselves either useful or invisible, and Delaunay made no move to send us away.

"What happened?" he asked quietly.

Over the course of the next hour, Gaspar laid out the story for us, as best he knew it. He had got it from a friend who was one of the King's lords-in-waiting, so it bode fair to be accurate. Gaspar had gone directly to Delaunay with the news, not knowing where else to turn for advice, but he believed his friend had spoken truly, being concerned only for his well-being.

The story he had heard was that Isidore d'Aiglemort had learned of the matter through the careless boasting of one of Baudoin's Glory-Seekers, deep in his cups after a fruitless patrol of Camlach's borders. D'Aiglemort had investigated, and upon obtaining proof of it, gone straight to the King with the matter, riding day and night to reach the City in all haste. With typical Camaeline bluntness, he hadn't even bothered to request an audience, but gone directly to a public hearing and made his accusation: Lyonette de Trevalion had conspired with Foclaidha of Alba and her son, the new Cruarch, to join forces. Backed by a Pictish army, she planned to seize the regency of Terre d'Ange and place Baudoin on the throne. In exchange, she would put the forces of Azzalle at the disposal of Foclaidha and her son to hold the kingdom of Alba against the disposed heir and his allies among the Dalriada. To accomplish this, the Azzallese fleet would sail directly against the Master of the Straits. While they had little hope of defeating him they could perchance distract him long enough to ferry the Pictish army across the Strait at its narrowest point. Once they had secured the throne, they would have the whole of the royal fleet at their disposal to achieve their return.

"It was a clever plan," Gaspar concluded, wiping his brow with a velveted sleeve and holding out his wineglass for a refill. "Dangerously clever. If d'Aiglemort hadn't proved loyal . . . Baudoin was his friend, after all. He might have stood to gain."

I thought of Melisande Shahrizai's smile, and the dark glitter of the Duc d'Aiglemort's eyes behind the jaguarondi mask. I was not so sure he did not still stand to gain.

Delaunay had to ask; he did it gently. "What about Marc?" There was no love lost between Gaspar and Lyonette, but Marc de Trevalion was his cousin and his friend. Gaspar shook his head somberly, eyes shadowed.

"My friend, if I could answer you truly, I would. It is in my heart to say that Marc would never do such a thing, and yet . . . he is at odds with the King over the matter of Quintilius' fleet, and there is a question of pride at stake. He has long disapproved that Ganelon will not see his granddaughter wed and the fate of the realm settled. If Lyonette presented her plan to him all of a piece . . . I do not know."

"I understand," Delaunay said, and pressed the matter no further. "How did d'Aiglemort get the letters?"

Gaspar gave the answer; it was one he had at the ready, and one we already knew. "Melisande Shahrizai."

I opened my mouth to speak. Delaunay gave me a look, warning me not to divulge what I knew of her involvement, but I knew that well enough. It was another question that puzzled me. "Baudoin was in her thrall. Why would she give him up, when he stood to gain the throne?"

"I would like to say it is because House Shahrizai is loyal," Gaspar said, and gave a short laugh, running a hand over his salt-and-pepper hair, still disheveled from his ride. "But I think it more likely that Melisande knew full well that Lyonette would never allow Baudoin to wed her. Lyonette seeks a biddable daughter-in-law, preferably one who brings a formidable alliance with her. If Baudoin has not defied his mother in this yet, he would surely not do it when she had it in her power to win him the throne. Melisande Shahrizai is formidable in her own right, but she's no match for the Lioness of Azzalle."

The former rang true enough, but as for the latter . . . If I had not been her farewell gift to Baudoin de Trevalion, I might even have believed it. But Melisande Shahrizai had known long weeks before Isidore d'Aiglemort had supposedly gained his "proof." That the treachery was real, I had no doubt, nor the proof of it. But I had no doubt, either, that the plans for its exposure were laid with more cunning and subtlety than the treachery itself. There was naught we could do; an ambiguous word spoken carelessly to a Servant of Naamah was proof of nothing. Only I knew for certain what Melisande had meant by it—Delaunay, Alcuin and I. No, we would hold our silence on this, I thought, and Melisande Shahrizai would gain praise for having done the right thing.

And the young Duc d'Aiglemort, already a war hero, would unexpectedly rise again in prominence. Someone had said, I remembered, that all scions of Camael thought with their swords. I did not think this one did.

In the days that followed, matters fell out in accordance with Delaunay's prediction. Parliament was convened, and a High Court trial summoned. While the royal army, under command of the Comte de Somerville, swept through Azzalle toward Trevalion, the King heard Gaspar's petition and granted clemency to the estate of Fourcay provided Gaspar place himself under the aegis of the Palace Guard until the trial was called to order.

Nothing travels faster than gossip. A full day before de Somerville's messenger arrived, we had learned that Trevalion had surrendered after a short, pitched battle, headed in the main by Baudoin and his Glory-Seekers. It was his father, Marc de Trevalion, who had ordered the surrender. Percy de Somerville accepted his sword, left a garrison in charge of Trevalion and set out for the City with Lyonette, Marc, Baudoin and even his sister Bernadette in his custody, along with their entourage; all the principles of House Trevalion.

When they arrived at the Palace, the trial began.

Because Delaunay would be called to testify on behalf of Gaspar Trevalion—for his loyalty remained in question—we were able to attend, Alcuin and I, somberly attired in Delaunay's colors. No seating was allocated for the retinues of attending nobles, but we found standing room at the sides of the Hall of Audience. At the far end, a great table stood. The King sat in the central seat, his granddaughter Ysandre at his right hand, and flanking them were the twenty-seven nobles of Parliament. Members of the Palace Guard lined the hall, and two Cassiline Brothers stood motionless behind the King, grey shadows in the background, only the glint of steel at their wrists betraying their presence.

There are individuals who relish a spectacle, and who dote on seeing those on high brought low. Though I am not sorry to have witnessed this trial, I am not one of them, and I took no relish in the proceedings. Lyonette de la Courcel de Trevalion was foremost among the accused, and the first brought for questioning. I had glimpsed her only once, from Cecilie's balcony, but I had heard tales all my life of the Lioness of Azzalle. She swept into the Hall of Audience attired in a splendor of blue-and-silver brocade, the colors of House Courcel, reminding anyone rash enough to forget it that she was sister to the King; and bearing, prominently, the shackles of her confinement. At the time, I was surprised to see that Ganelon de la Courcel had demanded his sister enchained. Later I learned that this dramatic touch came at Lyonette's insistence; but it mattered naught.

Never let it be said that the Lioness of Azzalle lacked for pride. Of her part in the scheme, she denied nothing. The evidence was brought forth; her chin rose, as she stared defiantly at her brother. He was a full twenty years her elder—she was born late and they are long-lived, the scions of Elua—and it was plain that neither bore each other a great deal of filial affection.

"How do you plead to these charges?" he asked her, when the matter had been laid before Parliament. His voice strove for sternness, but nothing could hide its tremble, nor the palsy that shook his right hand, though he held it down at his side.

Lyonette laughed, tossing her greying head. "You dare ask me, brother dear? Let me charge you, and see how you plead! You cripple the realm with your lack of re-solve, clinging to the ghost of your dead son in a mur-deress' get, without even the decency to make her an alliance through marriage." Her eyes flashed, dark-blue, the same color as the King's. "And you dare question my loyalty? I admit it, I have done as I saw fit, to secure the throne for the D'Angeline people!"

The crowd murmured; somewhere, there were those who would voice approval, if only they dared. But the faces of the King and the lords and ladies of Parliament remained stern. I chanced a look at Delaunay. He stared at Lyonette de Trevalion and his eyes burned, though I could not say why.

"Then you plead guilty," Ganelon de la Courcel said softly. "What part did your husband play in it, and your son and daughter?"

"They knew nothing," Lyonette said contemptuously. "Nothing! It was my doing, and mine alone."

"We shall see." The King looked to his left and his right, his expression sad and weary. "How will you sentence her, my lords and ladies?"

It came in a whisper, the answer, accompanied by the ancient Tiberian gesture. One by one, they lifted their hands, thumbs extended, and turned them downward. "Death," came the answer.

Ysandre de la Courcel was the last to give her vote. Cool and pale, she gazed at her great-aunt, who had named her a murderess' get before the peers of the realm. With slow deliberation, she lifted her fist, rotated it downward. "Death."

"So be it." The King's voice was as thin as the wind rattling the autumn leaves. "You have three days to name the manner of your choosing, Lyonette." He nodded once, and the Palace Guard came to escort her from the Hall of Audience, accompanied by a priest of Elua.

She offered no struggle, and went with her head held high; and her husband, Marc de Trevalion, was called onto the floor.

The Duc de Trevalion looked much like his kinsman Gaspar: older, a trifle taller and more slender, but with the same raven's-wing hair streaked with grey. Lines of age and sorrow were engraved on his face. He made a gesture, before the accusation was read, holding the King's gaze and lifting his empty, shackled hands.

"In the writings of the Yeshuites, the sin of Azza is named as pride," he said quietly. "But we are D'Angeline, and the sin of angels is the glory of our race. The sin of Blessed Elua was that he loved too well earthly things. I have sinned against you as they do, brother, in pride and love."

Ganelon de la Courcel's voice shook. "Do you say you aided my sister and conspired against the throne, brother?"

"I say I loved her too well." Marc de Trevalion's gaze never wavered. "As I love my son, who shares your blood. I knew. I did not countermand her orders to the admiral of my fleet, nor the Captain of my Guard. I knew."

Again the vote; again the thumbs turned downward, and it came at last to Ysandre de la Courcel. I watched her, and her face showed no more emotion than a cameo on a brooch as she turned it to her grandfather. Her voice was like cool water. "Let him be banished," she said.

I grew up in Cereus House; I knew well how to reckon steel beneath a fragile bloom. That was the first time I saw it in Ysandre de la Courcel. It was not the last.

"What say you?" asked the King of his Parliament. None spoke, but with judicious nods, their hands opened, turned palm outward. The King spoke again, his voice stronger. "Marc de Trevalion, for your crimes against the throne, you are banished from Terre d'Ange and your lands are forfeit. You have three days to clear the border, and if you return, there shall be a bounty of ten thousand ducats on your head. Do you accept these terms?"

The once-Duc de Trevalion looked, not at the King, but at his granddaughter, the Dauphine. "You jest," he said, his voice trembling.

She made no reply. The King drew his chin into his beard. "I make no jest!" His voice echoed in the rafters. "Do you accept these terms?"

"Yes, my king," Marc de Trevalion, murmured, bowing. The Palace Guard closed round him. "My lord . . . my daughter knew nothing! She is innocent in this matter."

"We shall see," the King repeated, weary again. He waved his hand without looking. "Begone from my sight."

A whispered consultation took place at the table. They had planned to call Baudoin next, I knew; Delaunay had had it from a friend who drew up the lists. But they changed their minds, and called instead Bernadette de Trevalion, his sister.

I would have known her for Baudoin's sister, for they looked much alike, but her manner was as shrinking as his was wild. It was not easy having the Lioness of Azzalle for a mother, I thought, if one was not the favored cub. Within several minutes of questioning, it was obvious that she had known as much as her father, and done as little. I watched closely this time, saw the old King look to his granddaughter, saw her faint nod. The vote fell out the same: banishment. Father and daughter would survive, albeit cut off forever from the land that nurtured us, whose glory ran in our veins like blood. I thought of Thelesis de Mornay's poem, and wept. Unseen in the crowd, Alcuin put his arm about me and steadied me.

Baudoin de Trevalion was summoned.

Like his mother, he made the most of his chains, letting them clank as he strode into the Hall. He was beautiful, and magnificent in duress. A sigh echoed through the room.

"Prince Baudoin de Trevalion," the King said aloud. "You stand accused of high treason. How do you plead to these charges?"

Baudoin tossed his hair. "I am innocent!"

Ganelon de la Courcel nodded to someone I could not see. From the wings, Isidore, Duc d'Aiglemort, approached the floor.

His face was like a mask as he inclined his head to Baudoin, then bowed to the King and gave his testimony before the High Court. Only his eyes glittered, dark and impenetrable. It was the same story Gaspar had told: a soldier's drunken boast, a loyal Duc's investigation. Baudoin flushed, and stared at him with hatred. I remembered that they had been friends. Isidore d'Aiglemort withdrew, and Melisande Shahrizai was summoned.

It is so clear in my memory, that day. How much of it they knew, I am not certain—nor have I ever known—but House Shahrizai had come out in her support, and Melisande was surrounded by her kindred. As so often happens in the old lines, they bore the stamp of a common heritage, and the Shahrizai made a splash amid the Hall of Audience, with their blue-black hair and their long, brocaded coats of black-and-gold. All of them had the same eyes, too; set like sapphires in pale faces. In none did Kushiel's flame burn as fiercely as it did in her, but it burned in them all, and I was grateful for Alcuin's arm.

I do not think Melisande Shahrizai could ever manage a true semblance of modesty, but she came closer than I would have reckoned. With downcast lashes, she answered the questions of Parliament, laying out a tale of an ambitious Prince in the thrall of his powerful mother, allies to be made, and a throne to be won. The letters, she said, he had showed her in boast, to make good on his claim.

Whatever the truth of it, she spoke naught he could dispute. If Baudoin had glared his hatred at the Duc d'Aiglemort, it was nothing to the rage that purpled him as he listened to her litany. In the end, it was enough and more. With stern remorse, the nobles of Parliament voted. One by one, while Baudoin stared, incredulous, their thumbs turned down.

Death.

It came at last to Ysandre. She looked at Baudoin, unmoved as ice. "Tell me, cousin," she asked him. "Would you have wed me off to a foreign potentate, or killed me outright?"

He had no answer at the ready; and it was answer enough. Her hand moved, thumb pointing downward. There would be no reprieve for Baudoin.

There was too much evidence; no sighs echoed the King's. "So be it," he said, and no one doubted that he grieved to say it. "Baudoin de Trevalion, you are sentenced to death. You have three days to name the manner of your choosing."

He did not make as good an exit as his mother. I watched him go, and his feet stumbled, disbelieving. Thus the fate of the son of too fierce a mother, whose ambition outpaced the law. Perhaps it was not so easy, I thought, to be the Lioness' favorite cub.

The trial of Gaspar Trevalion went smoothly; there was no evidence, and no accusation save his bloodline.

I watched Delaunay give his testimony, saying how Gaspar had known naught of the plot and brought word straight to him, heeding his advice to make a clean breast of it to the King, and I was proud to be a member of his household. In the end, Gaspar was absolved of any wrongdoing, and his title and estate affirmed in public forum.

Delaunay had regained his composure; his face gave nothing away. But I marked, all the while, how Ysandre de la Courcel hung on his every word, and there was a hunger in her gaze I could not name.

TWENTY-THREE

In the end, the executions were held privately.

It was a matter of much speculation, for the Lioness of Azzalle had threatened to grieve her brother through the final minute of her life by whatever means she could, and surely a public execution would have raised much ill-feeling against him; but at the last, her pride won out. She would die with dignity, and not on display for the masses. It was a swift-acting poison, I am told; she drank it straight off, and laid down to wake no more.

Of Baudoin, it was said that he died well. When he was told that his mother had chosen a private death, he called for his sword. The King ordered his bonds struck, and his own Captain of the Guard to stand at second. But whatever his flaws, Baudoin de Trevalion was a Prince of the Blood and no coward. When he fell on his sword, he aimed true, the point positioned directly over his heart. The Captain of the Guard sheathed his blade unused.

A strange and somber mood held the City in the aftermath of the trial and execution. I felt it myself. To mourn their deaths would have been to sympathize with high treason; yet mourn we did. For as long as I could remember, the Lioness had ruled in Azzalle, and her wild boy had been the D'Angelines' darling: the Sun Prince, the daring war-leader. Now they were gone, and her husband and daughter wandered in exile. The shape of our world was forever changed.

Even Hyacinthe, by nature cynical about the fate of nobility, was touched by it. He had placed a considerable wager on the manner of death Lyonette and Baudoin de Trevalion would choose, but a morbid superstition was on him when he collected his winnings on the following day.

"It is blood-cursed," he said with a shudder, holding up a silver regal. "Do you see, Phèdre? There is a shadow on it."

"What will you do?" I asked. "Give it away?"

"And pass on the curse?" He looked at me in shock. "Do you think I have no more scruples than that?" He shook his head, dispelling the idea. "No, I cannot use this profit for gain. I'll use it to make an offering to Azza and Elua. Come, let's see if there are mounts to be had at the stable."

The youth tending the stables that afternoon was familiar, a long-time errand boy and message-runner. He left off dicing with a groom and jumped up with a grin. "Off to play the lordling about town, Hyas? Good day for it, it's quieter than Cassiel's bedchamber around here."

"It'll pick up, once they set out to drown their sorrows," Hyacinthe said, sounding certain of it. With a sidelong glance at me, he added in a less confident tone, "Just bring out the quietest two, will you? And fetch a lady's saddle for Phèdre nó Delaunay."

The lad hadn't seen me standing in Hyacinthe's shadow, but he moved with alacrity at mention of my name, which made me smile. In Night's Doorstep, the D'Angeline streetfolk knew better than to stand in awe of the self-styled Prince of Travellers, but Delaunay's *anguissette* was another matter. I wore the dark-brown cloak and not the *sangoire*, but Hyacinthe took care that his friends knew who I was. It added to his prestige, and they in turn took care that I was well-guarded, so both of us gained by it.

Once mounted, we struck out through the City at a careful pace. In the distance behind us, I heard a skittering of hooves and a muttered curse, and turned to see if I could catch a glimpse of Guy, wondering if he had been forced to lease a mount from Hyacinthe's stable. Though he was nowhere in sight, I did not doubt but that he was there.

The streets were largely empty, and where people were, they stood about in small groups, talking quietly. I saw black armbands on not a few D'Angeline arms, but their bearers turned away quickly, not wanting their faces marked.

"Do you grieve for him?" Hyacinthe asked softly. A carter approached from the opposite direction, and I did not answer immediately. I was no more skilled a rider than Hyacinthe.

"Prince Baudoin?" I asked, when the street was clear. Hyacinthe nodded. I thought of his careless arrogance, his insulting manner, his hand at my neck pressing me against the table. And I thought of my first sight of Baudoin, bright with wine and merriment, the mask of Azza askew on his brow. He had named me joy-bearer, and kissed me for luck, I remembered; and nine years later, Melisande Shahrizai had presented me to him with a kiss of death. I had known, and I had kept my silence. Truly,

I had brought him all the luck of my ill-chosen name. "Yes."

"I'm sorry." He touched my arm lightly, his gaze questioning. "Is it that bad?"

I had not told him everything, nor could I. Even now, I merely shook my head. "No. Never mind. Let's go on, to the temple."

We rode in silence for a while. "There will be other princes," he remarked presently, glancing at me. "And one day, when you have made your marque, you will no longer be a *vrajna* servant, you know."

The temple of Azza beckoned in the distance, slanting beams of sunlight setting its copper dome ablaze. I cocked my head at Hyacinthe. "And will I then be worthy, O Prince of Travellers?"

Hyacinthe flushed. "I didn't mean . . . oh, never mind. Come on, I'll share the offering with you."

"I don't need *charity* from you," I spat at him, digging my heels into the mare's sides. She obliged by breaking into a brief trot, which set me to bouncing ungracefully in the saddle.

"We give each other what we can spare, and what we can accept," he said cheerfully, grinning as he drew alongside. "And that is as it ever has been between us, Phèdre. Friends?"

At that, I made another face, but he was right. "Friends," I agreed reluctantly, for I loved him dearly despite our quarrels. "And you will share the offering by half, yes?"

So it was that we came, bickering mildly, to the temple of Azza, and gave our horses into the hostler's keeping. I was not surprised to see that the temple was well-attended that day. House Trevalion was of Azza's lineage, and I had seen the black armbands. Inside the temple, hundreds of candles burned and banks of flowers lined the walls. The priests and priestesses of Azza wore saffron tunics with the crimson chlamys, or half-cloak, fastened with bronze brooches. Each of them wore the bronze mask of Azza, individual features lost behind the mask's forbidding beauty; though none, I daresay, was so finely wrought as the one Baudoin had worn to the Midwinter Masque.

We gave our offerings unto a priestess, who bowed, and gave in turn to each of us a small bowl of incense, and we took our places in line to await our turns. I gazed at the statue of Azza upon the altar as we waited. The same face echoed in a dozen masks about us gazed forth above the altar, proud and beautiful in its disdain. Azza held one hand open, palm upwards; in the other, he held a sextant, for that was his gift to mankind. Knowledge, forbidden knowledge, to navigate the world that was.

Hyacinthe went first, and then it was my turn. I knelt before the offering-fire, and the priest at the altar sprinkled me with his aspergillum, murmuring a blessing. "If I have sinned against the scions of Azza, forgive me," I whispered, tilting my bowl. Grains of incense spilled like gold into the flame, which burned briefly with a greenish tinge. The rising smoke stung my eyes. Mindful of the line behind me, I rose and gave my bowl over to the waiting acolyte, then hurried to join Hyacinthe.

The temple of Elua was quieter. No doubt people bore in mind that if Lyonette and Baudoin de Trevalion were scions of Elua, so much the more so was House Courcel, against whom they had committed treason.

There is no roof on Elua's temples, only pillars to mark its four quarters. Always, by tradition, the inner sanctum itself stands open beneath the heavens, unpaved, free to grow as it will. In the City's Great Temple, ancient oak trees flank the altar and a profusion of growth flourishes amidst the temple grounds, flowers and weeds alike lovingly tended. By the time we arrived, it was nigh-dusk, and the sky overhead was a deepening hue, the first stars emerging as pinpricks of light.

Barefoot and robed in blue, a priestess met us with the kiss of greeting, and an acolyte knelt to remove our shoes, that we might walk unshod in the presence of Blessed Elua. Our offerings were taken, and scarlet anemones pressed into our hands, to lay upon the altar.

The statue of Elua that stands in the great temple is one of the oldest works of D'Angeline art. By some reckoning, it is crude, but I have never thought so. It is carved of marble, and vaster than the size of a man. He stands with unbound hair and an eternal smile, gaze cast down upon this world. Both hands are empty. One is extended in offering, and the other is scored with the mark of his wound, the blood he shed to mark his affinity with humankind. Birds and an occasional bat flitted about the trees as Hyacinthe and I approached under the darkling sky, the advent of night leeching all color from the scarlet anemones we bore. The earth was moist beneath my feet.

Again I let Hyacinthe precede me, but this time no words came as I made my offering. In the presence of Elua, all was known, and all forgiven. I touched the fingers of the marble hand he extended, knelt and laid my blossoms at his feet. Stooping, I pressed my lips to the cool marble of Elua's foot, and felt peace pervade me. I do not know how long I lingered, but a priest came, hands on my shoulders bidding me to rise. He met my eyes as I did so, and his gentle smile did not falter. In his kind gaze, I saw knowledge and acceptance of all that I was. "Kushiel's Dart," he murmured, touching my hair, "and Naamah's Servant. May the blessing of Elua be upon you, child."

Though Hyacinthe waited in the grove beyond, I knelt

again, taking the priest's hands and kissing them in gratitude. He allowed me a moment, then drew me to my feet once more. "Love as thou wilt, and Elua will guide your steps, no matter how long the journey. Go with his blessing."

I went, then, grateful for the respite and finding my heart eased by the offering. "Thank you," I said to Hyacinthe, joining him once more. He looked curiously at me.

"For what?"

"For giving what you had to spare," I said, as we reclaimed our footware from the acolyte at the gate. I leaned over to kiss his cheek as he drew on his boots. "For being my friend."

"Patrons you can count by the score." Hyacinthe tugged at a boot and grinned at me. "But I reckon there are few enough can claim friendship of Delaunay's *anguissette*."

It was true, which did not stop me from slapping him on the shoulder for saying so, and thus we left as we had come, bickering, but with our hearts—and our purses—lighter for it. The hostler of the temple stables brought our mounts around, and we rode back toward Night's Doorstep in good spirits, making wild dashes through the alleyways in an effort to lose Guy, always unseen, but omnipresent.

Thus it was that we came upon the Shahrizai.

We emerged into the market square of Night's Doorstep. Hyacinthe saw them first and checked his mount, moving without thinking, his hands sure on the reins. I drew my horse up, and gazed past him.

Flanked by servants bearing torches, the Shahrizai rode together, gorgeous in their black-and-gold brocade, singing with Kusheline accents as they rode, swinging their whips and crops, bound for Mont Nuit. The women wore their hair loose; the men wore it in small braids, falling like linked chains around their pale, gorgeous features. Darkness was full on us and the torchlight glimmered on their blue-black hair, picked out highlights on their brocaded coats. I stared at them over the neck of Hyacinthe's bay horse, picking out Melisande in their midst effortlessly.

As if an unseen bolt connected us, her gaze found mine, and she raised her hand, halting their band.

"Phèdre nó Delaunay," she called, voice rich with amusement. "Well met. Will you come with us, then, to Valerian House?"

I would have answered, though I know not what I would have said, if Hyacinthe had not heeled his bay, dancing sideways between me and the Shahrizai.

"She is with me tonight," he said, his voice tight.

Melisande laughed, and her Shahrizai kin laughed with her, tall and beautiful, brothers and cousins alike. If I could not match the faces, I knew the names, all of them, from Delaunay's long teaching: Tabor, Sacriphant, Persia, Marmion, Fanchone. All beautiful, but none to match her. "So you are her little friend," Melisande mused, her gaze searching Hyacinthe's face. "The one they call the Prince of Travellers. Well, and I have it on good authority, you have never been beyond the City walls. Still, if I cross your palm with gold, will you tell me of what will be, Tsingano?"

At that, the Shahrizai laughed again. I saw Hyacinthe's back stiffen, but his face as he replied, I never saw. It mattered naught; I had heard it in his mother's voice, and I heard it in his. "This I will tell you, Star of the Evening," he said in a cold voice, bowing formally to her, the distant tone of the *dromonde* in his telling. "That which yields, is not always weak. Choose your victories wisely."

If ever I had doubted that Melisande Shahrizai was dangerous, I doubted it no more that night, for alone among her kin, she did not laugh and jest, but narrowed her eyes in thought. "Something for nothing, from a Tsingano? That is something indeed. Marmion, pay him, that there be no debt between us."

One name, at least, to a fair Shahrizai face; a younger brother or cousin, I guessed, from the good-natured speed with which he obeyed, digging in his purse for a gold coin and tossing it in Hyacinthe's direction. The coin flashed in the torchlight, and Hyacinthe plucked it neatly from the air, bowing with a flourish and tucking it into his purse. "My thanks, O Star of the Evening," he said in his normally unctuous Prince of Travellers tone.

At that, Melisande did laugh. "Your friends never fail to amuse in their honesty," she said to me. I made no reply. Someone gave an order to the servants, and the Shahrizai began to move onward, taking up their song. Melisande joined them, then wheeled her horse. "As for Baudoin de Trevalion . . . you grieve in your way," she said, her gaze making contact with mine once more, "and I in mine."

I nodded, glad of Hyacinthe's presence between us. Melisande smiled briefly, then put heels to her horse, catching up to her party with ease.

Hyacinthe let out his breath in a long sigh, brushing his black ringlets back. "That, if I am not mistaken, is the jewel of House Shahrizai, yes?"

"You spoke the *dromonde* without knowing?" My placid mare tossed her head; I glanced down and saw that my hands trembled on the reins.

"One's future knows one's name; it matters not if the teller knows," he said absently. "That *was* Melisande Shahrizai, wasn't it? I've heard songs about her."

"Whatever they sing, it's no more than the truth, and only a portion of it at that." I watched them disappear around a corner at the end of the street. "Stranger to tell, she knew who you were, and they sing no songs about you, Hyacinthe."

His white grin flashed in the darkness. "They do, actually. Haven't you heard the one Phaniel Douartes wrote about the Prince of Travellers and the Wealthy Comtesse? It's a great favorite at the Cockerel. But I take your meaning." He shrugged. "She is a friend of Delaunay's; mayhap he told her. Still, it is something, to so catch the interest of a Prince's consort. I suppose you should be flattered."

"Her interest is first in Delaunay's intrigues," I murmured. "As for the rest, she is Kushiel's line. It is writ in her blood as surely as mine is writ in my gaze."

"That much is obvious," Hyacinthe said dryly. "Only Kushelines would do their grieving at Valerian House, and only you would be fool enough to go with them."

"I didn't—"

"Nor would you," a third voice said behind us, flat and inflectionless in the dark. I twisted in the saddle to see Guy, unmounted, leaning against the alley walls with his arms folded. He raised his eyebrows at me. "I'm sure you wouldn't betray Lord Delaunay's trust in such a way, would you, Phèdre?"

"I thought you were on horseback," I said, for lack of a better response. Guy snorted.

"The way the two of you ride? Easy enough to follow on foot. Though you've a knack for it, when you forget to think about it," he added to Hyacinthe. To me, he said, "You, Delaunay should have taught. And if you've had enough of leading me on a merry chase, I'll take you home to him and tell him so."

There was no gainsaying Guy once his mind was settled. We returned the horses to the stable, and he had the coach brought round. Hyacinthe grinned at my annoyance, and it galled me, as it usually did not, to be subject to Delaunay's will. Guy merely gave me a resigned shrug, and called to the driver to take us home.

Delaunay was not even there, I discovered when we arrived, and was galled twice over by the knowledge that Guy had dragged me out of Night's Doorstep of his own wishes.

The fact that he might have other things to do with his time than spend it shepherding his master's headstrong, thousand-ducat-a-night *anguissette* through one of the most unsavory quarters of the City never crossed my mind. For that, I can only say that I was young, and filled with all of youth's self-regard. If I had known what was to come, I would have acted differently toward Guy that night, for he had been kind enough, in his fashion, but I am ashamed to say that I treated him with sullen disregard.

Restless and irritated on my return, I prowled the house as if it were a prison and came upon Alcuin in the library. I was on the verge of giving vent to my frustration, but something in his face stopped me as he looked up from the letter he was reading.

"What is it?" I asked instead.

Alcuin folded the letter carefully, smoothing the creases. His white hair gleamed about his face as he bent to the task. "An offer. It came by messenger this evening, from Vitale Bouvarre."

I opened my mouth, and closed it. He glanced up sharply at me. "You know?" Alcuin had always been better than I at hearing the unsaid. I nodded.

"I overheard you, the night of Baudoin's natality." I paused. "I'm sorry. I didn't intend to eavesdrop, truly. I've said nothing of it."

"It doesn't matter." He tapped the folded letter against the desktop, lost in thought. "Why now, I wonder? Does he have somewhat less to fear, now that House Trevalion has fallen? Or does he fear he's outlived his use to the Stregazza?"

I perched on a chair opposite him. "He has seen peers of the realm point fingers at one of the Great Houses, Alcuin, and live to gain by it. It has made him bold, and if the profit outweighed his fear, he would do it publically." I shook my head. "He is sick with desire, and these events have made him rash enough to seek a cure, no more. Have a care with him."

"I will have care," Alcuin said grimly, "this once, and never again."

"Will you . . . tell that to Delaunay?" I asked hesitantly.

Alcuin shook his head. "Not until it's done. The letter says only that Vitale agrees to my request regarding a patron-gift. Let Delaunay think it's an assignation like any other; if he knew how I felt, he'd not let me go." His dark eyes dwelled intently on me. "Promise me you won't say anything?"

It was not much to ask, and he had never asked me for anything before; it was not Alcuin's fault he had been offered his freedom the very night I was chafing at my own bonds.

"I promise."

TWENTY-FOUR

Though it was not my art to do it in the bedchamber—indeed, my gift lay in my very inability to do so—I am fairly well-skilled at dissembling. In all this time, for example, no patron of mine ever suspected the nature of my education as Delaunay's *anguissette* save Melisande Shahrizai, but she was a separate matter. Even Childric d'Essoms, who knew in his bones that Delaunay had a game at stake, never fathomed my part in it until the day I told him.

But if I thought my skills considerable, they were nothing to Alcuin's. I had heard in his voice and seen in his face the depth of his loathing for Vitale Bouvarre, yet in the days before his final assignation, no trace of it reflected in his demeanor. He was the same as he had always been, gentle-spirited and gracious, calmly accepting whatever fate dealt his way.

That which yields, I thought, is not always weak.

True to his word, Guy told Delaunay that Alcuin and I should be taught to sit a horse properly. Delaunay agreed, and Cecilie Laveau-Perrin graciously offered the usage of her country estate. It was still maintained by the seneschal appointed by her late husband, the Chevalier Perrin, when he had accepted his post as a counselor to the King.

We spent four days at Perrinwolde, and when I think back upon it, they were four of the happiest days of my life. Something in Delaunay eased in the country, a reserve that was so much a part of him I scarce noticed it. The manor was rustic, but clean and well-kept. The food was simple but good, and the seneschal's wife, Heloise, prided herself on having a hand in its preparation.

The riding lessons themselves were a pain and a delight at once. To Alcuin's and my mutual chagrin, we were placed in the charge of a grinning lad of eleven who sat bareback atop his shaggy pony as if he'd spent his whole life astride it. But once we put our dignity aside—which incident, I am happy to say, involved a headlong spill, a midden-heap and Alcuin, rather than me—we found him to be an excellent tutor. By the third day, we were neither of us as sore as we had been, and Delaunay gauged us proficient enough to be taught a few of the niceties of a nobleman's seat.

Our last morning, the seneschal called for a hunt in the early hours, to put a final test to the skill Alcuin and I had gained. The sun rose in the east, long rays slanting over the fertile earth. Green fields scarce touched with autumn's gold rushed past as we hurtled over them; peasants shouted, waving their hats. Far ahead, the hounds belled on the trail of scent.

We caught up with the front-runners in the orchard; the fox had gone to earth, and the hounds nosed about its den, giving mournful tongue while the riders milled in the open air. One of the men-at-arms whooped, and wheeled his mount; amid shouting and hallooing, half the hunt dashed back the way it had come, and I saw Alcuin among them, dark eyes shining, his white hair loosed from its braid, lashing his cheek like sea-foam as he turned his horse so sharply it near sat in its haunches. For this, like other things, he had a natural gift.

By the time we gained the manor, Delaunay's ease had perceptibly lessened. Surely he was no less cordial, but there was a measure of distance in his manner as he laughed and jested, paying the promised sum to the winner. We took our leave after the noon meal was served, and I daresay it was a regretful one on all sides.

There are those who hold that there is a pattern to all that is said and done in this world, that no thing happens without reason nor out of time. As to that, I cannot speak, for I have seen too many threads cut short to believe it, but of a surety, I have seen too the weft of my fate shuttled on the loom. If there is a pattern, I do not think there is anyone among us who can stand at a great enough distance to discern it; yet I will not say that it is not so. I do not know. This, though, I know is true:

If Alcuin had not learned to ride in that week's span, events would likely have fallen out differently. And if Hyacinthe had not placed his wager as he had . . . if he had not decided his earnings were blood-cursed, and Guy had not been forced to chase us through the City . . . who can say? I would not second-guess fate.

True to my word, I said nothing of Alcuin's assignation with Vitale Bouvarre. Delaunay had given his approval and the contract had been signed before ever we left for Perrinwolde. When the night arrived, there was some minor confusion over the matter of conveyance—Bouvarre sent his coach, when Delaunay thought to send Alcuin in his own—but the matter was easily settled. Delaunay accepted Bouvarre's offer of conveyance, on the contingency that Guy accompanied Alcuin.

This was a matter of course; indeed, a part of our contract, so no one thought anything of it.

If Bouvarre thought twice about it, I do not know. The contract specified merely that Alcuin or I would be accompanied by a liveried servant of the Delaunay household. Because Delaunay was not landed—so we believed—he was not officially entitled to have men-at-arms, and Guy was never sanctioned thusly. He was a quiet man, always, and there was nothing about him that marked him as a man of weapons. Many men affect a dagger at the waist; if he wore two, still, there was nothing else about him to suggest he had been trained by the Cassiline Brotherhood. I had known him for years, and never suspected.

The matter of the coach resolved, Delaunay gave Alcuin his blessing. As we never took assignations for the same night, I was there to see him off. He wore the same garb he had worn for his debut, the fawn breeches and the white blouse; Vitale's request, I assumed. His expression, calm and tranquil, never faltered, but his hands when I grasped them were ice-cold. I drew his head down to kiss his cheek—he had grown that much taller than I—and murmured, "Be well." Alcuin's lashes flickered, but he gave no other sign of hearing.

Thus he left us for the arms of Vitale Bouvarre.

It was well into the small hours of the morning when he returned.

Sound asleep, I thought that I dreamed, and in my dreams Gaspar Trevalion returned, shouting in the courtyard for Delaunay, loud and terrible. Even after I woke, it took me some moments to place the voice, for I had never heard Alcuin raise his. Then I scrambled out of bed at all speed, throwing on the first garment that came to hand and racing downstairs.

Half the household was there already, shocked and bleary-eyed behind raised torches. Delaunay had dressed as hastily as I, and his shirt was half-askew, caught up in the sword-belt he had lashed round his waist. "What is it?" he was shouting, as I emerged into the courtyard.

Alcuin was astride one of the coach-horses, legs clamped to her sides, wrestling with the severed reins. Maddened with fear, she plunged wildly, her traces dangling, nostrils flaring. Alcuin struggled to hold her in check, and his face was grim. "The coach was attacked," he cried, hauling back sharply on the reins. The mare's head came up, foam flying from her mouth where the bit sawed at her lips. Alcuin's white shirt was amber in the torchlight, but I could see a spreading dark stain across the ribs. "By the river. Guy's holding them off, but there are too many. He cut the traces."

For a split second, Delaunay stared, then turned to the nearest man, shoving him. "Get my horse!"

Already there were lights kindling in the stable. Now wide-awake, Delaunay grabbed the carriage-horse's bridle, bringing her to a standstill by force of arm and will.

Alcuin swung his leg over and dismounted, grimacing as he hit the ground.

"Are you . . . ?" Delaunay reached out a hand to him.

With startling speed, Alcuin struck his hand away, face set with rage. "This wouldn't have happened if you had taught me to use a blade!"

At that moment, a lad emerged from the stables at a run, leading Delaunay's saddle horse. Delaunay turned away, mounting in a flash and grabbing up the reins. "Where?" he asked coldly.

Alcuin pressed his hand to his side. "Near the elm grove."

Without a reply, Delaunay wheeled his horse and set out, striking sparks against the flagstones. With a sound somewhere between a laugh and a sob, Alcuin sagged to the floor of the courtyard. A bulging purse at his belt struck the stones, gold coins spilling out. I hurried to his side. "My marque, Phèdre," he gasped as I pushed untold wealth out of the way. "Unless I am wrong, Guy will bear the cost of it."

"Shhh." I held him in my arms, and unbuttoned his shirt deftly; if I was good at nothing else, that much, at least, I could do. I slid my hand inside and felt the wound, covering it with my palm, holding back the pulsing blood. Torches stooped low around us, faces peering to look. I wished we were at Perrinwolde, where Heloise would surely know what to do. "Get a physician!" I shouted. "Hovel, Bevis . . . send for the Yeshuite doctor! Now!"

I do not know how long I held Alcuin against the chill flagstones of the courtyard that night, while footsteps raced around us and voices muttered. It seemed like hours. His blood seeped warm between my fingers and his face grew pale, while I whispered prayers above him and apologized to Elua and all his Companions for every jealous thought I had ever had. When I saw the dark, solemn face of the Yeshuite doctor bending over Alcuin, it was the most beautiful sight I had ever seen.

"What is he doing on the cold stones?" he asked, clicking his tongue in disapproval. "Do you want him to take a chill and die, if this wound doesn't kill him? You . . . and you, there, carry him into the house."

I relinquished my burden with gratitude, my fingers stuck together with Alcuin's blood. He rolled his eyes in my direction as they lifted him, thanking me without words, and I gathered up the fallen coins and followed them into the house. Alcuin was esconced on the nearest couch, and the doctor cut his shirt away with expert shears.

The wound was long and deep, but not mortal. "You have lost much blood," the Yeshuite said matter-of-factly, threading a long needle with silk, "but you will not die of this, I think, because I am here." He plied his needle without speaking for a time, and Alcuin hissed through his teeth. When it was done, he called for strong spirits, and washed the wound, then bandaged it and gave me a container of salve. "You know to use this, I think," he said, and the irony was not lost on me despite his strange accent. "Tell Lord Delaunay to send for me if it mortifies."

Alcuin fumbled at his purse, spilling out coins. I plucked one from the floor and gave it to the doctor. He took it, then glanced at me with raised eyebrows.

"It is a hard life you lead. I hope it is worth the cost." I had no answer for that, nor did Alcuin, had he strength to speak. The doctor bowed, and one of the servants showed him silently to the door.

It opened before he could make his exit, Delaunay entering with a dreadful look on his face and the limp form of Guy in his arms. The doctor paused, laying one hand on Guy's throat and feeling for a pulse. Delaunay looked at him without speaking. The doctor shook his head. "For him, it is too late," he said quietly.

"I know," Delaunay said. He paused, a shadow crossing his face as he searched for courtesy. "Thank you."

The doctor shook his head again, sidelocks swinging, and murmured something in his own tongue. "It is nothing," he said, and though his voice was curt, he touched Delaunay's arm briefly before he left. The door closed behind him. Delaunay laid Guy's body down carefully, arranging his lifeless limbs as if he could still feel discomfort.

"You should have told me," he said to Alcuin. "You should have told me the bargain you made."

"If I had told you," Alcuin whispered, "you wouldn't have let me make it." He closed his eyes, and the tears that the Yeshuite's needle hadn't bidden seeped from beneath his lids. "But I never meant anyone else to bear the price."

Delaunay sank down on his knees, bowing his head over Guy's body and pressing his hands against his eyes. I hovered between staying and leaving, wanting to leave him to grieve alone, and not knowing if I should. But his head rose, a terrible imperative in his gaze that outweighed even guilt and grief. "Who was it?" he asked, voice scarce more than a whisper.

"Thérèse . . . and Dominic Stregazza." Alcuin's eyes opened a crack, speech coming with difficulty. "Prince Benedicte's daughter."

Delaunay covered his eyes again, and a shudder racked him. "Thank you," he whispered. "Blessed Elua, I am sorry, but thank you."

TWENTY-FIVE

Alcuin was a long time recovering from his wound.

It was true that he had lost a great deal of blood, but I daresay it was the blow to his spirit which lay at the heart of the matter. He had known the risk he was taking, but he had never thought past the bedchamber, and Bouvarre's desperation. Unlike me, Alcuin had never seen Guy act in his capacity as an unofficial man-at-arms. He never reckoned on the coach being attacked nor Guy's role in the threat; and for that, he could not forgive himself.

Delaunay, half-mad with grief and guilt, would have tended him night and day, but he was the last person Alcuin wanted to see. I understood it, better than I let on. What Alcuin had done, he had done for love of Delaunay; he couldn't bear, now, to reap the reward of Delaunay's concern. So I tended him through his fitful recovery, acting as go-between for them, and gradually got from Delaunay the story of what had happened after he'd left that night.

He had arrived in time to find Guy still alive, fighting like a cornered wolf against four attackers. Bouvarre's coachman was cowering in the driver's seat, sniveling but unharmed. Delaunay's description of his own arrival was terse—he said only that he dispatched three of the footpads, while the other one fled—but having seen him leave, I can well imagine how he burst onto the scene. When all was said and done, he was a seasoned cavalry-soldier, and a veteran of the Battle of Three Princes.

At first he thought he had arrived in time; but when

he turned to Guy, he saw how many wounds he had taken, and the hilt of the dagger that stood out from his ribs. Guy took two steps toward him, then faltered and sank to the street. With a hurled curse at the coachman, Delaunay went to his side.

If I describe it as if I were there, it is because Delaunay told me, for he had no one else to tell. And if I have embellished, it is only because I know my lord too well, and know what he left out.

Of Guy's heroism, he spoke freely. Guy had known. He had felt the coach slow, heard the approach of booted feet racing across the street, and known. He shoved Alcuin out ahead of him, fending off the first attackers as he slashed the traces and got the lead mare free. That was when Alcuin had taken his wound, but Guy had boosted him astride, smacking the mare across the haunches with the broadside of his dagger.

All of this he told Delaunay before he died—or most of it, at least, for some parts Alcuin filled in later. Of a surety, though, Guy told him they were Bouvarre's men, for as he said, "My lord, the coachman knew." As Delaunay told it, he knelt by Guy's side all the while, and both of them had their hand on the hilt of the fatal dagger. When Guy had told all he knew, his breath came short, and his skin grew cold and pale. His grip grew limp, fingers falling away from the hilt. I daresay I understood his final words as well as Delaunay, if not better. "Draw out the dagger, my lord, and let me go. The debt between us is settled."

Delaunay did not tell me that he wept as he obeyed, but I can guess it well enough, for I saw him weep at the telling. Blood enough to kill him, Guy had lost already, but the dagger had pierced a lung. Quickly enough, it filled; a bloody froth came to his lips, and he died.

As for the coachman, I daresay he thought his end was upon him as Delaunay rose and made toward him, bloodstained sword naked in his hand. But Delaunay did not kill him; it was never his way, to slay the weak. "Tell your master," he said to the coachman, "he will answer to me before the King's justice or on the dueling field, but answer he will."

Delaunay said the coachman gave no reply but to cringe. He gave the man no further heed, gathering Guy in his arms and laying him over his saddle, making his slow way home.

For many days, the household was in a state of cautious turmoil; cautious, for all were mindful of both Alcuin's convalescence and Delaunay's mood, yet the turmoil was unavoidable. The servants and I tended Alcuin, while the embalmers came to work their art on Guy, whose body lay in state in his humble room. Delaunay left for a time on the second morning, returning tight-lipped and angry.

"Bouvarre?" I asked him.

"Gone," came the curt reply. "Packed up and fled to La Serenissima, with half his household."

However extensive Delaunay's web, it was built of information, and not influence; if his knowledge extended beyond the bounds of Terre d'Ange, his reach did not. Vitale Bouvarre was safe enough in the Stregazza stronghold. Delaunay paced the library like a tiger, whirling to glare at me.

"No assignations," he ordered. "Until Bouvarre is brought to justice, I won't risk either of you."

Either of us, I thought, and stared at him. "You don't know?"

"Know what?" Too restless to give his mind over to one matter, he had paused at his desk, tracing the lines of a half-written letter and stabbing his quill at the ink-well.

I drew my knees up, wrapping my arms around them. "Bouvarre's patron-gift paid the remainder of Alcuin's marque," I said softly. "It was the other half of his price."

Delaunay looked at me, quill suspended in midair. "He *what*? Why? Why would Alcuin do that?"

My lord, I thought, you are an idiot. "For you."

Delaunay set the quill down slowly, taking care not to blot the letter. I had seen the address, it was to the Prefect of the Cassiline Brotherhood; to ask if Guy could be buried as a member of their order, I assumed. He shook his head, denying my suggestion. "I would never have asked him to take such a risk. Never. Either of you. Alcuin knew that!"

"Yes, my lord," I said cautiously. "We both of us knew; it is why he did not tell you, and swore me to silence. But the service of Naamah is not in his blood, as it is in mine. He swore himself to it to . . . to settle the debt between you."

Guy's words; I saw the blood leave Delaunay's face to hear them. "There was no debt between us," he whispered. "My duty to Alcuin lay elsewhere."

"In the promise of Prince Rolande de la Courcel?"

"He was my liege-lord!" Delaunay's voice was harsh. I shrank back at it and he saw, relenting. "Ah, Phèdre . . . I have trained you too well. Alcuin should have known, there is no debt between us."

"Then perhaps he is right, and you should have trained him to arms rather than bedchambers and intrigues, if you would have honored the memory of your liege," I said remorselessly. If my words were cruel, well, I make no apology. That night was too fresh in my mind, the cold stones and Alcuin's blood ebbing between my fingers.

"Perhaps," Delaunay murmured, no protest at my unkindness, gazing past me at some memory beyond my ken. "Perhaps I should."

I loved him too well to make him suffer. "Alcuin chose knowing what he did, my lord. Do not belittle what he has done for you. He grieves that Guy paid the price for it. Allow him the dignity of his grief, and he will come around. You will see."

"I hope you have the right of it." His gaze sharpened. "Nevermore, then. Alcuin's marque is made. And you . . ."

"I am pledged to Naamah, my lord," I reminded him gently. "You cannot absolve me of that, no more than Alcuin could break his own pledge."

"No." Delaunay picked up his quill. "But my words stand. No assignations, until Bouvarre is settled." He dipped his quill; I had pressed him to the limit of what he would discuss. Reluctantly, I cleared my throat. "Yes?" he asked, glancing up.

"There is the delegate posted to Khebbel-im-Akkad," I reminded him. "The one who developed . . . exotic tastes . . . in his posting? He is reporting to the King in some ten days' time, and I am contracted for his pleasure."

"The lordling from L'Envers' retinue." Delaunay tapped the pinion-end of the quill against his lower lip, lost in thought. "I had forgotten about him. D'Essoms must have commended you." He glanced down at his letter. "Bide, then, and we will see. If it come to it . . . well, we can claim tragedy in the household, and truly enough. But we shall see."

I bowed my head in silent acknowledgement, having

no desire to press him further. Only the weight of his regard forced me to look up again.

"Do not do this thing for my sake, Phèdre," he said gently. "If it is only for love of me . . . I beg you, let us beseech the priesthood of Naamah, and find another way to absolve you of your oath. Surely there is a way, for Naamah is compassionate."

I gazed at his beloved face, and the red haze rose in my vision uncompelled, moving from my left eye to obscure the whole of my sight. Behind Delaunay, Kushiel's face floated, stern and uncompromising, and in his hands he bore the rod and flail. In my skin, I shivered. I thought of Alcuin, and Guy. "No, my lord," I murmured, and blinked. My vision cleared. "It is you who put a name to what I am and made it a glory, and not shame, but it is Kushiel who chose me for it. Let me serve as I was made to do, whether it be in your name or Naamah's."

After a moment, Delaunay acceded with a curt nod. "Then let it be, only wait upon my word," he said, and returned to his letter.

Thus was the matter settled between us, and if I was at fault, it was only in failing to mark the significance when I saw that the courier who came for his letter bore the insignia of House Courcel. When no reply was forthcoming, I put it out of my mind, and indeed, Delaunay seemed reconciled. There was no funeral service—there was no family, and it would have been cruel, with Alcuin unable to attend—but he paid for full rites, and Guy was buried in the grounds of the sanctuary of Elua outside the City.

In a week's time, Alcuin's wound had begun to knit and bid fair to heal cleanly, although it would leave a fierce scar. I checked it daily, soaking off the bandage with warm water tinctured with valerian, to dull the pain.

If I had no skill at healing, at least I was trained to be deft, and he was grateful for it.

Alcuin was a good patient; he never complained, which was no surprise, as it was not his nature to do so. On the seventh day, he even essayed a laugh to see me sniff at the wound, checking to see that it didn't mortify.

"Some physician you make," he said faintly, pushing himself upright against the pillows and grimacing as the motion caught at his stitches.

"Lie quiet," I retorted, dipping my fingers in the pot of salve and spreading it over his wound. The gash looked quite dreadful as it curved across his pale torso, but for all that, it was healing. "If you want better tending, let Delaunay see it."

Alcuin shook his head mutely, stubborn and unrelenting. I glanced at his face and sighed. Nothing could take away his unearthly beauty, but still, he looked drawn and haggard.

"Guy made his own choices, too," I told him, folding a fresh linen pad over his wound. "He knew the risks, better than either of us. He was the one hired to kill Delaunay, after all; and it was Delaunay who forgave him and took him in. You diminish his repayment of that debt if you take the blame all unto yourself."

It was the first thing I had said that got through to him. "It does not excuse my folly," he said stiffly.

"Ah, no," I said, winding the bandages back over the pad. "Others may err, but not Alcuin nó Delaunay. Well, and if you think you are berating yourself for the failure, how much the more so do you guess Delaunay does for failing to discern that you despised the service of Naamah? I tell you, you should speak with him, Alcuin."

I thought for a moment that he would soften, but his lips hardened, and he gave another brief shake of his head, withdrawing from conversation. Undismayed, I busied myself about his room, moving the washing bowl, folding bandages, corking the doctor's salve.

"Now, which one of the Stregazza is Thérèse?" I asked, when I gauged that he was no longer paying attention to me. "Is she the firstborn? Prince Benedicte's daughters are House Courcel, I thought."

"They're of the Blood by birth, like Lyonette de Trevalion, but Thérèse married a Stregazza cousin. Dominic." I had caught his interest; his voice ran a little ahead of his thoughts. Alcuin had always been better than I at royal genealogies. "A bad match, by all reckoning; he's a minor Count, but then she was second-born. First is Marie-Celeste, who wed the Doge's son. It's her son stands to inherit La Serenissima. Once Prince Rolande died, I wager Dominic Stregazza thought to poise his family near the D'Angeline throne, though."

"And found his path blocked by House L'Envers," I mused. "How disappointed he must have been. But why would Delaunay care who killed Isabel L'Envers? By all counts, she was his enemy."

Alcuin shrugged, lifting up one hand and letting it fall. "That, I don't know."

"Perhaps it was her he loved, and not Edmée de Rocaille," I suggested. "Perhaps her betrayal lay not in causing the death of Prince Rolande's first-betrothed, but in becoming his second."

His eyes widened. "You can't think it, Phèdre! Delaunay would never condone murder. Never! And why would he honor the Prince's promise concerning me, if it were true?"

"Guilt?" I suggested. "He grew angry enough when I mentioned Rolande's name, the other day. Perhaps we have had it wrong all the while, and this feud between Delaunay and Isabel L'Envers de la Courcel was not enmity, but a love affair turned deadly bitter."

Alcuin gnawed his lower lip, mulling over my words while I concealed a smile. I had proposed it only to distract him, but it was too plausible to ignore. "You're mad to think it," he repeated, visibly distraught, color risen in his pallid cheeks. "It isn't in Delaunay to so dishonor himself, I know it."

"Well." I sat back and folded my arms, favoring him with a long glance. "You'll never know, if you won't speak to him. And you've a better chance than I of getting the truth out of him, by a far shot."

We were trained by a master, both of us; it was only seconds before Alcuin realized what I had done and laughed. It was his true laugh, free and unfettered; the very one that had greeted me the first day I had arrived at Delaunay's house. "Ah, no wonder they pay again and again for your charms! I laid my price before Vitale Bouvarre like a farm-wife in the market, while you coax secrets from their tongues and leave them none the wiser. Would that I'd had half your gift for it."

"I would that you had, too," I said ruefully. "Or found at least half the pleasure in it that I do."

"Even half might kill me." He smiled, quieting, and ran a fold of my gown through his fingers. "Your pleasures are too strong for my taste, Phèdre."

"Talk to him," I said, giving Alcuin a kiss and rising.

CWENTY-SIX

Healing of all kinds maintains its own pace, but there was no putting off the visit of Rogier Clavel, the lordling from Barquiel L'Envers' entourage. For one long day prior to our assignation, I thought Delaunay would cancel the contract, but at the last, he came home with a mercenary in tow: a man with the unlikely name of Miqueth, an Eisandine *tauriere* who had grown bull-shy after an incident which left a scar gouged into his left temple.

My new guard had parlayed his skill with weapons into a lucrative sideline, and Delaunay gauged him reliable enough. He was slight and dark, with brows that drew together in a perpetual half-frown, and while I had no doubt of his skill with a blade, I was surprised to find how greatly I missed Guy's silent presence. We rode together in Delaunay's coach and Miqueth grated on my nerves with his restlessness.

My assignation with Lord Clavel was at the Palace itself. To my relief, my guard remained blessedly silent as we traversed its marbled halls, contenting himself with hovering behind me and scowling at everyone we passed. We were in one of the lesser wings, where minor dignitaries are housed, so we encountered no one I knew, although there were a few who saw my *sangoire* cloak and gave me secret looks, knowing who I was and what it betokened.

Lord Rogier Clavel received me eagerly. He had the D'Angeline looks, but had been living a soft life in the court of the Khalif, and gone a little plump with it. Still, he had the haughty manners of a courtier, and dismissed Miqueth quickly enough, for which I was grateful. Delaunay and I had gone over our strategy enough times, but still, I needed no distractions.

"Phèdre nó Delaunay," Rogier Clavel said, putting on a formal voice that didn't quite disguise a quaver of eagerness, "I would appreciate it if you would put these items on." He snapped his fingers for a servant, who came bearing the flimsy gauze gowns of a hareem girl. I bit my lip to keep from laughing; it was a scenario straight out of a standard Night Court text, the Pasha's fantasy. I had expected more from a man who'd been satiated in the courts of Khebbel-im-Akkad.

Still, I knew what was expected of me, and donned the transparent robes. Rogier disappeared, and I was ushered into a bedchamber, which was arrayed with genuine Akkadian appointments. It was more than nice, with luxuriant silk tapestries of elaborate, abstract designs and worked pillows fringed in gold. I sank down on these and knelt *abeyante,* waiting. The first of my lessons, and still among the most valuable. In time, Rogier Clavel entered, magnificent in his Pasha's attire. I kept from laughing at how his jowels quivered in his soft face beneath the splendid turban, kneeling to kiss the turned-up toes of his kidskin slippers.

They guard their women well in Khebbel-im-Akkad. So I had heard, and so I came to understand, from the despite and desire mingled in him. Lord Clavel had been denied access, and he raged at it. Once I discerned this, we got on well enough. If he had been denied the hareem, he had gold enough and had paid it for this afternoon's pleasure. There was no question of exotic tastes learned abroad. He bore a gilt-handled quirt, and it roused him to a fury to punish me with it, chasing me about the cushions and flailing at my buttocks, breathing hard to see the thin red welts that ensued. I turned to the *languisement* when he groaned, kneeling solicitously, unbuttoning his voluminous pantaloons and taking him into my mouth. I thought that would be the undoing of him, but he surprised me, spilling me onto my back and tossing my legs into the air, performing the act of giving homage to Naamah with two years' pent vigor.

It surprised him, to bring me to climax; and made him solicitous afterward, which also might have made me laugh. "You paid for an *anguissette*, my lord," I murmured instead. "Are you unhappy to have gotten one?"

"No!" he said, caressing my hair, eyes wide with startlement. "No, Elua's Balls, no! I thought it was a myth, that's all."

"I am not a myth," I said, lying against him and gazing up so he might better see the scarlet mote in my eye. "Are there no *anguissettes* in Khebbel-im-Akkad, then? 'Tis a cruel land, I am told."

"Kushiel's Dart does not strike, where Elua and his companions have not laid their hand," Rogier Clavel said, tracing the curve of my breast through the thin gauze of my robes. "It is a harsh land indeed, and I am glad enough for a respite from it." A shadow crossed his face, " 'The bee is in the lavender,' " he quoted *The Exile's Lament* in a lovely, melancholy voice, " 'The honey fills the comb' . . . I never understood the sorrow of it until I, too, was far from home."

It was easier than I had reckoned. I smiled and twisted away, sitting back on my heels to put up my hair. "Is it so, then, with all D'Angelines? Does even the Duc L'Envers long for home?"

"Oh, my lord the Duc," he said, watching me hungrily. "He is of Elua's line, and would prosper anywhere, I think. The Khalif has given him lands and horses and men of his own. Yet even he misses the soil of Terre d'Ange, it is true; and word has reached us of the fall of House Trevalion. The Duc would return home, once his daughter is wed, and relinquish his appointment. I have come to petition the King on his behalf."

My hands stilled on my hair, and I made myself resume, twining it into a loose coil and thrusting an Akkadian hairpin in place. "The Duc's daughter is to be wed?"

"To the Khalif's son." Rogier Clavel reached for me, plucking out the hairpin and filling both hands with my hair. "Do . . . do that again, what you did before," he ordered, drawing my head down. "Make it last longer this time."

That I did, and well enough; he was no patron I would have chosen, for he had no true spark of Kushiel's fire in him, only a frustration so great he thought he burned with it. If I knew better, I would never say it aloud. Delaunay wanted this connection made; and anyway, it never pays to be rude to a patron. Besides, I didn't mind. Having spent long years under Cecilie Laveau-Perrin's tutelage, betimes it pleased me to be able to put that training to good use. I was born an *anguissette*, and can take no credit for that gift; but skills worthy of the finest adept of the First of the Thirteen Houses, I had acquired on my own merits, and I was justly proud of them.

"Ah, Phèdre," Rogier Clavel groaned when it was done. He lay sprawled on the cushions, his plump limbs slack with languor. He looked vulnerable and rather sweet, watching me with doting eyes as I rose to don my own gown. "Phèdre nó Delaunay . . . you are the most splendid thing ever I have known." I smiled without answering, and knelt gracefully to help him into a robe, covering him modestly. "If . . . Phèdre, if the Duc L'Envers' request is granted, and I am able to return with him, may I see you again?"

Even after he had gained my consent, Delaunay had delayed some time before accepting Lord Clavel's offer, for just this reason. I sat back and looked grave. "My lord Clavel, it is not for me to say. It is my lord Delaunay's desire to cull my patrons from among the Great Houses. Was it one such who commended me to you?"

"It was . . ." His expression, tinged with worry by my words, changed. I had wondered if he would dare name Childric d'Essoms, but he didn't. "It was someone highly placed at court. Phèdre, I have gold aplenty, and will surely be landed if we are allowed to return. The

King will be grateful, for the Duc has done much to advance D'Angeline relations with the Khalif."

Yes, I thought; and succeeded in wedding his own daughter to the Khalif's heir, which does much to advance L'Envers relations with Khebbel-im-Akkad. I did not say that, but murmured instead, "Indeed, and there is somewhat for which my lord Delaunay would be grateful."

"What?" Rogier Clavel clutched eagerly at my hands. "If it is in my power, I will do it gladly."

"There is an . . . old quarrel . . . between my lord and the Duc," I said, raising my eyes solemnly to meet his gaze. "I do not say it may be easily set aside, but my lord would take it kindly if it were made known to the Duc that he is not averse to the idea of peace between their Houses."

"Delaunay is not a noble House," Rogier Clavel said thoughtfully; I saw a sharpness in him, and took note of the fact that, doting or no, he was not a fool. "Anafiel Delaunay . . . never mind." I bowed my head silently, and he reached out to raise my chin. "Is your lord prepared to give his earnest word in this?"

"My lord Delaunay guards his honor well," I answered truthfully. "He would not speak of peace if he intended ill."

He debated with himself, gaze wandering over me, then nodded. "I will make mention of it, if I am given occasion. You will see me again, then?"

"Yes, my lord." It cost me nothing to agree, and his answering grin was like dawn breaking. I watched him rise and go to a coffer atop a high table, belting his robe as he went. He opened the coffer and plunged his hands into it, filling them both with gold coins bearing an unfamiliar Akkadian stamp. While I remained kneeling, he returned, spilling a nobleman's ransom in gold over my lap.

"There!" he exclaimed breathlessly. "If you should forget your promise, that should give you something to remember me by! I will light candles to Naamah in your honor, Phèdre."

Gathering my skirts into a pouch to hold the gold, I rose and kissed his cheek. "You have done her a mighty homage three times already this day, my lord," I told him, laughing. "Surely your name rings in her ears."

He blushed at it, and called for the servants.

It was but early in the night when I returned home. Delaunay thanked Miqueth for a job well done—little enough he had to do, although his scowl had kept everyone at bay—and dismissed him with pay. I was glad he was not to be taken on as a member of the household, though no doubt I'd be seeing him or his like soon enough again, if I was ever to have another contract. Perhaps Hyacinthe would be able to find someone I would like better, I thought.

"Come out to the courtyard," Delaunay said. "It's warm enough, with a brazier lit."

The courtyard was tolerably comfortable, and lovely as always by torchlight, the autumn foliage in bloom. To my surprise, Alcuin was there, carefully ensconced on a couch with a blanket tossed over his lower body to keep any touch of chill from his wound. He looked a shade less haggard, and smiled briefly at meeting my eyes.

"Sit down." Delaunay waved his hand at a couch, and took another for himself, leaning forward to pour me a glass of cordial. "Tell me," he said, handing me the glass. "How fares Barquiel L'Envers?"

I sipped the cordial. "The Duc L'Envers is minded to relinquish his appointment and return to Terre d'Ange,

ny lord. He would leave in his stead one daughter, wed
o the Khalif's son."

Delaunay's eyebrows rose. "Khebbel-im-Akkad allied
with House L'Envers? The Lioness of Azzalle must be
spinning in her grave. Well, no wonder Barquiel is ready
o come home. He's gotten what he went for."

"And the Khalif's heir will be kin-by-marriage to the
D'Angeline heir," Alcuin mused. "Not a bad alliance for
him."

"My lord." I set down my glass and looked quizzically
at Delaunay. "Is that why you wish to make peace with
House L'Envers?"

"I knew naught of it until tonight," Delaunay said,
shaking his head. "No, it's not that." He gazed at a torch,
wearing the look he bore when he contemplated something neither of us could see. I glanced at Alcuin, who
moved his head slightly in denial; he knew no more than
I. "We have never been friends, Barquiel and I, but he
stands to gain by the goals I seek. Time enough to put
an end—or at least a truce—to the bad blood between
us. Did it fall out as we planned? Was Lord Clavel
agreeable to your suggestion?"

"He will speak to L'Envers of it if he may, though he
gave no promise." I picked up my cordial and took another sip, smiling. "Still, I think memory of this day's
pleasure will goad him to it. I made it clear enough
where your interests lay, my lord; though for my part, I
am not averse to his gold."

"And his company?"

I shrugged. "He is easy to please. I have passed duller
afternoons, and had naught to show for it in the end. My
marque will gain two inches, from his patron-gift alone."

"Well, then, you may keep your word to him, if he
should return; but once only, I think, unless he rises in
the King's regard by this venture, to a title worthy of

patronage. Still, I would that all your patrons were so
harmless," Delaunay said ruefully, his gaze falling on
Alcuin.

"Any man may be dangerous when cornered," Alcuin
murmured, "or any woman. That is a lesson I have
learned well, if late. My lord, what will you do now?"

"Now?" Delaunay asked, surprised. "Naught, but to
wait on word of the King's response to L'Envers' petition, and . . . somewhat else. Then we will see."

TWENTY-SEVEN

It was some days before we heard official word of the
wedding of Valere L'Envers to Sinaddan-Shamabarsin,
heir to the Khalifate of Khebbel-im-Akkad. The King
had chosen to give his blessing to the union, and the
request of the Duc L'Envers was granted, although with
one unspoken caution. If House L'Envers had hoped to
maintain a monopoly in Khebbel-im-Akkad, it was not
to be. Barquiel L'Envers' replacement as ambassador
was one Comte Richard de Quille, who bore no love for
the L'Envers clan.

Interesting as these matters were, they took place very
far away in a country to which D'Angeline ties were at
best tenuous, and I failed to see what Delaunay's stake
in the matter was. When word of L'Envers' impending
return came, I thought he would reveal it, but he kept
his silence.

Whatever Delaunay waited on, he made it clear that I
would have no assignations until it arrived, and worse,
I was forbidden Night's Doorstep and Hyacinthe's company. When I proposed that Hyacinthe could find a suitable guard, Delaunay merely laughed. Condemned to

idleness, I made do as best I could, tending to my studies. My old tumbling-master would have been pleased to see I had not forgotten everything I had ever learned, and I practiced diligently on the harp and lute and kithara, but being forced to it, these pleasures paled quickly.

Alcuin mended more quickly these days, and the atmosphere in Delaunay's house had eased, for which I was grateful. I do not think they had fully resolved matters between them, for Guy's death was an open wound still, which we did not discuss, but the dreadful tension had broken. When Alcuin was well enough to travel, Delaunay brought him to the sanctuary of Naamah, where I had gone betimes with Cecilie Laveau-Perrin.

What passed between Alcuin and the priests and priestesses of Naamah, I do not know. He did not offer to tell me, and I did not ask. But he was three days in that place, and when he returned, I knew they had absolved him of any sin against Naamah. A portion of the guilt that had clouded him was gone, and it shone freely in his every word and gesture. The healing waters of the springs had done him good, too. Though he wouldn't allow Alcuin to venture into the City unattended any more than he did me, with the Yeshuite doctor's approval, Delaunay made Alcuin a gift of an elegant grey saddle horse. I was glad enough of Alcuin's recovery that I wasn't even jealous; anyway, it is customary to present an adept with a gift when they have made their marque, and I am sure Delaunay was aware enough of the traditions of the Night Court to know it.

To be precise, Alcuin's marque was not actually made. His still-healing wound prevented it, as it would be a lengthy business lying on his belly. But the necessary sum was in his coffer, and there was no question that his tenure was done. I made mention of it to Master Tielhard when I put Rogier Clavel's patron-gift to good use. Delaunay at least allowed me that much, though he ordered Hovel and another manservant to accompany me. They spent the time dicing in the wineshop, a freedom I envied. By this time, I was suffering a tedium so deadly I would have gladly scrubbed the Marquise Belfours' chamber pot, for the distraction of a scathing punishment at the end of it.

In this state of mind, I luxuriated under the marquist's ministrations, lulled by the exquisite pleasure of the tight-needled tapper. Master Tielhard shook his head and muttered under his breath, but I kept from twitching and gave him no cause for real complaint. Instead I concentrated on the isolated pain, letting my mind still so that it became the center of my being. The session passed all too quickly, and I was surprised when Master Tielhard gave my buttocks a light slap. "You're done, child," he growled, and I had the sense he'd already told me once. "Don your clothes, and be on your way."

I sat up, blinking; the interior of the marquist's shop was hazy beneath a veil of red. It cleared quickly and I made out Master Tielhard's apprentice coming toward me with averted eyes, blushing as he proffered my gown. He was nearly a man grown now, but no less shy than the first time I'd come. The new ink of my extended marque burned like fire, and I wondered what Master Tielhard would say if I took his apprentice into the back room and relieved him of a measure of his shyness. *I'm sure you wouldn't betray Lord Delaunay's trust in such a way, would you, Phèdre?* With a sigh, I dressed, and hoped that Delaunay would allow me to return to the service of Naamah in short order.

When I arrived at the house, my wine-cheered escorts in tow, I was met by one of the maidservants. "Lord Delaunay would see you in the library, Phèdre," she murmured, not quite meeting my eyes. Sometimes I missed my days at Cereus House, when I knew all the servants by name and called them friend; I'd felt it more than ever during this confinement. But I was heartened by the summons, thinking perhaps my hopes had been answered.

Delaunay was waiting for me. He glanced up as I entered, shielding my eyes from the late-afternoon sun that slanted through a window, bathing the many volumes on his shelves with a mellow glow.

"You sent for me, my lord?" I said politely.

"Yes." He smiled briefly, but his eyes were serious. "Phèdre . . . before I speak further, I would ask you somewhat. You have some idea that there is a purpose in what I do, and if I have not revealed it to you, you know well enough that it is because I would afford you as much protection as ignorance allows. But I am reminded, of late, of how very slight that protection is. What you do is dangerous, my dear. You have said it once, but I ask again. Is it still your will to pursue this service?"

My heart leapt; he was offering another assignation. "My lord, you know it is," I said, making no effort to disguise my eagerness.

"Very well." His gaze drifted past me, seeing again whatever it was Delaunay saw, then returned to my face. "Know then that I am not minded to take the same risk twice. Henceforth, your safety will be assured by a new companion. I have arranged that you will be warded by a member of the Cassiline Brotherhood."

My mouth fell open. "My lord will have his jest," I said faintly.

"No." A glimmer of amusement flickered in Delaunay's eye. "It is no jest."

"My lord . . . you would set some, some dried-up old stick of a Cassiline Brother to trail after me?" Between outrage and astonishment, I nearly stammered it. "On an *assignation*? You would set a crochety, sixty-year-old celibate to ward a Servant of Naamah . . . an *anguissette*, no less? Name of Elua, I'd rather you brought back Miqueth!"

For those who are unfamiliar with D'Angeline culture, I will explain that the Cassiline Brotherhood, like Elua's Companion Cassiel, are alone and united in their disapproval of the ways of Blessed Elua. Like Cassiel, they serve with steadfast devotion, but I cannot imagine anything more off-putting to a patron of Naamah than their cold-eyed disdain.

Aside from that, they are dreadfully unfashionable.

Delaunay merely raised his eyebrows at my tirade. "Our lord and King, Ganelon de la Courcel, is attended at all times by two members of the Cassiline Brotherhood. I would have thought you'd be honored by it."

It is true that I had never, in the wildest of tales, heard tell of a Cassiline Brother serving as companion to anyone not born to one of the Great Houses, let alone a courtesan. It would have given me pause, had I not been so shocked; but I could not think beyond the grim effect the ascetic grey presence of a Cassiline Brother would have on a hot-blooded patron. "Guy was trained by the Cassiline Brothers," I shot back at Delaunay, "and look what happened to him! What makes you think I would be any safer?"

Delaunay's gaze strayed past me again.

"If this man Guy was expelled at fourteen," an even voice said from behind me, "he had only begun the merest part of the training to become a Cassiline Brother."

Sparing a glare for Delaunay, I whirled about.

The young man standing in the shadows behind me bowed in the traditional manner of the Cassiline Brotherhood, hands crossed before him at chest level. Warm sunlight gleamed on the steel of his vambraces and the chain-mail that gauntleted the backs of his hands. His twin daggers hung low on his belt and the cruciform hilt of his sword, always worn at the back, rose above his shoulders. He straightened and met my eyes.

"Phèdre nó Delaunay," he said formally, "I am Joscelin Verreuil of the Cassiline Brotherhood. It is my privilege to attend."

He neither looked nor sounded as though he meant it; I saw the line of his jaw harden as he closed his mouth on the words.

It was a beautiful mouth.

Indeed, there was very little about Joscelin Verreuil that was not beautiful. He had the old-fashioned, noble features of a provincial lord and the somber, ash-grey garb of a Cassiline Brother adorned a tall, well-proportioned form, like the statues of the old Hellene athletes. His eyes were a clear blue, the color of a summer sky, and his hair, caught back in a club at the nape of his neck, was the color of a wheatfield at harvesttime.

At this moment, his blue eyes considered me with scarce-concealed dislike.

"Joscelin assures me that what happened to Alcuin, and Guy, would never occur to someone under his warding," Delaunay said in a calm tone. "I have measured my blade against his daggers, and I am satisfied that it is true."

A Cassiline Brother never draws his sword, unless it is to kill. I had heard of it once, when an assassin attacked the King. I turned my head toward Delaunay, considering. "He bested you with daggers alone?"

Delaunay made no answer, nodding toward Joscelin, who gave his formal bow, arms crossed. He was not, I gauged, much older than I was.

"In the name of Cassiel, I protect and serve," he said stiffly.

Wholly unbidden, I took a seat, choosing one where I could see both of them. The back of the chair stung the new lines of my marque. If I agreed to this, Delaunay would allow me to return to the service of Naamah. If I did not . . . well, Delaunay had not offered a choice in the matter. I shrugged. "My lord, at least he is pretty enough to be an adept of Cereus House wearing fancy dress. If you will, then so be it. Is there an offer to entertain?"

From the corner of my eye, I could see Joscelin Verreuil glare at being compared to an adept of the Night Court. Delaunay's mouth twitched, and I was sure he'd seen it too, but he answered seriously. "Offers aplenty, if you wish them, Phèdre. But there is a matter I would have you attend first, if you would hear it."

I inclined my head. "In the name of Kushiel, I—"

"Enough." Delaunay raised his hand, silencing me, but his glance took in Joscelin Verreuil as well. "Phèdre, you of all people should know better than to mock the service of Elua's Companions. Joscelin, your Prefect has gauged this matter worthy of your order's attendance, and you stand in danger of heresy if you question his judgment."

"As my lord bids," Joscelin said with restraint, bowing. It would have grated on my nerves, this constant bowing, were his every motion not such a damnable pleasure to behold.

"What is it?" I asked Delaunay. He gazed steadily at me.

"The Duc L'Envers is due to return in a fortnight's time. I would have you request of Lord Childric d'Essoms that he send word to Barquiel L'Envers that I desire a meeting with him."

"My lord." I raised my eyebrows. "Why d'Essoms?

We have laid the groundwork with Rogier Clavel."

"Because Barquiel will listen to him." Delaunay shook his head. "Clavel is a minor functionary; Barquiel would dismiss him out of hand. He has served his use. Barquiel L'Envers has grown large with this new alliance, and I cannot afford to to have him dismiss my request. D'Essoms got him the appointment in the first place; Barquiel will heed his words. And I need you to convince Childric d'Essoms."

"Then he will know," I said simply.

"Yes." Delaunay rested his chin on a fist. "That's why I waited for the Prefect's answer. Do you think he will act against you?"

I glanced sidelong at Joscelin Verreuil, finding a sudden comfort in the quiet menace of his ashen Cassiline attire, the daggers that hung at his waist. He looked straight ahead, refusing to meet my gaze. "Perhaps . . . not. D'Essoms has known from the beginning that I was part of your game. It is which part that he has not known." And that had comprised the greatest part of his pleasure, the endeavor to extract that knowledge. I felt a pang of sorrow at the idea of losing him as a patron. He had been my first.

"Then you will go to him," Delaunay said. "Ganelon de la Courcel ails, and time grows short. Let it be done."

"There is no assignation?"

He shook his head. "I would sooner surprise him with it. Do you think he will see you uninvited?"

I thought of Childric d'Essoms, the gifts he had sent after the time he had burned me. "Oh yes, my lord, he will see me. And what bait is it I am to dangle?"

The lines of Delaunay's face grew stern, sterner than Joscelin Verreuil's in all his disapproval. "Bid him to tell Duc Barquiel L'Envers that I know who killed his sister."

~WENTY-EIGHT

Delaunay wasted no time, dispatching me on the errand that very day. D'Essoms had quarters in the Palace in addition to his house in the City, and I had met him there before—it pleased him, at times, to flaunt me under the noses of his peers—but I had never sought him out. I had never sought out any of my patrons, and it was strange to be doing so.

In the coach, Joscelin was as silent as Guy had ever been, but a good deal more noticeable despite his subdued Cassiline attire. That he despised me, I had no doubt. Resentment at the role into which he had been forced shouted from every line of his body, glared from his summer-blue eyes. I did my best to ignore him, having considerably more important matters on my mind than his impaired dignity, but it wasn't easy.

We made a strange couple, entering the west wing of the Palace. I wore the *sangoire* cloak over my gown— a modest one of brown velvet—and had my hair caught up in a black mesh caul, but I might as well have come tumbled straight from the bedchamber. Next to Joscelin's solemn height, ashen garb and plain steel vambraces, everything about me cried Servant of Naamah. I tried to determine if he had ever been in the royal Palace before, and failed. If he was overwhelmed by its majesty and its bustle, he didn't let it show.

At d'Essoms' quarters, the servant who answered the door recognized me and took a step back, startled. I saw his gaze slide sideways to take in the presence of a Cassiline Brother beside me.

"My lady Phèdre nó Delaunay," he said, collecting

himself and bowing. I held no title, but I was of Delaunay's household, and servants found it best to err on the side of caution. I owed that respect to Guy, I thought, and grieved for him. "My lord d'Essoms is not expecting you," d'Essom's man said cautiously.

"Yes, I know." Joscelin Verreuil would be no help in a matter of protocol; I wrapped the *sangoire* cloak around me and summoned what dignity I could, raising my chin. "Will you send to Lord d'Essoms, and ask if he might spare a moment of his time for me?"

"Yes, of course, my lady." He hastened to usher us into the antechamber. "If you will be seated . . . ?"

I took a seat gracefully, as if I did this sort of thing every day. Joscelin followed without a word and remained standing, at ease in the Cassiline manner, which consisted of a relaxed stance, arms crossed low, hands resting on the hilts of his daggers. I tried to catch his eye, but he gazed straight ahead, scanning the antechamber imperceptibly for danger.

In a short while, Childric d'Essoms entered with two men-at-arms in attendance, a curious look on his face. Seeing me, he halted. "Phèdre. What is it?"

I rose only to sink into a low curtsy, holding it until he gestured impatiently at me.

"I've no time for games," he said. "What brings you here? Is it Delaunay?"

"Yes, my lord." I straightened. "May I speak to you in private?"

D'Essoms glanced at Joscelin, who stood impassively and looked at nothing. D'Essoms' brows rose a fraction. "Yes, I suppose you may. Come with me."

I followed as he beckoned, and his men stood back and fell in behind me, cutting off Joscelin's route.

"My lord." The Cassiline Brother's voice was quiet and even, but it held a tone that stopped even d'Essoms

in his tracks. He turned around and looked back. Joscelin
gave his formal bow. "I have sworn an oath."

"Oaths." Childric d'Essoms' face twisted at the word.
"I suppose you have. Accompany her if you must, Cassiline."

Another bow—how someone so rigid could make
obeisance look as fluid as a river-bend, I will never
know—and Joscelin stepped to my side. We retired, the
five of us, to d'Essoms' receiving room. He took his
chair and drummed his fingers on the armrests, waiting,
watching me with his hawklike gaze. Knowing better
than to presume, I remained standing. His men-at-arms
flanked him, hands hovering conspicuously over their
sword-hilts.

"My lord d'Essoms." Uttering the words, I sank down
to kneel, *abeyante*. It was engrained in me as deeply as
Joscelin Verreuil's Cassiline watchfulness. "My lord Delaunay sends me to beg a boon."

"A boon? Delaunay?" D'Essoms eyebrows rose to full
arch, all the more marked by the way his taut braid drew
back the dark hair from his face. "What does he want of
me?"

One sentence, and he would know. I clasped my hands
together and fought back another shiver, thankful of Joscelin's grey-clad legs behind my back. "He desires a
meeting with Duc Barquiel L'Envers. He asks that you
act as go-between in this matter."

I looked up, as I said it; I saw d'Essoms' face change.
"How does . . . ?" he began, puzzled. It changed. "You."

Childric d'Essoms was trained to arms, and a skilled
hunter besides; still, it took me by surprise, how swiftly
he moved. It shouldn't have, I'd seen from the first the
unerring aim with which he toppled the *plastinx* in Cecilie Laveau-Perrin's game of kottabos. But I failed to
gauge it, and he had me in an instant, back straining

beneath his knee, his blade at my throat. I felt it score a fiery line against my skin, and gasped.

"All this time," d'Essoms hissed, "you have played me false. Well, the King maintains his own justice against treachery, and so do I, Phèdre nó Delaunay. There is no contract between us now, and no word you may speak to bind me from acting."

"There is one." From my strained position, I could see Joscelin give his damnable bow; only this time, his daggers flashed free of their sheaths as he gave it. "Cassiel."

Would that I could have seen it clearer. From the far edges of my vision, I saw d'Essom's men-at-arms step up to the attack. Joscelin moved calmly, and steel glinted in an intricate pattern; he whirled as smoothly as silk, no haste in his motions, and yet the men-at-arms spun away from him like a child's toys. D'Essoms' gold-hilted dagger came away from my throat as he rose, then Joscelin moved again and it was flying through the air with a ringing sound. D'Essoms shook his hand and cursed. A line of red scored his palm. Joscelin bowed and sheathed his daggers.

"I protect and serve," he said without inflection. "Phèdre nó Delaunay was speaking."

"All right." D'Essoms sank back into his chair, waving his scored hand at his men, who staggered to their feet and fumbled for their blades. The predatory curiosity doubled in d'Essoms' gaze as he watched me collect myself to kneel with some semblance of dignity. "First an *anguissette*, now this. He's as real as you are, isn't he? Anafiel Delaunay is serious indeed, if he's contracted a Cassiline Brother as your companion. What makes you suppose I serve Barquiel L'Envers?"

"My lord, you spoke of it." I touched my throat unthinking, feeling a trickle of blood. "The night you . . . the night you took up the poker."

Behind me, I heard Joscelin's sharp intake of breath. Whatever his training had prepared him for, it was not this. D'Essoms' brows shot up toward his hairline. "You *heard* that?" he asked, astonishment unfeigned.

From my kneeling position, I stared at him, and the red haze clouded my vision. "My lord d'Essoms, you have known from the first that Anafiel Delaunay fished with interesting bait," I said, citing his own words. "Did you suppose Kushiel's Dart had no barbs?"

One of the men-at-arms made a sound; I don't know which. I held d'Essom's gaze as if my life depended upon it, which perhaps it did. After a moment, he gave a short laugh. "Barbs, yes." His mouth twisted wryly. "I've known since that night yours were sunk in me. But these you speak of are Delaunay's crafting, and not Kushiel's."

I shook my head. "Delaunay taught me to listen, and cast me on the waters. But what I am, I was born."

D'Essoms sighed and gestured at a chair. "For Elua's sake, Phèdre, if you would petition me on behalf of a peer, do it seated." I obeyed, and d'Essoms gave his wry smile as he watched Joscelin move to take up his post at my elbow. "Now what does Anafiel Delaunay want with Barquiel L'Envers, and why on earth should the Duc listen to what he has to say?"

"What my lord Delaunay wants, I could not say," I said carefully. "He holds my marque, and I do as he bids; he does not explain himself to me. I know only what he offers."

"Which is?"

It was the only card I held, and I hoped I was playing it wisely. "Delaunay knows who killed the Duc's sister."

Childric d'Essoms sat unmoving. I could trace the play of his thoughts behind his still gaze. "Why does he not take it to the King?"

"There is no proof."

"Then why should the Duc L'Envers believe him?"

"Because it is true, my lord." I saw as I said it the pattern of Delaunay's ploy unfolding before me, and gazed at d'Essoms. "By the same token by which I know you serve Barquiel L'Envers, I swear it is true."

"You?" he asked. I shook my head.

"Not I, but by the same token."

"The white-haired boy. It must be." D'Essoms moved restlessly; I sensed rather than saw Joscelin tense, then relax. "Still, they have been enemies a long time, my Duc and your lord. Why would Delaunay . . . ?" I saw the answer come to him, but he bit it off unspoken, gaze moving from me to Joscelin. "Delaunay." He uttered it like a curse, and sighed. "Very well. My lord the Duc would have my head if I didn't bring him word of this. I make no promises, but tell Delaunay I will accede to his request. And unless I am mistaken, the Duc will wish to hear what he has to say."

"Yes, my lord," I said, bowing my head. "Thank you."

"Don't thank me." D'Essoms rose smoothly; Joscelin shifted, but I motioned him to stillness as d'Essoms approached. He traced the line of my cheek with his knuckles, ignoring the Cassiline. "You will have a great deal to answer for, should I choose to see you again, Phèdre nó Delaunay," d'Essoms said, making a menacing caress of his voice. I shuddered at his touch, half-overcome with desire.

"Yes, my lord," I whispered, turning my head to kiss his knuckles. His hand shifted, closing hard on the back of my neck. Joscelin quivered like an overtight bowstring, unsheathing several inches of steel from his daggers. D'Essoms gave him an amused look.

"Know what it is you serve, Cassiline," he said contemptuously, giving my neck a brief, hard shake. I drew in a sharp breath, not exactly in pain. "You'll need a strong stomach, if you're to be companion to an *anguissette*." Releasing me, d'Essoms stepped back. His men eyed Joscelin warily, but the Cassiline merely bowed, his face like stone. "Tell Delaunay he will hear word," d'Essoms said to the both of us, bored by his own game. "Now get out of my sight."

Escorted by his men-at-arms, we obeyed quickly; indeed, Joscelin couldn't oblige him quickly enough. The moment the door to d'Essoms' quarters closed behind us, he turned on me, livid with revulsion.

"You call . . . *that*," he said savagely, "You call *that* service to Elua and his Companions? It's bad enough, what most of your kind do in Naamah's name, but that . . ."

"No," I hissed, cutting him off and grabbing his arm. A pair of passing courtiers turned to look. "I call *that* service to Anafiel Delaunay, who owns my marque," I said in a low tone, "and if it is offensive to you, then I suggest you take it up with your Prefect, who ordered you into the same service. But whatever you do, do not blather it about the halls of the Palace!"

Joscelin's blue eyes widened and white lines formed at the sides of his nobly-shaped nose. Effortlessly, he pulled his arm free of my grip. "Come on," he said in a tight voice, turning to stride down the hall. I had to hurry to catch him, cursing under my breath.

At least he was easy enough to keep in sight, the dim grey robe of his mandilion coat swinging with the speed of his pace, the hilt of his broadsword rising over his shoulder and the blond hair clubbed at his neck. If we had looked a sight entering together, side by side, I couldn't imagine how much stranger it looked to have me chasing after him as we left.

"Phèdre!"

A woman's voice, low and rich, with a hint of laughter in it like music; it was the only one I knew that could stop me in my tracks, my head turning like it was on a string. Melisande Shahrizai stood with two peers just inside an arched doorway. I approached at her beckon, while she bid farewell to the two lords with whom she had been conversing.

"What brings you to the Palace, Phèdre nó Delaunay?" With a smile, she reached out to stroke the scratch d'Essoms' dagger had scored on my throat. "Anafiel's business, or Naamah's?"

"My lady," I said, struggling for reserve, "you must ask it of my lord, and not me."

"I shall, when I see him." Melisande ran a fold of my *sangoire* cloak through her fingers. "Such a beautiful color. I'm glad he found someone who could recreate the old dye. It suits you." She watched me with amusement, as if she could see the pulse quicken in my veins. "I mean to visit, soon. I've been in Kusheth, but I heard of your household's misfortune. Convey my regards to that sweet boy, will you? Alcuin, isn't it?"

I would bet my marque she had no doubt of his name; the number of people outside Delaunay's household who even knew of the attack could be numbered on one hand. "I will, my lady, gladly."

Footsteps sounded behind us, quick and sure. I saw Melisande's graceful brows arch and turned to see Joscelin, frowning. He made a swift bow, and rose with hands resting on his dagger hilts, standing at ease by my right elbow.

Melisande glanced from my face to his, then back again, framing a question. "You?" she asked me, astonished. "The Cassiline Brother serves you?"

I opened my mouth to reply, but Joscelin's bow and

answer came quicker. "I protect and serve," he said flatly.

It was the only time I ever saw Melisande Shahrizai startled into true laughter. It rang from the vaulted roof of the salon, free and spontaneous. "Oh, Anafiel Delaunay," she gasped, gaining composure and wiping her eyes with a lace-edged kerchief. "You priceless man. No wonder . . . ah, well."

The white lines were back at the sides of Joscelin's nose and I could nearly hear his teeth grind. As if oblivious to his discomfort, Melisande patted his cheek, then traced a line on his chest with one finger. "It seems the Cassiline Brotherhood has been robbing the Night Court's cradles," she murmured, regarding him. He stared over her shoulder, the blood rising in a tide to heat his face. "Lucky brethren."

I thought Joscelin might well explode, but he held his stance fixedly and stared into the distance. It is a long discipline, the Cassiline training. Even Melisande Shahrizai couldn't breach it with a touch. No, it would take somewhat more, I wagered; five minutes, perhaps even ten.

"Well, then." Her eyes sparkled with the aftermath of laughter; a darker blue than Joscelin's, the starry hue of sapphires. "You will carry my regards to Alcuin, and my everlasting admiration to Delaunay?" I nodded. She had not given me the kiss of greeting, but she kissed me now in farewell, knowing it would set me off-balance with Joscelin watching.

It did.

"Who," he said when she had left us, "is that?"

I cleared my throat. "The Lady Melisande Shahrizai."

"The one who testified against House Trevalion." He continued to gaze after her. I was surprised he knew that much about the affairs of the realm. He shuddered, as if shaking off a spell; I actually sympathized with him, for a moment. "Will you be leaving now?" he asked then, polite and toneless. He had defaulted on his duty once through haste, I thought; it would not happen again.

My feeling of sympathy evaporated.

TWENTY-NINE

When we returned, Delaunay was waiting for us in his receiving room, unusual in itself. I wondered if the formality was for Joscelin's benefit, and grew further irritated with him to think it. Alcuin was there, sitting cross-legged and quiet on a low couch; he had been watching Delaunay pace for the better part of an hour, I guessed.

"Well?" Delaunay asked as we entered. "Will he do it?"

As I made ready to speak, once again Joscelin beat me to it.

"My lord," he said in his most impassive voice, unbuckling his baldric and slinging the sheathed sword off his shoulder, "I have failed in your service. I beg you to accept the blade of this unworthy one."

I stared at him open-mouthed as he went to one knee before Delaunay and proffered the blade across the back of his vambraced left arm. Even Delaunay looked startled.

"What in Elua's name are you talking about?" he asked. "Phèdre looks well enough to me, and I ask no more than that."

"Show him," Joscelin said, not looking at me.

"What, this?" I touched the trickle of blood that had dried at my throat and laughed, uncomprehending.

"From Childric d'Essoms, this is no more than a love-scratch, my lord," I said to Delaunay. "And 'twas Joscelin kept him from giving me worse."

"D'Essoms grew violent toward you?" Delaunay raised his eyebrows.

"When he learned that I had betrayed his patronage to you. But Joscelin—"

"He laid a blade against her and drew blood," Joscelin interrupted me, adamant in his profession of guilt. "I failed in my warding, and then in my anger, I let her out of my sight."

I caught Delaunay's inquiring glance. "Melisande." Her name sufficed as explanation. "She sends her greetings, and her regrets upon your injury," I added to Alcuin. To Delaunay, I said, compelled by fairness, "Joscelin did not fail you. He protected me well. D'Essoms took him by surprise, that's all."

Joscelin didn't rise, still holding out his sword, head bowed. "I have never drawn blade against any save on the practice-field," he murmured. "I was unready. I am unworthy."

Delaunay drew a deep breath, then released it. "An untried Cassiline," he muttered. "I should have known the Prefect would salt his gift thusly. Well, lad, I have measured your skill myself on the practice-field, and if you succeed thus well against Childric d'Essoms unready and untried on the proving-ground of D'Angeline intrigue, I am not displeased." Joscelin's head came up, blue eyes blinking. He tried to offer his sword once more. Delaunay shook his head. "To fail and persevere is a harder test than any you will meet on the practice-field. Keep your sword. I cannot afford its loss." Dismissing the matter, he turned his gaze back to me. "Now what of the Duc L'Envers?"

"D'Essoms was convinced," I said, unclasping my

cloak and taking a seat. "As you intended. He will convey your request, and convey word if L'Envers accedes."

"Good." A measure of tension left Delaunay. I wished I knew what it was he had invested in this. Retribution against Vitale Bouvarre and the Stregazza, of course—any fool could guess as much—but why? He had sought it even before Guy's death and Alcuin's injury. In the silence, Joscelin rose and strapped on his baldric, slinging the sword back over his shoulder. Two spots of color glowed on his cheeks, and shame made his movements awkward. I nearly pitied him again. The motion caught Delaunay's eye. "You are dismissed," he said, nodding with absent courtesy.

"My lord," I said. "Now that—"

"No." He cut me off. "No assignations, not until I have met with Barquiel L'Envers. We have shaken the game-board, and I will take no risks until the players have realigned."

I sighed. "As you will, my lord."

Once again, I was condemned to a life of tedium. As if to make matters worse, Alcuin and Joscelin struck up a friendship. It began watching Joscelin at his morning exercises, a novelty which paled quickly for me—I was willing to admit it was a thing of beauty to behold, but even the most avid music lover tires of hearing the same song—but Alcuin's fascination endured. One afternoon, drawn by the clatter, I walked onto the terrace of the rear garden to find them sparring with wooden practice swords, the kind boys use at play.

To my surprise, Joscelin was a gentle and patient teacher. He never laughed at Alcuin's clumsy efforts to thrust and parry, but waited on him when he lost his grip, demonstrating strokes over and over again in slow, flowing movements. Alcuin followed his lead with a good will, never out of temper, laughing at his own mistakes—and stranger indeed, Joscelin sometimes laughed with him.

"I should have known," Delaunay murmured at my elbow; I hadn't heard him come onto the terrace. His gaze tracked their progress. "A pity it's too late for him to learn it in truth. Alcuin's temperament is better suited to the Cassiline Brotherhood than the Service of Naamah."

It must have been he who gave them permission, and the wooden blades. "He is *not* suited to the Cassiline Brotherhood, my lord," I said sharply, rendered out of sorts by their laughter. "After all, he is in love with you."

"Alcuin?" Delaunay's voice rose, and he blinked at me. "You cannot mean it. If anything, I have stood as a father to him, or . . . or at the least, an uncle."

There is no folly like the folly of the wise. I eyed him wryly. "My lord, if you believe that, I have a vial of the Magdelene's tears I would sell you. You are Alcuin's rescuer from sure death, as you are mine from ignominy, and you could have either one of us by crooking your smallest finger. But I have watched Alcuin, and he would happily die for you. There is no one else in the world for him."

It was something, at least, to see Delaunay dumbstruck. I sketched him a curtsy which he did not see, and took my leave with haste. Alcuin, I thought, sorrow in my heart, never say I have not done you a kindness. If my lord will not have you, at least he cannot plead ignorance as an excuse.

After that, I could not stay in the house. Let Delaunay stripe my hide if he would—which I knew he would not—but if I was forbidden the service of Naamah, I had to escape from this eternal confinement. With everyone at the rear of the house, it was easy enough to slip out through the side gate.

I had the sense to take my brown cloak, and not the *sangoire*, and to bring some few coins that had not gone to pay the marquist. It was a simple matter to pay coach-fare to Night's Doorstep; for a smile, the coachman undercharged me.

Hyacinthe was not at home, but I endured his mother's too-knowing stare, and found him quickly enough at the Cockerel, dismissing the coach.

After long days of tedium, my heart leapt at the rollicking music and blazing light spilling out onto the street. I entered into pandemonium, its apparent source a game of dice at the back of the inn. A mass of guests was clustered about a table, most dressed in courtiers' finery, while a fiddler played on the dais. Below his frantic playing, I heard the sound of dice rattling in the cups, being cast upon the table. Groans rose from some of the watchers, and shouts from others, and ringing over them all, a familiar triumphant cry.

The crowd dispersed to mill around the inn and I saw Hyacinthe with several of his friends about him, grinning as he swept his winnings into a pile. "Phèdre!" he shouted, seeing me. Shoving the coins into his purse, he vaulted over a chair to greet me. I was so happy to see him, I threw both arms around his neck. "Where have you been?" he laughed, returning my embrace then holding my shoulders to look at me. "I've missed you. Was Guy so wroth after the last time that Delaunay wouldn't let you come?"

"Guy." The word caught in my throat; I had forgotten, for a moment. I shook my head. "No. I've a lot to tell you."

"Well, come in, sit down, I'll clear those louts away from the table." He flashed his grin, teeth white against his dark skin. He was wearing finer clothes than before, in a wild array of color—a blue doublet with gold brocade on the front and saffron sashes in the sleeves, over scarlet hosen—and looked absolutely splendid to my eyes. "I'll buy us a jug of wine. Naamah's Tits, I'll buy everyone a jug of wine!" He shouted to the innkeeper. "Wine for everyone!"

Good-natured cheers rose, and Hyacinthe laughed, sweeping a bow. No question that they loved him here, and no question why. If the Prince of Travellers won more at dice than an honest man ought, he returned nine centimes out of ten in his extravagance, and no one grudged him the tenth part. I never knew if he cheated or not; Tsingani are reputed to be lucky. Of course, they are also reputed to cheat, lie and steal with considerable skill, though I had never known Hyacinthe to do worse than filching tarts from the pastry-vendors in the market.

His friends made room for us at the table, and the noise made a shield for conversation as I told him all that had happened. Hyacinthe listened without comment, shaking his head when I was done.

"Delaunay's mixed up in House Courcel's business, that's for sure," he said. "I wish I could tell you how. I found a poet who'd a friend with a copy of Delaunay's verses, you know."

"You did?" My eyes widened. "Can you—"

"I tried." Hycinthe's tone was regretful. He sipped his wine. "He'd sold them not a month prior, to a Caerdicci archivist. I would have bought them for you, Phèdre, I swear it, or a fair copy at least, but my friend's friend swore he sold the original and kept no copy. Too dangerous, he deemed it."

I made a noise of disgust. "It doesn't make any sense. Why does House Courcel aid him with one hand, and gag him with the other?"

"Well, you know why they gag him." Hyacinthe leaned back in his chair, propping his boot-heels on the table. "He blackened their faces, when he made a song about Isabel L'Envers. I heard the Lioness of Azzalle named her a murderess in front of the High Court."

"She did." I remembered Ysandre de la Courcel, casting her vote for death. "So why aid him?" There were too many threads, too tangled to sort. "Phaugh! I've no head for riddles, and had naught to do for days on end but think on them. If you were truly my friend, you'd ask me to dance," I said, teasing him.

"There is someone who will be jealous if I dance with you," he said, a gleam in his eyes. He nodded to a woman across the inn, a cool blonde in an ice-blue gown. Cool as her demeanor was, I saw indeed that she smouldered to watch us.

"Do you care?" I asked him. Hyacinthe laughed and shook his head, black ringlets dancing.

"She is wed to a Baronet," he said, grinning, "and if I have danced with her before, it does not mean I will dance to her every tune." He took his feet off the table and rose, bowing and extending his hand. "Will you do me the honor?"

The fiddler doubled his vigor to see us join the dancing, winking at Hyacinthe, and we danced with good will. It brought more guests onto the floor, and with the exception of the Baronet's sulky wife and a couple of her companions, everyone not dancing laughed and clapped the time. I danced twice with Hyacinthe, then once each with several of his friends, and then the fiddler struck up a switch-reel, and everyone traded partners in a rush, whirling from one to the next, while those not dancing hastily moved chairs out of the way. When it was done, we were all breathless and flushed with merriment, and the fiddler bowed with a gasp, stepping down to wipe his brow and catch his wind with a mug of ale.

We had not yet taken our own seats when a commotion from the street drew a handful of people outside. A slight young man with curly hair darted in to catch Hyacinthe's sleeve. "Hyas, come on, you've got to see this," he said, laughing. "It's better than baiting badgers!"

Hyacinthe looked inquiringly at me.

"Why not?" I agreed, high-spirited and ready for anything.

A crowd of spectators had already gathered along the sides of the street, watching the entertainment taking place in the middle of it, but Hyacinthe pushed his way through to a stack of empty wine-barrels and upended one that we might stand upon it and gain a good view.

I saw and groaned in dismay.

It was a party of drunken young nobles, perhaps a dozen lords and ladies in all, returning to Mont Nuit with four adepts from Eglantine House, whom I knew by the green-and-gold of their attire. Their open carriage was turned sideways across the street, blocking the passage, and a distance behind it the young lords ranged in a semicircle, with hilarious expressions and drawn swords.

In the center of the space they had created was one very uncomfortable young Cassiline Brother, being taunted mercilessly by the Eglantine adepts.

"Joscelin," I sighed.

An Eglantine flautist perched on the back of the carriage, playing a merry, skillful tune while another adept sang unabashedly bawdy lyrics, her well-trained voice so lovely it took a moment for listeners to realize the vulgarity of her song. The other two Eglantines were tumblers, male and female, and it was they who pressed Joscelin the hardest. As I watched, the male tumbler knelt and the female sprang off the balls of her feet in a neat somersault, landing atop his shoulders. He stood as she straddled his neck, and her rising cleavage was thrust nearly under Joscelin's nose.

His face a study, he took a step backward, only to be prodded forward by the points of the lordling's swords. The female tumbler stood atop her partner's shoulders and he placed his hands beneath her feet, aiding her with a boost as she somersaulted over Joscelin's head. The male promptly went to a handstand, wrapping his ankles around Joscelin's neck and hanging suspended, ducking his head between the Cassiline's legs and grinning at the cheering crowd.

With a look of disgust, Joscelin pried the tumbler's crossed ankles loose, and the Eglantine caught himself on his hands, rolling and bounding to his feet. Joscelin took a step in the direction of the carriage, only to be confronted by the other tumbler, who leapt up to wrap her slim legs around his waist, grabbing his face in both hands and kissing him. Disengaging himself from her, he turned back toward the lordlings, laughing faces and gleaming steel arrayed against him. The male tumbler snuck up behind him, pulling a pin from his neatly clubbed hair. A swatch of wheat-blond hair trailed loose.

"Name of Elua," I muttered. "If you won't draw your sword, at least use your daggers, you idiot!"

"He can't," Hyacinthe said beside me, eyes bright with amusement. "They're just having fun, and Cassilines take an oath to draw steel only to defend their lives or protect their companions."

I sighed again. "I suppose I have to do it, then." Before Hyacinthe could protest, I hopped down from the barrel and squirmed my way through the crowd, stumbling into the open street in front of the sword-baiting lordlings. Joscelin caught sight of me with a startled look, and the flautist missed a beat.

"Heya, leave off," one of the young lords complained,

catching my arm and trying to pull me away. "We're just having fun with him!"

I raised my arm, his hand still gripping it. "Joscelin? Serve and protect?"

His vambraces flashed as he bowed, and both daggers rang free from their sheaths; I don't think he'd taken two steps before the lordling dropped my arm and the others began backing away, hastily sheathing their steel. The Eglantine flautist continued to play, no less merry with this new entertainment, and the singer took up a tambor while the tumblers threw tricks.

"Enough, enough!" cried one of the ladies of the party, traces of hilarity still in her voice. She curtsied in Joscelin's direction. "Cassiel's Servant has amused us enough for one evening, I think."

His glare could have chiseled stone, but their laughter echoed on the air as they departed. He turned his glare on me instead.

"I suppose Delaunay sent you?" I asked reluctantly.

"You are to return with me." His jaw clenched as he nodded toward Delaunay's coach, parked some distance away. The coachman looked apologetic. *"Forthwith."*

Hyacinthe leapt down from the barrel and ran over to give me a hasty farewell kiss. "Come when you can," he said, trying not to turn his laughing gaze on Joscelin, whose expression made it quite clear that that would be never, if he had any say in the matter. I prayed he didn't. "I always miss you."

"Me too." I made a point of kissing him again, grabbing his black ringlets in both hands. "Take care, Prince of Travellers."

We didn't speak in the coach, though Joscelin radiated fury like a forge. His ash-grey clothing had been pulled askew, and a hank of hair fell along his face; I am certain he never in his life imagined a Cassiline Brother could be subjected to such indignity, and it was obvious that he held me to blame.

Which gave me cause to think about facing Delaunay. I did not look forward to it.

If I expected to meet Delaunay's cold, implacable anger, I was mistaken, though not through any saving grace of my own. Joscelin conducted me to the library, hand at my back, nearly marching me along—and by this time, I was sufficiently aware of my guilt to make no protest. But when we arrived, Delaunay merely glanced up, raising a letter in one hand.

"It's come," he said briefly. "Barquiel L'Envers will see me in two days' time."

"My lord." I kept my voice steady with an effort. "Good news indeed."

"Yes." He studied the letter as if dismissing us, then looked up again and this time his gaze held all the emotionless resolve I had feared. "Phèdre. I warned you once; I will not do it again. If you leave these walls again without my permission, I will sell your marque. That is all."

"Yes, my lord."

My knees were trembling, and it took all the strength I had to turn and walk out without giving Joscelin Verreuil the satisfaction of seeing it. Before I closed the door behind me, I gained some measure of reparation in hearing Delaunay say to Joscelin, in quite a different tone, "What in the seven hells happened to you, lad?"

It was a pity I didn't dare stay to hear his reply.

THIRTY

There were terms, it seemed, to the Duc L'Envers' agreement. He would meet with Delaunay on his own territory, on the L'Envers estate an hour's ride outside the City; not the seat of his duchy, which lay in northern Namarre, but a pleasure-retreat he used when attendant on the Palace. In addition, there was to be an escort of twenty of L'Envers' men-at-arms. The Duc was taking no chances with Delaunay.

This much we knew, so it was no surprise when the escort arrived en masse and the Captain of L'Envers' Guard knocked on the door. Delaunay's horse was saddled and ready; although Joscelin was prepared to accompany him, he was minded to go alone. If it went well, he had said, there would be no need of Joscelin's aid; if it did not, then one Cassiline Brother alone would not suffice to protect him, not against those odds. A half-dozen might, or even four, but not one.

Delaunay's plan, however, was laid in vain; Barquiel L'Envers had made other plans. The Captain of the Guard looked Delaunay up and down, folding his arms. He wore light chain-mail, under a tunic of deep purple with the L'Envers' crest on it in gold: a stylized bridge over a fiery river. "I was told to bring the others."

"What others?"

"D'Essoms' girl and the other, the boy who claims to know." The Captain looked smug; Barquiel L'Envers had done his schoolwork. Delaunay paused, then shook his head.

"I vouch for their word. They stay here."

"Then so do you." Turning on the doorstep, the Captain gave his men a hand-signal, and they wheeled their mounts.

"Wait." Alcuin pushed past Delaunay. "I'll go." He turned before Delaunay could speak. "There is a score to be settled. Do you deny I have the right to be there, my lord?" he asked coolly.

He wanted to, I could tell; but it was not in him to deny Alcuin this last ounce of pride. "Very well." He gave a brief nod, then looked back at me. "No. Don't even say it."

"My lord." I lifted my chin and gambled. "I have risked as much as anyone to gain you this audience. If you would jeopardize it by going without me, do not think to find me here when you return."

Delaunay took a step in my direction and lowered his voice. "And do not think I will fail to do as I have threatened."

It was hard to look him in the eyes, but I did. "Will you, my lord?" I swallowed, then pressed onward. "To whom? Melisande Shahrizai, perhaps, who would use me as I've been trained in a game even you cannot guess at?"

"Agh!" Delaunay threw up his arms in disgust. Behind him, I could see bemusement on the Captain of the Guard's face. "I taught you too well by half," he snapped at me. "I should have known better than to buy the marque of someone who *enjoys* risking her life!" He turned to Joscelin, hovering in the entryway. "You'll come too, then, Cassiline, and ward them both well. By Cassiel's Dagger, it's on your head if you don't keep them alive!"

Joscelin made his impassive bow, but I saw a hint of apprehension flicker in his blue eyes. Still, I had to admit, he made for an impressive companion; the L'Envers Captain took a startled step backward when he emerged.

The team was hitched to the coach and Alcuin's horse saddled for Joscelin in short order, and we were under way, our breath rising in clouds of frost in the chill morning air. The purple-and-gold L'Envers standard rose above our small party, and the gleaming mail the men-at-arms wore gave us a martially festive air—I was naive enough, then, to find it thrilling. Besides, four or five of the men, I was sure, were not D'Angeline. They rode with a particularly wary air about them, and dark burnouses wrapped their heads and swathed their faces. The Khalif of Khebbel-im-Akkad had given L'Envers land and horses and men; I was willing to bet these riders were Akkadian.

The Duc L'Envers' country estate was surprisingly charming. I had never been to a country estate save Perrinwolde, but this was no working manor. We crossed a small river—the arched bridge echoed the design on L'Envers' arms—and rode through fanciful grounds, where gardeners labored over all manner of imported trees, binding them with burlap against the cold.

Still, we were seen from the parapets of the modest chateau, there was no doubt of that. The standard-bearer rode a little ahead and hefted the banner three times; there was an answering flash from atop the walls, and the gate was raised to admit us into the courtyard. And if we were politely received, we were nonetheless conducted by our full escort into the Duc's receiving room.

The room was beautifully appointed with Akkadian tapestries and furniture of unusual design, low and cushioned. One chair, with carving elaborate enough for a throne, was clearly the Duc's, but it stood empty. One of the men-at-arms—one of those I guessed to be Akkadian—left, while the Captain and the others lined the walls and stood at attention. I watched Delaunay, taking my cue from him. He was calm and watchful, betraying no sign of unease. It heartened me to see it. In a few moments, we heard the sound of booted strides in the hallway, and the Duc L'Envers entered the room.

Though I'd never seen him, I'd no doubt who it was; his men made him instantaneous bows, and Delaunay and the three of us followed suit.

To my surprise, when I straightened from my deep curtsy, I saw that the Duc himself was dressed in Akkadian style. A burnouse of L'Envers purple shrouded his face, and instead of a doublet, he wore loose robes over his breeches, with a long, flowing coat. Only his eyes were visible, but I knew them, once I had the chance to look him full in the face. They were a deep violet, House L'Envers' coloring; the color of Ysandre de la Courcel's eyes, who was his niece.

"Anafiel Delaunay," the Duc drawled, taking his seat and unwinding the long scarf of his burnouse. He had the white-blond hair, too, and pale skin, though it was sun-darkened around his eyes and his hair was cropped shorter than I'd ever seen a nobleman's. "Well, well. So you've come to apologize for your sins against my House?"

Delaunay stepped forward and gave another bow. "Your grace," he said, "I have come to propose we put that matter behind us, in the past, where it belongs."

Barquiel L'Envers sat at his ease, legs crossed before him, but I did not doubt for an instant that he was a dangerous man. "After you named my sister a murderess for all the realm to hear?" he asked smoothly. "Do you suggest I simply forgive this slight?"

"Yes." Delaunay said it without losing an inch of composure. I heard several of the men-at-arms murmur. The Duc raised his hand without looking to see which ones.

"Why?" he asked curiously. "I know what you have

to offer, and I wish to hear it. But it settles nothing between us, Delaunay. Why should I forgive?"

Delaunay drew a long breath and something smouldered in his voice. "Do you swear, your grace, on Elua's name and your own lineage, that my song was untrue?"

His question hung in the air. Barquiel L'Envers considered it, then moved his head slightly, neither a nod nor a shake. "I do not swear either way, Delaunay. My sister Isabel was ambitious, and jealous in the bargain. But if she had aught to do with Edmée de Rocaille's fall, I will swear she never intended her death."

"The intent does not matter; the cause alone suffices."

"Perhaps." Barquiel L'Envers continued to study him. "Perhaps not. Because of your words, a traitoress may name my sister a cold-blooded killer to the King's own face, and no one will gainsay it. You have not given me sufficient reason to forgive. Have you more?"

"I have sworn an oath," Delaunay said softly, "by which you stand to profit."

"Oh, *that*!" L'Envers' voice rose in surprise. He laughed. "You mean to stand by *that*, after the way Ganelon's treated you?"

"I did not swear it to Ganelon de la Courcel."

I wished, fervently, that one of them would say more of the matter, but neither did. Delaunay stood tautly upright, while L'Envers' thoughtful gaze wandered over the three of us, pausing longest on Joscelin.

"Well, Ganelon takes it with some degree of seriousness, it would seem," he observed. "Though I have never seen a stranger retinue. Two whores, and a Cassiline Brother. Only you, Anafiel. You always had a reputation for being unpredictable, but this is downright eccentric. Which one knows who killed my sister?"

Alcuin stepped forward and bowed. "My lord," he said calmly, "I do."

I had never been prouder of him, not even when he made his debut; I could swear, he was more composed than Delaunay. Even when L'Envers pinned him with his violet gaze, Alcuin didn't flinch. "Do you?" the Duc mused. "Which one of the Stregazza was it, then?" He saw a flicker of consternation on Alcuin's face, and laughed. "I have ears in the City, boy. If Isabel was killed, it had to be by poison, and no true D'Angeline would resort to such means. I hear tell you were attacked, and one man killed; now Vitale Bouvarre, who trades with the Stregazza, is nowhere to be found . . . and I hear from d'Essoms he paid an unheard-of sum for your virgin-price. Who was it?"

One flicker was all the Duc would get out of Alcuin; he looked to Delaunay as coolly as could be. "My lord?"

Delaunay nodded. "Tell him."

"Dominic and Thérèse," Alcuin stated simply.

I'd not seen the face of a man deciding to kill before, but I saw it then. A stillness came over Barquiel L'Envers, a look of intensity and hunger, all at once. He sighed, and there was release in it. "Did Bouvarre offer proof?"

"No." Alcuin shook his head. "He had none. But he carried a gift of candied figs from the Stregazza to Isabel de la Courcel. They were put in his hand by Dominic, but it was Thérèse who knew how she loved them. Bouvarre delivered them himself."

"There was an empty salver in her rooms," L'Envers said, remembering. "I suspected, we all did. But no one knew what had been in it, nor from whence it came."

"He tried to tell me it was Lyonette de Trevalion," Alcuin murmured, "but I laughed, and guessed it for a lie; it was too safe an answer, as she no longer lived to refute it. I do not think he would have tried to kill me, nor fled the country, had he lied the second time."

"You knew I have a cousin who has some sway in La Serenissima," L'Envers said to Delaunay. "My arm is longer than yours, and considerably more powerful, yes? But why do you care who killed Isabel? I might almost have thought you'd seek allies among them."

"You insult me," Delaunay said, flushing with anger. "If Isabel and I were enemies, you know well the only weapon I wielded against her was words."

"All too well. Why do you care who killed her?"

"Did you know that Dominic and Thérèse Stregazza have four children? All of the Blood by way of descent, and all fostered in one of the D'Angeline Great Houses."

"Yes, and Prince Benedicte is yet hale whereas the King's health fails, and his brood is powerful in La Serenissima, while certain parties whisper in certain circles that Baudoin de Trevalion was innocent, and the Dauphine's name is sullied by virtue of the slur with which her mother's was tainted." Barquiel L'Envers rested his chin on one fist. "Will you teach me to play the game of thrones? I think not, Delaunay."

"No, your grace. And I have not yet congratulated you on the marriage of your daughter," Delaunay added with a bow.

"Indeed." A brief smile touched L'Envers' face. "Well, perhaps you're right. It seems our interests do run the same course in this matter. You are aware that any actions I take against the Stregazza may not be entirely . . . honorable?"

Delaunay's gaze drifted over the line of men-at-arms, taking in the veiled features of the Akkadians. "You have sufficient leverage to insist that Vitale Bouvarre be taken into custody and questioned. He would confess, in exchange for his life. Benedicte would see that justice was done."

"Do you think? Ah, yes, you are old comrades, aren't

you, from the Battle of Three Princes. Well, perhaps he would, at that. Benedicte always had a name as an honorable man; he should never have married into that Caerdicci vipers' nest. I swear, if it can be done justly, I will do it." Barquiel L'Envers drummed his fingers idly on the elaborate arms of his chair and turned his attention to me. "So you're Childric's *anguissette*, hm? Spying on him for Delaunay's sake?"

I curtsied. "Your grace, I am the Servant of Naamah. My lord Delaunay merely sought a way to gain your ear. He is grieved at the dissent between you."

"Oh, indeed." A corner of L'Envers' mouth twitched in another faint smile. "As grieved as he was at Vitale Bouvarre's silence, I've no doubt. Well, I'd a mind to see these chits who outwitted one of my best counselors and the shrewdest trader in Terre d'Ange, and to see too if Delaunay was desperate enough to risk you both. It seems he is." The violet gaze turned back to Delaunay, thoughtful. "So it's the old promise, is it, Anafiel?"

"If you would speak of this matter, your grace," Delaunay said quietly, "I ask that we do it in private."

"They don't know?" Barquiel L'Envers' brows rose and he laughed aloud. "What loyalty you command! Ah, I'm envious, Anafiel. Then again, those who loved you always did remain true, didn't they? In some measure, at least. What about you?" He looked curiously at Joscelin. "Surely you don't serve him out of love, Cassiline. What binds you here?"

Steel glinted as Joscelin bowed. "I am vowed to serve as Cassiel did, your grace," he said in his even voice. "I, too, take my vows in earnest."

The Duc shook his head, mystified. "They say the old blood runs purer in the provinces. You're Siovalese, lad? Is your House of Shemhazai's line?"

Joscelin hesitated a moment. "A Minor House, yes.

But I am the middle son, and sworn to Cassiel."

"Yes, I can see that," L'Envers said dryly, then to Delaunay, "Well, it must be nice for you to have a fellow countryman in your household, Anafiel."

"Your grace." Delaunay lifted his brows.

"All right, all right." Barquiel L'Envers waved his hand. "You are dismissed. Beauforte, take them to the kitchens, bid them well-fed. We must not be remiss in attending to our guests. Oh, and give word that Lord Delaunay and his companions are indeed to be considered guests." He gave a wolfish grin. "No doubt it will set their mind at ease. So, Anafiel Delaunay, shall we converse?"

I didn't think I had any appetite, after the tension of the day and the audience with the Duc, but I was wrong. We were given a table and served warm, crusty bread, sharp cheese and a good stew—fit provender for the Duc's men, though not meant for the Duc's table, I guessed—and I set to almost as heartily as Alcuin and Joscelin.

No one spoke for some time, unavoidably conscious of the presence of L'Envers retainers bustling around the kitchen. Alcuin and I would not have risked it in any case, but we hadn't reckoned with Joscelin's naïveté. On his second helping of stew, he burst out with it, dropping his spoon with a clatter.

"Who *is* he?" he demanded of us. "There's no House Delaunay in Siovale! Who is he, and why am I commanded to attend him?"

Alcuin and I exchanged glances and shook our heads warningly at Joscelin. "Delaunay does not wish to tell us that which could get us killed," I said, adding wryly, "beyond what we already know. If you think perhaps he will confide in a, a fellow countryman, by all means, ask him."

"Maybe I will." There was a stubborn light in Joscelin's blue eyes.

Alcuin laughed. "Good luck, Cassiline."

THIRTY-ONE

I cannot say what passed between Delaunay and Barquiel L'Envers after we were bidden to leave, but it seemed that some form of accord had been reached, albeit an uneasy one.

The days of autumn grew shorter, and brought no word save the rumor of Skaldi glimpsed once more in the passes of the Camaeline Range. Delaunay waited on the matter's resolution, and once more I cooled my heels, while my coffer stayed empty and my marque grew no longer. I knew there was no malice in it, but even so, it galled me when Alcuin's final appointment with Master Tielhard was made, and his marque completed. He was free, as I had never been, in all my life.

Still, it was not in me to be cruel, not to Alcuin. I accompanied him to the marquist and made all the proper sounds of admiration. Indeed, it was a thing of beauty. The light of the braziers in the marquist's shop warmed Alcuin's fair skin, and the supple lines emphasized his straight, slender back. The delicate spray of birch-leaves that formed the finial ended at the very nape of his neck, where the first down of his white hair began. Master Tielhard actually wore a look of satisfaction as he inspected his handiwork, and his apprentice forgot for a moment to blush. Joscelin, hovering in the background, did blush, looking ill at ease and singularly out of place.

When one looks back at one's life, it is easy to mark the turning points. It is not always so easy to know them when they arrive; but this one, I daresay I knew well enough. It had been a long time in coming, and in some part of me, I had accepted it. Even so, it was another thing when it happened.

I was restless that night, and though I retired early, I found sleep eluded me. Thus it was that I wandered down to the library, with the thought of reading some verse or a diverting tale. When I saw Alcuin slip into the library ahead of me, I nearly went back, being in no mood to be reminded of the change in our status. I don't know why I didn't, save that he had a strange look of resolve and I was trained to curiosity.

As he hadn't seen me, it was a simple matter to stand at an angle to the doorway, where the lamplight didn't reach, and watch. Delaunay was there, reading; he marked his place with one finger and glanced up as Alcuin entered.

"Yes?" His tone was polite, but there was reserve in it. I knew Delaunay, and he had not forgotten what I'd told him.

"My lord," Alcuin said softly. "You have not even asked to see my marque finished."

Even from a distance, I could see Delaunay blink. "Master Robert Tielhard does excellent work," he said, at something of a loss. "I've no doubt it's well-limned."

"It is." There was a rare amusement in Alcuin's voice. "But my lord, the debt is not concluded between us until you acknowledge it. Will you see?"

He spoke truly; in keeping with the traditions of the Night Court, the Dowayne of the House must acknowledge an adept's marque before it is recorded as finished. How Alcuin knew this, I don't know. It may have been a fortunate guess on his part, though he always surprised me with what he did know. At any rate, Delaunay knew it, and set down his book. "If you wish," he said formally, rising.

Alcuin turned without a word, unbuttoning the loose shirt he wore and letting it slip off his shoulders. His hair was unbraided, and he gathered it in one hand, drawing it over his shoulder so it fell, white and shining, in a thick cable over his chest. His dark eyes were downcast, shadowed by long lashes the color of tarnished silver. "Is my lord pleased?"

"Alcuin." Delaunay made a sound that might have been a laugh, but wasn't, not quite. He raised his hand, touching the fresh-limned lines of Alcuin's marque. "Does it hurt?"

"No." With the simple grace that marked everything he did, Alcuin turned again and laid both arms around Delaunay's neck, raising his gaze to meet Delaunay's. "No, my lord, it doesn't hurt."

In the hallway, I drew in my breath so sharply it hissed between my teeth, though neither heard. Delaunay's hands rose to rest on Alcuin's waist, and I more than half expected him to push Alcuin away; but Alcuin expected it too, and instead tugged Delaunay's head down to kiss him.

"Everything I have done," I heard him whisper, "I have done for you, my lord. Will you not do this one thing for me?"

If Delaunay answered, I did not hear it; I saw that he did not push Alcuin away, and that was enough. A grief I'd not known was in me rose to blind my eyes with tears, and I walked backward, feeling the wall with one hand, wanting to hear no more. I was no romantic fool, to moon over what was not to be, and I had known since my first year of service to Naamah that my gifts were not to Delaunay's taste. Still, it was another matter to know that Alcuin's were. Somehow I found the stairs, and stumbled my way to my bedroom, and I am not to proud to admit that I shed a good many bitter tears before at last I slept, exhausted with weeping.

In the morning, I felt husk-hollow, emptied by the force of my own emotions. It made it easier to bear, seeing the faint shadows beneath Alcuin's eyes, and the smile he had only worn once before, after his night with Mierette nó Orchis. I almost wished I could hate him for it, but I knew too well what he felt for Delaunay.

Too well indeed.

For Delaunay's part, he took it quietly, but something in him had loosened. I cannot put it into words; it was the same thing I had seen in the countryside. Some part of himself which Delaunay held tightly at bay was given rein to breathe. It was in his voice, in every motion, in the way he was quicker to smile than to cock a cynical brow.

I don't know what I would have done had there not been news from La Serenissima that day; between boredom and despair, I was ready to test Delaunay's tolerance and cared little enough if he sold my marque. It's funny, how one can look back on a sorrow one thought one might well die of at the time, and know that one had not yet reckoned the tenth part of true grief. But that came later. Then, I was merely miserable enough to be morbid with it.

It was the Comte de Fourcay, Gaspar Trevalion, who brought the news. His friendship with Delaunay was stronger than ever since the trial, and he had weathered the ordeal with admirable dignity. The taint of treachery had not touched Fourcay.

The news he brought from the Palace was mixed. Vitale Bouvarre had indeed been taken into custody by

Prince Benedicte; but he had been found hanged in his cell before a confession could be obtained, and rumor had it that the regular gaoler had been replaced by a man who owed gambling debts to Dominic Stregazza. When that man was sought, his body was discovered floating in a canal. There was no question of his drowning. When they pulled him out, they found his throat had been cut.

It seemed Prince Benedicte was no fool; he sent for his son-in-law, Dominic. But Barquiel L'Envers—or perhaps his cousin—must have feared the slippery Stregazza would succeed in lying his way out of any wrongdoing, which like as not was true. At any rate, Dominic's party was assaulted en route by a group of masked riders. They were deadly archers, who fled uncaught, leaving behind four dead, one of whom was Dominic Stregazza.

"There's a rumor," Gaspar said shrewdly, "that one of the survivors saw Akkadian trappings on one of the horses; tassels on the bridle or some such thing. And it's said that the Duc L'Envers went a bit native during his posting to the Khalifate. Do you know aught of it, Anafiel?"

Delaunay shook his head. "Barquiel L'Envers? You must be jesting, old friend."

"Perhaps. Though I also heard that Benedicte added a private postscript to his letter, begging Ganelon to bring in L'Envers for questioning." He shrugged. "He might press the matter, too, if it weren't for other concerns in La Serenissima. Some rumor of a new Skaldi warlord. All the city-states of Caerdicca Unitas are frantic to form military alliances of a sudden."

"Truly?" Delaunay frowned; I knew he was worried, having heard nothing from Gonzago de Escabares since he sent a polite thanks for the translation I had made him. "Does Benedicte take it seriously?"

"Seriously enough. He sent word to Percy de Somerville, warning him to keep an ear cocked toward Camlach. We're fortunate to have young D'Aiglemort and his allies holding the line there."

"Indeed," Delaunay murmured; I knew by the sound of it that he held a measure of reserve. "So there's no talk of Stregazza retribution?"

"Nothing immediate." Gaspar Trevalion lowered his voice. "I will tell you privately, my friend, I do not think Benedicte de la Courcel will mourn the death of this son-in-law overly long. It is my belief that he would have drawn that one's fangs himself, had he not been wary of venom."

"And wisely so." Delaunay did not elaborate on the comment—I knew what he meant by it, and I daresay Gaspar Trevalion knew too—but turned the conversation to another matter.

I waited out their visit, attending on it with more than half my mind elsewhere. It is the discipline of the Night Court that stays with me at such times, rather than Delaunay's training. A useful thing, to be able to smile and pour with a graceful hand when one's heart is broken. When at last the Comte de Fourcay had gone, I had a chance to confront Delaunay.

"My lord," I said politely. "You said I might return to the service of Naamah when the matter was resolved."

"Did I?" He looked a little startled; it hadn't been uppermost in his mind, and I guessed he was a little short of sleep. "Yes, I suppose I did. Well, and I am willing to abide by it, on the strength of this news—though you will go nowhere without the Cassiline, mind."

"Yes, my lord. Are there offers to entertain?"

"Some few," Delaunay said dryly; there had been many. "Had you somewhat in mind?"

I drew a breath and steadied myself to say it. "I have a debt to settle with Lord Childric d'Essoms."

"D'Essoms!" Delaunay's russet brows arched. "He made an offer this week gone by, Phèdre, but I am minded to let his anger cool before he sees you. D'Essoms has served his purpose; we'll get no more of him, unless Barquiel's up to somewhat I cannot fathom. I doubt it, though. He's made his alliance and had his vengeance; he's clever enough to keep his head down for a time."

"Send me where you will, my lord," I said and meant it, "but I am Naamah's servant too, and I owe a debt to Childric d'Essoms for what I have done in her service."

"Well enough." Delaunay gave me a curious glance. "I'll not gainsay you in this. I'll have the other offers sent for your consideration, and sign the contract with d'Essoms." He rose to stroke my hair, the curiosity in his gaze turning to concern. "You're sure of this?"

"Yes, my lord," I whispered, and fled his touch before tears could choke me.

Of that assignation, perhaps the least said, the better. Suffice it to say that d'Essoms' anger had not cooled, and I was glad of it, for it suited my mood. Never before had I used my service to escape any woes that troubled me, but I did that day. There was no artistry in what passed between us; given license by his rage and my contract, d'Essoms greeted me with a powerful blow across the face. It knocked me sprawling to the floor, and I tasted blood, the red haze of Kushiel's Dart claiming me with blessed relief.

I did all that he ordered, and more.

When he bound me to the whipping-cross, I felt the grain of its wood caress my skin like a lover. I cried out at the first stinging kiss of the flogger, shuddering with helpless pleasure, and d'Essoms cursed me and wielded the lash with fury until pain overwhelmed the pleasure and I wept out of both, buffeted by pain, guilt and rage, sorrow and betrayal, no longer knowing the nature of the release for which I pleaded.

D'Essoms was tender when he was done; I hadn't expected that. "Never again, Phèdre," he whispered, holding me gently and sponging the blood from the morass of welts he'd laid across my back. "Promise me, you'll never betray me like that again."

"No, my lord," I promised, dizzy with agony and catharsis. In some distant part of my mind, I hoped Delaunay was right, and there was naught more to be obtained from Childric d'Essoms. "Never again."

He murmured something—I don't know what—and continued to tend to my weals, squeezing the sponge. Warm water ran over my skin, and I felt good, languid with the aftermath of it all, and happy that the first of my patrons still wanted me. I loved him a bit for that; I could not help it, had always loved my patrons at least a little bit. I never told Delaunay, though I think he guessed it.

I cannot guess at my appearance as I entered d'Essoms' receiving room. I stumbled a bit, I know, but it must have been worse than that alone, for Joscelin's eyes widened in shock and he sprang to his feet.

"Name of Elua!" he breathed. "Phèdre . . ."

It may have been pain or weakness, though I tend to think the sheer unexpectedness of hearing him say my name like that that made my knees buckle; either way, Joscelin was at my side in two strides. Without ceremony, he scooped me into his arms and headed for the door.

"Joscelin." Irritation cleared my head. "Joscelin, put me down. I can walk."

He shook his head, stubborn as any of his Brethren. "Not while I attend you!" He nodded to d'Essoms' liveried servant. "Open the door."

I was glad, as we emerged into the courtyard, that we were at d'Essoms' townhouse and not his quarters in the Palace; there was no one to see save a startled stableboy as Joscelin Verreuil, in his Cassiline drab, carried me to Delaunay's coach, my *sangoire* cloak trailing over his ashen-and-steel arms. I tried to ignore the strength of those arms, and the firmness of the chest against which they held me. "Idiot!" I hissed as he set me carefully within the coach. "This is what I *do*!"

Joscelin gave the homeward command to the coachman and got in opposite me, folding his arms and glaring. "If this is your calling, would that I knew what sin I'd committed, that I should be ordered to witness it and stand idly by!"

"I did not ask to have you here." I winced as the coach lurched into motion, throwing me back against the seats.

"And you call me an idiot," Joscelin muttered.

Thirty-two

Delaunay offered little comment on my condition afterward save to say in his very driest tone that he was glad to see I was in one piece, and to bid me use the Yeshuite doctor's salve unstintingly, which I did. As I have said before, I have good-healing flesh, and the marks of Childric d'Essoms' wrath soon faded from my skin.

During the time of my convalescence from this assignation—for whether I ailed or no, it would not do to go to one patron with the tracks of another still on me—Delaunay held a small dinner-gathering for a number of his friends. Thelesis de Mornay was among them, and when she returned some days later, I assumed it was to visit Delaunay, but I was wrong.

Instead it seemed she had come to invite me to a performance by a troupe of players, staging a play written by a friend of hers.

No one except Hyacinthe had ever made me an invitation for the pleasure of my company, and I was thrilled by it. "May I go, my lord?" I asked Delaunay, not caring that he heard the note of pleading in my voice. He hesitated, frowning.

"She will be safe with me, Anafiel." Thelesis gave the gentle smile that warmed her dark, luminous eyes. "I am the King's Poet, and under Ganelon's own protection. No one would be fool enough to trifle with that."

A faint twinge, as of an old wound, crossed Delaunay's face. "You're right," he conceded. "Very well, then. Only you," he added, pointing at me, "will behave yourself."

"Yes, my lord!" Forgetting I was still upset with him, I kissed his cheek and ran to get my cloak.

I had seen players often enough in Night's Doorstep, and heard them declaim bits of this and that from the season's newest plays, but I had never, in truth, seen an actual performance. It was enthralling. The play was performed in the old Hellene style, with the players in gorgeous masks, and the verses were resonant with poetry. All in all, I enjoyed it most thoroughly. When it was over, I was fair glowing with the excitement of it all, and must have thanked Thelesis a dozen times at least.

"I thought you would like it," she said, smiling. "Japheth's father was an adept of Eglantine House, ere he wed; 'tis the first play written outside the Night Court to tell Naamah's story thusly. Would you like to meet him?"

I went with her to the players' quarters, behind the

stage. In contrast to the well-orchestrated performance, it was chaos in their dressing rooms. The masks were treated with care—players are superstitious about such things—but garments and props were thrown hither and thither, and the sounds of players squabbling mingled with a triumphant rehashing of the night's performance.

I knew the playwright straightaway, for he was the only one in sober garb. Spotting Thelesis, he came toward her with arms outstretched and eyes aglow. "My dear!" he exclaimed, giving her the kiss of greeting. "What did you think?"

"It was wonderful." She smiled at him. "Japheth nó Eglantine-Vardennes, this is Phèdre nó Delaunay, who very much enjoyed your play."

"It is my pleasure." Japheth kissed my hand like a courtier. He was young and handsome, with curly chestnut hair and brown eyes. "Will you join us for a drink at the Mask and Lute?" he asked, shifting his attention eagerly back to Thelesis. "We were going to celebrate the triumph of our debut."

Before she could answer, there was a stir at the door. One of the players gasped, and a hush fell over their quarters as a tall man in courtier's finery entered. I knew him by his long, clever face and his habit of waving a perfumed kerchief under his nose: Lord Thierry Roualt, the King's Minister of Culture. Japheth composed his features and bowed.

"My lord Roualt," he said carefully. "You honor us."

"Yes, of course." The Minister of Culture waved his kerchief, sounding bored. "Your play was not displeasing. You will perform it for His Majesty's pleasure five days hence. My undersecretary will see to your needs." Another flourish of the kerchief. "Good eve."

They held their breath until he had departed, then

burst into cheers and hugs. Japheth grinned at Thelesis. "Now you *must* join us!"

The Mask and Lute is a players' house, and only Guild-members and their guests are allowed. As the King's Poet, of course, Thelesis de Mornay would have been welcome at any time, but I would not have been admitted alone, and so was happy at the chance. I sat and sipped my wine, marvelling at how the players carried on like children with their quarrels and dramas, when they held such power onstage. It reminded me of the bitter rivalries that went on behind the scenes among the adepts of Cereus House.

Thus I paid little heed while Japheth and Thelesis spoke of poesy, but when their talk turned to politics, it caught my Delaunay-trained ear. "I heard a rumor," he said, lowering his voice. "One of my troupe had it from the steward of the Privy Chamber, who is enamored of her. It is said that the Duc d'Aiglemort met in secret with the King, to bid for the Dauphine's hand. Is it true?"

Thelesis shook her head. "I had not heard it. But I have no contacts in the Privy Chamber," she added with a smile.

"Well, indeed." Japheth made a face. "Who would, were it not for the merits such gossip may afford? But I bade her keep it silent, for the nonce. I've no wish to jeopardize our chances of playing before the King."

"And you shall, splendidly."

I held my tongue for all of three seconds, but could not resist. "What was the King's answer?" I asked as innocently as I could.

"He declined, and would give no reason." Japheth shrugged. "As he has to every suitor. That is what I heard. Mayhap d'Aiglemort thought he was owed a boon, for bringing House Trevalion to justice. And mayhap he is, but not this one." With that, he turned the talk to other matters.

Though I was neither poet nor player and could not follow all their talk, I am well enough read that I enjoyed it and the whole of the evening most heartily. When Thelesis' coach took me back to Delaunay's house, I thanked her again. She gave me her warm smile and took my hands.

"It gladdened me to cheer your spirits, Phèdre," she said kindly. "I have known Anafiel Delaunay a long time. If you have care in your heart for him, do not judge him too harshly for it. He has lost a great deal in his life, and not the least of it is his verses. Were it not for . . . well, for several things, he, and not I, might be the King's Poet. Alcuin is good for him, though Delaunay himself may not know it. Allow him this small happiness."

"I will try, my lady," I promised, abashed by her goodness. She smiled again, and bid me good night.

If it had not been for what happened later, I might have taken no notice of the playwright's bit of news. Of a surety, I told Delaunay, who heard it without surprise; he was only surprised, I thought, that it had taken Isidore d'Aiglemort this long to ask. What he thought of the King's response, I do not know, save that it was no more than he expected. And with that, I would have put it out of my mind, save that a day later, an invitation arrived for Delaunay, bidding him to attend the royal staging of Japheth nó Eglantine-Vardennes' *Passion of Naamah*.

Being Delaunay, he made little of it; it was hardly the first time he had been invited to court. But I saw the invitation, and it bore the seal of House Courcel.

As matters fell out, I was contracted the very day of the performance to fulfill my promise to Lord Rogier Clavel, who had returned from Khebbel-im-Akkad with the Duc L'Envers. I half looked forward to it, for it would be easy work, and I had hopes that his second patron-gift would equal his first. He had offered to send his own coach, an offer Delaunay had declined, but he sent word to accept Clavel's conveyance after the invitation arrived. He gave me no reason for it, but I knew he had need of his team. It would not do to arrive sweated and on horseback for a royal audience.

Joscelin, of course, would accompany me. We had spoken little since my assignation with Childric d'Essoms, though I knew he was no happier with his posting than before. Well, I thought, he should be glad enough of Rogier Clavel, then, whose desires were so simply met.

So it was that Joscelin cooled his heels in Lord Clavel's quarters—rather finer than the ones he'd had before, I noted—while we disported ourselves. I daresay Lord Clavel was well enough pleased, and if a good portion of my mind was elsewhere, he never noticed it. For my part, I could not help but think of Japheth's play being staged in the Palace theatre, and Delaunay's mysterious invitation to attend it. Rogier Clavel favored afternoon assignations, and I knew full well when the hour arrived for the performance to commence. 'Twas early evening by then, and we had finished with our sport; I fanned him while he lay on soft cushions, the sheen of exertion drying on his skin. By the time he donned his robe and went to his coffer, I had an idea.

"Thank you, my lord," I murmured, tying the generous purse to my girdle.

"You've kept your word, and more." He looked eagerly at me. "So've I, Phèdre. The King has awarded me an estate in L'Agnace. Do you think your lord Delaunay might allow me to see you again?"

"Perhaps." I eyed him thoughtfully. "My lord Clavel,

tell me this; is there another exit from your quarters?"

"There is the servants' route to the kitchens, of course." He blinked at me. "Why do you ask?"

I had thought about it, and had an answer ready. "There is . . . someone . . . I must see, who made an offer to Delaunay," I said, putting a hesitation in my voice that suggested it was a patron I dared not name. "He would take it amiss, to have a Cassiline Brother on his doorstep, but they are rigorous in their service. Still, Delaunay bid me deliver word, if I chanced to do it without the Cassiline present."

"I could send word for you."

"No!" I shook my head in alarm. "My lord, the Servants of Naamah are known for discretion. I pray you, do not put mine to the test. But if you would send your coach to the west wing, and bid Brother Verreuil to meet me there, I . . . and perhaps others . . . would be indebted to you."

Rogier Clavel mulled it over, and I could see him assessing the risks and possible gain. The gain won out and he nodded, his plump chin wavering. "Easily enough done. You'll put in a good word for me with Delaunay?"

"Of course." I swung my cloak about my shoulders and smiled, kissing his cheek. "I will do so gladly, my lord."

I do not pretend to know the Palace so well as those who live there, but I thought I knew it well enough to make my way to the King's theatre in the west wing. It is a vast and impressive construction, which even a provincial would be hard-put to miss. Still, I was unfamiliar with the servants' passages, which were far narrower and more poorly lit than the main hallways, and managed to lose my way in them. At last I found an exit into the Palace proper, and stumbled into an empty hall, blinking at the light.

Around the corner, booted footsteps were approaching; two men, I gauged by the sound, and moving swiftly. I heard their voices before I saw them.

"Camael's Sword!" one of the voices exclaimed, livid with disgust. "It's not so much to ask, for the protection of the realm. You'd think the old fool owes me somewhat!"

"Mayhap he's right, Isidore. Do you really think the Glory-Seekers would follow you, after you betrayed Baudoin?" the second voice asked diffidently. "Anyway, they're not Camaeline."

"They're a hundred warriors, trained to fight in the mountains. They'd have followed, if I led; all but a handful, and we'd have soon been rid of them. Never mind, I'll recruit in the villages if I have to. Let Courcel see how he likes it, when D'Angeline peasants start dying in his name. He'll give me the Glory-Seekers." Isidore d'Aiglemort strode around the corner and halted, seeing me. "Hold, Villiers," he said, putting up a hand to his companion.

With no other course of action open to me, I gave a quick curtsy and continued forward, my head bowed, but d'Aiglemort caught my arm and gave me a hard look. "Who are you and where are you bound?"

"I am on Naamah's business, my lord."

He took in my cloak and studied my eyes, and it was the latter he recognized. "So it would seem. I've seen you before, haven't I? You offered Baudoin de Trevalion *joie*, the night of the Midwinterfest." He released my arm, which felt as if it still bore the impress of his fingers. His gaze glittered at me like ice over black rock. "Well, keep Naamah's silence and take care you don't bring me the same luck, little adept, for I'm about Camael's business."

"Yes, my lord." I curtsied again, truly frightened, and

thankful for once that a peer of the realm had no cause to recognize me as Delaunay's *anguissette*. They continued onward, his companion—the Comte de Villiers, I guessed—casting one quick glance back at me. Then they were gone.

Had I not been lost, I might have been shaken enough to abandon my plan, but as it was, I'd no choice but to make my way to the west wing. By the time I arrived, my nerves had settled and curiosity had the uppermost.

One thing, however, I had forgotten; this was the Palace, and members of the King's Guard stood at every entrance to the theatre, standing firm with spears upright. Beyond their reach, I gazed into the darkened theatre and saw the players onstage, lit by an ingenious system of torches and lamps, but I couldn't make out faces in the audience. Still, I could see the royal box, and it was empty. Disappointed, I turned to make my way to the western doors exiting the Palace.

I was just in time to see Delaunay emerging from the theatre, glancing at a note in his hand.

If I went forward, he would see me. Thinking quickly, I took off my *sangoire* cloak and folded it over my arm, walking purposefully around toward the rear of the theatre. If its design was anything like the other, I could hide in the players' quarters, for I didn't like to think on Delaunay's anger if he caught me at this. I'd sooner take my chances with Isidore d'Aiglemort, if it came to it.

As luck would have it, I guessed aright, and found the first chamber of the players' dressing rooms to be open and untenanted, save for the now-familiar heaped disarray of props and garments. Beyond the next door, I could hear an urgent commotion, but it seemed this room was far enough from the stage to go unused during the performance. Indeed, the quarters were likely more generous than those to which they were accustomed. This one held a great bronze-framed mirror, taller than I was, which must have come dear. I paused to glance in it and compose my features, when the mirror began to swing open like a door on cunningly hidden hinges.

Between Delaunay in the hall and whatever lay beyond the mirror, my choices were few. If I hadn't been in the King's own Palace, I'd have trusted Japheth nó Eglantine-Vardennes to hide me, but I dared not risk it here. I took the only refuge I could, crawling under a chair heavily draped with clothing. Reaching between the legs of the chair, I dragged a pasteboard shield in front of it. Cramped and confined, I prayed to Elua that it was refuge enough to hide me. There was a gap between the edge of the shield and a trailing gown of tawdry fabric. I reached out to twitch the fabric to cover it, then stayed my hand and peered through it instead.

The mirror swung outward, giving back a crazily angled reflection of the dressing room. I could see my own hiding place, nothing of my person visible in the gaudily cloth-hung shadow beneath the chair. A woman, tall and slender, slipped into the room. She wore a heavy cloak with a deep hood, rendering her features invisible, but I gauged her to be young by the way she moved as she closed the secret door behind her.

Anafiel Delaunay entered the chamber.

I nearly betrayed myself with a gasp, and held my breath to contain it. Delaunay gave the room a careful study, then inclined his head to the hooded woman. "I am here in answer to this message," he said simply, holding it out.

"Yes." The woman's voice was young, albeit muffled in the depths of her hood. She folded her hands in opposite sleeves, not taking the note from him. "I am . . . my lady bids me ask you what news you have of a . . . a certain matter."

"A certain matter," Delaunay echoed. "How may I be sure of who you serve, my lady?"

From my hiding place, I could discern that her hands were working within the sleeves of her robe. She extended one, briefly, and handed him something that gleamed. It was a gold ring, that much I saw. Delaunay took it, and she withdrew her hand quickly. "Do you know this ring?" she asked.

Delaunay gazed at it, turning it over and over. "Yes," he murmured.

"I . . . my lady bids me ask, is it true that you have sworn an oath upon it?"

Delaunay looked up at her, and the emotions writ on his face were too many and too complex to decipher. "Yes, Ysandre," he said gently. "It is true."

She drew in her breath sharply, then raised her hands and pulled down her hood, and I saw the pale gold hair of Ysandre de la Courcel. "You knew," she said, and I knew her voice too, now that it was no longer muffled. "Then tell me what news you have."

"There is none." Delaunay shook his head. "I wait on word from Quintilius Rousse. I would have told Ganelon, the minute it arrived."

"My grandfather." There was an edge in her voice, and the Dauphine moved restlessly, though I could tell her gaze stayed on Delaunay. "My grandfather would use you, and keep you from me. But I wanted to see for myself. I wanted to know if it was true."

"My lady," Delaunay said, in that same gentle tone, "it is not safe for you to be here, nor for us to speak of . . . this matter."

She laughed, a trifle bitterly. "It is the best I could manage. I have the Queen's quarters, you know, since my mother died. There was a Queen, once, some hundred years gone, who was enamored of a player. Josephine de la Courcel. She had this passage built." She crossed to the mirror-door, and pressed the hidden catch to open it. I could see Delaunay's brows rise a fraction. "My lord Delaunay, I am alone in this, with no friends to aid me and no way of knowing who I can trust. If you honor your vow, will you not give me counsel?"

Delaunay bowed, as he had not done when she'd drawn back her hood. Straightening, he returned the ring to her. "My lady, I am at your bidding," he said softly.

"Come with me, then." She stepped behind the mirror, and I could see her no more. Without hesitation, Delaunay followed. The mirror closed behind them, once more blending seamlessly into the wall.

Cramped and uncomfortable, I remained crouching beneath the chair for some minutes, until I was certain they had gone. Then, pushing the pasteboard shield out of the way, I crawled out of my hiding place and glanced in the mirror to see if I looked as dumbstruck as I felt. I did.

Taking a deep breath, I gathered my composure and steeled myself to find the western doors and deal with the next confrontation.

This one came in the form of a very irate Cassiline Brother. I had seen Joscelin white with rage; this time, waiting with Rogier Clavel's coach, he was apoplectic.

"I will *not*," he began in a tight voice, "have my vows compromised because *you*—"

"Joscelin." Weary with the exhaustion that prolonged tension can bring, I cut him off. "Is not your order vowed to protect the scions of Elua?"

"You know it is," he said uncertainly, unable to guess my intent in asking.

I was beyond caring. "Then hold your tongue and ask me nothing, because what I have seen this day might endanger House Courcel itself. And if you're fool enough to mention it to Delaunay, he'll have both our heads for it." With that, I climbed into the coach, settling myself for the homeward journey.

After a moment, Joscelin gave the coachman the order and joined me. His glare was no less furious, but it held something new besides: curiosity.

THIRTY-THREE

Delaunay returned some time in the small hours of the night, and was quiet and pensive the next morning. I more than half thought Joscelin would betray my disappearance to him, but I was wrong. He performed his exercises with a particularly single-minded focus, heedless of the cold air, the twin blades of his daggers weaving elaborate steel patterns.

I stood bundled in my warmest garments and shivered on the terrace, watching him. When he was done, he sheathed his blades and came to speak with me.

"Do you swear to me that what you ask in no way dishonors my vows?" he asked in a quiet voice. All of that, and he wasn't even winded; I was hard put to catch my breath just standing in the cold.

I nodded. "I swear it," I said, trying to keep my teeth from chattering.

"Then I will say nothing." He raised his mail-backed hand, one finger extended. "This once. If you will swear not to deceive me again while you're in my protection. Whatever I may think of it, I'd not keep you from honoring your pledge to Naamah, Phèdre. I'm pledged to Cassiel to protect and serve, and I ask only that you respect my vows as I do yours."

"I swear it," I repeated. I hugged myself against the cold. "Shall we go in now?"

There was a blazing fire laid in the hearth in the library, which was always one of the warmest rooms in the house, so it was there that we gathered. There was no sign of Delaunay, but Alcuin was reading at the long table, tomes and scrolls strewn across its surface. He gave a brief smile as we entered. I sat down opposite him and peered at his research, seeing references in several different languages and by as many names to the Master of the Straits.

"You think to solve the riddle of him?" I raised my eyebrows. Alcuin shrugged and grinned at me.

"Why not? No one else has."

"You mean Delaunay?" Joscelin asked, surveying the shelves. He took a volume out and pondered it, shaking his head. "One thing's certain, this is a Siovalese lord's library. He's got everything in here but the Lost Book of Raziel. Can Delaunay actually read Yeshuite script?"

"Probably," I said. "Do all Siovalese treasure learning?"

"There was an old Aragonian philosopher who would cross the mountains every spring to visit our manor," Joscelin said, putting the book back and smiling at the memory. "While the cherry trees were in blossom, he and my father would spend seven days solid arguing whether or not man's destiny is irrevocable. Then he would turn around and go back to Aragonia. I wonder if they ever settled it."

"How long since you've been home?" Alcuin asked curiously.

As if he'd been caught out at something, Joscelin's formal manner returned. "My home is where duty bids me."

"Oh, don't be such a damned Cassiline," I grumbled.

"So are we to take it you didn't succeed, as a fellow countryman, in prying any further information out of Delaunay?"

Joscelin paused, then shook his head. "No," he admitted ruefully. "My eldest sister would know. She once charted every one of Shemhazai's lines, every House, Major and Minor, in Siovale. She could tell you in three minutes whose line ends in a mystery." He sat down and scratched absently beneath the buckles of his left vambrace. "Eleven years," he added softly. "Since I've seen my family. We swear our vows at twenty. I'm allowed a visit at twenty-five, if the Prefect gauges I've served well my first five years."

Alcuin whistled.

"I told you it was a harsh service," I said to him. "And what about you? What can you add to the mystery of Anafiel Delaunay these days?"

I had tried to be mindful of Thelesis de Mornay's advice, but that had pertained to Delaunay, not Alcuin, and the banked jealousy smouldered beneath my words. If I'd not had enough questions before, I had a score more after what I'd seen yesterday. What was Delaunay to House Courcel, that Ganelon would use him; and how? What did Ysandre de la Courcel want of him, and what was the "certain matter" she wished to discuss? What oath had he sworn, and upon whose ring?

If Alcuin had no way of knowing what questions roiled around my mind, he knew well enough from whence my hostility came. But he merely sat and regarded me with his grave, dark eyes.

"You do know," I said in sudden comprehension. "He told you." My anger flared, and I shoved at the books nearest me. "Damn you, Alcuin! We always, *always* promised we would share with the other what we learned!"

"That was before I knew." Quietly, he moved the most brittle of the scrolls out of my reach. "Phèdre, I swear to you, I don't know the whole of it. Only what I need to aid him in this research. And I promised only not to tell you until your marque was made. You're near to it, aren't you?"

"Will you see?" I asked him coldly.

They were the words he had asked Delaunay. I saw him remember, and flush, the color as visible as wine in an alabaster cup. He'd known I knew; he hadn't known I'd seen. But it wasn't in Alcuin to evade the truth, and blushing or no, there was no guile in his eyes as he held my gaze. "You were the one who told him, Phèdre. He might never have let it happen, if you hadn't put it in his thoughts."

"I know. I know." My anger died, and I held my head in my hands and sighed. Joscelin stared at us, blinking and perplexed. It was no easy thing, to follow a quarrel between students of Anafiel Delaunay's. "I saw too well how you loved him, and for all his cleverness, Delaunay was as simple as a pig-herder where you were concerned. He'd have let you starve your heart out in his shadow before he saw. But I didn't think it would hurt so much."

Alcuin came over to sit beside me and put his arms about me. "I'm sorry," he murmured. "Truly, I'm sorry."

From the corner of my eye, I saw Joscelin rise silently and give his formal bow, withdrawing tactfully from the room. In that distant part of my mind that was ever calculating, I regretted that we had driven him away, the first time that he had relaxed a little in our presence. But Alcuin and I had been too long together in Delaunay's household not to have this conversation, and it had been long days in coming.

"I know," I said to him. I laughed, and my breath

caught in my throat, but I had no tears left for this. "I wish there were a little unkindness in you, Alcuin, so I could hate you for it. But I suppose I'll have to settle for wishing you well, and hating you for what you won't tell me."

He laughed too at that, his breath warm at my ear. His white hair spilled over my shoulder, mingling with my own sable locks. "Well, I'd have done the same."

"Yes," I said, "you would." I stroked his hair where it lay against mine, then drew out two lengths and braided them together, dark and white intertwining. He kept his head next to mine and his arms about me, watching. "Our lives," I said. "Bound together by Anafiel Delaunay."

Who, having entered the room, cleared his throat.

Alcuin, startled, jerked his head up. My hair, braided with his, tugged at my scalp and made me wince.

I can't imagine how foolish we looked; Delaunay's mouth twitched with amusement, but he managed to keep a straight face. "I thought you might like to know, Phèdre," he said, working hard at keeping his voice solemn, "that Melisande Shahrizai has come to visit, and would like to make an offer of an assignation."

"Name of Elua!" I yanked at the braid, dragging Alcuin's head back down with a yelp, and began undoing it frantically. "Why can't she send a courier, like normal people?"

"Because," Delaunay said, still amused, "she is an acquaintance of long standing, and likely most of all, because she enjoys seeing you discomfited. Be thankful I bid her wait in the receiving room while I summoned you. Shall I say you'll join us presently?"

"Yes, my lord." I got the braid unbound, and endeavored hurriedly to restore some semblance of order to my hair. Alcuin laughed; he ran his fingers through his hair once, and it fell glistening into its customary river of white silk. I glared at him, and wondered if I had time to change into a different gown. Delaunay shook his head and left us.

In the end, I elected to appear as I was, in the warm woolen gown I'd worn to watch Joscelin practice. It would merely have served Melisande Shahrizai's entertainment, to suggest that I was unsettled enough to need to arm myself in my best attire. She had arrived unannounced; well, then, I would receive her accordingly, even as Delaunay had.

I could hear the laughter before I even entered the room; whatever else they had been to each other, she and Delaunay made each other laugh. I prayed he wasn't describing the scene he'd witnessed, though it wasn't like Delaunay to be thoughtlessly cruel. He beckoned me into the room, and I obeyed. "My lord, my lady." I kept my voice level, made a curtsy and took a chair. Melisande shot me one amused glance that nearly undermined all of my composure.

"Phèdre," she said, cocking her head thoughtfully. "I have made Anafiel an offer he deems acceptable. My lord the Duc Quincel de Morhban is visiting the City of Elua for the Midwinter festivities, and he is minded to host a masque. His is the sovereign duchy of Kusheth, and I am minded to make somewhat of a statement on behalf of House Shahrizai. A genuine *anguissette*, I think, would be just the thing. Are you contracted for the Longest Night?"

The Longest Night. In the Night Court, no contracts were made for the Longest Night; but I was not of the Night Court any longer, nor ever had been in the service of Naamah. My mouth grew dry and I shook my head. "No, my lady," I answered her, not without difficulty. "I am not contracted."

"Well, then." Her beautiful lips curved in a smile. "Do you accept?"

As if there were some question of it, or I could summon the will to decline. I had been waiting for Melisande Shahrizai to offer me an assignation since I was scarce more than a child. I would have laughed, if I could have. "Yes."

"Good," she said simply, then glanced at Joscelin, who had arrived before me to stand at ease by the door in his cross-vambraced stance. "A long, dull vigil for you, I'm afraid, my young Cassiline."

His face was expressionless as he bowed, but his eyes blazed like a summer sky. I hadn't realized, when they'd met at the Palace, that he quite despised her. I wondered if it was because she had mocked his vow of celibacy, or for somewhat else. "I protect and serve," he said savagely.

Melisande arched her brows. "Oh, you protect well enough, but I'd ask better service, were you sworn to attend me, Cassiline."

Delaunay coughed; I knew him well enough to know it hid a laugh. I don't think Joscelin did, but he was filled with enough ire at Melisande's teasing that it hardly mattered. Oddly enough, it cheered me to know that despite consorting with House Courcel and Cassiline Prefects, Delaunay's sense of humor was undiminished. I liked Joscelin a little better for keeping my secret and his brief moments of humanity, but he needed to unbend a bit further if he wanted to avoid making a fool of himself in Delaunay's service.

Or of me, I thought glumly.

"The Longest Night, then," said Delaunay aloud, collecting himself enough to divert attention from poor Joscelin and smooth the awkward moment. He grinned at Melisande. "You don't do anything by halves, do you?"

"No." She smiled complacently back at him. "You know I don't, Anafiel."

"Mmm." He sipped at a glass of cordial and eyed her thoughtfully. "What's your game with Quincel de Morhban?"

Melisande laughed. "Oh, that . . . as to that, it's nothing more than Kusheline politics. The duchy of Morhban holds the Pointe d'Oeste, and reckons its sovereignty thusly, but the Shahrizai are the oldest House in Kusheth. Phèdre's presence will remind him that we trace our line unbroken to Kushiel, no more. I may wish a favor some day; it is good to remind one's Duc that there is merit in boons granted to ancient Houses."

"No more than that?"

"No more than that for the Duc de Morhban." She toyed with her glass and smiled idly in my direction. "My other reasons are my own."

Her smile went through me like a spear. I shuddered, and knew not why.

Thirty-four

When poets sing of the winter upon whose threshold we stood, they call it the Bitterest Winter; indeed, so it was, and I pray never to know one more bitter. But as the days grew ever shorter, we knew naught of what was to come. Betimes I have heard people bewail the fact that our destinies are shrouded in mystery; I think, though, that it is a blessing of sorts. Surely if we knew what bitterness fate held in store, we would shrink back in fear and let the cup of life pass us by untasted.

And mayhap there are those who would claim 'twere best were it so, but I cannot believe it. I am D'Angeline to my core, and we are Elua's chosen, descendants of his seed, born to the soil where his long wandering ended and he shed his blood for love of humankind. So I think, and betimes I believe it. I cannot do otherwise. Though I think they would have laid long odds on my chances in Night's Doorstep, I survived the Bitterest Winter, and I must believe, as survivors do, that there is reason in it. Were there not, the sorrow would be too much to bear. We are meant to taste of life, as Blessed Elua did, and drink the cup of it to the dregs, bitter and sweet alike.

But these beliefs came later, and are the fruit of long thought. Then, life was sweet, spiced only with apprehension, and tempered only by the gall of petty jealousy.

In the days before the Longest Night, my coming assignation was much on my mind, and I fretted over the preparations until Delaunay, exasperated, sent word to Melisande, who replied—by courier, for once—that she would see to all that was needful for my attendance at the Duc de Morhban's Midwinter Masque. I remembered the cloth-of-gold gown she had sent for my assignation with Baudoin de Trevalion, and was comforted in part; in another part, I was no less uneasy in mind, for the fate of Prince Baudoin remained fresh in my memory.

Delaunay, for his part, was amused by my worries, when he paid them heed, which was seldom. Whatever the game in which he was immersed, Melisande Shahrizai played no direct part in it by his reckoning, and there was naught he wished of my other patrons. The game, it seemed, had moved to another level, one to which I had no access.

With snow in the mountain passes, there came the resumption of Skaldi raiding parties, and the Allies of Camlach began to ride once more under the Duc d'Aiglemort's banner. This we heard, and in slow, creeping whispers the name Waldemar Selig surfaced in the salons of the City: a rumor still, nothing more, a name heard too oft to be ignored on the lips of fur-clad raiders who rushed Camaeline villages with axe and torch, sometimes escaping with loot of grain and stores, sometimes dying at the end of a D'Angeline sword.

These stories Delaunay heard with interest, cataloguing them in a record he kept; and another story too, from Percy de Somerville, of how the King had commanded him to send the Azzallese fleet against the island of Alba. Ganelon de la Courcel had not forgotten how the usurping Cruarch—whose name, it seemed, was Maelcon—and his mother had conspired to aid House Trevalion in treason.

As a reward for his loyalty, the King had deeded the duchy of Trevalion to the Comte de Somerville, who gave it over to his son, Ghislain, to rule in his name. And on the King's order, Ghislain de Somerville had set the Azzallese fleet to gain Alban shores, but the waves rose up four times higher than a man's head, and after several ships capsized, Ghislain de Somerville gauged failure to be the better part of wisdom, and shouted orders for a retreat, staying behind on his flagship until the last man still afloat could be rescued.

I am no fool; I marked at hearing it how Alcuin continued to pore over the most obscure of books and treatises for references to the Master of the Straits, sending word to libraries in Siovale and even to the scholars of Aragonia and Tiberium for copies of materials. Maestro Gonzago de Escabares arrived one day with a pack-mule full laden with fair copies of books and old parchments for Alcuin, and whispers of a direr rumor. The city-states of Caerdicca Unitas had formed strong alliances, and the north wind bore rumor, they said, that Waldemar Selig looked to Terre d'Ange, a riper plum for the plucking, and one fair rife with dissention.

I do not think, then, that we were quite so rotten-ripe; Ganelon de la Courcel held the throne, and no one challenged it. He had the support of Percy de Somerville, at command of the royal army, a powerful ally still in his brother, Prince Benedicte, and the interest of the Duc L'Envers, who held the favor, distant but lucrative, of the Khalif of Khebbel-im-Akkad.

But Ganelon was old and doddering, and de Somerville's hold on the duchy of Trevalion was tenuous, for the Azzallese had loved their Prince Baudoin, and did not take kindly to having a scion of Anael rule them. Courageous or no, Ghislain's compliance with the King's order was held by some to be folly, causing disquiet in Azzalle. Most of Prince Benedicte's attention was still devoted to La Serenissima, and where it was not, his new enmity with the Duc L'Envers undermined them both, for where one said yea, the other said nay, and neither would both support the King at once.

And all the while, Ysandre de la Courcel remained a shadow in the wings, heir to a throne that looked increasingly unstable.

There is a power in naming things. I do not doubt that the rumors from the Caerdicci city-states weakened Terre d'Ange; and I knew it for certain when I learned from whence they came, though that was yet to come. But of a surety, the political unrest that had marked the realm all the days of my life drew ever more pointed as the Longest Night drew nigh.

I do not pretend I saw it all at the time; these pieces of the great puzzle I put together later, when the pattern was clear to see. That I had the wherewithal to do even that much is a credit to Delaunay's teaching. I daresay if he'd known how matters would fall out, he'd have armed me with better knowledge, but at the time, I think he was glad enough to have me safely ignorant and out of harm's way.

And I, of course, had my own concerns.

In the past, Delaunay had always briefed me before an assignation, reminding me of the patron's connections and influences; with Melisande Shahrizai, he shrugged, turning his hands palm upward. "Melisande is Melisande," he said, "and anything you may learn of her game may be useful. But I think she is too chary, even with you, my dear, to let anything slip unwitting. Still, learn what you may, and pay heed to the guests' conversation at the Duc de Morhban's Masque."

"I will, my lord," I promised.

He kissed me then on my brow. "Have a care, Phèdre; and may you have joy on the Longest Night. It is the time for it, after all, and even Kushelines rejoice to see the Sun Prince woo the Winter Queen into loosing her grip on the darkness."

"Yes, my lord," I said. He smiled and adjusted my cloak. Already I could see his thoughts turning elsewhere. He would attend Cecilie Laveau-Perrin's private Midwinter Masque, he and Alcuin.

Thus did Delaunay advise me, and then there was no more time, for Melisande's coach arrived, and a livery servant in Shahrizai black-and-gold stood at the door, bowing. It was a new coach, a cunning little trap I'd not seen before, black trimmed in gold, with room only for two in the plush velvet seats. The door panels bore the insignia of House Shahrizai, three keys intertwined, nigh lost in the elaborate pattern. I knew the legend; Kushiel was said to have held the keys to the portals of hell. A matched team of four white horses drew the trap, beautiful creatures with arching necks, picking up their hooves daintily on the flagstones.

Joscelin Verreuil was like a dire shadow, accompanying me to the coach. Twilight came early these short days, and a hoarfrost lay on the courtyard, making everything but the Cassiline sparkle under the evening stars. He helped me into the coach and sat beside me glowering, while the livery servant climbed into the driver's seat and snapped his whip. Bells jingled on the harnesses.

"How would you pass this night, were you not in Delaunay's service?" I ventured to ask him.

"Meditating," he said. "In the temple of Elua."

"Not Cassiel?"

"Cassiel does not have temples," Joscelin replied shortly, and after that, I made no further effort to engage him in conversation.

We arrived at Melisande's home in short order. One thing I will say about her; she never failed to surprise. We were greeted not only by Melisande herself, but also by the Captain of her modest Guard and four of his best men, and the Guard bowed low as we were admitted— not to me, but to Joscelin.

"Well met, Brother Cassiline," the Shahrizai Captain said as he straightened, and there was nothing but sincerity in his handsome face and resonant voice. "I am Michel Entrevaux, Captain of the Shahrizai Guard, and I am bid make you welcome this Longest Night. Will you honor us with your company?"

It caught Joscelin unprepared; I daresay he was ready for anything but respect in Melisande Shahrizai's home. He had quarreled with Delaunay thrice this week about accompanying me on this assignation, since Delaunay was minded that Joscelin remain here, and not travel to the Duc de Morhban's Masque.

We who are well-trained react out of reflex; in Joscelin's case, he responded with his cross-vambraced bow. "The honor would be mine," he replied formally.

Melisande Shahrizai, at once resplendent and demure in a long coat of black-and-gold brocade, her hair braided in a crown, smiled warmly. "There is a niche in the garden, Messire Cassiline, if you wish to maintain Elua's vigil. Phèdre, well met." She stooped to kiss me in greeting, and the scent of her perfume surrounded me, but her kiss was no more than perfunctory, and left me able to stand.

It made me more nervous than the other kind.

"Young men," Melisande murmured when they had left, smiling faintly. "Such a sense of honor. Is he a little bit in love with you, do you think?"

"Joscelin quite despises me," I said. "My lady."

"Oh, love and hate are two sides of the same blade," she said cheerily enough, motioning for a servant to take my cloak, "and an edge finer honed than yon Cassiline's daggers divides them." Her servants led the way to her receiving room, gliding silently ahead to open doors; she took my arm as we went. "You despise your patrons a little, and love them too, yes?"

"Yes, my lady." I sat down in the chair held for me and accepted a glass of *joie*, eyeing her warily. "A little."

"And how many of them do you fear?"

I held my glass without sipping, as she did, and answered honestly. "One, at least, not at all. Most of them, sometimes. You, my lady, always."

The blue of her eyes was like the sky at twilight when the first stars appear. "Good." Her smile held promises I shuddered to think on. "Be at ease in it, Phèdre. This is the Longest Night, and I am in no hurry. You're not like the others, who are trained to it from birth, like hounds cringing under the whip for a kind touch from their master's hand. No, you embrace the lash, but even so, there is aught in you that rebels at it. Let others plumb the depths of the former; 'tis the latter that interests me."

At that, I did shudder. "I am at my lady's command."

"Command." Melisande held her glass to the light, inspecting the sparkling cordial. "Command is for captains and generals. I have no interest in command. If you would obey, you will discern what pleases me, and do it unasked." She lifted her glass to me, smiling. "Joy."

"Joy." I echoed it unthinkingly, and drank the *joie*. It burned, sweet and fiery, blazing a trail down my throat, evoking memories of the Great Hall at Cereus House, a blazing hearth and the smell of evergreen boughs.

"Ah, you do please me, Phèdre; you please me a great deal." Rising, Melisande set down her empty glass, and reached down to stroke my cheek. "My attendants will make you ready. We leave for Quincel de Morhban's Masque in an hour's time."

With that, she swept from the room, leaving only the lingering scent of her perfume, and a maidservant with downcast eyes came to lead me away.

There was a hot bath awaiting, fresh-drawn, with wreaths of steam still curling above the surface of the water, candles set all around and two more attendants waiting. I luxuriated in the bath, while one of Melisande's attendants rubbed fragrant oil into my skin and another tended to my hair, brushing it out at length, merely twining a few sprays of white ribbons in my dark curls. When the maidservant brought in my costume, I rose from the bath, letting them wind a linen sheet about my damp body, and looked at what she had brought.

I am used to fine clothing and not easily impressed, but the overgarment took even me aback. It was a loose-fitting gown of transparent white gauze with trailing sleeves—and it was spangled all about with tiny diamonds, sewn with exquisite care onto the sheer fabric. "Name of Elua! What does it go over?"

The maidservant fussed with a half-mask, a white-and-brown feathered osprey with the eye-holes trimmed in black velvet piping. "You, my lady," she said quietly.

In the candlelight, I could see right through the gauze. I would be as good as naked in it, before half the nobles of Kusheth. "No."

"Yes." Her manner may have been meek, but no one in Melisande's service was going to gainsay their mistress. "And this." She held out one other item, a velvet slip-collar, with a diamond teardrop suspended from it, and a lead attached. I closed my eyes. I had seen such things, in Valerian House. In the privacy of the Night Court, it would not be so bad.

But Melisande meant to display me before the peers of the realm.

Gently and inexorably, her attendants helped me dress, putting on the sheer garment, adjusting my hair so that it spilled down my back, drawing the slip-collar over my head and settling it so the diamond fell just so in the hollow of my throat, and placing the mask on me. When they were done, I looked at myself in the long mirror.

A captive creature gazed back, masked and collared, naked beneath a scintillating curtain of gauze.

"Very nice." Melisande's voice, amused, startled me; like Joscelin, I reacted out of reflex. A Cassiline bows in defense, and an adept of the Night Court kneels. I knelt and gazed up at her.

As I was in sheerest white, she was in densest black, velvet skirts sweeping the floor, the bodice tight to her torso, white shoulders rising above it, and black gloves above the elbow. Her mask was black, night-black feathers with a dark rainbow sheen upon them, sweeping up in points to mingle with her elaborately styled hair. A band of black opals on velvet encircled her throat, like the colors that glimmer 'round a cormorant's neck, and I knew what her costume was then, and mine. There is a Kusheline legend of the Isle of Ys and its dark Lady, who commanded the birds of the air and kept a tame osprey about her. Ys drowned, they say; I do not know the legend well enough to remember why, only that there was a Lady, and her cormorants may still be seen fishing the waters above the sunken isle and crying out for their lost mistress.

"Come," Melisande said, and held out one gloved hand for my lead. Truly, there was no command in her voice, only the simple expectation of obedience.

I rose and followed her with alacrity.

*C*HIRTY-FIVE

I knew not what to expect from a Kusheline gathering, but in the end, it was not so different from other fêtes, only a shade darker in tone, with an unfamiliar undercurrent and a preponderance of Kusheline accents, at once harsh and musical.

It all fell to a hush when we entered.

The Duc de Morhban's herald gave our names; both of them, though I had not heard what Melisande had said to him. For those who heard, even anonymity was stripped from me, marking me not as some nameless Servant of Naamah willing to contract on the Longest Night, but a member of a peer's household, collared and bound to Melisande Shahrizai of my own free will.

We moved among the guests, and a murmur followed. I could not but feel my nakedness beneath the sheer gauze with every step. Masked faces, feathered and

furred, turned to watch our progress. Melisande glided
smoothly between them and I trailed, tethered, in her
wake.

And to my chagrin, with a hundred eyes upon me and
Melisande's hand at the end of my velvet lead, I felt a
desire such as I had never known stir in the distant
reaches of my being, like the wave that had drowned Ys
gathering force in the far depths of the ocean.

"Your grace." Only Melisande could make a curtsy
seem the gesture of a queen receiving homage. A tall,
lean man in a wolf mask inclined his head and looked
gaugingly at her.

"House Shahrizai arrives," he said dryly. "And what
have you brought?"

She made no answer but to smile; I sank deeply in a
curtsy. "Joy to your grace on the Longest Night," I murmured.

His fingers lifted my chin and he searched my eyes
through the holes of my mask. "No!" he exclaimed,
glancing at Melisande, then back at me. "Is it true?"

"Phèdre nó Delaunay," she said, with her faint smile.
It curved like a scarlet bow beneath the black mask that
hid her features. "Did you not know Elua's City boasted
a genuine *anguissette*, your grace?"

"I cannot credit it." Without removing his sharp gaze
from mine, he reached forward and gathered up the sheer
folds of my gown, slipping his hand beneath them.

I cried out then, out of pleasure and shame both. The
Duc de Morhban regarded me from behind his mask, an
amused wolf. Melisande twitched the line and I staggered, dropping to my knees in defense. The tiny diamonds sewn into my sheer gown bit into my flesh.

"The Duc de Morhban is not your patron," she reminded me, one hand twining in my hair in a gesture
that was half caress, half threat.

"No, my lady," I breathed. Her hand grew gentler, and I found myself leaning into it, pressing my cheek to the velvet of her skirts and inhaling her scent as if it were a sanctuary. Her fingers trailed down my throat, and I heard as if from a great distance my own answering whimper.

"You see, your grace," Melisande said lightly. "Kushiel's Dart strikes true."

"Well, have a care where it strikes!" he snapped, turning away. I could feel her low laugh thrumming through her, and a crimson haze rose to cloud my vision.

I could not say what transpired during the remainder of the Duc de Morhban's Midwinter Masque; and I tried, for Delaunay queried me at some length, having never known my wits to thus falter. I can only say that my time there passed as if in a fever-dream. As Blessed Elua is my witness, I tried to pay heed to what passed about me and what conversations I overheard, but the slender velvet rope Melisande Shahrizai had set about my neck had severed at last my connection with that far part of my mind that was ever thinking and analyzing at Anafiel Delaunay's behest, and I was aware only of her hand on the far end of it. When I reached for that calculating corner, I found only the indrawn susurrus of the great wave gathering, and knew myself doomed when it broke.

If you were to ask me what I remembered of that Masque, it is only this: Melisande. Every laugh, every smile, every movement, all thrummed along the velvet cord that bound us, till I was nearly gasping with it.

There was a pageant; I remember nothing of it, except the outcry of the horologer, Melisande clapping, and her smile. I see that smile still in my dreams.

And too many of them are pleasant.

It is a small mercy that Joscelin was not there to see me.

When at last we left, the guests were fewer. Now it seemed I stumbled in her wake, and when the coachman handed me into the trap, I was quivering all over like a plucked harpstring. The velvet lead-line grew tight between us; she had not released it, getting into the coach.

"Come here," Melisande whispered as the coach lurched into motion, and there was still no order in it, but the velvet cord twitched and I slid, helpless and obedient, into her arms. Elua knows, I had been kissed before, but never like this. Everything in me surrendered to it, until she released me and pulled off my mask, stripping off the last vestige of disguise. Hers she kept, glowing blue eyes flanked by the dark upsweep of cormorant wings. And then she kissed me again, until I could return it with no artistry, but mere craving, clinging to her and drowning under her mouth.

Until the coach stopped, shocking me with its suddenness. Melisande laughed as the coachman opened the door onto her own courtyard; I could not imagine that we had arrived so soon. He helped me out, face studiously averted—I cannot even think what I looked like, glaze-eyed, touseled and naked beneath the expanse of diamond-studded gauze—and the velvet line grew taut. Too far from her, I shivered with dismay until she disembarked, and guided me, gently, into her home.

It was the Longest Night. It had only begun.

What befell afterward, I relate without pride. I am Kushiel's chosen, as she was his scion; this had been a long time coming between us. With Baudoin, I had seen her pleasure-chamber. This time, I saw the inner sanctum that was her boudoir. Little enough I saw of it, at that first glance: lamps burning scented oil, a great bed, and from the highest rafter, a single hook hung. That much I saw, and then she bound my eyes with a velvet sash, and I saw no more.

When she took the slip-collar and lead from about my neck, I almost wept; but then I felt them again, the familiar cord binding my wrists as she raised them above my head and looped them securely about the dangling hook.

"For you, my dear," I heard her whisper, "I will not dally with lesser toys."

A sound, then, of a catch being lifted. I hung suspended, too high to kneel, too weak to stand, and wondered what.

"Do you know these?" The cold caress of steel against my cheek, a razor-fine edge tracing the line of the sash binding my eyes. "They are called flechettes."

Then I did weep, and it availed nothing.

The fine blade of the flechette, keen as a chirurgeon's tool, trailed down the length of my throat and brushed the neckline of my gown. How much that diamond-spangled gauze had cost, I could not guess, but the sheer fabric parted with a sigh, and I could feel the brazier-heated warmth of Melisande's bedroom against bare skin. The sleeves were pooled around my upwardly wrenched shoulders; the flechette traced the veins in my bound wrists, not breaking the skin, down the length of my arms to whisper effortlessly through the gauze. I felt the gown slither away, tangling about my ankles, the tiny diamonds clicking against each other.

"Much better." The fabric was withdrawn and tossed to one side; I heard it rustle and click in falling and turned my head after the sound. "You don't like having your eyes bound, do you?" There was deep amusement in Melisande's voice.

"No." My skin shivered all over involuntarily and I fought to remain still, fearful of the deadly point of the flechette. It was hard to do, suspended like that. The blade moved softly over my skin and the point of it pricked between my shoulder blades.

"Ah, but if you could see, the anticipation would be so much less," she said softly, drawing the flechette down the length of my spine. I didn't answer. I was shuddering like a fly-stung horse, and couldn't stop the tears that steadily soaked the velvet binding my eyes. Fear made my mind a blank, and a yearning so sharp it was like pain made breathing a struggle.

"Such desire," Melisande murmured, and the tip of the flechette danced over my skin, pricking my taut nipples. I gasped, bound hands clenching involuntarily, making the chain sway. Melisande laughed.

And then she began to cut me.

Any warrior wounded in battle has taken far worse from a blade than I had from Melisande's flechettes; I daresay it was nothing to the knife-slash Alcuin had endured. But the point of the flechette is not injury: it is pain. The blades are unimaginably sharp, and part flesh nigh as easily as gauze. One barely feels it, when first it pierces the skin.

That is why the subsequent cutting is done very, very slowly.

Blind and dangling, gripped by terror and longing, my entire consciousness narrowed to the scope of the flechette's blade as it harrowed my flesh with agonizing slowness, etching an unseen sigil on the inner swell of my right breast. I could feel the blood running in a steady trickle between my breasts and down my belly. My skin parted before the blade, and flesh was carved by it. It was like the pain of the marquist's needles multiplied a thousand-fold.

How long it continued, I could not say; forever, it seemed, until she stopped cutting and traced the point of the blade slowly down the path my blood had taken.

"Phèdre." Melisande's voice whispered softly at my ear. I could feel the warmth of her body. The tip of the flechette trailed downward from my belly, a cool and deadly caress, until I felt it hovering near my nether lips, and trembled like a leaf. I knew where next the blade would go. I could almost hear Melisande's smile. "Say it."

"Hyacinthe!" In a paroxysm of terror, I gasped the *signale*, and every muscle in my body went rigid against the force of the climax that overtook me. Not until it ended did Melisande laugh and withdraw the flechette, and I sagged, limp, at the end of the chain.

"You did very well," she said tenderly, removing my blind. I blinked upward in the lamplight, half-dazzled, as her beautiful face swam into focus. She had taken off her mask, and her hair fell loose, rippling in blue-black waves.

"Please." I heard the word before I realized I'd said it.

"What do you want?" Melisande cocked her head slightly, smiling, pouring warm water from a ewer over my skin. I didn't even glance as it sluiced away the blood.

"You," I whispered. I had never asked it of a patron before: never.

In a moment, Melisande laughed again, and unbound my hands.

Afterward, she was well-pleased and let me stay, toying with my hair. "Delaunay saw to your training well," she said in her rich voice, sending a thrill through every fiber of my being. "You could match your skills against any House in the Night Court, my dear." She drew one finger up the line of my marque and raised her brows. "What will you do when it's done?"

Even now, I shivered at her touch with the aftershocks

of pleasure. "I don't know. I've not decided."

"You should think on it. You're near enough to it."
She smiled. "Or has Delaunay some target left for you?"

"No," I said. "I don't know, my lady."

She wound a lock of my hair around her fingers. "No?
Perhaps he's satisfied, then. He used you to gain access
to Barquiel L'Envers, didn't he? And used the Duc to
gain revenge on the Stregazza." She laughed at my expression. "Who do you think taught Anafiel Delaunay to
manipulate others, my dear? Half of what he knows, I
taught him; he taught me in turn to listen and observe,
and the two skills together are more formidable than either alone could hope to be."

"He said you were well-matched in many ways," I
said.

"All but one." Melisande tugged gently at my hair and
smiled. "Sometimes I think we should have wed anyway,
for he's the only man who truly makes me laugh. But
then, his heart was given long ago, and I think a large
part of it died with Prince Rolande."

"Rolande?" I sat upright, staring at her, my wits
scrambled into a dazed sort of alert. *"Prince Rolande?"*

"You really didn't know, did you?" Melisande looked
amused. "I wasn't sure. Yes, of course, ever since they
were together at the University of Tiberium. Even Rolande's marriage couldn't come between them, though
of a surety, Delaunay and Isabel detested each other.
You've never read his poetry?"

"There's no copy to be found in the City." My mind
reeled.

"Oh, Delaunay keeps a book of his verse, locked in a
coffer in his library," she said idly. "But what's he up
to, then, if he's no longer using you as his eyes and
ears?"

"Nothing," I said absently, trying to remember. There

was a coffer; I'd seen it, atop a high shelf on the eastern side of the room. It was dusty and uninviting, and I'd never wondered what was in it. "Reading. Waiting for word from Quintilius Rousse. Nothing." Too late, I remembered where I'd heard him mention Quintilius Rousse, and glanced quickly at Melisande, but she was disinterested.

"Well, mayhap he'll have sent a message with the Duc de Morhban's party; Rousse's fleet is anchored just north of Morhban." She drew me back down, tracing the lines of a sigil carved into my skin. The bleeding had long since stopped, but the lines were clear. "He'll want to see you."

"De Morhban?" Delaunay, Prince Rolande, oaths and poems and coffers; Melisande's mouth moved on me, following the lines she had graven, and it all went out of my head.

"Mmm. He's a Kusheline lord, albeit a half-bred line." Melisande drew back and watched the flush mount to my cheeks, amused. "Choose as you will, but remind him who he has to thank for the knowledge of you." With no bonds, no blades, no pain to compell me, she parted me effortlessly and slid her fingers inside me. "Say your little friend's name again, Phèdre. Say it for me."

There was no reason for it, no reason to give the *signale*.

"Hyacinthe," I whispered helplessly, and the long-cresting wave broke over me once more.

In the morning, I woke in a guest-room, and one of Melisande's efficient servants drew me a bath and brought my own clothes to me, neatly laid out upon the bed. When I was conducted to the dining hall, Joscelin was there, and I was hard-put to meet his eye. For his part, he was inclined to ask no questions, seeing me apparently hale. Indeed, I had been in far worse condition—physically, at least—after my assignation with Childric d'Essoms, and I think Joscelin was somewhat relieved.

As she had before, after the night with Baudoin, Melisande came to bid me farewell. She greeted Joscelin graciously and he bowed stiffly in response. "Perhaps 'twould be best if you kept this, Cassiline," she said, tossing him a purse. "On Naamah's honor." To me, she turned smiling, and slid something over my head.

It was the velvet cord; she tied it off, and settled the teardrop diamond in the hollow of my throat. I felt the relentless tide of desire surge in me.

"That," Melisande said softly, "is for remembrance, and not for Naamah." Then she laughed, and gestured to a servant behind her. He came forward with a bow, and filled my arms with a tattered mass of diamond-studded gauze. "I've no need of rags," Melisande added, wickedly amused, "but I've a certain curiosity to see what an *anguissette* trained by Anafiel Delaunay will do of her own accord."

"My lady." It was all I could get out, meeting her gaze. She laughed once more, kissed me lightly, and left.

Across the table, Joscelin stared at me. With my arms full of gauze and diamonds, I stared back.

THIRTY-SIX

Delaunay's home was quiet; it was early enough yet that nigh everyone, the housekeeper told me, was asleep yet, including his lordship. The Longest Night, by tradition, was a late one. Joscelin handed me Melisande's purse and excused himself, with red-rimmed eyes, to get some sleep. He had slept not at all, maintaining Elua's vigil.

I'd had little enough of it myself, but my mood was strange and sleep seemed far away. I went to my room and put Melisande's patron-gift in my coffer, mulling over the amount it contained. Then I closed the lid and sat on my bed, holding the remnants of my costume.

It was enough. It would be more than enough.

I had no idea what to do.

Too much had happened in one night for my mind to compass. My gaze fell once more on my coffer. That, at least, I could learn for myself, I thought, and went down to the library.

I'd remembered rightly. Though I had to crane my neck to see it, there was indeed a coffer gathering dust atop a high shelf along the eastern wall. I listened for sounds of stirring and heard none. Dragging the tallest chair I could find over to the shelves, I stood atop it and reached for the coffer. I lacked a good foot of attaining it. With a whispered apology to Shemhazai and the scholars of the world, I piled several thick volumes on the seat of the chair, and clambered up to balance precariously on them. My fingertips grazed the gold fretwork adorning the coffer, and I succeeded in dragging it within reach.

Holding the coffer carefully, I dismounted from my perch and set to studying it. The rich wood was dimmed beneath a thick layer of dust, and the edges of the fretwork fuzzy with it. I blew gently upon it, raising a cloud, then examined the lock.

There are merits to befriending a Tsingano; Hyacinthe had long since taught me to pick simple locks. I fetched two hairpins from my room, bending the end of one into a tiny hook with my teeth. Manipulating them delicately, listening all the while for the sounds of the household rising, I soon caught the tumbler inside the lock and sprang open the latch.

An odor of sandalwood breathed into the still air of the library when I raised the lid of the coffer. Melisande had spoken truly; it held a slim volume, silk-bound and untitled. Opening the book, I saw page after page of verse in Delaunay's hand, younger and more painstaking than his current fluid scrawl, but clearly the same. Smoothing the pages open, I read the verses written in faded ink.

O, dear my lord . . .
Let this breast on which you have leant
As close in love as a foe in battle,
Unarmed, unarmored, grappling chest to chest,
Alone in the glade
Where birds started at our voices,
Laughter winging airborne, we struggled
For advantage, neither giving quarter;
How I remember your arms beneath my grip,
Sliding like marble slickened;
Your chest pressed to mine
Heaving;
As our feet trampled the tender grass
Your eyes narrowed with tender cunning
And I unaware
Until your heel caught my knee; I buckled,
Falling,
Vanquished; O sovereign adored,
To be pierced ecstatic by the shaft of victory;
Sweet the pain of losing,
Sweeter this second struggle . . .

O, dear my lord,
Let this breast on which you have leant
Serve now as your shield.

Melisande had not lied about the book. If Delaunay had written these lines, surely he had written them for Rolande de la Courcel, who had died at the Battle of Three Princes. Rolande, whose word Delaunay had upheld, when he went back for Alcuin. Rolande, whose wife Delaunay had branded a murderess, whose father the King had ordered Delaunay's poetry anathematized.

No wonder he hadn't dared banish him.

A small sound caught my ear, and I spun about to see Alcuin standing stock-still and open-mouthed. Too late, I closed the book.

"You shouldn't have done that," he said quietly.

"I had to know." I closed the coffer and latched the lock. "It's what Delaunay taught us to do, after all," I added, returning his gaze defiantly. "Help me put it back."

He hesitated, but the long bond of tutelage between us won out; Alcuin came over to give me a hand up, steadying me while I returned the coffer to its dusty resting-place. We replaced the other books and the tall chair, erasing the evidence of my trespass, then listened. All was quiet.

"So." I folded my arms. "Delaunay was Prince Rolande's beloved. What of it? Rolande de la Courcel has been dead fifteen years and more; why does House Courcel still traffic with Delaunay, and award him couriers and Cassiline Brothers and the like? And why does he make peace with the Duc L'Envers, who is brother to his equally dead enemy, the Princess Consort?"

Alcuin's gaze looked past me. "I don't know."

"I don't believe you."

He looked straight at me, then. "Believe as you choose, Phèdre. I made Delaunay a promise, too. Who told you? Melisande?" I didn't answer, and he frowned. "She had no business. Would that I could tell the difference between amusement and ambition in that woman. I'd sleep easier for it."

"What I now know," I said, "half the peers of the realm knew already, and I think no one is anxious to kill for it. Isabel de la Courcel had her revenge, when she had his verses banned. Thelesis de Mornay told me Delaunay might have been the King's Poet, if matters hadn't fallen out differently. It's what he became instead that is dangerous to know."

"And do you suppose Melisande Shahrizai isn't clever enough to send you fishing for it?" Alcuin raised his brows.

I felt a chill at the thought, and kept my silence. Alcuin had said he would tell me what he knew when I made my marque; he had promised not to speak of it before then. The long-ago prophecy of Hyacinthe's mother echoed in my memory, and I was suddenly afraid to tell him what Melisande had given me. "Will you tell Delaunay?" I asked instead.

He shook his head somberly. "It's your decision. I'll have no part of it, Phèdre. If you're wise, you'll tell him. But I'll leave it to you."

With that, he left me, feeling more alone than ever I had in Delaunay's service.

In the end, I temporized.

I told him everything, all that I could remember, except the part about Prince Rolande and the book. He made me go over the Duc de Morhban's Masque a dozen times over, at last giving up and turning his attention to the diamond-spangled cloth, turning it over in his hands and shaking his head.

"What will you do?" he asked at last.

I'd had a little time to give it thought, and clasped my hands together, gathering courage to voice it. "My lord," I said, keeping my voice steady. "In the Night Court, when an adept has made their marque, they may stay in the service of their House, and rise within its ranks until such time as they choose to retire. I don't . . . I don't wish to leave your household."

Delaunay's smile was like the sun rising after the Longest Night. "You wish to stay?"

"My lord." I swallowed against the lump of mingled fear and hope in my throat. "Do you permit it?"

He laughed out loud, drew me into his arms and kissed me on both cheeks. "Do you jest? Phèdre, you take enough risks to turn my hair grey with fright, but I'm the one who taught you to do it. Since you will take them whether I will it or no, I would sooner you do it under my roof, where I can safeguard you somewhat, than anywhere else in the realm." Delaunay stroked my hair. "I'd half-thought I might lose you to your Tsingano boy," he said, not entirely in jest. "If not House Shahrizai."

"If the Prince of Travellers thinks I've been waiting for the moment my marque was made, that he might deem me worthy, he's sore mistaken," I said, giddy with relief. "Let him court me, if he wishes it. And Melisande is too interested in seeing how far I will run with her collar on me," I added, fingering the diamond at the end of the velvet cord, color rising to my face.

Delaunay forbore to comment on it, for which I was grateful. "Phèdre," he said instead, his tone sober, "you are a member of my household, and bear my surname. If ever you doubted it, know well, I would never, ever cast you out."

"Thank you, my lord," I murmured, unexpectedly moved. He grinned at me.

"Even if your service fills Naamah's coffers and your own, rather than mine." He hefted the remains of my gown. "Shall I send this to a gem-merchant, then?"

"Yes, my lord," I said, adding fervently, "please."

It would be some days before the whole of the transaction could be completed; with Delaunay's permission, I took a sullen Joscelin as my escort and rode to Night's Doorstep, albeit by day. Alcuin lent me his saddle horse, and though the winter air was bitter, it was a pleasure to ride on horseback rather than cloistered in a coach. My last memory of a coach had too much of Melisande Shahrizai in it, and I welcomed the cold air clearing my thoughts.

I wore the diamond, though. I couldn't quite bear to remove it, and tried not to think too much about why.

Hyacinthe was supervising a handful of young men, easing a battered carriage into the stables he leased. "Phèdre!" he shouted, catching me in his arms and swinging me around. "Look at this. I've nigh got a full-fledged livery service now. A noble's carriage, and I bought it for a song."

Joscelin leaned against the weathered wall of the stable, ashen garments rendering him nearly invisible. "Then you paid a verse too high, Tsingano," he said, nodding at the warped wheels and missing spokes. "Stripping that fancy trim won't cover the cost of repairing the wheels."

"Happily, Sir Cassiline, I know a cartwright who will also work for a song," Hyacinthe said mildly. He turned back to me and grinned. "Delaunay let you out of your cage? Can I buy you a jug?"

"I'll buy you one." I jingled the purse at my belt. "Come on, Joscelin, it won't kill you to set foot in an inn. Cassiel will forgive you, if you stick to water."

Thus we ended at our familiar table in the back of the Cockerel, though with the unfamiliar addition of a Cassiline Brother seated in the corner with folded arms, steel glinting off his vambraces as he scowled at the other customers. The inn-keeper looked almost as displeased at Joscelin's presence as he did himself.

I told Hyacinthe most of what had happened. He fingered the diamond at my throat and whistled.

"Do you know what that's worth?" he asked.

I shook my head. "No. A fair amount."

"A lot, Phèdre. You could . . . well, you could do quite a few things with the money it would bring."

"I can't sell it." Remembering the cord taut around my throat, I flushed. "Don't ask why."

"All right." Hyacinthe regarded me curiously, his black eyes lively with intelligence. "What else?"

"Joscelin." I fished a coin from my purse and slid it across the table. "Will you buy a jug, and bring it to Hyacinthe's crew in the stable, with my regards?"

The Cassiline looked at me with flat incredulity. "No."

"I swear, it's nothing like the other time, and naught against your vows. It's just somewhat . . . well, you'd rather not hear. I'll not stir from this chair." I grew annoyed as he sat unmoving. "Name of Elua! Do your vows say you have to remain glued at my side?"

With a sound of disgust, Joscelin shoved his chair back and snatched the coin from the table, heading to the bar.

"Let's hope we don't find him in need of rescue," Hyacinthe said, watching him go. "What is it?"

I told him quickly about Delaunay and Prince Rolande, what Melisande had said, and the book of verse. Hyacinthe heard it out.

"No wonder," he said when I was done. "So he was neither brother nor betrothed to Edmée de Rocaille after all?"

"No." I shook my head. "No, he wasn't avenging her, he was protecting Rolande. I think. You never . . . you never looked?"

"I said I would not use the *dromonde* in this. You know why." It was the wholly serious tone I doubted many had heard in Hyacinthe's voice.

"Your mother's prophesy." I glanced at him, and he nodded briefly. "Either it came to naught, or it waits the day I know the whole of it."

"Pray it is the former," he murmured, then recovered his spirits, flaunting his white grin. "So you'll no longer be a *vrajna* servant, Phèdre nó Delaunay! You know what that betokens."

"It means I can aspire to heights on my own greater than I've reached as Delaunay's *anguissette*," I said coolly. "Mayhap one day I'll have my own salon, which might even surpass the fame of Cecilie Laveau-Perrin, who trained me. Who knows what suitors that will bring?"

It took the wind from his sails, momentarily gratifying, but it wasn't easy to discomfit Hyacinthe. He touched Melisande's diamond where it lay in the hollow of my throat. "You know what it will bring, Phèdre," he said. "The question is, what will you choose?"

Annoyed, I slapped his hand away. "I'll choose nothing, now! I've spent all my life at someone's bidding. I've a mind to taste freedom before I choose to give it up again."

"I'd put no collar on you." He grinned at me again. "You'd walk the long road with me, free as a bird, the Princess of Travellers."

"The Tsingani collared your mother with shame," I said, glowering at him, "and set her to washing clothing and telling fortunes for copper pennies. And if the stories are true, they'd collar your *dromonde*, Prince of Travellers, and set you to playing the fiddle and shoeing horses. So don't ply your O Star of the Evening wiles on me."

"Oh, you know what I mean." He shrugged, undisturbed by my ire, and plucked the velvet cord at my throat. "I'd not parade you half-naked before the peers of an entire province, Phèdre."

"I know," I whispered. "Hyacinthe, that's the problem."

I don't think, before that moment, that he truly grasped the nature of what I was. He knew, of course; had always known, and had been the one person who'd never cared for what, but only who I was. I saw him comprehend it now, and feared. It could change everything between us.

Then he flashed his irrepressible grin. "So?" he asked and shrugged, miming the crack of a whip. "I can learn to be cruel, if that's what you want. I'm the Prince of Travellers," he boasted. "I can do anything."

At that, I laughed, and took his face in my hands and kissed him; and caught my breath when he returned it, kissing me back with unexpected skill and sweetness—they'd taught him well, the married noblewomen with whom he dallied—until Joscelin's mail-backed fist slammed my change onto the table and both of us jumped, guilty as children, to meet the Cassiline's dour gaze.

Riding homeward beside him in the gloaming winter twilight, I glanced at Joscelin's forbidding profile and ventured to speak of it. "I told you there was no harm in it, and no concern of yours," I said, irritated by his silence. "My marque is made; I've no bond to betray now."

"Your marque is not yet limned, Servant of Naamah," he said stiffly, and I bit my tongue; it was true. He looked straight ahead. "Anyway, it's naught to me where you bestow your . . . gifts."

Only a haughty Cassiline could have summoned that much contempt for the word. He set spurs to Delaunay's saddle horse and left me scrambling to keep up, detesting him once more.

THIRTY-SEVEN

In due time, the deal with the gem-merchant was concluded, each tiny diamond assessed for its quality and worth, and when all was tallied and counted, I was presented with a goodly sum of money.

With Joscelin's rebuke still stinging, I wasted no time in arranging a final appointment with Master Tielhard. I confess, I looked forward to the day with no small excitement. Like most Servants of Naamah, I had made my marque in slow, agonizing inches; to have it done in one blow, as it were, was a coup indeed.

Alcuin had done it, of course, but Alcuin had forced his patron's hand to it, and done penance to Naamah for it. Melisande's gift, whatever motivated it, was genuine. Whatever strings were attached to her gifts lay in the one about my throat, and not the one to be limned on my back.

Until the day of my appointment arrived, I dwelled in a strange hinterland, neither bond-servant nor free D'Angeline citizen. For once, though, I did not chafe at my confinement, but strove to make sense of all that had happened, not the least of which was my last encounter with Hyacinthe. I had a strange longing then to see his mother.

I wish, now, that I had seen her; Delaunay would decry it as superstition, but there was a grim truth in her prophecies. Perhaps things might have fallen out differently, if I had.

The wisdom of hindsight is always flawless. I know, now, that I should have told Delaunay the whole of what had befallen between Melisande and I; I should have told him that I knew about Prince Rolande. Indeed, I should have guessed it for myself. Of all the shadows that darkened Delaunay's soul, that had always been foremost among them: the Battle of Three Princes.

Rolande had fallen; Delaunay had failed to save his liege-lord. I had thought that was all it was. But now, I looked at him differently, remembering the words of his poem. *O, dear my lord, Let this breast on which you have leant, Serve now as your shield.* He had loved Rolande, and failed him. "Rolande was always rash," Delaunay had said, his voice bitter. "It was his only flaw, as a leader."

I should have known.

So I think, and doubt, and second-guess myself. But in truth, would it have mattered? I cannot know. I never will.

The day of my final appointment with Master Tielhard dawned cold, crisp and bright. Delaunay, half his mind elsewhere, was expecting a visitor; he agreed unthinking to the loan of his horse and Alcuin's, so my surly Cassiline companion and I rode to the marquist's shop.

Master Tielhard was not a greedy man. He was an artist, and no question about it. But artists, no less than other mortals—and betimes more—aspire to heights unreached by their peers, and I saw his aged eyes glimmer at the sight of the gold I offered, and the prospect of an *anguissette*'s marque fulfilled. I was the first, in his lifetime.

We spent a fair amount of time in the stifling-hot back room of his shop, confirming the design and the lineaments of my marque. I could see Joscelin through the curtain, waiting with outstretched legs and folded arms. Well, then, let him wait; I was not about to rush the completion of my marque upon a youthful Cassiline's impatience.

I had only just disrobed, and felt the first blow of Master Tielhard's tapper pierce my skin, when the commotion arose in the front room. As it was no business of mine—so I thought—I remained upon the table while Robert Tielhard sent his apprentice to investigate.

I wish, now, that I had known Master Tielhard's apprentice's name; I never did, and I am sorry for it now. He came through the curtain, eyes wide.

"There is a man, Master," he said. "He insists upon seeing m'lady—upon seeing Phèdre nó Delaunay. The Cassiline has him well in hand. Shall I call for the King's Guard?"

I sat up, then, wrapping a sheet about me. "Who is he?"

"I don't know." He swallowed hard. "He says he bears a message, which you must deliver to Lord Anafiel Delaunay. My lady, shall I call for the Guard?"

"No." I was too long Delaunay's pupil to turn away information; I scrambled for my gown, pulling it over my head in haste. "Send him in, and Joscelin with him. Master Tielhard . . . ?"

The old marquist held my gaze a moment, then gestured with his head toward the rear of his shop, where he and his apprentice ground their pigments. "See him, then, *anguissette,* and give me no cause to regret it," he growled.

I had barely laced my stays when Joscelin came through the curtain, driving before him at knife-point a youngish man with a sailor's queue and a discomfitted look on his face.

"Call off your Cassiline hound," he said to me, grimacing as Joscelin shoved him into the marquist's studio. "I've word that needs be delivered to Lord Delaunay!"

For what it was worth, I put on my sternest expression as I followed them through the far curtain. Joscelin gave the sailor one last shove, then sheathed his daggers efficiently, standing between me and the messenger. "Who are you?" I asked the man.

He rubbed at his midsection and made a face. "Aelric Leithe, of the *Mahariel*. I'm oath-sworn to the Admiral, Quintilius Rousse, and here under the standard of the Comte de Brijou of Kusheth. I'm supposed to be meeting with your lord, Delaunay."

I paused. "How do I know this?"

"Elua's Balls!" He rolled his eyes. "There's a password, isn't there? What is it? I swear it, on the Prince's signet, his only born."

The Prince's signet. I thought of the ring that Ysandre de la Courcel had showed Delaunay, and schooled my features to expressionlessness. "Very well, then. Why are you here?"

"There are men, watching the Comte's manor." He bent over, still trying to catch his breath. "Damn you, Cassiline, for a hasty fool! I saw 'em, and scryed out the situation at Lord Delaunay's; he's being watched too, they're waiting for me. Someone slipped up, and gave 'em word. I saw you leave, and followed you here."

It chilled me to realize that Delaunay's fears had merit. Motioning Joscelin to bide, I pressed the sailor. "What word, then, from Quintilius Rousse?"

Aelric Leithe drew in his breath, and loosed his message with it. "When the Black Boar rules in Alba, Elder Brother will accede. That's my message. That's the whole of it."

I fumbled at my purse, trying to cover my consternation, and found a coin at hand; it was a gold ducat, but I'd no doubt Delaunay would reimburse me for it. "My thanks, lord sailor," I murmured. "I will relay your Admiral's message to my lord Delaunay, and of a surety, he will send word."

Aelric Leithe was no coward, I am sure of that; no man who sailed with Quintilius Rousse could be. But he was out of his element here, and fair frightened. He took the coin, bobbed a bow with fist to brow, and fled. Through the curtain I saw Master Tielhard and his apprentice staring after his disappearing figure.

Then I looked at Joscelin Verreuil, and the terrible expression on his face.

"The house," he said, and headed for the door.

I had seen Joscelin move quickly, and I have seen it since; but that day, he rode as if seven devils were after him, and I have never seen him move faster. How I kept apace of him, I don't know, save that terror gave my heels wings, and Alcuin's horse, whom I rode, seemed to sense it when I mounted and laid into his sides. We laid a trail of sparks from the marquist's shop to Delaunay's door, skittering amid a shower of them into the courtyard.

It didn't matter; it wouldn't have mattered how fast we'd ridden. We had dallied too long at Master Robert Tielhard's, the sailor, the Cassiline and I.

It was too quiet in the courtyard, and no stable-boy came to take our mounts.

"No!" Joscelin shouted, dismounting in a flash and charging the door, both daggers drawn. "Ah, Cassiel, no!"

I followed him into the silent house.

Whoever had been watching it, they had been there before us.

Delaunay's men lay where they had fallen, weltering

in their own gore. They'd killed the housekeeper too, and thrown her apron over her face; I couldn't look. So many servants, and I'd never bothered to know them all, why they'd chosen to share their lives with Anafiel Delaunay.

We found him in the library.

There must have been a dozen wounds or more on him; which had killed him, I do not know. His sword was still in his hand, blood-crusted the length of it. Delaunay's face, unmarked, was strangely peaceful, at odds with the awkward sprawl of limbs. I stood in the doorway while Joscelin knelt and felt for a pulse. His expression, when he looked up, said all that was needed.

I stared uncomprehending, my world crumbling.

In the dimness of the unlit library, something moved, making a scraping sound.

Joscelin moved quicker than thought, shoving a path through the disarray, volumes and tomes strewn hither and thither. When he saw what it was, he cast his daggers aside, frantically clearing debris away from the source of the sound.

I had seen a swatch of hair like moonlight glimmer amid the strewn books. I followed slowly.

I saw Alcuin's eyes, dark and flooded with pain.

Joscelin cleared away the books that had been tossed heedlessly across him, and I heard his breath hiss between his teeth to see the damage. He pressed both hands to Alcuin's stomach, to the fine cambric shirt drenched with red blood, and shot me an agonized glance.

"Water." Alcuin's voice was no more than a thread. I knelt beside him and fumbled for his hand. "Please."

"Get it," I murmured to Joscelin. He opened his mouth, then nodded, and disappeared. I held tight to Alcuin's hand.

"Delaunay?" His dark gaze searched my face.

I shook my head, unable to say it.

Alcuin's gaze wandered away from mine. "Too many," he whispered. "Twenty, at least."

"Be quiet!" My voice came out fierce with tears. Joscelin returned with a ewer and a sponge. Dipping the sponge, he squeezed a trickle of clear water into Alcuin's mouth.

Alcuin's lips moved; he swallowed, feebly, grimacing. "Too many . . ."

"Who?" Joscelin's voice was low and calm.

"D'Angeline." Alcuin's wandering gaze sharpened, focusing on him. "Soldiers. No crest. I killed two."

"You?" I stroked his hair, heedless of the tears spilling down my face. "Oh, Alcuin . . ."

"Rousse," he whispered, and grimaced. "Get him word."

"Quintilius Rousse?" I exchanged a glance with Joscelin. "His messenger found us. Me. He said the house was being watched."

Alcuin whispered something; I strained to hear, leaning close, and he repeated it. "Password?"

"No." My wits were utterly scrambled. "Yes, yes, he gave one. The Prince's ring . . . the Prince's signet, his only born."

Alcuin twitched, and gasped for air. Joscelin gave him more water, sponging his face. I saw then, incredibly, that he was trying to laugh. "Not a ring . . . cygnet . . . swan. Courcel. Delaunay . . . oath-sworn to guard her. Cassiel's oath . . . Rolande's daughter."

"Anafiel Delaunay stood as oath-sworn protector of Ysandre de la Courcel?" Joscelin asked quietly. Alcuin's head moved in a faint nod.

"Swore it . . . for . . . Rolande's . . . sake," he murmured, licking his lips. Joscelin squeezed another trickle of water over them. "What . . . of . . . Rousse?"

"When the Black Boar rules in Alba, Elder Brother will accede." I held Alcuin's fading gaze, pleading. "Alcuin, don't go! I need you! What do we do?"

The thread of his voice was fraying, the dark eyes dim and apologetic. "Tell . . . Ysandre. Trust . . . Rousse. Trevalion. The . . . Thelesis knows . . . about Alba." He stirred again, a slight cough, and blood frothed on his lip. Such beauty, ruined; I was clutching his hand too hard. "Not Ganelon . . . slipping. It's the Dauphine." His head moved, and I knew he was looking for Delaunay. "He kept his promise." Alcuin's voice, for a moment, rang clear; he gasped, his eyes rolled upward, and his hand clenched on mine. "Phèdre!"

How much time passed, I do not know. I held his hand for a long time, long after it lay limp in my own, and the final spasm of pain had smoothed itself from his features. It was Joscelin who pulled me away, raising me stumbling to my feet and shaking me. I let him do it, boneless in his grasp, feeling the broken pieces of my heart rattle as he shook me. Beyond the still figure of Alcuin lay Delaunay. I could not bear to look. Gone, all gone, his noble features deceptively calm in the gentle repose of death. The auburn coils of his braid, streaked with silver, lying so seemly over his shoulder, as if no pool of blood clotted beneath him.

"Elua curse you, Phèdre, listen to me!" The sharp retort of a slap echoed in my hearing; I raised my head, dimly aware of the blow, and met Joscelin's eyes stretched wide with terrified urgency. "We have to leave," he said, his voice high and tight. "Do you understand? These are professionals, they took their dead with them. They'll trace their steps, they'll come back. We have to deliver Rousse's message to the Dauphine before they do." He shook me again, and my head lolled. "Do you understand?"

"Yes." I pressed the heels of my hands into my eyes. "Yes, yes, yes! I understand. Let me go." He did, and I moved without thinking, clutching my cloak about me, the wheels of my mind turning remorselessly. Kushiel's chosen, but Delaunay's pupil. "We'll go . . . we'll go directly to the Palace. If we can't gain access to the Dauphine, we'll seek Thelesis de Mornay." I dropped my hands, looking at Joscelin. "She knows me. She will see me."

"Good." His face settled into hard lines, and he caught my wrist, dragging me out of the abattoir that had once been a library. "Come on."

THIRTY-EIGHT

Of the ride to the Palace, I remember next to nothing. That we arrived, I am sure; but I could not say how long it took, nor what the weather, nor who we passed in the streets. Later, I saw men in battle fight on for a time after having received their death-wounds. I understood, then.

Delaunay had laughed, saying mine was an ill-luck name. It amused him, that my mother, Night Court-taught, had been ignorant enough to choose it. He should not have laughed. He had given me his name; would that he'd given me better luck with it. Instead, I had given him the luck of mine, the same luck Baudoin de Trevalion had had of me.

I cannot second-guess my own luck; even now, I know, had my fate not been in Elua's hand, matters might have fallen out differently. All I know is that, at that time, I would they had.

Ysandre de la Courcel's Guard turned us away.

In the past, I had worried about the spectacle we made, I in my *sangoire* cloak and Joscelin in Cassiline grey. This time, I could not have cared less, until I noted the look in the eyes of Thelesis de Mornay's servants, who politely informed me that the King's Poet was engaged, and like to remain so for some hours yet. Her verses, it seemed, soothed the King, and such sessions were not to be disturbed.

I pressed my hands to my eyes, and remembered the mirrored passage to the Dauphine's quarters.

There are those who map the influence of the stars, and claim that our destinies may be charted within. Doubtless such would claim this meeting was fated; but I, who know better, could have guessed that there was no chance to our encounter. It is not such a difficult thing, to set a watch on those who guard. No trouble, to have word sent whenever an audience is sought.

So I know now; then, I merely started dumbly at the sound of Melisande Shahrizai's voice.

"Phèdre?"

Joscelin's hands sought his hilts. I simply looked up, feeling her voice like a tug on a bond I'd forgotten I wore. Her brow was furrowed with concern.

"What is it?"

Her compassion undid me; I felt the tears rise unbidden. "Delaunay," I said at a gasp. I tried to say the words, but they wouldn't come; it didn't matter. I saw her comprehend it. "Alcuin. All of them."

"What?"

I doubt many things in life. Even now, still. But I do not doubt that my news took Melisande Shahrizai by surprise. That was one emotion she never rehearsed; she had too little cause for genuine surprise. I heard the instrument of her voice in one word unstrung, untuned. Even Joscelin heard it, releasing his hilts.

The nature of her surprise, however, was another matter.

When she spoke again, her voice was under control, though she was pale. "You're in search of the King's Guard?"

"No," Joscelin said, at the same time I answered, "Yes."

Nothing, not even this, could render me so far out of my senses as to blindly trust Melisande Shahrizai. I dashed the tears from my eyes, impatient with them. "Yes," I said, repeating it more strongly, ignoring Joscelin at my side. "Do you know where they're quartered?"

"I can do better than that." Melisande turned to an attendant in Shahrizai livery, standing some paces behind her. "Summon the Captain of the King's Guard to my rooms; the Captain, and no less, you hear? Tell them it's urgent." He gave a quick bow and headed off purposefully. Melisande turned her attention back to us. "Come with me," she said gently. "They should be there in a moment."

I had never seen the Shahrizai appointments in the Palace. They were luxurious, I remember that; the rest is lost. We sat at a long marble table in the great room, waiting for the Guard.

"Drink this." Melisande poured two glasses of cordial herself, handing them to us. "Both of you," she added, seeing Joscelin hesitate. "It will do you good."

I drank mine at a gulp. It had a clear fiery taste, with a faint aftertaste of honey and thyme and a hint of something else. It did seem to settle my nerves a little. Joscelin coughed at the burn of it, and a little color rose to his face. He looked better for it. Melisande refilled my glass unasked, but when she reached for his, he shook his head. "Tea, perhaps?" he asked faintly.

"Of course." She went to the door and summoned a servant, speaking in a low tone, then sat down, gaze dwelling on my face. "Do you want to tell me what happened?"

"No." I started shaking, and cupped both hands around my cordial glass. "My lady, I don't know. We were . . . we were at the marquist's shop, making the final arrangements for my marque." My mind raced desperately as I improvised; even my vision seemed out of focus. "I had to approve it, Master Tielhard had changed the design of the finial. It was . . . I don't know how long."

"Three-quarters of an hour," Joscelin said, supporting my story. His voice was a little unsteady, but it sounded like it was due to shock, and not the half-truth. "Mayhap a little bit longer." The servant came with the tea, and he thanked her, sipping it. "When we arrived back at the house . . ." His hand trembled, and tea spilled into the saucer. He set it down, then willed both hands to steadiness and picked it up, taking a long drink. "There were signs of battle all over the house," he said grimly. "And no one left living to tell of it."

"Oh, Anafiel," Melisande murmured. She glanced toward the door, looking, I thought, for the King's Guard. I looked too, but there was no one.

A thud sounded at the table.

Joscelin lay slumped, his cheek pillowed on cold marble. The teacup had overturned, and steaming liquid puddled under one limp, mail-clad hand. I felt dizzy staring at him, his oblivious, unconscious features swimming in my vision.

"No," I said. My grip loosened on the cordial glass, and I pushed it away, looking at Melisande with mounting horror. "Oh, no. No."

"Phèdre, I'm sorry." Her beautiful face was composed

and quiet. "I swear to you, I never gave an order to kill Delaunay. That wasn't my decision."

"You knew." The horror of it crawled over my skin. "You used me. Ah, Elua, I told you, I told you myself! Rousse's messenger!"

"No. I already knew Delaunay was awaiting word from Quintilius Rousse." With chilling care, Melisande reached out and righted the overturned teacup, setting it neatly back on the saucer.

"Why, then?" I whispered. "Why did you tell me about Prince Rolande, if you already knew? I thought you wanted to find out what it meant."

She smiled, smoothing an errant lock of hair out of my dazed eyes. "That Delaunay was oath-sworn to protect the life and succession of Ysandre de la Courcel? Oh, my dear, I've known that for ages. My second husband was a great friend of the King's, and a terrible gossip. Not clever enough to guess that Delaunay meant to keep his promise, but then, of that scant handful who knew it, precious few were. No, it's what he's *up* to that I needed to know. Why Quintilius Rousse, and what has it to do with the Master of the Straits?"

"But why . . . why me?" It was hard to keep my head upright; whatever she had put in Joscelin's tea, there must have been somewhat in the cordial too, in a lesser quantity.

"Do I need a reason?" Still smiling, Melisande traced the line of my brow over my left eye, the one with the dart-stricken mote. If I had known horror before, it was nothing to this; the power of her touch remained unaltered. "Perhaps I do, for Delaunay's pupil. It's a bit like flushing pheasants, you see, when they send the beaters into the brush. I wanted to see which of de Morhban's lordlings startled at the mention of your name. It wasn't hard to guess that the Comte de Brijou harbored a messenger for your lord, Phèdre nó Delaunay."

The blood ran like fire in my veins, a scalding betrayal. I struggled against it, her cord like a noose around my neck, trying to put the pieces together. Whose men, then, had killed Delaunay? Melisande's? She didn't command an army; the Shahrizai dealt in money and influence, not men-at-arms, not beyond their personal guard. Alcuin could have done it, I thought, he could have fit the pieces, and my tears were as scalding as the terrible desire. Clinging to the thought of Alcuin, I saw the shape of the pattern. "D'Aiglemort."

A spark kindled in Melisande's deep blue eyes; she was proud of me for guessing it. "Delaunay did teach you well," she said with satisfaction. "I'm sorry Isidore wasn't here himself, he'd have had sense enough not to kill Delaunay without finding out what he was about. I wouldn't have relayed word, if I'd known how they would botch it, but it's true, you know, most Camaelines do think with their swords."

"Not d'Aiglemort."

"No." Rising, she went to the door and gave an order I couldn't hear; I had already guessed that no Captain of the King's Guard would be forthcoming. Melisande returned, standing behind me to rest both hands on my shoulders. "No, Isidore d'Aiglemort thinks with more than his blade. He was fostered for three years in Kusheth, did you know? In House Shahrizai."

"No," I whispered. "I didn't know."

"It's true." Her hands continued to move on me, horrible and compelling. I had never truly understood, until then, that Kushiel's victims dwelt in the flames of perdition. Joscelin lay slumped before me, dead or unconscious, I could not know, and nothing, not even the thought of Delaunay lying in his own blood, not even the memory of Alcuin's dying breath gasping my name, could stop the tide of longing that threatened me.

"Don't," I said, weeping and shuddering. "Please, don't."

For a moment, she paused; then I felt her breath, warm at my ear. "Why did the Cassiline Brother say no, Phèdre?" she murmured; her voice sent a shiver through the marrow of my bones. "When I asked, you said yes, and he said no. If you weren't looking for the King's Guard, what were you doing?"

The room reeled in my vision; I saw a red haze, and in it Delaunay, Alcuin, everyone I had loved, and behind it the face of Naamah, compassionate and giving, and the stern bronze features of Kushiel, in whose hand I dwelt. "I don't know." My own voice seemed to come from a great distance. "Ask Joscelin what he meant, if you haven't killed him."

"Ah, no; you've warned him, my dear. A Cassiline would sooner die than betray his oath," Melisande whispered, so close I could feel her lips move. I closed my eyes and shuddered. "And anyway, I would rather ask you."

THIRTY-NINE

It was the jolting of the cart that woke me.

My first impressions were purely sensory, and none of them pleasant. It was cold and dark; I lay atop straw, prickling my cheek, beneath rough-spun woolen blankets, and from the incessant lurching motion and the sound of hooves, it was a cart in which I rode, lashed over with a canvas tarpaulin. That much I apprehended, before a wave of nausea gripped my belly. I, who had never known a sick day in my life, scarce knew what it was. It was pure instinct that sent me crawling across the straw to the farthest corner of my confines, where I promptly spewed up the meager contents of my stomach.

Afterward the sick feeling gripped me less urgently. Shivering with cold and lightheaded, I made my way back to the nest of blankets in which I had awoken, seeking the measure of miserable comfort they offered. It was then that I saw the second figure half-buried under the woolens, blond hair blending into straw, dim grey clothing rendering him nearly invisible in the faint light that filtered around the lashed edges of the canvas above us.

Joscelin.

Memory returned in a relentless surge.

I barely made it back to the corner in time to vomit bile.

This time, the noise of it woke him. I wrapped my arms around myself and huddled shivering, watching him glance around the darkened interior of the cart, frowning. A good Cassiline warrior, he took stock of his weapons first. They were gone, daggers and sword both, and the steel vambraces from his forearms. Then he saw me.

"Where . . . ?" Joscelin's voice cracked. He paused and cleared his mouth, drug-dried, working his tongue and swallowing. "Where are we?"

"I don't know," I whispered, not sure if it was true. Outside, hoofbeats; a team of four? There were too many beats, steel-shod and martial. Soldiers rode with us, a dozen at least.

"Melisande," he said remembering. "Melisande Shahrizai."

"Yes." That, too, I whispered. Memories crowded my mind, beating like dark wings. I had never, until that awakening, known what it was to despise the very nature of what I am. Even now, in cold and pain and misery, I could feel the residual languor of my body's infinite betrayal.

Naive as he was, Joscelin was no fool; he was young enough to learn, and he had served a time in Delaunay's household, where even a fool might gain some measure of wisdom. I saw understanding dawn on his clear-cut features. "Did you give her Rousse's message?" he asked quietly.

"No." I shook my head as I said it, and couldn't stop, shaking and chattering, huddling in onto myself. "No. No. No."

This was beyond his ken. Alarmed, Joscelin reached out for me, drawing me back to the warmth of the blankets, piling them around me and at last, when my shaking continued unabated, wrapping his own arms around me and rocking me to stillness, murmuring meaningless sounds.

It was true.

Everything, everything else she had desired of me, every betrayal flesh could afford, she had had. Numb and heartsick and broken, I had yielded it all.

But not that.

I think, at the last, she even believed it. I remembered her relenting, lifting up my drooping head by a clutch of hair, that beautiful face and merciless, gentle smile. I had pleaded my voice raw; I could only shape the word and beg with my eyes. "I believe you, Phèdre," she had said, caressing my face. "Truly, I do. You have only to say the word, if you want it to end. You have only to say it."

If I had, if I had said it, given the *signale*, I would have given her the rest. So I didn't.

And it didn't end. Not for a long time.

I remembered it all now, but I had stopped shaking. I

carried the memory of it inside, like a cold stone in the center of me. Joscelin grew suddenly aware of the situation and awkward with it, giving my shoulders a brusque chafing and withdrawing his embrace. He didn't move far away, though; we had nothing here but each other. I watched him repress a shiver and silently unwrapped one of the blankets, handing it to him. He didn't refuse, but drew it around him and blew on his hands.

"So you don't know what's befallen us?" he asked eventually. I shook my head. "Well," he said resolutely, "let's see what we can learn." He blew once more on his hands to warm them, then pounded on the side of the cart and shouted. "Heya! You, outside! Stop the cart!" The wooden clapboards rattled under his assault; outside, I could hear the shuffle of riders, and a muttering. "Stop the cart, I say! Let us out!"

A tremendous blow from the other side shocked the boards. A quarterstaff or a mace, at least; Joscelin snatched his hands back, stung by the reverberation of the wood. Another fierce blow descended onto the taut canvas, landing on his shoulder with a dull thud. Grimacing, Joscelin rolled out of the way of a second blow.

"You in the cart, keep it down," a male voice said in a soldier's clipped tones, "or we'll beat you like badgers in a sack. Understood?"

Joscelin crouched low beneath the canvas, eyeing it warily as he tried to track the shadow of a weapon above him. "I am Joscelin Verreuil, son of the Chevalier Millard Verreuil of Siovale, member of the Cassiline Brotherhood, and you are holding me against my will," he called. "Do you understand that this is both heresy and a crime punishable by death?"

The weapon—a staff, by its reach—came down on the canvas again with another muffled thump. "Shut up, Cassiline! Next time, I aim for the girl."

I caught Joscelin's arm and shook my head at him as he opened his mouth to retort. "Don't," I murmured. "Don't make it worse. There are a dozen or more fully trained, armed and mounted soldiers out there. If you're going to play the hero, at least pick a moment when you're not outnumbered and trapped like a . . . like a badger in a sack."

Joscelin stared at me. "How do you reckon the odds?"

"Listen." I nodded around the cart. "Horses, and armor creaking. Four before and four aft, two on the sides, and I've heard at least two riding scout. And if they're under Melisande's orders, likely they're D'Aiglemort's men."

"D'Aiglemort?" He was still staring, but he had the sense to keep his voice low. "What's he to do with it?"

"I don't know." Cold, sick and weary, I huddled under my blankets. "But whatever it is, they're in it together. They brought down House Trevalion, and his men killed Delaunay and Alcuin. He bid for Ysandre's hand. I think he means to have the throne, one way or another. And if they're D'Aiglemort's men, you may be sure they're well-trained."

His face showed perplexity in the dim light. "I thought you were but a Servant of Naamah."

"Did you learn nothing of what we were about in Delaunay's house?" I asked bitterly. "Better if I was and had stayed in the Night Court, gone to Valerian to be a whipping-toy to ham-fisted tradesmen. Then Melisande Shahrizai would not have had me to use as her hunting dog, and flush out Delaunay's allies."

"Is that what happened?" He checked himself, shaking his head. "Phèdre, you couldn't have known. Anafiel Delaunay should have, to use his bond-servants that way. It's not your fault."

"To blame or no," I said softly, "it doesn't matter. I was the cause. Delaunay is dead, and Alcuin too, who never harmed anyone in his life, and everyone else fool-hardy enough to serve him. I caused it."

"Phèdre . . ."

"It's getting darker." I interrupted him, holding my hand out. It was harder to see than before. "Mayhap they'll make camp, come nightfall. We've been going north, I think. It's colder than in the City."

"Camlach." He said it grimly.

"It may well be. They would be wary, inside the borders of L'Agnace; they ordered us to be silent, not still. They fear detection. If it's so, they might be less cautious in their own province."

"Delaunay taught you well," he murmured.

"Not well enough."

Worn out with fear and pain, I dozed for a time, waking only when the cart came to an abrupt halt. Utter darkness surrounded me. Then came the sound of men and chains rattling, and the rear gate of the cart opened. I squinted into blinding torchlight, flames streaking my vision.

"Come out," a harsh voice said from behind the swimming flames. "You first, girl; come out slowly."

Still clutching my blankets around me, I crawled out the back of the cart to stand blinking and squinting in the firelight, half-frozen and covered with straw. Rough hands took hold of me, guiding me toward a campfire. A helmeted soldier handed me a waterskin, and I drank greedily.

"All right, all right, easy, Cassiline." They were more cautious, allowing Joscelin to emerge, but he came docilely enough, his first concern for my safety. He was a Cassiline Brother and I was his charge; no matter what had befallen him, obeying that oath was foremost. I saw it in the relief in his face.

As my eyes adjusted to the firelight, I saw I had

guessed near enough. There were some fifteen soldiers, in unmarked gear, but professionals all. One tended a stewpot over the fire, while others saw to the horses, and a full half-dozen surrounded Joscelin with drawn blades. Our encampment was in a rocky valley, mostly frozen turf with a dusting of snow, and wooded mountains rising all around. Searching the mountainsides, I saw no other fires flickering. We were alone here.

"Come on, Cassiline. That's right." From his tone of command, I took the soldier chivvying Joscelin along at sword-point to be their leader. "Here, give him a drink," he added, catching a waterskin that someone tossed him. "There you go."

Joscelin drank, but I could see the banked fury in his face. He handed the waterskin back to the leader. "In the name of the Prefect of the Cassiline Brotherhood," he said quietly, "I demand to know who you are, and why you have done this to us."

Laughter rose around the campfire.

"In the name of the Prefect of the Cassiline Brotherhood," the leader echoed him in mincing tones, then struck Joscelin a sharp blow to the head with one gauntleted fist. "In the borders of Camlach, the only order we obey is the order of steel, Cassiline!"

Joscelin's head snapped back at the blow, and his eyes glittered. "Then give me mine, and try its mettle!"

Encouraging shouts came from the soldiers, but their leader shook his head regretfully. "I'd like to, boy, for you're angry enough to try for my head, and it would be an entertaining challenge. But my orders are to keep you alive." He jerked his chin at me. "You, girl; you need to use the latrine?"

Unfortunately, I did. For anyone who has never had to relieve themselves in the watchful presence of an armed guard, I do not recommend it. Joscelin had an escort of six, but he is a man, and considerably more accustomed to such company.

Thus humiliated, I was ushered back to the campfire and issued a bowl of stew. I ate it and said nothing; silence is the first skill I learned. In the Night Court, silence is common wisdom for a child; in Delaunay's household, it was taught us for other reasons. Joscelin followed my lead and held his tongue, until the leader beckoned for a flask one of his soldiers carried.

"You're to drink some," he said, holding out the flask.

It gleamed in the firelight. I could guess what was in it; more of the drug we'd been given before. Joscelin looked up remotely beside me, and I could sense his body coiling.

"No," he said mildly, and exploded into action, lunging forward to deliver a sharp chop to the leader's throat. The man staggered backward, struggling for breath, and the flask fell with a faint chink to the ground. The other soldiers moved belatedly to surround the whirling Cassiline as Joscelin fought with hands and feet, limbs moving in a blur of precisely executed movements.

He might have succeeded, against fewer men; six or eight, I would even believe. He'd taken them by surprise. But their leader got his wind back and his voice. Roaring, he waded into the fray, kicking a loose blade away from Joscelin's reaching grasp. "Ware your swords, you idiots! Don't let him get armed!" They surrounded him, pressing him hard, and then someone brought the pommel of a dagger down hard atop his head, and Joscelin sagged to his knees.

Cursing, one of the soldiers he'd injured stepped up and drew back his blade to run him through.

"Stop!" I hadn't even realized I was on my feet until I heard my own voice shout fiercely. The man stayed his hand; they were all staring at me. I had remembered the rest of it, and drew up the few ragged ounces of dignity I could summon. "If this man dies, you'll be accountable to Melisande Shahrizai for it," I said coldly. "Sooner or later, one way or another. Do you want to take that chance?"

The soldier considered it and glanced at his leader, who nodded. He sheathed his sword. At a word, the leader had the flask retrieved. "Hold him," he ordered, and two men wrenched Joscelin's arms behind his back, while two others held him. The leader uncorked the flask and grabbed Joscelin's chin, forcing the neck of the flask between his teeth and tipping it while another soldier pinched his nostrils shut.

Joscelin choked and sputtered, clear liquid spilling out the corners of his mouth, but a good deal of it went down his throat. It took effect quickly, and he pitched forward onto the ground.

"Tie his arms behind him," the leader ordered. "He'll give us less trouble." He came toward me, holding out the flask. "Lady, I hope you'll not give me the same."

"No, my lord." It was the first time I could recall using a formal address sarcastically. I took the flask from his hand and drank.

He took it back, eyeing me wryly. "You needn't take that tone, you know. I've treated you fair and kept my men off you, and it's the last kindness you're like to see, where you're going, lady. It's a strange way to keep someone alive, that's all I've to say."

That much I heard, and then darkness claimed me. I was vaguely aware of being lifted and slung back into the straw of the cart, feeling Joscelin's limp form near me and hearing the gate chained behind us. Slipping down into unconsciousness, I heard again what I had remembered: Melisande's voice, at the end, tender and rich.

"Don't worry, my dear, I'd no more kill you than I'd destroy a priceless fresco or a vase," she had said, somewhere beyond my failing vision. "But you know too much, and I can't afford the risk of keeping you here. It may not be much, but believe me when I say I'm giving you the best chance I can to stay alive. I'll even leave you the Cassiline, and pray he does a better job protecting you than he's done so far." Her fingers, twining in my hair, cruel and sweet. "When it's over, if you live, I'll find you. That much, I promise, Phèdre."

Elua help me, but then, even then, there was a part of me that hoped she would.

The Night Court taught me to serve, and Delaunay taught me to think; but from Melisande Shahrizai, I learned how to hate.

My memories of the remainder of our journey are blurred. Wishing to take no further risks, the Camaeline leader kept us confined to the cart and drugged, allowed full consciousness and freedom only long enough to eat, drink and relieve ourselves. I knew that the terrain grew harsher and we entered the mountains from the steep angle of the cart and the swearing of soldiers. I knew that we went further north from the cold that gripped me night and day, even in my drugged and bloodstained dreams.

But I didn't know where we were bound until they released us, stumbling and blinking in the bright light of day, on a snowy plain beyond the Camaeline Mountains.

Eight men, thewed like iron and clad in furs, sat arrayed in a semicircle atop tall, shaggy horses, watching us. One of them, whose yellow hair was bound with a bronze fillet and whose mustaches flowed luxuriantly, tossed the Camaeline leader a stained leather sack that clinked with coin and made a comment to him in a gutteral tongue. Joscelin's lips parted and he frowned, straining to understand.

I understood. It was Skaldic.

He had just paid the purchase-price for two D'Angeline slaves.

FORTY

From the speed with which the transaction occurred, I had no doubt that it was prearranged. The Camaeline leader handed the bag of coins to his second to count; at his affirmative nod, the leader cut the thongs that bound Joscelin's wrists and ordered one of his men to leave our baggage. He fetched a wrapped bundle, the hilt of Joscelin's sword protruding, and dumped it unceremoniously to the ground. At a word, they wheeled their party and struck out toward the mountain pass, the rearguard keeping a vigilant eye on the Skaldi, who watched them go impassively.

Joscelin glanced from the retreating Camaelines to the impassive Skaldi to me with a look of utmost bewilderment. "What is it?" he asked me at last. "Have you any idea what they've done?"

"Yes." I stood ankle-deep in snow, shivering under the bright sun. The sky overhead was a remarkable blue. "They've just sold us to the Skaldi."

If his response was singular, Joscelin's reactions were always swift. The words were scarce out of my mouth before he was scrambling for the pack and his sword, boots skidding in the snow.

The Skaldi leader loosed a shout of laughter, whooping to his men. One of them spurred his shaggy horse forward, intercepting Joscelin, who dodged. Another drew a short spear and thundered past the bundle, his mount's hooves spraying snow as he leaned down to pluck the pack neatly from the snow on the tip of his spear. Joscelin veered toward him, and the Skaldi jerked his spear, tossing the pack to a comrade.

They surrounded him, then, laughing with ruddy cheeks and high spirits, tossing the bundle back and forth across the circle while Joscelin spun about hopelessly, floundering in snow. The Skaldi leader sat apart, grinning with strong white teeth as he watched the entertainment. I wondered if the Camaelines had unbound Joscelin's hands knowing what would follow.

It was worse than the Eglantine adepts taunting him in Night's Doorstep, and I stood it as long as I could before I threw away our one advantage.

"Let him be!" I called to the leader in fluent Skaldic, raising my voice so it carried across the snow. "He does not understand."

His yellow eyebrows rose, but he betrayed no other sign of surprise. Joscelin, on the other hand, had ceased his futile efforts and stood gaping at me as if I'd grown a third eye. The Skaldi leader waved negligently to his men and moved his horse over to stare down at me. His eyes were a light grey, and disconcertingly shrewd.

"Kilberhaar's men didn't tell me you spoke our tongue," he mused.

"They didn't know," I replied in it, doing my best to hold his gaze despite my shivering. Kilberhaar; Silverhair, I thought, and remembered Isidore d'Aiglemort's pale, shining hair. "There are many things they do not know."

The Skaldi gave his roaring laugh, tossing back his head. "Those are true words, D'Angeline! You say your comrade does not understand. Do you?"

I knelt in the snow, as gracefully as my cold-stiffened

joints would allow, and kept my gaze on his face. "I understand I am your slave, my lord."

"Good." A look of satisfaction spread across his face. "Harald," he shouted to one of his men, "give my slave a cloak! These D'Angelines are frail creatures, and I would not have her die of cold before she has a chance to warm my bed!"

It got a laugh; I didn't care, for a young man whose mustache was barely started rode over grinning and tossed me a thick garment of wolfskin. I wrapped it around me and pinned it with frozen fingers.

"Thin blood," observed my Skaldi lord, "though they say it runs hot." Reaching down with one brawny arm, he lifted me into the saddle behind him. "You ride with me, little one. I am Gunter Arnlaugson. Tell your companion to be wise."

He wheeled his horse, bringing us broadside of the still-staring Cassiline.

"Joscelin, don't," I said through chattering teeth. "They won't kill us out of hand; they paid too dear. Skaldi value their slaves."

"No." His blue eyes were fixed and wide, nostrils flared. "I failed you with Melisande Shahrizai, and I failed you with d'Aiglemort's men, but I swear it, Phèdre, I won't fail you here! Don't ask me to betray my oath!" He lowered his voice. "The Skaldi's sword is in your reach. Get it to me, and I swear I will get us out of here."

I didn't look; I could feel it, the leather-wrapped hilt protruding from Gunter's sword-belt near my left elbow. Joscelin was right, it was in my reach.

And we were alone, in a frozen wasteland. Even armed, the Cassiline was still outnumbered eight to one, by mounted Skaldi warriors.

"I have lived in servitude all my life," I said softly.

"I'm not willing to die for your oath." I touched Gunter's shoulder. He looked back at me, and I shook my head. "He is too proud," I said in Skaldic. "He will not heed."

The shrewd grey eyes narrowed and he nodded. "Bring him!" he called to his men. "And have a care he does not hurt himself on your spears," he added with another roar of laughter.

It took all seven, and I had to watch it.

I daresay Joscelin himself had never known, until that moment, what true battle-fury was. He fought like a beast at bay, bellowing with rage, and for a time I could see nothing but horses' bodies and thrashing limbs. He succeeded in wrenching a short spear loose from one of them and kept them all at a distance then, jabbing and threatening; if it had been a more familiar weapon . . . I don't know. I cannot afford to guess.

"He looks like a girl," Gunter commented, his expression lively with interest, "but he fights like a man. Like two men!"

"He is trained to it from childhood," I said in his ear. "D'Angelines have betrayed him, the man you call Kilberhaar. Make him your friend, and he may fight for you against him."

It was a risk. Gunter's gaze slewed around to me, considering. "Kilberhaar is our ally," he said. "He pays us gold to raid your villages."

The shock of it went through me like a knife, but I kept it from showing on my features. "To have a traitor for an ally is to have an enemy-in-waiting," I said solemnly, silently blessing the number of hours I had spent translating Skaldic poetry. Gunter Arnlaugson made no reply, and I kept my mouth shut, leaving him to think on it. His men, half of them dismounted, finally succeeded in bringing down the thrashing Joscelin, wrestling the spear from his grasp and forcing him facedown in the snow.

"What shall we do with him?" one of them called.

Gunter thought about it a moment. "Tie his hands and let him run behind your horse, Wili!" he called. "We will tire the fight from this wolf-cub before we reach the steading."

It was quickly done, and we set out, riding beneath the bright blue sky. I clung awkwardly behind Gunter, pathetically grateful for the fur cloak and his burly frame blocking the wind, and trying not to look back at Joscelin. They had bound his wrists before him, attaching a long thong like a lead, and one of the Skaldi held the end, forcing the Cassiline to run behind his horse. Joscelin floundered in the snow, sometimes losing his footing and being dragged, until the Skaldi halted and gave him time to gain his feet. His breath came raggedly and his face was bright red with cold, but his eyes glared fierce blue hatred of everything and everyone around him.

Including me.

Hate me, I thought, and live, Cassiline.

It was nearing nightfall when we reaching the steading, our shadows stretching long and black before us across the deep snows. Gunter made up a song as we rode and sang it aloud in a powerful voice, about how he had outfoxed Kilberhaar and captured a D'Angeline warrior-prince and his consort; it was a good song, and I didn't bother to correct him. By that time, I was so cold, I could barely think.

There were a handful of snug cottages in the steading and a great hall. The doors to the hall were flung open wide as we approached, and men and women alike poured out shouting congratulations. Gunter dismounted, beaming, firelight from the hall catching the bronze fillet that bound his hair. He lifted me down from his horse and shoved me toward a knot of Skaldi. "See my new bed-slave!" he roared. "Is she not fine?"

Hands grasped at me, prodding and examining; too many faces, crowding close, ruddy and rough-hewn. I struggled free, searching for Joscelin.

He had sunk to his knees behind the Skaldi's horse, exhaustion compelling the obedience that nothing else would. Whoever said the Cassiline Brotherhood was a humble order, lied. His chest heaved, and his hair had come completely loose from its tidy club, rimed with frost. He glared through it at me.

"Joscelin," I murmured, cupping his cold face in my hands. He jerked his head away and spat at me. I felt Gunter's hands on my shoulders, drawing me away, tucking me under one massive arm.

"Look at him!" he said jovially. "A proper wolf-cub, he is! Let him spend the night with the hounds, then, eh?"

There was no shortage of willing hands to wrestle the Cassiline into submission. Laughing and shouting, a group of young men dragged him away; to the kennels, I could only surmise. I was spun around again by Gunter's grasp, propelled staggering into the warmth of the great hall.

"Shame on you, Gunter Arnlaugson!" The exclamation came from a woman, against whom I fetched up like a bit of flotsam, stumbling away awkwardly. She was young, and pretty enough by Skaldic standards, with sun-colored hair and sharp blue eyes. At this moment, she had both hands planted firmly on her hips, and her eyes were narrowed. "The poor thing's half-frozen and terrified to death, and you're bragging about bed-rights! No wonder you've not found a woman to warm it before this."

A round of laughter echoed from the rafters, and my fiercesome Skaldi lord looked down and shuffled his feet, before coming up with a retort. "Ah, Hedwig, you know I'd no need to go raiding over D'Angeline borders if you would have me, lass!" he said, grinning. "Now there's no telling what this little one can teach me, and you'll be sorry for the loss of it!"

"Not tonight, you won't." Despite the laughter his retort won, her reply was no less acerbic. "A bowl of warm soup, and a turn by the fire, that's what you need, isn't it, child?" she said kindly.

"She's a barbarian, Hedwig, she can't understand a word of it," someone said good-naturedly.

"I understand," I said in Skaldic, struggling to make my voice heard. Still shivering under my fur cloak, I sank to my knees and grasped her work-roughened hand, kissing it. "Thank you, my lady."

Embarrassed, Hedwig snatched her hand away. "Gods above, we'll have none of that here, child! We're not savages, we don't make slaves crawl on their knees!" Gunter had not said as much, I thought, rising, and filed the thought for future usage. Clapping her hands, she shouted for a bowl of soup and ordered room made at the hearth for me. There was grumbling, but she was obeyed.

I was in no shape to protest, even if I'd been minded to, which I was not. I took my seat by the fire, and the roaring heat of it slowly thawed the ice at the marrow of my bones. I could see Gunter in the hall, half a head taller than any other man there, boasting and making the best of the situation.

Later I learned what that night should have been obvious; Hedwig's father had been the lord of the steading, until his death. Gunter had won the leadership by might of arms, but had failed thus far in his campaign to win

Hedwig's heart, and some of her father's legacy of command still clung to her.

If I do not love the Skaldi—and I cannot, for what they sought to do to the land to which I was born, and which is ever a part of me—it is not in me to hate them, either: I knew kindness at their hands. If I knew cruelty—and I did—it was no more and no less than the cruelty they inflicted upon each other, for theirs is a harsh and warlike culture. But it is not without its beauty, even if it is born of blood and iron; and as I have learned, it is not without compassion.

Skaldi drink deep when celebrating, and they celebrated that night. Enough mead to drown a village flowed, and there were songs and fights and constant laughter. No one kept a close watch on me, and I daresay if I had wanted to slip away, I could have done so. But where would I have gone? I was in no condition to flee across miles of snowy wastes, through hostile territory. I thought of finding Joscelin, freeing him, and attempting the flight, and I shivered.

So it was that I stayed, while my new Skaldi masters sang and boasted and drank, and worried about Joscelin freezing in the cold, until a hand shook my shoulder and I woke with a start, to realize I was drowsing. It was Hedwig, who took me kindly to her room, shooting baleful looks at an only semi-abashed Gunter. There she made up a pallet for me, of straw ticking and heaped blankets, alongside her own bed, and I curled up like a dog myself and let sleep, honest sleep, claim me.

FORTY-ONE

Thus began my period of slavery under the ownership of Gunter Arnlaugson, Skaldic chieftain of one of the westernmost steadings held by the tribe of the Marsi—under the aegis, I would learn, of the great warleader Waldemar Selig, Waldemar the Blessed.

I was roused that morning by Hedwig, who showed me, to my immense joy, the bathing room. The bath itself was nothing more than a tub of battered tin, but it was sized for Skaldi, which meant I had ample room to sit and wash myself. Hedwig showed me how to fetch water and stoke the fire to heat it, marvelling that I had no knowledge of such things.

I may have been a servant all my life, I reflected, struggling with a heavy pail of water, but of a surety, I had been a privileged one. Still, I had never known a bath so sweet as that first one I drew for myself in Gunter's steading. Even the lack of privacy—for Hedwig perched on a stool and observed, while other women came and exclaimed—could not diminish its pleasure.

"What do you call this?" Hedwig asked, pointing at my marque; still unfinished, of course. I was glad, at least, that I had paid Master Tielhard in advance. If ever I returned to the City of Elua, surely he would honor our contract. I gave its name, translating as best I could into Skaldi, and explained that it was the sign of a Servant of Naamah. This too required considerable explanation, which the women heard with puzzled looks. "And these?" Hedwig asked then, her hovering finger indicating the fading lines of Melisande Shahrizai's handiwork. "This is part of the . . . the rituals?"

"No," I said shortly, pouring a dipper of warm water over my skin. "That was not part of Naamah's rituals."

Something in my tone stirred Hedwig to pity, and she shooed the other women out of the bath, remaining to help me out of the water and into a rough-spun woolen gown, so long on me that it dragged on the floor. "We will have it hemmed," she said pragmatically, and loaned me her own chipped comb for my damp, tangled hair.

Washed and combed, I felt more properly myself than I had since Rousse's messenger had entered the marquist's shop, and I endeavored to take the measure of my situation.

The great hall of the steading was a busy place. It is, I learned, the heart of any Skaldi community. The outlying fields were held by Gunter's thanes, or warriors, and farmed by their carls, who I took to be a class of peasants or bondsmen. For this privilege, they supported the thanes and paid a tithe in herds and grains to Gunter. When Gunter and his thanes were not out raiding or hunting, they spent their time carousing in the hall, wagering on contests of strength and song.

For all of this, Gunter was not a bad lord as such things are reckoned. The Skaldi have an elaborate system of law, and he heard complaints twice a week, deciding fairly and impartially as he could. When a decision went against one of his thanes and he was ordered to make reparation to one of his own carls for the unlawful stealing of a yearling bull-calf, he did it without grumbling.

These things I observed over time; then, on that first day, I merely kept my eyes open and my mouth closed, trying to make sense of it all. Of Gunter himself, I saw nothing during the daylight hours. His thanes abounded in the hall, honing their weapons and working thick bear-grease into their leather footware, laughing and joking. They made comments aplenty, elbowing each other and eyeing me, but made no move to molest me, so I ignored it, silently thanking Elua that it seemed I was Gunter's property alone, and not to be held in common among his men.

While the men idled and jested, the women worked tirelessly. There is a great deal to be done to keep the great hall in a steading functioning smoothly; tending the hearths, preparing food, cleaning up after drunken warriors, mending and spinning and sewing. There were housecarls who helped with the heavier work, but much of it the women did themselves. Hedwig ordered them about with a tone much accustomed to being obeyed, not shirking to labor herself. When I asked her what my duties were to be, she waved me away, saying it was for Gunter to say. I asked then if it was permitted for me to leave the hall, for I was concerned for Joscelin and wished to find him. She bit her lip and shook her head. Of her own accord, I think, she would have permitted it, but she dared not cross Gunter so far as that.

So I was confined to the hall, and the attentions of Gunter's thanes. One of the youngest—Harald the Beardless, who had given me his cloak—was the most daring of them, and a skilled poet in the bargain. If my heart had been less like a stone in those days, I might have blushed at some of his verses, which gave an exceedingly detailed inventory of my charms.

It was amid one of the latter that Gunter burst into the hall, attended by a couple of his men, shouting for mead. I don't know where he had been all day, but he was glowing with the cold, snow clinging to his cloak and leggings. When he unclasped his cloak and slung it aside, I saw Melisande's diamond about his neck and gasped aloud.

It was an incongruous thing, that glistening teardrop lying in the hollow of his powerful throat. I hadn't even had the sense to wonder about its loss; it had been amid our baggage, it seemed, as untouchable to d'Aiglemort's men as Joscelin's Cassiline weapons had been. No small wonder, I thought. I would sooner steal from the Cassiline Prefect than Melisande Shahrizai. The sight of her diamond drew exclamations, and Gunter laughed, running one thick forefinger beneath the black cord.

If I had thought about it, I would have welcomed its disappearance; but here it was now, again, dangling from the throat of my Skaldi master. I felt Melisande's presence in my life like a touch, and despaired.

"D'Angeline!" Gunter shouted, catching sight of me sitting by the fire. I rose with an automatic curtsy, awaiting with bowed head as he strode across the hall. "I have a powerful hunger upon me!" Strong hands closed about my waist and he lifted me into the air, planting a loud kiss on my less-than-willing lips. Gunter roared with laughter, holding me suspended. "Look at this!" he shouted to his men. "These D'Angeline women weigh no more than my left thigh. Think you she knows what a real man is?"

"Nor like to, at your hands," Hedwig retorted sharply, emerging from the kitchen with a ladle held in one hand like a sword. "Put the child down, Gunter Arnlaugson!"

"I'll put her down, flat on her back!" he declared, setting me back on my feet with another resounding kiss. I had never known such a hairy man, and it was strange to be kissed by him. "There! What do you think of that, D'Angeline?"

I had never hated any patron, having entered every contract freely, in homage to Naamah. I hated this man now, who would take me without consent, by virtue of an ownership he held through betrayal. "I am my lord's servant," I said stoically.

Gunter Arnlaugson was in high spirits; sarcasm was

lost on him. "And a cursed fine one at that," he agreed cheerfully, picking me up once more and slinging me over his shoulder like a sack of meal. "If I'm not back in two hours, send in a barrel of ale and a rasher of meat," he called to his thanes, striding out of the hall.

I hung, helpless as a child, over his shoulder, listening to the shouts and jibes of his men as we left. I could feel his muscles working beneath his woolen jerkin; I swear it, by Elua and his Companions, Skaldic warriors are unnaturally hale. In his modest quarters, he set me down and turned to build up the fire in the hearth. His room was simple timber, and held nothing but a rough-hewn bed covered with furs and a pile of tangled equipage, bits of steel and leather peeking from behind the edge of a shield, in one corner.

"There," he said with satisfaction, rubbing his hands together. "That should be warm enough for your thin blood, D'Angeline." He eyed me, the unnerving shrewdness back in his gaze. "I know what you are, D'Angeline, that you are trained to serve your goddess-whore. Kilberhaar's men told me, that I would pay the purchase-price, when I could have had a village girl for free but for the cost of a raid. We have done it before, you know."

"Yes," I said. I knew. I thought of Alcuin, whose village had been burned by the Skaldi. I thought of how the screams of the women had echoed in his ears, as he rode astride Delaunay's pommel. "What do you wish of me, my lord?"

"What?" Gunter Arnlaugson grinned, stretching his massive arms wide in the firelit bedroom. Light glittered on Melisande's diamond. "Everything, D'Angeline! Everything!"

It is funny how despair can so soon become an old companion. What he asked, I gave; not everything, not everything I had to offer, but everything he might desire. I was not fool enough to spend the coin of my skill all at once—and indeed, he was too young and too crude in the ways of Naamah to have grasped its value. But what I gave him, you may be sure, was beyond any price he had known to ask.

If I thought before that I knew what it was to serve Naamah, I learned that evening that I had grasped only the smallest part of it. On their wandering, Naamah lay in the stews with strangers for love of Elua, and Elua alone; I had done it for coin, and my own pleasure. Only now did I grasp what it was she had done. For my own part, I would not have cared overmuch if I lived or died. Joscelin thought I had betrayed him, but it was for his sake, and for Alcuin and Delaunay and his oath to Ysandre de la Courcel, I had to live, by any means I could.

I had nothing else to live for, save vengeance.

The arousement alone was enough for my Skaldi lord; I had barely begun the *languisement* when he gave a mighty whoop and toppled me onto his fur-clad bed, harpooning me with the gusto of a starving whaler. Melisande's diamond dangled from his neck and brushed my face as he plunged into me, burning like a brand. There is a point, always, where I no longer control either my patrons' desires nor my own. I gazed over Gunter's shoulder, the room swimming red in my vision, gritted my teeth and wept at my body's inevitable betrayal. Delaunay had lied, when he had set his value upon me. *I can make of her such a rare instrument that princes and queens will be moved to play exquisite music upon her*, he had said. A rare instrument I was, that sang at a Skaldi's crude thrusting. Pinioned under my master's hairy, heaving bulk, I came shuddering to climax, and despised all I was, and most especially the part that savored the humiliation of it.

In the hall, I had to endure his strutting and boasting, and the envy of his thanes. It was not so hard, compared to what had gone before, but still it galled me. Hedwig saw, and paused in passing to lay a kind hand upon my arm.

"His mouth is large," she said gently, "but his heart is larger. Don't take it so ill, child."

I looked at her without answering. If I found compassion in my soul later for Gunter Arnlaugson, I had none that night. Whatever she saw in my eyes, it sent her hurrying away.

I cannot recall the verses that Gunter sang that night; well-trained as my memory is, there are times when there is a kind of healing in forgetfulness. It sufficed that my reputation was made, there in the great hall. That, I remember all too well. D'Angeline I was, they said, and kin to the spirits of the night, that visit a man in exquisite dreams, summoning forth his seed for their own pleasure by the most delightful wiles; only Gunter had mastered me, by force of his prowess, and made me cry out his name, binding me to his will.

So they thought, and I let them think it. And this I remember, that it was the first I heard the murmurs, among his thanes who thought I listened not, that Gunter was minded to give me to Waldemar Selig at the All-thing, the great meeting of the tribes, and thus win the favor of the Blessed.

Once again, then, I would be a gift fit for a prince. Well, and it was no consolation. I wondered at a man that even Gunter Arnlaugson spoke of in tones of awe, and I feared. I thought of Joscelin, somewhere, shivering in the cold, and prayed he kept the wit to stay alive, for I feared I wouldn't survive this alone. I thought of Alcuin and Delaunay . . . Delaunay most of all, his beautiful, noble face, the intelligent eyes forever dimmed, and

I wept for him, alone by the fire, for the first time. Great, tearing sobs racked me, and the raucous Skaldi grew strangely silent.

Their eyes, curious and sympathetic, watched me with strangers' gazes. I gulped for air, and rubbed the tears from my eyes. "You do not know me," I said to them in D'Angeline, looking defiantly at their uncomprehending faces. "You do not know what I am. If you mistake the yielding in me for weakness, you are fools for it."

Still they stared, and there was no cruelty in it, only curiosity and incomprehension. I had a longing then, so acute I felt it in the marrow of my bones, to be home, to have my feet on D'Angeline soil, where Elua trod with his Companions. "There," I said in Skaldic, reaching out to point to a crude lyre in a warrior's hand. I didn't know the word for it. "Your instrument. May I borrow it?"

He gave it over wordlessly, though his closest companions laughed and shouted. I bowed my head and tuned it, as my old music master had taught me, running in my head the lines of a poetic translation. I had a gift for it, Delaunay's studies had taught me that much. When I had done, I lifted my head and looked around me. "By right of your laws, I am bond-slave to Gunter Arnlaugson," I said softly. "But by the laws of my own country, I have been betrayed and sold against my will. I am D'Angeline, and born to the soil on which Elua shed his blood. This is the song we sing when we are far from home."

I sang then *The Exile's Lament* of Thelesis de Mornay, the King's Poet. It was not written for the Skaldic tongue, which is harsh to the ear, and I had not worked properly on the translation, but the Skaldi of Gunter's steading understood it, I think. I have said it, and it is true, that I have no great skill at song; but I am

D'Angeline. I would pit the lowliest D'Angeline shepherd against the mightiest singer among the Skaldi, and wager on the shepherd each time. We are all of us, no matter how faint the thread of blood, the scions of Elua and his Companions. We are what we are.

So I sang, and put in the words as I sang them my farewell to Alcuin and Delaunay, and my promise to Joscelin Verreuil that I had not forgotten what I was, and my love for all those who yet lived, for Hyacinthe and Thelesis de Mornay and Master Tielhard, Gaspar de Trevalion, Quintilius Rousse, and Cecilie Laveau-Perrin, for the Night Court in all its faded glory, and for all that came to mind when I conjured the word, "home."

When I was done, there was silence, and then a roar of approval. Hardened warriors shook tears from their eyes, clapping and shouting for me to sing again. It was not the response I had expected; I had not reckoned, then, on the deep streak of sentimentality that runs in the Skaldi nature. They love to weep, as much as they love to fight and wager. Gunter was shouting over the din, flushed with triumph, prouder than ever of his conquest.

I shook my head and passed the lyre; I had no other tunes to hand that I could work into Skaldic, and I was wise enough to rest on these laurels. Whatever cost I had paid that night, I had gained some small advantage. Though for that, too, there would be a price. I heard it again, in the murmurs when Gunter proceeded with me from the hall, his face beaming, his hand in the small of my back as he steered me back to his room.

He was a young man, Gunter Arnlaugson, and tireless after their fashion. There was no shame among the Skaldi, and I could feel his eagerness when he brushed up behind me, his considerable phallus erect and straining at the front of his trews. It would be some time before he wearied of this. To my dismay, I felt the answering moisture begin between my own legs. I would have wept again, but my eyes, at least, were dry. I concentrated instead on the murmurs. "He would be a fool not to give her up," I heard. "Even Waldemar Selig has nothing like *that*."

A gift fit for princes, I went obediently toward my own personal hell.

✌ORTY-TWO

Embers smoldered in the hearth in Gunter's bedroom. He lay beside me, deep in slumber, rumbling sounds emanating from his broad chest. This too was a strangeness to me; never, in all my days as a Servant of Naamah, had I shared sleep with a patron. He had fallen soundly asleep with one arm flung over me, but hadn't woken when I'd cautiously moved it. As well to know it; there was no lock on the bedroom door, likely I could slip out without waking him.

Gunter seemed to have no fear of my trying to escape. Rightly so, since I feared the snow and the journey as much as capture . . . but mayhap there was some merit in his casual trust. As I lay awake, considering the possibilities, I saw it.

It was not, I feared, an option I liked; I liked it not at all, in truth, and the prospect of success was as terrifying in its own way as failure.

Still, it had to be tried.

Unfortunately, this was easier said than done. In the morning, I attended Gunter at his breakfast, serving him with the unobtrusive grace that was a hallmark of Cereus House. It pleased him well enough, and I had hopes that he was in a generous mood, but when I asked permission to see Joscelin, he slewed his gaze round at me with that canny look.

"Nay, he's a hellion, that one. Let him stew in the kennels a while longer. I'll not show him softness till he learns to heel to the hand as feeds him," he said, laughing. "Leastwise he's making some new friends a D'Angeline lordling doesn't often get to meet, eh?"

Poor Joscelin, I thought, and let the matter go for that day. Gunter patted me on the head and went out from the great hall to do whatever it was he did while away—betimes hunting, I later learned, and betimes making the rounds of the farms on his steading, seeing that all was well with his carls.

So I was left to idle once more, only now there was some resentment in the glances of the women, whose labors seemed more onerous than mine. I would have traded places with any one of them, but they had no way to know it, and no reason to understand it. Hedwig resisted him, but Gunter was accounted a handsome man, I learned, and no small prize for the woman who would get him to plight his troth with her.

Never skilled at doing nothing, I asked for pen and paper, that I might work out more translations of D'Angeline songs for my meager repertoire. They stared at me uncomprehending—the Skaldi have no proper written language, but for a magical system of runic sigils they call *futhark*. Odhinn the All-Father gave them to his children, they say, and there is virtue in them. I do not laugh at this, for it was Shemhazai who taught the D'Angelines to write. It is my thought that he made a better job of it, but then, I am biased. At any rate, there was neither pen nor paper to be had in the steading, so I made due with a clean-swept table and a burnt twig.

Happily, the Skaldi women were intrigued by my

charcoal scratchings, and their hostility eased as I explained what it was I did. They taught me songs, then, that I had never heard: Skaldic songs, but not of war . . . songs of life, of the harvest, of courtship, of love, of childbearing and loss. Some I still remember, but I wish I'd had paper to write them down. What the Skaldi lacked in melody and tone, they made up for in surprisingly beautiful imagery, and I do not think any scholar has catalogued these homely poems of house and hearth.

So it was that I had more songs to sing that night, D'Angeline and Skaldic alike, and they were well received. Gunter dandled me on his knee and beamed; I was something of a luck-charm to the Skaldi, it seemed, with this sorcerous gift of tongues.

The second night passed much like the first. I saw that Gunter was well pleased and slept the sleep of deep exhaustion, and repeated my request in the morning. Again he denied it, and I bided, to ask again after the third night.

"When he is tamed, I will show him kindness," he repeated to me, tugging at my curls and grinning. "Why do you persist, little dove? Have I not pleased you well enough between the furs? Your cries say as much." He shared his grin with the room, then.

"That is my gift from my patron-god, my lord," I said somberly to him. "I am marked with his sign." I touched the outer corner of my left eye.

"Like the petal of a rose, floating on dark waters," Gunter agreed, drawing me forward to plant kisses on both eyelids.

"Yes." I pulled away from him, kneeling and gazing upward. "But I am bound to Joscelin Verreuil, by his oath to his patron-god. And if I may not see him, our gods may turn their faces away in disfavor. Such gifts as I have will turn to dust in my mouth." I paused, then said, "It is a matter of honor, my lord. He will die, rather than answer to your hand. But if he sees that I have yielded to you and Kushiel favors me still, he may relent."

Gunter considered it. "All right, then," he said, and hoisted me to my feet, clapping me on the behind. "You may see the boy, that he may make peace with his gods. But let him know, eh, that if he does not calm soon, I'll have no use for him! He eats more than a hound, that one, and less value in his service!" He shouted for his thanes. "Harald! Knud! Take her to see the wolf-cub, eh? And see that he doesn't harm her," he added ominously.

They sprang up grinning, eager to escort me anywhere. I retrieved my fur cloak, and went with them as the doors of the great hall were opened.

It was not far to the kennels, and the snow was trodden solid. Still, Harald and Knud escorted me with care, helping me solicitously over the rough patches. Whatever I was here, I was something to be valued. The dogs were penned in a crude fence, and had a low building to shield them from the weather. Harald the Beardless leaned over and pounded on the roof of it, shouting. I heard the sound of chains stirring from within.

When Joscelin emerged, I gasped.

The Cassiline looked awful, his long hair was matted and wild, his eyes glaring through it. He bore a manacle about his neck that had chafed him raw, and his ashen attire was wholly unsuited to the cold. He crouched on his haunches in the packed snow, ignoring the dogs that sniffed around him, treating him as one of their own.

For all of that, he was D'Angeline and beautiful.

"Let me in to see him," I said to Knud. He gave me a dubious look, but opened the latch on the gate. I went in and crouched opposite Joscelin. "Joscelin," I murmured in our shared tongue. "I need to talk to you."

"Traitor!" he spat at me, scrabbling at the fetid snow of the kennel-yard and hurling a handful at me. "Skaldic-speaking treacherous daughter of a whore! Leave me alone!"

I dodged most of the snow, and wiped the rest from my face. "Do you want to know the face of treachery, Cassiline?" I retorted angrily. "Isidore d'Aiglemort is paying the Skaldi to raid Camaeline villages. How do you like that?"

Joscelin, who had turned away to dig up another handful of snow, turned back to me, a questioning—and thankfully human—light in his eyes. "Why would he do that?"

"I don't know," I said softly in D'Angeline. "Save that it has allowed him to rally the Allies of Camlach around his flag again, and build up his own armies. He even asked for command of Baudoin's Glory-Seekers, you know. I heard it."

On his haunches, Joscelin sat still and stared at me. "You really think he seeks to overthrow the Crown."

"Yes." I reached forward and took his hands. "Joscelin, I don't think I can make it through these lands. You can, and I can free you. Gunter has no guard on me, no chain. I can get out of the great hall tonight. I can get you arms, and clothing and a tinderbox, at least. You have a chance. You can make it to the City, and deliver Rousse's message, and tell them what d'Aiglemort is about."

"What about you?" He was still staring.

"It doesn't matter!" I said fiercely. "Gunter means to bring me to the Allthing, to give me to Waldemar Selig. I'll learn what I can, and do what I may. But you have a chance to escape!"

"No." He shook his head, looking sick. "No. If you

are no traitor . . . Phèdre, I can't. My oath is to Cassiel, and not the Crown. I cannot leave you."

"Cassiel bid you protect the Crown!" I cried. Harald and Knud glanced over, and I lowered my voice. "If you would serve me, do this thing, Joscelin."

"You don't know." He bowed his head, pressing the heels of his hands into his eyes, despairing. "You don't understand. It has naught to do with thrones and crowns. Cassiel betrayed God because God Himself had forgotten the duty of love and abandoned Elua ben Yeshua to the whims of Fate. To the point of damnation and beyond, he is the Perfect Companion. If you are true, if you are true . . . *I cannot abandon you*, Phèdre nó Delaunay!"

"Joscelin," I said, tugging his hands down. I glanced around at Harald and Knud, waving them back. "Joscelin, I ask you to do this thing, with all that is in me. Can you not obey?"

He shook his head, miserable. "Do you not know what we call Elua and the other Companions, in the service of Cassiel? The Misguided. Ask me anything but this. Cassiel cared naught for lands and kings. I cannot abandon you."

Thus was my plan, which was a good one, resigned to the midden-heap. "All right," I said sharply, in a tone that brought his head up so quickly it rattled his chains. "Then if you would serve me as Companion, do so! You merit naught, chained in the kennel like a dog!"

He gulped, and swallowed hard. Humility does not come easy to Cassilines. "How may I serve, then, my lady Phèdre, O slave of the Skaldi?"

Harald and Knud were leaning on the fence, watching with interest. They may have understood none of what passed between us, but they saw Joscelin willing to listen, something none of them had seen before.

"First," I said relentlessly, "you will learn to be a good slave, and make yourself useful. Cut wood, fetch water, whatever is needful. Gunter Arnlaugson has half a mind to slay you as a waste of food. Second, you will learn Skaldic." He moved in protest, chains sounding. I held up my hand. "If you would be my Companion," I said ruthlessly, "you will serve your lord, and win his trust, and make of yourself a gift fit for princes! Because if you do not, Gunter will give me to Waldemar Selig anyway, and kill you for sport. I swear to you, Joscelin, if you will do this much for me, and live, I will make my escape with you, and cross the snows without one word of trepidation! Will you obey?"

He bowed his head, matted blond hair hiding his proud D'Angeline features. "Yes," he whispered.

"Good," I said, and turned to my escort. "He comes to understand his position," I said in Skaldic. "He consents to receive the gift of tongues. I will teach him, that he may comprehend and obey my lord Gunter Arnlaugson. Do you say it is fairly done?"

They glanced at each other, and shrugged. "He stays among the hounds, until he has proved his worth," Knud called. I nodded my assent.

"Listen well," I said to Joscelin, who attended my words with a faint light of hope in his eyes. "This is the word for 'I' . . ."

So began my third role among the Skaldi, although they themselves may only have counted two. Consort, bard . . . and teacher.

To his credit, Joscelin learned quickly. It is harder to learn as an adult than as a child, but if he had lost the ease that childhood affords, he made up for it in stubborn persistence. By virtue of having accompanied me on that first outing, Harald and Knud had appointed themselves my permanent escort, and it amused them to watch our lessons. Joscelin, I learned, they regarded as a genuine barbarian, wild and untamed, hitherto lacking even rudimentary speech. I could not, in truth, entirely blame them for this; if I had seen no more of the Cassiline than they had, I too might have thought him a savage.

It is a fine line, in all of us, between civilization and savagery. To any who think they would never cross it, I can only say, if you have never known what it is to be utterly betrayed and abandoned, you cannot know how close it is.

Gunter turned an indulgent eye to the proceedings. He had paid good coin for a D'Angeline warrior-prince, and if I thought I could transform the snarling captive he'd gotten instead into something worthy of serving a Skaldi tribal lord, he was willing to let me try.

Through the kindness of Hedwig and the other women of the steading, I was able to smuggle a few bits of comfort to Joscelin: a woolen jerkin from one, worn but still serviceable; rags to wrap his hands and his feet inside his boots; even a poorly cured bearskin, which stank, but afforded considerable warmth. Unfortunately, the dogs tore it to shreds and Joscelin was badly bitten on his left arm when he sought to rescue it, but Knud, swearing me to silence, gave me a bit of salve to put on the wounds. He said he'd gotten it from a village witch, who'd put the virtue of healing in it. Whether or not it was true—it smelled much like any other ointment I'd know—Joscelin's arm healed without festering.

I think it pleased Gunter to wait to evaluate Joscelin's progress. I was hard-pressed to track the days passing, but I think it was nigh onto two weeks before he put Joscelin's learning to the test. In all the time before that, he paid heed to him only once, visiting the kennels to greet his favorite dogs, tossing them scraps of dried meat to fight over. But for the glint in his eye, it might have been no more than robust Skaldic humor that made him toss one to Joscelin. I was not there, but I heard about it later; Joscelin caught the scrap neatly in midair and gave his Cassiline bow, forearms crossed.

After that, I gauged him ready enough to meet Gunter as a D'Angeline, and not the feral creature I'd seen him. We rehearsed a greeting, to smooth over his rudimentary Skaldic, and continued to work on the rest. When Gunter chose to acknowledge him, Joscelin was prepared.

It was a dim afternoon, on a day that had threatened snow, and Gunter and his thanes had idled in the hall drinking for some hours when he took it in his head to visit Joscelin. He took me with him, wrapped in fur, and with a few of his men went out to the kennels. They sang and jested and passed a skin of mead. When they reached the kennel, Gunter put his arm around me and shouted for the D'Angeline. Amid a swirl of bounding dogs, Joscelin emerged. He caught himself briefly at the sight of me under Gunter's arm, but kept his features expressionless, standing and giving his bow.

"So, D'Angeline, what have you learned, eh? Has my little dove taught you to speak like a proper man?" Gunter asked, squeezing my shoulders.

"I am at my lord's service," Joscelin said in carefully accented Skaldic, bowing again and standing at Cassiline ease, hands where the hilts of his daggers would have been.

"Ah-ha, so the wolf-cub does more than growl!" Gunter laughed, and his thanes laughed with him. "What will you do if I set you loose from the kennels, eh D'Angeline?"

I had given him a bit of thong to tie back his matted locks. Somehow, in rags and squalor, Joscelin managed to look every inch a Cassiline Brother. "I will do as my lord commands," he said, bowing again.

"Will you?" Gunter looked skeptical. "Well, there is water to be drawn and wood to be fetched and Hedwig has been complaining about the housecarls, so mayhap we have a use for you, wolf-cub. But how do I know you will keep your word, hm? How do I know you'll not try to flee, nor assault us in our sleep if I give you half a chance? I've not men to waste, setting a guard on you all day!"

It was too much Skaldic too fast; I saw Joscelin blink in consternation. "He wants your word that you'll not try to escape nor attack the steading," I said in D'Angeline.

Joscelin thought. "Tell him this," he said to me. "While he keeps you safe, I will protect and serve this . . . steading . . . as if it were my own. I will do aught he asks, save turn on my own people, unless they be d'Aiglemort's men. This I swear, upon my oath."

I repeated his words to Gunter in Skaldic, slowly, so that Joscelin could follow the gist of it and nod agreement. Gunter scratched his chin.

"He has a mighty hatred for Kilberhaar," he said thoughtfully. "So much I fear he may choose vengeance over honor, no matter how he swears. What do you say, little dove? Will the wolf-cub honor his oath?"

"My lord," I said honestly, "he is more bound by this oath than words can compass. Mountains will fall and cattle will fly before he breaks it."

"Well, then." Gunter grinned at Joscelin. "It seems my dove has tamed the wolf, where all my dogs have failed. I will give you one night to say farewell to your new friends, and in the morning we will see what kind of servant you make."

The Cassiline followed the sense of his words, if not the exact meaning. He bowed again, then sat cross-legged in the snow, ignoring the dogs that milled around sniffing him. "I will wait my lord's command," he said in Skaldic.

"Is he going to sit there all night?" Gunter asked me curiously.

"I don't know." I'd had my fill of stubborn Cassiline honor, and despaired of understanding the logic that drove it. "He might."

Gunter roared with laughter. "What a man! Some prize I will have to show at the Allthing, if he will serve! The wolf and the dove, yolked in tandem at Gunter Arnlaugson's steading! Even Waldemar Selig might envy such a prize." In high good spirits, he urged his thanes back to the hall, singing loudly about the honor he would win.

I glanced back once. Sure enough, Joscelin sat without moving, watching us go.

Forty-Three

Boisterous and crude he might be, but Gunter was a man of his word, and he had Joscelin's chains struck the following morning. Knud, who harbored a fondness for me, took me to see it. I'd no doubt that Joscelin would keep his own word, but still, freedom was a heady thing to one who'd been kept in chains. He started briefly when the manacle about his neck was unlocked, muscles quivering with the urge to strike out.

But Cassiline discipline prevailed quickly, and he regained his composure, bowing obediently.

"Well, we will see, eh?" Gunter said. He jerked his thumb at one of his thanes. "Thorvil, you will stay with him today, and keep a watch. Let him do a carl's work. Only, give him no weapons, eh? If he need break ice on the stream to fetch water, let him use his hands. Mayhap when he's proved himself, we'll let him chop wood or somewhat."

"Aye, Gunter." Thorvil fingered the hatchet in his own belt and grinned, showing a gap in his teeth, knocked out in a friendly contest of strength. "I'll keep my eye on him, never fear."

From what I could see that day, Joscelin gave him no cause for concern. Indeed, he worked with a will, hauling buckets of water tirelessly from the stream to refill the cisterns of the great hall; no small task. Thorvil sauntered behind him, whistling and cleaning his fingernails with the point of his dagger.

And the women of Gunter's steading stared.

None of them had seen Joscelin, save for a brief glimpse that first night, when he'd been brought in at the end of a line, half-wild and snow-covered. They got a good look at him now. Filthy and disheveled, smelling of the kennels, Joscelin was still, undeniably, a D'Angeline.

"He must be a prince in your land!" Hedwig whispered to me, awed, watching him emerge from the kitchen with his buckets empty. "Surely all the men do not look so!"

"Not all, no," I said wryly, wondering how Gunter would contend with this reaction. One of the younger women—Ailsa, her name was—contrived to brush into Joscelin, giggling when he blushed and dropped his buckets. Of the two men, I reflected, Joscelin might have a harder time of it.

Gunter and his thanes returned from the hunt flushed and triumphant, dragging a good-sized hart with them. He was minded to celebrate and we had a feast that night. Gunter got roaring-drunk, but not so drunk he didn't have the presence of mind to have Joscelin chained by the ankle to a great stone bench by the hearth. At least, I thought, both admiring and despising his foresight, it was warm and indoors. Joscelin curled up in the rushes on the floor, exhausted beyond caring. Even if it hadn't been for his oath, I don't think he would have fled that night if Gunter had left him free with the door standing wide open.

As the cold winter days passed and Joscelin gave no indication of untrustworthiness, matters settled into a routine. One day, when Gunter and his thanes were out, Hedwig and I conspired to see Joscelin bathed. If I had been grateful for my first bath in the steading, I cannot even begin to fathom how much more so Joscelin was. We emptied the water twice, so filthy was it. And if I thought my bath had been well-attended, it was nothing to his. Women of all ages, from the giggling Ailsa to dour old Romilde, whom I'd never seen smile, crowded into the bath-room to peek at him.

The Joscelin of my earliest acquaintance would have died of mortification; now, he merely blushed and looked politely away, trying to preserve what little dignity they allowed him. Even the most retiring of the women, dark-eyed Thurid, came to see, shyly offering a clean woolen jerkin and hose that had belonged to her brother, killed in a raid.

He looked dismayed to see his grey Cassiline rags piled for discard, so I gathered them carefully. I understood; it was all he had left of home. "Don't worry," I promised him. "I'll see them washed and mended if I have to do it myself."

I spoke to him in Skaldic, as I tried always to do when others were about. His understanding had improved, and his speech. "I would thank you," he grinned at me, "only I hear talk of your sewing."

The women giggled. It was true, Hedwig had been

teaching me, that I might help with the endless mending, and my skills were thusfar deplorable.

"I will mend them," Ailsa said slyly, taking the clothing from me and making eyes at Joscelin. "There is virtue in a kindness dealt to strangers."

Joscelin blinked helplessly at me, drawing his knees up further in the bathing tub to hide his privates. "Serves you right," I said to him in D'Angeline, then in Skaldic to our putative mistress of the steading, "Hedwig, I would see him groomed, if you would loan me your comb."

She eyed him doubtfully. "See that he is soaped and dunked once more," she said. "I'm not minded to share fleas with Gunter's dogs. 'Tis hard enough to contend with them as it is." For all that, she brought the comb, and had the grace to order the others out of the bathing room so Joscelin could dress in peace. I combed his hair then, taking pains to ease through the mats and snarls.

It was strangely soothing, putting me in mind of my childhood at Cereus House. Properly washed and combed, Joscelin's hair fell, blond and shining, halfway down his back. I didn't try to bother with the Cassiline club, but twined it in one thick braid, binding it with thong. He endured the process with patience, for it was the closest thing to luxury either of us had known in a long time.

"There," I said, unconsciously falling back into D'Angeline. "Let them see you now!"

He made a face, but went out from the bathing room. If the women had stared before, now they gaped. I could understand why. Clean and groomed, he shone like a candle in the rude, timbered interior of the great hall. Seeing him among the Skaldi women, I thought, it was no wonder Gunter's thanes made of me what they did, if I looked so to them.

Having nigh emptied them with his bath, it was Joscelin's job to refill the house cisterns. He did it with quiet grace, making trek after trek with the yolked buckets across his shoulders, stamping the snow from his boots before he entered the hall.

Ailsa, sewing in a corner, watched him and smiled.

If Gunter had not noticed before, he noticed it that night. He remarked on it to me as we lay in bed, afterward. It had surprised me, that he liked to talk after pleasure, when he'd not drunk heavily before it.

"He is pleasing to the women, your D'Angeline," he mused. "What do they see, so, in a beardless boy?"

So that was why he thought Joscelin a boy still. "We do not grow hair like the Skaldi," I said to him. "Some of the old lines, where the blood of Elua and his Companions runs strong, grow none on the face. Joscelin is a man grown. Perhaps women are less easily misled than men in this," I added, smiling.

But Gunter was in no mood to be teased. "Does Hedwig find him pleasing?" he asked me, yellow brows scowling in thought.

"She finds him pleasing to behold," I said honestly, "but she does not make eyes at him, as does Ailsa, my lord."

"Ailsa is a trial," he muttered. "Tell me, is the D'Angeline trained as you are? Kilberhaar's men did not say so."

I nearly laughed, but smothered it, as he was minded to take it wrong. "No, my lord," I said instead. "He is sworn to lie with no woman. It is part of his oath."

At that, his brows shot up. "Truly?"

"Yes, my lord. It is true that he is a lord's son, but he is a priest, first; a kind of priest, as you know it. That is the nature of his oath."

"So he is not trained to please women, as you are to please men," Gunter said thoughtfully.

"No, my lord. Joscelin is trained to be a warrior and companion, as I was trained to please in bed," I said, adding, "Men and women both."

"Women!" His voice rumbled with surprise. "Where is the sense in that?"

"If my lord has to ask," I said, somewhat offended, "there is no merit in answering."

I thought perhaps I had annoyed him then, and he would turn over and speak no more that evening, but Gunter was considering something. He lay gazing at the ceiling, running one finger beneath the cord of Melisande's diamond. "I please you," he said eventually. "But you say it is the gift of your patron-god."

"A gift, or betimes a curse," I muttered.

"All the gifts of the gods are like that," he said dismissively, pinning me with his shrewd look. "But I thought maybe you only said it that I would let you see the D'Angeline boy, eh?"

It was hard, sometimes, to remember that he was a clever man, for all his Skaldi ways. I shook my head. "What I said was true, my lord." It wasn't, of course, exactly true; I'd no idea if Kushiel's Dart could be unstricken. But of a surety, it was true that I was its victim.

"So you say that I would not be pleasing to a D'Angeline woman who lacked your curse of a gift?"

"I am the only one with this gift," I murmured. "Does my lord wish me to answer him truly?"

"Yes," he said bluntly.

I remembered what Cecilie had said about Childric d'Essoms. "My lord makes love as if he is hunting boar," I said; it was not as much of an insult to a Skaldi as it would be to a D'Angeline. "It is a heroic act, but not necessarily pleasing to women."

Gunter thought about this, absently smoothing his mustaches. "You could teach me," he said cannily. "If you are trained as you say."

I nearly laughed at that, too, albeit bitterly. I would be dead now, were I not pleasing to Melisande Shahrizai, whose skills I would match against any adept of the Night Court. "Yes, my lord," I said. "If it is your wish."

"It would be a mighty thing to know." He still had that canny look on his face, though in this, he wasn't nearly as shrewd as he thought. I knew well enough that Hedwig had refused him three times. If he meant to give me to Waldemar Selig at the Allthing, surely he would ask her a fourth. After his time with me, I did not think Gunter Arnlaugson would be one to welcome a cold bed for long.

"It is a dangerous thing to know," I said without thinking. But Gunter's mood had turned, and he laughed uproariously at my words.

"You will begin to teach me this tomorrow, eh?" he said, adding cheerfully, "And if you speak of it, little dove, I will send your friend back to the kennels."

Matters resolved to his own satisfaction, Gunter rolled over, and was soon snoring. I lay awake, rolling my eyes at the prospect, and prayed to Naamah for aid and guidance.

It would be, I thought, a formidable task.

So began my second tutorship among the Skaldi, and I daresay it went well enough, at least as the Skaldi would measure such things. I never heard, afterward, that Gunter had any complaints. It brought to light, though, a deeper danger.

If the greatest danger one faces as a slave is displeasing one's masters, this is the second: pleasing them. All too soon, it becomes all too easy to forget doing aught else. Skaldi reckon time differently than we do, but the

meeting of the tribes they named the Allthing was still
some weeks away; and once we had found our feet, Joscelin and I, on solid ground at Gunter's steading, we
began sliding into the trap of growing too comfortable
in our roles. Wearing the mask of obedience so long, I
saw Joscelin forget at times that it was but a mask.

And for my part, to my dismay, I found myself falling
asleep at times thinking with pride—and even pleasure—
upon Gunter's progress at our private lessons.

Until the next time they raided.

The shock of it was like ice-cold water. Gunter and
his thanes arose in the small hours of the morning, rousing the entire household to service as they armed themselves for the raid, laughing and jesting and testing the
edges of their weapons. They wore little in the way of
armor, but wrapped themselves well in furs, and each
man carried a shield as well as a sword or axe, and the
short spear they favored.

The horses were brought round, stamping and blowing
frost under the faint stars. They would ride through the
waning hours of the night, bursting through the pass at
dawn to descend upon a hapless village in full daylight.
Amid the clangor and bustle, Joscelin and I stared at
each other, pale with horror. I saw him begin to shake
all over with repressed rage, and turn away to hide his
face from Gunter and his thanes. He made himself
wisely scarce, and I did not see him until Gunter came
striding, sheathing his sword, to bid me farewell, shouting as he came. "I ride into battle, little dove! Kiss me
and pray to see me alive come nightfall!"

I believe, in truth, that he had forgotten for the moment who I was, and where I came from. I had not, and
froze.

And then Joscelin was between us, brushing Gunter's
reaching hands aside with a sweep of his forearms, ef-

fortless as thought. His blue eyes locked with Gunter's. "My lord," he said softly. "Allow her one ounce of pride."

What passed between them, I do not know. But Gunter's eyes narrowed, gauging the measure of Joscelin's rebellion, while the Cassiline kept his face calm. After a moment, Gunter nodded. "We ride!" he shouted, turning and beckoning to his thanes.

They streamed out of the great hall, brawn and fur and iron, mounted and rode, while those left behind cheered them on. Joscelin sank to his knees and gave me a sick look. I, I just stood, gazing out through the open doors of the hall, and wept.

They came back after nightfall.

They came back victorious, boisterous and half-drunk and singing, staggering under the spoils they'd taken: meager enough stuff, sacks of grain, and stores of winter roots and fruit. I heard Harald boasting about the number of D'Angelines he had slain; when I caught his eye, he fell silent, blushing. But he was one among many.

Piecing the story together, I gathered that they had met with a party of warriors; Allies of Camlach, riding under the sign of the flaming sword. There had been a second banner, someone said, with a red forge on brown. Not d'Aiglemort's men, then, I thought. Two thanes had fallen—Thorvil among them—but they had won the day, slaying half the D'Angelines before retreating through the skirling snows.

If Gunther had been mindful of my sensibilities upon leaving, he took no such niceties upon his victorious return, and I had had the wit to caution Joscelin not to intervene. Thanks to Elua, he did not, for I think Gunter in a drunken state might have set upon him. When the celebration had reached its apex and besotten warriors sprawled about the hall, Gunter hoisted me over his shoulder amid roars of approval, carrying me away.

It was not a night for lessons.

When he was done, I left him snoring and crept from his bed, into the great hall, where his thanes slept off their mead, rumbling and murmuring. Someone had remembered to secure Joscelin's leg-irons. I thought he too slept, there by the hearth-bench, but his eyes opened at my near-soundless approach.

"I couldn't stay there," I whispered.

"I know." He moved over, cautious not to clank his irons, and made room for me on the rushes. It was one of his duties, to see that they were replaced when the hall was swept. I sank down to the floor and curled up next to him. His arm came around me, and I laid my head on his chest and stared into the dying embers of the fire.

"Joscelin, you have to leave," I murmured.

"I *can't*." Low as it was, I could hear the agony in his voice. "I can't leave you here."

"Damn your Cassiel to hell, then!" I hissed, eyes stinging.

His chest rose and fell beneath my cheek. "He believed he was, you know," Joscelin said in a low voice. He touched my hair lightly with one hand, stroking it. "I learned it all my life, but I never truly understood it until now."

A shudder ran through me. "I know," I whispered, thinking of Naamah, who had lain with strangers, who had lain with the King of Persis, thinking of Waldemar Selig, the Skaldi warleader. "I know."

We did not speak then, for a long time. I had nearly fallen asleep when I heard Joscelin ask softly, "How can d'Aiglemort bear it? He is sending D'Angelines to die against the Skaldi."

"Ten may die, and a hundred more rally to his banner," I said, staring into the embers. "And he can blame the King for Camlach's losses, for not sending him further troops. That was his plan, with the Glory-Seekers. He is building an empire. How he can do it, I don't understand, but I can see the why of it. What I would like to know is, why does Gunter have no fear of him?"

"Because d'Aiglemort pays him," Joscelin said bitterly.

"No." I shook my head against his chest. "It's more than that. Gunter knows something that d'Aiglemort doesn't; he laughed, when I told him there were things Kilberhaar didn't know. Gonzago de Escabares said it, a year ago. The Skaldi have found a leader who thinks."

"Elua help us all," Joscelin whispered.

After that, neither of us spoke, and then I did sleep, and wakened only to a light tug on my sleeve. Opening my eyes, I met the worried features of Thurid, the shy one, who had risen early to her chores. Dim light filtered into the great hall from the oiled skins over the windows, and slumbering thanes still snored around us, stinking of stale mead.

"You must go," she whispered to me. "They will wake soon."

It was the first moment, I think, that I realized how things had begun to change between Joscelin and me. In the shock and horror of the night, it had only seemed natural that we held to each other for comfort. The faint awe on Thurid's face made something different of it. I sat up, brushing away bits of rush tangled in my hair and caught in my skirts. Joscelin's eyes were open, watching me. What he thought, I could not say. Neither of us dared speak now, for fear of rousing the thanes. I squeezed his hand once and rose, stealing after Thurid, who picked her way carefully among the snoring warriors, to slip back into Gunter's room and between the warm furs of his bed.

He made a rumbling noise in his sleep and turned over, drawing me into his embrace. I lay wide-eyed in the curve of his massive arm, despising him.

FORTY-FOUR

After the raid, matters settled back into familiar routine, though neither Joscelin nor I were likely to succumb to its comforts any time soon. The raid had served its purpose as a bitter reminder of the reality of our situation.

Winter in the City of Elua is not a pleasant time; it grows chill, and betimes a sweeping wind blows that drives everyone indoors, and halts trade and leisure alike. But it is nothing to life on a Skaldi steading. Here, we were truly snowbound, for at times the weather grew so fierce, not even the Skaldi would venture out for any length of time. And even when it was fair, there was nowhere to go, and precious little to do. In some ways, I think, the tedium was easier on the women and carls, for even in winter there was work to be done. But when they could not hunt, Gunter and his thanes were oft condemned to idleness. If the Skaldi are overly fond of wagering, bickering and drinking among themselves, I learned why: When the men are winter-bound in the confines of the great hall, there is naught else to be done.

They have their poetry, of course, and of that, there was an abundance. In addition to the Skaldi war-songs I knew and those homelier tales I learned from the women, I heard endless heroic sagas, humorous stories, epic lays that related tales of warring Gods and Giants, and a new, growing body of verse—the rise of Waldemar Selig.

Of him, many wonderous things were told. It was said that when his mother died in childbirth, a she-wolf was heard scratching at the door of the great hall in his steading, of which his father was the lord. When his thanes opened the door, they saw the wolf, and none dared harm her, for her fur was as white as snow and they knew her for a supernatural creature. She padded through the hall and straight to the infant Waldemar, lying beside him, and he reached for her fearlessly, taking hold of her white fur with his chubby fists and nursing.

They said that when he was still a lad, though half a head again taller than any man in the steading, and fully as broad, his father gave him a handful of gold and bid him to see the land. Thus did Waldemar travel disguised, with only two loyal thanes to accompany him. To all who gave him hospitality, he revealed himself and paid them in gold. Those who shunned him, he challenged, and defeated every one, revealing himself only after the victory.

So did his name and his fame spread across the far-flung Skaldic territories, and he came to be spoken of in terms of awe. He freed an owl caught up in a trapper's lines, who turned into a wizard and gave him a charm that would blunt the edges of his enemies weapons so they would deal him no wound. He met a witch, they said, whose son was of Giant blood; him he slew by discovering that his life was held in a gnarled root-ball the witch kept in her cupboard, which Waldemar threw upon the fire. He threatened to slay the witch as well, but she begged for her life, and gave him a charm to make him proof against poison.

When he came home at last to his own steading, he found his father slain, and the most powerful of his thanes, Lothnir, had wed his sister and laid claim to the steading and the leadership of the tribe. Lothnir met him with an embrace, and offered him a poisoned cup in welcome. Waldemar drank it down and threw the cup upon the snow, where it hissed and gave forth fumes, but he was unharmed. Then Lothnir came upon him at night while he slept, and struck at him with a dagger, but the edges of the blade turned dull and slid from his skin as if from a stiff-cured hide, and Waldemar only sighed in his sleep. In the morning, he challenged Lothnir and slew him with one cast of his spear, so mighty it split his shield and pierced his heart. He was acclaimed as leader, and gave his sister to one of his steadfast companions to wife.

These were the tales of Waldemar Selig, and if I was not naive enough to believe them the literal truth—indeed, I recognized in some the echoes of ancient Hellene tales—the glee with which the Skaldi heard and told them made me uneasy. Of a surety, they reckoned this man a hero; and not, from what I knew, without reason. If no other part of these stories was true, one thing was. He had united the contentious Skaldi tribes in their admiration of him.

Soon enough, though, a new dispute rose out of the cloistered life we led, providing the steading with a new distraction from the tedium of winter. And this dispute, unfortunately, had Joscelin at its center.

The young Skaldi woman Ailsa persisted in her interest in him. True to her word, she had washed and mended his Cassiline garb, presenting it to him with an insinuating smile. Joscelin blushed and smiled, there being naught else, as a slave, he could do. When he did not don it, but continued to wear the woolens given him by Thurid, Ailsa pouted and flounced about the hall, flaunting her displeasure until he put it on to quiet her.

I know Hedwig had a sharp word with the young woman, reminding her that Joscelin was a slave, and Gunter's property. Ailsa, however, was clever enough in her own right, and pointed out that as a D'Angeline lord's son—and it had been Gunter himself who'd put about word that Joscelin was a warrior-prince—he was as much a hostage as a slave, and therefore of a worthy status.

Gunter kept a wary eye on these proceedings and had no great trust of Ailsa, but the prospect of a ransom intrigued him. When he asked Joscelin if his father would pay money for his safe return, Joscelin, all un-witting, promptly answered that he was sure he would, as would the Prefect of the Cassiline Brotherhood, al-though, he added, not unless I accompanied him.

The matter gave Gunter somewhat to mull over, and Ailsa no reason to desist in her pursuit. I had little hope of the prospect of ransom coming to fruition—fierce though they were, Gunter and his thanes weren't likely to succeed in fighting their way across the whole of Camlach to deliver the message, and d'Aiglemort was hardly like to carry it for him—but it sufficed to give me concern.

For the other point in this triangle of dispute was one Evrard the Sharptongued, a surly thane who'd come hon-estly by his nickname and harbored a jealous fondness for Ailsa.

It did not help that she was a terrible flirt, reckoning herself the belle of the steading, and it did not help that Evrard was a homely man, albeit a wealthy one. Evrard's persecution of Joscelin was blatant. Echoing Ailsa's own unsubtle techniques, the thane made a point of putting himself in the Cassiline's path; but instead of a flounce or an incidental brush, he dealt in trips, shoves and taunts. Time and again, Joscelin attempted to step out of his way, only to find himself mocked or sent sprawling. It got so bad that he could not even go to spread new rushes on a clean-swept patch of floor without finding Evrard's boot-heels propped on the spot, while the thane cursed and swatted at him for the inconvenience.

If Joscelin had given no reason for Gunter and his thanes to mistrust him, he had not incited their love either; his effect upon the women of the steading had provoked too much resentment for that. And when they saw the white lines of silent fury etched on his face, they remembered his early days, and taunted him further, hoping to kindle him to wild rebellion for their sport.

Eventually, they succeeded.

It fell on an evening of blizzard, when everyone was confined to the hall and Joscelin came in shivering from the outdoors with an armload of wood for the cookstove. Catching his eye, Ailsa blew him a kiss and made an unsubtle gesture, hoisting her bekirtled breasts at him to show off her considerable cleavage.

Blushing and distracted—he had not wholly lost his Cassiline prurience—Joscelin failed to see when Evrard thrust a booted foot in his path and tripped over it accordingly, measuring his length on the floor of the great hall, scattering kindling as he fell.

Even that, he endured. I was playing the lute quietly at the time, and saw him kneel, head bowed, gathering up the fallen wood. Gunter sat in his chair by the fire, watching idly.

"Look at that," Evrard said contemptuously, flicking Joscelin's braid with one brawny hand. "What man has such hair, and none upon his chin? What man blushes like a maid, and takes no offense at being treated like a carl? No man, I say, but a woman!" It drew a laugh from the thanes, although I saw Hedwig's lips thin from across the room. Joscelin's shoulders stiffened, though he continued to ignore the thane. "He's pretty enough for one, eh?" Evrard continued. "Maybe we ought to check!"

Everyone has their own particular genius; Evrard the Sharptongued's was for goading others, and he saw from Joscelin's tense stillness that he'd landed a bolt that stung. "What do you say?" he asked two of his comrades, bluff and boisterous. "Give me a hand, eh, and we'll skin this wolf-cub of his drabs, see if he's a bitch after all, shall we?"

I stopped playing, and looked at Gunter, hoping he would stop it. Alas, he was bored enough to see it as good sport.

So it was that Evrard the Sharptongued and a handful of thanes set upon Joscelin, intent on wrestling him to the ground and stripping off his clothing. Of their intent, I've no doubt; how it played out was another matter. The moment the first hand closed on his shoulder, Joscelin was on his feet, a stout length of branch in each hand.

It was the first time, I believe, they had occasion to witness him fight in the Cassiline style of combat. The edge of Joscelin's skill had not dulled; if anything, the weeks of hard labor and smothered rage had honed it. He fought with calm, deadly efficiency, the impromptu staves moving in a blur, whirling and warding. Within moments, the rest of the hall was in an uproar, thanes rushing into the fray and staggering back out, clutching bruised limbs and battered skulls.

I understand some little about the two-handed Cassiline fighting style. It is designed to afford the most protection to one's ward, making an armed human shield of the wielder. With no companion to protect, Joscelin grimly protected himself, holding nearly the entire fighting force of Gunter's steading at bay for a goodly amount of time. For his part, Gunter watched it with the same interest he'd shown when they first captured Joscelin. It took some seven or eight men to bring him down at last, muscling with brute force past the reach of his staves and bearing him to the floor, where he continued to thrash as they roared with laughter and tugged at his clothing.

I had drawn breath to shout, though my mind was empty of words, when Gunter did it himself, raising his voice to a bellow of command.

"Enough!" he shouted.

He had mighty lungs; I could swear the very rafters trembled. His thanes grew still, and allowed Joscelin to rise. He gained his feet, disheveled, his clothing askew, fair shivering with rage—but to his credit, he stood his ground, crossing his arms and bowing stiffly in Gunter's direction.

If anything, it was that which saved him. Gunter took on his canny look, drumming thick fingers on the arm of his chair and looking thoughtfully at the infuriated Evrard. "So you claim injury of this man, eh, Sharptongue?"

"Gunter," Evrard said with bitter eagerness, quick to take the bait, "this carl, this *slave* of yours, has made a cuckoo's nest of this steading! Look," he said, pointing an accusatory finger at Ailsa, "look how he woos the very women from under our noses, into his servile embrace!"

"If there is wooing being done," Hedwig called, casting a direful glance at Ailsa, who sniffed, "look to yon vixen, Gunter Arnlaugson!"

It got a greater laugh than Evrard had done. Gunter rested his chin in one hand and gazed at Joscelin. "What do you say of it, D'Angeline?"

If Joscelin had learned anything in Gunter's steading,

he had learned somewhat of how the Skaldi measure such things, and the vocabulary with which they speak of them. He tugged his garments into order and met Gunter's gaze evenly. "My lord, he questions my manhood. I beg your leave to answer him with steel."

"Well, well." Gunter's yellow brows rose. "So we've not drawn the wolf-cub's teeth, eh? Well, Sharptongue, I nearly think he's challenged you to the holmgang. What do you say to that?"

I knew not this word, but Evrard paled at it. "Gunter, he's a housecarl at best! You cannot ask me to fight a slave. I will not stand for the shame of it!"

"Maybe he is a carl, and maybe he is not," Gunter said ambiguously. "Waldemar Selig was taken hostage by the Vandalii, and he fought their champions one by one, until they made him their leader. Do you say Waldemar Selig was a carl?"

"Waldemar Selig was no D'Angeline fop!" Evrard hissed. "Do you mean to make a mockery of me?"

"Oh, I think no man will mock you, for fighting this wolf-cub in the holmgang," Gunter laughed, glancing around the hall. "What do you say, hm?"

Rubbing their bruised parts, the thanes met his query with dour glares. No, I thought, none of them would make mock of the challenge. Gunter grinned, slamming his fist down on the arm of his chair. "So be it, then!" he announced. "Tomorrow, we will have the holmgang!"

If they did not favor Joscelin, there was no great fondness for Evrard the Sharptongued either; young Harald shouted his approval, and cried out the first wager, putting good silver coin on the D'Angeline wolf-cub. It was promptly taken by one of Evrard's backers, and in the general uproar, the matter was approved.

With quiet dignity, Joscelin gathered up his armload of kindling and continued into the kitchen.

The following day dawned clear and fair, and the thanes, grateful for sport, made a holiday of it. I'd no idea, still, what they were about. With great ceremony, a vast hide was brought forth, and a square field trampled flat in the snow. The hide was pinned flat with broad-headed pins, and four hazel-rods set out from the corners, marking an aisle around the hide.

For all that Evrard was not well-loved, he was Skaldi, and the bulk of the thanes supported him, crowding round him, testing the edge of his blade and offering advice and extra shields alike. Joscelin watched the preparations with perplexity, at last approaching Gunter and asking respectfully, "My lord, may I ask the manner of this fighting?"

"What, you the challenger, and not knowing?" Gunter teased him, and laughed at his own jest. "It is the holm-gang, wolf-cub! One sword to each man, and three shields, if you can find those who will lend them. The first to shed the other's blood upon the hide is the victor; and he who sets both feet onto the hazeled field is reckoned to flee, and forfeits the victory." Good-naturedly, he unslung his own sword. "You defended your honor well, D'Angeline, and for that I give you loan of my second-best blade. But for a shield, you must go begging."

Joscelin took the hilt in his hand and stared at it, then raised his gaze to Gunter's. "My lord, my oath forbids me," he said, shaking his head and offering it back, laying the blade across his arm and proferring the hilt. "I am bound to draw my sword only to kill. Give me my daggers and my—" there was no word for vambrace in Skaldic, "—my arm-shields, and I will fight this man."

"It is the holmgang." Gunter clapped him cheerfully on the shoulder. "You should kill him if you can, wolf-cub, or he will surely challenge you again tomorrow or the next day. Anyway, I have a bet on you." He wandered off then, shouting at one of the thanes who had mismeasured the placement of a hazel-rod. I stood shivering under my fur cloak, while Joscelin stared back down at the sword in his hand. He'd not held a blade since we were captured. He looked helplessly up at me.

"He would take your life, Cassiline," I said to him in D'Angeline, struggling to keep my teeth from chattering, "and leave me unprotected. But I cannot tell you what to choose."

Knud, my kind and homely guard, sidled up to us. "Here," he said gruffly, thrusting his own shield at Joscelin. "Take this, boy. There's no honor in forcing a slave to fight unguarded."

"Thank you," Joscelin said to him, bowing awkwardly with sword and shield. Knud nodded brusquely, moving away from him and whistling as though he'd naught to do with it. Joscelin settled the shield in his left hand and hoisted the sword, testing its balance, eyeing it with a kind of awe.

On the far side of the hide, Evrard essayed a few darting jabs and doughty strokes with his own sword, to shouts of laughter and encouragement. Sharptongued he might be, but he was a Skaldi warrior, in the prime of life, and a veteran of a dozen raids. It would be no easy match. His second stood by with a replacement shield, and another close at hand.

"Any last bets, eh?" Gunter shouted, having satisfied himself regarding the pinning of the hide and the placement of the hazel-rods. "We are ready, then! Let the holmgang begin, and he who is challenged may strike the first blow!"

Grinning through clenched teeth, Evrard stepped onto the hide and scraped his feet against it, testing the surface. Joscelin stepped soberly up to meet him. The women of the steading had gathered to watch, and no few of them sighed at the sight of him.

"Take his pretty head off, Sharptongue!" one of the thanes yelled; other laughed.

"He has the first blow," Gunter cautioned Joscelin, who nodded, bracing his shield.

I remember well how the sky overhead was the deep, brilliant blue that the Skaldi sky turns on clear winter days, the ground beneath it eye-blindingly white with snow. Evrard warmed to his attack with a prolonged roar, a rumble that began in the depths of his chest and gathered momentum as he swung his blade, issuing from his mouth in a powerful bellow as he rushed forward. All around, fur-clad Skaldi shouted and gasped; I think Joscelin and I were the only two silent.

Joscelin raised Knud's shield; it took the blow, but shattered beneath it, leaving worthless bits of painted wood. He cast the broken shield aside, as Evrard, still bellowing, made ready to launch a second blow.

I had never seen the Cassiline fight with a sword, save in his practice bouts with Alcuin. He held the hilt in a two-handed grip, slanted across his body, and moved like a dancer. The blade of Gunter's sword whirled, and Evrard's blow was parried; Joscelin spun lightly into the backstroke, and Evrard's shield broke beneath it.

"Shield!" Evrard shouted, scrambling backward. "Shield!" Joscelin allowed him to take his second shield, settling it on his arm, waiting with the hilt of his sword at shoulder-level now, the blade still angled to ward his body.

The Cassiline Brotherhood is, at its most basic level, an elite bodyguard. They are trained to work in tight situations, not battlefields, and do not bear shields; that is why they wear the vambraces. If Joscelin lacked his, he did not need them that day. He feinted once, moved smoothly away from a wild swing of Evrard's, and thrust forward. This time, Evrard's shield stuck on the point of his sword. He dislodged it swiftly, yanking it from the Skaldi's grasp, and snapped the cracked wood in two with one quick stamp of his foot.

"Shield," Evrard whispered, groping blindly.

I do not know what Joscelin was thinking, but I saw his face as he swung, and it was empty of everything but a calm at once serene and blazing. He turned beneath that bright sky, moving his head only slightly to avoid Evrard's blow, and the two-handed stroke he dealt held all of his momentum. The blade flashed like a star, crashing through the third and final shield, and splinters flew like rain.

"No." Evrard's voice trembled; he put up one hand, and took a step backward off the hide, setting one foot in the hazel-rod aisle. I might have pitied him, were it not for the thought of D'Angelines dying under his spear. "Please." Joscelin held the raised sword-blade angled high, and sunlight glinted off it to cast an edge of brightness across his face.

"I will not be foresworn, Skaldi," he said softly, taking care with the words in a strange tongue. "Step off the hide or die."

If it had only been the two of them, I think Evrard the Sharptongued would have retreated. But he was among Skaldi, warriors with whom he'd ridden cheek to jowl, and all were watching; and not only them, but the women. If he feared to lose face by fighting a slave, how much more did he stand to lose by running from one?

I did not like the man, but I will say this for him; he met his death bravely. Forced to choose between the watching Skaldi and the waiting Cassiline, Evrard summoned his courage and loosed it in a final roar, charging, swinging his sword like a berserker. Joscelin parried the blow, pivoting, following through on his own swing, the edge of his blade catching Evrard full across the midriff, angling upward.

It was a death-blow, and no mistake. Evrard crumpled to the hide and lay unmoving, a pool of blood spreading slowly beneath him. For a moment, there was silence; then Gunter pumped one fist skyward and shouted his approval, and his thanes echoed it. It had been a fair fight, and a good one, by their standards. Joscelin stood watching blood seep from Evrard's corpse, his face pale. I remembered then that he had never killed a man before, and I liked him better for taking it hard. He knelt then, laying down his sword and folding his arms, murmuring a Cassiline prayer beneath his breath.

When he was done, he rose and cleaned his blade, walking over to present it hilt-first to Gunter, who took it back with a shrewd look.

"Thank you, my lord, for allowing me to defend my honor," Joscelin said carefully, and bowed. "I am sorry for the death of your thane."

"Sharptongue brought it on himself, eh?" Gunter said cannily, putting a meaty arm about Joscelin's shoulders and giving him a shake. "I tell you, wolf-cub; how is it if you take his place?"

"My lord?" Joscelin shot him an incredulous look.

Gunter grinned. "I'm minded to take a risk on you, D'Angeline! They seem to pay off, hm? If I give you your irons back, does your oath still bind you? Are you still minded to protect and serve; my life with your own, if need be?"

Joscelin swallowed hard; it would be harder, a harder chore and temptation than he'd been given before. He met my eye, and resolve hardened his features. "I have sworn it," he said. "Do you keep my lady Phèdre nó Delaunay safe."

"Good." Gunter gave his shoulders another squeeze and shake. "Give him a cheer, eh?" he cried to his thanes. "The boy's proved himself a man this day!"

They cheered then, and came around, clapping him on the back and boasting or bemoaning the bets they'd laid on the holmgang, while Evrard lay dead and cooling nearby. Someone began to pass around a skin of mead, and the singing began, one of the wits beginning to make a story of it: The epic battle of Evrard the Sharptongued and the D'Angeline slave-boy.

I watched a while longer, still shivering, then went inside with Hedwig and the women to prepare for the boisterous carousing to follow. Whether things had just gotten better or worse, I could not have said.

FORTY-FIVE

It was passing strange to see Joscelin attendant on Gunter in full Cassiline regalia; his mended grey garments, the vambraces on his forearms, daggers at his belt and sword at his back. Allowed a measure of freedom, he resumed the practice of his morning exercises, flowing through the intricate series of movements that formed the basis of the Brotherhood's fighting style.

The Skaldi beheld this oddity with a mix of awe and scorn. Their own combat skills were straightforward and efficient, reliant on might-of-arms, sheer ferocity and the fact that most Skaldi warriors are taught to wield a blade from the time they can lift one.

Their attitude toward Joscelin's discipline was consistent with their feelings toward Terre d'Ange as a whole, and I will admit, it is something I never quite fathomed. It was a strange commingling of derision and yearning, contempt and envy, and I mused upon these things while the steading began to prepare for its journey to the All-thing, for my survival depended largely on my ability to comprehend the Skaldi nature.

Would that I'd had a map in those days, to mark our place in the steading, and the meeting-place decreed by Waldemar Selig. Delaunay had taught me to read maps, of course, and I daresay I could do so as well as any general, but I had no skill to chart my way by the stars, as navigators do. I knew only that we were close to one of the Great Passes through the Camaeline Range, and that we would ride east to the Allthing; seven days' ride, Gunter said, or perhaps eight.

That I would accompany them, he took as a matter of course, although he had still said nothing to me of being a gift for Waldemar Selig. Twenty thanes would go with him to represent the steading, and Hedwig and three others, to speak for the women. They had not the say of the men, but there was an old tale—there is always an old tale, among the Skaldi—of how Brunhild the Doughty wrestled Hobart Longspear and took him two falls out of three, to win the right for women to speak at the Allthing. I suspected Gunter was minded to travel without them, but even he was wary of Hedwig's wrath. I do not know if she wrestled, but of a surety she wielded a mean ladle, and had no compunctions about raising knots on the skull of any man to oppose her.

As for Joscelin, it was simply assumed that he, too, would make the journey, as Gunter's body-servant. Gunter Arnlaugson had a fondness for the trappings of power, and it made him strut not a little to have the Cassiline attendant, with his deft bow and D'Angeline elegance.

So we made ready to go, and I had my first taste of Skaldic augury. An old man, the priest of Odhinn, was fetched to the great hall, and led the steading in procession to a stand of winter-barren oak, their sacred grove. He spread a cloak of stainless white wool upon the snow, and mumbled over bits of rune-carved rods, casting them upon the garment. Three times he did this, then proclaimed in a loud voice that the omens were favorable.

Gunter's thanes cheered at the announcement, banging their short spears on their shields. I, shivering as always in the Skaldic cold, prayed silently to Blessed Elua for protection, and to Naamah, and Kushiel, whose sign I bore. A raven lighted near me on one of the leafless branches, ruffling its feathers and cocking one round, black eye at me. At first it gave me fear, then I remembered that when Elua wandered through the Skaldic hinterlands, the ravens and wolves were his friends, and it heartened me somewhat.

A false spring thaw had broken the ice upon the stream, and we would take our leave in the morning. Much of the remaining day was spent in final preparations, in which I had little part, save to watch the bustle and bundle of it all. Gunter, a seasoned campaigner, had the prudence to retire early, taking me with him. I thought he would leave me be that night, to be all the fresher in the morning, but he tumbled me instead with a soldier's vigorous efficiency, spending himself with a heroic shout and rolling off me to snore within minutes.

I'd taught him better than that, of course, but he had determined in his naively crafty way that it didn't matter with a slave when he was minded to have his simple pleasures; and of a surety, it mattered naught with me, dart-stricken and cursed. I lay awake in the darkness, throbbing with the aftermath of a pleasure I despised, and wondered what the coming fortnight would bring.

We arose with the dawn and made ready to leave. He came beaming into the bed-room with a bundle of woolen undergarments and fur wrappings, a gift for me against the cold. To my surprise, he even knelt to wrap the leggings on himself, showing me how to lace the leather thongs to keep them secure. When he was done, he did not rise immediately, but lifted my skirts and thrust his head beneath them, parting my thighs to bestow a kiss upon my pearl of Naamah, as I had taught him.

"I will not ever forget you," he said gruffly, smoothing my skirts in place and looking upward. "Maybe your gods have cursed you, but Gunter Arnlaugson counts it a blessing, eh?"

The last thing I ever expected of him was tenderness; but lest it undo me, Melisande's diamond glinted at his throat, reminding me of things I had rather forget. I put my hands on his head and kissed him, thanking him for the gift of clothing.

It seemed it was enough. He rose, pleased, and went about his business, seeing to the equipage of the horses.

Well, that is that, I thought. He means to do it.

The journey to the Allthing took a full eight days, and if it was not the hardest thing I have ever endured, I thought it was at the time. I had a horse of my own to ride, for Gunter was mindful of our mounts, and I spent interminable hours hunched in the saddle in my woolens and furs, the reins slack, trusting to my sturdy mount to follow the others. A cold snap followed the false spring, and the snow, softened by warmth, hardened with a brittle crust that made riding slow and bit at the horses' legs. When we made camp at night, the Skaldi tended their mounts first, rubbing their legs down with a salve made of bear-grease.

Our camp was made with rude tents of cured hide that afforded some protection against the cold. Although he made no move to touch me, Gunter kept me with him, and I am not ashamed to say that I huddled against him at night for warmth. We survived on a fare of pottage and dried strips of meat, of which I grew heartily tired.

The lands through which we rode were splendid, though I was hardly minded to appreciate them. The Skaldi seemed not to mind the cold as I did, singing as they rode, breath frosty on the chill air. Hedwig's cheeks were rosy with cold, her eyes sparkling like a girl's.

Even Joscelin fared better than I did; I should have guessed it, for Siovale is mountainous, and he was born to it. Like most men, he was happier in action than still-ness. Someone had given him a bearskin cloak and he seemed warm enough in it, riding with high-spirited élan. They say there is Bodhistani blood in the torrid lineage of Jasmine House, and I thought of my mother for the first time in many years, wondering as I shivered if this aversion to the cold came through her.

On the eighth day, we reached the meeting-place. It was set in a great bowl of a valley, ringed about with forested mountains, with a lake at the bottom, around which the camp was arrayed.

This, I understood, was Waldemar Selig's steading, which he had inherited through birth and right of arms, and built into greatness. Indeed, though still crude by our standards, the great hall was thrice the size of Gun-ter's, and there were two outbuildings near as big. And all around the lake, throughout the whole of the basin, were pitched encampments, bustling with the activity of varying Skaldi tribemen.

We had been seen before we came within a mile of the steading. The forest had seemed virgin and silent to me; but for the occasional snap of a twig bursting in the cold, but Knud, who had much skill at woodcraft, laid a finger alongside his nose and nodded wisely at Gunter. Still, I think even he was taken by surprise when three

Skaldi rose from the snow in front of us, cloaked and hooded in white wolfskin, spears at the ready.

In a flash, Joscelin turned his horse sideways to the Skaldi, making a rolling dismount and fetching up before them on his feet, vambraces crossed, daggers at the ready. It startled them as much as they had us, and they blinked at him, looking momentarily silly beneath the empty white wolf-masks that draped their brows.

Gunter laughed uproariously at the sight, waving his thanes and the rest of us to bide behind him. "So you would defend me, eh, wolf-cub?" he asked. "Well and good, but don't do it at the cost of the Blessed's hospitality!" He nodded cheerfully to the blinking Skaldi. "Hail and well met, brothers. I am Gunter Arnlaugson of the Marsi, summoned to the Allthing."

"What is this fighting thing you have brought to our midst, Gunter Arnlaugson?" their leader asked sourly, annoyed at being caught out. "Surely he is no Marsi, unless the maids of your steading have been straying over the border."

Hedwig sniffed loudly, and one of Waldemar's Skaldi glanced in her direction. Catching sight of me, he dropped his jaw and stared, tugging at his comrade's sleeve.

"What I have brought, I reveal only to Waldemar Selig himself," Gunter said shrewdly. "But they are loyal to me, eh, wolf-cub?"

Joscelin gave him a bland look, bowing and sheathing his daggers. "I protect and serve, my lord."

"You will answer for them, then," the leader said, and shrugged. "We will lead you down."

"Lead on," Gunter said magnanimously.

So it was that we descended to the meeting-place with our escort, who picked their way carefully while our horses plunged through the snow, sinking chest-deep at times.

If the mass of encampments seemed vast from above, on the valley's floor they sprawled endlessly. A veritable city of tents had sprung up to host the Allthing, clamoring with innumerable Skaldi. They do not practice heraldry as we do, but I saw subtle differences marking the tribes in their manner of dress; the cut of their garments, the colors of their woolens, how they laced their furs. This tribe wore bronze disks for adornment, that one bears' teeth rattling on bared chests, and so on.

Undeniably, there was tension amid the gathering of Skaldi tribes. I could feel it as we rode down the broad, snow-packed aisles between encampments, passing from one territory to the next. The thanes watched, honing their weapons, and the women, who numbered fewer, eyed us speculatively. Only children and dogs seemed oblivious to the covert menace, racing shrieking or barking from camp to camp in a sort of endless game of chase, the rules of which are known only to children and dogs.

Everywhere, though, murmurs followed us. Joscelin and I had been oddities among the folk of Gunter's steading, who dwelt a day's ride from the D'Angeline border. Here, we were as misplaced as a pair of Barquiel L'Envers' desert-bred steeds amid a stable of plowhorses.

"You will find lodging there," our guide said to Gunter, pointing to one of the smaller halls, "and you may take two of your thanes. Your headwoman and two others may lodge there, and the rest must remain in camp with your thanes." He pointed to the other lesser hall. "Make camp where you will. You may draw one armload of wood a day from the common pile, and one bowl of porridge at dawn and night, or forage where you will. Your horses you must tend yourselves."

The thanes grumbled, although they'd expected little better, and Gunter looked displeased at being relegated to a lesser hall. "I wish to see Waldemar Selig," he announced. "I have much of import to relate."

"You can tell it at the Allthing, that all might hear," the leader said, unimpressed. "But the Blessed will receive tribute in the evening, if you wish it." He pointed to the horizon. "When the sun is a finger's width above the hill, the doors of the great hall will open."

He has a sense of ceremony, then, I thought; he understands how the hearts of men are ruled. It was an uneasy thought.

"Thank you, brother, for your courtesy," Gunter said softly; there was irony in it, and the leader flinched slightly before it, but nodded and departed. Gunter took Hedwig aside then, speaking to her in a low voice while the rest of us milled about. She looked at me once with sorrow in her eyes, but I saw her lips move in a word of assent. "Well, then!" Gunter said loudly, looking at the rest of us. "You will stay with me, wolf-cub, and you, Brede. For the rest, you will do what is needful, and we will meet here when the sun is two fingers above the hill, eh?"

I was left unsure of my own role, but Hedwig and another woman—Linnea, her name was—both dismounted, and Hedwig beckoned me, a kindness in her face. My homely Knud reached over to take the reins of my mount, and would not meet my eyes.

Gunter and Brede had dismounted as well, and Gunter made an impatient gesture at Joscelin. He remained in the saddle, blue eyes darting, his horse dancing a little at the pressure of his knees. If I was hard-put to guess what was happening, it must be ten times worse for him;

he had come quickly to grasp rudimentary Skaldic, but it was hard to hear, with everyone milling about in the open air. "My lord, my oath is based on my lady's safety," he reminded Gunter.

"She will be safe, wolf-cub," Gunter said quietly. "She goes to a King, and you with her."

Joscelin met my eyes, and I nodded. He dismounted and tossed his reins to one of the thanes.

And then Hedwig took my arm and led me away, and I could only glance over my shoulder, watching as the men went the other way, and people stared and murmured.

In the women's hall, they stared no less, and there was venom in the whispering that followed. I cannot help but be grateful, in my deepest heart, for the kindness of Hedwig and the example she set for the women of Gunter's steading. And though she had neither seniority of place nor age in the women's hall, she commanded it as if she did, bustling others out of her way and securing the bathing room for our usage.

It was warm in there, and humid. Linnea busied herself with filling the tub. Like Knud, she would not meet my eyes. Hedwig stood waiting, and did not look away. I loosed the pin on my fur cloak and let it fall to the floor.

"What did he bid you, Hedwig?" I whispered.

"To polish your beauty so it shone," she said gently.

I undid the bindings on the furs about my legs, then unlaced the kirtle of my woolen gown, stepping out of it. "Did he tell you why?" I asked, shrugging off my underskirts of undyed wool and stepping into the tub.

"Yes," she said, even more gently, then shook her head. "Child, if I could do aught about it, I would. But 'tis a man's world we live in, for all that they give us a voice in it."

I reached out for her hand then, and kissed it as I had the first day. "Hedwig, you have given me kindness, and that is more than I deserve," I murmured. This time, she did not snatch her hand away, but laid it open against my cheek.

"You brought beauty to my steading, child," she said. "Not just in your face, but in your manner. You listened to our songs, and made them beautiful. I thank you for that."

So I had meant something to her, to the folk of the steading, and not just as Gunter's plaything. It made me weep to hear it, though I poured water over my face and showed it not. I could not afford, then, any more pity. I finished my ablutions, and when I had done, Linnea helped me into a gown of combed white wool. Where they had hid it, I do not know. It was a little crumpled from the journey, but the heat of the bathing room eased the creases. I sat quietly then on a stool while Hedwig combed out my hair, teasing out the tangles of eight days of travel until it fell in a wealth of dark, shining curls.

"Mark the sun where it stands," Hedwig said to Linnea. She gave a quick nod, and slipped out of the room.

"Am I ready, then?" I asked.

Hedwig gave one last flounce to my hair. "If Waldemar Selig has seen anything like you," she said with satisfaction, "I will eat my shoes." It was unexpected, and it made me laugh. She smiled then, and hugged me roughly. "I'll miss you, child, I will at that. You and that beautiful lad both."

And then Linnea came scurrying back, an alarmed look on her face. "They're gathering," she gasped, picking up our things.

If I was a gift fit for princes, surely I was fit for barbarian kings. I donned my fur cloak, and left the women's hall with Hedwig and Linnea, ignoring the murmurs.

Outside the great hall, representatives of several steadings had gathered. We stood together, the folk of Gunter's steading, and tried to stand tall in our pride; I daresay even Joscelin and I were no exception in this, and if I had not the height to match the Skaldi, at least I had the pride.

The slanting sun cast a blaze upon the tall wooden doors, bound in brass. The air grew ever more chill as it lowered. Surely enough, when the sun stood a thick finger's breadth above the treeline, round and orange, the great doors swung slowly open.

Waldemar Selig awaited us.

FORTY-SIX

Waldemar Selig may have grasped the uses of ceremony, but when it came to showmanship, Gunter wasn't entirely lacking in a sense of style. With his usual cunning, he allowed the members of other steadings jostling for position to precede us into the great hall. As a result, my initial impression was simply that of a great many Skaldi in one place at one time, most of them male. From my vantage point, I could see little more than a sea of brawny forms, clad in furs and woolens.

Apart from its size, which was impressive, the hall had nothing to distinguish it. In design, it was much like Gunter's hall; there, I found myself thinking, was the kitchen, there the storerooms, and there a handful of private chambers. Still, the hearth was higher than a man, and I was hard-put to imagine the girth of the trees whose timber formed the rafters high overhead.

Representatives from four steadings awaited audience with Waldemar Selig that evening: two of the tribe Marsi, including us, one of the Manni, and one of the Gambrivii. Many of the other tribes, including the powerful Suevi and Vandalii, had arrived earlier.

All, it seemed, had brought tribute; Gunter had not been alone in his thinking, or perhaps it was custom. The Gambrivii steading, a wealthy one, brought gold and much envy. Though I could not see it, I heard from the talk around me. The other Marsi steading, which had a woodcarver of great skill among its number, brought *futhark* rods reckoned no mean gift.

We followed the Manni of Leidolf's steading, who brought a gift of wolf-pelts, a full dozen of them, snow-white and flawless. This drew a low murmur of acclaim, for the white wolves of the north are notoriously hard to hunt, and Selig's totem-animal beside. His hand-picked thanes who wore the wolf-pelt were called the White Brethren; I learned it there, waiting in the great hall, behind the Manni.

If my vision was blocked, my ears were not, and the first I learned of Waldemar Selig was his voice as he greeted those who paid him tribute. I heard it best with the Manni, being closest. He had a deep voice, and even; well-tempered, I would say, which meant he knew how to use it, and he had that good leader's trick of making every man feel singled out for welcome. Then the folk of Leidolf's steading made way, and it was our turn to come before the man who would unify the Skaldi.

Gunter stepped forward, and his thanes ranged about him in a loose formation, alertly attentive. Hedwig and the women would stay behind, as would Joscelin and I; this was a matter for Skaldi warriors first and foremost. Thus it was that my first glimpse of Waldemar Selig came between the shoulders of Gunter's thanes. I could not see his face, only that he was a large man, broad-shouldered, seated in a sizeable wooden chair, like enough to a throne that it might as well have been one.

A D'Angeline would have knelt; the Skaldi did not. Gunter stood straight before his warleader.

"Gunter Arnlaugson of the Marsi, well met, brother," Selig's rich voice said, warm and welcoming. "It raises my heart to see you here, whose steading wins us glory on our western borders."

"We come in good faith to the Allthing," Gunter said expansively, "and to pledge our loyalty to the great Waldemar Selig. I bring you these thanes, whose spears are keen for your enemies, and Hedwig Arildsdottir, who keeps the hearth of the steading alight."

Behind him, Hedwig bobbed nervously; so, the Skaldi were not immune to the trappings of ceremony. I moved, to better catch sight of Waldemar Selig. I saw his eyes, a greenish hazel, and thoughtful. "Be welcome among us, folk of Gunter Arnlaugson's steading."

"We, too, bring tribute, oh Blessed," Gunter said cunningly, stepping back. Hands propelled me forward, and Joscelin beside me. "These two D'Angeline slaves, purchased with gold won by Skaldi blood, I give unto you, warleader."

That Waldemar Selig had heard rumors of our arrival, I do not doubt. There was no startlement in his face at Gunter's words; but at the sight of Joscelin and me, his eyebrows rose. This I saw clearly, for we stood full before him now, no Skaldi to bar our way. I met his curious eyes and curtsied; not the reflexive obeisance of the Night Court, but a different gesture, one that Delaunay had taught me, the salute one makes to a foreign prince.

He knew it, somehow. I saw it, saw it in his measuring gaze. He was handsome enough, for a Skaldi, was Waldemar Selig. Tall and hale, in his middle thirties, with eyes that thought in a strong-featured face. His hair was a tawny brown, bound with a gold fillet, his beard combed to two points, both twined with gold wire. He had a sensual mouth, for a warrior. For a Skaldi. But his eyes, they kept their own counsel.

Joscelin swept his Cassiline bow, which served all purposes for him; it mattered naught. For the moment, it was me upon whom Waldemar Selig's thoughtful gaze rested. I saw his eyes shift to study my own, the left one. He saw the scarlet mote, and noted it.

"You give me two more mouths to feed, Gunter Arnlaugson?" he asked lightly; laughter answered, and Gunter flushed. I understood it. He did not know what we betokened, but he had not mismeasured our value. He had simply not determined whether or not he wished to acknowledge it.

But Gunter was no fool, nor a man to be taken lightly. "She is trained to please kings," he said, and paused. "My lord."

Sovereign words, and ones I uttered so thoughtlessly. Gunter did not. He had said what the Skaldi had not yet voiced. He knew. He had said as much to Joscelin. It was something else, to say it before Skaldi, who had never had a sole ruler. I understood, then, the full import of his gift. He was acknowledging Waldemar Selig a King.

Waldemar Selig shifted in his thronelike chair, still temporizing. He didn't need exotic furs to set him off; his movement shifted the flames in the great hearth behind him, casting light like shadow. "And the lad?"

"A lord's son," Gunter said softly, "and an oath-sworn warrior-priest of the D'Angelines, bound to the girl. He will guard your life as his own, do you but keep her safe. Ask your thanes, if you do not believe."

"Is it so?" Waldemar Selig asked the White Brethren, his thanes with the snowy wolf-pelts draped over their shoulders, wolf-masks over their own heads. They stirred and muttered. His gaze fell back to me, curious and wondering. "Is it so?"

I do not think he expected an answer; Gunter had not told him I spoke their tongue. I curtsied to him again. "It is so, my lord," I said in clear Skaldi, once again ignoring the sound of surprise about me. "Joscelin Verreuil is a member of the Cassiline Brotherhood. Ganelon de la Courcel, who is King of Terre d'Ange, does not stir but two Cassilines attend him."

It was a gamble, truly. But in his demeanor, in his very self-control, I saw a hunger for a more civilized society, to impose upon his people the structures that allowed for a glory not wholly won by iron and blood. Joscelin, following my lead, merely bowed again.

"You speak our tongue," Waldemar Selig said softly, "and trained to serve kings. What does it mean?" Another man might have said it for effect; he meant it. His gaze probed my face. "I would send one such as you, if I wished to tempt my enemy to foolishness. How do you say, then, that you came to be a slave?"

It was not a question I had anticipated, though I should have, knowing as much as I did of him. There is a time to dissemble, and a time to tell the truth. Looking at his eyes, I gauged it was the latter. "My lord," I said, "I knew too much."

My whole history lay naked in those words, for one who knew to read it. If Waldemar Selig did not, still he recognized the language in which it was written. He nodded once, as much to himself as to me. "That may happen," he remarked, "if one is trained to serve kings." The great hall stirred at that; he had acknowledged Gunter's words, and my own, for truth. But no one disagreed.

"And what of you?" he asked, then, switching his focus suddenly to Joscelin. "How do you come before me?"

If I had had reason to doubt the Cassiline's quickness of wit—as opposed to his propensity for swift belligerence—I could only praise him now. Joscelin turned to me and spoke in D'Angeline. "Tell him that I am oathsworn to guard your life," he said. "Tell him that it is a matter of honor."

I turned back to Waldemar Selig, who held up one hand. "I . . . speak a little . . . of your tongue," he said haltingly in D'Angeline. "You must speak . . . a little of mine, to hear this." He switched then to near-fluent Caerdicci. "Do you speak the scholar's tongue, D'Angeline? I understand what you say."

Joscelin bowed, unable to keep his eyes from widening. "Yes, my lord," he replied in Caerdicci. "It is as Gunter Arnlaugson has said."

"So." Waldemar Selig considered Joscelin. "And do you swear as Gunter Arnlaugson has said, to guard my life as your own, Joss-lin Ver-ai?"

He had marked Joscelin's name when I spoke it, and remembered; he spoke somewhat of our tongue—albeit with a barbaric accent—and Caerdicci in the bargain. The more I saw of this man, the more I feared him. Gonzago de Escabares had been right; Waldemar Selig was dangerous.

Joscelin had recovered his composure and his face was cool and unreadable, a mask of Cassiline discipline. Of those in the hall, only Gunter and his thanes, who stood behind us now, knew his skill. He stood scant yards from the Skaldi leader, fully armed and on his feet. In three moves, I thought, he could kill Waldemar Selig; and of a surety, the tense unity that held the Skaldi at the Allthing would not survive Selig's death. Fractured and leaderless, the Skaldi would be what they had always been, a threat to our borders, but one that could be pushed back by a concerted effort.

And he would be foresworn, and both of us slain or worse. Cassiel had chosen damnation to remain at Elua's side; Joscelin would do no less.

"I swear it," he said in Caerdicci, "on the safety of my lady Phèdre nó Delaunay."

"Fay-dra," mused Waldemar Selig, glancing at me. I curtsied, conscious of the weight of his gaze. "That is how you are called?"

"Yes, my lord."

"Fay-dra, you will teach me D'Angeline. I wish to learn more." His glance moved back to Joscelin. "Josslin, we will see what kind of warrior you are." Selig nodded to one of the White Brethren, making an oblique gesture with two fingers.

With a battle-cry, the thane sprang at his leader, short spear extended for a killing thrust. Waldemar Selig sat unmoving. It may have been staged; I don't know. But I believed then and I believe now that the thane's attack was in earnest. From his own men, he commanded that much obedience. Even in this, they would obey.

I could see Gunter's smug grin as Joscelin went into action. Smooth as oiled silk, he slid himself between Selig and the thane, twin daggers rising to catch the shaft of the spear with its pointed head an inch shy of his heart. With a subtle twist of shoulders and wrists, he turned its course harmlessly, and in the same motion landed a level, well-planted kick to the abdomen that sent the White Brother staggering backward, his breath leaving him with a huff.

With a brief bow, Joscelin presented the spear to Waldemar Selig. To the accompaniment of snickers, the defeated thane scowled and adjusted his pelt, taking his place with his brethren once more.

"So." The Skaldi leader's eyes glinted with amusement. He rose, holding the spear, and placed a comradely arm about Gunter's shoulders. "You have given me a mighty gift, Gunter Arnlaugson!" he announced loudly.

Waldemar Selig had given his approval, and the Skaldi cheered. Looking about the great hall, however, I made no mistake. They were cheering Selig and Selig alone; there was no welcome in their voice for two D'Angeline slaves. Except for the members of Gunter's steading, gazing at their faces I saw naught to thaw my heart. Among the women, there was only envy and hatred. Among the men, hatred and hunger for me, hatred alone for Joscelin.

If I had ever doubted it, I knew it now. We were among the enemy.

That night, Selig feasted the assembled leaders of the steadings, and you may be sure, Gunter sat in close proximity to the warleader. It was a Skaldi gathering, and the mead flowed freely; there was song and boasting and politicking alike. I was there, for Waldemar Selig ordered me to attend that night, pouring mead for Skaldi chieftains from a heavy earthenware jug. I cannot tell how many times I had to refill my jug.

I could count, though, the number of times I refilled Selig's tankard, for they were few. The rest of them got roaring-drunk, no question, and he allowed it, but Waldemar Selig remained sober. I watched his calculating eyes, and saw how he gauged the manner of his chieftains. They had presented themselves to him on their best behavior, and he had gauged them then; now they let their true natures show, and he watched them all the closer for it.

It gave me the shivers.

I noted too, how his gaze followed me, and sensed rather than saw his appreciation for the niceties of

D'Angeline service: the linen cloth I held beneath the jug, the line of the arm as one pours, the proper angle of approach, the thousand and one details one is taught in the Night Court with which to serve with unobtrusive grace. It mattered naught to the other Skaldi, who held out their tankards at will and didn't care if the contents slopped over the sides, but it mattered to Waldemar Selig.

He had Joscelin attend, too, in the Cassiline manner; three paces behind his left shoulder, hands crossed at ease on his hilts. He must have asked what was proper. Clever, but not foolish; I could see that Waldemar Selig was aware of his every move, and that two of the White Brethren kept a careful watch on Joscelin. He hungers for our customs, I thought. He would set himself up as a King, but this nation of brawling drunkards is not fit for the sort of kingdom he wishes to rule. I thought of my homeland, and my blood ran cold.

There was no talk, that night, of why they were assembled; only boasting, and tales of what they had done already. Two of the leaders, a Suevi and a Gambrivii, fell to quarreling over an ancient blood-feud, and it wasn't long before their swords were out. Drunken and excited, the Skaldi cleared way for the fight. I saw Gunter among them, bawling out a wager which was quickly accepted.

It was the sound of Waldemar Selig's tankard being slammed onto the table that caught their attention and commanded silence. "Are you men," asked the Skaldi warleader into the abashed stillness, his hazel eyes glinting, "or dogs, to quarrel over a dry bone? I have a rule, in my household. Any man who bears a grudge, let him bring it to me. And any man who would settle it by might of arms, let him take up his cause against me. Is that your wish? You, Lars Hognison? You, Erling the

Quick?" They fell to shuffling and muttering, for all the world like two boys caught quarreling. "No? Good, then. Make peace among you, and behave yourselves as brethren ought."

Skaldi are easily moved to emotion. The two men, who moments before were like to tear out one another's throats, fell on each other's shoulders and embraced like brothers.

"Well done," Waldemar Selig said softly, levering himself to his feet, using his height and the breadth of his shoulders to dominate the hall. "You are here," he told them, "because you have learned to lead, among your own folk. If you would truly be leaders of men, you must learn to unite, and not to divide. Divided, we are but so many dog packs, squabbling in the kennel-yard. United, we are a mighty people!"

They cheered him, then, but Waldemar Selig was too canny to rest on his laurels. "You," he said, pointing at Gunter. "Gunter Arnlaugson of the Marsi. Did I hear you cry out a wager?"

Gunter had the sense to look embarrassed. "It was the heat of the moment, Blessed," he protested. "Surely you have done as much, to warm a long winter's cold."

"If a man does wager on a dogfight," Waldemar Selig said calmly, "how does his hunting pack fare come spring?" He sat down and thrust up the right sleeve of his jerkin, baring one mighty arm. "A wager is a challenge, Gunter Arnlaugson, and you are a guest in my hall. What will you wager, then? That stone which sparkles so prettily about your neck? A D'Angeline trifle, if I make no mistake."

Caught out unwitting, Gunter glanced at me. I could not help but pity him; Melisande's diamond was ill luck for anyone. "Do you admire it?" he asked brashly, lifting it from about his neck and holding it out to Selig. "Then it is yours!"

"Ah, no." Waldemar Selig smiled. "I would win it as honestly as your respect, Gunter Arnlaugson. Come, if you would wager, try your luck against my arm." He beckoned, and the muscles in his arm shifted like boulders beneath the skin. Deprived of a fight, the Skaldi applauded the prospect of a test of strength. Clever Selig, I thought, to catch them out with shame, then shame them with strength. They didn't know what he was about, but I did.

Making the best of a bad situation, Gunter clasped his hands above his head and shook them, flashing the diamond as he stepped up to the table. Skaldi admire courage, and they rewarded his with shouts of approval. Waldemar Selig merely gave a wolfish grin. They sat down then across from each other, and Gunter laid the diamond on the table before they gripped hands and leaned into it, pitting sheer force against one another.

It was not a pretty sight, that much I will say. As I had cause to know, Gunter Arnlaugson was a powerful man, and no easy match, even for one of Selig's stature. Their faces reddened and the tendons stood out on their necks, while their arms bulged and corded with effort. Eventually, though, it had to happen. Gunter's wrist bent back slowly, while Waldemar Selig's curved over the top of it; inch by inch, Gunter's arm was forced to the table, until at last it struck wood.

Selig's White Brethren cheered the loudest, but they were not alone in it. Even Gunter had the grace to grin, wringing his hand. You are well shed of that thing, I thought, as he picked up Melisande's diamond and presented it to Waldemar Selig.

I thought too soon.

Waldemar Selig dangled the diamond on its cord from

one finger. "Never let it be said," he remarked to the Skaldi, "that we are cruel masters, who fear to give the D'Angelines their due, their baubles and trinkets. Let them keep what they will! Who fears a race trained to serve?" He raised his voice to a shout. "Fay-dra!"

Trembling, I set down my pitcher and approached, sinking without thought to kneel before him. I could feel the heat coming off him without looking. "My lord," I murmured.

The cord settled over my head, Melisande's diamond returning to rest between my breasts. "See," Waldemar Selig said, "how the D'Angeline kneels, to receive with gratitude what is hers by right from my own hand. See it and mark it, for it is an omen!" He grasped the hair atop my head then, raising it for all to look on my face, and they cheered. "Look well at our future!"

Gunter had given me to him as a symbol, and he was clever enough to use me as such. The Skaldi shouted and pounded their mugs, while Waldemar Selig smiled at their approval. I understood, then, the measure of his ruthlessness. What he hungered for, he would grasp, though he destroyed it in the process. Beneath his hand, I trembled like a leaf.

And inevitably, damnably, in the wake of this casual humiliation, came desire. If Waldemar Selig had chosen to take me in front of four dozen assembled Skaldic chieftains, I would have cried out encouragement. I knew it, and knowing it, wept, despising what I was.

Behind it all, Joscelin's face swam in my vision, a clear and impassive D'Angeline noble's profile, staring straight ahead. I fixed my eyes upon it and prayed.

FORTY-SEVEN

On the following day, the Allthing met.

Waldemar Selig did not entertain me that night, to my silent relief. I was accorded a pallet among the serving-women of the great hall, which I took to with gratitude, ignoring their sullen stares. Selig was not done with me—of that, I had no illusions—but for the moment I was content to curl up on straw and ticking, letting oblivion claim me.

A sober mood prevailed after the excesses of the night. I do not know how Joscelin fared, but we found ourselves cast together, herded into a small storeroom off the great hall while the Allthing met and the house-carls slipped about cautiously, attending to them. Each leader of a steading was allowed to bring two thanes, and his headwoman; that much, I had gathered. To my dismay, the room which held us muted sound, so that neither Joscelin nor I could hear clearly what was spoken.

If Blessed Elua accorded us any mercy, it was the fact that we were alone together in the rough-timbered store-room. The White Brethren had bolted the door against us. Whatever symbol Waldemar Selig would make of his D'Angeline slaves, we would play no part at the Allthing. What would be spoken there was not for barbarian ears to hear; the meeting was for Skaldi alone.

I listened to the rumble and murmur of voices, echoing in the vaulted rafters. Joscelin paced about our small enclosure, testing the door, examining stored grains and ale with disgust until determining that there was no way out and naught of use to be found.

"How bad was it?" he asked me eventually, leaning against a barrel and keeping his voice low.

"Be quiet," I whispered, concentrating. It was no good. I could almost hear, but not quite. One word in ten was not enough; understanding evaded me. I shot Joscelin a fierce glance, then checked, looking from him to the barrel to the rafters. I remembered him in the street with the Eglantine tumblers, and how Hyacinthe and I had stood atop a barrel to watch. "Joscelin!" Urgency pervaded my voice; I was already clambering atop a barrel. "Get up here, and help me!"

"You're mad," he said uncertainly, but he was already rolling another barrel into place. I stood on my toes, reaching overhead and gauging the height.

"They are planning somewhat," I said calmly. "If we manage to escape and reach Ysandre de la Courcel, do you wish to tell her the Skaldi have some dire plan . . . but, so sorry, we couldn't hear it? Hoist that up, we need to get higher."

He did it, protesting all the while. It took some time, for they were heavy. I kept my gaze upon the rafters.

"Do you remember the tumblers?" I asked him when the barrels were in place, kneeling on the topmost. "I want you to lift me onto your shoulders, and boost me to the rafter. I'll be able to hear, then."

He swallowed at that, hard, gazing up at me from the second tier of barrels. "Phèdre," he said gently. "You can't."

"Yes," I said steadily, "I can. What I *can't* do is lift you. This is what Delaunay trained me for, Joscelin. Let me do it." I held out my hand to him.

He cursed, then, with unwonted Siovalese fluency, took my hand and scrambled up to stand beside me. "Take my coat, at least," he muttered, shrugging out of it and forcing my arms into the sleeveless grey mandilion. "Those rafters must be filthy; there's no need to tell them where you've been." Once I had it on, he bent one knee for me to mount to his shoulders.

I did it quickly, not looking down at the floor of the storeroom. It was a long way down, and though the barrels were steady as a rock, it was a precious small space on which to stand. For all of that, we might have been partners of long training; he bowed his head as I steadied myself, gripping my ankles as I rose to stand upon his shoulders.

The rafter was a few inches shy of my fingertips.

"Lift my feet," I whispered down to him. I felt his hands, shifting carefully, as he planted his legs under him, and his fingers gripped my ankles until the bones fairly squeaked under the pressure. I rose steadily as his arms extended, into the open air, until I could wrap my hands about the great beam and swing myself up.

They were mighty timbers, that had built Waldemar Selig's hall. Once I had myself in place, I peered down, and Joscelin seemed far below me atop our pyramid of barrels, his upturned face pale and nervous.

So be it; I was there. Lying flat on my stomach—the beams were that broad—I drew myself forward, rough splinters under my nails reminding me, with an odd nostalgia, of Childric d'Essoms' whipping-cross. A layer of grime and soot covered the rafter, and I was grateful that Joscelin had given me his coat. Inch by slow torturous inch I progressed, until I could peer over the partition that divided our storeroom from the vast confines of the great hall. This I did, letting my sable locks fall over my face to shadow my fair skin lest anyone glance upward.

By all accounts, I should have been terrified—and I was, truly. But mingled with the terror was a strange exhilaration, born of defiance and the knowledge that, no matter how futile the outcome might be, I was at last pitting my skills against our enemies. It was like what I had felt betimes with clients, but a thousand times stronger.

The great hall was full to bursting, and it was cursedly warm atop the rafter with the heat of the fire and so many bodies. Some had taken seats where they could, but most were standing, including Waldemar Selig, who stood taller than any man there. I had not missed much, it seemed. A priest of Odhinn had asked the blessing of the All-Father and the Aesir, and the assembled Skaldic chieftains and thanes swore loyalty to Selig, one by one; they were just finishing, when I began to listen.

Selig waited for them to quiet, his hands on his hips. A half-dozen of the White Brethren surrounded him, making a dark spot in a pool of white, seen from above.

"When our forefathers met at the Allthing," he began, pitching his voice to carry, "it was to settle disputes among the tribes, to make trade and marriage perhaps, to meet old enemies in the holmgang, or to affirm the borders of the territories each had carved out for himself. That is not why we meet." He turned slowly, surveying them all; I could see by their rapt attention that he held them in his palm. "We are a nation of warriors, the fiercest the world has known. Caerdicci nursemaids tell their children to hush, lest the Skaldi take them. And yet the world ignores us, safe in the knowledge that our savagery is contained within our borders, turned in upon itself, that while nations rise and fall, great palaces are built and crumble, books are written, roads are built and ships are sailed, the Skaldi snarl and bite and kill each other, and make songs about it."

That drew a grumble of protest; he'd cut to the heart of sacred Skaldi tradition. I could see Selig unmoving, though he raised his voice a notch. "It is a true thing I speak! Across our border, in Terre d'Ange, the lordlings dress in silk from Ch'in and eat pheasant from silver plates in halls of Caerdicci marble, while we brawl in our wooden halls, dressed in hides and gnaw meat from the bone!"

" 'Tis the marrow that's sweetest, Selig!" some wag cried; from my perch, I saw him receive a sharp elbow to the ribs. Waldemar Selig ignored him.

"In the name of the All-Father," he continued, "we are better than that! Do you seek glory, my brothers? Think on it. What glory is there in slaying one another? We must take our place in this world, and make a name for ourselves; no mere bogeymen to scare children, but a name such as the armies of Tiberium won long ago, to be spoken in fear and reverence across the face of a thousand lands! No more will the Skaldi be fighting dogs on a chain, bought for hire to safeguard the passage of Caerdicci or D'Angeline caravans, but rulers at whose passage the sons and daughters of conquered nations will kneel and clutch their forelocks in respect!"

He had won them over; I shuddered at the resounding cheer, gazing down at their flushed faces. Even the women, I saw with sorrow, shouted approval. Even kind Hedwig, whose eyes shone at Selig's words, imagining herself, no doubt, mistress of a marble hall, swathed in silks and velvet.

I cannot blame them, in truth, for desiring. To glory in the splendor of one's homeland is a magnificent thing. But they were like children, who have only just begun to grasp the idea of a thing. And like children, they had no notion of laboring to create, but only of having . . . and no thought given to the cost, to others, of taking it.

One man, some forty years of age, fully as broad through the shoulder though not so tall as Waldemar Selig, spoke up. I did not know who he was then, but I learned it later: Kolbjorn of the Manni, whose thanes had been foremost in gathering information to the south. "How do you propose we achieve this, Selig?" he asked pragmatically. "This I know, the city-states of Caerdicca Unitas are on guard against us and have made treaties to defend against invasion. There are watch-towers and garrisons from Milazza to La Serenissima, and swift roads all the way south. Tiberium may no longer command an empire, but she can still summon five thousand foot-soldiers at a courier's word."

"We showed our hand too soon to the Caerdicci," Selig said calmly; I remembered Gonzago de Escabares' story, of how King Waldemar of Skaldia had bid for the Duke of Milazza's daughter's hand. I hadn't fully credited it, till now. Selig must have learned somewhat from that, and grown more circumspect. "But they are political creatures, the Caerdicci. It is the only way they retain a shadow of the glory that was Tiberium. Once we have established ourselves, they will treat with us, and where might cannot prevail, cunning will."

He was right, of course; any alliance among the city-states would be fractious at best. They would stand united against a common enemy, but if there was political advantage to gain . . . well, I could guess how quickly they would outbid each other, to secure the goodwill of a new potentate.

Which left Terre d'Ange, my beloved homeland.

"Then where and how do we prevail?" Kolbjorn asked, a frown in his voice. "The D'Angelines hold their passes, and we have never won through in great numbers."

In the crowd, I could see Gunter shifting about with eagerness. Waldemar Selig withdrew a letter from his belt and tapped it against his palm. "The D'Angeline King is weak and dying," he said with satisfaction, "and has no heir but a mere woman to succeed him, and her not even wed. This offer is from the D'Angeline Duke of Day-gla-mort, whom men call Kilberhaar. He would be King, with our aid. Will you hear his offer?"

They cried out assent, and he read it slowly, translating from Caerdicci, in which it was written, to Skaldic. I will not repeat it verbatim, save to say that it made the blood run cold in my veins. It is enough to summarize. The gist of Isidore d'Aiglemort's plan was this: The bulk of the Skaldi would be allowed through the two southerly Great Passes, to lure the Royal Army into action and engage them in lower Camlach. A smaller detail of Skaldi, under the command of Waldemar Selig, would assail the northernmost pass, ostensibly to confront d'Aiglemort and the Allies of Camlach, who would be waiting for them. They would parley and hammer out terms of peace. The Skaldi would withdraw, in exchange for a beneficial trade agreement, the coastal flatlands lying north of Azzalle and the acknowledged sovereignty of Waldemar Selig as King of Skaldia.

The price of the peace, for Terre d'Ange, would be Isidore d'Aiglemort on the throne. And if Ganelon de la Courcel would not agree to it, Isidore d'Aiglemort wrote privately, they would fall upon the Royal Army from behind and eradicate it, taking the throne by force.

Lying atop my rafter, I wept in horror, that any D'Angeline could so betray his country, and I wept in fury, for the sheer, arrogant idiocy of it. Below me, Waldemar Selig folded the letter and tapped it against his palm once more, grinning at his thanes. "It is an interesting offer," he said, "and one that would greatly increase our status. But I have a better idea!" He waved the letter in the air. "This Kilberhaar, he is a cunning man and a bold fighter, but he does not know the Skaldi if he thinks we are fool enough to settle for a piece, when the whole is there for the taking! If you agree, I will answer this man, and say we will take his offer and he may lay his plots. Enough men will we send to the southern passes that he thinks we have done so; and we will take ground and hold it, then retreat, and draw the D'Angelines into the passes, which can be held only by a handful, so they never need guess our true numbers." He shoved the letter back into his belt and his hands sketched the movements in the air. "Then we will come in numbers through the northern pass, and we will fall upon Kilberhaar when he thinks to make the false parley! And it shall be *we* who sweep down upon the rearguard of the D'Angeline army and trap them against the mountains, and *we* who prevail!"

They were all on their feet then, roaring approval, so that the hall thundered with it. I clung to the rafter and shuddered. Waldemar Selig waited for them to settle.

"What do you say?" he asked, when it was quiet enough to make himself heard. "Shall we do it?"

There was no question of it; they were for it, the men shouting and stamping, rattling their swords. I saw here or there, among the women, quieter faces as they began to think of the reality of war and the numbers who would be killed. Hedwig was among them, I was glad to see. Still, none spoke against it. For the part of the men, they were all for setting out the next day. It took some doing for Selig to calm them.

"We cannot fight this war in winter," he said rationally, once they would listen. "I have read books." He paused to let that sink in and impress them; few Skaldi had seen a book, and most knew only *futhark* if any written tongue at all, simple symbols carved on wood and stone. "I have read books by the greatest tacticians of Hellas and Tiberium. One thing all agree upon, that an army travels on its belly. If we are to hold the passes, we cannot do it starving and freezing, on mounts we cannot feed. It must wait until summer, when the hunting is rich and the crops coming, with good grazing and no need to build the fires high at night. Let every man go forth from the Allthing and prepare for this day. Let the forges begin to work, that every man be keenly armed. Let every woman count the household stores, and make plans to supply our campaign. Do you say it shall be so? Then we will vote upon it."

I was surprised that they did this, after the loud acclaim, but they did. Selig was clever; King some had named him and he would even call himself, but he was yet uncrowned. Needless to say, the vote passed without dissent.

"If you have quarrels among yourselves," he said then, softly, "let it be a matter of pride to settle them now. We must go into this conflict as brethren all, a glorious army. We do not go as squabbling tribesmen. Who has a case that would be heard before the Allthing?" There was some shuffling; there were quarrels, no doubt. Anyone could see it. Waldemar Selig's gaze swept the crowd. "You, Mottul of the Vandalii? It is said Halvard killed your sister-son. Do you accuse him?"

These were Skaldic matters, and of no concern to me; by the pricking of the hair on the back of my neck, I knew it was time to withdraw. I began to wriggle backward along the rafter, using my knees and elbows as best I could. It was a great deal more difficult than going forward, and my skirts encumbered my progress. Melisande's diamond hung free from about my throat, bumping against the wood; I was terrified that the glitter of it would give me away. It seemed an eternity before I was safely above the storeroom, and peered over the edge to see Joscelin tracking my progress with worried eyes.

"Get *down*!" he hissed at me, holding up his arms. Now that I was out of sight of the Skaldi, the shock of what I'd witnessed struck me, and I found myself trembling. Still, there was nothing else for it. I clung to the rafter by my fingertips, lowering my body until I felt Joscelin's hands graze my ankles. "Let go," he whispered, and I did, falling to slide through his grasp until his hands caught me hard about the waist, and he set me down carefully on the barrel.

We stood there like that for a moment, pressed close with nowhere else to stand, and I shuddered in his arms, face against the warmth of his chest. If anyone had told me a year ago that my sole comfort in life would be a Cassiline Brother, I would have laughed. I pulled back and looked up at him. "They mean to invade," I whispered. "They mean to have it all, and that cursed d'Aiglemort's given them a way to do it. Joscelin, this goes far beyond border raids. We have to find a way to warn them."

"We will." He said it quietly, but with all the implacable strength of a Cassiline vow. With unaccustomed gentleness, he took my face in his hands and brushed away the traces of my tears. "I swear to you, Phèdre, I'll get us out of here."

Because I needed to, I believed him and took strength from it. The sounds of the Allthing rumbled and quieted on the far side of the wall. "The barrels," I said, and drew hastily away to clamber down a tier. Joscelin followed quickly, hoisting down the topmost barrel. We worked in tandem, urgent and silent, he doing the heavy lifting while I rolled barrel after barrel along its rim back to an approximation of its original place.

Our fear, while prudent, proved needless; we finished, and still the Allthing continued, no one coming for us. I gave Joscelin back his grey coat. He sat on his heels, working out the worst of the dirt and soot, while I scrubbed at the grime ground into my sleeves and skirts. I stole glances at him while I worked, taking solace in the haughty D'Angeline beauty I had first despised in him, the proud, provincial features and his clear, summer-blue eyes.

He must have been thinking along the same lines, for after a time he looked up at me. "You know, when I was assigned to attend you," he said softly, "I thought it was a punishment of some sort. I thought you were nothing but an expensive plaything for the worst of the scions of the Misguided."

"I was," I murmured bitterly. I touched Melisande's diamond. "I still am. Were I not, we wouldn't be here, and Delaunay and Alcuin would still be alive."

Joscelin shook his head. "If Melisande had one plan, she had others; I've no doubt she could have gotten the information elsewhere. It fell on you, that's all."

"And I let it. And Waldemar Selig will do the same." I leaned back against a barrel, closing my eyes. "And Elua help me, I'll welcome it when he does. While I eat my heart out with anguish, I'll prove to him a thousand times over exactly how debauched and yielding a D'Angeline whore can be, and I'll thank him for it when he's done."

I opened my eyes to see Joscelin blanch; he was enough of a Cassiline to look as sick as I felt at it. But his voice, when he spoke, was fierce. "Then do it," he said, "and live! And when he crosses onto D'Angeline soil and I'm there to meet him and plant ten inches of steel in his guts, I'll thank *him* for the pleasure of it."

It made me laugh; I don't know why, except for the absurdity of his oath, given our present circumstances. I can't explain it to one who has never been a captive. Sometimes absurdity is the only thing that keeps one sane. After a moment, Joscelin saw the humor of it and smiled wryly.

And then the bolt of the storeroom door was thrown back, and the White Brethren came for us. The Allthing was ended, and the Skaldi were ready to prepare for war.

FORTY-EIGHT

The news rioted through the Skaldi encampment and the fires burned long into the night, casting a flickering orange glow on the snow-covered mountainsides, while shouted war-songs and the clash of spears beaten on shields rose up to challenge the distant stars.

Waldemar Selig not only let them have their celebration, but opened the doors of his storerooms. Barrel after barrel of mead was rolled out—indeed, Joscelin and I would have had naught to stand on by morning—and hauled to distant tents by thanes staggering under the weight. I've no doubt Selig had planned for this day and laid provisions in store.

In the great hall, the celebrants were hand-picked among those leaders whom Selig judged key to his plans; he was careful, too, to include the steading's head-women among them. Gunter, grinning like a boy, was among those chosen. He had made his mark with his gift of D'Angeline slaves, and his partnership with Kilber-haar—d'Aiglemort—was useful. He was not the only Skaldi chieftain to have raided for Kilberhaar's gold, but he was the most successful at it.

Hedwig was there, and excitement still flushed her cheeks, but there was a shadow on her too, that touched her when she glanced in my direction. For her kindness, I was grateful, but she had no words to speak against the invasion of my country, and that I could not forgive.

There was no hiding the news from us, and Selig made no effort to do so, secure in the belief that we had no knowledge of the details of his plan. He kept a close watch on Joscelin, who stood at his guard-position without expression, only his pallor betraying his emotions. The White Brethren watched him closely too, and I had the impression that they were prepared to run him through if he so much as twitched.

Me, Selig kept near him, as if I were a trophy marking a victory already won. It made an impact on the Skaldi, which doubtless he intended. He was not crudely possessive, as Gunter had been, but he let it be known in a dozen subtle ways that I was under his ownership; stroking my hair as one would pet a dog, or feeding me choice tidbits from his plate and suchlike.

I endured it, having no choice. In truth, I would sooner have been tossed over Gunter's shoulder again. Better simple ravishment than this calculating dominion, which eroded my will and filled me with fear. Always in my mind was the knowledge of the Skaldi invasion plan. I guessed well that Selig would have killed me if he discovered I knew it. It amused him to assume a degree of risk in probing the D'Angeline character; the Cassiline's armed presence at his back was proof of that. Personal risk was one thing; his legend was built upon it. But he was a leader who thought. He would do what was necessary to eliminate the risk of having his entire plan betrayed.

It looked as though the reveling would continue far into the night, and I began to relax somewhat against my most immediate fears, thinking Selig would again dismiss me to the care of the serving-women.

This time, I was wrong.

He rose after the third round of songs, bidding a good

night to his people, and ordering them stay and be welcome as long as they wished. Taking his leave, he paused to speak to two of the White Brethren. "Bring her to my room," he murmured, nodding in my direction.

Fear filled me like water in a drowning man's lungs.

I remained in the great hall, serving mead as I had been bidden. They came for me soon, two of them, taking my arms to lead me from the hall. The Skaldi bawled out cheerful obscenities and banged their mugs. I could hear Gunter's voice among them, roaring a colorful litany of my skills, making the most of his loss.

I am Phèdre nó Delaunay, I thought, born of the Night Court proper, trained by the greatest living courtesan of Terre d'Ange, dedicated to the service of Naamah. I will not go crawling to this barbarian king like a slave.

So it was that I walked from the hall with my head high, between my guards. What the Skaldi saw in my face, I do not know, but the jests fell silent as I passed.

And then they brought me to Waldemar Selig.

One of the White Brethren scratched at the door in a particular sequence. They have a code among them, I learned later; I committed this one to memory. Selig opened the door, and they left me to him.

I don't know what I had expected. A room like Gunter's, I suppose, only larger, which it was. There the resemblance ended. Waldemar Selig's room held a hearth and a great bed, the headboard elaborately carved with a scene I recognized from one of the sagas. It held a great deal else, beside: books, whole shelves full of them, and cubbies for scrolls. A steel breastplate and helmet on a stand, which I later discovered was in part the source for the legend that he was proof against arms. Most Skaldi warriors fight unarmored; Selig had won his in a bout against some tribal champion who'd fought in the arenas of Tiberium. There was a map pinned to the wall, inked on well-scraped hide, which had the Skaldic territories as its center and showed the borders of Caerdicca Unitas and Terre d'Ange in excellent detail. A desk, oft-used by the look of it, with other maps and correspondence strewn about.

Waldemar Selig stood in the center of his room, tall and imposing, watching me look about. There was a book on the corner of his vast desk, worn and much-mended. I picked it up. It was Tullus Sextus' *Life of Cinhil Ru*.

"He is a great hero to me," Selig said quietly. "A model of how one should lead a people, do you not think?"

I set the book down; my hand was trembling. "He united his people to save his land from conquest, my lord," I replied softly. "I see no invaders here."

It took him aback a little. His color rose slightly. No one, I thought, answered back to Waldemar Selig, and I was in the least position of all to do it. But if ever I had a gift, it was for knowing how to engage my patrons, and I knew, in my bones, that Selig would not be long engaged by mere subservience.

"You read Caerdicci then," he said, turning the subject. He came over to stand beside me, pointing out other books on the shelves. "Have you read this? It is one of my favorites." It was Lavinia Celeres' tale of the wandering hero Astinax; I told him I had. "You know, there are no books in Skaldic," he mused. "We've not even a written tongue to our name."

"There are some, my lord." I felt like a child next to him; my head came no higher than the pit of his arm. "Didimus Pontus at the University of Tiberium translated Skaldic phonetically into the Caerdicci alphabet some forty years ago," I added.

I felt his gaze from above. "Truly?" he asked, startled.

"I'll have to find those. Gunter did not say you were a scholar, Fay-dra. A witch, perhaps. It is beyond them to understand more."

"I am a slave, my lord," I murmured. "Nothing more."

"You are a very well-trained slave." I thought he might say somewhat more, but his pointing finger moved over the books. "Have you read this? It is a D'Angeline book."

It was a Caerdicci translation of the *Trois Milles Joies*; I might have wept. I had read it under Cecilie's tutelage, of course. It is one of the great erotic texts, and required reading for every adept of the Night Court. "Yes, my lord," I said. "I have studied this book."

"Ahhh." He shuddered with the force of his sigh, plucking the book out from the shelf and smoothing the cover. "I learned Caerdicci from this book," he said, eyes bright with amusement and desire. "My tutor was a grizzled old Tiberian mercenary who had a fancy to see the northlands. I bribed him to stay here and teach me, when I was nineteen years old. It was the only book he had. He said it kept him company on cold nights." His long fingers stroked the cover. "I paid dear to keep it. But I have never found a woman who knew of such things." He set the book down and tipped my face upward. "You do."

"Yes, my lord," I whispered, helpless under his touch and hating him. Still he did not act, but searched my face with his gaze.

"Gunter says you are gifted by your gods so that any man must please you," he said. "That it is marked upon your eyes. Is this so?"

I could have lied to him, but some spark of defiance made me answer the truth. "I am marked by the gods to be pleased by suffering," I said softly. "That, and no more."

He touched my face with surprising delicacy, running the tip of one finger over my lower lip, watching intently as I drew in my breath sharply and my pulse grew faster, the inevitable tide of desire rising. "But I am causing you no suffering," he said gently. "And I see you are pleased."

"Does my lord say so?" I closed my eyes, willing my voice to be steady. "I am a free D'Angeline enslaved. Do not speak to me of suffering."

"I will speak to you as I please." He said it matter-of-factly, not intending to hurt. It was a simple truth. Releasing me, he tapped the book he had set upon his desk. I opened my eyes to look at him. "I would know what it is to be served by one trained to please Kings in this manner. You will begin on page one."

Bowing my head, I knelt in obeisance.

That is how one begins.

In the morning, Waldemar Selig had a sleek, satisfied look about him. There were the inevitable murmurs and jests, which I ignored. Joscelin took one look at my shadowed eyes and asked no questions, for which I was grateful.

I had pleased him, at least; that much was sure. Unlike Gunter, his ardors were not untutored, at least in his mind. Waldemar Selig had had a dozen years or more to pore over the finer points of D'Angeline lovemaking. He hungered for sophistication that Gunter never dreamed existed.

Selig had been married once; I didn't know it then, but learned it later. From what I gathered, she'd been nigh a match for him too, a quick-tempered and passionate Suevi chieftain's daughter. He used to read some of the *Trois Milles Joies* aloud to her, and they would experiment together, laughing and falling over one another in his great bed. But she got quickly with child, and it was a breech birth; the child lived only a day, and she took septic and died.

Perhaps he would not have been driven to conquest, had she lived. Who can know such things? It is my observation, though, that happiness limits the amount of suffering one is willing to inflict upon others. I like to think it might have been so.

Despite the pervasive aftermath of too much mead, the Skaldi encampments were beginning to break up that day. Waldemar Selig rode hither and thither, speaking to one and all. He cut a splendid figure atop a tall dark-bay horse, gold gleaming on the fillet that bound his hair and the tips of his forked beard. I don't deny him that. Clear-eyed from having abstained from overindulgence, he went efficiently about his business, arranging for the swiftest rider from each steading to stay encamped, setting in place a network of communications.

Since I had no orders to remain in the great hall, I went out amid the camps that day, thinking to bid Hedwig farewell. I don't know why, save that it was better than enduring the resentment of Selig's folk. The mood among the camps was markedly different than it had been upon our arrival. Men who'd eyed each other with veiled loathing clasped arms like brothers, vowing to guard each other's backs in battle when next they met. Selig has done this, I thought, and wondered how Isidore d'Aiglemort could ever have been so foolish. I knew, though, in my heart. He did but make the same mistake with Selig that the realm had made with him. "Camaelines think with their swords," I remembered someone saying dismissively at Cecilie Laveau-Perrin's fête so long ago. So we had thought, while the Duc d'Aiglemort plotted and secured his army. I wondered if he had said the same words of Waldemar Selig. Maybe not. I never heard a fellow D'Angeline credit any Skaldi with thinking, with or without a sword.

Thinking these thoughts, I failed to pay heed to my course and wandered straight into the path of a Gambrivii thane as he emerged from his tent. He grinned, showing bad teeth, and caught my wrist, shouting. "Look, Selig's decided to give us an early taste of victory, eh? Who's for swiving like a King, lads? First luck to me, and seconds for the rest!"

It happened too fast, between one instant and the next. One instant I was still gaping at his rot-toothed face, drawing breath for a reply, and the next he bent my arm behind me with a quick, expert twist and shoved me down in the snow, one hand pinning the back of my neck. Shouts of encouragement rang out—and a few cautionary protests—as my face was pressed hard against the trodden snow. Even then, it wasn't until he dragged my skirts up, exposing my bare buttocks to the cold air, that I believed it was happening.

One must understand, rape is not merely a crime in Terre d'Ange—as it is in all civilized countries, and indeed, even among the Skaldi, for their own women—it is heresy. Love as thou wilt, Blessed Elua said to us; rape is a violation of that sacred precept. As a Servant of Naamah, it was always mine to give consent; even for an *anguissette*, which is why no patron would have dared transgress the sanctity of the *signale*. Even Melisande honored it, within the bounds of Guild-law. What she did to me that last night . . . she would have ended it, if I'd given the *signale*. I do believe that. It was my choice to withhold it.

With Gunter and with Selig, I'd been taken against my will with no choice at all, and I thought I knew some measure of the horror of it. As the packed snow melted and froze against my cheek and the Gambrivii thane fumbled with his breeches while yelling Skaldi gathered around, I knew I had grasped only the smallest part of it.

And then another voice roared into the fray, and the weight was lifted from my neck. Scrambling out of the way and yanking my skirts down, I gazed up to see Knud—whose homely face looked positively beautiful to me—lifting the Gambrivii up by the scruff of the neck, landing two solid left-handed punches to his face.

It lasted that long, and then the other Gambrivii swarmed him, all brotherly goodwill forgotten. Knud went down struggling. Forgetting my own terror, I grabbed the nearest thing at hand—a cooking pot—and dashed it against the back of the closest Gambrivii head. One of their thanes caught my arms and held me back, rubbing himself against me and laughing.

In the melee, no one noticed Waldemar Selig's arrival.

He sat atop his tall horse staring down at the struggle with supreme annoyance, drawing breath to order an end to it. What he would have said, I don't know, for Joscelin was behind him amid the White Brethren, and he was off his horse before Selig could voice a command, shouting my name like a battle-paean.

It was his sword he drew.

Two Gambrivii died, I think, before anyone knew what had happened. The one who held me dropped my arms with a curse, drawing his sword and running forward. Red blood stained the snow. What had been a brawl turned abruptly into a deadly battle, with Joscelin at its center, a moving dervish of grey and steel, sparks striking from his sword and vambraces. Another man went down before Waldemar Selig dismounted and drew his sword, wading shouting into the violence. I watched with my hands over my mouth.

I had not seen, before then, why the Skaldi revered

him. I saw it now. He didn't have a Cassiline's skill and grace. He didn't need it. Waldemar Selig wielded a sword as simply and naturally as he breathed. The Gambrivii thanes fell back before him, while continuing to engage Joscelin.

"D'Angeline, I order you to *stop!*" Selig shouted fiercely, his face pale with rage. A Gambrivii spear darted at Joscelin, who dodged, striking back at the thane with a well-aimed blow.

It never landed. Waldemar Selig shoved the Gambrivii out of the way with one powerful shoulder, bringing his own blade up for a parry that sent Joscelin's wide, then stepped inside the Cassiline's guard and struck him on the temple with the pommel of his sword.

Joscelin went to his knees as if poleaxed, nerveless fingers releasing his hilt. He knelt there, swaying, amid fallen Skaldi bodies bleeding silently onto the white snow. Some distance away, Knud groaned and climbed dizzily to his feet. No one spoke. Waldemar Selig gazed at Joscelin and shook his head in disgust.

"Kill him," he said to the White Brethren.

"No!" It was my voice. I knew from the sound of it. I flung myself between them, kneeling before Selig, pleading with clasped hands. "My lord, please, let him live! He was only honoring his vow to protect me, I swear it. I will do anything, anything you wish, in exchange for his life!"

"You will do it anyway," Selig said impassively.

I did not say the words: Not if you kill him. I thought it, though, and he saw it in my face. Kushiel's Dart or no, I could have and would have, I believe. We are mostly human, Elua's children. Like Joscelin, who had drawn his sword, I had been pushed to the limits of my nature.

It didn't come to it. Knud, blessed Knud, limped over,

rubbing a lump on the side of his head. With one toe, he nudged the body of a fallen Gambrivii, whose blackened teeth were bared in a grimace. His breeches were undone, his phallus lying pale and shrunken on his thigh, a sorry sight. "Found him like this trying to get atop the lass, Lord Selig," Knud said bluntly. "It's true, the boy's sworn to protect her. It's his vow. Gunter used 'em that way, one to tame t'other."

Waldemar Selig considered us as we knelt, Joscelin nigh insensible, I frozen in plea. "Who spoke against this?" he asked then of the gathered Gambrivii. The leader of the steading had stepped forward, and stood trembling. "No one? Would you urge a man to steal my horse? My sword? No? This woman is as much my property, and more." He reached down and gathered a handful of my hair, shaking my head. Behind me, Joscelin made an inarticulate sound of protest, then slumped sideways. Selig released me. "For your plea of clemency and the injury you have suffered," he said formally, "I will see the boy spared, and merely struck in chains. Vigfus." His gaze flicked to the Gambrivii chieftain. "I will pay were-gild for the death of your thanes. Are you satisfied?"

"Yes, my lord." The Gambrivii chieftain's teeth chattered; no doubt he feared Selig would call him out for it. "It is just."

"Good." Selig glanced around. "Go about your business," he said calmly, and the Skaldi hastened to obey. He reached down then, and drew me to my feet. My teeth were chattering too, between the cold and the dawning shock. "Where were you bound?" he asked, plainly annoyed. "What in Odhinn's name were you doing amid the camps?"

"My lord." I hugged myself, shivering, near tears at the stupid, simple truth of it. "I went to bid farewell to the folk of Gunter's steading. They were kind to me, there, some of them."

"You should have told me. I would have given you an escort." He beckoned to one of the White Brethren. "Take her to Gunter's camp."

"I'll do it, Lord Selig," Knud called out gruffly. Selig arched a brow at him, and he shrugged. "I'm fond of the lass. There'll be no more trouble once this word spreads."

It was, by now, the last thing I wanted to do; all of my concern was for Joscelin, now unconscious and breathing shallowly in the snow. But I had won his life, if he could hold onto it, and I feared to push Selig further.

"Fine." Waldemar Selig was done with the matter, and impatient to move on. "Bring her back within the hour." He nodded to two of the White Brethren. "Take him to the smithy, and have him shackled. That should keep him out of trouble." His cool green gaze rested on me a moment. "And you too, I trust."

I knelt, kissing his hand. He shook me off and strode to his horse, leaving with his remaining thanes. Knud helped me up gently, leading me away. I turned back, watching over my shoulder as the White Brethren hauled Joscelin to his feet. He doubled over, vomiting, then straightened and staggered away with them, toward the edge of the lake where the forges blazed. One of the Brethren picked up his sword, sticking it in his belt as if it were fair-won spoil.

"You've done all you could for him, lass," Knud said kindly. "He'll live, if he doesn't force Selig's hand. He's a fair sight tougher than he looks, that lad. No one else I know has survived Gunter's kennels. 'Course, no one else I know has had the pleasure." He chuckled at that, as if it were a great witticism. Perhaps it was, for Knud;

all I know is that I burst into tears. With awkward tenderness, he held me and patted my back, glowering over my head at the stares of the watching Skaldi.

When I had somewhat regained my composure, he led me on, to bid farewell to the last folk who bore me any trace of goodwill in this enemy land.

FORTY-NINE

It was an awkward moment, saying good-bye to the Skaldi of Gunter's steading; not merely for what had immediately preceeded it, but for the fact that they had just, unanimously, declared war on my people. Since there was nothing else for it, I put a good face on it. Harald the Beardless—whose beard was beginning to come in and would soon need a new cognomen—would be staying as Gunter's best rider and of a surety it wouldn't hurt to have one voice that spoke well of me.

So it was that we had hugs and tears all around, and my emotions were in such a jumble that I needn't feign sorrow at their leaving; I had sorrow to spare.

"If Gunter asks you a fourth time," I whispered to Hedwig, "tell him yes. He's tender feelings for you, for all his bluster, and the two of you are too well matched to settle for less. And if he's learned a trick or two of pleasing women, light a candle to Freja in my name." I had learned some little of the Skaldic pantheon, and reckoned this goddess the closest in nature to Naamah. Hedwig nodded and sniffled, turning away.

And then Knud gave me safe-conduct back to Selig's great hall, limping gamely from the beating he'd taken on my behalf, and bid me farewell, kissing my hand when none of Selig's thanes were watching. Less cautious, I took his head in both hands and kissed him upon his brow, offering a silent prayer to Elua that he would emerge unharmed from the coming battles. Blessed Elua would understand. Love as thou wilt, I thought, watching Knud hobble hurriedly back to camp, a glowing smile on his unlovely features. Yeshua ben Yosef of whose blood Elua was born bid his followers to love even their enemies; I understood then, a little, what he meant.

But I could not love them all.

There was no sign of Joscelin. I dared ask Waldemar Selig when he returned in the evening, weary from a long day's labors. He told me curtly that Joscelin was safe, and I had no choice but to take his word for it.

It was three full days before I learned more, and in those three days it was made manifestly apparent to me that I was unwelcome by the denizens of Selig's steading. Always I felt the eyes of his thanes, watching me with hunger and scorn; from the women, I received resentment, scarce veiled even in Selig's presence. Only the children treated me as an equal. Remembering a trick Alcuin had used to charm them at Perrinwolde, I braided the hair of a few, making do with bits of thong and scraps of fur instead of ribbons. The children delighted in it—all children delight in being made much of—but I saw the women glaring, undoing my work with quick, angry gestures while the children squirmed, and I tried it no more.

Selig himself was not unaware of it, but he didn't understand the nature of his people's dislike. When he tried to soften matters by complimenting me on my appearance or some nicety of service, they only saw that he set me above them, and hated me for it.

In response, he kept me closer by him, which made it the worse. Still, I was glad when he set me to the chore of recreating an approximation of Didimus Pontus'

Skaldic alphabet. It allowed me to stay out of sight in his chamber. At other times, he had me pore over maps of Terre d'Ange with him, correcting and clarifying the topography as best I could. I am not ashamed to say that I lied with as much invention and conviction as I dared, reckoning any misinformation was to the good. When he bade me teach him D'Angeline, though, I didn't dare lead him astray. Errors in geography, if he learned of them, he could ascribe to ignorance; in the teaching of my native tongue, I had no such defence.

During the nights, it was another matter as we worked our way steadily through the *Trois Milles Joies*. It is not necessary to speak of what services I performed for him; they are written down in that book, for any who wish to know. I am trained in all those suitable for a woman to perform, and some few that are not, to the exacting standards of Cereus House. Those are the things I did, excepting those feats which the Skaldi reckon unmanly.

It was on the fourth day that Waldemar Selig said to me, frowning, "It has been some days, and Josslin Verai will not eat. Maybe you should see him."

My heart plummeted; I'd gotten through the previous days believing him safe and well, albeit confined. I hurried to fetch my fur cloak, and went with Selig to where Joscelin was held.

It was a mean little hut, some distance from the great hall; it had been a woodcutter's, I think. One of the White Brethren was on guard, lounging before the hide strung across the door and tossing a dagger for amusement. He sprang to his feet when we approached.

Inside, it was cold and dingy, warmed only by a tiny brazier in which a few coals smoldered. There was a straw pallet and a blanket, but Joscelin knelt huddled on the floor, shivering, his arms crossed. His hands and feet were shackled, with a chain run from his ankles to an iron ring pounded into the floor. It was long enough to allow him to walk and reach the pallet; he knelt by choice.

He looked horrible. His face was wan and haggard, lips cracked, hair lank. While Selig leaned against a wall, I ran to Joscelin, kneeling before him and peering at his ravaged face.

What came out of my mouth, in D'Angeline, was, "You idiot! What are you doing?"

Joscelin raised his head, staring at me with bloodshot eyes. "I dishonored my vow," he whispered in a cracked voice. "I drew to kill."

"Blessed Elua! That's all?" I sat back on my heels and pressed my hands to my face. Remembering Selig, I dropped them and glanced at him. "He grieves for his wrongdoing," I said in Skaldic. "He is atoning."

Waldemar Selig nodded soberly; he understood this. "Tell him to live," he said. "I have made atonement in were-gild for the lives of the men he killed. And I wish him to teach me his manner of fighting." He paused, recalling, and repeated it slowly in Caerdicci to Joscelin.

Joscelin gave a laugh that scared me, wild and half-mad. "My lord has bested me," he said to Selig in Caerdicci. "Why would you want to learn what I know?"

"You did not expect to battle me. You have given me your pledge. And you did not expect me to step inside your guard," Selig said deliberately. "Another time, it might be different."

"I cannot teach him to fight like a Cassiline," Joscelin said to me in D'Angeline, shaking his head over and over. "I have failed you, too many times. I've dishonored my vow. Better I should die!"

I shot a quick glance at Selig, then looked fiercely at Joscelin. "How many times do you need to discover your humanity, Joscelin? You're not Cassiel reborn, but you're vowed to me, and I have never needed your service more!" I shook his shoulders, quoting Delaunay's words at him. "Do you remember this? To fail and persevere is a harder test than any you will meet on the practice-field. Keep your sword, I cannot afford its loss."

Joscelin laughed again, despairingly, then caught it with a gasp. "I can't, Phèdre, I swear I can't! I've not even a sword to keep." He gazed up at Selig from his huddled pose. "I am sorry, my lord," he said in Caerdicci. "I am not worthy to live."

I swore at him then, in D'Angeline, Skaldic and Caerdicci alike, shoving him so he lurched sideways in his chains and fell sprawling, gaping at me. "Elua curse you, Cassiline, if that's all the courage you've got!" I railed at him, in what tongue I know not. "If I live through this, I swear I'm writing to the Prefect of your order, and telling him how Blessed Elua was better served by a courtesan of the Night Court than a Cassiline priest!"

What Selig thought of my diatribe, I don't know; if I'd thought to look at him, I wouldn't have dared, but it never crossed my mind. With scarce the strength to get upright, still Joscelin's eyes narrowed at my harangue. "You will *not!*" he retorted with febrile intensity, scrabbling to rise to his knees.

"Then stop me." I stood up, hurling the last words at him. "Protect and serve, Cassiline!"

It must sound, I know, as if I had no pity for him; it wasn't true. I was angry because I was terrified. But there are times when a curse is more bracing than an endearment. Dragging at his chains, Joscelin struggled to a kneeling position, shivering, staring at me with tears standing in his bloodshot eyes. "It's hard, Phèdre," he said pleadingly. "Elua help me, but it's hard!"

"I know," I whispered.

Selig stepped outside then and said something to the

guard. I didn't know what until the White Brethren thane returned scowling some minutes later, carrying a wooden bowl of broth. Selig nodded, and he shoved it at Joscelin. "You eat," Waldemar Selig said to him in his rudimentary D'Angeline. "You live."

We left him then, holding the bowl in two trembling hands. I looked back as Selig held the hide back from the door for me, catching sight of Joscelin lowering his lips to the rim of the bowl.

He would live, I thought with relief. It gave me one less reason to die.

After that, Joscelin continued to take nourishment and grew stronger, although he had developed chilblains on his hands and on his wrists where the manacles chafed. They itched and pained him mercilessly, but he used it as a reason to postpone teaching Cassiline swordplay to Waldemar Selig. Having invested somewhat in keeping his tame D'Angeline warrior-priest alive, Selig acceded to my pleas to be able to visit Joscelin once a day, rightly reckoning that once Joscelin had chosen to live, my presence would give him incentive to continue living. He had his vow.

It was the one thing I looked forward to each day. Selig had other business to attend to, so he set one of the White Brethren to escort me. It was well that Joscelin had kept the extent of his fledgling Skaldic hidden, for it aroused no suspicion when we spoke in D'Angeline, and I quickly determined that, unlike Selig, his thanes had no knowledge of our tongue.

Unfortunately, there was little we could do in the way of plotting an escape. The steading was simply too well guarded. Still, we spoke of survival, and kept each other's spirits from flagging.

Never long on tolerance when he suspected delay, Selig grew impatient for Joscelin's hands to heal, and sent for a priest of Odhinn who was also a healer to see to him.

"In truth," he confessed to me the night before, "I am curious to see what Lodur will make of you. He is my oldest teacher, and I have great respect for his wisdom."

I should add that by that point, unrest over Selig's patronage of me had continued to grow and it was commonly put about that I was a witch, sent from Terre d'Ange to ensorcel him, as evidenced by the red mote in my left eye—a sure sign of a witch.

Selig laughed at the rumor. "Lodur's mother was a witch too, so they said. They said she could cure a man of any wound, mortal or no, if she found him favorable. Truth is, she was a skilled healer. As you are skilled at . . . other things."

I don't know what I said to that; something flattering, you may be sure. If I added a touch of defiant spice sometimes, for the most part, I told him what he wished to hear. But so it came to pass that I rode with him and two of his White Brethren to the home of Lodur the One-Eyed, on a shaggy pony Selig had given me as my own to ride.

My first glimpse of the healer was of a wiry old man standing bare-chested in the snow, a fur vest over his scrawny torso. His hair was white and wild. He held a carved staff in one hand, and on the other fist, a raven perched. We saw him at a distance speaking to it, but it flew away at our approach. I thought it was Skaldi magic at the time. Later I learned he'd nursed it broken-winged, and it was still half tame. Lodur glanced up, unsurprised, and I saw that he bore a patch over his right eye; I hadn't know, then, that he was called One-Eyed.

"Waldemar Berundson," he said calmly, using a patronymic I'd never even heard spoken. Selig, they called him, Blessed, as if the gods themselves had named him.

"This is Faydra nó Delaunay of Terre d'Ange, old master," Selig said respectfully. He dismounted and bent his head to the old man, so I did the same, and noticed that his thanes did too. "She has a companion who has the cold-wounds, that will not heal."

"Indeed." Lodur came to meet us across the snow, moving with a quickness that belied his age. His one eye was a pale, fierce blue, but it did not look unkindly on me. Unlike every other Skaldi male I'd seen, he was beardless, a grizzled white stubble on his leather-tanned face. "You like it, eh?" He saw me looking and stroked his chin, grinning. "I met a girl once who fancied a clean face. Got into the habit, I suppose."

Priests aplenty I have known, but never one like him; I stammered some reply. "No matter," he said casually, and felt me all over with firm hands, an impersonal patting. I stood still for it, bewildered. Selig looked approving. "D'Angeline, eh?" Lodur fixed me with his solitary ice-blue gaze, gazing thoughtfully at my face and my own mismatched eyes. The cold didn't seem to touch him. "What do they call it, that?" He nodded at my left eye.

"Kushiel's Dart," I said softly.

"You're god-marked, then. Like me, you think?" He laughed, pointing to his patch. "One-Eyed, they call me, like the All-Father. Do you know the story?"

I knew it; I'd heard it sung at Gunter's steading often enough. I could even sing it myself. "He gave his eye in exchange for a drink from Mimir's fountain," I said. "The fountain of wisdom."

Lodur clapped, tucking his staff beneath one arm. Selig's thanes muttered. "Me, now," the old priest said conversationally. "When I was a fool apprentice, I took my own eye, offered it with prayer, reckoning to become wise like Odhinn. You know what my master told me?"

I shook my head. Lodur cocked his and gazed at me. "He told me I had gained a valuable piece of wisdom: No one can bribe the gods. What an idiot I was!" He chuckled at the memory. Only a Skaldi could laugh at such a thing. "But I got wiser," he added.

"Old master . . ." Selig began.

"I know, I know." Lodur cut him off. "The cold-wounds. And you want to know what I think of the girl. What can I tell you, Waldemar Berundson? You take a weapon thrown by a D'Angeline god to your bosom, and ask me for wisdom? As well ask the mute to advise the deaf. I'll get my medicine bag."

Selig stared at me, frowning. I kept my countenance as open as I could, frankly as bewildered as he. All along, I had thought myself Kushiel's victim, marked out for the awful divinity of his love. It was something else, to think of myself as his weapon.

The old priest fetched his medicines and mounted up behind Selig, spry as a boy. We rode that way back to the steading, through the spectacular forests. Lodur hummed to himself and sang a snatch of song, but no one else spoke. Selig's brow was dark with thought.

At the hut, Lodur rapped three times on the threshold with his staff and gave a loud invocation before stepping inside. He seemed to bring a clean scent of snow and pine needles into the close, dim air of the hut. Joscelin, engaged in some Cassiline meditation, stared at the apparition.

"Like a young Baldur, eh?" Lodur said casually to Selig, naming their dying-god, who is called the Beautiful. "Well, let's see 'em, boy." He squatted on his shanks next to Joscelin, examining the swollen red flesh of his hands and wrists. They were cracked and suppurating, weeping a clear fluid and refusing to heal. "Ah, I've one of mother's recipes will do for that!" the priest-healer laughed, digging around in his bag. He drew out a small stoneware jar of balm and unstoppered it. What was in it, I don't know, but it stank to heaven. Joscelin made a face at it, then looked questioningly at me over Lodur's head as the old man began slathering his hands and wrists with it.

"He is a healer," I said in Caerdicci, for Selig's benefit; we kept up the pretence that Joscelin's Skaldic was inadequate for conversing. "Lord Selig wishes that you become well enough to teach him your manner of fighting."

Joscelin bowed his head to Selig. "I look forward to it, my lord." He paused. "To teach the Cassiline style, I require my arms, my lord; or at least my vambraces. Wooden training daggers and sword will suffice."

"The Skaldi do not train with wooden toys. I sent your arms to my smith, to duplicate their design. You shall have them when we spar." Selig cast a scowl at one of the White Brethren; he'd reclaimed Joscelin's sword, then, and been annoyed at its loss. "Are you done, old master?"

"Oh, nearly." Lodur worked deftly, winding bandages of clean linen about Joscelin's balm-smeared skin. "He'll heal quickly. These D'Angelines, they've gods' blood in their veins. It's old and faint all right, but even a mere trace of it's a powerful thing, Waldemar Berundson."

If I did not miss the warning in his words, Selig could not fail to heed it. "Old and powerful, and corrupted with generations of softness, old master. Their gods will bow their heads to the All-Father, and we will claim the magic of their blood for our own descendants, to infuse it with red-blooded Skaldi vigor."

The old man glanced up at him, his one eye as wintry and distant as a wolf's. "May it be as you say, young Waldemar. I am too ancient to strong-arm the gods."

I felt a chill run through me at his words. Whatever else was true, the old man had power, that much I knew. I felt it in that hut, creeping over my skin, whispering of the dark earth and the towering firs, of iron and blood, fox, wolf and raven. Lodur rose then, patting Joscelin kindly on the head, and gathered his things.

At the center of the steading, he refused a ride back to his home in the woods, saying he would welcome the walk. I, shivering as always, could not credit his hardiness, but truly, his bare skin seemed unaffected by the cold. Selig was speaking to the White Brethren about some matter, so I took the chance to approach Lodur as he made ready to leave.

"Did you mean it?" I asked him. "About the weapon?"

No more than that did I say, but he knew what I meant and considered me, standing ankle-deep in snow. "Who knows the ways of the gods? Baldur the Beautiful was slain with a sprig of mistletoe, cast by an unknowing hand. Are you less likely a weapon?"

I had no answer to that, and the old man laughed. "Still, if I were young Waldemar, I'd take the risk of you too," he added with a wicked grin, "and if I were not much younger at all, I'd ask you for a kiss."

Of all the unlikely things, it made me blush. Lodur cackled again and struck out across the snow, staff in hand, walking briskly back the way we'd come. A strange man; I'd never met stranger. I was sorry not to see him again.

For his part, Waldemar Selig responded to the whole encounter by regarding me with a new suspicion. It came out that night in bed, when he did not bid me to please him, but regarded me instead, tracing with one finger the lineaments of my marque. "Mayhap there is rune-magic in these markings, Faydra," he said, deceptively. "Would you say so?"

"It is my marque, that says I am pledged to Naamah's service. All her Servants bear such, and there is no magic in it save freedom, when it is made complete." I held myself quiet, kneeling before him.

"So you say." He laid his hand open across my back; it spanned a great expanse of my skin. "You say you were sold into slavery because you knew too much. I, I would merely kill you, were it so. Why do you live?"

Melisande's voice came back to me, calm and distant. *I'd no more kill you than I'd destroy a priceless fresco or a vase.* "My lord," I whispered, "I am the only one of my kind. Would you kill a wolf with fur of purest silver, if it wandered into your steading?"

He pondered it, then drew away from me, shaking his head. "I cannot say. Perhaps it was led by Odhinn, to my spear. I do not understand this thing you say you are."

It was true, and a mercy to me. Even he, the least unsubtle of Skaldi, understood pleasure in its simpler terms. It was not much, but I was grateful for it. "I am your servant, my lord," I said, bowing my head and setting the rest aside. It was enough. He reached for me, then, running his fingers through my hair, and drew me down to him.

𝒥IFTY

As Lodur had predicted, Joscelin healed quickly. Selig had his arms brought to their training-sessions, and sought to learn this new D'Angeline skill.

I'd paid little heed to Joscelin's sessions with Alcuin in the garden. Now I watched more closely. The forms through which Joscelin flowed so effortlessly in his morning ritual were at the heart of it. Watching, I saw them broken down and how each one had a purpose. No matter that the Cassilines had given them poetic names, they were strikes and feints, blocks and parries, all of them, designed to lead and anticipate an opponent's blows—or multiple opponents, as it were.

Members of the Cassiline Brotherhood begin their training at ten, when they are inducted. Day after day, for long years, they practice nothing else, until the forms are so deeply embedded in them that they can do them backwards and forwards, waking or sleeping. And even so, they do them every morning, lest the memory etched in their bones begin to flag.

I'd thought, when Joscelin said he couldn't teach it to Selig, that he meant it was against his vows; I saw then that he meant it was impossible. With Alcuin, it had been play, and he'd naught to unlearn. Waldemar Selig, acknowledged champion of the Skaldi, thought to add to his skill. But what Joscelin sought to teach him ran contrary to the simple, brutal efficiency bred and trained into him. When he found himself floundering, awkward as a stripling lad, he grew impatient and displeased.

The lessons ended. Joscelin's arms were locked away in Selig's cupboard, and his shackles returned permanently.

And Selig's suspicions mounted.

Kolbjorn of the Manni came to meet with him, bearing news from the south. There are Skaldi there, I learned, who live near the border of Caerdicca Unitas nigh unto Tiberian nobles, with proper houses and vast estates worked by slaves. The Caerdicci reckoned them almost civilized, and still maintained some measure of trade and correspondence with them. It was from them that Kolbjorn came, bearing a letter for Selig.

Even in the bustle of the great hall, I knew how to

make myself invisible, kneeling motionless in a corner. Selig supposed me working on some new translation for him, and paid me no heed; taking their cue from him, the others ignored me. I was too far to read, but I saw his face as he broke the seal and opened the letter. It held relief. "Kilberhaar suspects nothing!" he exclaimed, clapping Kolbjorn on the back. "He will take our bait, and move his armies as we agreed. Good news, eh?"

Kolbjorn of the Manni rumbled something in agreement, I couldn't hear what. I saw, instead, the letter lying open on the table between them, the cracked seal impressed in gold wax. Broken or no, I knew the design, even at a distance. Three keys intertwined, almost lost in the intricate pattern; the emblem of Kushiel, who was said to hold the keys to the portals of hell.

It was the insignia of House Shahrizai.

Of course, I thought, kneeling in silent agony. Of course. Melisande Shahrizai was clever enough to bring down House Trevalion; she was too clever to fall with House d'Aiglemort. She would play both sides, and claim the victor's part. I clutched the diamond at my throat, grasping it until I could feel every facet impressed into my palm. Even here, I was not beyond her reach.

It was then that I heard, through a distant haze, Selig tell Kolbjorn in a casual tone that there would be a great hunt on the morrow. The Skaldi place great stock in hospitality, and Kolbjorn was a valuable ally; the hunt would be held in his honor, and a feast to follow.

That was when the plan came to me.

Withdrawing silently, I returned without subterfuge, approaching Selig and kneeling. He acknowledged me with a nod, and I begged his permission to visit Joscelin. He granted it absentmindedly, sending one of the White Brethren with me. Trudging across the snow, I studied the lay of the steading and the encampment, my mind working feverishly. It would work, perhaps. If sufficient numbers of Selig's thanes turned out for the hunt. If Joscelin would cooperate.

That was the sticking point.

I ducked through the doorway of the hut, my escort following. Joscelin was exercising insofar as his shackles permitted, hard at press-ups against the floor. He had little else to do, save meditate. He got to his feet when we entered, chains rattling. The White Brethren guard gave the hut a cursory scan, then went to wait outside the door, preferring the fresh cold air to the sullen, smoky chill inside.

"Look," Joscelin said to me, nudging the iron ring staked into the raw wooden planks of the floor. It wobbled, obviously loose in its hole. I was glad, for it was one less obstacle. "What's been happening?" he asked me then. "I've heard the camps stirring."

"Kolbjorn of the Manni is here," I said. "Joscelin, he brought a letter from the south, routed through Caerdicca Unitas. I saw the seal. It was from Melisande."

He was silent, then, taking in the extent of her betrayal. I knew the shock of it. "What did it say?" he asked eventually. I shook my head.

"I'd no chance to see. But I know she told him d'Aiglemort doesn't suspect anything."

"Do you think it's true?"

I hadn't considered it, too stunned to question it; seeing the possibility, I smacked my forehead. "I don't know. She might be playing Selig into d'Aiglemort's hands. It could be." We stared at each other. "Either way," I said softly, "the Crown falls, and she stands to gain. Joscelin, could you kill a man with your hands?"

He turned pale. "Why do you ask?"

I told him my plan.

When I was done, he paced the hut with shackled

steps, circling at the length his chain allowed. I could see the thoughts chasing themselves across his features. "You are asking me to betray my vow," he said at last, not looking at me. "To attack, unprovoked . . . to kill . . . it goes against all the tenets I have sworn to honor. What you ask, Phèdre . . . it's murder."

"I know." There were a great many things I could have said. I could have pointed out to him that we were both dying by slow degrees, he in chains, I serving Waldemar Selig's pleasure against a rising tide of hatred. I could have argued that we were at war and trapped behind enemy lines, where the common rules of decency no longer apply. I could have said these things, and did not. Joscelin knew them as well as I did.

It was still murder.

After a long moment, he looked at me. "I will do what you ask," he said softly, his voice inflectionless.

Thus our plan was laid.

All that day, I was restless, my heart beating at an unaccustomed pace and a sick, nervous feel in the pit of my stomach. I hid it with smiles and pleasantries, going quietly about the business of Selig's orders, wearing subservience like a mask. I must have done it well; he was in good enough spirits to set aside his suspicions during the day, making a point to compliment my service in Kolbjorn's presence. Glad that Selig would be wholly given over to Skaldic pursuits and not D'Angeline corruption on the morrow, his thanes and the White Brethren made no trouble over it.

He had me that night. By chance, it happened that we had come to a passage in the *Trois Milles Joies* called "The Rutting Stag," and Selig took it as a good omen, for they would hunt deer the next day. On my hands and knees, I shuddered beneath him, staring at the carved headboard and despising him as he thrust himself into me, head thrown back, hands clutching hard at my shoulders. Enjoy it, my lord, I thought, it is the last you will have of me.

Afterward he slept, while I lay wide-eyed in the darkness. Only a faint glimmer of orange came from the shifting embers, glinting where it struck metal. I stared at the nearest gleam, my mind occupied with a thousand details, not realizing what it was until the shape of it resolved itself out of darkness and made sense to my eyes.

It was Selig's dagger, laid upon the far night table when he undressed.

Of course, I thought, and relief suffused me. Of course there was another way. The price was higher, but the end . . . oh, the end was sure! Turning my head, I gazed at Selig as he slept, picking out his features by the faint emberlight. His face was peaceful in repose, as though no bad thoughts troubled his dreams. He breathed deeply, his powerful chest rising and falling with even, regular motions. There, I thought; my eyes had grown quite accustomed to the dark. There, in the hollow at the base of his throat, laid bare by his forked beard. Shove the point in there, and twist. I knew little of weapons, but it would suffice.

All I had to do was reach the dagger.

I shifted cautiously, reaching one arm across his body.

The bed creaked on its timbers, and I felt a hand grasp my wrist. Gazing down, I saw Selig's eyes, open and awake. He was not Gunter, to sleep like the dead through any manner of disturbance . . . Waldemar Selig, they called him, Blessed, proof against steel. What I did then, I did without choice. I had nearly been caught attempting to assassinate the apparent King of the Skaldi. With a murmuring sound of protest, I shifted my arm to reach around him in embrace, laying my head upon his shoulder.

It pleased him, to think I had come unwilling to tenderness. He gave a drowsy chuckle, which echoed like a drum beneath my ear, and let me stay, nestled into him. His breathing settled back quickly into the rhythms of sleep. I lay awake for a long time, forcing my limbs to pliancy, willing away the rigidity of terror. At last, exhausted by fear, I slid into restless dreams.

The morning dawned crisp and bright, and the great hall bustled with all of the activity attendant on a hunt. I moved through it all in wooden shock, feeling like I had stumbled, dazed, into some strange theatre. Refreshed by sleep, my terror had returned, split between horror at what had nearly befallen last night and the fear of what was to come. I remember very little of that morning. The Skaldi arming to hunt, the women at their labors, the horses brought round stamping against the cold; it blurs in my mind with the morning Gunter's folk went raiding and came back singing of slain D'Angelines. Even Harald the Beardless was there, fingering the new growth on his chin and giving me a cheerful wink, not knowing I was in disfavor among Selig's folk. Only the yelping of dogs was different; that, and the White Brethren drawing straws to see who would stay to guard me. Those were Selig's orders. A thane named Trygve drew the short straw, grumbling amid good-natured jeers from his comrades. He cut it short at a warning glance from Selig. I kept my eyes downcast, not wanting to look at the man whom fate and a short straw had marked for death.

And then they were off, and the great hall nigh empty. The housecarls went about their work. Trygve sprawled at his leisure on a bench, flirting with one of the women. I withdrew into Selig's room; he saw where I was headed, and nodded, knowing I did work for his lord there.

Alone in Selig's room, I took the brooch from my wolfskin cloak and opened it, taking the sharp end of its bronze pin between my teeth. With careful pressure, I bent the very tip of it into a tiny hook. It took some doing, but I was able to catch the tumbler on the lock on Selig's cupboard, opening it to reveal private correspondence, a locked coffer of coin, a jumble of clothing and Joscelin's arms piled at the bottom. The letter from Melisande Shahrizai was there. I sat down to read it.

It was her hand; I knew it, having seen it often enough in letters to Delaunay, though she wrote now in Caerdicci. The letter itself was brief, little more than confirmation of what Selig had said aloud. *I trust we understand one another*, she wrote at the end.

Selig's leather saddle-packs stood in the corner, unnecessary for a day-long hunt. I hauled them out and shoved the letter in an inner pocket, then rummaged through the cupboard for the warmest garments I could find, stuffing them into the packs. There was a tinderbox too, and I took that gratefully. There was little else I could do, at this stage. I put on my cloak and pinned it with difficulty. Drawing a deep breath, I walked into the great hall and approached Trygve, still engaged in dalliance. He glanced up, displeased. "What is it?"

"I would visit my friend, please, my lord," I said softly. "Lord Selig permits me to do so, once a day."

It was true, and he knew it; still, Selig was not there. "I'll take you later," he said dismissively, turning back to the woman, resuming his interrupted tale.

I knelt, keeping my eyes down. "If it please you, my lord, I can go alone. The steading is empty, and I will be safe. I need not trouble your day with this."

"Oh, let her go," the Skaldi woman—Gerde, her name

was—said impatiently. "She'll be back soon enough, she knows where her profit lies!"

Another time, I might have bridled at her comment, but now I held still. Trygve sighed, swinging his sprawling legs down from the bench and tossing the pelt that marked him White Brethren over his shoulders, draping the hood over his head. "And have word get to Selig after some carl tells him he saw the D'Angeline unescorted? Never mind, I'll go." Standing, he picked up his shield and took my arm ungently. "Come on. And make it brief this time, mind?"

I was glad, walking behind him in the cold, that he hadn't been kind. It made it easier. The worst of the terror had passed, now that it was happening. Warriors say that the waiting is always the hardest, before a battle. I understood it that day. The grounds of the steading were as sparsely populated as the great hall, no one coming or going from the other halls, only a few figures amid the handful of tents that still dotted the broad swath of land around the lake.

And then we reached Joscelin's hut, and Trygve gestured for me to preceed him. Drawing back the hide, I entered. My eyes were sun-dazzled, and it took a second to see that there was no one in the center of the hut, only a hole in the planks where the ring had been pounded. Turning my head, I saw Joscelin motionless beside the door, a length of chain in his shackled hands. Neither of us spoke. I moved away, allowing Trygve to enter.

He got two steps inside the door, before Joscelin moved, looping the chain over his head and twisting it ruthlessly. I had made him do it; I made myself watch it. Partially protected by the hood of his white pelt, Trygve struggled, gasping for air, his hands dragging at Joscelin's arms. Joscelin kneed him sharply from behind, and Trygve's legs collapsed. As he slid down, drawing breath to shout, Joscelin dropped the chain, took his head in both hands and gave it a sharp twist.

I heard the sound of his neck breaking. The shout died unuttered in his mouth, and the spark of life faded from his eyes. It was that quick.

"Give me your hands." I tore the brooch from my cloak, working swiftly as Joscelin stood with arms extended. The clasps on the manacles were simple. "Thank you, Hyacinthe," I muttered, kneeling to free his ankles. I glanced up. Joscelin was rubbing his wrists, his expression tightly under control. "We need to strip him."

Joscelin nodded curtly. "Let's do it."

Dead weighs heavier than living; it took some doing to undress Trygve's corpse, but we did it, neither looking at the other. Without comment, Joscelin turned away and stripped, donning the Skaldi garments in place of his threadbare Cassiline garb.

"Let me see you." Studying him, I unbound his single braid, then stooped to the brazier to gather a handful of ash. This I rubbed into his hair, altering its color to dun, and his face, giving him a layer of grime that did somewhat to hide his D'Angeline features. I glanced at Trygve's hair and copied the manner of it, twining small braids in the sides of Joscelin's hair, tugging it forward to further shadow his face. "Here," I said then, holding out the white wolf-pelt. Joscelin drew it over his shoulders, tying the skin of the forelegs together as they did, then pulled the hood over his head, the empty-eyed wolf-mask low on his brow.

It would work. At a distance, he would pass for one of the White Brethren.

"Are you ready?" I asked. He took a deep breath and nodded. "The great hall will be the worst. I couldn't bring a sack without arousing suspicion, but we need clothing and a tinderbox, and Melisande's letter is there. We can get stores from the lesser hall, there's fewer folk about."

"I need my arms."

"They're not Skaldi. Take Trygve's."

"I need the vambraces. I'm not trained to fight with a shield, you saw it in the holmgang." He paused, then added quietly, "They were given me by my uncle, and his uncle before him, Phèdre. Let me keep that much."

"All right. Take Trygve's for now, it will look strange if you don't have them." I feared to waste time in arguing. "Keep your head down, and look sullen. If anyone speaks, shake your head. If they persist, say this: 'Selig's orders. He's making camp.' " I gave him the words in Skaldic, made him repeat it again and again until he had the accent right. He'd not forgotten what he'd learned. "And treat me like dirt," I added, still in Skaldic. We would be lost, if I forgot and addressed him in D'Angeline.

"One moment." He knelt on the wooden floor next to Trygve's body, pallid and bluish in the cold hut. Crossing his arms, Joscelin murmured a Cassiline prayer, the same he had for Evrard the Sharptongued. It looked strange, to see a Skaldi warrior pray like a Cassiline Brother. He stood up then, putting on Trygve's sword-belt and settling his shield over his shoulder. "Let's go," he said to me in Skaldic.

I drew back the hide and stepped out into the dazzling winter sun.

FIFTY-ONE

At every step of the way I was certain an alarm would be sounded, that Trygve's dead body would somehow shout our crime to the skies. We walked across the snowy expanse toward the heart of the steading, and the distance seemed to grow longer with every step. I have dreams, still, of crossing that space. The day was mercilessly clear, threatening the illusion of Joscelin's Skaldic attire. He kept his head low, glowering under the wolf-mask, a harsh grip on my upper arm.

Surely, though, the White Brethren did not walk so fast; or did they amble, coming back this way? I couldn't remember, I who was trained to note such things. My very wits felt frozen.

We stopped first at the lesser hall, where my presence was less known. A few stared curiously, and one of the housecarls came up gaping, touching his forelock to Joscelin, respecful of the insignia of the White Brethren. "What do you desire?"

Joscelin jerked my arm, nodding at me. "Tell him," he growled, sounding for all the world like an annoyed thane. Not the words I'd given him, but they would work; perhaps it would arouse less suspicion this way.

"Lord Selig has decided to make camp with Kolbjorn and a few men," I said. "He's sent for a skin of mead, two sacks of pottage and a cook-pot. Bring them to the stable; my lord Trygve will ride to meet him."

"Only one skin of mead?" the carl wondered aloud, then gulped with fear, glancing at Joscelin.

"Three," Joscelin retorted, giving my arm another shake, turning away as if in impatience and drawing me after him. I wasn't sure it had worked, until I heard the carl shouting for assistance.

My knees trembled as we made for the great hall. When Joscelin pushed me through the doors, I nearly stumbled, and found myself angry at him for it. It gave me strength enough to stand upright, glaring at him. He glared back, following close on my heels as I headed for Selig's room.

Gerde was not in sight, Elua be thanked. In Selig's room, I shut the door and pointed to the cupboard, which I'd not bothered to relock. Joscelin threw it open and gathered up his arms quickly, buckling his vambraces in place, replacing Trygve's belt with his own, settling the daggers in their sheaths. He took off the wolf-pelt to put on his baldric, hiding his scabbard back under the pelt when he was done. I tangled the hilt of his sword with a length of his abundant hair, and prayed no one would notice a Skaldi warrior bearing Cassiline-style arms. Joscelin grabbed up the saddle-packs and nodded at the door.

"Melisande's letter!" I gasped, struck by a sudden awful realization.

"I thought you had it." He stood waiting, leathern packs in one hand.

"I do." I tore the packs from his hand and wrenched open the one with the letter, rummaging frantically until I found it. "Selig doesn't know we know his plan to betray d'Aiglemort," I said grimly. "If we take the letter, it will tip our hand. He'll alter his plans accordingly, and any advantage will be lost. We'll have to forego proof." I placed the letter back where I'd found it, on a high shelf in the cupboard. My hands were trembling, and I wiped them on my skirts, taking a deep breath. "All right. Let's go."

We weren't so lucky in leaving.

Halfway to the door, Gerde emerged from the kitchen and caught sight of us. "Where are you going *now*?" she asked querulously, walking toward us. "Trygve, you *promised*!"

"Selig's orders." Joscelin muttered it, keeping his eyes on the door and towing me forward.

"*I* never heard anything about it!" Gerde kept walking, hands on her hips, irritation in her voice. Another few yards, and she'd realize it wasn't Trygve beneath the wolf-hood. I shook Joscelin's hold off my arm and stepped between them.

"And why would you?" I asked, letting my voice fill with scathing contempt. "Does Lord Selig send for you, when he is minded to have pleasure? Does he send for any woman in his steading?" I swept my gaze across the hall, meeting gaping stares. At least no one was looking at Joscelin now. "No, he does not," I continued haughtily. "He is worthy of the name King, and he sends for one worthy of pleasing a King. And if it is his pleasure to make camp this evening and send for me to join him, anyone who would remain long in his favor would be well-advised not to question it!"

I spun on my heel and marched toward the door. Joscelin gave a disgusted shrug in the general direction of the hall, moved ahead of me and shoved the door open, following me through it. I could hear the furor rising behind us, like a kicked hornets' nest. If we were caught, there would be no mercy spoken anywhere in Selig's steading on my behalf.

"Not so fast," Joscelin said under his breath when we were outside. I had been hurrying. I forced myself to slow to a more measured pace, grateful for his sense.

Selig's stables, if they could be called such, were merely a long row of lean-tos erected against the wind in a large paddock. The Skaldi do not coddle their animals, reckoning to keep them hardy. A few horses remained in the paddock, huddled together for warmth; my shaggy pony was among them. One of the carls came running, seeing a White Brother approach.

"The stocks were sent," he said breathlessly, "and we've your horse near saddled, sir. Is it true Waldemar Selig is making camp?"

"Selig's orders," Joscelin repeated brusquely.

"Lord Selig has sent for me as well," I said imperiously. "You will bring my horse and see him saddled."

The carl glanced at Joscelin, who shrugged and nodded. He ran off shouting, and a couple of boys raced into the paddock to round up my pony. The carl returned, touching his forelock.

"Fodder for the horses." I looked at Joscelin. "How many did Lord Selig say? A dozen?"

He gave a glare under the wolf-mask. "Fodder for a dozen," he echoed.

"Yes, sir." The carl gave a nervous bob, and whirled off again. We watched in a kind of shock as Selig's folk made ready the manner of our escape, loading the horses with supplies. They even led the horses out of the paddock for us. Joscelin secured Selig's saddle-packs on his mount, lashing them atop the packs already in place. He swung himself into the saddle, snapping his fingers at me. It was a Skaldi gesture, but I saw the steel glint of his vambraces beneath the sleeve of his wool jerkin and held my breath. No one noticed. I mounted and took up the reins. My hands shook. They will put it down to the cold, I thought, waiting for Joscelin until I remembered that he'd no idea which way the hunt had gone. So many small details to give us away! I nudged my pony forward, leaning down to whisper in its ear. "Ride to the north end of the lake, and up the mountain trail," I murmured in D'Angeline.

It was enough. Joscelin gave a curt nod to the carl and said to me in Skaldic, his tone impatient, "Go!" He set heels to his horse, trotting briskly toward the verge of the lake, and I followed.

We had to ride past the tents of the other steading riders, where some few remained; only the favored ones had been invited to the hunt. I was thankful that Harald numbered among them. Alone among those encamped here, he knew Joscelin by sight, maybe well enough to pick out his seat on a horse, to know him in disguise by the glint of steel at his wrists, the twin daggers, the protruding hilt.

But Harald was with Selig, and there was no one else who would see, at a distance, that the White Brother who rode with me was no Skaldi. A handful of thanes shouted greetings and cheerful obscenities; Joscelin laughed in response, and once responded with an obscene gesture I'd no idea he knew. Gunter's men used to do it behind my back, and laugh like boys if I caught them out at it.

The day was perishingly cold, and the air made my lungs ache, stiffening my face to a mask. I thought of the night, when the temperature would drop, with terror. We should have procured a tent, I realized. The Skaldi would not have taken them on a hunting party or an overnight raid, but Selig might have sent for one, if he sent for me. If we freeze to death, I thought, it will be my fault.

We made it around the north end of the lake, and picked out the trail leading out of the valley, clearly marked by the passage of mounted men and dogs. It was steep, but at least the horses didn't have to flounder through unbroken snow. We threaded our way up, both of us listening intently for sounds of Selig's hunters in the distance. There was nothing but the sound of the forest, occasional birdsong and the faint noise of snowy branches shifting. I turned to look behind us at the top, and Selig's steading lay far below, the lake like a blue bowl. Joscelin blew on his fingers.

"How shall we do this?" he asked.

I considered the view behind us again. "We'll follow their trail a little further, until we're well out of sight from the steading. Then we go west." I drew my fur cloak tighter around me and shivered. "Joscelin, this was as far as my plan went. I know where we are, thanks to Selig's maps. And I know where home lies. How we get from here to there alive, I've no idea, except that we'd best get as much of a start as we can, before they find us gone. And I didn't think to get a tent."

"You found us a way out. I'll find us a way home." He gazed around the forest, his blue eyes familiar and strange beneath the hood of the White Brother. "Remember," he added, "I was raised in the mountains."

I took heart at that, and blew on my hands as he had. "Let's go, then."

We rode some distance along the hunters' trail, then veered off sharply to the left, heading westward. Joscelin made me wait, holding the reins of his horse, while he retraced our steps through the snow and erased them with a pine broom.

"They'll not see it if they're not looking," he said with satisfaction, hurling his pine branch away and remounting. "And not if they ride at dusk. Come on, let's put some distance between us."

There was only one thing we had forgotten.

It happened not long afterward. We rode in silence, as best we could; only the creaking of leather and the blowing and snorting of the horses gave us away.

Enough for the White Brethren who guarded the boundaries of Selig's territory to hear.

They are well concealed in snow, with their white pelts. Knud might have known they were there, but we did not, until they sprang up, spears ready to cast, crying out a challenge.

And seeing Joscelin attired at one of their own, fell confused.

"Well met, brother," one called cautiously, lowering his spear. "Where are you bound?"

I do not think Joscelin had any choice in the matter; there was no lie convincing enough to explain our presence here and gain us passage, even if they didn't penetrate his disguise. I heard him murmur one anguished word, and then his sword was out and he clapped his heels to his mount, charging them.

The one who'd spoken barely had time to frame an expression of astonishment before Joscelin rode him down, sword flashing in a killing stroke. The other scrambled backward, cocking his spear, as Joscelin swung around toward him. His eyes flickered frantically, trying to decide: the horse or the rider? He flung his spear at Joscelin, aiming at his heart. Joscelin dropped low along his horse's neck, and the spear passed cleanly over him. Swinging himself upright, he rode down the second of the White Brethren. This one got his shield up; it took several blows to finish him.

There is nothing redder than fresh-spilled blood on virgin snow.

Joscelin rode slowly back toward me, his expression stricken. His eyes, that had looked so young when first he gazed at the forest, looked sick and old.

"It had to be done," I said softly.

He nodded and dismounted, cleaning and sheathing his sword. Without looking at the man's face, he went to the nearest of the White Brethren, the first one, who wore crude fur mittens on his hands. One still clutched his unused spear. Joscelin drew them off gently, bringing them to me. "Don't say anything. Just put them on."

I obeyed him without question. My hands swam in them and I could scarce grasp the reins, but they were warm. Joscelin remounted and we set out again.

No one else challenged our path, and it grew evident as we journeyed that we were in uninhabited territory. We pressed the horses as hard as we dared, forging through snow that at times was nigh breast-high on my shaggy pony. For all that, he seemed hardier than Joscelin's taller mount. Once we had to cross a quick-flowing stream, that ran with such vigor between its narrow banks as to render it unfrozen. We let the horses drink, holding them to small sips; it would have given them colic, Joscelin said, to fill their bellies all at once. He emptied out two of the meadskins there, filling them with clean water.

We paused only to rest the horses, and then only briefly. Our midday meal was a handful of pottage oats, chewed dry and washed down with icy water. From time to time, Joscelin would dismount and lead his mount, breaking a path and giving it a respite from his weight. He made me do it once too, when I was turning blue with cold. I cursed him for it, but the exertion warmed me. He was right, of course. If the horses foundered, we'd be caught for sure.

I had in my head a clear map of the route we must take to reach the lowest pass of the Camaeline Range. It was something else, though, to measure it against the vast, trackless expanse we travelled; and I was no navigator. When at last the sun began to sink in the west, throwing tree-shadows long and black toward us, I realized we'd angled off-course. We corrected our course, then, trudging westward toward the lowering orange glow.

"That's far enough." Joscelin's words broke a long silence between us. A scrap of light remained to be glimpsed through the trees, and no more. "Any further, and we won't be able to see to make camp."

He dismounted, then, tying his horse's reins to a nearby branch. I followed suit, trying not to shiver at the encroaching darkness. "Do you think it's safe to make a fire?" I asked through chattering teeth.

"It's not safe not to, unless you want to freeze in your sleep." Joscelin tramped down a patch of snow, then set about gathering dead branches, stacking them efficiently. I helped as best I could, lugging wood to the fire site. "We need to tend to the horses first," he said, digging out Selig's tinderbox and kneeling to strike a spark. Once, twice, three times, it failed to catch. My heart sank. Unperturbed, Joscelin drew one of his daggers and carefully shaved wood from a dry branch, then struck another spark. This time, it caught. He nurtured it tenderly, feeding it with twigs, until a tidy blaze resulted.

"What do you want me to do?" I felt hopelessly inadequate.

"Here." Joscelin handed me the cook-pot. "Fill it with one of the skins, and water the horses. We can thaw snow to refill it. When you're done, set the pottage to cooking."

Circumstance is everything. In Delaunay's household, I'd have balked at eating a meal cooked in a pot from which horses had drunk; now, it couldn't have mattered less to me. My hardy pony dipped his muzzle and drank deep, lifting his head when I drew the pot away lest he guzzle too much at once. Droplets of ice formed on the whiskers that grew from his soft muzzle, and he looked at me with dark limpid eyes under his forelock.

While I went about my assigned chores, Joscelin worked with a tireless efficiency that humbled me, removing the horses' saddles and rubbing them down with a bit of jersey-cloth, rendering makeshift hobbles from a length of leather he scavenged from one of the packs, giving each a measure of grain fodder—which smelled, in truth, better than our pottage—and erecting a wind-break from deadfalls and gathering a night's supply of wood. He gathered more pine boughs, green ones, hacking them down with his sword while I stirred the pottage, and made a springy bed of them upon the snow. Rummaging among Selig's clothing, which I'd taken, he found a woolen cloak which he spread over the boughs.

"It will keep the snow from stealing the heat of our bodies," he said by way of explanation, sitting on the pine-bed and drawing his sword. "We'll . . . we should sleep close, for warmth."

There was an awkwardness in his tone. I raised my eyebrows at him. "After all we've been through, that embarrasses you?"

He bent his head over his sword, running a sharpening stone that had been among his things the length of the blade. His face was averted, fire-cast shadows flickering in the hollow eyeholes of the wolf-mask on his brow. "It does if I think on it, Phèdre," he said quietly. "I've not much left to hold on to, by way of my vows."

"I'm sorry." Abandoning my burbling pottage, I came over to sit beside him, wrapping both mittened hands around one of his arms. "Truly, Joscelin," I repeated, "I am sorry." We sat there together, staring into the fire. It burned merrily, melting a hollow into the snow and throwing dancing branch-patterns into the night above us. "I tried to kill Selig last night," I told him.

I felt the shock of it go through him, and he turned to look at me. "Why? They'd have killed you for it."

"I know." I gazed at the shifting flames. "But it would have been sure, that way. The Skaldi wouldn't unite under another, he's the one holds them together. And you wouldn't have had to betray your vow."

"What happened?" His voice was soft.

"He woke up." I shrugged. "Maybe it's true, maybe he really is proof against harm. It was that old priest made me think it, who called me Kushiel's weapon. But he woke up. I was lucky, he didn't know what I was about."

"Phèdre." Joscelin drew a shuddering breath, and loosed it in a sound almost like a laugh, but not quite. "Plaything of the wealthy. Ah, Elua . . . you put me to shame. I wish I'd known Delaunay better, to have created such a pupil."

"I wish you had too." I drew off one of my mittens and plucked a twig from his hair, toying with it to feel its fineness. "But in all fairness, when I first met you, I thought you were—"

"A dried-up old stick of a Cassiline Brother," he finished, shooting me an amused glance. "I remember. I remember it very well."

"No." I gave his hair a sharp tug and smiled at him. "That was before I met you. Once I did, I thought you were a smug, self-satisfied young prig of a Cassiline Brother."

He laughed at that, a real laugh. "You were right. I was."

"No, I was wrong. The man I thought you were would have given up and died of humiliation in Gunter's kennels. You kept fighting, and stayed true to yourself. And kept me alive, thus far."

"You did that much for yourself, Phèdre, and for me as well," he said soberly, prodding the fire with the tip of his sword. "I've no illusions on that score, trust me. But I swear, I'll do what's needful now to get you alive and whole to Ysandre de la Courcel. If I'm to be damned for what I've done, I'll be damned in full and not by halves."

"I know," I murmured. I'd seen his eyes when he killed the White Brethren. We sat in silence together, until I broke it. "We should eat."

"Eat, and sleep. We need all the strength we can muster." Heaving himself to his feet, he sheathed his sword and fetched our pottage from the fire. We had but one spoon between us, and took turns with it, filling our bellies with warm, albeit tasteless, food. When it was gone, Joscelin scraped the bowl clean and filled it with snow to melt, while I sat part-frozen, part-warm and drowsy with exhaustion, huddled in my cloak.

We laid down then together on the pine-bed, piling every spare bit of hide and wool upon us. I lay curled against Joscelin, feeling the warmth of his body seep into my limbs. "Sleep," he whispered against my hair. "They'll not find us tonight. Sleep."

After a while, I did.

FIFTY-TWO

I awoke in the morning alone, stiff and cold.

If I had thought the voyage from Gunter's steading to Selig's was hard, it was nothing to this. Whether I had known it or not, I endured that journey as a cherished and pampered member of the tribe. I did not think, then, on the fact that I'd no need to saddle my own horse, to cook my own meals, and make do for myself in every way possible.

Now, I needs must shift for myself, for speed was of the essence, and Joscelin—no matter how efficient—was but one man, and not bred to the Skaldi wilderness, where the cold cuts deeper and the snow drifts higher than in the mountains of Siovale.

We came to a new language together on that deadly journey, one of quick gestures, nods and grimaces. I learned things I had never known, nor ever thought it would be needful to know, such as the most efficient way to pack a horse and the best way to pick a trail through dense growth where twining branches hidden beneath the snow formed traps to entangle horses and humans alike.

I learned to wrap my head in wool as if in a burnouse, saving precious heat, draping a length across my face to protect it from the wind. I learned to crack the ice from my garments and press onward without pausing. I learned to dig ice out of my pony's hooves, when the tender pad inside cracked and bled. I learned to carry a dagger—Trygve's dagger, that Joscelin had kept—at my waist and to use it for simple chores.

These things I learned, and quickly, for we travelled as fast as we dared, pushing ourselves and our horses close to the point of foundering. Our flesh grew numb, and we had to check our extremities for signs of the dead white flesh that betokened frostbite. On the second night, a pack of wolves circled round while we made camp, close enough that we caught glimpses of them through the trees. Joscelin worked frantically to build the fire and raced around the edges of the camp shouting when it was lit, brandishing a torch. They withdrew, then, into the forest, but we caught sight of their eyes reflecting fire in the night.

Still, we saw no one on the second day, nor on the next. That was the third day, when we lost a precious hour in a near disaster. It befell us atop a snowy ridge, where we dismounted and paused to get our bearings. Shading my eyes against the snow glare, I pointed to the distant north, where a thin trail of smoke threaded into the blue sky behind a twin-forked mountain peak.

"Raskogr's steading," I said, my voice muffled through the wool shroud across my face. "One of the Suevi. We need to bear a little south and follow the ridge."

Joscelin nodded and took one step forward.

The ledge of snow crumbled beneath his feet, nothing under it. With a shout, he went down, tumbling head over heels in a sliding sheet of snow. I flung myself backward in terror, scrabbling for solid rock, and found myself clinging to a rough boulder that thrust out of the snow, empty air inches beyond my toes. My faithful pony tossed his head and snorted in alarm, while Joscelin's horse bolted some yards away and stopped, rolling the whites of its eyes.

Trembling, I leaned forward to look.

Far below, Joscelin was pulling himself out of the snow, apparently unharmed. As I watched, he tested his limbs, checking himself for injury, then felt for his weapons. His daggers were at his waist, but his sword had come out of its sheath. I could see it protruding from the snow, a length of blade and the hilt, halfway up the ridge.

Seeing me peer over the ledge, he signalled he was well. I waved back and pointed at his sword. Even from here, I could see his disgust.

It took him the better part of an hour to climb back up the ridge, for thrice the sliding snows gave way beneath him, casting him back down half the distance he'd gained. Much of the time I spent stomping after his recalcitrant horse, that blew out its breath in a frightened cloud of frost and floundered away through the snow when I got near. Finally I remembered what the children of Perrinwolde had done, and lured it with a handful of oats. When at last I captured its reins, I was so cold and tired and frustrated that I leaned my face against its warm neck and wept, until my tears froze bitter and icy on my cheeks. Joscelin's horse munched its bit of fodder and nuzzled my hair as if it hadn't been the cause of such dismay.

Joscelin, upon gaining the summit, simply lay on his back and stared at the sky, exhausted. I gave him the waterskin without speaking, and he drank.

"We have to keep going." His voice was reedy, lungs seared by his exertions in the cold air, but he heaved himself to his feet.

I nodded. "At least the horses are rested." It was a feeble witticism at best, but that was how we kept ourselves going.

And onward we went.

Neither of us spoke that night about the time we had lost, but we were both on edge, jumping at the sounds of the forest: shifting snow, the sharp crack branches will make when the sap freezes in their woody veins. Joscelin stared moodily at the fire, poking at it as he did when he was thinking.

"Phèdre." His voice startled me, and I realized the extent of my nerves' fraying. I met his sober look. "If . . . when . . . they catch us, I want you to do something. Whatever I say, whatever I do, play along with it. Here, I want to show you something." Rising, he went to our packs, and came back with Trygve's shield. It was a simple round buckler, hide-covered, with a steel disk at the center and straps to go over one's arm. I'd wondered why he hadn't discarded it, when he fought better without one.

Under the Skaldic night skies, he showed me how to wield it, slipping my arm into the straps and covering my body.

"If you have a chance," he said quietly, "any chance, to get away, take it. You know enough to survive on your own, while the supplies hold out. But if you don't . . . use the shield. And I will do what I can."

"Protect and serve," I whispered, gazing up at him, silhouetted against the starry night. He nodded, tears in his eyes, glimmering in the dark. I felt a pain in my heart I had never felt before. "Ah, Joscelin . . ."

"Go to sleep." He murmured it, turning away. "I'll take the first watch."

On the fourth day, it snowed.

It was the sort of weather that played with us as a cat will play with a mouse between its paws, battering us with whipping wind and a flurry of whiteness, then drawing back to allow us enough of a respite to press forward, sometimes huddled over our mounts' necks, sometimes wading through snow waist-deep, until the next blast came, swiping at us with wintry claws.

I fell into a cold dream, numb and frozen, huddled in the saddle or stumbling in Joscelin's trail, only his curses and exhortations keeping me moving. I don't know how long we travelled that way. Time becomes meaningless, measured out in lengths of endless staggering in a frigid daze, broken only by brief moments of lucidity when the snows broke and the landscape lay visible before us, showing our markers.

There is a sound the wind makes when it gusts, a high keening sound, as it bends around rock and tree. I grew so used to it, I scarce noticed when it changed, no longer rising and falling but rising steadily, rising and rising.

"Joscelin!"

The wind tore the word from my lips, but he caught it, turning back, a strange and hoary figure under the wolf-pelt. I pointed back along our trail with one mittened hand.

"They're coming."

He threw his head back in alarm, gaze sweeping our surroundings. There was nothing for the eye to see, nothing but swirling snow. "How many?"

"I can't tell." I made myself be still, straining to hear the distant yells over the keening wind. "Six. Maybe eight."

His face was grim. "Ride!"

We rode, then, blindly, the way one flees in a nightmare. I hunched in the saddle and clung to my pony's neck, the air gasping in my lungs like knives as my mount struggled gamely in Joscelin's wake, plunging and churning the snow. I could hear them now, clearly, a bloodthirsty Skaldic war-chant that rose above the wind and battered our ears like raven's wings, urging us onward, onward, into the madness of flight.

It was too much, and we had too little left to give. I heard the sound of howling Skaldi pursuers string out, half their number circling around our forefront. I rode, floundering, alongside Joscelin and shook my head at him as we burst into a clearing, near a promontory of rock. His horse was nigh done in, and I could feel my pony's sturdy sides heaving under me.

Joscelin drew up his horse, then, a serene calm settling over his wind-burned features. "We will make a stand, Phèdre," he said to me, very clearly. I remember that so well. He nodded at the promontory, dismounting and handing me Trygve's shield. "Take this, and guard yourself as best you may."

I obeyed, getting down from my exhausted mount and settling the shield on my arm, my back against the rock. Our horses stood without moving, heads low, trembling as the lather turned to ice on their coats. Shield-armed and settled, I stood watching while Joscelin drew his sword and walked out into the middle of the clearing to meet them, a lonely figure half-lost in the swirling snows.

I'd been right; there were seven of them. Volunteers, Selig's best, the fastest riders, the most skilled trackers. It was something, that it had taken them four days to catch us. The howling had stopped when we ceased to flee, and they rode silently out of the snows, dark and ominous. Seven. They halted before Joscelin, ranged in a semicircle. He stood alone, his sword hilt at shoulder-height, the blade angled across his body in the Cassiline defensive pose.

And then he threw it down, and clasped his hands in the air above his head.

"In Selig's name," he cried in passable Skaldic, "I surrender!"

I heard laughter, then a gust of wind came, and snow-devils obscured my vision. When it died, I saw four had dismounted and approached him on foot, swords drawn, and one battle-axe among them. Two riders hung back.

The third rode toward me.

Joscelin, hands clasped above his head, waited un-moving until the nearest Skaldi reached him, poking his chest with the tip of his sword.

Then he moved, and steel rang in the clearing as he swept the Skaldi blade away with one vambraced fore-arm, both daggers suddenly in his hands, moving as un-expectedly as the skirling winds. No one will ever write of the strange poetry of that battle, the Cassiline's ballet of snow and steel and death in the Skaldic hinterlands. Figures moved like wraiths in the snow-veiled clearing, only the clash of arms giving the deadly lie to their dance.

And the Skaldi rider approaching me drew nearer, un-til I shrank back against the rock and threw up my shield in defense.

It was Harald the Beardless, of Gunter's steading.

I stared, astonished; in two heartbeats, he was off his horse and inside the reach of my shield, wrapping one arm around me and setting the point of his dagger to my throat. "D'Angeline!" he cried, pitching his voice toward the battle. "Let be! I have the girl!" I struggled in his grip, and he tightened it. "Don't worry," he muttered under his breath. "I'll not do it, Selig wants you alive."

On the field, I could see one of the figures pause; Joscelin, it had to be. He had his sword back, and I knew it by the angle at which he wielded it. Two of the Skaldi were down, but as I watched, one of those still mounted spurred his horse forward, axe sweeping for a blow.

"Joscelin!" I filled my lungs to bursting with the shout, willing it to reach him. "Don't listen to him!"

Harald swore at me, clamping a hand over my mouth. I stamped on his foot and nearly broke free, but he regained his grip, shifting the dagger so I felt its edge. From the corner of my eye, I could see that Joscelin was down, rolling, but he fought still; the mounted Skaldi was slumping sideways in the saddle.

"I traded places with one of Selig's thanes to come after you," Harald hissed. "Don't make me harm you, D'Angeline! I mean to regain the honor of our steading with your return."

He held me hard against his side, my shoulders pinned, the shield awkward between us. Fumbling at my waist, I slid my hand out of my oversized mitten and felt the hilt of Trygve's dagger beneath me. I wrapped my fingers about it and eased it from its sheath.

Joscelin was on his feet again, dodging through the snow, quick and agile. If nothing else, he had learned to maneuver on this terrain, the hard way. Two Skaldi yet opposed him on foot, and one on horseback. None of them had ever been forced to run over miles of wasteland behind one of Gunter Arnlaugson's horses. The Cassiline sword flashed through the snow-laden air, and another of the unmounted Skaldi went down.

"Let me go, Harald," I said softly, twisting to gaze at his face. So young, the golden stubble of his first beard just thickening. Despite the cold, my hand was slippery with sweat, clenched about the hidden dagger hilt. "I am a free D'Angeline."

"Don't try to sway me!" He looked away stubbornly, refusing to meet my eyes. "I'll not fall under your witch-craft, D'Angeline. You belong to Waldemar Selig!"

"Harald." My hand was trembling, holding the dagger so near his vitals, hidden behind the shield bound so awkwardly to my left arm. Pinned against him, I could feel his warmth. He had given me the fur cloak I still wore and been the first to sing songs about me. My vision was blurred with tears. "Let me go, or I swear I will kill you."

Intent on the battle, he shouted a warning to the last mounted Skaldi, who narrowly avoided having his horse hamstrung by Joscelin. It was a measure of our desperate straits, that he would attempt such a thing.

As was what I did.

"Forgive me," I whispered, and pushed the dagger into Harald with all my strength.

I do not think, at first, he knew what had happened; his eyes widened, and his arms fell away from me. He looked down, then, and saw between us what the shield had hidden. With a gasping sob, I forced the dagger up-ward toward his heart and let go the hilt. Harald took a step backward and looked up at me, his eyes quizzical as a boy's. What have you done? they seemed to ask of me. What have you done?

I gave no answer, and he crumpled to the ground and lay unmoving.

The last Skaldi rider saw, and gave a cry. Turning away from Joscelin, he spurred his horse toward me, looming through the snow. With nowhere to run, I waited, dumb and silent. In the distance, Joscelin dispatched the lone unmounted warrior and raced for a horse, any horse.

In dreams, things happen slowly. It was like that still, this unending frozen nightmare. I could see the Skaldi's face, distorted with rage, shouting curses I couldn't make out in the rising wind. Selig wanted me alive, Harald had said; I could guess his second choice. He would take me dead. At twenty yards, I saw the Skaldi cock his arm, spear at the ready. At fifteen, he cast it.

I closed my eyes and lifted Trygve's buckler.

The impact jarred my arm to the bone, knocking me off my feet. Opening my eyes, I saw him above me, blotting out the winter sky atop his horse. Still strapped to my arm, the shield was useless, cracked beneath the force of the blow, the lethal, leaf-shaped tip of the spear gone clean through to the inside.

If he had had a second spear, I would have died then. I know this. But what spears he'd had, he had already cast. He dismounted and drew his sword.

"No!" Joscelin's shout split the air, and the Skaldi turned, hesitating at the now-mounted Cassiline's approach. I struggled to free myself from the useless shield, scrambling backward through the snow. Face grim, Joscelin lashed his borrowed horse forward, nigh on us.

Too hard, too fast. The horse stumbled, slid, losing its footing; it went down hard, head low, the mighty body crashing to the snow-covered earth. Sword in hand, Joscelin was flung free and fell no less hard, some distance from the thrashing horse.

The Skaldi looked back at me and grinned, the fierce, savage grin of a warrior with nothing left to lose. "You first," he said, and raised his sword high above his head, preparing to bring it down two-handed upon me.

"Elua," I whispered, and prepared to die.

The blade never fell.

It slipped, instead, falling away from his nerveless fingers to fall with a soft thump into the snow. The Skaldi stared down at himself, where the bloody tip and a handspan of Joscelin's sword protruded. No one, I think, fails to be surprised at the death-blow when it comes in battle. He turned about slowly, his hands going to the blade's tip. I saw the hilt and the rest of the blade standing out from between his shoulders. Joscelin was still down, propped on one arm; he'd thrown it from where he'd fallen. The Skaldi stared at him in disbelief, sinking slowly to his knees. Still clutching the tip of the sword lodged in him, he died.

It was quiet then, but for the wind and snow. Joscelin got painfully to his feet and came toward me, staggering. I saw when he drew near that he had a cut on one cheekbone, already frozen, and runnels of blood in his hair. He turned the last Skaldi on his stomach and tugged his sword free, bracing one foot on the body to get it loose. I stood wearily, and we held each other upright.

"Do you know what the odds of making that throw were?" Joscelin murmured, wavering on his feet. "We don't even train for it. It's not done."

"No." I swallowed, and nodded at Harald, motionless by the promontory, a dusting of snow already covering him. "Do you know he gave me his cloak? He never even asked for it back."

"I know." With an effort, Joscelin released me and stood on his own, passing one hand to his side. "We have to keep moving. Take . . . take anything we can use. Food, water, fodder . . . we could use more blankets. We'll take a pack-horse, use whichever mounts are freshest. We need to gain some distance before we rest."

FIFTY-THREE

Stripping the dead of spoil is a grim business. I have heard that Skaldi women sing as they do it. I tried to imagine kind-hearted Hedwig doing it, and could not; then I remembered how the women of Selig's steading hated me, and I could. We did not sing, Joscelin and I, working together in numb horror. We did not even speak, but only did what was needful.

One of the Skaldi horses, the one that had fallen, had broken a leg and had to be put down. Joscelin did it with his daggers, cutting the large vein on the neck. I could not watch. We took two of their horses, and left the others to fend for themselves, hoping they would find their way to a steading before the wolves found them; they were nigh as tired as our own mounts. I kept my pony, though, unable to bear leaving him for the wolves. And in truth, he was hardier than the horses, quicker to regain strength. I learned, later, that the breed was native to the Skaldic lands; they'd bred for the larger mounts with strains of Caerdicci and Aragonian horses, better for battle, but not for enduring the cold.

So it was that we set out once more.

It had been my intention, when we reached it, to follow the Danrau River, keeping it in sight until we reached the Camaelines. It was Joscelin's idea to follow the riverbed for a time, rendering our trail invisible, then cut to the south and throw off any other pursuers. We had no way of knowing whether there were others, or how many or how far behind they might be, but I suspected Selig would send more than one party.

We followed his plan, our horses picking their way

cautiously through the cold, fast-flowing water, and he did as he had before, backtracking to erase our trail where it emerged from the river. How he did it, I do not know, for by then the cold and exhaustion were so deep in my bones that I could barely think. It wasn't until he returned, hollow-eyed, that I realized he was worse off than I. It is a strange thing, human endurance. After the river, I would have said I was done in, but when I saw his condition, I found a bleak pocket of strength that kept me going, taking the lead to forge a trail through the gathering dusk. The wind had picked up again and there was no shelter to be found, only barren rock and thin trees. I knew, by then, how to look for a campsite. There was no place to be found, so I kept going.

I don't know what all I thought of, trudging through the endless winter, leading my horse while Joscelin followed, hunched in his saddle, the heavily laden pony trailing. A thousand memories of home, of fêtes I had attended, of patrons, of Delaunay and Alcuin. I thought of the marquist's shop, of the healing springs of Naamah's sanctuary, of Delaunay's library, which I had once thought the safest place in the world. I thought of Hyacinthe and the Cockerel, and the offering we had made at Blessed Elua's temple.

At what point I began to pray, I don't know, for it was a prayer without words, a remembrance of grace, of Elua's temple, scarlet anemones in my hands, the earth warm and moist beneath my bare feet, cool marble beneath my lips, and the priest's kind voice. Love as thou wilt, he had said, and Elua will guide your steps, no matter how long the journey. I clung blindly to the moment, along my endless journey, until I could go no farther and stopped to look about me, realizing in the gloaming and snow that I had walked straight into a wall of stone.

This is the end, I thought, putting out my hands and feeling the stone before me. I can go no further. I dared not look behind me.

My left hand, sliding sideways, met no resistance. Darkness opened in the rock before me. Groping, I felt my way forward, trusting that my mount was too exhausted to run.

It was a cave.

I went into it as far as I dared, sniffing the air for scent of wolf or bear. The sound and force of the wind died inside the stone walls, leaving a strange black stillness. There was no sense of any living thing. I emerged, fighting my way through the snow to Joscelin's side. He looked blearily at me through frost-rimed lashes.

"There's a cave," I shouted, cupping my mouth against the wind, then pointing. "Give me one of the torches, and I'll look."

Moving as though it hurt to do so, he dismounted, and we led the horses into the overhang. With a faint, dim light still filtering through the opening, we unpacked the tinderbox and the branches swathed in pitch-soaked rags we'd taken from the fallen Skaldi. I struck a spark and a torch flared into light.

Holding it aloft, I ventured deeper into the cavern.

It went farther than I'd guessed, and was vaster. Alone in a dark arena, I turned about, letting torchlight illuminate the walls. I'd been right, it was empty; but there, in the center, were the remains of an ancient campfire. Glancing up, I saw high above a small rift in the stone ceiling, a hole for smoke to escape.

It would do. It would more than do.

I wedged the torch in a crevice, and went back for Joscelin. This time, it was I who did the lion's share of the work, tending to the horses, who huddled gratefully out of the gale, gathering scrub branches and laying a fire on the site of ancient ashes. I even found a massive deadfall and devised a crude hitch for the pony, dragging the better part of a small tree into the cavern itself. The wood was dry and burned without much smoke, until the space was suffused with welcome warmth and light.

No pine-bough bed for us tonight, but we'd no need of it for once, the stone floor of the cave warmer than snow. Joscelin had laid out our things, and we'd furs and blankets to spare, with what we'd taken from the Skaldi. We sat together without shivering, and dined on pottage and strips of dried venison, which we also had in plenty now, courtesy of Selig's stores.

When we had eaten, I cleaned the cook-pot and set it full of snow to melt, stoking up the fire once more. I hauled the one meadskin Joscelin hadn't emptied over then, and a container of salve one of the Skaldi had carried. With a careful touch, I cleaned the cut on his cheek and the deeper gash on his skull with hot water and a bit of cloth, then washed them with mead.

"I wondered why you kept this," I said, smiling at his grimace. "That was clever."

"It wasn't that." He winced again as I dabbed at the cut on his cheek. "I thought you might need it. The Skaldi drink it against the cold."

"Do they?" I tried it, squirting a stream into my mouth. It tasted of fermented honey, and burned pleasantly in my belly. Warming indeed, so that it grew almost hot within the cavern. "It's not bad." I sat back on my heels and gazed at him. "So how bad are the wounds you're hiding?"

He smiled then, wry in the firelight. "Is it that obvious?"

"Yes. Don't be an idiot." I softened my voice. "Let me see."

Without speaking, he stripped off his upper garments.

I caught my breath. His torso was a mass of bruises, and his jerkin beneath the furs was stiff with dried blood from a gash in his left side, a handspan above his hip. Even now, it was still seeping dark blood. "Joscelin," I said, biting my lip. "That should be sewn."

"Give me that meadskin." Tilting it back, he squeezed a long draught into his mouth and swallowed. "I took a kit from one of Selig's men. It's in the pack."

I am neither chirurgeon nor seamstress, and by the time I was done, a good bit of mead had found its way down Joscelin's throat. When it was over, my black stitch-marks straggled across the flesh of his side, but the wound was closed.

"Here," he said, handing me the meadskin as I stretched out alongside him, exhausted beyond words. "You did a good job," he said softly. "Through all of it. Phèdre . . ."

"Shh." Propping myself on one arm, I laid my fingers across his lips. "Joscelin, don't. I don't want to talk about it." Silent behind my hand, he blinked his blue eyes at me. I took my hand away then, and kissed him instead.

I don't know what I expected. I hadn't thought about it. My hair fell loose about us, curtaining our faces. His lips parted under mine, and our tongues touched, only the tips, soft and tentative. I felt his arms slide around me in an embrace, and kissed him harder.

The fire burned untended and the horses murmured and whickered in the forefront of the cavern, their drowsy stirrings and the occasional stamp of a hoof the only backdrop to our lovemaking. I would have thought he would be uncertain—a Cassiline, and celibate—but he came to it with wonder, taking all that I offered with a kind of reverent awe. His hands slid over my skin and I wept at his touch, that had such love in it, tasting the salt of my own tears as I kissed him. I had never, ever, chosen before. When he came into me, I shuddered, and he held off until I drew him back down, fiercely, burying my face against his shoulder and losing myself in him.

At the end, though, I had to look, to see his face, D'Angeline and beloved, above my own. Chosen. He cried out at the end, a sound of wonder and amazement.

Afterward, he rose and walked away, standing alone.

I could only watch, lying in furs beside the fire, that same strange pain twisting at my heart. Joscelin, my Cassiline, my protector, his beautiful body bruised and torn in my service. Somewhere, in the distant part of my mind, I was astonished at it all, not the least that we were here, together, like this; both of us alive, naked in this cavern and not freezing to death.

"We have dreamed this day," I said aloud. "Joscelin, we dream still, and tomorrow will wake from it."

He turned about then, his face grave. "Phèdre . . . I am Cassiel's servant. I cannot cling to that vow, no matter how I've betrayed it, and be otherwise. And without the strength of it, I've not the strength to endure. Do you understand?"

"Yes." Tears stung my eyes, which I ignored. "Do you think I would have survived this long, were I not Naamah's servant, and Kushiel's chosen? I understand."

At that, he nodded, and came back to sit with me on our makeshift bed.

"You're bleeding again." I rummaged in our things for a length of clean cloth, making a pad and binding it over the wound in his side, not meeting his gaze as I did it. It was different, now, touching his flesh.

"I thought . . ." he began to say, then stopped, and cleared his throat. "It's not only pain that pleases you, then. I didn't know."

"No." I glanced up at him, smiling slightly; he looked

so earnest and disheveled, naked and battered, his wheat-streaked hair tangled in Skaldic braids. "Did you think that? I answer to Naamah's arts, and not Kushiel's rod alone."

He reached out and touched Melisande's diamond where it hung, still, about my throat. "But the latter calls louder," he said gently.

"Yes." Unable to lie, I whispered the word. My hand rose to clutch the diamond, and I jerked it hard, breaking the knot that bound the lead. "Ah, Elua! I would be free of it if I could!" I said in disgust, hurling it away from me. It fell with a faint chink against the cavern well. Joscelin gazed after it into the darkness beyond the firelight.

"Phèdre," he said presently. "We've nothing else of value to our names."

"No." Obstinacy overcame me. "I would rather starve."

"Would you?" He looked soberly at me. "You made me choose life over pride."

I was silent a moment, thinking on it. "All right," I said. "Fetch it back, and I will keep it. I will wear it, and remember. If we need it to buy life, we will use it." My voice rose, ringing. "And if we do not, I will wear it, until the day I throw it on the ground at Melisande Shahrizai's feet. And then she will have her answer to her question: It is Kushiel's Dart throws truer than Kushiel's line!"

Joscelin retrieved the diamond without comment, tying it back around my neck. Better him, I thought, twining my hair forward, than anyone else who'd put it there. When he was done, he brushed the length of my spine with a light touch. "I'm sorry you had to leave your marque unfinished," he murmured. "It's beautiful, you know. Like you."

I turned round at that to meet his eyes; he gave me his wry smile.

"If I had to fall from Cassiel's grace," he said softly, "at least I know it took a courtesan worthy of Kings to do it."

"Ah, Joscelin . . ." I leaned forward and took his head in my hands, kissing his brow. "Go to sleep," I told him. "We've a long way to go, yet, and you've healing to do. I'll tell you a story, if you like . . . do they tell Naamah's temptation of Cassiel, in the Brotherhood? They tell it in Cereus House . . ."

I told him the story, then, and he fell asleep smiling before the end; as well he did, I thought, for it is one of those stories that ends without an ending, that the listener may judge for him or herself what happened.

Tales of gods and angels may end that way, for they continue, we know, in the land beyond the end of the world, the true Terre d'Ange. Alas for we who are mortal, and are denied the luxury of dramatic license. We must live, and go onward.

In the morning the fire had burned down to cold ashes and a few buried embers, and we dressed shivering in the chill. Of what had befallen us in the night, we did not speak. What would we have said, if we did? The romances would have it otherwise, but this I will say: There is no point in speaking of love when survival is at issue. I had spoken truly, when I said that we dreamed. It was only the waking that was grim. We went about the business of making ready to leave.

The snows had ended, and the day bid to be overcast, but the lowering clouds held no more in store. A grey light filtered into the cavern from outside. I worked quickly to lash the last of the packs onto my pony, holding my fur mittens between my teeth and working with frozen fingers. Joscelin, much recovered from his wounds, checked the horses' hooves.

"Phèdre!" I heard him gasp as he released the foreleg of one of our Skaldi remounts. The horse stomped, the sound ringing off the stony walls. I looked up to see where he was pointing.

There, etched in rock above the mouth of the cavern, was Blessed Elua's sigil. Caught by some trick of refracted daylight it gleamed, silvery, in the hard stone. I stared without speaking, then closed my mouth, realizing it gaped. Joscelin and I looked wildly at each other.

"You know what this means?" he asked breathlessly. "They sheltered here, crossing the Skaldic hinterlands! Elua, Cassiel, Naamah . . . all the Companions!" Approaching the cavern mouth, he laid his hands reverently upon the rock. "They were here."

"They were here," I echoed, gazing at the silvery lines, remembering my wordless, snow-bound prayer. We had dreamed, I thought, in a sacred place. "Joscelin," I said. "Let's go home."

Tearing himself away from the cavern wall, he glanced at me and nodded, settling the wolf-pelt of the White Brethren in place about his shoulders. "Home," he said firmly, leading the way.

A dream, and the promise of our long-ago celestial begetters, who had not forgotten the distant generations of their children, in whose red blood a thin thread of ichor ran still. Home, a golden memory, from which we were separated by mile upon icy mile.

Outside, the cold of a Skaldic winter awaited us.

Home.

FIFTY-FOUR

In the days that followed, no further pursuit came upon us. The weather was our only enemy, but of a surety, it was enemy enough. With horses somewhat fresher than our own had been, we pressed harder, stopping when the light failed and setting up camp to fall into an exhausted sleep.

Betimes we encountered steadings along the way, but our senses had grown keen living in the wilderness, and each time either Joscelin or I detected signs of human habitation well in advance. We gave all steadings a wide berth, and never made camp within less than an hour's ride from the nearest man-sign. Once or twice more, we saw wolves at dusk, and one terrifying time, we disturbed a fierce bear from its winter slumber in a cave that proved not to be abandoned. I thought my gallant pony lost that time as we fled, the longer-legged horses churning snow in their terror, but he floundered in our wake, making a horrid squeal of fear, his hindquarters inches away from swiping claws the length of my whole hand. I have heard the fabled oliphaunts of Bhodistan are the largest creatures living, but if I never see a doughtier beast than a Skaldic bear, I will rest well content. In this one thing, winter proved our friend, for the bear gave up the chase after a short distance and turned to lumber back into the depths of its shelter, and sleep.

Thus did we reach the Camaeline Range without further incident.

There is no easy way to cross from the Skaldic territories into Terre d'Ange. Where the Camaelines give way in the north, the Rhenus River takes over, too deep and fast to be forded, and seldom bridged since the days of the Tiberian Empire. They, with their legions of engineers, could muster a bridge-building brigade in a matter of a day, given sufficient timber. Since then, D'Angelines have held the river border.

If we dared, I would have ridden clear up to the flatlands and begged passage through Azzalle, for I've no doubt there were loyal adherents to the Crown there, if only in the person of Ghislain de Somerville, who, to the best of my knowledge, still held command of Trevalion. But to cross the heart of Skaldi wilderness was one thing; to ride the borders during wartime—albeit a war Terre d'Ange didn't know was coming—was another. No, it had to be the mountains, and expedience demanded that we attempt the southernmost of the Great Passes.

We rode in the shadow of the tall peaks of the Camaelines for a day, and camped beneath them at night. The snow was deeper here, and it was hard going. Still, we were close enough to sense that the air of home lay on the far side of those cruel mountains, and it gave us heart.

In the morning, we came upon a sight that dashed our hopes.

I had feared that Selig would take further measures against us, and my fears were well-founded. Joscelin, heeding them, made a reconaissance on foot and returned grim-faced, leading me to a secure vantage point. On the snowy plains before the southern pass, we saw them: A party of some two-score Marsi raiders, encamped between us and the pass.

Harald had said he'd traded places with one of Selig's hand-picked thanes. I saw now what he meant. Selig had sent the steading-riders as well, turning out the Marsi tribe to guard the passes against us.

I looked once, hoping against hope, at Joscelin.

"Not a chance," he said ruefully, shaking his head. "There are too many and on open ground, Phèdre. I'd be slaughtered."

"What, then?"

He met my eyes reluctantly, then turned, gazing up at the vast mountain peaks, towering high above us.

"No," I said. "Joscelin, I can't."

"We have to," he said gently. "There's no other way."

On the plain below us, the Skaldi of the Marsi built up their fires, singing and holding games, drinking and shouting and dashing at each other in mock combat. For all of that, they kept scouts posted, watching the horizons. There were probably men of Gunter's steading among them, I thought; men I'd known, men I'd served mead. We could hear them, occasionally, the clear thin air carrying their shouts. If word of what we'd done to Selig's thanes had reached them, they'd kill us without blinking. We couldn't go through them, and we couldn't go around them.

He was right. There was no other way.

I pulled my wolfskin cloak tight around me and shivered. "Then let's go. And may Elua have mercy on us."

I will not tell every step of that treacherous journey. It is enough to say that we survived it. Joscelin rode back the way we'd come, flogging his poor mount, and returned in the lowering orange light of sunset to report that he'd found a trail, a mere goat-track, winding up among the crags beyond where the eye could follow. Turning our backs on the Skaldi, we rode back to make camp in the foothills, daring only the smallest of fires. Joscelin fed it all night with twigs, and I daresay it would have fit within his cupped hands. It kept the warmth of life in our flesh, though barely.

In the morning, we began to ascend.

After a certain point, it was no longer possible to ride, and we needs must dismount and climb, using frigid hands and feet to find holds, leading the horses scrambling after. I lost my mount on the first day. It was a horrible thing, and I do not like to think on it; he sheered away from a crag when it loosed a small avalanche of snow and lost his footing. If I'd been mounted, I'd have gone over the precipice too. As it was, we lost half our stores, and I was sick at the poor creature's demise.

"Never mind," Joscelin said through frozen lips, his eyes looking as sick as I felt. "We've enough for two more days, and if we don't live that long, it won't matter."

So we kept on, shifting the bulk of our packs to the pony. I was glad I'd kept him with me, for he was surer-footed in the mountains than the tall horses.

Joscelin's mount we lost on a mistep.

It happened after we had reached the summit, where the air was so thin we could not seem to fill our lungs, but gasped in breath like knives. It is beautiful in the mountains; so they say, and I daresay it is true. If I fail to describe the beauty of the Camaelines, do not think it is for lack of poetry in my soul. I fought for my life with every step, and could not spare the strength needed to lift my head and take in the view. We reached the top, and headed down.

It is easier to go down than up. It is also more dangerous. A pocket of snow, a hidden crevice; Joscelin's horse snapped a foreleg. It was the second he'd had to put down, and no easier than the first. This time, he held the cook-pot to the vein when he cut it.

"One of Barquiel L'Envers' men told me the Akkadians make blood-tea when they're caught out in the desert," he said without looking at me. "They can live for days, and the horses too. He's dead anyway, Phèdre."

I did not argue; it was true. We drank blood-tea. We survived the mountains, and descended into Camlach.

The province of the traitor Duc, Isidore d'Aiglemort, and the Allies of Camlach.

It was too much to ask, that we should pass unnoticed through the D'Angeline borderlands. When they sing of this winter, the poets—none of whom stood atop the Camaelines, you may be sure—call it the Bitterest Winter. The Skaldi had been raiding all winter, braving the passes. The border was well patrolled.

The Allies of Camlach found us that night.

We were careless, it is true, relieved to be alive. Our campsite was secluded and our fire small, but it might as well have been a beacon in those lands, which are little kinder than the Skaldi territories themselves, so close to the mountains.

It was a small scouting party that found us, riding out of the darkness with a faint jingle of bit and harness, the firelight gleaming on mail shirts. Joscelin sprang to his feet with a curse, kicking snow at the fire, but too late; they were on us.

They expected us no more than we did them; less, I daresay. No more than a score of men, mounted D'Angeline warriors all, staring in perplexity at the sight of us. My heart bounded and sank, all at once, and I looked frantically for their standard-bearer.

There, the burning sword, emblazoned on sable. Allies of Camlach. Not d'Aiglemort's men, though; Elua favored us. Beneath it flew a standard of a mountain crag and fir, argent on green. Whose House, I wondered desperately, searching the archives of my mind.

From the corner of my eye, I saw Joscelin begin the sweeping Cassiline bow, reaching for his daggers. With a shout, I threw myself at him, cutting his knees out from under him. We rolled on the snowy ground together, while the Allies of Camlach stared. Whatsoever House they belonged to, I didn't want word out that a lone woman and a Cassiline Brother were travelling through the wilds of Camlach.

One of their number stepped forward, a seasoned warrior in well-worn arms. "Identify yourselves!" he snapped curtly.

It wasn't until then that I realized how we must look, the both of us, wind-and snow-burned, swathed in Skaldi furs, venturing alone through the worst of Camlach's winter, with only a heavily laden Skaldi pony to accompany us.

"My lord!" I gasped, signing Joscelin urgently to silence. "I am sorry, we meant no harm! Do we trespass here?"

He settled back in the saddle, eased by my tone, my voice and accent clearly D'Angeline. "No, lass, you've the right to passage. But it's not safe this close to the border. Who are you and where are you bound?"

Not to be easily swayed, then. I swallowed hard, and lied through my teeth. "Suriah of Trefail, my lord. This is my cousin, Jareth." I trembled, not dissembling; to be undone now was unthinkable. "Our village was destroyed by Skaldi raiders some days past. We ... my cousin took a blow to the head, I hid him in the empty granary, they never found us, my lord. We took these things from those who'll need them no longer, and fled for the City. Was that wrong?"

It was a gamble. I couldn't be sure of where we were, nor how well these scouts knew all the mountain villages. One thing was sure, though. Trefail had been destroyed by the Skaldi. I knew, because it was the village where Alcuin had been born.

"No, no, not wrong." The scout's face was unreadable in the shifting firelight, embers scattered across the snow by Joscelin's attempt to extinguish it. "You thought we were Skaldi?"

"You might have been." I shuddered and stole a glance at Joscelin. He was silent under the shadow of the wolf-mask on his brow. "We didn't know, my lord. My cousin got scared." Joscelin nodded without speaking, somehow managing to make it seem a dumb-show, for which I was grateful.

The leader chewed at his lower lip, ruminating. I saw his gaze wander over us, assessing our garb, our gear. I kept my head slightly averted, trusting to the flame-cast darkness to hide the tell-tale mark of Kushiel's Dart. For a moment, I thought we'd get away with it; but the scions of Camael are too martial to trust wholly to the element of chance in a chance encounter.

"There's nothing for you in the City of Elua," he said cannily. "Winter's been hard, and it's fever-stricken. You'll ride with us to Bois-le-Garde. The Marquis le Garde won't turn away Camaeline refugees, you'll be well taken care of." He turned to one of his men. "Brys, ride on and tell the castellan we're coming in. Be sure to give him the details."

He stressed the last words; there was no mistake. The le Garde rider began to turn his horse's head northward.

Joscelin moved like lightning; and what's more, he did it more like a Skaldi than a Cassiline, with brutal efficiency. One dagger—one dagger only—flashed from his sheath as he grabbed the leader of Bois-le-Garde's scouting party, setting his blade to the man's throat.

"Everyone," he said tersely. "Dismount. Now!"

They obeyed, eyes glaring fury. He set his teeth and held the dagger steady; their leader stood unmoving.

I didn't need orders. Working frantically, I stowed our gear, lashing the packs onto our Skaldi pony.

"Two horses." Joscelin held himself rigid; I could see

the effort it cost him, to hold a dagger on a fellow D'Angeline. He was breathing hard. "Scatter the rest."

I did it, though over a dozen armed warriors stood frozen in hatred, unwilling to sacrifice their leader by interfering with me. The horses scattered reluctantly, trained to obey; I had to shout and wave my arms, slapping at their hindquarters with ferocity. They ran, then, in all directions, save the two whose reins I'd lashed to a tree. They tugged at their restraints, large eyes rolling to show the whites.

"Ph . . . Suriah, mount up." Joscelin cursed at his near-slip, jerking the dagger. The leader inhaled sharply.

"You won't get away," he said bitterly. "We'll come after you."

"Our kin in Marsilikos will protect us!" I said defiantly. "You've no right to detain free D'Angelines!"

"Quiet!" Joscelin hissed at me. "Suriah, get out of here!"

He'd followed my lead; I followed his, freeing one of the Camaeline horses, swinging into the saddle and plunging headlong through the woods, trailing the pony on a lead-rope.

To any who've not tried it, I do not recommend a blind flight through the wilds on horseback. We blundered, crashing through the undergrowth, both animals caught by the contagion of my fear. Joscelin caught up with us no more than half a mile out, a dark blurred figure on horseback, and we rode for our lives.

It was a clear night, Blessed Elua be thanked, the stars standing distant and frosty overhead; if not for that, we would surely have been lost, but the Great Plow and the Navigator's Star stood clear in the black skies above us, guiding our way and shedding their faint silvery light over the snowy landscape. Fixing a map in my mind, I headed us grimly south, hoping to intersect one of the great roads of the realm: Eisheth's Way, that the Tiberians call the Via Paullus.

Eisheth's Way leads south, to the coast; Marsilikos is her greatest city—founded long ago by Hellenes, even before Elua's time—and because it is a harbor city, a great many wanderers end there. I hoped the Marquis le Garde's men would take our bait, and follow our trail south.

We reached Eisheth's Way come dawn, our Camaeline mounts staggering with exhaustion, foam-flecked and winded. The pony trotted behind us, sides heaving, still game; half-dead with tiredness as I was, it put me to shame.

There is little trade at this time of year. Now, in the Bitterest Winter, the road stretched open and empty before us, gilded with the pale gold light of dawn.

The Allies of Camlach could not be more than a mile behind us.

"A side road," I said to Joscelin, lifting my voice with an effort. "Any road, leading west. And pray they keep on toward Marsilikos."

He nodded wearily; we pressed the horses, demanding speed they didn't have to give. An hour along Eisheth's Way, we saw it, a nameless road, only the signpost with Elua's sigil indicating that it led to the City.

"There." Joscelin pointed.

I cocked my head and listened. In the distance, I could hear hoofbeats, an erratic multiple beat. A dozen men, riding horses nigh as tired as our own. "Ride!" I gasped, setting heels to my mount.

Once more, we fled.

A mile along the route, we came upon the Yeshuite wagon.

We nearly ran them down, in truth, coming hard around a bend. It was a narrow road. The horses, done in, balked and wheeled; the team of mules set their ears and showed their teeth. Joscelin shouted something, I don't know what, and a young girl poked her head out of the rear of the wagon even as the driver turned round to look at us.

I'd not known, until that moment, that it was a Yeshuite family, but I knew him by his sidelocks, long and dangling, while the rest of his hair was cropped at the neck. I would have said something then, but Joscelin spoke first.

"Barukh hatah Adonai, father," he said, at once breathless and respectful, giving his Cassiline bow from the saddle before I could protest. "Forgive our intrusion."

"Barukh hatah Yeshua a'Mashiach, lo ha'lam." The Yeshuite driver said the words automatically, keen dark eyes gauging us. "You are a follower of the Apostate, I think."

He spoke to Joscelin, who bowed again. A second face peered through the curtains at the back of the wagon, with a markedly girlish giggle. "Yes. I am Joscelin Verreuil of the Cassiline Brotherhood."

"Indeed. And who is chasing you so hard?"

I drew breath to answer, but Joscelin cut me off. "Men who are apostate even from the teachings of Blessed Elua, father, fruit of Yeshua ben Yosef's vine. Stand aside, and we will go. Ya'er Adonai panav—"

"And why do they chase you?"

"To kill us, most like, by the time they catch us," I broke in impatiently. "My lord . . ."

"Your horses, I think, will not go much further."

It was true and I knew it, but they would go a little further, and right then, my only thought was to put as much distance as possible between us and our pursuers, whose mounts must surely be as tired. For after them would come fresher riders, and if we could get beyond the borders of Camlach ahead of them, we would be safer. "Yes, my lord, but—"

"Shelter us." Joscelin's voice was abrupt, his eyes intense with the plea. "The men who follow us, father, they'll not think to look in the heart of a Yeshuite family. They think we are rebels, perhaps, Skaldi spies. I swear to you, we are not. We are free D'Angelines, escaped from captivity, and we bear information on which the freedom of our nation hinges."

I drew in my breath, terrified by the trust with which he revealed our secret. The Yeshuite nodded slowly, then glanced at the back of the wagon. "How do you say, Danele?"

The curtains clashed open, and a woman with kind eyes and a shrewd face emerged, shooing the two girls into the depths of the wagon. She sized up Joscelin and me and her face softened, especially for Joscelin. "He is one of the Apostate's own, Taavi. Let him in." Raising her voice, she called into the wagon. "Girls! Make room!"

And so we came to join the Yeshuites.

ℱIFTY-FIVE

I had not known, before this, of the relationship that existed between the Cassiline Brotherhood and the Yeshuites. It is obvious, and I should have seen it; but it is not a thing which is discussed outside the society of Cassilines. For although Cassiel was apostate, as the Yeshuites name him, he never broke faith with the One God, but only turned his face away in sorrow. Alone among the Companions, he kept the commandments of his Lord and did not commingle with mortals.

Of course, the Cassilines believe he took on the duty that the One God neglected—love of the son of Yeshua's blood—and the Yeshuites do not see it that way, but still, it is enough for a common bond. For as I well knew, even the Cassilines believe Cassiel chose damnation when he became Elua's Companion, the Perfect Companion.

We turned the horses of Bois-le-Garde loose, driving them southward. Unexpectedly, Danele and Taavi's girls grew instantly enamored of our Skaldi pony, and begged their father not to loose him. With a thoughtful mien, he acceded, and our faithful pony was tied behind the wagon.

"A little truth seasons a lie like salt," he said pragmatically. "You have turned the horses free; we will say we found the pony wandering, if they ask. If they find us."

They did.

It happened a scant hour after we'd come upon them, and not long after we'd been ushered into the back of the wagon, our gear stowed and hidden. Danele supervised our concealment with level-headed efficiency, marshalling her giggling daughters to move skeins of wool and fabric to hide us; Taavi, it transpired, was a weaver, and she had some skill as a dyer. They made space for us in the tidy, well-ordered wagon, the girls giggling and nudging each other. Joscelin, charmed, smiled at them; they giggled all the harder.

My ears sharpened by Delaunay's training, I was the one who heard the hoofbeats.

For all that had befallen us, I'd never felt so helpless, crouching in the dark behind bolts of fabric while Taavi answered the riders' questions—two of them, by the sound of it—with disarming frankness. No, they were not bound for the City, but for L'Arène, where they had kin. Yes, they had found the pony on Eisheth's Way, wandering alone and packless. No, they'd not seen anyone else. Yes, the Camaelines were welcome to look in the wagon. The curtains were yanked aside, and three Yeshuite faces gazed at the Bois-le-Garde riders, silent and apprehensive.

From my hiding place, I caught a glimpse of one of the scout's faces, weary and uninterested. The curtains clashed closed; we were free to go onward.

The girls gave muted squeals of excitement as the mules trotted stolidly forward. Danele shushed them, her arms around them both. I sighed, quietly, and felt Joscelin do the same beside me.

We were three days with the Yeshuites.

There are those who do not hold that there is any innate goodness to mankind. To them I say, had you lived my life, you would not believe it. I have known the depths to which mortals are capable of descending, and I have seen the heights. I have seen how kindness and compassion may grow in the unlikeliest of places, as the mountain flower forces its way through the stern rock.

I had kindness from Taavi's family.

They asked us no questions, only shared with us wholeheartedly what they had to give. I learned a little bit of their story; I wish I knew more. They came from one of the inner villages of Camlach, where their families had settled a generation ago, filling a need for village weavers and dyers. But fever came to the village, and the Yeshuites were blamed, for all that a courier had clearly brought it from the City of Elua. So it was that they fled, southward, the whole of their livelihood packed in that wagon.

It was a strange thing to me, to see a family entire.

I'd never thought, before then—save at Perrinwolde—how such a thing formed no part of my life. I remembered my parents, vaguely; the road and the caravanserai, and after that, the Dowayne of Cereus House. For Joscelin, it was different. Until the age of ten, he'd been a part of a family, a loving household. He'd had brothers, and sisters. He knew how to play with children, to tease and tickle them.

And they adored him for it.

Taavi and Danele smiled, well content that they'd chosen aright in aiding us. Me, they regarded with a gentle pity, and spoke to with soft words.

Such kindness; such misunderstanding.

I grieved at what I was.

Some miles shy of the City of Elua, we parted ways. We had discussed it, the four adults, over the past night's fires. They had no wish to enter the City, where it was rumoured that fever still raged; we had no choice.

"We would take you to the gates," Taavi said, worried. "It is not so far out of our way, I think, and you will be safe with us. Is it not so? No one will trouble with a poor weaver and his family."

"You've done enough, father," I said fondly; I understood, by then, that the title was of respect to an elder, for all that Taavi and Danele had but a handful of years on us. "We don't know what welcome awaits us. Go to L'Arène, and prosper. You've done more than enough."

The girls—Maia and Rena, their names were, six and eight years of age—played in the background. Maia had Joscelin's white wolf-pelt on her head and chased her younger sister, shrieking with laughter, while Rena ducked behind the placid pony and giggled. Danele watched them complacently. Such sounds of fearless innocence, rising up to the dusky sky. If Waldemar Selig had his way, the laughter of children, D'Angeline or Yeshuite, would no longer ring freely under these same emerging stars.

"Still, I would—"

"No." Joscelin said it gently, smiling, but with a firmness that said he would not be swayed. "We will ride with you to the crossroads, father, and the last miles we will walk. Not for love of Cassiel himself would I put your family in any further danger."

Taavi opened his mouth for a final protest, and Danele laid her hand on his arm. "Let be," she reprimanded him kindly. "It is their will, and for the best." He nodded, then, reluctantly. On an impulse, I withdrew Melisande's diamond from around my neck and held it out to him. The diamond glittered in the firelight.

"Here," I said. "For all you have done. It will go a long way to enabling you to establish yourselves in L'Arène."

They looked at each other, then shook their heads, while the diamond hung glittering from my hand. "It is too much," Taavi said. "And we did not help you for gain." Danele, her fingers still laced around his arm, nodded agreement.

"But—" I protested.

"No." Taavi was firm. "Thank you, Phèdre, but no. It is too much."

"You're stuck with that thing," Joscelin said wryly, looking past me to where Maia and Rena hugged our Skaldi pony, their chase forgotten. "But mayhap there is some small thing we may give you, father," he added, grinning.

So it was that we took our leave of them, with tears and blessings on both sides. Perched high in the driver's seat, Taavi clucked to the mules, and they set off southward at a steady pace. Danele and the girls waved from the rear of the wagon, and the shaggy pony trailed behind on his lead, trotting gamely. He had been the most loyal and steadfast of companions, and though it grieved me to part with him, I was happy that he would be rewarded by such tender fondness.

Ahead of us, to the west, lay the white-walled City of Elua, my home. Joscelin blew out his breath, frosty in the chill morning air, and shouldered our packs. We'd not much to carry, having left the bulk of it with Taavi's family. I kept my wolfskin cloak and Trygve's dagger, while Joscelin had the pelt of the White Brethren stowed in a bag along with some foodstuffs Danele had provided and a pair of waterskins. These things were all we had by way of proof of our sojourn.

The ease that we'd found among the Yeshuites slipped away as we walked toward the City. It was months we'd been away. Who ruled from Elua's throne? How deep-laid was the conspiracy that had felled Delaunay? Who was part of it, and who was not? I realized, with mounting anxiety, the pitfalls that awaited us. What had Alcuin said? Trust Rousse, Trevalion. Thelesis de Mornay. The Dauphine, and not the King.

The odds of Quintilius Rousse being in the City were slim; he would be wintering with his fleet. Trevalion . . . perhaps. But he would be quartered at the Palace, as likely would Thelesis de Mornay—the King's Poet— and of course, Ysandre de la Courcel. And I remembered all too well what had happened when we tried to reach her at the Palace.

Blessed Elua, I prayed fervently, let Melisande Shahrizai be elsewhere.

Yet even if she were, I'd no idea who her allies were, the extent of her network. There was no way to approach the people Alcuin had named without running the gauntlet of the Palace, and no one else I dared trust.

Except Hyacinthe.

I shared my thoughts aloud with Joscelin. He heard me out and gave no answer.

"You don't like it."

He walked steadily, eyes on the horizon. There was some bit of traffic on the road now, not much, as it was winter, but the occasional carriage passed, the occupants glancing curiously at us. Roadworn and disheveled, our attire a mix of rude woolens and fur pelts lashed with thongs or pinned with bronze, Joscelin's Cassiline hilt protruding over his shoulder; no wonder they stared. It made me increasingly uneasy.

"There is no one else," Joscelin said finally, "that you can turn to? No patron, no friend of Delaunay's?"

"Not without risk." A gust of wind blew, and I tugged my cloak reflexively about me. "We aren't talking about a simple favor, Joscelin. Whomever we approach will hold our lives in their hands. I trust Hyacinthe with mine. No one else."

"The Prince of Travellers." He pronounced it with irony. "How much gold could he get for it, do you think?"

Without thinking, I struck him across the face with my open palm. We stopped on the road and stood staring at each other. "Tsingano or no," I said softly, "Hyacinthe has been a friend to me, when no one else was, and never asked a centime for it. When Baudoin de Trevalion was executed, it was Hyacinthe who gave me money to make an offering in his memory at the temples. Did you know that I was Melisande's farewell gift to Prince Baudoin before she betrayed him?"

"No." Joscelin's face was pale beneath the wind-burn, save for a ruddy patch where I'd slapped him. "I'm sorry."

"If you have a better idea," I said grimly, "then say it. But I'll not hear you speak against Hyacinthe."

He glanced toward the City. It was not far now, we could see the distant glint of its walls. "I can approach the Captain of the King's Cassiline Guard. He is a Brother, he would have to give me audience. He is oath-sworn, and may be trusted."

"Are you sure?" I waited until he looked back at me. "Are you sure beyond doubt, Joscelin? You disappeared from the City with your charge—a notorious Servant of Naamah and plaything of the wealthy—leaving behind the slaughtered household of Anafiel Delaunay. Do you know what poison's been spread in our absence? Are you sure of your welcome by the Cassiline Brother-hood?"

My words struck him like blows; it had never oc-curred to him, I could see, that his honor as a Cassiline could be impugned.

"No one would dare suggest such a thing!" he gasped. "And even if they did, no Cassiline would believe it!"

"No?" I asked wearily. "But I thought of it, and if I could, others would. As for believing . . . what is easier to credit? A simple murder driven by greed and lust, or a vast, deep-laid conspiracy to betray the throne into Skaldi hands, known only to you and me?"

After a moment, he gave a curt nod, adjusted his back, and set his face toward the City. "Your way, then, and pray your trust isn't misplaced. Anyway, we still have to make it through the gates."

I looked at the distant walls and shivered.

For all of our fears, gaining admittance to the City proved the easiest of our trials. Two tired-looking mem-bers of the City Guard halted us at a distance, glanced up and down at our bizarre attire, and demanded our names without much interest. I gave false names and a history, citing Taavi and Danele's village; they asked a few cursory questions, mostly about our health, then bid us to stick out our tongues for examination.

Bemused, we obeyed without protest, and one of the guards drew near enough to look, then waved us through.

"It's true, then," Joscelin said in a low voice. "There's sickness in the City."

I said nothing, overwhelmed at being once again within the City walls. It didn't mean as much to him; it wasn't his home, he'd not been born and raised here, as I had. The beauty of the place made me want to weep, the elegance of the cobbled streets, lined with gracious trees, now barren in winter. And the people, ah! Despite the cold and the rumored fevers, there were people about, D'Angelines all, and the sound of their voices was music to my ears.

As twilight fell, we made our way on foot to Night's Doorstep, winding through the poorer districts, where our appearance went largely unremarked. The scent of food cooking in homes and inns made my mouth water; D'Angeline cuisine, real food! We reached Night's Doorstep in good time. The street-lamps were fresh lit, and the first revelers taking to the streets, their numbers thinner than I remembered, but still glorious in their silks and velvets, brocade and jewels shimmering in the lamp-light.

"Joscelin, we can't go inside," I murmured, as we stood in a shadowed alley across from the the Cockerel. "The place would be turned upside down, and word would reach the Palace by midnight. Tongues wag faster than you can blink, in Night's Doorstep."

"Do you have an idea?"

"I think so. Listen," I said, and told him.

Hyacinthe's stable was quiet, too early for business, the horses drowsing in their stalls with the smell of good hay all around. There were two attendants on duty, boys of twelve or thirteen, tossing dice; we took them by surprise. One of them squeaked, seeing Joscelin with drawn sword, and then both cowered. I couldn't blame them for being terrified. Even without the pelt of the White Brethren, with his clothing and his tangled hair, he looked more like a changeling Skaldi warrior than a Cassiline Brother.

"You work for Hyacinthe?" I asked them; they nodded. "Good. You." I pointed to the one who hadn't squeaked. "I need you to do something, and your friend's life depends on it. Find Hyacinthe, and bid him to come here. Privately. Tell him an old friend needs his help. If he asks who, tell him we used to eat tarts under the bridge at Tertius' Crossing. Have you got that?"

He nodded again, rapidly. "Old friend," he said breathlessly. "Tarts. Tertius' Crossing. Yes, my . . . yes."

"Good." I wouldn't have accorded me a title either, not in this state. "If you breathe a word of it, a *word*, mind you, or if anyone overhears, your friend will die. Do you understand?"

"Yes!" His head bobbed so fast his forelock flopped in his eyes. "Yes, I swear it!"

"Good," I repeated, adding ominously, "and if we don't kill you, you may be sure Hyacinthe will, if you make a mistake in this. Now go!"

He was out the door like a bolt, and we heard the sound of his running feet in the street. Joscelin sheathed his word. "You're safe if he keeps his word," he said to the other lad, who stared white-faced at us. "Just don't think of following him."

Hyacinthe's stable attendant shook his head in fervid terror.

We waited, strung tighter than harpstrings. Ever since I'd awakened in the covered cart, it seemed, aching and soul-sick, I'd been listening for approaching steps. I knew these. I knew the sound of Hyacinthe's casual stroll, boot-heels scraping against the cobblestones.

And then he entered the stable and closed the door, and any pretense of ease disappeared. He turned around, his expression strained with hope and disbelief.

"Phèdre?"

I took two steps, and threw myself into his arms.

It fell to Joscelin to guard the door, sword drawn once more, against both anyone seeking entrance, and escape by Hyacinthe's assistants. The boy we'd sent had slipped in behind him, and stood staring with his fist pressed against his teeth. To my shame, I was worse than useless, weeks' worth of pent terror releasing itself in shaking sobs, my face pressed to Hyacinthe's shoulder. He held me hard and made soothing noises, his voice trembling a little with astonishment. When I could, I regained my composure and stepped away from him, wiping the tears from my eyes.

"All right?" Hyacinthe raised his eyebrows at me, and I nodded, taking a deep, shuddering breath. He beckoned to the boys, and fished in his purse. "Listen to me, you two. What you saw tonight, never happened. Understand?" Both nodded silent acquiescence. "Here." He gave them both a silver coin. "You did well. Take these, and keep your mouths shut. Don't even talk to each other about it. If you do, I swear, I'll call the *dromonde* upon you, and curse you so you wish you'd never been born. Understand?"

They did. He dismissed them, and they ran, with fearful glances at Joscelin.

Hyacinthe hadn't looked closely at him. He glanced over now as Joscelin sheathed his sword and blinked hard. *"Cassiline?"*

Joscelin smiled wryly, inclining his head. "Prince of Travellers."

"Blessed Elua, I thought you couldn't draw your blade . . ." Hyacinthe shook himself, as if waking from a dream. "Come on," he said decisively. "I'll take you to the house. You were right, it's not safe for you to be seen."

I closed my eyes. "Do they think . . . ?"

"Yes. You were tried and convicted in absentia," Hyacinthe said, his voice unwontedly gentle. "For the murder of Anafiel Delaunay and the members of his household."

ℱifty-six

Hyacinthe lived still in the same house on Rue Coupole, but alone. To my sorrow, I learned that the fever of which we'd heard rumors had claimed his mother's life. She'd taken pity on a Tsingani family whose youngest was ill, and caught it from them; there were no tenants now, and Hyacinthe was grimly set against taking others until the sickness had run its course. It manifested first, we learned, with white spots on the back of the tongue; that was why the City Guard had examined ours, and had little interest in anything else.

It was strange, to be in that house without the presence of Hyacinthe's mother, muttering over her cookstove. He used it to heat water for the bath, sending one of his runners to the Cockerel for hot food, with word only that he was entertaining in private that night.

To be warm and clean and safe seemed a luxury beyond words. We sat around the kitchen table and ate squab trussed in rosemary, washing it down with a rather good red wine Hyacinthe had procured, taking turns telling what had happened between famished bites, sketching in the events. To his credit, Hyacinthe never interrupted once, listening gravely as Joscelin and I unwound our tale. When he learned of d'Aiglemort's betrayal and the Skaldi invasion plan, he looked sick.

"He wouldn't," he said. "He *couldn't*!"

"He thinks to pull it off." I gulped a mouthful of wine, and set down my glass. "But he has no idea of the numbers Selig can muster. We have to talk to someone, Hyacinthe. The Dauphine, or someone who can reach her."

"I'm thinking," he murmured, reaching for his own glass. "Your lives are forfeit, if anyone knows you've set foot in the City."

"How . . . why? Why would they think we did it?" Joscelin had had a bit of wine too, and was impassioned with it. "What possible gain would there have been?"

"I can tell you the popular theory." Hyacinthe swirled the wine in his glass, gazing into its depths. "Rumor has it that Barquiel L'Envers paid a fabulous sum for you to betray Delaunay—and you your oath, Cassiline—and admit his Akkadian Guard into the house, to settle the old score for Isabel, and set you both up in Khebbel-im-Akkad. There's no proof of it, of course, and he's not been formally charged, but the stories about the assassination of Dominic Stregazza haven't helped his cause."

"I would never—" I began.

"I know." Hyacinthe raised his gaze, dark eyes meeting mine. "I knew it for a lie, and told whoever would listen. There were a few others who spoke on your behalf, I heard. Gaspar Trevalion, and Cecilie Laveau-Perrin both did, and the Prefect of the Cassiline Brotherhood sent a letter protesting his order's innocence." He inclined his head to Joscelin. "But Parliament wanted a conviction, and the courts obliged. It won't do to have people thinking D'Angeline nobles could be slain out of hand, and their killers go unpunished."

"Melisande?" I asked; I had already guessed.

Hyacinthe shook his black curls. "If she was behind it, she kept her hand well hidden."

"She would. She played that card at Baudoin's trial, she's too canny to play it twice." I fingered the diamond without thinking. "It would look suspicious," I added dourly.

Hyacinthe began to clear away the remains of our dinner without comment, stacking the plates in a washtub for later. "All I have is at your disposal, Phèdre," he said presently, returning to sit at the table, propping his chin on his hands. "Poets and players go everywhere, know everyone; I can get word through them to whomever you like. The problem is, not a one of them can be trusted to keep silence."

I looked instinctively at Joscelin, who frowned.

"You say the Prefect sent a letter?" he asked Hyacinthe, who nodded. Joscelin shook his head. "I don't know," he said reluctantly. "If he protested the order's innocence and not mine . . . if he wrote rather than came to speak in person . . . no. I wouldn't trust him not to call the Royal Guard on us. I'll go to him myself, rather. Can you provide a mount?" The last was addressed to Hyacinthe.

"Yes, of course."

"No." I pressed my fingers to my temples. "It's unsure, and would take days. There's got to be another way." A thought struck me, and I raised my head. "Hyacinthe, can you find someone to deliver a letter to Thelesis de Mornay?"

"Absolutely." He grinned. "A love letter, perhaps? A message from an admirer? Nothing easier. The only thing I can't guarantee is that it will arrive with the seal intact."

"It doesn't matter." My mind was racing. "Do you have paper? I'll couch the real information in Cruithne. If any one of your poets can read Pictish, I'll eat this table whole."

After rummaging in a chest, Hyacinthe brought me pen and paper, shaving the quill with a sharp knife and setting the inkpot at hand. I penned a quick, fervid note of admiration in D'Angeline, then added a few lines of Cruithne, structuring them to look like verse to the uneducated eye. *The last student of he who might have been the King's Poet awaits, at the home of the Prince of Travellers, begging your aid in the name of the King's cygnet, his only born.*

I read it aloud, in D'Angeline then in Cruithne, stumbling over the pronunciation.

"Cruithne," Joscelin murmured; he'd thought himself beyond surprise. "You speak Cruithne."

"Not well," I admitted. I'd glossed over the fact that I knew neither the word for cygnet nor swan; I had translated Ysandre de la Courcel's emblem, in truth, as something closer to "long-neck baby water bird." But Thelesis de Mornay spoke and read Cruithne, and moreover, it was she who'd told me that Delaunay might have been the King's Poet, had matters not fallen out as they had. "Will it do?"

"It'll do, and more. Leave it unsigned." Hyacinthe, idling with his chair tipped back, moved into action, snatching the letter from my hand and grabbing a taper to seal it deftly with a blob of wax. "Give it me now, there's a party bound for the Lute and Mask later this evening. I'll see it in Thelesis de Mornay's hand by noon tomorrow, if I have to bribe half of Night's Doorstep to get it there."

He was out the door within seconds, swirling his cloak around him.

"You were right to trust him," Joscelin said quietly.
"I was wrong." I met his gaze across the table; he gave
me his wry smile. "I can admit that much."

"Well, and you were right about Taavi and Danele,"
I said to him. "I never told you, but I could have killed
you when you asked their help. But you were right."

"They were good people. I hope they're well." He
stood up. "If there's naught more to be done this
night . . ."

"Go, get some sleep." I stifled a yawn at the thought
of it. "I'll stay awake until Hyacinthe comes back."

"I'll leave you alone, then. I'm sure you want a chance
to talk with him." The same wry smile, but something
caught at it, twisting at my heart.

"Joscelin . . ." I looked up at him. It seemed impossible to believe, here in this childhood haven, all that
we'd been through together. All of it. "Joscelin, whatever happens to us . . . you did it. You kept your vow to
protect and serve. You brought me home safe," I said
softly. "Thank you."

He swept his Cassiline bow, and left me to wait.

Hyacinthe was some time returning, and entered the
house quietly, turning the key carefully in the lock. I
started, having fallen into a doze, slumped at the kitchen
table.

"You're awake." He came to sit with me, taking my
hands in his. "You should be in bed."

"How did it go?"

"Fine." He inspected my hands, turning them gently.
"Thelesis should have the letter by tomorrow, unless
young Marc-Baptiste has a terrible quarrel with Japheth
nó Eglantine-Vardennes, which is not likely. He thinks
I'm sheltering Sarphiel the Reclusive, who is indeed mad
enough to send the Prince of Travellers with an unsigned
love note to the King's Poet. Thelesis was ill, you know,

but the King's own physician attended her, and she's on the mend. Phèdre, it looks like you've been working as a galley-slave."

"I know." I pulled my hands away. They were red-roughened and chafed by cold, scratched and torn, with dirt engrained that a single bath couldn't remove. "But I can build a fire with a single sodden log in the middle of a snowstorm."

"Ah, Elua." Emotion flooded his face, his dark eyes liquid with unshed tears. "I thought I'd lost you, truly. Delaunay, Alcuin . . . Phèdre, I never thought to see you again. I can't believe you survived what you did. To return here, and find yourself branded a murderess . . . I'd have fought harder against it, if I'd known you were alive. I'm so sorry."

"I know." I swallowed, hard. "At least it's home, though. If I have to die anywhere . . . Oh, Hyacinthe, I'm so sorry about your mother."

He was quiet a moment, gazing unthinking toward the cookstove that had seemed so eternally her domain, rife with muttered prophecy and the chink of gold coins. "I know. I miss her. I always thought she would live to see me claim my birthright among the Tsingani, and not this sham I play at in Night's Doorstep. But I waited too long." He rubbed at his eyes. "You should sleep. You must be exhausted."

"Yes. Good night," I whispered, kissing him on the brow. I felt his gaze follow me as I made my way to a warm and waiting bed.

There is a point beyond exhaustion, where sleep is hard in coming. I had reached it that night. After so long sharing a bed, it seemed strange to be alone in one, in clean linen sheets with a warm velvet coverlet atop them. Even after the strangeness of it wore off, giving way to drowsing familiarity, something seemed to be missing.

The realization of what it was struck me with a shock, just before the tidal wave of sleep finally claimed me and dragged me under to the depths of oblivion, erasing the thought as the waves erase a line drawn in the sand by a child's stick.

It was Joscelin.

I slept late into the morning, and awoke remembering nothing of it. Hyacinthe had been up and about and busy already, and the modest house gleamed; he'd brought in a girl he could trust, the daughter of a Tsingano seamstress his mother had known, to cook and clean. She went about her business with ducked head, eager to please and fearing to meet the eye of the Prince of Travellers or his mysterious friends.

"She'll say naught," Hyacinthe assured us, and we believed him. He had found clothing, too; or bought it, rather, from the seamstress. I bathed again, murmuring a prayer of thanksgiving as the hot water steeped further traces of the Skaldi from my skin, and dressed afterward in the gown he'd provided, a dark-blue velvet that did not fit too ill.

Joscelin, in a sober dove-grey doublet and hose, struggled to drag a comb through his hair, damp and clean, but matted with Skaldi braidwork. He made no protest when I went to aid him with it, easing out the tangles.

His daggers, vambraces and sword lay in a tangle of steel and leathers on the kitchen table.

"You're not . . . ?" I began to ask; he shook his head, hair sliding over his shoulders.

"I may have kept you alive, but I've broken my vows nonetheless. I don't have the right to bear arms."

"Do you want me to put it in a single braid, then?" I gathered his hair in my hands, feeling the fair, silken mass of it.

"No," he said resolutely. "I'll put it in a club. I've still the right to that much, as a priest."

He was that, though I had forgotten it. I watched as his hands moved deftly, binding his hair into a club at the nape of his neck. Even without his arms, he looked a Cassiline again. Hyacinthe observed it all without comment, only the arch of his brows reminding me how far it was from where we'd begun.

"We should burn those," he said aloud, wrinking his nose at the pile of garments, furs and woolens, we'd shed.

"No, leave them," I said quickly. "Elua, the smell alone will testify to our story! And we've naught else to prove it."

Joscelin laughed.

Shaking his head in bewilderment, Hyacinthe glanced out the window onto the street and tensed. "There's a carriage drawing up to the doorstep," he said, his voice tight. "You'd best get in the back, there's an exit out the postern gate. If it's not de Mornay, I'll hold them off as long as I can."

We moved quickly, Joscelin sweeping his gear off the table, and hid ourselves in the scullery, where there was a passage to the rear of the house.

It didn't take long. I heard the door open and one person enter, Hyacinthe's courteous greeting. The voice that answered was unmistakable; fainter than I remembered, but rich and feminine.

Thelesis de Mornay.

I remember that I stumbled out of hiding weeping, even as she drew back the hood of her cloak, revealing the familiar plain features illumed by her dark eyes, which held grief and welcome alike. She took me in her arms, her embrace quick and fierce, unexpectedly strong.

"Ah, child . . ." her voice whispered at my ear. "I'm

so glad to see you alive. Anafiel Delaunay would be proud of you." She grasped my arms then, shaking me a little. "He would be so proud," she repeated.

I gulped back my tears, gathering myself, fighting the shudder in my voice. "Thelesis . . . We need to speak to the Dauphine, to Gaspar Trevalion, Admiral Rousse, to whomever you trust. The Skaldi are planning to invade, they've a leader, and the Duc d'Aiglemort plans betrayal—"

"Shhh." Her hands at my arms steadied me. "I got your message, Phèdre. I knew you were no traitor. I'm taking you now to an audience with Ysandre de la Courcel. Are you ready to bear that much?"

It seemed sudden, too sudden. I looked around for an instant, frantic and uncertain. Joscelin stepped up to my side, empty-handed, but armed in Cassiline rigor.

"She will not go alone," he said in his softest, most deadly tone. "In the name of Cassiel, I will bear witness to this."

"And I." Hyacinthe bowed gracefully in his best Prince of Travellers manner, but his eyes when he straightened were cold and black. "I have lost Phèdre nó Delaunay once already, my lady, and protested too little. I do not propose to let the same mistake happen twice. And mayhap it will be that my small gift of the *dromonde* may be of service in this matter."

"It may be, Tsingano." Thelesis de Mornay gazed at him with her intent, dark eyes, laying one small hand upon his sleeve. "I pray that it may."

FIFTY-SEVEN

It was at once like and unlike the old days, a covered carriage bearing me to the Palace, to meet in secret with one of Elua's line. But no longer was I the darling of Naamah's patrons, garbed in exquisite finery, awaited in breathless anticipation. Now I was a condemned murderess and an escaped Skaldi slave, awaiting the judgment of the heir-apparent of the realm, the very gown on my back there only by courtesy of the scapegrace of Night's Doorstep.

Only the scarlet mote in my eye and the unfinished marque that twined my spine gave tongue to what I was; Delaunay's *anguissette* the only such born in three generations.

We told our story, Joscelin and I, to Thelesis de Mornay in her carriage. Not the whole of it nor the details of our escape, but the gist of what mattered to the throne of Terre d'Ange. She listened intently, turning aside now and then to cough.

She believed; of that, I had no doubt. But would Ysandre de la Courcel? I had not met her, and could not guess.

The carriage drew round to a seldom-used entrance to the Palace, where we were met by guards in House Courcel livery, midnight-blue with the silver insignia. Delaunay's lessons were not lost on me; I looked closely, and observed somewhat. Each of them bore on the small finger of his left hand a silver ring.

"The Dauphine's personal guard," Thelesis said, stifling a cough. She'd seen me looking. "They may be trusted."

The Courcel guards checked us for weapons. Joscelin handed them the bundle of his Cassiline arms with a curt bow, and Hyacinthe gave them the dagger at his belt, sliding another out of his boot and gave it over with a shrug. I bore no weapons, but I had Trygve's dagger in a sack with the other Skaldic items, and protested its removal, for those were our only proofs.

"I will take custody of these things," Thelesis said firmly, and the guards did not demur, nor did they search her. She was the King's Poet and the Dauphine's confidante, and above suspicion.

Thus were we issued into the presence of Ysandre de la Courcel.

I had seen her at a distance, from hiding, and at the trial of House Trevalion; still, I knew not what to expect. It was a formal audience room to which we were conducted, albeit a small one. I learned later that we were in the King's quarters, and not the Dauphine's. I learned why, too. But for now, my worst fear was allayed; no other D'Angeline nobles were present. We would be heard, at least, and not seized upon entry.

Ysandre de la Courcel sat on a high-backed chair, flanked by a half-dozen guards in royal Courcel livery, all bearing the silver ring. Her face was cool and impassive, with all the pale beauty of her L'Envers mother's line. Only her long, slender neck bore the stamp of House Courcel, who took the swan as their emblem.

"Your highness." Thelesis made a deep curtsy. "From the bottom of my heart, I thank you for granting this audience."

"We appreciate your service to our House, King's Poet. Who do you bring before us?" Ysandre's voice was as I remembered it, light and controlled. She knew. The question was a formality.

"Phèdre nó Delaunay. Joscelin Verreuil of the Cassiline Brotherhood. And . . ." Thelesis de Mornay hesitated at Hyacinthe, not sure how to name him. He stepped forward and bowed.

"Hyacinthe, son of Anasztaizia, of Manoj's *kumpania*."

A Tsingani designation; I'd never heard him use it before. I'd never known his mother's name. But I'd no time to sorrow, for Ysandre de la Courcel's gaze was fixed on me, deep violet eyes burning like embers in her pale face. If we were guilty, mine was the gravest betrayal in her mind, that was clear.

"You," she said. "You, to whom Anafiel Delaunay gave his name, stand convicted of killing him, who was oath-sworn to ward me with his life. How do you plead to *that, anguissette*?"

It gripped me like a wave, a nameless emotion, rising from the souls of my feet to lift the very hair on my head. I had lost nearly all that I loved, had been through torture and slavery and the brutal killing cold of Skaldi winter to meet this accusation. I held her gaze and gave it back, a wash of red filming my vision, the words I'd been entrusted with so long ago coming to my tongue. "In the name of the King's cygnet, his only born, I bring you a message, your highness. When the Black Boar rules in Alba, Elder Brother will accede!"

The words rang in the small room, oddly resonant. The Courcel guard shifted, and a curious expression crossed Ysandre's face. "Yes," she said. "I know. Quintilius Rousse sent another messenger. Is that all you have to say?"

"No." I drew a deep breath. "But it is the message I was charged to bring, many weeks gone by. I am innocent of the death of Anafiel Delaunay and his household, may the earth rise and swallow me if I am not. Joscelin

Verreuil of the Cassiline Brotherhood is innocent." He bowed silently in response. I kept my gaze on Ysandre's. "You have been betrayed, your highness. The Duc Isidore d'Aiglemort plots to bring down the throne, and conspires with the Skaldi warlord Waldemar Selig. I have been two months and more a slave and a refugee among the Skaldi. They plan to invade. And they plan to betray d'Aiglemort. And unless they are stopped, they will succeed."

Whether or not she believed, I do not know, but the blood drained from her face, leaving her like a marble statue in her high-backed chair. Only those eyes continued to blaze. "You charge Isidore d'Aiglemort, hero of the realm, leader of the Allies of Camlach, with this terrible crime?"

"Not alone." I held my ground in the face of her awful stare. "I charge the Lady Melisande Shahrizai of Kusheth, who is d'Aiglemort's ally. It was her word that betrayed Delaunay, and it is her word, conveyed in writing, that assures Waldemar Selig of the Skaldi that his plan will succeed."

Ysandre turned away, whispering something to one of her guards. He nodded and departed. She turned back to me, expressionless. "Tell me what you claim to have witnessed."

We told the whole story then, Joscelin and I both, beginning with the Longest Night, telling of the slaughter at Delaunay's house, Melisande's betrayal, and our sojourn among the Skaldi. The Dauphine of Terre d'Ange listened and stared into the distance, her chin propped on one fist. Thelesis de Mornay spilled the contents of our pack on the marbled floor at the appropriate time, displaying our worn Skaldi pelts and Trygve's dagger. Hyacinthe stepped forward and testified to our condition, finding us in his stable.

"And that is all you have to offer?" Ysandre de la Courcel mused, contemplating the items on the floor. "A wild tale, and a heap of stinking hides as proof?"

"Summon Melisande Shahrizai, then," Joscelin said, his blue eyes flashing, "and let her be questioned! I swear by my oath that all we have told you is true!"

The guard sent on an errand returned unobtrusively, slipping through the door and closing it carefully behind him. Ysandre arched her fair brows at him, and he shook his head.

"The Lady Shahrizai," Ysandre murmured, "is not in residence, it seems. But if what you say is true, why would she let you live?" The cool gaze turned back to me. "No member of House Shahrizai is a fool, and that one least of all, I think."

I opened my mouth to answer, and found myself unable to frame a reply. How did one say such a thing to the King's daughter? The blood rose to my face, a hot blush overtaking me. Her gaze never wavered as I began to stammer out a response. Hyacinthe and Thelesis spoke simultaneously. To my mortification, I heard his words clearly, "The answer, your highness, is worth a thousand ducats and would take some time to give"; while the King's Poet quoted an Eisandine fishing proverb, "If you catch the speaking salmon in your shrimp-net, cast him back."

"Ah." One syllable, and the merest arch to the brows.

"Your highness." Joscelin bowed, having regained his composure, his voice coming calm and level into her pointed silence. "Even were that not so, for a scion of Kushiel to kill one marked by Kushiel's hand would bring a curse upon the House," he said reasonably. "Nor is it counted lucky to murder a priest. Melisande Shahrizai did not kill us, but she deemed our survival a slender chance at best. That we would escape and return uncaptured, she never dreamed. No one in their right mind would have dreamt it," he added soberly. "That we stand before you is a measure of Blessed Elua's grace."

"So you say. You have naught else?"

Thelesis de Mornay stepped forward. "They have my word, your highness. I knew Anafiel Delaunay. I knew him well. He trusted his pupils with his life."

"Did he trust them with his secrets?" The arched brows turned toward the King's Poet. "Did he tell Phèdre nó Delaunay that he was my oath-sworn protector?"

Thelesis made a slight, helpless gesture, glancing at me. She knew, I think, that he had not.

The feeling returned, the wave lifting me out of myself. "No, my lady," I whispered. "He did not. But you would have been better served if he had." I had given no thought to what I uttered, and it terrified me to hear my own words, for there was bitterness in them. "Anafiel Delaunay taught me and used me and kept me in ignorance, thinking to protect me. And if he had not, mayhap he would not have died, for I might have guessed Melisande Shahrizai's game, if I'd known what was at stake. I was the only one close enough to see it. But I did not, and he is dead." Joscelin stirred next to me, willing me to silence; we understood these things, who had been slaves together. Too late, and I was too far gone in my anger. I stared at the Dauphine and a connection formed in my mind, so simply that I almost laughed with relief. "The guard, your highness question the guard!"

Joscelin moved again, this time with a jolt. "Your highness! We sought an audience with you, then with the King's Poet, the night of Delaunay's murder. Both times we were turned away." He grinned, the flash of white teeth unexpected. "A Cassiline Brother and an *anguissette* in a *sangoire* cloak. Surely one of them would remember."

For a moment, I thought she would refute the idea, then Ysandre de la Courcel nodded to the guard she'd sent before. "Go," she said. "Be discreet." She looked back at us, and I saw for an instant a frightened young woman gazing from behind the mask of authority. "Ah, Elua!" she said, grief in her voice. "You're telling the truth, aren't you?"

I understood, then, the nature of her anger and her fear, and sank to my knees, gazing up at her. We had brought to her the last news any ruler wished to hear, of war, war incipient, and treason at the heart of her realm. "Yes, my lady," I said softly. "It is true."

She was silent a moment, accepting the truth of it. I saw in that moment something else surfacing in her, a dreadful resolve that she drew from some inner depths, hardening the planes of her lovely young face and firming the line of her mouth. Ysandre de la Courcel would stare unblinking at this terror. I remembered, then, that she was the daughter of Rolande de la Courcel, whom Delaunay had loved.

"And my uncle?" Ysandre asked, coming back to herself. "The Duc L'Envers?"

Still kneeling, I shook my head, then rose in the fluid movement I had first learned at Cereus House. "To the best of my knowledge, Barquiel L'Envers had naught to do with it, your highness. He and Delaunay had settled the score between them."

"Is it true that he had Dominic Stregazza killed?"

Ysandre de la Courcel would be ruthless in acknowledgement of the truth, I saw that much. "I believe it to be true," I said quietly. "The name of your mother's murderer was the coin Delaunay paid for the truce between him and the Duc L'Envers. He reckoned it worthwhile to protect you from the same fate, your highness."

She absorbed it without blinking. "And you gathered this intelligence for him."

"I had a companion; we both did." Grief sank its claws into my heart, fresh again now that I was home in the City. "His name was Alcuin nó Delaunay. It was he who garnered the Stregazza's name. He died with my lord Delaunay."

"You weep for him." Ysandre looked curiously at me, saddened. "I wish I had known him better. I wish there had been time." She glanced at the door through which the guard had left, then rose, beckoning. "Come here."

We followed her, then, the four of us and her guard, through two doors, into a cloistered bedroom. It was heavily guarded, and two elderly Cassilines stood aside at her command, opening the door. Joscelin took care not to meet their eyes. The Dauphine stood in the doorway and looked within; pressed close behind her, we gazed over her shoulder.

Ganelon de la Courcel, the King of Terre d'Ange, lay in a canopied bed, his face waxen and unmoving, fallen into deep lines. He was more ancient than I remembered. At first I thought he slept the long sleep of death, then I saw his breast rise and fall, disturbed by a long breath.

"So lies my grandfather the King," Ysandre said softly, twisting a heavy gold ring on the finger of one hand. I knew it; it was Rolande's signet, on which Delaunay had sworn his oath. "So lies the ruler of our fair realm." She backed out of the doorway, and we hastened to get out of her way. "He suffered a second stroke in this Bitterest Winter," she murmured, closing the door and nodding to the Cassilines, who took up their pose, arms crossed at ease. "I have been ruling in his name. Thus far, the nobles of the realm have endured my pretence. But if we stand upon the brink of war . . . I do not know how long I can last before someone wrests the reins of control from my hands. I do not even know if it is a mercy or a curse that he lives still. How long can this last? I do not know."

Someone gasped for air. I glanced, startled, at Hyacinthe. He leaned against the wall, fumbling to unfasten the velvet collar of his doublet, and his skin beneath its rich brown tone was a deadly grey.

"Hyacinthe!" I uttered his name in fear, hurrying to his side to aid him. He waved me away, doubling over, then straightening with a great indrawn breath.

"Three days," he said, his voice faint. He steadied himself, reaching for the wall, and repeated it. "The King will die in three days, your highness." His gaze slid over toward Thelesis. "You did bid me to use the *dromonde* my lady."

"What do you say?" Ysandre's voice had gone as cold and hard as a Skaldi winter. "You claim the gift of prophecy, son of Anasztaizia?"

"I claim the *dromonde*, though I do not have my mother's skill at it." He passed his hands blindly over his face. "Your highness, when Blessed Elua was weary, he sought sanctuary among the Tsingani in Bhodistan, and we turned him out, with jeers and stones, predicting in our pride that he and his Companions would ever be cursed to wander the earth, doomed to call no place home. It is not wise to curse the son of Earth's womb. We were punished, the fate we decreed sealed as our own, condemned to walk the long road. But in her cruel mercy, the Mother-of-All granted us the *dromonde*, to part the veils of time, that next time we might see truer."

Ysandre stood unmoving, then turned purposefully to the Cassiline Brothers on guard. "You will say nothing of this. I bid you by your oaths." They bowed, both of them, identical Cassiline bows. "Let us return."

Her man-at-arms had come back by the time we arrived, a nervous-looking Palace Guard in tow. He took one look at Joscelin and me, eyes widening.

"Those are the ones," he said, certainty in his voice. "Him in grey, and her in that dark red cloak. Asked to see the King's Poet. But I thought—"

"Thank you." Ysandre de la Courcel inclined her head to him. "You have done us a service. Understand that this is a matter of utmost secrecy, and to speak of it is treason and punishable by death."

The guard gulped, swallowed and nodded. I didn't blame him. She dismissed him then, and had a quiet word with one of her own guardsmen. He would be followed, I guessed. We all stood quietly, forgotten while Ysandre paced the audience room, her face strained with grief.

"Elua have mercy," she murmured to herself. "Who do I trust? What must I do?" Remembering us, she caught herself, and paused. "Forgive us our ingratitude. You have done us a service, a mighty service, and endured great hardship to do it. We are grateful, I assure you, and will see that your names are cleared, and reinstated with glory as heros of the realm. You have the word of the throne upon it."

"No." The word came automatically to my lips. I cleared my throat, disregarding Joscelin and Hyacinthe's incredulous stares. "My lady . . . your highness, you cannot," I said reluctantly. "Isidore d'Aiglemort is your first and closest enemy. He has an army at his command, assembled and at the ready. You have but one advantage: He does not know you know him for a traitor. If you reveal it now, you force his hand. Now, before he does, gather those peers you trust and seek their counsel. If you do not marshal your strength, he will strike. And he may win. Even if he does not, it will lay Terre d'Ange bare for the Skaldi to plunder at will."

Those cool purple eyes considered me. "Then you will still be named a murderess, Phèdre nó Delaunay, the engineer of your lord's demise. And your companions with you."

"So be it." I straightened my backbone. "Hyacinthe's part is unknown, he is safe enough. Joscelin . . ." I glanced at him.

He bowed to me, with sorrow in his wry smile. "I am already condemned. I have broken every vow but one to get us here alive, your highness. I do not fear the judgment of Terre d'Ange, when a greater judgment awaits me," he said quietly.

Ysandre stood silent, then nodded. "Understand that I am grieved at this necessity." There was dignity in her words and her bearing; I understood, and believed. I could see in her the echo of the Crown Prince that Delaunay had revered. I wondered what he had made of Rolande's daughter. Then a calculating light lit her eyes. "But you are too valuable to discard into safe exile, and you no less than the others, if your gift tells true, Tsingano. In the name of my grandfather, I place you all under the custody of the throne."

So it was done.

Fifty-eight

Hyacinthe had spoken truly: Ganelon de la Courcel, King of Terre d'Ange, died in three days' time.

I have little firsthand knowledge of what it was like in those days, being cloistered in the Palace under the express care of Ysandre's personal guard. Some news we gained from them, and from her chirurgeon, who examined us, treating Joscelin's half-healed wounds and prescribing a rich diet to counter the toll of deprivation our long flight had taken, but for the most part, it felt as though I were confined in a dream, while the real world passed by me. We heard the mourning bells toll, that had not rung since I was a child at Cereus House. We saw the solemn faces of the guards, and their black armbands. For all of that, it seemed unreal to me.

One thing was sure, though; I could feel the uneasiness of the City—and the greater realm beyond it—on my very skin. Although they knew not the true threat that awaited, reports of Skaldi invasion increased, and Isidore d'Aiglemort and a half-dozen other Camaeline nobles begged off attendance at the King's funeral and Ysandre's coronation, claiming they dared not leave the province unguarded.

The coronation itself was a hasty affair; after so long, no one truly believed Ganelon would die and, too, illness had thinned the ranks of D'Angeline nobles as well as the common folk. There were five empty seats or more in Parliament alone. And among those who remained to fill them, there was grave mistrust of the worth of a young and untried Queen, who yet stood unwed and alone.

These things I learned in some detail from Thelesis de Mornay, who was permitted to visit us. She continued to mend from her bout with the fever, but slowly, and I cringed to hear her wracking cough.

Above all, I dreaded to hear word of Melisande Shahrizai. Though she was reported to be in Kusheth—one of the cousins, Fanchone, came bearing flowery condolences on the part of House Shahrizai—it was within the Palace walls that I had last encountered her, and it preyed on my mind in that place. I fingered her diamond that lay still at my throat, a talisman of vengeance, that somehow I dared not discard, and thought of her, too often. Survival in a hostile land takes up all of one's thought; now, I had too much time to think, and remember. I had withheld the *signale,* it was true, but with Delaunay's blood as good as on her hands, I had given up everything else. She had played me like a harp, and I had sung to her tune. I could not forget, and it sickened me.

It was Joscelin who found a way out for me.

He knew; he had walked with me into her hands, and been there when I'd awakened from it, retching and soul-sick. And he was that thing I ever forgot with Cassilines: A priest. What he said, he said somberly, not quite meeting my eyes.

"Phèdre, you give Elua his due, and Naamah, whose servant you are. But it is Kushiel who marked you, and Kushiel whose will you challenge when you despise what you are." He looked at me then, expression undecipherable. "You will break, to challenge the will of the immortals. I know, I have been at the verge of it, and it was you who drew me back. But I cannot help in this. Beg leave to attend the temple of Kushiel. They will accept your atonement."

This I did, and Ysandre de la Courcel granted me leave, provided I went hooded in the attendance of her personal guard.

Of that, I will say little. Those who have had need of Kushiel's harsh mercy know; those who have not, need not know. Of all of Elua's Companions, Kushiel's disciples can be trusted beyond death with their vows of secrecy. Were it not so, no one would atone. Even his priests wear robes and full bronze masks, so that their identity cannot be discerned, nor even their gender. They looked at my face through the eyeholes of their masks when I raised my hood, saw the mark of Kushiel's Dart, and took me in without question.

It is a terrifying place, though a safe one, from all but the evil that one carries within oneself. I endured the rituals of purification, and then, cleansed and purged and stripped naked, knelt at the altar before the great bronze statue of Kushiel himself, serene and harsh, while two priests bound my wrists to the whipping-post. There I made my confession.

And was scourged.

I am what I am; I can say now without shame that I wept with release at the first blow of the flogger, the iron-tipped lashes searing my skin. Pain, and pain alone, pure and red, flooded me, washing away my guilt. Before me, Kushiel's stern face swam in the blood-haze of my vision; behind me, the same face was echoed in the bronze mask of the priest wielding the flogger, with a cruel and impersonal love. My back was ablaze with agony, awful and welcome. I do not know how long it lasted. An eternity, it seemed, and yet not long enough. When the priest stopped, the leather straps of the flogger were wet with my own red blood, and drops of it spattered the altar.

"Be free of it," he murmured, voice muffled behind the mask. Taking up a dipper, he plunged it into a font of saltwater, pouring it over my flayed skin. I cried out as the pain multiplied five-fold, salting my open weals; cried out and shuddered, the temple reeling in my vision.

Thus did I make my atonement.

When I returned to the safekeeping of the Palace, I was calm with it, empty of the terrible sickness that had eaten at my heart for many days, suffused with the simple languor of childhood after the Dowayne's chastiser had done with me. Joscelin glanced at my face once, then looked away. At that moment, I did not care. I was content.

"News," Hyacinthe informed me; it wasn't news that

would wait. "The Dauphine . . . the Queen, I mean, has given out that she's retiring to one of the Courcel estates to mourn for a fortnight. She's summoning a council of the peers she dares to trust. And we're to attend it."

We went.

The numbers, I sorrow to say, invited to attend that council were pathetically small. If it were a simple matter of state, I daresay Ysandre would have trusted others, but the matter of d'Aiglemort's betrayal was too grave. Thelesis was there, simply because the Queen trusted her. Gaspar Trevalion, whom Delaunay had trusted. Percy de Somerville, who looked older than I remembered, and less hardy. Barquiel L'Envers, whom would not have trusted, were the choice mine. There were two only whom I did not know by sight, for they came seldom to the Palace, though I had heard Delaunay speak of both with respect; the Duchese Roxanne de Mereliot of Eisande, who is called the Lady of Marsilikos, and Tibault of Siovale, the scholarly Comte de Toluard. Were it not for Ganelon's funeral and Ysandre's coronation, they would not likely have been summoned so quickly.

Also present was the Prefect of the Cassiline Brotherhood, tall and severe, with a face that looked carved of ancient ivory and eyes like a stooping hawk's. Bound in a tight club, his hair was entirely white, with the yellow tinge that age sometimes brings, but his carriage was as erect as a young man's.

The estate that Ysandre de la Courcel had chosen was one of the King's hunting lodges in L'Agnace. It was well done, I thought, for it was gracious and secluded, with a discreet staff that was removed from the arena of politics. Also it was not far from de Somerville's estate, and his long history of loyalty to the throne was beyond reproach.

L'Agnace, in the person of de Somerville; Azzalle, in the person of Trevalion, and de Somerville's son Ghislain by proxy; Namarre, represented by L'Envers, and Eisande and Siovale. Kusheth, I thought, was not represented. Nor was Camlach. There was no one Ysandre had dared trust.

These tallies I made later, when the council had begun, for they assembled first, waiting on the Queen's arrival. She had chosen one of the larger rooms, comfortable and well-appointed, but informal; there were chairs and couches both, that guests might situate themselves as they chose. Light refreshments were served and the wine poured, and then the servants withdrew.

I was there when Ysandre de la Courcel entered, for she kept the three of us in attendance, not wanting word to leak in advance of her arrival. She bid her Cassiline guards—for she had inherited those who served the King—to await her outside, then stood before the doors and gathered herself, schooling her features to calm. No older than I am, I thought, and pitied her.

But she was the Queen.

Ysandre entered the room, the unlikely three of us in tow, and the Queen's Council was met.

It was strange, standing behind her, to see these seven peers come instantly to attention, offering deep bows and curtsies.

"Rise, gentles," Ysandre said. "We will not stand on ceremony here. You may find it difficult indeed, when I have told you why I've asked you here."

"Phèdre!" Gaspar Trevalion's voice rang out with unadulterated surprise, and to my gratitude, joy. He crossed the room with long strides, embracing me. "You live," he said, taking my shoulders and looking to make sure it was I. "Blessed Elua, you live!"

Barquiel L'Envers approached, with a smile that did

not reach his eyes. "Delaunay's *anguissette*," he drawled. "And the Cassiline. Didn't you enjoy my largesse in the Khalif's court? I heard I sent you to Khebbel-im-Akkad after paying you to betray your master."

I turned toward him, but Joscelin stepped forward. "Your grace," he said in his even tone, "it is not a matter for jesting."

L'Envers gave him a long gauging look. "You've grown some spurs, lad. Well, I hope you've brought them to clear my name, Ysandre."

"It is one reason, but the least of them, I fear," she murmured.

"My lord Rinforte!" Joscelin's voice held all the relieved surrender I'd felt at Kushiel's temple; I looked, and saw why. He had recognized the Prefect. He went to kneel at the Prefect's feet, crossing his forearms and bowing his head. "My lord Rinforte," he said formally, "I am in violation of my sworn vows. I remand myself to your justice."

"You stand condemned of betraying the household you swore to protect and serve, Joscelin Verreuil," the Prefect said grimly. "That is no mere violation, young Brother."

"Of that he is innocent." Ysandre de la Courcel raised her voice; it carried clearly, reminding them that they stood in the presence of the Queen. "My lord Rinforte, the integrity of your Order is unbreached. Believe me when I tell you that I wish it were not so. Hear their story, and judge."

And so we told it once more.

They listened in silence and varying degrees of disbelief. For that, I did not blame them. Ysandre had been right, they took to their seats as the tale unfolded. I didn't blame them for that, either. It was a long story and hard to hear. When we were done, there was silence.

I could not read most of their faces, not even Gaspar Trevalion's, who had been like an uncle to me. Those I could, did not bode well.

"Surely, Ysandre," Barquiel L'Envers said with deceptive insouciance, "you don't expect us to believe this ludicrous confabulation?" Of all of them, he lounged at his ease on a couch, dangerous as a hunting leopard, toying idly with the ends of his burnouse that lay unwrapped around his neck. I could see only the danger in him, but he was Ysandre's nearest kin.

"Not on their word alone." Her voice held firm, and she lifted her chin on her elegant Courcel neck. "My guard has asked questions, as discreetly as they dared. There are four among the Palace Guard who saw them that night, seeking audience as they claim, and one indeed who saw them in the presence of Melisande Shahrizai. They were examined by my own personal physician, who has attended me since childhood, and he will testify that their condition was consonant with the hardship they claim to have endured, from exposure to direst cold down to the weals on Joscelin Verreuil's wrists, where he was confined in chains."

"And yet these things may have other explanations, and other causes," murmured the Comte de Toluard, his expression thoughtful.

"They may," Ysandre said. "Yet the most damning piece of evidence in their conviction was their absence. Here they stand before us."

"Is there no other evidence that we may consider?" Roxanne de Mereliot inquired. Past the age when suitors battened the walls of Marsilikos, she retained a lush, rounded beauty, streaks of white in her coal-black hair. I liked her, for her dark eyes were both kind and clever.

"Yes, my lady," I said, curtsying to her. "You may

send to the Comte de Bois-le-Garde of Camlach, whose men came upon us in the woods. Or," I added, glancing dourly at Barquiel L'Envers, "you may venture into the Skaldi lands, if you wish. I can point out Gunter Arnlaugson's steading on a map, it is no difficulty. Ask him about the D'Angeline slaves he bought from Camaeline soldiers, if you so desire."

"And if it's true, either way we show our hand to d'Aiglemort, if we're not killed for our troubles," Barquiel remarked, scratching his cropped fair hair, so odd to see on a D'Angeline nobleman. But whether I trusted him or no, he was no fool. "A pretty trap, if you've laid it. Delaunay taught you well. If it's not, Elua help us all."

"Elua help us, indeed," Gaspar Trevalion said quietly. "I have known Phèdre nó Delaunay since she was a child, and I cannot believe she would be party to Anafiel Delaunay's murder. If that is so, then she tells the truth, as she believes it. And as for the Cassiline . . . look at him, Barquiel. He bears his honesty on his face. I do not know you," he added to Hyacinthe, "but I see no gain in this for you."

Hyacinthe cleared his throat, flushing slightly at the company he addressed. "I have known Phèdre longer than anyone," he said. "Even Delaunay. I saw her the night they returned to the City. She does not lie."

"But why," Tibault de Toluard said in his thoughtful manner, "would Isidore d'Aiglemort desire Delaunay's death?"

Gaspar Trevalion and Thelesis de Mornay exchanged a glance, but it was Ysandre de la Courcel who answered, color rising to stain her alabaster skin.

"Because," she said with dignity, "I asked his aid in a certain matter, which d'Aiglemort may have believed dangerous to his plans."

"No." Barquiel L'Envers came upright on his couch. "Oh, no. You can't mean to abide by it!"

"I can," she said, eyes blazing at him, "And I do!"

"No." He glared back at her. "If there's a measure of truth to this tale . . . Ysandre, I can arrange a union with a Prince of the royal House of Aragon, who can bring two thousand spears to your aid!"

"The Lioness of Azzalle," Gaspar Trevalion remarked conversationally, "came a great deal closer to overthrowing the Crown than anyone realized. If she had succeeded in bringing the army of Maelcon the Usurper, the old Cruarch's son, across the Strait, they would have swept across the country like a scythe."

Percy de Somerville shook his gold-grey head, speaking for the first time. "They'd have taken us unprepared, but they wouldn't have made it across. Ghislain tried near the same tactic, at the King's command. The Master of the Straits left no vessel unturned."

"No one can say why the Master of the Straits chooses as he does," Tibault de Toluard mused. "He let the old Cruarch cross, and no one knew why. If they *had* succeeded . . ." A thought came to him, and he paled. "But they did not, because of Isidore d'Aiglemort and Melisande Shahrizai. My lady Ysandre, what have you to do with that fateful island of Alba, and what has it to do with the death of Anafiel Delaunay de Montrève?"

I repeated the name silently, wondering: Montrève?

Ysandre de la Courcel folded her hands in her lap, lifting her chin again. "At the age of sixteen," she said quietly, "I was promised to the Cruarch's heir, his sister-son Drustan mab Necthana, the Prince of the Cruithne."

There is a thing that happens when a truth suddenly comes clear, a white blaze in which the pattern of it all manifests. I saw it then, in the presence of the Queen's council.

"Delaunay!" I gasped, the word an agony of grief. "Ah, Elua, the message, Quintilius Rousse, the Master of the Straits . . . you sought passage for him, for the Pictish Prince, to D'Angeline soil! But why . . . why turn to Delaunay?"

"Anafiel Delaunay de Montrève." Ysandre gave me the ghost of a smile. "You never even knew his proper name, did you? His father, who is the Comte de Montrève, abjured him, when he tied his fate to my father's and forebore to get heirs. He took his mother's name as his own, then, for she loved him nonetheless. My lord de Toluard would know, being of Siovale."

"Sarafiel Delaunay," Roxanne de Mereliot, the Lady of Marsilikos, said unexpectedly, smiling. "She was Eisandine by birth. There is an old story in Eisande, of Elua and a fisher-lad named Delaunay. Sarafiel would have understood. She sent Anafiel to me to be fostered when he was a child."

"Blessed Elua!" It was almost too much information to bear, and I pressed the heels of my hands to my eyes. I felt Hyacinthe steady me, gripping my arms, and was grateful for it.

"My grandfather was already using Delaunay," Ysandre said, continuing ruthlessly. "He didn't favor him, but he knew the strength of his oath, and the extent of his discretion. It was his will to learn if there was any merit left in an alliance with a deposed heir. I wanted somewhat else." Her composure slipped a little bit, and she whispered the last words. "Drustan mab Necthana."

Her words created a silence almost as great as Joscelin's and mine had, broken by Barquiel L'Envers' abrupt laugh. "The *blue boy*?" he asked, disbelieving. "You really want to wed the blue boy?"

Ysandre's eyes flared into life. "I want to wed the rightful heir to the Kingdom of Alba, to whom I am betrothed! Yes, uncle. And it is to that end that Anafiel Delaunay worked, and it is to prevent it that he was killed."

"But what . . ." It was Lord Rinforte who spoke, the Prefect of the Cassiline Brotherhood, his jaw working as he attempted to make sense of what had been said, "What has this to do with the Skaldi and the Duc d'Aiglemort?"

"Nothing," Ysandre said gently, "or everything."

It was then that I knew we would be a long time meeting.

A very long time.

ƆIFTY-NINE

I will confess, like the others, I could not fathom Ysandre's will in honoring her betrothal to the Prince of the Picti. A year ago, the romance of it might well have swept me away, but I had since been a barbarian lord's bed-slave, and my blood was soured on the romance of the exotic.

Still, when she spoke of it, I came to some sympathy, for she spoke with precision and passion, rising to pace restlessly.

"All my life," she announced, her hands clasped behind her back as she walked, chin tilted, "I have been a pawn in the game of alliance by marriage. I have been courted and besuitored and fêted by D'Angeline lordlings who saw in me only a path to the throne, grasping inbred creatures, jaded to everything but power. The Cruithne did not come for power. They came following a dream, a vision so strong it swayed the Master of the Straits to allow them passage."

Ysandre glanced at Thelesis de Mornay as she said those words, and a memory sparked in me: Delaunay's courtyard, after the audience with the Cruarch. I heard Alcuin's voice echo in my mind. *Still, I heard somewhat of a vision, of the King's sister; a black boar and a silver swan.*

A black boar. I mouthed the words to myself, repeating them silently in Cruithne. Black boar.

The Queen's council stirred, most of them uncomfortable with talk of visions.

"Drustan mab Necthana does not desire rulership of Terre d'Ange," Ysandre said firmly. "We spoke of it, laughing, in broken tongues; a dream of the two of us grown, ruling our kingdoms in tandem. The idle dreams of romantic youth, yes, but there was truth in it. And I saw in him somewhat that I could love, and he in me. When he spoke of Alba, his eyes lit like stars. I am not prepared to abandon this alliance for mere political expediency."

"You are the Queen, my dear," Roxanne de Mereliot murmured. "You may not have the luxury of choosing."

"The House of Aragon—" L'Envers began.

The Lady of Marsilikos cut him short. "The House of Aragon will send aid, if we are invaded by the Skaldi, for they know where the Skaldi would turn next if Terre d'Ange falls. But the immediate danger lies within our own borders." She looked at Ysandre, her dark eyes rich with sorrow. "The simplest solution, my dear, is for you to marry Isidore d'Aiglemort."

"And set a traitor on the throne?" The Comte de Somerville was outraged. "If what they say is true . . ."

"*If* it is true," Roxanne interrupted, "and our first duty is to determine if it is, then we have no choice but to bind his loyalty, by any means possible. It is that, or conquest."

There were murmurs, grudging ones, of agreement. Ysandre paled, the blood draining from her face.

"No," I said, whispering the word. Conversation halted, and they stared at me. "That would not be the end of it. The Skaldi threat remains, and it is ten times more dire than anything Isidore d'Aiglemort could muster. And there is Melisande. She has . . . she has a private correspondence with the Skaldi, with Waldemar Selig, routed through Caerdicca Unitas. I have seen their numbers. If they know themselves betrayed . . . not even the full loyalty of the Allies of Camlach can save us."

"Then we will take Melisande Shahrizai into custody," Lord Rinforte, the Prefect, said brusquely. "It is a simple enough matter."

I laughed hollowly. "My lord . . . oh, my lord, there are no simple matters with Melisande Shahrizai. Do you think it is an accident that she is in Kusheth and not the City? I would not wager upon it."

"But why?" Tibault de Toluard pulled at his braid, a scholar's abstract gesture, frowning. "Why would she betray the realm? What stakes are worth such risk?"

They looked at me, then, all of them. My hand stole up to close around her diamond, and I closed my eyes. "Not one realm, but two lie at stake; but it is the game, and not the stakes," I murmured. "When you come to it. The Shahrizai have played the Game of Houses since Elua's footsteps echoed across the land, and Melisande plays it better than anyone." I opened my eyes, and gazed back at them. "She has made her mistake. I am the proof of it, and this slight advantage we bear as its sole outcome. Do not count on her to make another. And if you take the Duc d'Aiglemort to be our greatest foe, I fear it will be our undoing. Waldemar Selig is no fool either."

"We cannot ignore a province in revolt," Percy de Somerville protested.

"And we cannot know for sure that Camlach is in rebellion," Barquiel L'Envers said pragmatically. "That, then, is our first order of business. Establishing the truth of this confabulation."

"Without, of course," de Toluard reminded him, "tipping our hand."

"Of course." L'Envers inclined his head, only slightly sardonic.

Gaspar Trevalion scratched his chin. "Where," he asked Percy de Somerville, "are Prince Baudoin's Glory-Seekers now? D'Aiglemort petitioned the King for them."

"You ought to know," the one-time Royal Commander said sourly. "In Trevalion, under Ghislain's command, making trouble. I wonder Marc suffered their insubordinacy."

"My cousin was always a patient man." Gaspar grinned. "He survived marriage to Lyonette, didn't he? This is my thought. Send d'Aiglemort the Glory-Seekers, let him think the Queen is softer than her grandfather was. Baudoin's Guard bear no love for Isidore d'Aiglemort, who brought down their Prince and disgraced their name. Let them dissemble, let them ride the length of Camlach and see where loyalties lie."

"And what is to guarantee their loyalty?" Roxanne de Mereliot inquired. "It was House Courcel that had Baudoin de Trevalion executed."

"Ah," Gaspar said softly. "Yes. Ganelon de la Courcel. But it is Ysandre de la Courcel who could recall Duc Marc de Trevalion and his daughter Bernadette from exile."

"And strip my son Ghislain of his estates?" Percy de

Somerville asked dangerously. Gaspar Trevalion looked evenly at him.

"I have heard great things of your son, my lord de Somerville. But he is a scion of Anael, and they will never love him in Azzalle, whose sin is pride; never, unless he were to become one of them. To wed, let us say, a Trevalion."

"Bernadette."

"Even so."

Ysandre followed the exchange with acute attention, her face grave. "Azzalle holds the flatlands, and we cannot risk dissention there," she said calmly. "My lord de Fourcay, your cousin has committed a crime against the throne, in withholding knowledge of Lyonette's plan. If he were given a chance at redemption, would he take it?"

"Your majesty." Gaspar Trevalion, the Comte de Fourcay, bowed to her. "He is a D'Angeline in exile. Yes, he would take it. And this I swear to you, upon my name, that he would be twice fierce in his loyalty, for being given a chance to prove it. Never while you live will House Trevalion give you cause to regret this clemency."

She was young; she bit her lip, then nodded. "Let it be so, then. You know where he resides?" She glanced at Gaspar, who inclined his head. "We will communicate with him, then. But let the offer be made to Baudoin's Guard first, and let them understand that upon their loyalty—and their discretion—rests the redemption of their House. Will you undertake this, my lord?"

"I will," Gaspar said firmly.

"Good." Ysandre looked stronger for the resolution. "Now, I have spoken with Prince Benedicte of these matters, insofar as I dared. You should know he and my uncle the Duc have made peace between them." She glanced at Barquiel L'Envers, who nodded curtly, no mockery in his expression. It was well done, I thought, impressed that she had brought them to concord. Oh, they had underestimated her direly, those D'Angelines who had called for Baudoin to replace her; there was steel indeed in Ysandre de la Courcel! "La Serenissima cannot aid us with men," she continued. "They are too near the Skaldic border, at too great a risk themselves. But they can aid us with intelligence, and that Benedicte has sworn to do." She gazed round at the others. "We require knowledge, my lords and ladies. Knowledge of Aragonia's support, and the other Caerdicci city-states. Knowledge of the movements of the Skaldi. Knowledge of the loyalties within our own realm. Knowledge of the extent of the forces we can marshal, and the degree of their readiness. This knowledge we require, and we require that it be obtained in secrecy. What are you prepared to do?"

I will not detail the conversation that followed, for it was lengthy and complicated. In the end it was resolved that each of them would take various measures toward these ends, moving with the utmost of discretion. The Cassiline Brotherhood would serve as the conduit for this intelligence, forming a network of couriers to carry information to all the provinces. This was well-conceived, for no one would suspect the Cassilines of politicking. Indeed, I think the Prefect would not have agreed were he not anxious to remove the taint that Joscelin's actions had cast upon his order. It was resolved too that no word would be given on the matter of the alleged traitors, until such time as there was proof at hand, and an advantage to be gained in revealing it.

When it was done, it was Barquiel L'Envers who returned to the topic of Alba. "Well, Ysandre," he said wryly, "we have planned our first steps toward handling civil war and invasion as best we may. What of your blue lad? How stand matters on fair Alba?"

It was Gaspar Trevalion who answered, rubbing at the bridge of his nose. Everyone was weary by this time. "Drustan mab Necthana escaped the bloodbath and fought his way, with his mother and sisters and a handful of warriors, to the western side of Alba, to seek refuge among the Dalriada. This we know. If the Dalriada would fight for him, it is likely that he could retake the throne from his cousin Maelcon, but thus far they have refused."

"Yes," Barquiel replied sarcastically, "I'm aware of this, as is much of the realm, as was Ganelon, which is why he was inclined to break their betrothal, which, of course, was never made public in the first place. Is this the extent of your vast intelligence, for which Anafiel Delaunay was slain?"

"No." Thelesis de Mornay intervened softly, but with the poet's command of tone that summoned their attention. "Delaunay was in contact with Quintilius Rousse, who carried a request to the Master of the Straits. We pleaded that he grant passage to Drustan mab Necthana and his folk. Were they to gain D'Angeline soil, he and Ysandre could wed. Terre d'Ange would aid him in regaining the throne of Alba, and Alba would aid Ysandre in retaining the throne of Terre d'Ange."

"The very plan of the Lioness of Azzalle," Roxanne de Mereliot murmured.

"Which nigh succeeded," Gaspar reminded her. "Yes. Except we sought the compliance of the Master of the Straits."

"Which," Tibault de Toluard observed, "I take it he did not give."

"He answered thusly," Thelesis said, and quoted. " *'When the Black Boar rules in Alba, Elder Brother will accede.'* Those were the words of Quintilius Rousse, and the message for which Delaunay was killed."

I knew the words, knew them well; and yet they tugged at my mind, an echoing memory.

"A message which makes no sense," L'Envers said acerbically.

"Not so." Thelesis shook her head. "There are dozens of tribes in Alba and Eire, but they fall into four peoples. The folk of the Red Bull, to whom Maelcon and Foclaidha are born; the folk of the White Mare, whom the Dalriada follow; the folk of the Golden Hind, to the south, and the folk of the Black Boar, to whom Drustan mab Necthana was born, Cinhil Ru's line. The Master of the Straits is saying that he will grant our request if Prince Drustan can reclaim Alba."

"Ah, well then." L'Envers shrugged. "Likely he would grant our request if Blessed Elua returned from the Terre d'Ange-that-lies-beyond and asked him a boon. It is a moot point."

The memory that had evaded me at last came clear.

"Do not discount the Cullach Gorrym," I said aloud. "Hyacinthe!" I shook him in my excitement. "Do you remember? Your mother said it to me. Do not discount the Cullach Gorrym." I repeated it. "Don't discount the Black Boar!"

He frowned. "I remember. It didn't make any sense."

"It does now," I said. "It means Prince Drustan."

"You say your mother had this gift?" Ysandre asked, bending her gaze on Hyacinthe.

"Yes, your majesty." He bowed. "Greater than I. And she said this, it is true."

"What do you see?"

He stared into the distance, his black eyes going blank and filmy, and finally shook his head. "I see a ship," he said reluctantly. "Nothing more. Where the paths branch in many ways, I cannot see far. It is only the straight road I see clearly, majesty. Such as your grandfather the King's."

"Anyone could have foretold that," Percy de Somerville muttered. "Ganelon was on his deathbed."

"The young Tsingano foretold the day of it," Ysandre reminded him. She looked thoughtful. "If the Dalriada knew of the Master of the Strait's pledge, mayhap they would lend Drustan their aid. Anafiel Delaunay would have gone, had he not been killed. It is a pity, for he spoke Cruithne, and his young pupil as well. And there is no one else I trust." She glanced apologetically at Thelesis. "I do not speak of you, of course; I trust you with my life, Queen's Poet, and I know your spirit is willing. But I have spoken with the physicians, and a winter voyage across land and sea would be the death of you, Thelesis."

"So they tell me," Thelesis de Mornay murmured; and I did not doubt that she was willing to go anyway, though the ravages of the fever were clearly marked on her strained features. But her dark, luminous gaze fell on me instead. "My lady," she said to Ysandre, "Anafiel Delaunay had two pupils."

The shock of it went clean through me. "What are you saying?" I whispered.

"I am saying . . ." She had to pause, overcome by a fit of coughing. "Phèdre nó Delaunay, *you* could take Anafiel's place as the Queen's ambassador."

"My lady," I protested, looking from Thelesis to Ysandre, not sure which one of them I was addressing. My mind was reeling. "My lady, I am an *anguissette*! I am trained to be a Servant of Naamah! I'm not trained to be an ambassador!"

"Whatever you're trained to do, you apparently do it damnably well," Barquiel L'Envers remarked laconically. "Did you know Rogier Clavel went into mourning for you and lost some twenty pounds? He's as thin as a rail these days. Any pupil of Anafiel Delaunay's is considerably more than a Servant of Naamah, little *anguissette*. You're the first whore I've heard of to double-cross a Skaldi warleader and survive to warn a nation of treason."

"My lord!" I heard the terror in my own voice. "What I did to survive, I hope never to do again. I do not have the strength to live through it twice."

"The Cruithne are not the Skaldi," Ysandre said reasonably. "And you would be under the protection of Quintilius Rousse, who is one of the greatest admirals ever to set sail. Phèdre, for what you have done, I am grateful. Never think it is not so. I would not ask this thing if our need were not urgent."

I sat without answering, unseeing with shock. Near to me, Joscelin rose, giving his smooth Cassiline bow to the Queen. He turned to me, then, and I gazed up at him, his face shining with bright fearlessness. "Phèdre," he said, his voice ringing with a hero's courage. "We have survived worse adventures. I will go with you. I have sworn it. To protect and serve!"

For a moment, his courage kindled my own. Then the Prefect's voice came hard on the heels of Joscelin's ringing tones, like a dash of icy water.

"Brother Joscelin!" he said crisply. "We are glad that your innocence has been established in the matter of Anafiel Delaunay's death. But you have confessed yourself in violation of your vows and remanded yourself to our justice. For the salvation of your soul, you must atone and be shriven. Only those who strive to be Perfect Companions are fit to serve the scions of Elua."

Joscelin blinked, staring at him open-mouthed, then regained his composure. "My lord Prefect," he said with a bow. "I am sworn still to the household of Anafiel Delaunay." There was a note of anguish in his voice. "If there is salvation to be found for me, it lies in honoring that vow!"

"You are relieved of your vow to Delaunay's household," the Prefect said flatly. "I decree it so."

"My lord!" Joscelin winced as if struck. "My lord Prefect, please, no!"

The old Prefect leveled his hawk's glare at Joscelin. "What transgressions have you committed, young Brother?"

Joscelin looked away, unable to hold the Prefect's gaze. "I have failed to safeguard my charge," he said dully. "I have slain in anger instead of defending. I have . . . I have committed murder. And I have . . ." He looked at me for a moment, his expression grave. I remembered Elua's Cavern, and what had happened between us there. Then his gaze slid away from mine and he glanced at Hyacinthe. "I have drawn my sword merely to threaten," he finished.

"These are grave sins." The Prefect shook his head. "I cannot allow it, Brother Joscelin. Another will go in your stead."

It was very still in the King's hunting lodge. No one, not even Ysandre, would intervene in a Cassiline matter. Joscelin stood alone, lost in thought. He raised his blue gaze toward the ceiling, then looked once again at me. I remembered him standing alone in the deadly veils of snow, casting down his sword before the Skaldi. He had made choices no other Cassiline ever had faced. He had been tempered, by chains and blood and ice, and not broken. I did not want any other protector to stand in his stead.

"Your majesty." Joscelin turned to Ysandre with a bow, speaking with the utmost formality. "Will you accept my sword in your service as the protector of Phèdre nó Delaunay?"

"Do it and be damned, young Brother!" the Prefect said harshly. "Cassiel's vows bind for a lifetime and beyond!"

Ysandre de la Courcel sat in consideration, her face expressionless. At last she inclined her head. "We accept your service," she said formally. To the Prefect, she said, "My lord Rinforte, we grieve to cross your wishes. But we must follow the precepts of Blessed Elua in such matters, and not the will of the Cassiline Brotherhood. And by Elua's teaching, he is free to choose his course."

"There will be a reckoning upon the Misguided!" the Prefect muttered through clenched teeth. "So be it. Is that your will, Brother Joscelin?"

"It is." Joscelin's voice sounded hollow, but he stood unwavering.

The Prefect gave an immaculate Cassiline bow, then made a gesture with both hands, as though breaking something. "Joscelin Verreuil of the Cassiline Brotherhood, I declare you anathema." He bowed again, to Ysandre. "I remand this man into your service, your majesty."

"Good," she said simply. "Phèdre nó Delaunay, do you accept this charge to take up your lord's duty and carry my words to Prince Drustan mab Necthana of the Cruithne?"

After what Joscelin had done, it left me little choice. I stood, my stomach a mix of sinking terror, pride and excitement, and made obeisance to my Queen. "Yes, your majesty. I will go."

"Good," Ysandre repeated, adding thoughtfully, "Then the only problem that remains is how to get you safely to Quintilius Rousse."

"Where is he?" I knew where he had been. I dreaded the answer.

"Kusheth." The word fell like a stone.

"Your majesty," Hyacinthe said unexpectedly. "I have an idea."

Sixty

It seemed that there was a Tsingani route to Kusheth, something neither I nor anyone else in the Queen's Council had known. The Tsingani live among the D'Angelines and travel our roads, and yet we know little of their ways. Hyacinthe knew. It had always been his half-secret passion, while he played in Night's Doorstep at being the Prince of Travellers, to claim his birthright from his grandfather's *kumpania*. I think, other than his mother, only I knew it.

They are great horse-traders, the Tsingani, and breeders as well. Eisande boasts the most famous, for they are dearly sought after by the *taurieres* who perform their deadly games with the great Eisandine bulls, but inland Kusheth holds another great center of Tsingani horse-breeding. And some few of the *kumpanias* journey there in early spring to have their pick of the first foaling.

This was the essence of Hyacinthe's plan: that we should journey to Kusheth along Tsingani-marked roads, seeking his people, the *kumpania* of Manoj. And when we found them, he reckoned, we could beg or buy their aid in travelling as horse-traders to the Pointe d'Oest, where Rousse's fleet was beached.

It was a dangerous plan, for it meant we would be isolated and vulnerable. And it was an excellent plan, for it cast us in a guise no one would expect.

That, more than anything else, was what swayed the odds in favor of Hyacinthe's plan. If there was one thing that terrified me above all others, it was not daring the wrath of the Master of the Straits nor the dangers of distant Alba and the blue-tattooed Cruithne. It was venturing through Kusheth, the homeland of House Shahrizai. But no Kusheline lordling, I thought, not even Melisande, would think to examine the eyes of a young Tsingano woman for the tell-tale scarlet mote.

So it was decided.

The details of the matter were established after the Queen's council had adjourned, all of us sworn to secrecy and loyalty. We met after a fine dinner, only a handful of us—Gaspar and Thelesis, who had been party to the Alban plan since the beginning, and Joscelin, Hyacinthe and I. It would be a week's time before we could set out, for it was early yet, and only the eagerest of the *kumpanias* would be on the road. And too, there were some arrangements to be made. Hyacinthe and Thelesis would return to the City, to procure what was needful.

When all was decided, we had some leisure to talk.

"Phèdre," Gaspar Trevalion said, taking my hands in his, "I've not had time to tell you how deeply grieved I am at the death of Anafiel Delaunay. He was . . . he was my friend, and a finer one I never had. The world is the less for the loss of his brilliant mind and his great heart. And Alcuin . . . I knew him from a boy, you know. He was a rare jewel."

"Thank you, my lord." I wrung his hands in gratitude, tears stinging my eyes. "Delaunay always counted you one of the best among men."

"I thought he was a fool sometimes," Gaspar said gruffly, "honoring an oath sworn to a dead man. It demanded a great deal, that honor of his."

"Yes." I thought of the bitter words I'd spoken to

Ysandre de la Courcel, at our first audience. "But," I said, "I loved him for it, too."

"We all did," Thelesis said, and smiled. "At least those who did not hate him, for he drew strong emotions, Delaunay did. Phèdre, his house and his things were seized by the court. Have you nothing to call your own?"

I shook my head, fingering Melisande's diamond. "Only this," I said wryly, "which surely I earned. It seems I will wear it until the day I may throw it back at her who gave it me. But I lost little to the courts. Nearly all that I had went to Master Robert Tielhard, to contract for the finishing of my marque." I looked over my shoulder, and shrugged. "That loss, I lay at the doorstep of Melisande Shahrizai and Isidore d'Aiglemort."

"I swear," Gaspar Trevalion said solemnly, giving my hands another squeeze, "on the memory of Anafiel Delaunay, while I live, you will never lack for aught, Phèdre. And when this matter is done, I will see your name cleared." He glanced at Joscelin. "Both of yours."

"Thank you." I leaned forward and kissed his cheek, which had grown seamed with age since I had known him. Joscelin, silent and introspective, nodded his gratitude.

"It seems to me," Hyacinthe remarked, "that we might claim a considerable reward from the Queen for this service, yes?" He looked at our startled faces and grinned. "If you are to travel among Tsingani, you must begin thinking like one."

I could see the distaste on Joscelin's face. "Better than thinking as one of the White Brethren," I said to him in Skaldic. His blue eyes widened for an instant, shocked to hear words in our slave-tongue, then he smiled reluctantly.

"Will you teach me to speak Cruithne as you did Skaldic?" he inquired lightly.

"I don't know," I said. "Do I have to have you chained in a kennel to make a willing pupil of you?"

"No," he said wryly, and ran his hands absently over his hair, which fell wheat-gold and loose over his shoulders, unbound from its Cassiline club. "I think I have learned the merits—and the dangers—of paying heed to your words, Phèdre nó Delaunay. Your lord would be proud of you."

"Mayhap." I met his eyes. "Thank you," I said softly.

We had not spoken of the choice he had made. Joscelin looked away, picking with his thumbnail at a flaw in the carven arm of his chair. "Well," he murmured. "I could not leave you to suffer the guardianship of some dried-up old stick of a Cassiline." He looked at Hyacinthe and smiled. "And the Brothers would despair of you, Tsingano. I may at least hope to survive our companionship without being driven mad."

"I hope so." Hyacinthe flashed his imperturbable grin. "You've come a long way since Phèdre had to rescue you from the degradations of Eglantine tumblers, Cassiline. I hope we face nothing worse together."

"Elua grant that it's so." Joscelin stood, bowing, catching himself out with crossed arms. He shook his head. "Forgive me. It's late, and I've need of sleep."

We bid him good night, and watched him go.

"You know," Thelesis said in her soft, compelling voice, "I had a great-uncle who was a Cassiline. There is a name for what he did today." She looked at me with those darkly luminous eyes in her wasted face. "They call it Cassiel's Choice."

I did not need her to explain. I understood.

The days that followed passed in relative isolation, as our forces dispersed to the four corners of the realm. At my request, Ysandre had several volumes sent from the Royal Library, texts on Alba and books in Cruithne, and treatises on the Master of the Straits. I wished I had Delaunay's library at hand. I remembered how Alcuin was studying the history of the Master of the Straits, and wished he were there. I wished, too, that I had been present at that fateful audience, when Ganelon de la Courcel had received the old Cruarch. But no, Alcuin had gone with Delaunay, and I had been glad of it, going instead to Valerian House to dote over flagellaries and pleasure-chambers.

Such things seemed as child's play to me now. I knew firsthand the ravages that could be perpetuated against the soul. The torments of the flesh were as nothing to them.

On the fourth day, Ysandre summoned me into her presence.

"I have brought someone to see you, Phèdre," she said judiciously. "Someone whom I have gauged worthy of trust."

It was my first thought that it was Cecilie Laveau-Perrin, for I had missed her sorely since returning to Terre d'Ange, and Thelesis had confessed to me that she had confided in Cecilie, who had wept tears of joy to hear that I was alive. But Ysandre beckoned, and the frail figure that stepped forth was not Cecilie.

It was Master Tielhard, the marquist.

I knelt at the sight of him, my eyes blurred with tears, grasping his gnarled hands and kissing them. He drew them back, fussing.

"Always this," he complained, "with *anguissettes*. My Grandpère warned me it was so. Well, child, we have a contract unfulfilled between us, and my Queen commands me to see it finished. Will you disrobe, or have these old bones made this journey for nothing?"

Still kneeling, I gazed through tear-flooded eyes at Ysandre. "Thank you, your majesty."

"You should thank me." She smiled faintly. "Master Tielhard was not easy to persuade. But it is best to start a journey with all unfinished business concluded, and Thelesis de Mornay told me of yours."

She left us, then, and the servants of the lodge led us to a private room, where the marquist's things had been laid out for him. They even had a table made ready. I stripped naked and lay down upon it. He grumbled at the nearly healed weals left by the priests of Kushiel's Temple, but it seemed I would do.

"Where is your apprentice, Master Tielhard?" I asked him as he pottered muttering among his things.

"Gone," he said shortly. "The fever took him. You will be my last great work, *anguissette*. I am too old to start anew, training one to take my place."

"Naamah will surely bless you for the service you have given," I whispered. Master Tielhard grunted an unintelligible response and laid the tapper against my spine, striking it smartly.

A hundred needles pierced my skin, bearing pigment to limn it indelibly. I closed my eyes, awash in pleasure at the exquisite pain of it. And no matter what else happened, this much I was granted. My marque would be made. No matter that I ventured forth into certain danger; I would do it as that which I had claimed to be to Waldemar Selig: A free D'Angeline.

"At least you've learned to lie still," Master Tielhard said irascibly, and struck the tapper again.

Pain blossomed like a red flower at the base of my spinal column, suffusing my limbs. I gasped, clutching at the corners of the table, and proved him wrong. If Ysandre had told him I was a hero of the realm, it made no difference. Master Robert Tielhard was an artist, and I was his canvas. He swatted irritably at my writhing buttocks, ordering me to stillness.

"Damned *anguissettes*," he muttered. "Grandpère was right."

Later I had time alone in the room I'd been given to consider it. It was a well-appointed room, if a bit dark and frowsty for my taste, but it was a hunting lodge, after all. Still there was a great oval mirror, gilt-edged, in which I could gaze at my finished marque. I stood naked before it, twisting my hair out of the way and gazing over my shoulder.

In truth, the finished marque was stunning.

Thorny black lines, intricate and powerful, rose from the graceful scrollwork at the base to twine upward the full length of my spine, ending in an elegant finial. The teardrop-shaped scarlet accents had been used sparingly, serving as vivid counterpoints to the black lines and my own ivory skin. Echoing Kushiel's Dart, I had thought at the time; now it reminded me too of the Bitterest Winter, of the Skaldic wilderness, branches stark against the snow, spattered with crimson blood.

Stunning; and fitting.

A knock sounded at the door, and I slid on the silk robe that had been provided me. I opened the door to see Ysandre de la Courcel, and began to kneel.

"Oh, stop," she said restlessly. "I've ceremony enough in my life, and we're near bed-cousins after all, between Delaunay and my father." It was a startling thought, but Ysandre gave me no time to dwell on it. "Was it done to your satisfaction?"

"Yes, your majesty." I stepped back from the door, allowing her to enter. "It was a great kindness. Thank you."

Ysandre eyed me curiously. "May I see it?"

One does not refuse such a request from one's sovereign. Silently, I undid the sash of my robe and slipped it off, turning.

"So that is the marque of Naamah." Her fingers brushed the fresh-limned skin, light and curious. "Does it hurt?"

I repressed a shudder. "Yes."

"I beg your pardon." There was a trace of amusement in the cool voice. "Thank you. You may cover yourself."

I did, turning back to face her. "You have never seen a Servant of Naamah?"

"No." Ysandre shook her head. "My grandfather forbade me such contact. Virginity is too highly prized in a bride, especially among barbarians," she added wryly. "Akkadians, for example."

"Blessed Elua bid us to love as we willed," I said. "Not even the King can violate that precept."

"No." She moved restlessly around the room, her pale hair like a flame in the dim light. "But you should understand. When you were a bond-slave to Anafiel Delaunay, you could not spend the coin of your love as you willed, no? I am bond-slave to the throne, Phèdre. Still, I would obey Elua's Precept, and that is why I am sending you to Alba to bear word to Drustan mab Necthana. If you fail . . . I will still have the coin of my unsullied bridal bed. Elua grant I have somewhere to spend it."

"I will do my best," I whispered.

"You have a gift for survival." Ysandre leveled her violet gaze at me. "I can but hope it holds true." Her tone changed back to one of curiosity. "Tell me, why do Naamah's servants bear such a marque?"

"You do not know?" I smiled, shrugging my shoulders to feel the silk brush against tender skin. "It is said that Naamah so marked the backs of those lovers who pleased her, scoring her nails against their skin. They bore the traceries of those marks of ecstacy all the days of their lives. We do it in homage, and out of memory."

"Ah." Ysandre nodded once, satisfied. "I understand.

Thank you." She turned to go, then paused. "Your companion Hyacinthe will return on the morrow, and you will make ready to leave. I thought you might like to have this. 'Tis small enough to port." She handed me a small, slim volume, much mended. I took and opened it, glancing at the pages, writ in an unfamiliar hand. "It's my father's diary," Ysandre said quietly. "He began it at the University in Tiberium. It ends shortly after my birth. There's a great deal about Delaunay. That's what made me dare to approach him."

"In the players' changing-room," I said without thinking, remembering. I looked up at her shocked face, and colored. "It is a long story, your majesty. Delaunay never knew I was there."

Ysandre shook her head. "My uncle was right. Whatever it is you do, Phèdre nó Delaunay, you seem to do it very well." Her violet gaze deepened. "My father wed out of duty, and not love. Elua grant you spare me the same fate. I will pray for your safe return, and pray you bring the Prince of the Cruithne with you. No more can I do. I must protect the realm as best I can."

I grieved for her burden; mine own seemed light beside it. "If it is possible, I will do it, my lady."

"I know."

We gazed at each other, the two of us, both of an age, yet so different.

"Be well," Ysandre said, and took my head in both hands, laying the formal kiss of blessing upon my brow. "May Elua bless and keep you. I pray that we will meet again."

She left, then, leaving me alone with my finished marque and my book. Since I had nothing else to do, I sat and read.

In the morning, Hyacinthe arrived, returning from the City. He had with him three rather good horses, foodstuffs in abundance, and two pack-mules that would bear our gear.

And he had clothing.

For himself, he would wear his usual garb, garishly colorful, covered over with a saffron cloak that was the Tsingani travelling color. He had brought a like cloak for me, with a maroon-lined hood, that went over a blue velvet gown with a three-flounced skirt with a maroon underlining. It was very fine, though a bit much, and the fabric was well-used, the nap worn shiny in places.

"Tsingani discard nothing needlessly," he reminded me. "Phèdre, you will be my near-cousin, a by-blow gotten in one of the pleasure-houses of Night's Doorstep by a half-breed Tsingano trader. You've the eyes for it, anyway, at least excepting the one." He grinned. "As for you, Cassiline . . ." Hyacinthe held up a voluminous grey cloak, swirling it to reveal the lining.

It held an opalescent riot of color: madder, damson, ochre, cerulean and nacre. I laughed, covering my mouth.

"You know what it is?" Hyacinthe asked.

I nodded. "I saw one, once. It's a Mendacant's robe."

"It was Thelesis' idea, she conceived it with the Lady of Marsilikos." He handed the cloak to Joscelin, who received it expressionless. "You can't pass as Tsingani, Cassiline, not even a by-blow. And we need somewhat to explain your presence."

The wandering fabulists known as Mendacants come from Eisande. Among Elua's Companions, it was Eisheth who gave to mortals the gifts of music and story. So D'Angelines claim; our critics hold that she taught us to play and to lie. Be as it may, Eisandines are the finest storytellers, and the best among them the Mendacants, who are sworn to travel the realm, embroidering truth and fable together into one fabric.

If any D'Angeline would travel the long road with the Tsingani, it would be a Mendacant.

"Can you lie, Cassiline?" Hyacinthe was grinning again.

Joscelin swung the cloak over his shoulders. It settled around him, dove-grey and somber as his former priest's garb, until he shifted and a glimpse of swirling color was revealed. "I will learn," he said shortly.

"You can start with this." Ysandre de la Courcel had entered unannounced. She nodded at one of her dour Cassiline Guards, who held out an armload of gleaming steel.

Joscelin's gear—daggers, vambraces, sword and all. He gazed wide-eyed at the Queen.

"The arms belong to the family, and not the Cassiline Brotherhood, yes?" Ysandre said. "You offered me your sword, Joscelin Verreuil, and this is the sword I accepted. You will bear it, and your arms, in my service." A small smile played about her lips. "It is up to you to conceive a tale of why a wandering Mendacant should bear Cassiline arms."

"Thank you, your majesty," he murmured, bowing without thinking with arms crossed. He reached out then and took his gear from the scowling Brother, settling the belt around his waist, buckling on his vambraces and slinging on his baldric. With the hilt of his sword protruding from beneath the Mendacant cloak, he seemed to stand taller and straighter.

"You have done well," Ysandre said to Hyacinthe, who bowed. She surveyed the three of us. "All is in readiness for your journey. Phèdre . . ." She handed me an object, a heavy gold ring on a long chain. I took it and looked; it bore the Courcel insignia, the swan crest. "It is my father's ring," Ysandre said. She held up her hand, which bore its twin. "I wear my grandfather's now.

You may show it to Quintilius Rousse, if he doubts the truth of your word. And when you gain the distant shore of Alba, give it to Drustan mab Necthana, that he might know from whence it came. He will know it. I have worn it since my father's death."

"Yes, your majesty." I lifted the chain over my head and settled the ring under my clothing, where it lay below Melisande's diamond.

"Good," Ysandre said simply. She held herself proud and upright, letting nothing but courage show on her face. She was the Queen, she could afford to do nothing less. "Blessed Elua be with you all."

It was a dismissal, and our order to go. Hyacinthe and Joscelin bowed; I curtsied.

And thus did we set out.

Sixty-one

The place to which we were bound was called the Hippochamp. One thinks of Kusheth as a harsh and stony land, but, of course, this is only true of the outermost verges. Inland, it is as rich and fertile as any of the seven provinces, with deep valleys cut through by mighty rivers.

We would travel westward across L'Agnace, taking the Senescine Forest road into Kusheth; or so Hyacinthe believed. He could not be sure until we intercepted one of the *chaidrov*, the imperceptible markings the Tsingani leave along their route. It would not matter, overmuch, in L'Agnace, which was under the Comte de Somerville's rule and peaceful. Of the Companions, Anael's gift was husbandry, and he taught much to mortals of the growing of good things and the care of the land. It made for a peaceful province, although L'Agnacites are fierce as lions when roused to defend their land, as Percy de Somerville's noble history as the Royal Commander evidenced.

Good weather graced our leavetaking, a damp early thaw rendering the air moist and gentle. Despite my fear at the vastness of our undertaking, I found myself in good spirits to be riding once more. Truly, nothing is worse than waiting idle, while fear preys on one's mind like ravens upon a corpse. And after the frozen terrors of Skaldia, the Senescine seemed almost friendly.

Our first day proved uneventful. We saw no one save a few farmers at early tilling for spring crops, who nodded in taciturn acknowledgment. Once we gained the forest road, we rode in solitude.

Hyacinthe made for a cheerful companion. He had brought a handheld timbale, which he played as he rode, his nimble fingers drumming and jangling out a merry rhythm. After our terrible journey of desperate, hurried silence and secrecy, it seemed odd and dangerous to Joscelin and me, but I saw the wisdom in it. Tsingani do nothing quietly, and there is as much deception in noise as there is in silence.

It was after we had paused for a luncheon that we saw the first sign of Tsingani on the road, passing a campsite near a forest stream. Scorched earth and scraps of metal gave evidence that a travelling forge had been erected there, and the Tsingani are known to be smiths. Hyacinthe scouted the area and loosed a shout of triumph. We hurried to his side, and he pointed to a split twig planted in the ground, one side bent westward.

"A *chaidrov*," he said, nodding. "We are on the right route."

So we continued our journey, following such Tsingani signs as Hyacinthe espied; indeed, all of us grew adept at spotting them. I will not speak overmuch of these travels, for the days passed without incident. From Hyacinthe, we learned somewhat of Tsingani ways, preparing ourselves for what we might find. In turn, I taught a few words of Cruithne to both he and Joscelin. It is more difficult than Skaldic, for there are sounds in the Pictish tongue that come hard to D'Angelines. I had always despised the fact that Delaunay had made me learn it; ironic, that I should need it so direly now.

The remainder of the time, I passed in reading the journal of Prince Rolande de la Courcel, that with which Ysandre had gifted me.

From this slim book, I pieced together the great and fateful romance that had bound Anafiel Delaunay's fate to the protection of Ysandre de la Courcel, and indeed, made of me what I was, a courtesan equipped to match wits with the deadliest of courtiers.

They had met at the University in Tiberium, of course; that much I had known. But I glimpsed Delaunay now through another's eyes, as a young man, full of beauty and a splendid passion to *know*. I had never known Delaunay as a youth. It surprised me to read his poems, carefully recorded by Rolande de la Courcel; wicked, biting satires that lampooned fellow students and masters alike. And it was Rolande who began calling him Delaunay, after his mother's name and the Eisandine shepherd lad Elua had loved. Once they were together—and I blushed to read that passage, wondering how Ysandre had taken it—it was the masters of the University who nicknamed him Antinous, after a lad beloved by an ancient Tiberian Imperator.

Rolande's nature shone through it all, a generous and reckless spirit who loved freely without reckoning the cost, truer to the Precept of Blessed Elua and the archaic ideologies of glory than the political machinations of a monarchy. I could only imagine how Delaunay had adored and despaired of this careless nobility, incapable of subtlety.

It was the death of Edmée de Rocaille that had caused a rift between them, after the University, after Delaunay had been castigated by his father and formally taken his mother's name. Hyacinthe and I had not been too far wrong; there was a longstanding bond between the Houses Rocaille and Montrève—strange, still, to think of Delaunay as aught but Delaunay—and Edmée had been a childhood friend to Delaunay in Siovale, betrothed to Rolande out of goodwill and because her family had ties to the royal House of Aragon.

A good arrangement, it seemed; there was fondness between all of them, and Edmée understood that she was trading passion to be the eventual Queen of Terre d'Ange, mother of heirs.

Then came her hunting accident.

It was obvious that Rolande genuinely grieved for her, and obvious too that he was blind to the possibility that Isabel L'Envers had been involved, attributing Delaunay's vehemence to a mix of grief and jealousy. It is a human failing, to attribute the best of motives to those we know the least, and the worst to those we love best; he loved too well, Rolande did, and feared to be lenient in his judgment and favor Delaunay because of it. He heeded Isabel, who flattered and bewitched him. And they were betrothed, for House L'Envers was powerful; betrothed, and wed.

And Delaunay wrote his satire.

I think that Rolande knew, when Isabel sought to have him banished. I read what he wrote privately, for none to behold, of how he argued long and hard with his father the King on Delaunay's behalf. The agreement they reached was a bitter compromise. Delaunay would live, and retain status such as his father's repudiation had left him, but his poetry was declared anathema. To own it was tantamount to treason.

That much, I had known. I had not known that every extant copy of Delaunay's works was gathered and burned. Nor that Prince Rolande de la Courcel had wept at the conflagration. I daresay no one knew, save Ysandre, who read these same words.

Somehow, then, somewhere, they were reconciled, Rolande and Delaunay. It falls within a gap in Rolande's journal; he wrote only, *"All is forgiven, though nothing is the same. If we cannot have the past, Elua grant us a future."* One might argue that he wrote of Isabel and not Delaunay, but for what followed.

It came upon the heels of Ysandre's birth, an event heralded in Rolande's life with mingled joy and terror at donning the mantle of fatherhood. That his relations with Isabel had grown bitter was obvious to one trained to read between the lines. I hoped that Ysandre had not discerned as much, though I doubted it. There was another gap, then Rolande wrote, *"Anafiel has promised, swearing upon my ring, and my heart is glad for it though neither Isabel nor Father are pleased. But who among us is whole? He is the wiser half of my sundered soul, and I can give my firstborn no greater gift than to pledge my devotion entire."* And then, *"It is done, and witnessed by the priests of Elua."*

Shortly after this, Rolande's journal ends. I know why, for he was caught up in the affairs of the heir of Terre d'Ange, and rode not long afterward to Camlach, to the Battle of Three Princes, where he lost his life.

So many killed, I mused, sitting beside the campfire the night I finished my reading of his diary. So much bloodshed. I had been a child still in Cereus House when these things had shaped Ysandre's life. Mine too, had I known it; but that pattern was forming in the distant future. While I learned how to kneel uncomplaining for hours at a time and the proper angle of approach for serving sweets after a meal, Ysandre was learning how greed and jealousy corrupt the human soul.

No wonder she clung to a girl's dream of love. I glanced at the well-worn journal, then toward the west, where dim streaks of dying sun glowed between the trees. We were near to Kusheth now, if we'd not crossed the border already. It was hard to tell, in the forest. Somewhere beyond the ability of my vision to scry lay the Straits of Alba, that wind-whipped expanse of water as grey and narrow and deadly as a blade, separating Ysandre from a dream.

Not a mere girl's dream, I reminded myself, but a Queen's; Ysandre's blue boy might have hands that would lie lightly upon the Crown, but they came gripping a spear, a thousand spears. It was a dream to pit against a nightmare, of D'Angeline heads bowed before the Skaldi sword. Thinking of Waldemar Selig, I shuddered. It was hard to imagine any Pictish prince who could stand against him, in all his brawn and might and the teeming loyalty of tens of thousands of Skaldi.

And yet . . . the Skaldi had felt the hobnailed sandal of Tiberium upon their necks, while the Cruithne had never known defeat. And Drustan mab Necthana was of Cinhil Ru's lineage, who had cast the soldiers of Tiberium from Alba.

Such a slender hope, and all of it resting now upon our shoulders, this unlikely threesome. I clutched Rolande's journal to me like a talisman, lifting my gaze to the emerging stars, and prayed that we would not fail.

ꙅixty-two

The scale of the Tsingani horse-fair at the Hippochamp caught me unprepared.

Once we emerged from the Senescine, our route grew ever more obvious, despite the increasing number of roads. As the dank cold of false spring eased into the truer promise of spring-to-come, pale green buds emerged on the trees around us, and traffic grew steadily along the roads.

And amid the travellers, we saw Tsingani in numbers, the true Travellers, journeying always upon the Long Road.

There is another horse-fair at the Hippochamp that takes place in late summer, when the most promising of yearlings are green-broken, offered to the *gadje* noblemen for outrageous prices. That fair, Hyacinthe assured us, dwarfed this one, as did the fair in midsummer in Eisheth. This was primarily a Tsingani affair, when there were opportunities to be seized early, untried yearlings and stumbling foals at auction, only their bloodlines and the cunning gaze of their breeders to recommend them.

No one has ever made a count of the Tsingani in Terre d'Ange; they are too migratory to stand still for it, too suspicious to report honestly. I have seen them gathering and I can say that they are many, more than we reckon.

As we drew near to the Hippochamp, we passed caravans of Tsingani. It was a strange thing, to witness the change in Hyacinthe. For it was he whom they acknowledged, calling out greetings in their private dialect. And why not? He was young, bold and handsome, one of their own. Hyacinthe shouted back, waving his velvet cap, black eyes sparkling. Their tongue was mixed with D'Angeline, but I scarce understood a word of it.

"You didn't tell me I had to learn Tsingani," Joscelin muttered to me, riding close by my side.

"I didn't know," I replied, chagrined. Even Delaunay, scholar that he was, hadn't reckoned Tsingani a proper language. In all the time I had known Hyacinthe—through all the meals I'd eaten in his mother's kitchen—I'd never understood what it meant to him to be a Tsingano. In front of me, they spoke D'Angeline proper. I thought of all the casual cuffs and curses he'd endured, from the very beginning of our acquaintance, when the Dowayne's Guard had found me. I hadn't known. I hadn't understood. When he took a broken-down nag and built a profitable livery stable out of it, I hadn't realized how deeply rooted in Tsingani tradition it was. I'd merely thought him clever for it.

It is a funny thing, how one's perspective changes. I saw Hyacinthe through new eyes as we journeyed toward the Hippochamp. We passed Tsingani wagons, far more colorful and elaborate than Taavi and Danele's humble Yeshuite conveyance, though similar in design, and the young women hung out the back, making eyes at Hyacinthe. I learned to tell the unmarried ones, who wore their hair uncovered. They chattered and flirted as we passed, and Hyacinthe grew more desirable with every exchange.

If they seem shameless enough to make a D'Angeline blush—and some of them do, those Tsingani women—I will say that it is a deceptive thing, although I did not learn this until later. For all their licentious behavior, it is only show. Among their own, the Tsingani hold chastity in fierce regard. But I did not know this at the time, and I will admit that it galled me somewhat, to see the number of women who made free to bid for Hyacinthe's attention.

For Joscelin's part, his appearance was met with giggles and titters, whispers passed from lip to ear behind shielding hands. The Skaldic women had ogled him openly; Tsingani dared not. The law of *laxta* is fierce in their society. Hyacinthe could not translate this word exactly, but it is the unsullied virtue of a Tsingani woman. This may be lost in a hundred ways—suffice to say that if I'd ever had it, it was long gone—but foremost among them was the mingling of precious Tsingani blood with one of the *gadje*, the Others.

Once I understood the gravity of this law, I understood somewhat of the sin of Hyacinthe's mother. Not only had she allowed her body to be defiled, to become *vrajna* and unclean, but she had fouled her very bloodline. She had lost her *laxta*, all her worth as a Tsingano woman.

But they did not know this, the Tsingani en route to the Hippochamp. They knew only that Hyacinthe spoke and thought as one of them. If a D'Angeline fineness illumed his features, that keen, cutting beauty that is our blood-right, they saw in it only that he was a fine specimen, a veritable Prince of Travellers.

And so he was, with his bright, fine clothes, rich brown skin, his gleaming black ringlets, the merry light that danced in his dark eyes. When he called out that he was seeking the *kumpania* of Manoj, they laughed and called back, pointing. Manoj was there, the old patriarch, already a-field. Surely he would welcome Hyacinthe, blood of his blood, and all his uncles and cousins and aunts he had never met.

That was his dream, the old dream, and it bode well to come true. I saw it as we rode, drawing nearer, in the eagerness that marked him, the white grin that flashed out without warning.

It was a simple enough dream and a homely one: to be accepted, to find a family. I prayed for his sake that it would come true. Hyacinthe had risked much to come on this journey, and truly, that and that alone was the reward he sought. But Joscelin and I fell together as we approached, riding side by side and handling the pack-mules with the ease of our long, silent practice, and I saw the reserve in his blue eyes. He who had taken a simple vow knew well enough how things can twist and change.

We reached the Hippochamp.

It is a field, nothing more; a broad, green field, even now, so early in spring. A vast expanse of green, the grass new and tender, alongside the great Lusande River that burrows the length of Kusheth. We had timed our arrival well. A great many Tsingani *kumpanias* had already arrived, setting up wagons and tents and paddocks against the new green field; but a great many were still to come, and we found ourselves a space easily enough, staking it at the corners with the bright ribbons Hyacinthe had brought for that purpose.

And everywhere, there were horses: ponies, carriage-horses, palfreys and hunters, massive drays, and even war-horses, broad-backed and arch-necked, mighty enough to carry full mail, but long-legged and swift in battle. There were yearlings, gangly and slab-sided, and the early crop of foals, some of them still staggering drunkenly on tee-tering legs quick to tangle.

In the center of the field, where the most powerful of *kumpanias* had established themselves, was a common area set around a fire. Already a good-sized group of Tsingani had gathered to play music, sing and dance. I thought at first that it was a fête, but Hyacinthe said no, it was only their way. There were smaller gatherings too, in the outlying areas where we had made our camp.

As sunset drew nigh, cooking odors filled the air, rich and savory, making our staples—flatbread and cheese, nuts, dried fruit and meat—seem duller than usual, for all that they were bought with the Queen's coin. Hyacinthe, ever with a keen eye to chance, bartered with our nearest neighbors, trading a skin of passable wine for three bowls of a game stew spiced with fennel and last-year's carrots, with the assurance of meals to come.

It was wisely done, for we made a friendship over it, in the quick and easy way of Travellers. Our neighbors were a young family, not yet established as a proper *kumpania*; Neci was the *tseroman*, or headman, and introduced us to his wife, Gisella, her sister and brother-in-law, his cousin, who had thrown in his lot with them, and a passel of children, who ranged in age from still-suckling to ten or older. They wed young. The women all came forward to give me the kiss of greeting; the men nodded their heads, dark eyes gleaming with curiosity. I've a good ear for languages, and had begun to be able to follow the thread of D'Angeline that laced the Tsingani dialect. Hyacinthe had told them what we'd agreed upon, that I'd been gotten in a brothel by a Tsingano half-breed, adding—needlessly, to my mind—that his mother had taken me in out of pity when she found me taking to the streets.

Then he introduced Joscelin, who bowed, making his cloak swirl with a subtle riot of color. Neci's family laughed, and the children gazed wide-eyed.

After that, they invited us to join them around the nearest fire, where Gisella's brother-in-law—his name, I think, was Pardi—would play the fiddle, which we did.

The virtue of silence served me best there; I sat by Hyacinthe's side and listened while he spoke with Neci, struggling to filter meaning out of the Tsingani dialogue. In the background, to my surprise, I heard Joscelin spinning a tale in D'Angeline, and doing it fairly well. Gi-sella, her sister and all the children were listening, a small group that grew somewhat larger as the tale wove onward, through the skirls of fiddle-playing and nimble tambors.

"... and I said to the Skaldi princess, my lady, al-though you are more beautiful than the moon and all her stars, I cannot oblige you, for I am sworn to Cassiel. And she said to me, well, then, if you will not wed me, you must fight my brother Bjorn, for no man may refuse me and live. Now this Bjorn was a mighty warrior, who had once defeated a witch, and she gave to him a great magic in exchange for her life, a bearskin that had the power to transform its wearer into a bear . . ."

I shook my head, turning my attention back to Neci and Hyacinthe. A Cassiline turned Mendacant; truly, no one would believe it possible.

"If it is true that you are the grandson of Manoj," Neci was saying—or something very close to it, "then you must seek him out. The *baro kumpai*, the four mightiest *kumpanias*, are there." He pointed toward the great fire at the center, where the staked territories were vast, en-compassing impromptu paddocks filled with many horses. "But if you are only seeking Tsingani and *khushti grya* to travel west and trade . . ." Neci shrugged, strok-ing the tips of his elegant mustache. "Perhaps we would be interested, if there is *czokai* in it. Perhaps enough to make our *lav* as a *kumpania*."

"There is gold enough to make the name of whoever succeeds with me," Hyacinthe said noncommittally, switching to D'Angeline and glancing at me for corrob-oration. I nodded solemnly. "I have many important friends in the City of Elua. But none so important as blood, yes? I will see Manoj first."

"Well," Neci said, and grinned. "Do not see him tonight, *rinkeni chavo*, for the old *Tsingan Kralis* is a *gavvering* hellion when he drinks, and he's like to knock your *dandos* out with a kosh-stick if you go claiming to be Anasztaizia's son. So see him tomorrow, and remember who gave you good advice, hey *rinkeni*?"

"I will." Hyacinthe clasped hands with Neci, Tsingani-fashion, at the wrist. "Thank you."

Neci wandered away to reclaim his wife and dance with her. They made a striking couple, bold and handsome. "What's a gavvering hellion?" I asked Hyacinthe, watching them dance.

"You followed that?" he asked, and didn't answer for a moment. "I don't know. It doesn't translate. Strict. Belligerent."

"And khushti grya? Rinkeni chavo? Tsingan kralis?"

He eyed me sidelong. "Delaunay taught you to listen too well," he sighed. "Grya are horses. Neci says he has good horses to trade, khushti grya. Rinkeni chavo . . ." Hyacinthe looked wry. "Pretty boy. I didn't tell him I was half D'Angeline."

I waited, then asked again. "And Tsingan kralis?"

Hyacinthe shifted his gaze toward the central fire, where the tents stood tallest, the wagons were brightest, and the finest horses in the paddocks. "King of the Tsingani," he said finally, his thoughts elsewhere.

"You mean he really is?" I was startled, and the question came out rudely. "I'm sorry."

"Don't be." He shot me a quick glance. "I wasn't . . . I wasn't sure myself, until Neci said it. I always believed it, but . . ."

"I understand." I smiled ruefully and stroked his black curls. "Prince of Travellers."

Somewhere behind us, Joscelin's story continued. He was acting it out now, giving the bear-warrior's terrible roar. Shrieks of terrified glee answered; the children loved it. The old Prefect would have died of mortification. One of the young Tsingani women, long hair still uncovered, approached Hyacinthe to invite him to dance. He looked apologetically at me, rising. I understood, of course; it would have looked peculiar if he'd declined. Unless we were a betrothed couple—and if I were no longer a *vrajna* bond-servant, still, as a half-breed's by-blow, I had no claim to *laxta*, to being a true Tsingani woman.

Which made me unfit for the grandson of the *Tsingan Kralis*.

It is a strange thing, how pride may run the strongest among a people despised, as the Tsingani had been in so many lands. I thought about that, as I sat alone near the fire, watching the dancers, watching Joscelin spin his first-ever Mendacant's tale. It made no difference to our mission.

But it made a difference, I thought, to me.

SIXTY-THREE

In the morning, we went to see Manoj.

The horse-fair at the Hippochamp lasts for three days, and this was officially the first. The first day is for looking, the Tsingani say; the second for talking; the third for trading. While this is true, it is also true that by the third day, a handful of canny *gadje* nobles would have gotten word that the horse-fair was ongoing and come to buy, so the greater part of the trading would be all but concluded by the third day.

Hence, the deceptively casual undertone to the browsing and conversation, which was in fact deadly earnest. To see Manoj, we had to take part in it, for Hyacinthe was not so naive as to present himself and expect a welcome.

Instead, we strolled around the paddock surveying the horses. Joscelin, who had been entrusted with our funds—Mendacant or no, anyone wearing Cassiline daggers was the least likely target among us—had brought out the necklace Hyacinthe had provided. I knew it well, for it had been his mother's, an elaborate affair of gold coins strung together.

It provoked not a few whispers, that a *Didikani* woman would dare sport a Tsingano *galb*—I understood those words quickly enough, for "half-breed" and for coin-wrought jewelry—but it achieved its purpose. One of Manoj's many nephews spotted us in short order, and came over to lean on the woven saplings of the paddock fencing to talk with Hyacinthe. When he learned of our desire to contract horses and men alike to travel west for a lucrative trade, he brought us to meet with Manoj.

We met with the King of the Tsingani in his tent, which was brightly striped and well appointed. I'd been expecting another ancient, like Ganelon de la Courcel, I suppose, but I had forgotten how young the Tsingani wed. It was hard to gauge his age—they weather quickly, on the Long Road—but I think him not much over sixty. He had fierce, staring dark eyes, iron-grey hair and a resplendent mustache.

"You want to take my people and my horses *west*?" he demanded. "Who are you to ask such a thing? What is your *kumpania*?"

Those are not, of course, the words he used; like the rest, Manoj spoke in the Tsingani dialect. Some of it, I could follow. Some I gathered from the general nature of the exchange. Some I did not understand, and Hyacinthe translated later. What I recount now is as I recall it, woven out of whole cloth like a Mendacant's fable, only closer to the spirit of memory.

"I seek a handful of brave men and good horses to make a great bargain, *Kralis*," Hyacinthe said smoothly.

Manoj beckoned one of his nephews near and whispered in his ear, then shooed him away. "Tell me of this trade."

Hyacinthe bowed. "The Queen's Admiral and his fleet are docked at the Pointe d'Oeste. I have knowledge that they will be in need of horses."

It was true, actually; if Quintilius Rousse was going to take a single ship across the Straits, he would need to have a handful of men well armed and mounted to ward the remainder of the fleet and secure their beachhead. Kusheth was neutral territory at best. But none of us would divulge these details.

"I have not heard this," Manoj said dismissively. "Who are you to come by this knowledge? You have not given me your name or your *kumpania*."

"I come from the City of Elua, and I know many people there and hear many things." Hyacinthe held the patriarch's gaze. "I am Hyacinthe son of Anasztaizia. I am born to your *kumpania*, Grandfather."

A middle-aged Tsingano woman dropped an earthenware cup in the corner of the tent. It fell with a dull thud, unbroken. Otherwise there was no sound. Manoj blinked wrinkled eyelids under ferocious brows.

"Anasztaizia's son?" he said slowly, wondering. "Anasztaizia had a boy? A son?"

"I am her son," Hyacinthe said simply.

After that, pandemonium broke loose. It began with Manoj shouting for one of his nephews, a nervous man of around forty, who ran into the tent and threw himself upon his knees before the Tsingani patriarch. It ended with cries and embraces and Manoj weeping openly as he drew Hyacinthe up to kiss him on both cheeks.

I pieced the story together later, for it was at this point that I lost the ability to follow what was being said. It seemed that the nephew Manoj had summoned—Csavin, his name was—had run afoul of a Bryony House adept the one and only time the *kumpania* of Manoj had entered the City of Elua.

Bryony is the wealthiest of the Thirteen Houses, for wealth is their specialty, in all its forms, and there are those to whom nothing is more titillating than money. If one stripped the staff of the Royal Treasury, one would find a full half of them bear Bryony's marque, for her adepts' acumen is legend.

Bryony is also the only House whose adepts are willing to wager for their favors.

And they almost never lose. Not even to Tsingani.

I had believed—as Hyacinthe had—that his mother had fallen enamoured of a D'Angeline, for that was the story she had told him. It was out of love, to protect him from a more sordid truth; she had lost her virtue, her *laxta*, because her cousin Csavin had laid it as a wager upon the table with a Bryony adept, believing he could not lose. Tsingani know a thousand ways to cheat the *gadje*.

He had lost.

Not only had he lost, but in the face of the Dowayne's Guard of Bryony House, he had paid his debt with coin that was not his, deceiving his cousin—Manoj's daughter, who was young and desiring of adventure—into meeting with a patron who paid good coin to Bryony House for the pleasure of seducing a Tsingani virgin.

It appalled me as much as almost anything I have ever heard, for it hit close to home for me. If she had been D'Angeline and not Tsingani, it would have been a violation of Guild-laws; but the Guild covers only

D'Angelines, leaving Tsingani and other noncitizens to their own law. It was a violation of Tsingani law, and Csavin had forfeited all his possessions and rights to Manoj, living as a pariah among them. Still, I think Bryony House is liable for heresy, for what was done to Hyacinthe's mother violates the precept of Blessed Elua, which applies to everyone, D'Angeline or no. Naamah's service is entered willingly, or not at all.

As for Hyacinthe's mother, she was Tsingani, and bound by their law. She was *vrajna* and outcast, in sorrow and tears, never to be redeemed.

But now there was a son, Hyacinthe, and even if he was a *Didikani* half-breed, he had been raised as a true Tsingano, and he was the son of Anasztaizia, whose loss Manoj had never ceased to mourn, his only daughter, his only child, his precious pearl in the swarming mass of children his brothers and sisters had begotten, whose *mulo* had beseeched him on the winds since her death a month gone and more.

Prince of the Tsingani. Prince of Travellers.

The remainder of the day passed in a whirlwind as our campsite was struck and our things brought to join with Manoj's *kumpania*, where trade and celebration blurred into one. Joscelin and I trailed in its wake, bewildered and half-forgotten as Hyacinthe was drawn into an extended reunion with cousins and great-aunts and uncles he'd never known existed.

Manoj kept Hyacinthe close by him, drawing out the tale of his childhood and youth in Night's Doorstep, eking out the details of his mother's life. He was proud to hear of her fame as a fortuneteller, pounding his chest, proclaiming that no one had ever had the gift of the *dromonde* as Anasztaizia had had it, among all the women of her line.

I understood enough of this to raise my eyebrows at

Hyacinthe, who shot me a fierce warning glance, shaking his head. It was true, what Delaunay had said: The *dromonde* was the province of women only. For a man to practice it was *vrajna*, forbidden.

When night fell, the fires blazed, and the Tsingani drank and played, their music rising in wild skirling abandonment. Hyacinthe joined them, playing his timbales, dancing with the unwed women; there must have been a dozen of them vying for his attention. I sat on the outskirts and watched his white grin flash in the firelight.

So I sat, when an old crone hobbled over to me, wizened as one of last winter's apples, bent under the weight of the gold-bedecked *galbi* she wore.

"Good evening, old mother," I said politely.

She looked at me and cackled. "Not for you, is it, *chavi*? For all you've the evil eye to give, with that red mote you bear. Know you who I am?"

I shook my head, bemused. She pointed to her chest with a gnarled forefinger.

"Abhirati am I, and I was Anasztaizia's granddam. Her gift comes through my blood." She turned her pointing finger on me, taking me back to Hyacinthe's mother in her kitchen. "You've no drop of Tsingani in your veins, *chavi*, for all the lad may claim it. Don't you know the *dromonde* can look backward as well as forward?"

"What do you see, then?"

"Enough." The old woman laughed wickedly. "Pleasure-houses, indeed. The lad spoke that true, didn't he? Your mother was a whore, sure enough. But you're no by-blow, no, not you."

I watched Hyacinthe surrounded by his newfound family. "Better if I had been, mayhap. My father had a name, but he didn't give it to me. My mother sold me into servitude and never looked back."

"Backward, forward, your mother had no gift to look either way," Abhirati said dismissively. "His mother did." She nodded at Hyacinthe. "What do you suppose she saw, eh? The *Lungo Drom* and the *kumpania*, eh, or somewhat else, a reflection in a blood-pricked eye?" She gave another cackle. "Oh, what did my granddaughter see, for this son of hers? Think about that, *chavi*."

With that, she tottered off, bony shoulders hunching with laughter. I frowned after her.

"Trouble?" Joscelin asked, materializing at my side.

"Who knows?" I said, shrugging. "I think I'm fated to be targeted by Tsingani fortunetellers. I'll be glad when we're on our way. Do you think Manoj will give Hyacinthe the horses and escort he asked for?"

"I think Manoj would give him just about anything," Joscelin said wryly. "Including Csavin's head on a platter, if Hyacinthe hadn't granted him forgiveness." That scene, with many drunken tears, had taken place earlier. "I just hope he remembers why we're here."

"I'm not sure we're all here for the same reasons," I said softly, watching the Tsingani revel, Hyacinthe among them. "Not anymore."

The second day is for talking.

Manoj had a half-dozen likely young horses, three- and four-year-olds, hunters for the most part, glossy coats polished to a high gleam, that would do nicely for patrolling rough borders. And he had too a half-dozen young men men in his *kumpania* eager for adventure, willing to ride across the wilds of outer Kusheth on the promise of great trade, returning by slow wagon.

It was important that Hyacinthe appear astute; the haggling went round in circles, until I thought I would die of tedium. Then the horses were examined one by one. We rode each one of them around the Hippochamp, like hundreds of others, tearing about in spring madness, shouting and laughing, hooves pounding, a race without victors or losers, while the smiths glancing up from the dozen small forges that had sprung up on the outskirts of the field and grinned through soot-stained faces.

"Pulls up a little lame, this one does," Hyacinthe said breathlessly, slowing to a trot under a stand of willows along the river, greenish-yellow buds emerging on their long trailing branches. We had lost Joscelin somewhere in the aimless race. "I think Grandpa-ji's testing me."

"Maybe so," I murmured. The exertion of the ride had brought out a touch of color on his face. "Hyacinthe . . . you know you're not bound to go to Alba. If you can help us get to Quintilius Rousse . . . that's all you pledged to Ysandre, after all."

"I know." My words had sobered him. Hyacinthe gazed across the Hippochamp, the field bright and gay with his people. "I didn't . . . Phèdre, I didn't know they'd accept me like this. I just wasn't sure. I didn't know it would be like this."

"No." I looked at him with pain in my heart. "But it is. And you are free to choose, Prince of Travellers."

There was no need to spell out the fact that choosing the Tsingani meant losing me; our friendship, what it was, what it might grow into. Or not. The promise of one kiss exchanged in a busy tavern. We both knew it. And knowing, we rode silent back to Manoj's campsite, where the old patriarch delighted to hear that Hyacinthe was clever enough to have spotted the game-legged horse in the lot.

On the third day, they trade. But our trade was done, or as good as; our journey was set, with a half-dozen of Manoj's great-nephews ready to go forth with us on the morrow. I do not recall their names, but they were eager and bold, with dark flashing eyes that looked sidelong at me, elbowing each other in the ribs at the thought of being on the Long Road with a whore's daughter who had no *laxta* to lose, only the fear of the evil eye keeping open expression of it at bay. That, and Joscelin's hands straying toward his dagger-hilts when he caught them at it.

And true enough, on the third day, a handful of Kusheline nobles arrived, strolling the new grass of the Hippochamp, looking smug at having the cleverness to steal a march on their compatriots and skim the cream of the early Tsingani horse-crop.

We watched them with amusement, sitting on folding stools outside the tents of Manoj's *kumpania*. Some of the women had warmed to me enough to share with me the secrets of the *Hokkano*, the myriad ways the Tsingani had devised to part D'Angeline nobles from their precious coin. It was something to see, the way the proud, defiant Tsingani turned obsequious; helpful and unctuous, palms extended, silver lies flowing from their tongues. Out of kindness, I will not mention the name of the Kusheline Marquise—though I know it, make no mistake—who gave over a bundle of jewels and coin to one of Hyacinthe's female cousins, who swore that burying it under the birthing-spot of an all-white foal would remove the curse it surely held. Suffice to say that when the Marquise returned to the spot—neatly marked by a stake and a snow-white ribbon—three days hence, she and her escort would unearth an empty packet in an empty field.

"It is a kindness to liberate such things from the possession of a fool," Hyacinthe's cousin said complacently upon her return, drawing the bundle from her bodice and fingering its contents. "Of course," she added, "even among the *gadje*, there are those it is unwise to attempt." She pointed with her chin, Tsingani-style, across the field.

I followed her gaze, and that was when time stood still.

Four or five of them, no more, and a handful of the House Guard; riding slowly and gazing about, talking and laughing among themselves beneath the pale-blue sky. Fine mounts, as ever, and the devices that set them apart, long robes of night-black overlaid with ornate gold patterns, intricate and Eastern, always different, the Shahrizai, with long, rippling blue-black hair, faces as pale as carven ivory, set with sapphire eyes.

There were three men, buying war-horses. And two women.

One of them was Melisande.

I had forgotten—how could I?—how beautiful she was. Damnably and deadly, her flawless face, like a star among diamonds. Small and insignificant, a *Didikani* outcast girl among Tsingani, I stared across the Hippo-champ at her, hot and cold shivers running across my skin, turning me to stone, hatred, and ah! Blessed Elua help me, yearning. No one else, not even Delaunay, knew me as she did, knew what it was to be what I was. What I am, and ever would be.

Every movement, every shift in the saddle, every slight change of pressure on the reins; I felt it, on my skin, in my flesh and bones.

And on the heels of it came terror, for I was here not as a Tsingani half-breed nor a Servant of Naamah nor victim of Kushiel's Dart, but as Phèdre nó Delaunay, ambassador of Ysandre de la Courcel, the Queen of Terre d'Ange, and Melisande Shahrizai was the most dangerous traitor the realm had ever known.

I saw brightness and darkness, while my breath came in sharp white flashes and my heart beat like a frightened rabbit's, thumping fast and terrified in my breast. Voices surrounded me, speaking D'Angeline and Tsingani, none of it making sense, none able to penetrate the sound that beat at my eardrums like the ocean, low and vast and thralling, Melisande's careless laughter, that I could hear no matter how great the distance between us. Faces swam in my ken, none distinct. I was aware, somehow, sometime, of hands shaking my shoulders and Joscelin's presence, fearful and urgent, his hair streaming across the rising red tide of my vision as he shook me, sun-streaked wheat lashing a bloody haze.

But it fell away, and there was only her, Melisande's face poised in a three-quarter turn, careless and beautiful, waiting to finish the gesture at any second, turning to look full upon me, fifty yards away or more, and see, completing the connection between us. Her diamond a millstone around my neck, the velvet cord merely awaiting the touch of her hand on its lead.

I was lost.

"She will pass, and see nothing."

It was a voice, hollow and insistent, penetrating my terror, anchoring itself in my soul and drawing me back. The veil lessened; I blinked, seeing Hyacinthe's face swim into focus before me, his dark, beautiful eyes. His hands held mine, gentle and firm. In the background, the Shahrizai rode onward, small, ornate figures on prancing horses.

"She will pass, and see nothing," he said, repeating it.

Sorrow, in his voice.

The Prince of Travellers had chosen.

Sixty-four

It was true that the *Tsingan Kralis* cared deeply for his half-breed grandson, that I believe.

But a silence fell after Hyacinthe's words, like the silence when a great wave has broken, while another greater wave gathers. And then the outcry arose.

"*Vrajna!* He has been taught the *dromonde*! Anaistai-zia's son speaks the *dromonde*! He brings a curse upon us all!"

I will not recount the thousand voices that rose to vilify him; suffice to say that they did, these great-aunts and uncles and cousins who had taken him to their hearts. Hyacinthe stood beneath the onslaught, enduring, meeting my eyes in silent understanding. Not for me, I thought. Don't do this for me alone. He understood, shaking his head. It was not for me alone. Somewhere, in the distance, the scions of House Shahrizai glanced over, mildly curious at the Tsingani uproar, bent on trade, acquiring steeds for a war no one else in the realm knew was coming, taking no sides, merely hedging their bets against the need.

And somewhere an old crone smiled in vindication, a hundred gold coins draped around her withered neck.

Hyacinthe stood unmoving.

Joscelin's daggers were in his crossed hands, as he turned slowly in a circle, polite and deadly, warding me.

"Is it true?"

It was Manoj who broke the silence, fierce eyes anguished as he came forward, members of his *kumpania* falling away before the patriarch's approach.

Hyacinthe bowed his Prince of Travellers bow. "Yes,

Grandpa-ji," he said softly. "I have the gift of the *dromonde*. My mother taught me to use it."

"It is *vrajna*." Manoj caught his breath as if it pained him. "*Chavo*, my grandson, Anasztaizia's son, you must renounce it. The *dromonde* is no business for men."

If Melisande had looked, in that instant, to the disturbance in the *kumpania*, she would have known. Even if she had not seen me . . . the circle, the stillness, Hyacinthe at its center, and a Cassiline warrior-priest in a Mendacant's cloak . . . she would have known, somehow, that I was involved. Delaunay had taught her what he had taught me, to watch and listen, and see the patterns emerging from chaos. We were alike, in that. But Elua was merciful, and she did not look. The Shahrizai had already spared us one casual glance. They were there to buy horses.

And Hyacinthe shook his head with infinite regret, his eyes like black pearls shining with tears.

"I cannot, Grandpa-ji," he said quietly. "You cast my mother from the *kumpania*, but I am her son. If it is *vrajna* to be what she made me, then I am *vrajna*."

What did she see? A reflection in a blood-pricked eye? I do not know. Only, in the end, that we needed Hyacinthe. And the Long Road he chose was not the one the Tsingani had walked since Elua trod the earth.

"So be it," said the *Tsingan Kralis*, and turned his back on his grandson. "My daughter is dead. I have no grandson."

A wailing arose then and they mourned Hyacinthe, as if he were not standing alive before them. I saw the blood drain from his face, leaving him grey. It was Joscelin who held us together, then, shoving his daggers into their sheaths, gathering our things, herding us out of the camp of Manoj's *kumpania*. On the outskirts of the Hippochamp, we met Neci's folk.

"Are you still minded to make your name?" Joscelin asked Neci bluntly, speaking in plain D'Angeline.

The Tsingano glanced at us all, startled, then looked to his wife. She shrugged once, looked at the others, then nodded vigorously, beginning to summon the children.

Somewhere, in the background, the Shahrizai were concluding a deal, and I shivered as if with the ague.

"Good," Joscelin said in a hard tone. "Get your horses and your things. We're riding west."

And so we did.

It is a remarkable thing, the speed with with a Tsingani company can become mobile. I daresay most armies could learn a thing or two about efficiency from them. Neci's family had one wagon, a team to draw it, and five horses to trade. Only two were hunters; there was a broodmare and her foal, and a yearling besides. In a matter of minutes, Neci had concluded a deal for the mare and the younglings, trading for two more hunters and a rangy gelding of indeterminate ancestry. And in that time, Gisella and her sister had the wagon hitched and the family ready to move.

Enough time, however, for word to spread. By the time we set out, they knew Hyacinthe no longer existed in the *Tsingan Kralis'* eyes. I thought for a moment that Neci would back out of the deal, but then Joscelin paid him a deposit in gold as surety against the trade with Rousse, and greed and pride won out. They would take the risk.

We were four days riding with Neci's family, following the Lusande west toward the harsh, stony hills of outlying Kusheth. The Lusande Valley is lush and rich in the center of the province, and we saw a fair number of folk as we travelled. The Tsingani traded with them, mending pots and horseshoes in exchange for wine and foodstuffs. Sometimes we saw nobles and their retinues,

House Guards in gleaming Kusheline devices, but we had no fear of discovery. With Neci's family, our disguise was complete, more than it would have been even with Manoj's riders. Joscelin performed for small crowds more than once, growing confident in his Mendacant's trade, while the children went among the spectators with tins, begging copper coins. I had a quiet word with Gisella to ensure that no purses were lifted; if we landed before the judiciary, our quest would be in vain.

It was a strange thing, to sojourn with an eloquent Cassiline and a quiet Tsingano. I spoke with Hyacinthe the first night, the others leaving us to it in privacy.

"You could still go back, you know," I said, sitting beside him. "When this is done. Manoj would take you back, I think. They like to forgive."

Hyacinthe shook his head. "No," he said softly. "He never forgave my mother, you know, for all his tears. Some things are unforgiveable. Murder, theft, treachery . . . but not that which is *vrajna*. I knew this. I was swept up in it, Phèdre. I'd never known what it was like to have such a family, so many folk to call cousin and aunt and near-brother."

"I know." I slipped my hand into his. "Believe me, I do know."

So much to say, at such a time, and none of it adequate. We sat like that for a long time. Hyacinthe put his arm about me and I laid my head on his shoulder, falling at length into the white exhaustion that follows strong emotion, until at last I slept, and dreamed I was awake. At least I did not dream of Melisande, which I had feared; Hyacinthe's presence kept those dreams at bay. So I slept, and woke to find it morning, and Hyacinthe still asleep, the two of us entwined like twins, my hair spread like a silken drape across his chest. Someone had laid a blanket over us. I sat up blinking at the daylight. Across the camp, Joscelin glanced at me, and politely looked away. Hyacinthe stirred, waking.

It was hard to leave the warmth of him. I fumbled for Ysandre's signet, on its chain beneath my dress, beneath the deadly weight of Melisande's diamond.

A mission for the Queen; that, above all else.

Our caravan moved slowly, the pace dictated by the Tsingani wagon, which was not built for speed, but by the third evening we left behind the rich spring valleys for the rocky terrain of outer Kusheth, and on the fourth day our progress was torturously slow, as the wagon had to be pushed at times. The children bounced shrieking in the back while all the men—Neci, his brother-in-law and cousin, Hyacinthe and Joscelin alike—set their backs to it and shoved, grunting.

But when we made camp that night, we could smell salt air.

I had taken our landmarks from atop the tallest hill, and studied them against the map Ysandre had provided us—a luxury, after the Skaldic wilderness. Joscelin gazed over my shoulder.

"There," I said, pointing. "The Pointe d'Oeste lies there. Rousse's fleet is quartered three miles to the north. If we take the road that runs just south of that ridge, we should reach him before noon."

"Good." Hunkering on his heels, Joscelin sifted a handful of dirt through his hand. Opening his hand, he showed me the thin, pale grass sprouts taking root even in the rocky soil. "Spring's coming even here," he said softly. "How long do you think Waldemar Selig will wait?"

"We're months from the first harvest." Fear made my heart beat faster. "He can't possibly be provisioned. And he'll wait for that."

"Not so far off." Joscelin lifted his head, staring toward the darkening west. "And we've a long way to go."

"Tomorrow," I said, and repeated it more firmly. "We'll reach Quintilius Rousse tomorrow."

And indeed, so we should have done. Except that it was not to be.

Perhaps we had grown overconfident, secure in our disguise, travelling unimpeded the breadth of Kusheth; but truly, I think it would not have mattered. The guard that stopped us was there for a purpose, and they would have stopped any travellers, Tsingani or royal courier alike.

Laboring over a hillcrest, we didn't see them until we were nigh upon them, and one of the children shouted out a warning. *"Dordi-ma! Gavveroti!"*

A squadron of twenty guardsmen, arranged across the road, waiting for us. Behind them, a mile off, we could see the grey sea wrinkling. The day was overcast, and the light glinted dully on their armor. A breeze lifted the standard-bearer's flag. I knew its device, echoed on their livery. I had seen it, in another time and place.

A raven and the sea.

The arms of the Duc de Morhban.

Spurring his horse, Hyacinthe rode quickly to the head of the caravan. This much, we had discussed. Better that he should be our spokesman than Joscelin or I, who might be marked as unusual.

"Where are you bound, *Tsingano*?" The leader of the guard invested the word with scorn; I noticed it more, now.

"We have an agreement to trade with the Queen's Admiral," Hyacinthe said reasonably. "May we pass, my lord?"

The leader of the guard turned his head and spat upon the ground. "The Queen's Admiral sails where he will, but this is Morhban. No one crosses without the Duc's permission. You'll wait on his grace."

In point of truth, we'd been crossing Morhban for some time now; it is the sovereign duchy of Kusheth, and vast. I understood. It was access to the Queen's Admiral that Quincel de Morhban was controlling. Hyacinthe turned back as if to survey our party, meeting my eyes briefly. I gave an imperceptible nod. We dared not try to fight our way through, not with the rest of Morhban's troops a mere mile or two away.

"Then we will wait," Hyacinthe said calmly.

So wait we did, while de Morhban's men idled and a rider headed south. The adult Tsingani were scared, but bore it well; the children, our best disguise, carried the act for us. One of the little girls found a nest of baby rabbits, which kept them all occupied.

And in short order, Quincel de Morhban appeared, with a second squadron of his House Guard. Forty armed men, now; if ever we'd had a chance of fighting clear, it was gone now.

I kept my head low, watching him through my lashes.

I remembered him, tall and lean, with features that had the same harsh beauty as the terrain he ruled: ruthless and hard. Greying sandy hair, and eyes the color of iron, a dark grey without warmth. I remembered his sharp banter with Melisande on the Longest Night, and how he had touched me beneath the sheer diamond-spangled gauze.

"You seek passage through my lands?" he asked without preface, his tone tinged with irony. "What do the Tsingani want with a sailor?"

Hyacinthe bowed. "Your grace de Morhban, we have an agreement to trade with the Queen's Admiral."

"Since when does a sailor need a horse?" De Morhban's keen gaze swept over our group, resting on Joscelin. "What in Elua's name is *that*?"

"Your grace!" Joscelin dismounted, bowing with an elaborate flourish that set his cloak to swirling in a riot of color. "I am but a humble Mendacant, born in Marsilikos City. If you would be entertained, I will tell you of how I came to—"

"Enough." De Morhban cut him off with a word, settling wearily into the saddle. "I've no time to waste with talespinners. So Quintilius Rousse thinks to build himself a horse patrol, does he?" The grey eyes narrowed. "Perhaps I might make a better offer for these creatures, Tsingano. What do you say to that?"

A murmur of excitement arose among Neci's family, but Hyacinthe shook his head, as if in sorrow.

"Alas, your grace, I gave my word to the Admiral. I swore it upon my own mother's spirit, may she rest in peace."

De Morhban crossed his hands, resting them on his pommel. "Did you?" he asked wryly. "And what is a Tsingano's word worth? Double Rousse's offer, perhaps?"

Another murmur, quickly hushed, from Neci's folk.

"Perhaps," Hyacinthe said slyly. "Perhaps we may trade somewhat with your grace. A token for our passage, mayhap?" He shifted his horse. "This steed I ride, your grace, is a fine one . . . could you use such a mount?"

"Rousse must be offering a great deal." De Morhban's face was unreadable. "No, I don't think so, Tsingano. It's not in my interest to see the Admiral horsed. But I'll play you fair, I'll pay his price, and more."

Hyacinthe spread his arms and shrugged. "As your grace wishes. I ask only that you allow me to convey my regrets to the Admiral, and beg his forgiveness." He closed his arms and shuddered, putting a tremor in his voice. "For if you do not, my mother's *mulo* will ride the night winds and plague my sleep forevermore," he added pitiably.

It was a good performance; I daresay most people would have bought it. But Kushelines are suspicious by birth, and Quincel de Morhban had not held his duchy by being a fool. He sat in his saddle and surveyed our motley band, then slowly shook his head. "No, Tsingano, I think not. Unless there's somewhat else you'd like to tell me?"

"My lord!" Joscelin's voice rang out. Nudging his horse forward, he unsheathed his daggers, and with one quick gesture, offered both hilts-first across his forearm. "I offer you this, in exchange for trade-passage to the Admiral. Genuine Cassiline daggers, forged three hundred years ago. If you would care to listen, I will tell you how I came to bear them—"

"No." De Morhban raised his hand. "I've no need of priests' trinkets, Cassiline or Mendacant or whatever you are. So if you've no other business with the Admiral you'd care to discuss with me, and naught else to offer in trade, let us be done with it."

His guard ranged unobtrusively before us, spreading out, a full forty men positioning themselves between us and the not-so-distant sea, where I could see, now, Quintilius Rousse's fleet. To be so near and fail! Perhaps, I thought, we could return after nightfall and gain the fleet.

Joscelin must have thought it too, and shown it. "The sooner it's done, my friends," de Morhban said aloud in his wry tone, "the sooner you can be on your way. I'll give you an escort to the borders of Kusheth, that no harm befalls you."

That we didn't double back, he meant. I heard it plain. We had Ysandre's ring, of course, which would gain us passage if he were loyal. I thought of showing it to him. But if he were loyal, he wouldn't deny us access to Rousse in the first place, and if he were Melisande's ally . . . there had to be another way.

House Morhban was not so old as the Shahrizai in Kusheth, but old enough to have attained sovereignty. He was a scion of Kushiel. There was one offer he would consider.

"My lord." It is funny, how the tones and inflection of Cereus House remain with one. I lifted my head and rode forward to meet his eyes, close enough that he could not fail to see what mine contained. "My lord, there is somewhat else we may offer in trade for passage."

Quincel de Morhban drew in his breath sharply, and his horse danced under him. "You!" he said, quieting his mount. His eyes narrowed again. "Melisande's creature, I thought. But I heard you were condemned for the murder of Rolande's poet, Delaunay."

"No." Joscelin, realizing belatedly what I'd done, grabbed my arm. "Phèdre, no!"

I shook him off, holding de Morhban's gaze. "You know what I am, your grace. You know what I offer. One night. Free passage. And no questions."

His eyebrows rose, but otherwise his expression was unchanged. "In Elua's City, you could not dictate such terms, *anguissette*. Why should I not seek you there? I have coin."

"I own my marque and I dictate the terms I choose," I said evenly. "I have named my price. From you, I will accept no other."

De Morhban's gaze strayed to Joscelin, who sat taut with anguish. "There was a Cassiline involved, I seem to remember. What would the Queen pay for such knowledge?" His grey eyes returned to me, gauging my reaction. "Or House Shahrizai, perhaps? Melisande likes to know things."

Somewhere behind me, I could hear Hyacinthe muttering in black fury, could feel Joscelin's wild rage building. We were betrayed, they thought; I had erred. Delaunay used to think such things too, when I took dangerous risks with a patron. But if I had one confidence, it was in that: Never, yet, had I misjudged a patron's desire. I did not answer de Morhban's question, only sat beneath his gaze. You know what I am, my lord, I thought. And I am the only one of my kind, the only one born in three generations. I am born to serve such as you are. Kushiel's cruel fire runs in your blood, and I, and I alone, kindle to it. Choose now, or never know.

The tension mounted between us like heat. At last Quincel de Morhban smiled, a smile that sent a shudder the length of my spine.

"What business is it of mine if someone sends Tsingani horse-traders, whores and priests to the Queen's Admiral? Very well. Your offer is accepted." He bowed, sweeping one arm toward the south. "I give to your company my hospitality for one night. In the morning, you may ride to Quintilius Rousse. Is it agreed?"

"It is *not*—" Joscelin began heatedly, while Hyacinthe said, "Your grace, perhaps—"

"Yes." I said it loudly, overriding them. "We will draw up the contract in your quarters, your grace. Have you a priest to witness?"

Quincel de Morhban's face reflected bleak amusement at my caution. "I will send to the Temple of Kushiel on the Isle d'Oeste. Will that suffice?"

"It will."

Thus did we come to enjoy the hospitality of the Duc de Morhban.

Sixty-five

I have known worse. The castle of Morhban is set atop a rocky escarpment over the sea, impregnable on three sides, and well-guarded from the front. It was a cheerless place on a grey day, spring having gained but the most tentative of footholds in this outlying land.

All of us shivered on the ride, Neci's family—even the children—silent and fearful. But de Morhban's word was good, and he saw to it that they were well-housed, the horses stabled.

In this, he included Hyacinthe, who ground his teeth, but did not protest. He would have included Joscelin as well.

"Your grace." Joscelin controlled himself with an effort. "I am oath-sworn to protect my lady Phèdre nó Delaunay. Do not ask me to foreswear myself."

"So you say." Quincel de Morhban looked at Joscelin's Mendacant cloak. "Then again, it is the sort of mindless loyalty a Cassiline would voice. Do you actually perform as a Mendacant, priest?"

After a moment, Joscelin gave a curt nod.

"Fine. Then you may entertain my household."

A couple of de Morbhan's men-at-arms nudged each other, grinning like boys at the prospect; it was the only thing on that journey that made me smile. It had been a long, dull winter in Morhban, I suspected.

"Yes, your grace." Joscelin bowed, a Cassiline bow, unthinking. "Harm her," he said under his voice, "and you will die. That I promise."

"Do you?" De Morhban raised his brows. "But she was born to be harmed." At that, he turned, summoning his chamberlain. Joscelin grabbed my arm again, painfully hard.

"Phèdre, don't do this. I swear, I'll find another way—"

"Stop." I laid one hand on his cheek. "Joscelin, you made Cassiel's Choice. You can't keep me from making Naamah's." Reaching into my bodice, I fished out Ysandre's ring, pulling the chain over my head. "Just keep this safe, will you?"

I thought he might protest further, but he took it, his face changing, taking on the impassive expression I'd seen so often in Gunter's steading and then in Selig's, while he had to watch me serve as bed-slave to our Skaldic masters.

But that had been slavery; this was not.

De Morhban had not lied. He sent for a priest, who came in the black robes of Kushiel, unmasked, carrying the rod and weal. She was an older woman, whose look held all the terrible compassion of her kind. De Morhban treated her with respect, and I saw that he would honor our contract.

For the most part.

"And the *signale*?" he asked, courteously, pen at the ready.

It took me by surprise; I'd nearly forgotten, after Skaldia, that such things existed. I started to reply, then caught myself. "Perrinwolde," I said. It did not seem right, anymore, to use Hyacinthe's name.

Nor did it summon the safety it once had.

De Morhban nodded, writing it down. The priest put on her bronze mask, taking on Kushiel's face, and set her signet in the hot wax to seal it.

"You know I will ask questions upon your departure," de Morhban said, passing me the contract for my signature. "Our contract does not bind me from that. Nor from questioning Rousse and his men, who are on Morhban territory."

"Yes, my lord." I wrote my name in a flowing hand. "But questions are dangerous, for they have answers."

He looked curiously at me. "So Anafiel Delaunay taught you to think. I'd heard as much, though it was hard to credit. There was no thought in your pretty head the night *I* met you."

No thought, at least, that wasn't connected to the lead in Melisande's hand. I flushed, remembering. De Morhban nodded to the Kusheline priest, who bowed and departed silently.

"Are you Melisande's creature?" he asked me, musing. Reaching out, he took up the diamond that lay on my breast, drawing me to him. I stumbled a little, feeling my heartbeat speed. "I thought so, then. Now, I am not sure. What game is she playing? Tell me this much, at least; did she send you? Is this some strange ploy of hers, to see where my loyalties lie?"

"No questions, my lord," I whispered, my head spinning. "You have pledged it."

"Yes." He dropped the diamond. "I have."

There are things that one can see in patrons, when one serves Naamah. I saw it in him, the fear that could cut desire. He had come to doubt, since his decision. He had the ill luck to rule a province that contained House Shahrizai, and all its wiles. I took a step back and made another choice, as rash as the first.

"No," I said, and met his startled look. "One answer, my lord, and then you will honor our contract, or I will leave. No. If I am anyone's creature, it is Delaunay's. And if I am here, it is at his bidding."

"From beyond the grave." He made a statement, not a question of it. "He honored his vow to Prince Rolande, I heard. To the grave and beyond." De Morhban laid both hands on the table, considering our contract. "If that is true, then you are here at Ysandre's bidding."

I did not answer. "I am here to serve your pleasure, my lord," I said instead, nodding at the contract.

"So you are." He drew his attention away from it and looked wryly at me. "It would please me, Phèdre nó Delaunay, to have you bathed and attired. I've no taste for Tsingani wenches, if you don't mind."

"As my lord wishes." I curtsyed.

The women of Morhban were kind enough to me, hiding curiosity behind their habitual silence; they are not a talkative folk, those who dwell in outermost Kusheth. I was led away to a bath that was fairly sumptuous, then waited, drying in silken robes, while a seamstress brought in an array of garments to determine what would best fit and suit me. For all its bleakness, Morhban did not lack for finery. We found a suitable gown, a rich scarlet with a low back, that showed to good advantage my completed marque.

I confess, I admired myself in the mirror, tucking my hair into a gold mesh caul and turning this way and that to see how the striking black lines of my marque emerged from the base of the gown, rising to the finial, gazing at my face to see how the gown's color brought out the deep bistre of my eyes, the scarlet mote of Kushiel's Dart.

I suppose I should have dreaded this assignation, it is true; it was necessity that forced it upon me. But I had been pledged since the first bloom of womanhood to the service of Naamah, and in a way I cannot voice, a deep pleasure pervaded me at the thought of practicing my art. I thought of Joscelin and of Hyacinthe, and guilt wormed cold within me. I thought of Gunter and Waldemar Selig, and shame made me small. And yet, I remembered my vows in the Temple of Naamah, the offering-dove quivering in my hands.

This was what I was.

What strength I possessed, it stemmed from this.

Quincel de Morhban received me in his garden, something I never would have suspected, from either the man or the place. It was an inner sanctum, like Delaunay's, like I had known in the Night Court, only vaster. It was shielded from the elements, warmed by a dozen braziers and torches, with mirrors set to gather the sun's heat when it availed, and scrims of sheerest silk that could be drawn across the open roof to protect the delicate flora.

In all defiance of the early spring chill, a riot of flowers bloomed: spikenard and foxglove, azalea, Lady's slipper and Love-Not-Lost, orchids and phlox, lavender and roses.

"You are pleased," de Morhban said softly. He stood beside a small fountain, awaiting me; his eyes drank in the sight of me. "It costs me thousands of ducats to maintain this place. I have one master gardener from L'Agnace, and one from Namarre, and they are ever at odds with each other. But I reckon it worth the cost. I am D'Angeline. So we count the cost of pleasure." He reached out one hand for me. "So I count your cost."

I went to him unhesitatingly. He drew me against him, his lean body clad in black velvet doublet and breeches, with the de Morhban crest on his shoulder. I felt the dark tide of desire loose in my marrow, as one hand clasped hard on my buttocks, pressing me to him, and the other grasped the nape of my neck, entangled in the mesh caul, drawing my head back. He kissed me, then, hard and ruthlessly.

I had chosen this. For what had happened before, for Melisande, for Skaldi; I had repented, I had been scourged. With a relief so profound it was like pain, I surrendered to it, to this Kusheline lord, with his strong, cruel hands.

Lifting his head, Quincel de Morhban looked at me with something like awe. "It's true," he whispered. "What they say . . . Kushiel's Dart. It's all true."

"Yes, my lord," I murmured; if he'd told me the moon was locked in his stables, I'd have said the same, at that moment. De Morhban released me, turning away to pluck a great silvery rose, mindful of its thorns.

"You see this?" he asked, placing it in my hand and folding my fingers about the stem. "It exists nowhere else. My Namarrese gardener bred it. Naamah's Star, he calls it." His hand was still around mine; he closed it, tightening my clutch on the stem. Thorns pierced my skin and I gasped, my bones turning to water. The silvery rose blossomed between us, fragrant in the torch-lit night air, while blood ran, drop by slow drop, from my fist. De Morhban's gaze held me pinioned, his body close, rigid phallus pressed against my belly. He released my hand and I sank to my knees, divining his desire, unfastening his breeches, the rose falling forgotten as I took him in my hand, his hard-veined and throbbing phallus, slick with my own warm blood, and then into my mouth.

All around us his unlikely garden opened onto the night as I performed the *languisement* until he drew away at the end, spending himself on me, in the garden, drops of milky fluid lying on my skin, on the dark leaves and silken petals, pearlescent and salty. He groaned with pleasure, then gazed down at me, freeing my hair from the caul with a harsh twist, so that it cascaded about my shoulders and down my back.

"Dinner," he said, catching his breath. "And then I will show you my pleasure-chamber, little *anguissette*."

On my knees, I touched the tip of my tongue to my lips, catching a drop of his seed. Pleasure-chamber. My very skin shivered, anticipating the lash. "As you wish, my lord," I whispered.

It is not needful, I think, to detail what befell thereafter; it was a good meal, a very good one indeed, for de Morhban's cooks were the equal of his gardeners. We had fresh seafood, baby squids so new-caught they fairly squirmed, cooked in their own inky juices. And after that, a stuffed turbot that I weep to remember, with rice and rare spices. Three wines, from the Lusande Valley, and a dish with apples . . . I cannot recall it now. De Morhban's eyes were on me through the whole of it, keen and grey and knowing. He had the measure of it now, what I was. How desire ran like a fever in my blood.

"Why did Ysandre send you?" he asked softly, testing.

I pushed my chair back from the table, struggling to my feet, fighting the dark blood-tide. Somewhere, I thought, listening, somewhere Joscelin is telling tales to de Morhban's House Guard. I clung to the memory of him like a talisman, his deadly dance with Selig's thanes in a driving snowstorm, remembrance cooling my blood, shaking my head.

"No questions," de Morhban said quickly. "No questions. Phèdre, forgive me, sit."

"You have sworn it in Kushiel's name," I murmured, but I sat. He reached across the table, tracing the line of my brow above my left eye, the dart-stricken one. Calluses; a warrior Duc's fingertips.

"In Kushiel's name," he agreed.

So it began.

It ended as it always does, with such things; he had a full pleasure-chamber and flagellary, the Duc de Morhban, and he took me there, in the cool depths of the earth beneath his castle at the outermost edge of Terre d'Ange, setting the torches ablaze until it might as well have been Kushiel's domain, wringing me limp with blood and sweat, his face distorted behind the lash, and the sound of my own voice, begging, pleading, as he rode me at the end, bestriding me like a colossus.

He used flechettes, too. I hadn't counted on that.

A thousand deaths, of agony and pleasure, I died there in Quincel de Morhban's chamber. He was good, better almost than any patron I had known, when at last he laid civility aside for violent pleasure, the mask of lust obscuring his features. He was a Kusheline, it was in his blood. He wanted—oh, Elua, he wanted!—to hear me give the *signale*. If he gave up his questions, it was for that, waiting. And if I had given it, I would have answered.

But I had given the *signale* to one patron only, who had sundered me from myself. Quincel de Morhban could command me, shuddering, to give up my very flesh, quivering in abject climax. He could, and he did, snarling with victory.

Not my *signale*.

And in the end, his exhaustion defeated us both.

"Take care of her," he bid his servants, weariness and profound satisfaction draining his voice, shrugging into silk robes, bowing in my direction. "Treat her gently."

They did, I trust; I don't remember it, in truth. I saw faces approach, awe-stricken. They understand, in Kusheth, what it is to serve Kushiel. I hurt, in every part of me. And I was content. I closed my eyes, then, and let the deeper tide of unconsciousness claim me.

In the morning, I woke aching and sore, in clean linen sheets with stiff red bloodstains. De Morhban's personal physician entered the room before I'd risen, eyes averted. He'd tended to me the night before, I understood; he checked such dressings as he'd applied, and rubbed salve into those weals that had opened in the night and bled. I felt better before he was done, and dismissed him.

Quincel had provided new clothing for me: fine stuff, fit for travel, but of a good quality, such as Kusheline noblewomen wear. I thanked him when we breakfasted together.

"I thought mayhap you'd no further need of your Tsingani rags," he said, grey eyes gleaming. I raised my eyebrows, knowing it was best not to reply. "Here," he said then, brusquely, and pushed something across the table.

It was a ring, a flawless circle of black pearls set in silver, small and immaculate.

"It is customary, is it not, to give a patron-gift?" De Morhban's mouth quirked wryly. "It was my mother's; I'd planned on giving it to my wife. But there are many women among whom to choose for a bride, and I do not think I shall meet another *anguissette*. Wear it then, and think of me sometime. I hope you will not give up Naamah's service altogether, Phèdre nó Delaunay."

There are times to demur, and times not. This was not such a time. I slid the ring onto my finger, and bowed my head to the Duc de Morhban.

"When I think of you, my lord," I said, "I will think well."

He toyed with items on the table, restless and curious. "I shall await with great interest the resolution of the mystery you pose me," he said. "Pray that I do not regret my choice in this matter."

In truth, I did not know. All I had fathomed in our congress was that he had not determined where his loyalties lay. He was the sovereign Duc of Kusheth; whether the province stood with the Crown or against it was his to decide. In the end, I answered him simply.

"Your grace," I said, "I pray it too."

So we left it, crossed blades, unsure and unwary. He rang a bell and had Joscelin summoned, who burst into the room in a fury of agitation, eyes red-rimmed and sleepless, glaring accusations and fear at me. I looked mildly at him, over the rim of a teacup.

"Are you disappointed, Cassiline?" Quincel de Morhban asked, amused. "I am sorry. I would be curious, I confess, to try the mettle of one of your kind."

Joscelin shot him a look, then, that said he would be glad to try it, any time, any place, kneeling at my side. "Is it true, then? You're all right, Phèdre?"

"His grace de Morhban honored his contract," I said, looking at Quincel, absently twisting the ring on my finger. It was easier than meeting Joscelin's eyes, for he would see the deep languor in my bones, and disapprove, in his uniquely Cassiline manner. "And we are free to go, then, your grace?"

Quincel de Morhban made a face, at once frustrated and fulfilled. He gestured with one hand, setting us free, calling his servants to witness. "Our contract is complete," he said, brusque and formal. "You have free passage throughout Morhban, where you will. To the Royal Fleet and beyond." He paused, then added, "One day, Phèdre. I give you one day before I decide if it behooves me to question the Queen's Admiral."

"Thank you, your grace."

Sixty-six

Joscelin walked quickly through the stone halls of Morhban Castle, and I winced, hurrying to keep up. He paused to wait for me, the line of his jaw tight.

"Are you fit to ride?" he asked abruptly.

"I'll manage." The words came out through gritted teeth. Joscelin looked at me and shook his head, setting out at a pace only slightly slower.

"I will never understand," he said, gaze fixed forward as he strode, "why you do what you do, and call it pleasure."

"With your temper? You should."

That stopped him in his tracks and he stared at me in shock, blue eyes wide. "I do not have a temper! And what does that have to do with it?"

"You have a terrible temper, Joscelin Verreuil. You've just buried it in Cassiline discipline." I rotated my arm, rubbing my shoulder where the joint ached. De Morhban's stocks had been made for a taller person. "And not all that well," I added. "I've seen it, Joscelin, I've seen you lose it, against the Skaldi. I've seen you fight like a cornered wolf, when you had no chance of winning. What's it like, that instant when you let it go? When you lash out, with everything in you, knowing you're going to be beaten to the ground? Is it a relief, to surrender to that?"

"Yes." He said it softly, and looked away.

"Well." Something snapped faintly in my shoulder, and the soreness eased. "Imagine that relief compounding, ten times, a hundred times, with every blow, through pain, through agony, to become a pleasure so great and awful it fixes you like a spear." I shook my arm, finding it better. "Then," I said, "you will understand, a little bit, what it is to serve Kushiel."

He listened, and heard, then looked somberly at me. "Even among the Skaldi?"

"No." I shook my head, my voice turning hard. "That was different. I did not choose it. That is what it is, I think, to be used by an immortal."

"Kushiel's Dart." Something in the way he said it made me think of One-Eyed Lodur, the wild priest of Odhinn. Joscelin shuddered inexplicably. "Come on, we'd best be off. One day, he said. Will he keep his word?"

"Yes," I said. "For a day."

"Here." He drew Ysandre's ring on its chain over his head. "She trusted it to your keeping."

I took it back without comment, and we hurried onward.

In the courtyard, we met with Hyacinthe and the Tsingani, a roil of disorderly activity as adults, children and horses alike strained with eagerness to be on the open road. Tsingani do not like to sleep in stone walls, reckoning it unlucky. Neci's brother-in-law finished hitching the team, jerking his chin toward the gate.

"Let's go, *rinkeni chavo*, before the sea-*Kralis* changes his mind!" he said impatiently, looking to Hyacinthe as our leader.

Hyacinthe glanced inquiringly at me.

"I'm fine," I said, swinging into the saddle and managing to suppress a grimace. "We've one day. Let's ride."

De Morhban's men-at-arms watched us go, a few shouting and laughing. A few friendly calls were directed at Joscelin, who acknowledged them with a slight smile and bow.

"You really did entertain them," I said.

He shrugged. "What else was I to do? Go mad worrying about you? Anyway, it's good practice."

"I think you enjoy it," I teased him, my heart growing lighter as the walls of Morhban Castle fell steadily behind us.

"I wouldn't go that far." His tone was reserved, but the ghost of a smile still hovered at one corner of his mouth.

The day had dawned fine and clear, a hint of damp warmth in the brisk air, the sky above bearing only a few scudding clouds. We followed a winding coastal road, the blue-grey sea crashing on the rocks below us, sometimes near enough to send a plume of spray over our party. Seagulls wheeled overhead, filling the morning with their raucous cries. I strained to see across the waters and catch a glimpse of distant Alba, but we were too far, here. In Azzalle, they say, one can see the white cliffs across the Strait.

We'd been no more than an hour upon the road when we saw them, coming around a high outcropping. There, below us, a narrow bay cut into the coast, with a flat sandy beach skirting it. One of the Tsingani outriders gave the cry, and the children boiled out of the wagon, jumping and pointing.

The Queen's fleet was anchored in the mouth of the bay, forty-some ships, their masts bobbing against the horizon. Their sails were lashed, but they flew the Courcel pennant, the silver swan snapping in the sea breeze. It was a beautiful sight. And on the beach, a vast encampment was set, with the figures of sailors made small by our height moving to and fro. There must have been a hundred oar-boats beached there, while others dared the plunging waves, heading out to or back from the fleet.

We had found Quintilius Rousse.

"Come on!" Hyacinthe shouted, waving us onward. The Tsingani caught our exhilaration as we began our descent, scrambling incautiously down the steep, declining road. Rousse's men spotted us well before we reached the bottom, assembling in mass, hands hovering over sword-hilts and bemused expressions on their faces.

Near to the bottom, our impatience took its toll; the wagon, lurching too fast, ran off the road and got hung up on a ridge. The racket of scared, squalling Tsingani children bid fair to outdo the gulls. Gisella and her sister, sighing, counted heads and checked limbs, while Neci and the men rode back shame-faced to prod at the wagon and mutter.

"Go ahead, *chavi*," Gisella said kindly to me, adjusting the scarf on her head and watching the Tsingani men with a practiced eye. "They'll get it loose. You and the others go make the trade. Go make a name for Neci's *kumpania*, who rode to the outermost west for gold."

I nodded, gathering Joscelin and Hyacinthe. We picked our way down the remainder of the cliff road carefully. By the time we reached bottom, the Admiral himself had arrived, a burly, imposing figure who parted a path through his men as surely as the prow of one of his ships.

"What vagabonds have we here?" he bellowed, roaring out the question, bright blue eyes squinting. "Elua's Balls! Have the Travellers decided to push their Long Road across the sea?"

He was not, like Gaspar Trevalion, nearly an uncle to me, but he was Delaunay's friend and a figure from my childhood, and unexpected tears choked me.

"My lord Admiral," I managed, dismounting and curtsying with some difficulty, "my lord Admiral, I bear a message from the Queen."

I looked up, then, and he looked down, and an expression of astonishment split his scarred face.

"By the ten thousand devils of Khebbel-im-Akkad!" he thundered, causing his men to grin and the nearest to cover their ears. "Delaunay's whelp!" And with that, he grabbed me in a bone-cracking embrace that drove the wind from my lungs, leaving me unable to gasp with pain as his mighty arms enfolded my fresh-welted back. "What in seven hells are you doing here, girl?" he asked when he released me. "I thought those justice-mad idiots in the City convicted you of murder."

"They did," I said, wheezing. "That's . . . that's one of the reasons I'm here and not there."

Quintilius Rousse looked calculatingly at me, then at the Tsingani wagon stuck on the cliff road. "Go help them down," he said to a handful of his men, who set out grumbling. "What's the other?" he asked me.

I had regained my breath. "I speak Cruithne."

"Aahhhh." One long syllable, and a gleam of understanding in his shrewd eyes. "Come along, then. We've a great deal to discuss." He looked at Hyacinthe and Joscelin. "You too, I suppose?"

Both of them bowed.

"Let's to it, then." He glanced up the cliff road once more, rubbing his chin. "Glad you brought them. I could use a few horse, you know."

"We were counting on it," Hyacinthe said.

The Queen's Admiral received us in his tent, which was large, mainly to hold the vast number of chests filled with maps and books that he had accumulated; that, and treasure, which he had in abundance. "No time to stow it or even buy a respectable mistress," he grumbled, sweeping aside a King's ransom of jewelry from atop one of the chests. "Sit. And tell me why you're here.

Starting at the beginning. Who killed Anafiel Delaunay?"

We told him, Joscelin and I, starting at the beginning, in the marquist's shop.

"My lad Aelric Leithe made it back with his skin whole," Rousse interrupted us. "I knew as much. S'why I knew it wasn't you, child, or the Cassiline either. That, and the fact you always doted on him like a babe on a sugar-tit. Delaunay was already being watched. So who was it?"

"Isidore d'Aiglemort," I said, then took a deep breath, and told him the rest. This time, he listened without interruption, his face growing dark with outrage. When we were done, he sat gathering fury like a thunderstorm.

Until it broke, and he roared about his tent, raging, breaking and throwing things. One of his men poked in his head, then hastily withdrew it as a piece of crockery came flying his way. When it was over, Quintilius Rousse sighed. "Too much to ask that you're lying, I suppose?" he asked hopefully.

I shook my head and reached for Ysandre's ring, showed it to him lying on my palm. "She gave me this. To show you, and to give to the Prince of the Cruithne."

"Rolande's ring." The Admiral gave it a cursory examination, and heaved another sigh. "Oh, I know it, all right. No, there's no hope for it. But I don't mind telling you, I'd rather bring my fleet upcoast and sail up the Rhenus, set us in place to crack Skaldi skulls—and Camaeline, come to it—than go chasing off on a fool's errand to Alba."

"What if it's not a fool's errand?" I argued. Quintilius Rousse fixed me with his shrewd gaze.

"We tried it before, you know, sailing the long way 'round from lower Siovale, going leagues out of our way to avoid the Straits, to the far shores of Alba. Know what we met? A thousand lime-haired Dalriada, shrieking curses and casting spears. We never even made landfall."

"How many ships?" Hyacinthe asked abruptly.

"Fifteen," Rousse replied curiously.

"You need one. Only one." Hyacinthe swallowed, as if the words pained him. "That's what I saw, when Ysandre asked me to speak the *dromonde*. One ship."

Another mighty sigh. "A Night-Blooming Flower, a Tsingano witch-boy, and a . . . a Cassiline whatever. This is what Ysandre sends me. I must be mad." Quintilius Rousse rumpled his hair, a tangled, half-braided mane of reddish brown. "What do you say, Cassiline?"

Joscelin bowed. "My lord Admiral, I say that whatever you choose, you must do it quickly. Because by tomorrow afternoon, the Duc de Morhban will be here asking questions."

"Morhban." It was uttered in tones of disgust. "He's got me penned in like a fox with chickens. How'd you get past him, anyway? Aelric scarce made it through, and de Morhban's gotten more suspicious since the King died."

Hyacinthe looked at me. Joscelin looked at me.

I raised my eyebrows. "Naamah's way."

"Aahhh." Rousse grinned. "Delaunay's pupil to the end! Well, then, I must decide, and quickly. Too much to ask, I suppose, that the Queen has a plan for passing Elder Brother?"

Dismayed, I shook my head. "I thought you would have passage, my lord. You treated with him, you won an answer. When the Black Boar rules in Alba!"

"And nigh foundered to gain it." Quintilius Rousse scratched his chin. "I've no right of passage, child. That answer was all I gained; that, and the right to cling to my wretched life. Why do you think Delaunay was working so hard to unravel the mystery of him? And the white-haired lad, Alcuin."

Outside the tent, on the beach, the sound of fiddles and a tambor sundered our depressed silence, punctuated by rhythmic clapping from the sailors. Hyacinthe stirred.

"My lord, we promised the Tsingani a great trade, for the horses they bring. They've done us fair service as disguise. It worked all the way to Morhban."

"Might as well." The Admiral grasped a handful of Akkadian treasure, long strands of rubies and seed pearls spilling from his brawny clutch. "I've naught better to do with this, it seems, and like to rest on the bottom of the Straits ere I come to spend it. We'll set 'em back on the Long Road with something to boast of, eh?"

I am no gem-merchant, to gauge the worth of the wealth Quintilius Rousse bestowed on Neci's family, nor a horse-trader, to guess at the value of what he got in trade. Whatever it was, it was enough that the Tsingani stretched their eyes to see it, and fell into their most obsequious manner, swearing to bless his name at every crossroads.

It had taken some time to get the wagon onto the beach and conclude the deal, and dusk was falling when it was done. The Tsingani would stay that night, and depart in the morning. They set up their camp with their usual efficiency, and I noticed Gisella doing a good trade in spices with the D'Angeline sailors, weary of bland fish stew. Joscelin entertained the children with one last Mendacant's tale as the stars emerged, benign and distant over the vast, surging ocean.

Hyacinthe brought me with him to make his farewell to Neci.

"May the *Lungo Drom* prosper you, *tseroman* of Neci's *kumpania*," he said, bowing formally. "You have been a good comrade on the way."

Neci stroked the tips of his mustache, twiddling them to elegant points. "And you," he added, and grinned "*Rinkeni chavo.*" He looked solemn then, with one o those quick shifts of emotion of which the Tsingani are masters. "*Chavo*, I don't know if it's true that you speak the *dromonde* or not. I do not care. When people say Manoj has no grandson, I will say it is untrue. I wil speak your name and remember it. In my *kumpania* your name will always be spoken."

"Thank you." Hyacinthe clasped his wrist, hard and firm. "And yours."

"The great trade of outermost west." Neci gazed at the sea, the waves breaking on the shore. "It is true. It wil make our *lav*." He bowed to me. "And you, *chavi*, who was never born in a back alley, else I am a fool. We wil remember you, too."

"Thank you." I kissed him, on the cheek. "Be kind to women without *laxta*, then, if you would remember me.'

"I will remember you in my dreams." His white grin flashed, and he turned to stride back to his family, waving a last farewell.

"It's not too late," I said to Hyacinthe.

He gazed out at the sea, rippling silver in the dusk "What did Rousse say? Maybe he's right. The Long Road doesn't end where the sea begins. If anyone is to cross it, it should be the Prince of Travellers, yes?"

"Yes," I said, tucking one hand around his arm. We watched the sea together, endless and amazing, moving without cease. "If we're not still here when de Morhban comes," I added, spotting the unmistakeable figure of Quintilius Rousse pacing the shore, pausing and staring out at his fleet.

"No," Hyacinthe said certainly. "He'll go. He has to. One ship; I saw it." He was silent a moment, then asked drolly, "And how was the dear Duc de Morhban, anyway?"

"You really want to know?" I glanced up at his starlit face.

He laughed. "Why not? I always did."

"Good," I said, looking back at the sea. "The Duc de Morhban was very, very good."

"I thought so. You had that look." Hyacinthe wound a lock of my hair around one finger. "I'm not afraid of it, you know," he said softly. "What you are."

"No?" I touched Melisande's diamond. "I am."

We went back, then, to Rousse's encampment, and I left Hyacinthe to go speak with the Admiral, still pacing the shoreline like an angry lion, wisely avoided by his men. A gibbous moon had arisen by that time, standing overhead to set a shining path across the sea, as if to show where the Long Road lay. "My lord," I said, kneeling near him. The sand was cool and damp beneath me. Quintilius Rousse turned on me, glaring.

"Ah, don't waste your Night Court decorum on me, girl! I've a hard choice to make here."

"Yes, my lord," I said, remaining on my knees. "To obey the Crown, or not."

"It's not that!" His voice rose above the sound of the waves, then he lowered it, squatting in front of me. "Listen, child. Ysandre de la Courcel's loyal to the land, and she's the making of a good Queen. I know it, and Delaunay knew it, and Gaspar Trevalion, too. That's why we aided her. And it would be a grand thing, this alliance . . . if it stood a chance of happening. But the chance is precious slim, and the reality is, if you tell me true, that we face civil war and Skaldi invasion, all at once. So I must ask myself, you see, where can I do the most good? On a hare-brained mission nigh-doomed to fail, or fighting for my country? I've over forty ships and nigh a thousand men here, hand-picked, who can fight at sea or on land. Elua's Balls, they whipped the Akkadians, who fight like their ten thousand devils! Ysandre de la Courcel is young and untried, and knows little yet of statecraft, and nothing of war. How am I best to aid her? By obeying, or defying?"

Kneeling, *abeyante*, as I had been taught since earliest childhood, I lifted my face and gazed at him. "You have nothing," I said softly. Quintilius Rousse stared at me. "Do you think your ships will make a difference in a land battle? Do you think your men will count for aught? My lord Admiral, I have *seen* the Skaldi, and they number more than the grains of sand on this beach. A few hundred men . . ." I scooped up a handful of sand and let it trickle through my fingers. "How do you wish to die, Admiral? We are D'Angeline. At the hands of numbers, or dreams?"

With a sound of disgust, Quintilius Rousse rose and turned his back on me, standing at the verge of the gently breaking waves. "You're as bad as your master," he muttered, scarce audible amid the sea-sounds. "Worse. At least he didn't ply his words from a courtesan's lips." I remained silent. Quintilius Rousse sighed. "Elder Brother have mercy on us. We'll sail at dawn."

SIXTY-SEVEN

And so we did.

It was somewhat later than dawn, truth be told, when we set out in the oar-boat for Rousse's flagship. Once he'd made up his mind, the Admiral was nothing but efficiency, but there were a great many orders to be delegated before we left.

These I tried to follow as best I could, but Quintilius Rousse was in no mind to be tailed by Delaunay's *anguissette*, so all I caught was a confused impression. He would leave his lieutenant in charge, with orders to implement a shore brigade, guarding their borders. A quarter of the ships would sail upcoast to Azzalle and find berth at Trevalion, held loyal by Ghislain de Somerville, and send word to Ysandre. If royal couriers could not make it through Morhban, they could send word through Trevalion.

As for the rest, they would do their best to hold off de Morhban's inquiry, and sound out his loyalty. For de Morhban had a fleet of his own—I'd not known that—and if he turned traitor, he could use it to sail north and harry the whole of the Azzallese coast, forcing them to turn their attention away from the flatlands and guarding the Rhenus.

It was a fair bewilderment of possibilities and strategies. I had never appreciated, until his death, the narrow and dangerous path Delaunay trod among his allies and enemies. Then again, I thought, nor had he, not entirely. Melisande had played a deeper game, and blinded him to d'Aiglemort's betrayal. It was only my ill-luck to have stumbled upon it.

And now I was playing an even deeper game that she had not yet guessed. Thinking on it, I shuddered. Kushiel's Dart, cast against the blood of his line. Whatever befell us on the waters, at least it took me further away from her. I did not trust myself, after seeing her at the Hippochamp. I had withheld the *signale*, it was true, the last time . . . but I would not trust it a third time. I had come closer than I liked to think, with de Morhban. It was shock and the numbness of grief that had buffered me that terrible night with Melisande, the night of Delaunay and Alcuin's death. And even then, it had been so close.

Another time . . . I trailed my fingers in the water, as the oarsmen set to and the shore grew distant behind us. Another time, it would be different. And Elua help me, I longed for it. I could not help it, even as I despised her.

The edge between love and hate is honed finer than the keenest flechette. She told me something like that once, but I dared not think on such things, with her name so close to my tongue. She told me too that it was not my acquiescence that interested her, but my rebellion. That was the thing that set her apart from the others, who failed to see where it lay.

That was the thing that terrified me.

Well, then; if I could not free myself from her sway, I could do that much. I ran one finger under the velvet lead tied about my throat, considering the horizon. Melisande Shahrizai wanted to see how far I would run with her line upon me, how far my rebellion would take me. I do not think she reckoned on it taking me to the green and distant shores of Alba. Elua willing, it might even lead to the unraveling of her subtle and deep-laid plans.

So I prayed, facing the forbidding seas. And if I were to die on these deadly waters, I prayed my last thought wouldn't be of her.

Though somehow I feared it would.

While I occupied myself with these morbid thoughts, Rousse's strong oarsmen gained his flagship, scrambling aboard. And then I had no time to dwell on such things, as they lowered rope ladders for us and we had to clamber on board, hands and feet slipping on the salt-slickened rope. I count myself agile, but it was no easy feat, learning to balance on the swaying wooden decks of the great ship.

A pillar of compassion, Quintilius Rousse laughed at ur dismay, striding about with a rolling ease he didn't isplay on dry land. He shouted orders as he strode, beyed with alacrity, and we came to see quickly, all of s, why he was the Royal Admiral. He gave us unto the harge of his second-in-command, wiry, sharp-eyed Jean Marchand, who showed us to a cabin with four hammocks slung from the ceiling.

By the time we had stowed such gear as we brought, Quintilius was giving orders to hoist sail.

I freely confess, boats are a great mystery to me. Before yesterday, I'd never even glimpsed the sea, let alone et sail upon it. I cannot begin to fathom the myriad tasks he sailors performed, swarming up and down the masts, ashing and unlashing ropes in bewildering profusion, ranking a chain that raised the anchor, massive and ripping. All I know is that Quintilius Rousse gave commands, and they obeyed. Some thirty men went belowecks to set to at the oars, and the great flagship turned s prow slowly, swinging away from land and toward he open sea. And then the sails rose, steady and majestic, deep blue with the Courcel swan: three in a row, the reatest at the center, with smaller sails fore and aft. The ind filled them and they bellied out, snapping, setting he silver swan aflight.

It happens faster than one imagines. One minute, the hip is turning slowly, inching through its own backater, oars beating the sea into a seemingly futile roil. nd then, suddenly, the waves are slipping past, lapping t the sides with ever-increasing speed.

A cheer arose from the sailors, and Quintilius Rousse reached a keg of wine for toasts all around; it is traition, I learned later, at the start of each voyage.

In this, we shared. Hyacinthe tossed his down, gazing bout him exuberantly. I sipped mine, finding it warming against the chilly wind. Joscelin stared into his mug and looked rather green.

"I don't think I'm a sailor," he murmured.

Quintilius Rousse, strolling past, clapped him on the shoulder. "Drink it, lad," he said heartily. "If it comes back up, so be it. Just bend over the side, and give your toll to the Lord of the Deeps."

It proved to be prophetic advice. I winced with sympathy as Joscelin clutched the railing and leaned over retching. Hyacinthe grinned.

"Cassilines aren't fit for the Long Road," he said. "Not when it extends over sea!"

"He can start a fire with damp tinder in the middle of a blizzard," I said, feeling an obscure need to defend him. "I didn't see any Tsingani in the heart of the Skaldic wilderness, Prince of Travellers."

"We're not that stupid." Hyacinthe laughed, and wandered off to watch the sailors at work, already taking on a rolling sea-man's gait. I watched him sourly, left to tend to the heaving Cassiline. There is something innately pitiful about a man in vambraces spewing up his breakfast.

It was Rousse's plan to sail due west, running ahead of the wind that blows through the Straits. If we got a good-enough lead, he reckoned, we might outrun Elder Brother's reach, gaining the open sea and rounding the southern tip of Alba.

It was a good plan, and from what I understood, we took a good run at it. A full half a day we sailed, until we were well and truly betwixt shores, neither visible not Terre d'Ange that we had left, nor Alba that we sought. The weather held clear, and the wind blew true. As we headed west, nothing lay before us but open sea that made my blood run cold with its endless horizon and made the sailors sing. Truly, they are a different breed, seafarers. I fixed my inner compass by the points around me, even in direst straits, knowing where I was. It is different for them. The unknown, the empty vastness of the sea, beckons with a lure I can but imagine.

Outermost west, the Tsingani had called the far shores of Kusheth. I understood then that it was only the place where the outermost west began, for the sea stretched endlessly, onward and onward, toward where the sun dies each night. Outermost west is beyond our ken. It is there, somewhere, the priests say, that Mother Earth and the One God created a realm where the sun never dies, but only rests; the true Terre d'Ange, where Elua walks smiling, naked feet treading upon the soil, and green things grow in his wake.

So it may be; I can only believe, and trust that it was true. Our journey was but a day's, and even that met its end.

It came, as such things ever do, when we believed that we had passed the point of crisis, and our way lay clear before us. No one knows, for a surety, how far the reach of the Master of the Straits extends. Without a doubt, it was farther than Quintilius Rousse reckoned, for it came when he began at last to relax, swaying comfortably at the wheel of his mighty ship, ordering his sailors to take the soundings and gauging whether or not it was time to turn his prow toward the north.

It began as a wind ruffling the waves.

Such a thing, one might think, is normal at sea, where the wind is one's mistress, and dictates one's course. This is true. But this wind . . . I cannot explain. It ran contrary to the westerly breeze that blew us true, *lower* than that wind, blowing the waves backward, creating a cauldron of distress.

"Ah, no," Quintilius Rousse breathed, taking a firmer

grip upon the wheel and casting his gaze skyward. "Ah, no, Elder Brother, have mercy!"

I looked up, then, at the sky, which had bid fair for our journey, as clear as the day before. No longer. Clouds roiled above us, gathering with purpose and darkness, a roiling mix, blotting out the sun.

"What is it?" I asked the Queen's Admiral, dreading the answer.

Questions are dangerous, for they have answers. I had said as much to the Duc de Morhban. Quintilius Rousse looked at me with fear in his bright blue eyes, the old trawler-line scar dragging down one side of his mouth.

"It is him," he said.

And that is when the skies opened upon us.

For those who have never survived a storm at sea, I do not wish it upon anyone. Our ship, which had seemed such a safe haven on the vast breast of the waters, was pitched and tossed about like a child's toy. The contrary winds, one moment ago a mild phenomenon, turned to forces of destruction, boiling the sea into crests and troughs higher than our tallest mast. Night or day, there was no telling, the skies turned a horrid bruised color, split only by lightning.

"Drop sails!" Quintilius Rousse shouted, his powerful voice battered and lost in the winds and the lashing rain that followed. "Drop sails!"

Somehow, his men heard; I saw them, as I clung helplessly to the foremast, their silhouettes against the lightning-struck sky, high overhead, obeying the Admiral's orders. The sails dropped like stones, and I saw one man at least swept over, as the ship listed to starboard. Rain blew like veils across my sight; through it, incredibly, I saw Joscelin making his way to the foredeck, from grip to grip, a dim figure inching along with sheer determination. I prayed Hyacinthe had gained the safety of our cabin, though I doubted it; I remembered him last amid a group of sailors, too interested to go below. And it had come upon us too fast.

Gaining the mast, Joscelin took hold and crouched over me, sheltering me with his body from the buffeting winds. Drenched and sodden, I peered out from under him, my own rain-lashed hair obscuring my vision. "Do we turn back?" Joscelin asked the Admiral, shouting the question. "My lord Admiral! Do we turn back?"

"Here he comes!" Quintilius Rousse roared his answer, pointing with one shaking finger across the water.

He came.

The Master of the Straits.

Those who have not made this passage say I lie; I swear, it is true. Huddled under Joscelin's sheltering form, I saw him, a face upon the waters, moving toward us. Of waves was his flesh wrought, of thunderclouds, his hair; lightning, his eyes and, I swear, he spoke. His voice burst upon us like thunder, drumming at our ears, until we could but cower beneath it.

"WHO DARES CROSS?"

Like calls to like. Lashing himself to the wheel, the Queen's Admiral dared to reply, roaring like fury into the winds, shaking his fist. "I do, you old bastard! And if you want your precious Black Boar to rule in Alba, you'll let me go!"

There was laughter, then, and the face of the waters reared up three times the height of our mid-mast, dwarfing Rousse's defiance. A vast, watery face, laughing like thunder, until I clapped my hands over my drowning ears.

"THAT IS NOT *YOUR* DREAM, SEAFARER! WHAT TOLL WILL YOU PAY?"

"Name your price!" Quintilus Rousse howled his answer, hands clinging like iron to the straining wheel. The ship plunged into a trough; he held its course, hurling defiance into the winds. "Just name it, you old bastard! I'll pay what it takes!"

The ship climbed up the crest of a wave, toward the vast maw, dark and infinite, that had opened in the sky. Open, laughing like thunder, to swallow us forevermore.

This is the end, I thought, closing my eyes.

And felt the absence of Joscelin's sheltering body.

"A song!" I knew the voice; it was Joscelin's, strident and urgent with hope. His hand grabbed at my shoulder, hauling me erect, even as the ship teetered atop the pitch of a wave. "Such as you have never heard, my lord of the Straits, sung upon the waters!" he shouted at the wave-wrought face that loomed over us. "A song!"

"What song?" I asked Joscelin desperately, the ship pitching. The rain whipped his hair, dull and sodden, his hands anchoring me. We might have been the last two mortals left alive, for all that I could see. "Joscelin! What song?"

He answered, shouting; I saw it, though I could not hear. The wind ripped his answer away, rendered it soundless. But we had been together through all that humans might endure, through blizzard and storm, and all that the elements might hurl at us. We did not need to speak aloud. I saw his lips form the words.

Gunter's steading.

And because there was nothing else to do, except die, I sang, then, a song of Gunter's steading: a hearth-song, one of those the women had taught me, Hedwig and the others, a song of waiting, and longing, of a handsome thane dying young, in a welter of blood and sorrow, of reaping and sowing and harvest, of old age come early, and weaving by the fireside, while the snows of winter pile deep at the door.

I am not Thelesis de Mornay, at whose voice all present fall silent, listening. But I have a gift for language, that Delaunay taught to me. These songs I had committed to memory, scrawled by burnt twig next to the hearth-fire, never recorded by men. They were the homely songs of Skaldi women, to which no scholar ever paid heed. And I sang them, then, though the wind tore the words from my lips, for the Master of the Straits, whose face moved over the waters, impossibly vast and terrible.

And he listened, and the waters grew calm, the awesome features sinking back into the rippling waves.

No one, ever, had brought these songs to the sea before.

I kept singing, while the seas grew tranquil, and the waves lapped at the sides of the ship, and Joscelin's hand was beneath my arm, keeping me upright while my voice grew ragged. Those sailors quailing beneath the onslaught stirred, creeping onto deck. I sang, hoarsely, of children born and fir trees giving forth new growth, until Quintilius Rousse roused himself with a shake.

"Do you accept our toll?" he cried.

The waves themselves shuddered, a face forming on their surface, benign and complacent, yet vast, so vast. Its mouth could have swallowed our ship whole.

"YESSSSS . . ." came the reply, whispered and dreadful. "YOU MAY PASS."

And it was gone.

The withdrawal of resistance came like a blow, the restoration of calm, water dissipating into mere waves, rippled by a western breeze. The skies cleared; it was not even dusk. I drew in a great breath, my throat rasping.

"Is it done?" I asked Quintilius Rousse hoarsely, trusting to Joscelin to keep me upright.

"It is done," he confirmed, his blue eyes darting left

and right, scarce trusting to the evidence they saw. He looked at me then with something like fear. "Did Delaunay teach you that, then, to soothe Elder Brother's craving?"

I laughed at that, my voice cracking with exhaustion and hysteria. "No," I whispered, leaning on Joscelin's vambraced arm. "Those are the songs of Skaldi women, whose husbands and brothers may yet slaughter us all."

And with that, I collapsed.

When I awoke, I was lying in a dark cabin, enmeshed in a hammock as if in a hempen cradle, swaying. A single lamp lit the darkness, its flame trimmed low. A familiar figure drowsed beside it, sitting in a chair.

"Hyacinthe," I whispered.

He started, and lifted his head, white grin reassuring. "Did you think you'd lost me?"

"I wasn't sure." I struggled to sit upright, then gave up, resigning myself to the hammock. "I saw at least one go over."

"Four." He said it quietly, no longer smiling. "It would have been more, if not for Jean Marchand. He made us lash ourselves to whatever we could."

"You saw it, then." My voice was hoarse still. It is something, to sing down the sea. Hyacinthe nodded, a faint movement in the shadows.

"I saw it."

"Where's Joscelin?"

"Above." Hyacinthe yawned. "He wanted to see the stars, to gain his bearings. He's not vomiting anymore, at least."

I began to laugh, then stopped. It hurt my throat. "We owe him all our lives."

"You sang." He looked at me curiously through the darkness.

"He made me. He remembered the songs. Gunter's

steading." I lay back, exhausted again. "I never thought I'd be grateful to the Skaldi."

"All knowledge is worth having," Hyacinthe said, quoting Delaunay, whom I had quoted to him. "Even this. Even the *dromonde*." Rising, he smoothed my hair back from my brow and kissed me. "Go to sleep," he said, and blew out the lamp.

SIXTY-EIGHT

The following day dawned as calm and bright as one might wish, as if in apology for the Master of the Straits' dreadful storm. We had turned northward in the night, rounding the lower tip of Alba, and I could see her green coastline lying off our starboard bow, hazy in the distance.

"Where do we make landfall?" I asked Quintilius Rousse, standing on deck with him. The wind tugged at my cloak, but it seemed milder than yesterday, with less of a biting chill. I felt more myself, and thanked Blessed Elua for the thousandth time that I healed quickly.

"That," the Admiral said dryly, "is a very good question." He looked haggard and tired, having gotten but a few hours sleep, delegating the wheel to his helmsman once he'd determined we were well and truly clear of danger. He swept one brawny arm toward the coast. "There, in all its glory, lies Alba. Where Ysandre's deposed Cruarch bides is another matter."

"I thought you knew," I said, dismayed once more. "You sought him before, you said. Among the Dalriada."

"I know where the Dalriada lie." Rousse turned to spit, then remembered my presence, and refrained. "On the land that juts out nearest to Eire. Our sources *said* that's where Drustan mab Necthana fled. But it's a sizeable kingdom."

"How do we even know it's true?"

Rousse shrugged. "Delaunay said it was, and Thelesis de Mornay. They had some system of exchange, across the waters, with Alban loyalists. Folk that Thelesis had known, during her exile. Then the messages stopped coming, and they reckoned Maelcon the Usurper caught them. That's when I tried the coast. But I never caught sight of any Pictish Prince."

And I had doubted, when he called it a fool's errand. I sat down on a spar near his feet, thinking. In the prow, Joscelin was doing his Cassiline exercises, silhouetted against the sky. Sunlight flashed from his steel. He had found his sea-legs, it seemed.

"How long until we reach the kingdom of the Dalriada?" I asked.

"A day, no more." Quintilius Rousse shrugged again. "Then we take our chances, I reckon, and hope they can lead us to the Cruithne."

I was not entirely sure I liked his plan. I'd doubts enough about my own skill with the tongue—it is one thing to learn a language on paper, with tutors who speak one's own language, and another to deal with native speakers—and I wasn't sure the Dalriada spoke the same Cruithne I had learned. Eire is its own island, and separate from Alba; if their folk had established a foothold on Alba, would they speak a dialect I recognized? Or somewhat altogether different? The scholars do not say, for the armies of Tiberium never ventured so far before being ousted by Cinhil Ru. And if it were so . . . how could I make them understand? Ysandre's ring, Drustan mab Necthana's pledge, would mean naught to them.

So I mulled over the problem, until it came together in my mind. *All knowledge is worth having.* "Hyacinthe," I said. "Mayhap he can help. He can speak the *dromonde*, and tell us where to land."

"You believe it?" Quintilius Rousse glanced at me sidelong, profound doubt in his blue gaze. "It's enough that we come in a single ship, I think. Even Delaunay wasn't so credible, lass, and he could ferret out truth in the strangest of places."

Resting my chin in my hands, I watched the waves pass. "I know. But my lord Admiral . . . when I was but thirteen, his mother spoke the *dromonde* for me, unbidden. While I was trying to get at the truth of Delaunay's history. She told me I would rue the day I learned it."

"And you did, I suppose," Rousse said gruffly, when I ventured no more.

"There were two days." It was hypnotic, watching the sliding waves, unchanging, never the same. "I learned half of it the day Melisande Shahrizai contracted me for the Longest Night, and used me to flush out your messenger, my lord, whose liege led d'Aiglemort's men to Delaunay. I learned that he had been beloved of Prince Rolande. And I learned the balance of it the day he was killed, and all of the household with him, including Alcuin, who was like a brother to me. That was the day I learned that he was oath-sworn to protect Ysandre de la Courcel, which Alcuin told us, dying. Yes, my lord, I rue those days."

Quintilius Rousse was silent for a moment, tending to the wheel. "Anyone could say as much," he said finally. " 'Tis dangerous, to chase after buried secrets."

"It is," I agreed. "But she spoke the *dromonde* twice. The second time, she said, 'Do not discount the Cullach Gorrym.' Do you know what that means, my lord?"

Rousse paused, then shook his head, ruddy locks fraying in the wind.

"Neither did she," I said. "It means the Black Boar,

in Cruithne. And there is no reason, no reason at all, my lord, why she should have known those words, or linked them to me." I rose, stretching out my joints. "When we are in sight of the kingdom of Dalriada, then, will you let Hyacinthe speak?"

"Those were his mother's words." Quintilius Rousse's voice was rough, though I could see he believed, a little. No one could pass the Master of the Straits and not come to believe in things unseen. "Did the lad ever speak you true?"

"Not me," I answered truthfully. "He fears it, to speak for friends. But he spoke it for Melisande, once."

"What did he tell her?" The Admiral's hands lay slack on the wheel, caught up despite himself. All sailors love a good tale, I have learned. He looked at me with sharp curiosity.

"That which yields," I said, feeling a chill despite the mild wind and hugging my elbows, "is not always weak."

I walked away, then, close-wrapped in my velvet cloak, salt-stained now, a gift of the Duc de Morhban, feeling Rousse's sharp gaze still at my back. An easy enough prophecy, a skeptic might say; but not if one is that which yields. I made my way across the wooden decks, polished to a high gleam—Quintilius Rousse abided no idle hands on his ship—to find Hyacinthe trying his luck at fishing. He glanced up at me, boasting.

"Phèdre, look! Three to one, I've caught." He dangled a string of fish at me, bright silvery bodies jerking and twisting, drowning in dry air. "We had a wager, Remy and I," he added, nodding toward the sailor beside him, who looked more amused than not.

"Very nice." I inspected his fish cursorily. "Hyacinthe . . . If I asked you to see where the Long Road we travel touches land once more, could you do it?"

His black eyes gleamed wickedly in the sunlight, and he grasped the largest of the fish, offering it to me with both hands. "For you, O Star of the Evening, anything. Are you sure you don't want to ask your Cassiline? He may be jealous of such bounty."

I laughed, despite myself. "I'll risk it."

For a day and another night, then, we made our way up the coast of Alba, tacking against the slow winds. Our third day broke misty and strange, becalming us, until even the Courcel pennant hung limp from the tallest mast. Rousse set his men to oars, then, cursing them, and we moved torturously slow, the green coast appearing and receding out of the mists.

"Now, if ever," Quintilius Rousse said grimly, calling me on deck. "Bring on the Tsingano lad, Phèdre nó Delaunay. Let him point the way."

There was no mockery in Hyacinthe now. He walked slowly to the prow of the ship, his face raised to the mists that held us thick-clasped. His head turned from side to side, like a hunting dog casting about for a scent, sight-blinded, all his senses elsewhere. The sailors watched him closely, having decided he was lucky—no few had had the ill fortune of dicing with him, I learned later—and Quintilius Rousse, in all his doubt, held his breath.

"I cannot see it," Hyacinthe whispered, arms blundering outward in the thick mists. "Phèdre, I cannot see our road."

I went to him, then; they left us alone, muttering. Joscelin watched silently, offering no comment.

"You can, Hyacinthe. I know you can," I said, taking his arm. "It's only mist! What's that to the veils of what-might-be?"

"It is *vrajna*." He shivered, cold beneath my grasp.

"They were right, Manoj was right, this is no business for men."

Waves lapped at the sides of our ship, little waves, moving us nowhere. We were becalmed. The rowers had paused.

"Prince of Travellers," I said. "The Long Road will lead us home. Let it show the way."

Hyacinthe shivered again, his black gaze blurred and fearful. "No. You don't understand. The Long Road goes on and on. There is no home for us, only the journey."

"You are half D'Angeline!" I raised my voice unintending, shaking him. "Hyacinthe! Elua's blood in your veins, to ground you home, and Tsingani, to show the way. You can see it, you have to! Where is the Cullach Gorrym?"

His head turned, this way and that, dampness beading on his black ringlets. "I cannot see it," he repeated, shuddering. "It is *vrajna*! They were right. I should never have looked, never. Men were not meant to part the veils. Now this mist is sent to veil us all, for my sin."

I stood there, my fingers digging into his arm, and cast my gaze about. Up, upward, where the sun rode faint above the mists, a white disk. The ship's three masts rose, bobbing, to disappear in greyness. "If you cannot see through it," I said fiercely, "then see *over* it!"

Hyacinthe looked at me slowly, then up at the tallest mast, the crow's nest lost in the mists. "Up there?" he asked, his voice full of fear. "You want me to look from up there?"

"Your great-grandmother," I said deliberately, "gave me a riddle. What did Anasztaizia see, through the veils of time, to teach her son the *dromonde*? A horse-drawn wagon and a seat by the *kumpania's* fire, or a mist-locked ship carrying a ring for a Queen's betrothed? It is yours to answer."

He looked for a long time without speaking.

And then he began to climb.

For uncountable minutes we were all bound in mist-wreathed silence, staring into the greyness where Hyacinthe had disappeared, far overhead. The ship rocked gently, muffled waves lapping. Then his voice came, faint and disembodied, a single lonely cry. "There!"

It might have been the depths of the ocean he pointed to for all any of us could see. Quintilius Rousse cursed, fumbling his way back toward the helm. "Get a relay!" he roared, setting his sailors to jumping. "You! And you!" He pointed. "Move! Get up that rigging! Marchand, call the beat, get the oarsmen to put their backs to it! We follow the Tsingano's heading!"

All at once, the ship was scrambling into motion, men hurrying hither and thither, carrying out Rousse's orders. "Two points to port!" the call came, shouted down the rigging. "And a light in the prow, Admiral!"

The mighty ship turned slowly, nosing through the mist. Far forward, a lantern kindled, a single sailor holding it aloft at the very prow. Down came the shouted orders, and Rousse at the helm jostled the ship into position, until the lantern was aligned with Hyacinthe's pointing finger high in the crow's-nest, unseen by those of us below.

"That's it, lads!" he cried. "Now *row*! Out oars!"

Belowdecks, the steady beat of a drum sounded, Jean Marchand's voice rising in counterpoint. Two rows of oars pulled in unison, digging into the sea. The ship began to move forward, gaining speed, travelling blind through the mists.

I did not need to be a sailor to guess how dangerous it was, so close to a strange, unseen coast. I joined Joscelin, and we stood together watching Quintilius Rousse man the helm, his scarred face alight with reckless desperation, having cast his lot. How long we sailed thusly, I cannot say; it seemed the better part of a day, though I think it no more than an hour.

Then came another cry, and a change of direction. On Hyacinthe's lead, we turned our prow toward land, invisible before us ... but, the last time glimpsed, close by. The Admiral's face grew grim as he held the course, white-knuckled. For the first time all day, a wind arose, sudden and unexpected, filling our sails. The rowers put up their oars, resting, as we raced before the wind like a bird on the wing.

Out of the mists, and into sunlight, gleaming on the waters, heading straight into a narrow, rocky bay that cut deep into the shoreline.

A great cheer arose, dwarfing in sound the one that they'd given when first we set sail. High overhead, Hyacinthe clutched the railing of the crow's-nest, weak with his efforts.

Before us lay landfall, a stony beach, with green hills leading down to it, a bright silver river snaking through the green.

And on the beach, what looked suspiciously like a reception party.

Fully armed and awaiting us.

Sixty-nine

"Drop anchor!" Quintilius Rousse's roar split the sudden brightness, as sails were lowered and lashed with alacrity, the rowers dug in the oars, the ship slowing in the backwash of water they churned. Hyacinthe descended the rigging on shaking legs. With a mighty clang, the anchor was loosed, enormous links of chain rattling through the winch. The ship came to anchor in the deep waters of the bay, broadside to the shore, the Courcel swan fluttering from her mast. Quintilius Rousse muttered under his breath, reaching into his purse; a gold coin he drew out, tossing it overboard in a high arc. It glittered in the sun, and fell with a splash. It is a sailor's superstition, to pay tribute to the Lord of the Deep after a dangerous journey.

And then all of us found places along the length of the ship, staring landward.

It was a small enough party, no more than a dozen men, in bright woolen plaids. But they waved broadswords in the air, no mistake, sun flashing off steel.

"What do you make of that?" Rousse asked, pointing and squinting.

I followed his line of sight. Two figures, in the forefront, smaller than the others. The larger was still, unlike the others, dark-haired; the smallest leaped about, brandishing a spear. Gauging the weapon against the size of the men's swords . . . "A child," I said, "my lord Admiral. Two, perhaps."

His reddish brows drew down in a scowl. "You're the Queen's emmissary. What do we do?"

I gathered my cloak around me, clutching briefly at Ysandre's ring. "We go to meet them," I said firmly. "Bring six men, my lord, skilled at arms. I will take Hyacinthe and Joscelin."

"We'll be outnumbered," he said bleakly.

"It will show faith." I glanced wryly at Joscelin, gazing shoreward with keen interest, vambraces glinting as he leaned on the rail. "If it is a trap, my lord, all your men would not suffice. If it is not, we will not be outnumbered, not with one trained by the Cassilines on guard. And my lord, if you can spare it . . . somewhat to offer the Dalriada, from your hoard. The Queen will recompense your loss."

"So be it." Quintilius Rousse made his selections—Hyacinthe's fishing companion Remy among them—and gave orders, giving the helm over to Jean Marchand. He went into his cabin, returning with a coffer he showed to me, filled with silks and gems, and vessels of spice. I nodded approval, as if I had knowledge of such things. And then one of the oar-boats was lowered, the rope ladder descended, and I found myself handed down into the boat.

Rousse's six sailors set to at the oars and we began moving through the shining waves, each stroke bringing us closer to shore, farther from the safety of the ship, and all things D'Angeline. I held my head high, doing my best to look as if I knew what I was doing.

At some thirty yards, they came clear. The men were warriors and no mistake, fair-haired and ruddy, reminding me uneasily of the Skaldi, tall and thewed as they were. But I'd been right: one was a child, a young boy, with red-gold hair and a gold torque about his neck, jumping up and down in his eagerness and shouting in an unintelligible tongue.

And the other . . .

She was no child, but a young woman, slim and self-possessed, with black hair and nut-brown skin, and there was a little space around her, where the Dalriada warriors gave way.

"Be welcome," she said clearly as we drew in earshot, her voice giving tongue to the words in Cruithne, fluid and musical. She held out one hand and the Dalriada men waved their swords, shouting; then sheathed them, surging forward, wading heedless into the sea to grasp the sides of our oar boat, hauling us through the shallows unto the rocky shore. The boy raced back and forth, waving his toy spear.

"Be welcome," the young woman repeated; no more than a girl, really, with twin lines of blue dots etched along her brown cheekbones. Her dark eyes smiled, her hand still extended.

The D'Angelines sat stock-still in the boat, beached and no longer rocking on water. With a slight shock, I realized that I and I alone knew what she had said. I rose, taking care not to tilt the boat.

"I am Phèdre nó Delaunay," I said carefully in Cruithne, taking pains to mimic her inflections, "and I come as ambassador from Ysandre de la Courcel, the Queen of Terre d'Ange. We seek Drustan mab Necthana, the true Cruarch of Alba."

The warriors yelled at the sound of Drustan's name, rattling their swords and stamping. The young boy shouted. The girl smiled again, laying her hands on his shoulders and stilling him. "I am Moiread, his sister," she said simply. "We have been waiting for you."

"How?" I whispered, then remembered, turning to the others. "It's all right," I said in D'Angeline. "They are giving us welcome." Strong hands extended, helping me out of the boat; I nearly staggered, to catch my footing on solid land. Moiread's smile deepened and she came forward to take my shoulders in her hands, looking into my eyes. Hers were wideset and very dark, seeming even wider with the blue dots on her cheeks.

"I had a dream," she said calmly. "Brennan played on the beach, and a swan flew overhead. He threw his spear and pierced its eye. The swan fell to earth, and took off its skin of feathers. It plucked out the spear and spoke. So I followed Brennan, to see where he shook his spear at the gulls. When I found out, Eamonn's men came. We waited. And here you are."

I shuddered under her hands. "You followed a dream?"

Her dark eyes moved over our party, came to rest on Hyacinthe's face. "You followed a dream," she said, and left me to go to him, touching his face with slim, brown fingers. "A waking dreamer."

He started back at the touch, with a strange expression. Rousse's men and the Dalriada stared at each other and fingered weapons gaugingly. The boy Brennan tilted his head up at Moiread and asked something. I could almost pick out words in what he said, almost.

"May we meet your brother?" I asked Moiread, desperate to make sense of the encounter.

"Of course." She turned back to me, still smiling. "But you must meet the Twins, first. They are the Lords of the Dalriada."

It was a strange procession. Two of Rousse's men remained behind with the boat, to relay what had happened shipboard. The rest of us followed, as we wended our way along a narrow track through the green hills. The Dalriada were laughing and shouting, one of them taking the boy Brennan on his shoulders, playing at being a horse. The D'Angelines were silent and wide-eyed. I did my best to explain, with scant idea myself what had befallen us.

The seat of the Dalriada royalty is a great hall, set atop one of the highest hills. It echoes the hall of Tea Muir in Eire, I am told, where the High King of Eire rules. A stone building, filled with daub and whitewashed with lime, the roof thatch; but that is not to do it justice. It is vast, with seven doors, through which one enters according to rank. They have laws governing such things, the Eirans do.

We entered through the Sun Door, which was an honor, although I did not know it then. It is the second-highest rank they could have accorded us, the highest being the door of the White Mare, through which only the scions of Tea Muir may enter. There we were made to wait in a sitting room, while Brennan was sent scuttling on an errand and the Dalriada warriors lounged about in bright-eyed poses. Beyond the next door, we heard sounds of quarreling.

"You speak for the swan," Moiread said to me, nonplussed. "Who stands with you?"

"He does," I said without hesitation, pointing to Quintilius Rousse, who held the treasure-coffer. "And he, and he." I indicated Joscelin and Hyacinthe, who both bowed uneasily.

"That is well," she said, and disappeared. After a moment, she returned. "The Twins will see you."

I looked once at Quintilius Rousse, once at Joscelin and once at Hyacinthe, drawing strength from their steady regard. Taking a deep breath, I followed Moiread into the hall of the Lords of the Dalriada.

I don't know what I had expected; it had all occurred with such speed. But if it was anything, it was not this: The two of them, brother and sister, on their adjoining thrones.

Now, I know them well enough, the Twins. Then, I took refuge in what I knew best, taking the coffer from Rousse and offering it to them, then kneeling with bowed head. Grainne looked at me keenly, I saw through lowered lashes, toying restlessly with the gold torque about her neck and the jeweled pins scattered in her redgold tresses. Eamonn was the more suspicious, setting the coffer aside and raising his voice in a sharp query.

"They have come to see Drustan," Moiread said, and I understood the Eiran words, picking them out one by one in her liquid accent, piecing them together after she had spoken. *"They seek audience with the Cruarch."*

Eamonn frowned, but Grainne stood up, her grey-green eyes alight. She was a tall woman, and striking by their standards; her features were cruder than ours, but her hair and her eyes were quite lovely, and her generous mouth that smiled at us. She wore a sword at her waist, and I gauged her to be not too much older than Joscelin, in her late twenties, no more.

"Tell them they are welcome," she said. *"And fetch your brother."*

"My lady," I said haltingly, lifting my head, the half-familiar words twisting my tongue. "I understand, I think."

She gave me her sharp gaze, red-gold brows arching. Eamonn muttered on his throne; I caught only a word of it. *Trouble.* He was tall, like his sister, but his hair had a paler hue, his eyes a muddier tinge.

So that is how it is, I thought. To the others, I said in D'Angeline, "They are sending for the Cruarch."

We heard him before we saw him; a halting gait, among other steps. I had forgotten that. I heard Delaunay's voice in my memory, light and amused. *And Ysandre de la Courcel, flower of the realm, shall teach a clubfoot barbarian Prince to dance the gavotte.*

Drustan mab Necthana, Prince of the Picti, the deposed Cruarch of Alba, entered the hall.

He had with him an older woman and two younger, as well as Moiread, who could only be his mother and sisters, and a handful of warriors as well. They were cut from the same cloth, all of them, slender and dark, a handsbreadth shorter at least than the Twins. But Delaunay trained me to observe, and I noted well how the Dalriada fell back, creating a space for the Picti.

Truly, he bore their sign, in blue woad-marque, bisecting his brow, swirling on his cheeks, outlandish and barbarian. But it was not entirely displeasing, and his eyes gazed out through Pictish warrior's mask, fine and dark. A cloak of combed red wool hung from his shoulders, clasped with gold.

"You are the swan's voice," he said to me in Cruithne, those dark eyes cutting me through to the bone. "What does she say?"

If he had not spoken . . . he was strange enough, and fearful, that I might have doubted my answer. But there was somewhat in his voice, a slight break, hopeful and young, that only one trained to listen would hear. I rose to my feet, lifting the chain from about my neck, holding forth Rolande's gold signet ring. It swayed between us.

"My lord," I said, raising my voice. "Ysandre de la Courcel, the Queen of Terre d'Ange, would honor the covenant between you."

Drustan mab Necthana took the ring, closing his hand hard about it. He glanced at his mother, and his three sisters, who nodded, all in unison. A gleam flared and died in his dark eyes. "What is the price?" he asked me harshly.

I met his dark gaze, staring out from his blue-marqued face that had seen loss and betrayal, his father's murder. For a moment, we understood each other, the Pictish Prince and I. "Terre d'Ange stands under threat of invasion," I said softly. "If you regain the throne of Alba, the Master of the Straits will allow you to cross. That is the price. Your aid, to secure the D'Angeline throne. That is the price of wedding the Queen of Terre d'Ange, my lord."

Drustan looked at the Twins.

They shifted on their thrones, the Lords of the Dalriada. Grainne leaned forward, while Eamonn leaned back, not meeting the Cruarch's gaze.

"What do you say, my brethren?" Drustan asked it in Cruithne. His dark eyes gleamed. "You have waited for a sign, Eamonn. Here it is. Let us take up the sword, and Alba will flock to our side. Maelcon's men will run before us, and the Master of the Straits will reward us, laying the waters as calm as a carpet. What do you say?"

"*I* say—" Grainne drew a deep breath.

"No." Eamonn cut her off, tugging at his torque, speaking slowly in Cruithne. "No." He shook his head, stubborn as an ox. "The risk is too great, and the gain to little. Do they bring an army? Do they bring swords?" He opened the coffer, showing its contents, shimmering and harmless, redolent with spice. Grainne murmured appreciatively, drawing out a length of gold-shot green silk. "No!" Eamonn drew the coffer back, nearly closing the lid on his sister's hand. "Fair words and baubles!"

"Dagda Mor!" Grainne snapped at him, eyes flashing. "You are a coward and a fool! *I* say—"

"You say what you like!" he flared back at her, slipping back into Eiran. "Unless we both say it, the Dalriada go nowhere! We are hard-put enough to hold this piece of land!"

Too much to hope I was hearing wrong; I followed it well enough, looking between them. Rousse, Joscelin and Hyacinthe watched perplexed as the Twins quarreled.

"Eamonn." Drustan raised his voice, silencing them. "You hold this land now because my father chose to honor Cinhil Ru's old promise to the Dalriada, and the folk of the Cullach Gorrym will not move against me, no, nor many of the Tarbh Cró, even if Maelcon commands the Red Bull to war. But what of your children, and your children's children?"

"Who will know their father and grandfather for a coward!" Grainne said hotly. "If we do not—"

"Enough!" Eamonn shouted at his sister, clutching his head. He glowered at Drustan. "Think you that Alban will flock to a cripple's standard, my lord?"

The Cruithne warriors murmured and one of Drustan's sisters drew a soft breath; his mother touched her arm lightly, bidding her to silence. Drustan mab Necthana laughed, showing strong white teeth, and held out his arms. The red cloak he wore slipped back, revealing the elaborate whorls of blue that tattooed his bare shoulders, braceleted his arms. "What do you think, brother? They have done before. On horseback, I have four strong legs. It is enough."

I could not help but glance at his deformity, then, though I'd resisted until that moment. In truth, though he wore boots of soft leather to conceal or protect it, one could see that his right foot twisted at the ankle, and the stunted foot bent upon itself, so that the sole did not rest upon the ground. For all that, his right leg looked as hale as the left, with lean-knotted muscle.

"Will you try my sword and see if I am fit to follow?" Drustan asked softly, and Eamonn looked away. "Then you have answered your question, brother."

I took the moment to translate quickly for the D'Angelines, recapping what had transpired. Quintilius Rousse looked unhappy. Joscelin glanced at Eamonn. "I'll try his steel," he muttered, with un-Cassiline ire. "Let him see how he likes the baubles I carry."

In the pause, the hall had erupted with a great deal of similar talk, the Cruithne and the Dalriada shoving and quarreling. Grainne was in the midst of it, shouting at one of the Picti, her sword half-unsheathed. Strange to me to see a woman armed, but she was not the only one of the Dalriada women to bear a sword; only, as I learned later, the mightiest of them. It is not uncommon among the Picti, either, though Necthana and her daughters did not ride to battle. Indeed, they were the only serene figures there, watching the proceedings with four sets of identical, wide dark eyes.

At length Eamonn stomped down from his throne shouting, and the melee broke apart, while he and his sister argued until he threw up his hands.

"It is too great a matter to decide on a moment's whim," he announced, saying it in Cruithne for my benefit, glancing at me. "We receive you and your gifts with thanks, Phèdre of Terre d'Ange. Tonight, we feast in your honor, and tomorrow we will speak again of such things. Do you agree, my Prince?"

Drustan inclined his head, but it was his mother who answered.

"That is wisely spoken, my lord Eamonn," Necthana said, in a voice deeper and even more mellifluous than her daughter's.

"Oh, he can *speak*," Grainne said contemptuously, tossing her red-gold hair, "and speak and speak, until the brehons cover their ears and beg him to cease!"

Necthana's mouth twitched as if repressing a smile. "That is a great gift, child, and no doubt. But we have guests we have granted hospitality, and they are no doubt weary from their journey. Will you not offer them rest and refreshment?"

"Dagda!" Grainne looked us over with dismay, and interest. "Yes, of course." Clapping her hands, she began to summon serving-folk about. Leaving domestic matters to his sister's control, Eamonn wrapped his cloak around him and stalked out with his insulted dignity, taking the Dalriada men with him. Prince Drustan gathered his Cruithne, speaking to them in low tones. I caught a little of it; he was urging them to go among the Dalriada, and spread the spark of glorious battle.

"Do not fear." It was a low voice at my side, soothing and musical. I turned to see Necthana and her daughters, smiling at me, Moiread the youngest of them. "They are like an ill-matched team, the Twins," Necthana said, nodding at Grainne. "She pulls at the traces, while he digs in his heels. But if you can find the balance between them, they are strong in the harness."

"How do I do that?" I asked, pleading.

But she only touched my brow, gazing into my eyes and smiling. "You will find a way. For this you were chosen."

They turned away, then, proceeding with calm from the hall. I turned to my D'Angeline companions, shrugging.

"It seems we must find a way to balance the Twins," I said wryly. "If anyone has an idea, let me know."

SEVENTY

I was given a room to share with Breidaia, the eldest of Drustan's sisters, who would be the mother of his heirs, in the Cruithne manner. Even if he and Ysandre wed, her children would never sit the throne of Alba.

They would be heirs to the D'Angeline throne instead, half-Pictish scions of Elua, raised to House Courcel. I will admit, for one born and bred to Terre d'Ange, it was a discomfiting thought.

"We are the eldest children of Earth on this soil," Breidaia announced as if divining my thoughts. Directing a servant-maid to plump the pillows, she gave me a tranquil smile. "Many thousands of years before Yeshua's birth, before he bled on the wooden gallow, before the Magdelene shed tears and Elua walked the earth, we crossed to Alba. We are the folk of the Cullach Gorrym, those who followed the Black Boar to the west, before D'Angelines knew to count time upon their fingers. When the others came, tall and fair, the Fhalair Bàn, the White Horse of Eire, the Tarbh Cró of the north, the Eidlach Òr of the south, we were here."

The Dalriada were of the White Horse, and Maelcon the Usurper of the Red Bull. Of the Eidlach Òr, the Golden Hind, I knew naught.

"And they will follow Drustan?" I asked. "All of them?"

"If the Cullach Gorrym wills," she said simply.

I was not reassured.

Breidaia bent her calm gaze upon me. "All things will be as they will. Do not fear."

It was soothing advice; but I'd seen too much to be soothed by the words of a girl no older than I, if as much. I had seen Duc Isidore d'Aiglemort ride in triumph with the Allies of Camlach, and I knew, too well, the dangerous intelligence of Waldemar Selig, whose warriors numbered in the tens of thousands, and whose shelves bore texts of the greatest of military tacticians. It had been a long time since Cinhil Ru rallied the Cruithne against the armies of Tiberium; and a pair of quarreling twins, a tattooed Prince, and a rabble of undisciplined warriors did not inspire confidence. They are like children, I thought, who reckon they know danger, until they meet it face-to-face.

Then I remembered Moiread's dream, and was unsure.

"Come." Breidaia cocked her head, listening. "They are making ready to feast. Shall we join them?"

Such was my mood as we proceeded to the hall of the Lords of the Dalriada, as despairing and reckless as Quintilius Rousse at the helm, racing through the mist toward unseen shores.

If the Twins were at odds on their course, they were agreed on their display of hospitality. Full half the ship had been brought to land while we rested, and the hall was crammed with guests, D'Angeline, Dalriada and Cruithne alike, loud and celebratory. It was a strange thing, to mark the presence of so many D'Angelines among foreigners, honed features shining like cut gems among unpolished stone.

They got on well enough, I daresay; sailors are a garrulous lot, and more used than most to the barriers that language presents. We feasted well, for Alba is a fertile land, and the Dalriada boasted of the wealth of it. Simple fare, by D'Angeline standards, but in abundance; venison and fish stew, spring greens, a curded cheese that was surprisingly sweet, pottage and crude wine. There is a drink they make too, *uisghe*, that burns at first with a fiery harshness, but is smooth at the second sip, tasting of peat and herbs.

As the night wore on, the *uisghe* flowed freely, and the bards of Dalriada entertained us with long poems that I translated for the D'Angelines. They are mighty talkers, the Dalriada; I understood Grainne's insult better. Then Quintilius Rousse, ruddy with drink, responded with a D'Angeline sailor's song that I blushed to translate. If I was unsure before then, I'd no doubt when it was done; there was no shame among the Dalriada or the Cruithne as regards such things. They clapped their hands and shouted, picking up the chorus.

It reminded me, a little, of the Skaldi, but it was different, here. If naught else, I noted that the women were as bold as the men, eyeing the D'Angeline sailors with undisguised interest. No few of them left ere the night was over, Rousse's men following where they led with willing grins, or at least those with a taste for women. D'Angeline, Dalriada; it mattered naught, for they'd been a long time stranded in Kusheth, with no company save each other.

When Rousse's song was done, Eamonn's champion, Carraig, a Dalriada warrior who towered over the others, made a half-jesting challenge to Joscelin, poking with amusement at his vambraces and gesturing, then clearing a space in the center of the hall, drawing his sword and waggling it tauntingly.

The Twins shouted approval, quaffing *uisghe*; Dalriada and D'Angeline urged the fight. The Cruithne looked amused. Joscelin, with considerable forbearance, glanced at me with raised eyebrows.

On a whim, I looked to Drustan mab Necthana.

As before, there was understanding between us. I read the query in his dark eyes, so oddly grave in his blue-marqued features. Can your man win? I nodded, imperceptibly. His shoulders lifted in a faint shrug, one hand cautioning temperance. I rose to my feet and addressed the Twins.

"Let it be seen, then, what manner of sword the D'Angelines bring, my lords," I said, *uisghe* rendering my tongue fluent. "But let no blood be spilled, to stain our quest! Let he who is disarmed surrender with honor!"

They accepted the terms with cheers, and Joscelin rose smoothly, bowing with crossed arms. Quintilius Rousse made his drunken way to my side.

"Thought Cassilines only fought to defend," he said, slurring his words a little.

I shrugged. "The Prefect of the Cassiline Brotherhood abjured him. Joscelin's blade is sworn to Ysandre."

"Ahhh." His eyes gleamed, and we watched.

Carraig swung his sword over his head in a blur, roaring; it descended as he rushed forward, mountain-tall. Joscelin's daggers flashed free of their sheaths, crossed hilts catching and deflecting the blade. The revelers laughed as he spun gracefully out of the way, and Carraig staggered, gathering himself for a second charge. Steel clanged; the sword slid harmlessly off one vambrace. Joscelin moved sideways, evasive as water, reversing his grip; with a motion too subtle for the eye to follow, he brought the hilt of one dagger down on Carraig's sword-hand, which opened in anguish, while he swept his leg against the back of the Dalriada's knees.

It made a considerable clatter, Carraig falling, sword spinning from his grip. By the time he realized he was on the floor, Joscelin's crossed daggers were at his throat. Eamonn's champion yielded with better grace than I'd expected. When Joscelin bowed and sheathed his daggers, Carraig rose, seizing him in a roaring embrace and pounding his back.

"We've impressed them with that, at least." Hyacinthe appeared at my elbow, a lopsided grin on his face, black eyes bright with *uisghe*. Not an ounce of jealousy in his tone; I saw why, clear enough. Moiread stood at his side, calm and smiling. A waking dreamer, indeed. The daughters of Necthana had an interest in him. He swayed a little on his feet, looking at me as if he wondered whether I would bid him stay or go, and not sure which he hoped.

"We have that, at least." I brushed my hand over his hair. I'd drunk too much, or not enough, to have it out with him. "Go where you will, Prince of Travellers," I said, with scarce-impaired dignity, or so I thought. "I'm about the Queen's business." His eyes gleamed, and he made a bow, disappearing with Moiread.

I looked back; Joscelin was firmly ensconced among the Dalriada warriors, hardly displeased by their lauding, laughing and struggling for words as he attempted to explain the Cassiline discipline. Quintilius Rousse had vanished; in his place were three young Dalriada men, falling over each other and shoving to offer me another mug of *uisghe*.

To those who have never served, untrained, as a royal ambassador, I offer this advice: Be wary of strange drink.

Unfortunately, I had not the benefit of such wisdom.

Parts of that night run together in my memory; others, alas, stand out clear. I remember Eamonn wading into the fray, shoving his men aside to offer me a seat and *uisghe* and somewhat else. I remember Grainne quarreling with him, red-gold hair like a mantle on her shoulders, eyes sharp with amusement. They squabbled like children, the Twins, I remember that.

They squabbled over me.

I must have said somewhat, at some point; what, I do not know, but I acceded to one of them, or both. That was what set them to arguing, though they needed little excuse. "Everyone is prettier than you, Eamonn," I remember Grainne laughing. "I should know what it's like, for a change. Isn't that what D'Angelines do?" She looked at me for an answer; I must have said yes. It is true enough, after all. Eamonn said something surly, which I do not recall, and Grainne looked mockingly at him. "Anyway, it is for the guest to choose."

So I did.

In the morning, I woke with a splitting head.

"Are they all like that, D'Angelines? Taught to do so?"

The words were spoken in Eiran, which had seemed perfectly comprehensible to me the night before. Now, I had to grope at the meaning, puzzling out the dialect as I struggled to collect myself from the rumpled sheets and deal with one of the Lords of the Dalriada, already fully awake, alert and clothed.

"No, my lady," I said in reserved Cruithne, pushing

my hair back to meet her curious regard. "Not all."

"Pity," she said mildly, tying her kirtle.

A small figure raced into the room and leapt onto the bed, burrowing amid the coverings; the boy Brennan, who I had guessed by now was her son. I winced, my head pounding.

"Go gently," Grainne said indulgently to him. She sat on the edge of the bed, ruffling his red-gold hair, gazing amused at me. "I am not sure I like it, to know someone better than I at such things. You serve to remind me, though, that some things are best done in leisure, not haste. Is it how you are trained to acknowledge royalty?"

I would have laughed, if my head hadn't ached so. Brennan squirmed out from under his mother's hand and wormed behind me, small fingers tracing the marque up my spine with a child's curiosity. "No, my lady," I said again, pressing fingertips to my temples. "It is what *I* am trained to do." I thought ruefully of the night, of the further wedge I'd driven between the quarreling Twins. "I'm not fit for diplomacy. I told the Queen as much."

"You're adept at tongues." One corner of Grainne's mouth curled in a smile. She rose to regard herself in a small mirror, thrusting a jeweled pin in her glorious hair. "Anyway, I've given you the key to Eamonn."

"My lady?" The child's poking was distracting me from my headache, but I failed to understand.

"He could never bear for me to have aught that he lacked," Grainne said complacently. "A horse, a sword, a brooch . . . whatever it was, Eamonn must have as much, or finer."

"You say he will go to war for me?"

Her look was kindly condescending. "Left to choose, Eammon will not decide, neither yea nor nay, until Macha's bull gives milk. For you alone . . . no. But it will gall him, to be denied what I have had. That is the key,

Phèdre nó Delaunay." She took care with my name, saying it slow, then smiled. "Though you are almost, *almost* worth a war."

I dragged myself up to sit cross-legged, raking my hands through my hair. Melisande's diamond hung about my throat, the only thing to adorn me. "Did you do it for that?" I asked.

"No." Grainne smiled again, clapping her hands and summoning Brennan to her. He clung to her waist and grinned up at his mother. "For me." She touseled his hair, and gave me a considering look. "Do you think your ship-captain would breed strong sons and daughters?"

"Quintilius Rousse?" I laughed, then caught myself. "Yes, my lady. That, I do."

"Good." Her grey-green eyes glinted in the sunlight. "Tomorrow, we may die, so it is best to live today. And some things *are* best decided in haste. Maybe you can teach my brother as much."

If you can find the balance between them . . .

"It seems," I said, "I will have to try."

SEVENTY-ONE

Mercifully, I was not the only one suffering the after-effects of *uisghe* that day; most of the D'Angelines were bleary-eyed, and no few of the Dalriada. Not all, it seemed, had Grainne's constitution. Even some of the Cruithne nursed aching heads, although Drustan was not among them.

None of them, however, had to face Joscelin Verreuil's glare of disapproval.

"It is a *disgrace*," he hissed at me, as we sat to break

our fast. "Do you think every problem can be solved by falling into someone's bed? Do you think it's for *that* that Ysandre de la Courcel chose you?"

"Forgive me," I muttered sourly, propping my head in my hands. "I've not your skill with a sword, to resolve matters that way. Anyway, I might not have fallen there, if you hadn't left me, all of you. Mayhap you should try it. It might improve your mood."

"I have never—" he began grimly.

I looked at him.

"That was different." He said it quietly.

"Yes." I rubbed my aching temples. "It was. And this was what happens when you send a Servant of Naamah to do a diplomat's job, and ply her with strong drink."

Joscelin drew breath to speak, then looked at my miserable state. A muscle in his cheek twitched that might have been a repressed smile. "At least you had the choosing of it. Or so I hear."

"Oh, I chose, all right."

He glanced at Grainne, laughing at the head of the table and eating with good appetite, tearing bread from a loaf. "She does have a certain barbarian splendor."

I laughed, then stopped. It hurt my head.

By noon, I had recovered enough to accept Drustan's invitation to tour the Dalriada settlement, which was called Innisclan. We went on horseback, the Pictish Prince and four of his Cruithne, Joscelin and I. He pointed out the holdings, the smithy and the mill, the vast cattle herds of the Dalriada that spread across the land, grazing on the bright spring grass.

A peaceful scene; but the moist warmth in the air made my blood run cold. The season was hastening on, each day that fleeted past bringing us closer to summer and war.

"Where lies your home, my lord?" I asked Drustan.

"There." Turning his horse, he pointed unerringly to the southeast. Like all exiles, he carried within him a map that ever marked the way homeward. "Bryn Gorrydum, where Maelcon sits upon my throne." He bared his teeth in a white snarl, frightful in his blue-marqued face. "I will mount his head above my door!"

Elua help me, I could only pray he did. "Will Eamonn accede, do you think?" I asked him.

Drustan shook his head, losing his fearsome expression. "There is no fiercer fighter when he is cornered, but Eamonn does not ride into danger. If Maelcon ever came for me, Eamonn would fight until his dying breath. But his nature is to defend, not attack."

"If Grainne chose against him, would the Dalriada follow?"

He gave me a speculative look. "Some of them would, yes. Your warrior's skill has fired their hearts." He inclined his head to Joscelin, who smiled politely, not understanding. "But Grainne will not do this. Bold as an eagle she may be, but even she cannot cut the bond between them." Resting his reins on the pommel of his saddle, he looked back to the east, homeward and beyond, to the distant shores of Terre d'Ange, and his voice changed. "I dreamed of a bond, once. Two kingdoms, side by side, in open and free alliance. Two thrones, bound with the silken thread of love, and not the chains of necessity." He smiled a little. "So we said, in my very bad Caerdicci, that I have not voiced even to you, and her Cruithne, which was little better. But we understood one another. That is what we dreamed, Ysandre de la Courcel and I. Does she still?"

I had not, I think, understood what Ysandre had told me; she had spoken of it indirectly, couching the meaning in the words of politics. I understood, then. She loved him, with all the wayward fervor of the sixteen-year-old girl she'd been when they met.

And he felt the same.

"Yes, my lord," I whispered. "She does."

His dark eyes returned to mine, dwelling on my face. Earth's oldest children, his sister had said. Perhaps, after all, he was not such an unfit match for the Queen of Terre d'Ange. "I will wait a week," Drustan mab Nec-thana said calmly, "for Eamonn to decide. Then, if his heart is unchanged, I will leave, and take up the banner of the Cullach Gorrym to march upon Bryn Gorrydum. There are those who will follow, though not enough, I think, without the Dalriada. You will take your ship and return to Terre d'Ange. Tell Ysandre I will come if I live."

There was naught to say; I bowed my head. Drustan turned his horse, calling his men, and we set out for the Hall of Innisclan. I translated our conversation for Joscelin as we rode.

"I am going to do somewhat else," I said then, "that you will not like. Just . . . abide it, and hold your tongue. I swear to you, on Delaunay's name, I've a reason for it."

For three days, we met and talked. Word of our arrival had spread, and Dalriada clan-lords appeared daily in Innisclan, until the hall could scarce hold them. Tall and fierce, all of them, in many-colored woolens and the fine, ornate goldwork on which they pride themselves. Some came ready for war, hair stiffened into white crests with lime; Rousse had spoken of it, but it was the first I'd seen.

But the Twins were the Lords of the Dalriada, and while Eamonn held out, there would be no war. And that he did; not alone, either, for there were those among the

Dalriada who'd no will to risk war for the Cruithne's sake.

"A fool's errand, and one we're like to return from empty-handed," Quintilius Rousse said grimly, observing the proceedings. I'd spoken that day until my mouth was dry and my mind a tangled knot of words, D'Angeline and Cruithne coiled like a serpent's nest. Eamonn listened, and watched me with hot eyes, caring nothing for what I said. I am no orator, to sway men's hearts with words. My skills lie elsewhere.

"We've four days, yet." I pressed the heels of my hands to my eyes, fighting exhaustion. Three days of politely declining Eamonn's unsubtle interest, pretending not to notice. I couldn't even count the other offers. I dropped my hands and grinned at Rousse. "Are you so quick to leave the Lady Grainne's bed?"

He blushed all over his scarred face, muttering, "Wants to get a child."

"I know. She thinks you're good stock. She's very direct in her desires." Actually, they were rather well-matched, but I thought it privately.

"Sibeal had a dream," Hyacinthe announced, referring to Necthana's middle daughter. "She saw you, Phèdre. You were holding a scale, tipped all to one side."

"You understood this." I raised my brows at him.

He looked at me nonplussed. "They are teaching me Cruithne. And I am teaching them about the *dromonde*. *You* have been busy elsewhere, doing the Queen's business."

"Yes, well, tell your dreamers that the scale is not yet ready to balance," I said wryly. "Do they see you as well, in their dreams, O Prince of Travellers?"

Hyacinthe shook his head, frowning slightly. "Only once. Breidaia dreamed me on an island, and asked if I was born there. Naught else."

"Passing strange," I said, forgetting about it in the next instant, as Drustan beckoned me to spin tales of the glories of a D'Angeline alliance for an eager-looking Dalriada clan-lord. We'd done a good job of that, at least. I made my way across the hall, feeling Eamonn's gaze at my back. So it had been, ever since I'd bedded his sister.

But I'd spoken true to Hyacinthe. If I was no diplomat, still, I knew to gauge a patron. Eamonn was a slow man, as cautious and deliberate as his sister was impetuous. He'd cast his luck and lost the first night; he'd be wary of approaching the brink. And I needed him to be desperate.

Four days, and then five. Grainne and Eamonn had shouting matches, backed by their factions. I saw the first quarrel between Dalriada and Cruithne, when one of Drustan's men was set upon by three outlander Dalriada. And I saw then why Eamonn had declined to test Drustan's steel. Outnumbered and outsized, the Cruithne warrior fought with a cunning and speed I'd never witnessed, holding his own until Drustan came at a run, half-gaited and furious, shoving Dalriada swords aside with his bare hands.

They could have killed him, then; they didn't, looking with fear and respect at his blue warrior's marques, the red cloak and the gold torque of his birthright, the Cruarch of Alba.

"Tell them tomorrow," I said to him when the Dalriada had apologized and gone. "Not in council, but after, when they're feasting in the hall. Tell them what you have decided."

He looked at me and nodded. "I will do as you wish."

So it was that it happened on the sixth day.

As on the others, nothing was decided, the Twins at odds. Still, they honored the laws of hospitality, fêting their guests. It was in the hall, before the roaring fire, that Drustan rose to address Grainne and Eamonn.

"My lords of the Dalriada," he said, bowing. "You have given shelter to me and my people, and I am ever grateful. But I have sworn a pledge." He held up his right hand, firelight gleaming from the gold of Rolande's signet. "I must honor it, or die trying. A usurper sits upon my uncle's throne, mine by right, my father-slaying cousin, Maelcon. On the morrow, I ride east, to reclaim that which is mine. And if I live, we cross the Straits."

Pandemonium erupted in the hall, noisy and familiar. I waited, then made my way to the Twins' thrones.

"My lords," I said, kneeling. "We thank you for your hospitality. Prince Drustan has spoken. We will depart on the morrow, carrying his words to our Queen."

Grainne gave me a regal nod and turned away, concealing an amused glint in her grey-green eyes. She knew what I was about to try; she'd given me the key. I stood and made my curtsy, with all the grace of Cereus House, and turned to leave.

"Wait," Eamonn protested, following to catch my shoulder. "You need not depart in such haste, my lady! At least . . . at least drink with me, will you not? You have not . . . you *cannot* . . ." He shot an evil glance at his sister. "We are alike, she and I, born of one womb! You cannot favor one over the other!"

"My lord!" I shook off his hand. "I am the Queen's ambassador! Would you treat me so?"

"I have never forced any woman!" Snatching his hand back, he glared at me. "But how can you choose so? It is not right!"

I shrugged. "My lord," I said mildly, "as you desire D'Angelines for our beauty, so do we admire aught in others, boldness and daring. Such, your sister possesses."

"And you say I do not?" Eamonn was working himself into a fury, features wild and distorted. "You say I lack courage?"

A small crowd was beginning to gather. Joscelin worked through it unobtrusively, making his way to my side.

Feeling his reassuring presence at my shoulder, I looked at Eamonn and shrugged again, keeping my face expressionless. "I do not say it, my lord. Your actions speak for me."

"Rather louder than you imagined, Eamonn." That was Grainne's voice, sharp and mocking; it drew laughter. He turned to glare at her, his face near purple with anger, hands fisting at his sides. She looked back at him, her face a cool reflection of his, red-gold brows arched. "You have made your bed; do you cry now, that you lie in it alone?"

"If it is daring you want," he said through grinding teeth, "*I* will show you daring!" Thrusting one fist into the air, he cried out. "The Dalriada ride to war, at the side of Drustan mab Necthana!"

Cheers erupted; if there were groans, they were swept aside in the wave of jubilation. Eamonn pumped his fist, shouting, wholly caught up in it. For a moment, I think, he forgot about me; I had been a catalyst to this deep rivalry between the Twins, no more. But he remembered, and turned to me with bright eyes, grinning.

"What do you say to *that*, D'Angeline?" he asked, catching my arms. "Was *that* daring enough?"

A horse, a sword, a brooch . . . it was a boy's glee, at a victory won. It made me smile, despite myself. "Yes, my lord," I said, meaning it. "It is enough."

At my side, Joscelin heaved a sigh.

Thus did it come to pass that I bedded the Twins, Lords of the Dalriada. Eamonn kept his grin for days, going about the business of preparing for war with it plastered on his face, foolish and blissful. I daresay I served him better than I had his sister, having been considerably more sober. Although Grainne had no complaints, to be sure; she caught me in the hall one day and slid a gold bracelet over my arm, rich with the fine, intricate knotwork they do.

"For luck," she said, amused. "This goddess you serve, she is a powerful one."

I hoped so.

We were riding to war.

SEVENTY-TWO

No D'Angeline need march, of course; it was not *our* battle. We could have set sail, gone the long way around, avoiding the Straits to set course for lower Siovale. But it would have been a coward's course, and in truth, we'd have had no word to bear. By the time we made landfall and won through to Ysandre, the Cruithne would have crossed the Straits or died.

Drustan was willing to ride to the aid of Terre d'Ange; we D'Angelines could do no less for the Cullach Gorrym. Quintilius Rousse left half his men with the ship, with instructions to bring word to the Queen if we failed.

The rest of us would follow the battle.

The Dalriada ride to war as if to a party, laughing and shouting and jesting, decked out in splendour and finery. The lords fight in the old style still, with war-chariots; it was something to behold, a Hellene tale sprung to life. The Cruithne are quieter, but just as deadly, fierce eyes and battle-grins gleaming in their blue-whorled faces.

Twenty warriors, Dalriada and Cruithne paired in twos, rode in advance on the swiftest horses, leaving at angles in a vast semi-circle to compass Alba. They carried the twin banners under which they fought, the Fhalair Bàn, the White Mare of Eire, white on a green field, and the Cullach Gorrym, the Black Boar on a field of scarlet. We cheered as they left, twisting in the saddle to wave bold farewells, knowing themselves most likely to die. If they succeeded, they would spread word, bringing allies to swell our ranks as we marched eastward.

Some would succeed. Some would die.

Drustan watched them go in silence. Fifty men, no more, had come with him to Innisclan, fighting free of Maelcon's forces, protecting the Cruarch's heir, his mother and sisters. A full two hundred had begun the journey. His blood-father had been among them, slain at the hands of the Tarbh Cró. Maelcon's mother, Foclaidha, was of the Brugantii, who followed the Red Bull; it was her kin who came, overrunning Bryn Gorrydum, starting the bloodbath.

Setting Maelcon on the throne.

No wonder, I thought, the Lioness of Azzalle had sought to treat with Foclaidha and Maelcon. They would have understood one another. I wondered about Marc de Trevalion, then, and whether he'd been recalled from exile, whether or not his daughter Bernadette was willing to marry Ghislain de Somerville, whether or not Marc agreed. I wondered whether or not war was declared, if d'Aiglemort was at large, and about the deadly vipers of House Shahrizai. I wondered, indeed, if Ysandre still held the throne. Who was to say? I wondered if the Royal House of Aragon had sent troops, and how many.

I wondered what Waldemar Selig knew.

It was a terrible thing, to be so far and know so little, but I could not help wondering. I rode with Hyacinthe and Joscelin, Necthana and her daughters, and others of the Twins' household, behind the advancing army. We'd have choked on their dust, in a D'Angeline summer, but it was late spring in Alba and a rain fell near every day, damping the dust and greening the earth. A full mile wide, our front line stretched, straggling and undisciplined, travelling at the foot-soldiers' pace.

We marched and marched, and ate what we could, the army foraging while the peasants cursed. Drustan's Cruithne shot for the pot, their arrows finding game with deadly accuracy. None of his folk ever went hungry.

And the allies came, flocking to the banner of the Culloch Gorrym.

Handfuls of Decanatii and Corvanicci, Ordovales and Dumnonii, flying the Black Boar, and our numbers grew. And then a wild band of Sigovae and Votadae from the north, defiantly waving the Red Bull; fair-haired, with height and lime-crested manes like the Dalriada and the blue masques of the Cruithne; and bad news, too, of tribes among the Tarbh Cró loyal to Maelcon, and six of Drustan's outriders slain.

Maelcon knew; Maelcon was raising an army.

Maelcon was waiting.

A rumor reached us; the south had declared for Maelcon, and was rising up to burn the homesteads of those to the north who'd left to follow the Cullach Gorrym. We nearly had a mutiny, then, as half the tribes of the Cullach Gorrym bid to turn back, until we saw a large force on the horizon.

The Twins were ready to attack. It was Drustan made them wait, holding desperately in place, until he saw who approached: Trinovantii, Atribatii, Canticae—folk of the Eidlach Òr, flying the Golden Hind on green, and above it the Black Boar, declaring their allegiance. It was a false rumor. Battle they'd seen, and lost hundreds of warriors, but Maelcon's supporters had given way to those who remembered their ancient blood-debt to Cinhil Ru's line.

So we made our way toward Bryn Gorrydum.

"Boy's amazing," Quintilius Rousse said, settling by our fire with a grunt. He'd a pain in his joints that troubled him in damp weather. "He never sleeps. Maelcon's army out there, Elua knows where, and he's riding up and down the lines, a word for every man among 'em, and the women too. What kind of damn-fool people let their women ride to war?"

"Would you try to stop them?" I asked, thinking of Grainne. Rousse gave me a dour look.

"I would if I wedded one," he said sourly. "Listen, I've been thinking. Mayhap it would be for the best if I brought the lads in, had them guard you, my lady. When the battle breaks, you shouldn't be without protection."

Sibeal, Necthana's middle daughter, spoke.

Quintilius Rousse looked at me. I translated. "If you will not die for us," I said slowly, "you cannot ask us to die for you."

"I don't want anyone to die," Quintilius Rousse said, scowling at her, waiting for me to translate, little need though she seemed to have of it. "But least of all, my lady Queen's ambassador."

I wrapped my arms around my knees and gazed at the night sky, stars hidden under a blanket of cloud. "My lord Admiral," I said, "if you are asking me for the sake of your men, I say yes, let them do this thing, for I've no wish to see D'Angeline blood shed on foreign soil, nor to bring word of your death to Ysandre de la Courcel. But if you are asking for my sake, I say no." I looked at him. "I cannot countenance it. Not with what we are asking of them."

He cursed me, then, with a sailor's fluency. Delaunay's name was repeated no few times, with several choice comments about honor and idiocy. I waited him out.

"We will be well behind the lines of battle, my lord Admiral," I said. "I take no risk that the Prince's own mother does not share. And I have Joscelin."

Quintilius Rousse cursed some more, got up and paced, stabbing one thick finger at Joscelin. "You will stay with her?" he asked, brows bristling. "You swear it, Cassiline? You will never leave her side?"

Joscelin bowed, his vambraces flashing in the firelight. "I have sworn it, my lord," he said softly. "To damnation, and beyond."

"I ask it for your sake." Quintilius Rousse fetched up in front of me and drew a ragged breath. "My men are itching to fight Albans. They've seen no action since we fought the hellions of Khebbel-im-Akkad. But I swear to you, Phèdre nó Delaunay, if harm comes to you in this battle, your lord's shade will plague me until my dying! And I've no wish to have it on my head."

"She will not die." It was Hyacinthe's voice, hollow with the *dromonde*. He turned his head, black gaze meeting Rousse's, blurred and strange with sight. "Her Long Road is not ended. Nor yours, Admiral."

"Do you say we will be victorious?" Rousse's voice took on a jesting edge; Hyacinthe's gift made him uneasy, the more so since it had proved true. "Do you say so, Tsingano?"

Hyacinthe shook his head, black ringlets swinging. "I see you returning to water, my lord, and Phèdre as well. More, I cannot see."

Quintilius Rousse cursed again, at greater length. "So be it! We'll fight for Ysandre's blue lad, then. Let Alban blood taste D'Angeline steel." He bowed to me, his scarred features suffused with irony. "May Elua bless you, my lady, and your Tsingano witch-boy and Cassiline whatsit protect you. We will meet again on the water, or in the true Terre d'Ange that lies beyond."

"Blessed Elua be with you," I murmured, kneeling and rising. I embraced him and kissed his scarred cheek. "No Queen nor King e'er had a truer servant, my lord Quintilius Rousse."

He blushed; I could feel the heat of it beneath my lips. "Nor a stranger ambassador," he said gruffly, embracing me. "Nor better, girl. You've brought 'em here, haven't you? Elua be with you."

We slept that night under the clouded skies, while the camp stirred, sentries startled at the slightest noise and Cruithne scouts prowled the perimeter, searching for Maelcon's army. We were less than a day's march from Bryn Gorrydum.

No word had come when the crepuscular light that heralds dawn seeped over Alba, but Drustan roused the army all the same. They turned out in a formless horde: some six thousand foot, seven hundred horse, and fifty chariots or more. We were encamped at the verge of a young copse, alongside a deep valley. Beyond the valley, it was straight onward to Bryn Gorrydum.

Drustan sat his brown horse with a straight back, his head high, the scarlet cloak flowing over its haunches. He rode slowly back and forth, letting the army see him, letting them know he would not hide his identity from Maelcon's forces.

"Brothers and sisters!" he cried. "You know why we are here. We come to restore the throne of Alba to its rightful heir! We come to seize it from the hands of Maelcon the Usurper, whose hands are red with his own father's blood!"

They cheered, hoisting spears, rattling swords against their bucklers; the Dalriada, I think, cheered loudest of all. Eamonn and Grainne led their folk, war-chariots side by side, as if awaiting the start of a race, their teams baring teeth and snapping at one another.

"I am Drustan mab Necthana, and you know my line and my kin. But I tell you now, all who stand here with me today, you are my kin, and I name you brother and sister, each one. When the sun breaks over the trees . . ."

A hush spread through the army, men and women falling silent, one by one. We had climbed onto a narrow outcrop behind the lines, those of us not fighting, but Drustan's kin had the place of honor, at the highest part. I could see well enough to make him out over the crush of warriors, but not beyond.

It was his sister, Breidaia, who let out a cry and pointed.

We crowded to her side, all of us, and looked.

There, at the edge of the copse, where the young beech trees were leafing golden and a thin mist rose from the warm, moist ground, a black boar emerged.

It was enormous. How long boars live, I do not know, but this one must have been ancient to have grown to such size. Its bulk loomed against the slender trees. It raised its black snout, scenting the air; its tusks could have harrowed a field. Someone made a faint sound of disbelief, and I recognized my own voice. I swear, I could smell its rank odor on the morning mist. The black boar glared through the grey dawn with small, fiery eyes. Six thousand and some Pictish and Eiran warriors stared back at it in awe-stricken silence.

A shout arose; a single, choked shout. The mighty boar wheeled with a fearful grunt, heading back into the copse.

It ran half-gaited and lame.

Almost seven thousand throats, giving voice to a single cry. Drustan mab Necthana's face, blue-marqued and savage, his black eyes shining as he drew his sword, his

fierce shout rising over the vast wave of the army's ululation.

"Follow the Cullach Gorrym!"

With a fearful din, they charged.

There was no discipline to it, no strategy, no plan.
Drustan's army charged as they were assembled, a bel-
ligerant horde, foot-soldiers outracing the horse as they
reached the copse, the chariots wheeling, seeking broad
enough passage. The beech woods full, suddenly, of
howling soldiers, bursting onto the verge of the valley.

What they found there, I know, for I heard it later; at
the base of the valley, Maelcon's army, that had crept
stealthily through the night, hoping to surprise them at
dawn. In another ten minutes, they'd have done it, coming round to flank us on both sides; and Drustan had bid
fair to speak for that long, if not for the black boar.

Do not discount the Cullach Gorrym.

We heard the sound of it, those of us left behind, a
terrible clash of arms, death-cries arising, as steel beat
upon steel. Trapped at the base of the valley, Maelcon's
men died, as thousands of the followers of the Cullach
Gorrym poured down the green sides of the hill; and
Maelcon's men fought, desperate and caught, slaying
hundreds as they died.

Now, I know; then, I did not. I looked at Hyacinthe,
saw his face blurred and terrified, sight-blind eyes turned
toward the battle.

"What do you see?" I asked, shaking him. "What do
you see!"

"Death." He answered me in a whisper, turning his
dromonde-stricken gaze upon me. "Death."

I looked at him and past him and saw something else.

A party of the Tarbh Cró, red-haired Cruithne and fair,
faces tattooed blue, in well-worn arms and mounted, under the standard of the Red Bull.

"Maelcon was right," one said, drawing his sword and gesturing; they spread out to encircle us. "Take them hostage."

Not us, but Necthana; Necthana and her daughters, Drustan's mother and sisters. With whom we stood, all of us, trapped on our rocky vantage.

They were Cruithne, the women; if they did not ride to battle, still, they could shoot, as well as the men, and better. I'd seen it. But their bows lay at the campsite, only a few yards away. And between it, and us, stood Maelcon's men. We were none of us armed.

Except Joscelin.

Almost without thinking, I looked to him, knowing, already, what I would see. He was in motion, unhesitating, the morning sun reflecting bright steel as his daggers came free; his vambraces flashed like silver, and he picked a spot halfway down the outcropping and bowed.

"In Cassiel's name," he said softly. "I protect and serve."

And they attacked.

Two fell, then three, then five; there were too many, and they swarmed the sides of the rock, dismounting, blades out and swinging. Hyacinthe swore and scrabbled for stones, hurling them with a street-fighter's accuracy. A small figure, dark and quick, slipped over the side of the outcrop. One of the Tarbh Cró gained the summit and lunged at me, whirling his sword; I ducked and got behind him, I don't know how, and shoved. He stumbled back into his comrades, laughing.

"Joscelin!" I shouted. "Draw your sword!"

He paused, mid-battle, glancing at me; I saw it, in his quick blue gaze, the memory of Skaldia, his oath betrayed. Then his face hardened, he rammed his daggers into their twin sheaths, and his sword rang free of its scabbard.

A single lithe form slipped past Joscelin, swift and darting. He started, and caught himself, fighting like a dervish.

"Fall back!" the leader of the Tarbh Cró party cried in harsh Cruithne; they obeyed, retreating to their horse. He had guessed aright. Joscelin, unwilling to give up the advantage of height, awaited on the rocks, his angled sword reflecting sunlight across their faces.

That was when the arrows began to sing.

It was Moiread who had gained the camp; Moiread, Necthana's youngest, a full quiver at hand, shooting grim and deadly, little more than a girl. Two of the Tarbh Cró dropped before their leader cursed and fumbled for the butt of his spear. "Never mind hostages!" he shouted. "Kill them all!"

With that, he cast his spear.

At Moiread.

I saw it catch her, pierce her through the middle, both hands rising to circle the shaft, gasping as she fell backward. And I heard two cries: Hyacinthe's, broken-hearted, and a second cry, like the sound of dying— Necthana, hands covering her eyes. Moiread's sisters keened, low and grieving.

One other shout, clarion, splitting the morning.

I had seen Joscelin fight against the Skaldi; nothing, I thought, could match it. I was wrong. Like a falling star, he descended on the Tarbh Cró, a Cassiline berserker, his sword biting and slashing like a silver snake. They fell before him, wounds bursting open in bright splashes of blood; fell, and died, still scrabbling for their spears.

How many? Twenty, I had counted. Most fell to Joscelin, save the two Moiread had slain. Not all. Necthana and her daughters, Breidaia and Sibeal; they flung themselves into the fray, with keen little daggers. Four, I think, died at their hands. Maybe five, or six. There were two that Hyacinthe finished, drawing a boot-knife, the Prince of Travellers.

I, shaking, killed none.

So it was that Drustan found us, the Cruarch of Alba, woad-patterned arms splashed to the elbows with gore, his face grimly exultant, the brown horse lathered and blown. The victorious army plunged raggedly through the copse, shouting behind him. He drew up, looked at his mother and his living sisters, their similar faces telling the same grief; and Moiread, the youngest, her smile forevermore stilled. "Ah, no. No."

We gathered to one side; Joscelin kneeling in Cassiline penance, Hyacinthe with bowed head. Necthana rose, grave and sorrowing. "The Cullach Gorrym has taken his due," she said quietly. "My son, who rules in Alba?"

Drustan turned his head; a chariot plunged toward him, Eamonn's, his face streaked with dust and blood. Behind the chariot bounced a corpse, a large young man, red-haired, his dead face locked in a grimace, flesh abraded. Maelcon. "I do, Mother," Drustan answered softly. "The Usurper is dead."

"Slain by the Cruarch's own hand!" Eamonn shouted, lashing his team closer. Then he saw, and drew rein. "Dagda Mor, no."

"For every victory," Necthana whispered, her great dark eyes shining with a mother's tears, "there is a price."

$\mathcal{S}$EVENTY-THREE

We did not ride into Bryn Gorrydum that day, but remained at the battle-site.

Our poets do not sing of the dire aftermath of war, of the horror and stench of it, strewn bodies, entrails spilled beneath the sun and stinking, ravens plucking gobbets of flesh, the buzzing clouds of flies that gather—nor of mass graves, or the horrid effort of digging, warriors cursing flies and wiping the sweat from their brows.

Some twelve hundred of the Tarbh Cró survived to surrender; thousands had been killed. It had been a slaughter when the Cullach Gorrym had boiled over the edge of the valley; they'd been caught unprepared, on lower ground, by the very enemy they'd thought to surprise.

Only Maelcon's hostage-takers had succeeded at that, I thought, and they were all dead too.

I worked as one with Necthana and her daughters, her surviving daughters, bearing water into the battlefield, for the dying and the laboring alike. I came upon Joscelin among the latter, working grimly; the dead of Drustan's army had been gathered, eight hundred or more, and a good many of them Dalriada. They were building a cairn above them, stone by heavy stone.

He shook his head when I offered him the dipper. His face was haggard in its beauty, splashes of blood drying rust-brown and flaking on his skin, his clothing, even the thick wheat-blond cable of his braid. Poets do not sing of that, either.

"You did what you had to," I said softly to him, proffering the dipper again. "Joscelin, they drew to kill."

"I should have saved her too," he replied grimly, turning away and hoisting another stone. I let it be and moved on, offering my dipper to a Cruithne warrior who took it gratefully, gripping with both hands, throat working as he drank. And on, and on. The dying were the worst. I remembered the night Guy was killed, pressing my hands over Alcuin's wound in Delaunay's courtyard, desperately trying to staunch the warm, slick flow of blood. I remembered Alcuin, dying, in Delaunay's library, his hand clenching hard on mine.

I lived it over that day, many times. I wept for them all, Cullach Gorrym and Tarbh Cró alike, prolonging their lives with the cool water they craved, while the ravens waited to claim their due.

We made camp there that night, a thousand fires blazing. A great victory had been won; Drustan did not deny them that, their celebration, though Moiread lay on a bier in state. I heard the stories that night, from Quintilius Rousse, who came limping to the fire, eyes gleaming, a great swath of bandage about his head and one tied about the calf of his left leg.

"Blessed Elua, but it was something to see!" he said, accepting a skin of wine with a sigh of relief. "Ah, Phèdre, they scattered before us, like autumn leaves before winter's wind! And Drustan . . . Elua's Balls! He went through them like a scythe, shouting for Maelcon. Savages, they are, but . . . ah! Eamonn and Grainne, oh, you should have seen it. The foot-soldiers surrounded the chariots, and they tore into that valley like, like . . ." Words failed him, and he took a swig of wine, shaking his head. "*She* was magnificent," he said. "But Eamonn . . . he fought like a tiger, I don't mind telling you. Once that lad's made up his mind, there's no stopping him. But Drustan and Maelcon, oh, that was a battle."

He told it for us, then, how Maelcon came riding amid

the slaughter, tall and haughty atop his grey horse. How they fought, how Drustan prevailed. And how Eamonn came to lash the Usurper's corpse behind his chariot, Grainne his sister guarding him all the while, lashing her team so they raced in a circle about him.

It was a splendid tale, valiant and heroic.

Four of his D'Angeline sailors were dead.

"They knew, my lady," Quintilius Rousse said at last, catching my eye and hearing my silence. When had I become "my lady" to him? I tried to remember, and could not. "All those who sign on with me, you may believe it, know the risks. To die on land . . . it is a glorious thing. 'Tis the watery grave we fear." He looked sidelong at me in the firelight and cleared his throat. "I promised them somewhat."

"What?" He'd caught me wandering, I feared. "My lord Admiral?"

He cleared his throat again, and scratched at his bandaged skull. "I promised . . . I promised they'd be knighted, those that lived. At your own hand."

Doubly unawares, he'd caught me; I looked at him in surprise. "*My* hand?"

"You're the Queen's ambassador," he said gruffly. "They respect you. And you've the right."

"They do? I do?"

On the far side of the fire, Joscelin lifted his head. "You do, Phèdre."

It was the first he'd spoken since the cairn. I blinked at him. "If it is so, Joscelin, then you—"

"No." His voice was harsh. "Not I. I am Cassiel's servant, and a poor one at that. But they, they deserve it."

I looked bewilderedly at Quintilius Rousse. "Let it be done, then, if they truly wish it at my hands. They've earned as much, and more."

The Admiral grinned and rose awkwardly, wounded leg stiff. With one hand, he placed fingers to his lips and blew a piercing whistle. With the other, he drew his sword and gave it unto me. It weighed more than I guessed, a curved blade, clean, but the grip still slick with the sweat of battle. I stood holding it, feeling like a child at a Masque, while the D'Angeline sailors filed one by one out of the darkness beyond the firelight.

I did it, then; Rousse supplied the words and I repeated them. In Elua's name and that of Ysandre de la Courcel, Queen of Terre d'Ange, I bequeathed the title of Chevalier on twenty-odd D'Angeline sailors, feeling all the while an imposter. But their eyes, as they knelt, said I was somewhat else.

"Well done," Quintilius Rousse exclaimed, reclaiming his sword and clapping me on the back when it was done. "I'll give them a fighting-name, I will. Phèdre's Boys, I'll call this lot! Let 'em take pride in that!"

"My lord," I said, not sure if I were laughing or weeping, "I wish you wouldn't." Somewhere, beyond the fire, Joscelin's eyes shone, red-rimmed with dire amusement and unshed tears.

"We are at war, little Night-Blooming Flower," the Admiral said, his breath smelling of wine. "Or so you tell me. What did you expect? If they will fight for you, well and good. If they take pride in dying for your name, so much the better. What did you think, when you bid me on this mission?"

"I don't know," I whispered, and buried my face in my hands. I saw, in the darkness there, Waldemar Selig and twenty thousand Skaldi, the Allies of Camlach, glittering and fierce. It was not true. I had known. "Call them what you will."

He did, too. The name still stands, in the Royal Fleet. When Quintilius Rousse had departed, I sought out

Hyacinthe, who maintained an unspeaking vigil at Moiread's bier.

"I heard," he said dully, sensing my approach. "Congratulations."

"Hyacinthe." I said his name, once my *signale*, and touched his shoulder. "I never sought acclaim for it. You know that."

He heaved a sigh, shuddering all over, and his face took on an expression I recognized as human. "I know," he said softly. "It is war. But, ah, Elua! Phèdre, why? She was only a girl."

"You cared for her." I said the obvious.

"I cared for her." Hyacinthe smiled painfully, faint and wry. "Yes. Or I might have, at least. Waking dreamer, that's what she named me, isn't it? She said it, first. On the beach." Another profound shudder; I put my arms around him. His voice came muffled against my shoulder. "My own people, they cast me out for it . . . you believed, I know it's true, you talked the Admiral into as much . . . but she was the first, to touch me, to put a name to it, in welcome, Necthana's daughter . . ."

Hyacinthe wept, I wept; both of us did. War is a strange thing. All that lay unspoken between us, unaddressed, set aside for this business of war. *We are on a mission for the Queen. That, above all else* . . . I knew it, as well as he. And yet, when he turned his griefstricken face to mine, I kissed him, lowering my lips to his. His arms caught at me like a drowning man's.

At Balm House, in the Night Court, they say Naamah lay with the King of Persis out of compassion, to heal the pain in his soul. I grew up in the Night Court, I knew such things, yet never did I understand them until that night, when I drew Hyacinthe out of the circle of torchlight that surrounded Moiread's bier.

We err, those of us who have quarreled, fragmenting Naamah's desire into thirteen parts, Thirteen Houses. There are many threads, it is true, but all of one piece, woven together like a Mendacant's cloak. Comfort and atonement, sorrow and exhilaration; all of a piece, woven together on the green earth of Alba. The poets do not sing of this, either, how death begets the urge toward life. I, who knew how to take pain, took Hyacinthe's. Pain and delight, I took from him, and gave him back both, until we understood, the both of us, how they are intertwined, how one does not come without the other.

Friend, brother, lover . . . I shaped his face in darkness with my hands, his mouth with my lips, his body with my own.

He cried out, before the end; I had used somewhat of my art.

"Shhh," I whispered, stilling his cry with my fingertips, my own flesh sounding like a plucked harpstring. "Shhhh." Until I die, I swear, I will never grasp the whole of what it is to serve Naamah.

Afterward he drew away, guilt coming in the ebb of desire.

"Hyacinthe." I laid my cheek against his back, the warm brown skin, and put my arms around him. "The draught of poppies takes away pain, that the body might sleep and heal. So Naamah may send desire, that our hearts may forget for a time and heal."

"Is that somewhat else you were *taught*?" he asked, the last word harsh.

"Yes," I said softly. "By you."

He looked around at me then, turning in the circle of my arms, touching my face and shaking his head. "It wasn't supposed to be like this, Phèdre. You and I. Not like this."

"No." I smoothed his black ringlets, touched with silver by the faint starlight, and smiled ruefully. "We were to be the Queen of Courtesans and the Prince of Travellers, ruling the City of Elua from Mont Nuit to the Palace, not coupling on the sod of Alba near a blood-soaked battlefield, with six thousand wild Cruithne and grief in attendance. But here we are."

It made him smile too, a little bit. "We should go back," he said, gazing toward the torches and the blazing fires. The Dalriada and Drustan's Cruithne celebrated still. Somewhere, penned together and under guard, the remnants of Maelcon's army watched in sullen exhaustion. They'd buried their dead too, and a harder job it was, though no cairn marked their grave, for the dead were many, and the diggers few.

Others had taken up the vigil at Moiread's bier when we returned. Necthana and her daughters, who sang a mourning song, quiet and beautiful, a woven thread of chant they passed among the three of them, taking it up in turn, descant and rise. I stood and listened for a time, tears in my eyes, both for its sorrow and its loveliness.

And Joscelin, who knelt in a private Cassiline prayer. He lifted his head at our approach, giving me a bleak stare. Never mind him, I thought; taking Hyacinthe's face in both hands, I drew it down and placed a kiss on his brow.

"Grieve and be healed," I whispered. He nodded and took up his place. I too knelt, gazing at Moiread; her face serene in death as it had been in life. Necthana, Breidaia and Sibeal sang, weaving the threads of life together, victory and loss, birth and death, love and hatred. After a time, I dreamed a little, waking, as had not happened since I was a child in Cereus House, kneeling attendant for endless hours at some adult function. Another voice had joined theirs, deeper, sounding an earth-rooted refrain. I shook myself alert and saw Drustan, who had joined his mother and sisters.

He is quite beautiful after all, I thought, surprised at the thought, seeing for the first time what Ysandre had seen. His features beneath the tattooing were finely made, black hair falling straight and shining over his shoulders. Earth's oldest children. All of them sang together, poignantly lovely.

Barbarians, we call them.

When it was done, Breidaia started another melody; this, though, only the women carried. Drustan made his way to Joscelin, crouching at his side. I wondered if I should rise to translate, but the young Cruarch of Alba spoke in broken Caerdicci. *That I have not voiced even to you,* he had said to me; I understood why, hearing it.

"You . . . fight . . . for family," he said to Joscelin. "Brother."

Drustan held out his hand. Joscelin shook his head, eyes on the bier. "Your sister is dead, my King," he said in his flawless Caerdicci, learned at his father's knee. "Do me no honor. I failed you."

Shifting, Drustan met my eyes and nodded. I rose smoothly and went to join them, kneeling and bowing my head. "Thousands died this day and I could not save them," Drustan said in Cruithne, looking at Joscelin and not me. "I, born Cruarch, to give my life for my people. Do you say right was not done this day, Prince of Swords?"

I translated it all, even the title. Joscelin turned his gaze on Drustan. "My King, it is your birthright you have taken, and the death of your kin you avenged. It was rightfully done. It is I who have failed in my trust."

I translated for Drustan, adding somewhat about Cassiline vows. The Cruarch looked thoughtful and rubbed his misformed foot unselfconsciously, working at the cramped ligaments. Then he said, "You have sworn no vow to the Cullach Gorrym. Our lives we risked to regain Alba. Do not demean my sister's death in taking it from her."

Joscelin started at his words, when I spoke them. I swear, the arrogance of Cassilines, even outcasts—especially outcasts—is beyond my compass. It dawned on him though, slow and gradual, that Drustan was telling him he was overstepping the bounds of his responsibility. And even more slowly, that it might be true. Having said his piece, Drustan merely continued to look evenly at Joscelin, holding out his hand, blue-whorled and strong.

"Brother," Joscelin said in Caerdicci, and clasped Drustan's hand. "If you will have me."

No need to translate that; Drustan understood and grinned, standing and pulling Joscelin with him, embracing him.

"There you are!" A woman's voice ran out in Eiran; I looked up to see Grainne, Eamonn a step behind her. Not a cut on them, either one. It must be true that they fought like tigers. I didn't doubt it. "Ah, little sister," Grainne said sorrowing, gazing at Moiread. Plucking a jeweled dagger from her kirtle, she seized a lock of her own red-gold hair, cutting it. Approaching the bier, she laid it carefully beneath Moiread's folded hands. "We avenged you, little sister, do not doubt it, a hundred times over."

Eamonn followed suit, his hair paler than his twin's, still streaked with traces of lime. He touched Moiread's cold hands gently. "Be at peace with it, little sister. We will sing of your valor."

"Folk need to see you," Grainne said to Drustan in her direct way, eyes on a level with his. "To share your grief, to share the victory. They followed the Cullach

Gorrym and fought well for you this day."

Drustan nodded. "I will come."

"And you." Grainne looked at me, still kneeling, and smiled. "You come as the Swan's emmissary, you ask the Cullach Gorrym to follow you. They need to see."

"I'm coming," I said, and stood, small beside the Twins. Joscelin gave his smooth Cassiline bow, not quite meeting my eyes. I glanced at Hyacinthe. Our eyes met in a small silence, the old familiarity and the new.

"I will stay," he said softly. "Let the dreamers and the seers keep watch. It is what we do."

SEVENTY-FOUR

The next day we marched into Bryn Gorrydum.

It was a small city, which surprised me; I recognized the underpinnings of Tiberian stonework. We intersected with a mighty river and marched along its banks, toward a bay, for the city lay on the eastern shore of Alba. Commonfolk turned out and cheered. Maelcon had not been loved. When we reached the fortress proper, we found the gates open and the door lowered, the garrison turned out to surrender arms.

They had heard. And they gave us Foclaidha.

Maelcon's mother.

Later we learned that it was not only the defeat of Maelcon's forces that put the fear of the Cullach Gorrym into the followers of the Red Bull, but the numbers of commonfolk, especially within the fortress itself, servants who had escaped the slaughter of Maelcon's betrayal, whose black eyes gleamed to hear the news of the Cruarch's return.

Discretion is the greater part of valor; the Tarbh Cró surrendered.

So it was that Drustan mab Necthana took his throne. Down came the standard of the Red Bull; the Black Boar flew once more from the peaks of Bryn Gorrydum. The Cruarch's sister, Moiread, was buried in state. The head of Maelcon the Usurper was nailed above the gates of Bryn Gorrydum. Drustan had not spoken in jest.

We do not call them barbarians entirely without reason.

Seated on the throne, he heard Foclaidha's petition.

As a guest of honor, I was privileged to attend; a privilege I'd gladly have foregone. I stood, watching. It seemed a thousand years ago that I had stood in the Hall of Audience where Lyonette de Trevalion stood trial, Alcuin and I straining to catch a glimpse of the proceedings. Now I stood at the left hand of the throne of Alba, my Cassiline companion attendant, struggling to keep my features expressionless as I represented the Queen of Terre d'Ange. If I had felt a fraud bestowing knighthood on Quintilius Rousse's men, it was nothing to this.

I could not help but think, if Ysandre de la Courcel knew we would succeed thus far, she would never have chosen to send me. A whore's unwanted get, I remembered, the Dowayne's voice echoing in my memory.

But send me she had, and if I was a whore's unwanted get, I was Anafiel Delaunay's chosen pupil too, and *he* had deemed me worthy of his name, when my own parents sold my right to carry theirs. And this woman who stood before Drustan's throne, tall and unrepentant, had caused not only the bloodshed to which I'd born witness yesterday and that which had stained these halls, but the deaths I'd witnessed decreed that other day, when I stood on tiptoe in the Hall of Audience.

Baudoin de Trevalion, who'd given me my first kiss. He'd taken the luck of it with him; I'd been his parting gift.

From Melisande, who brought to light letters, written to Lyonette de Trevalion, from this woman.

Who stood before Drustan's throne.

The Tsingani are right; it is a Long Road.

Drustan let her speak, and she spoke well, impassioned, of the passing of the old ways, of the need to join the new, where son succeeded father. No betrayal, but a noble cause, she said in ringing tones, to sweep away the cobwebs of superstition that said no one may know a child's father, to acknowledge the sovereignty of paternity. A tall woman, Foclaidha, with red hair and the whorls of a Cruithne warrior tattooed on her cheeks. I heard later that she killed four men by her own hand when the garrison came for her.

The Lioness of Azzalle had been overpowering too, although she'd never held a sword. It had made Baudoin wild and daring and a little mad. I wondered if Maelcon had been the same.

It was a good speech, and there were men who would have listened, inspired to overturn the bonds of matrilinealism, to raise up the children of their blood and seed, making them heirs to all they owned, all they claimed.

Not Earth's eldest children.

Four sets of identical dark eyes watched, as they listened: Drustan, Necthana, Breidaia, Sibeal. It should have been five. I wondered, did we follow the old ways once? Elua's wandering put an end to it, if we did; our bloodlines we trace through mother and father alike, back to the shining linkages of the past, to Elua and his Companions, when they walked the earth. Our lineage we bear stamped on our faces, in our souls.

Isolated by the Master of the Straits, in Alba it is

ifferent. They trace heritage through the mother, be-
ond question, proof born in blood and tears. Necthana's
hildren had different fathers; warriors, dreamers. *Love
s thou wilt*. Blessed Elua too was Earth's Child, Her
ast-begotten, conceived in Her dark womb of blood and
ears.

Having listened, Drustan bent his head toward the
wins, at his right hand. "What say the Dalriada?"

Eamonn drew a deep breath. "Drustan Cru, you know
ur hearts and our minds. Your uncle was our friend. In
ire, we do not suffer a blood-traitor to live." Grainne
odded in accord, unwontedly somber. They keep the
ld ways too, I thought, remembering her son Brennan;
vho was his father? I'd never asked. Elua knew, the next
orn might be Rousse's get.

Drustan looked at me. "What says Terre d'Ange?"

I hadn't been expecting it, though I don't know why.
t is how such things are done, in the eyes of all assem-
led. I remembered Parliament voting at the trial of
House Trevalion, the Lioness of Azzalle and Ysandre de
a Courcel's cool face, her down-turned thumb signalling
leath. "My lord," I said to Drustan, my voice sounding
s if it belonged to someone else. "Foclaidha of the Brugantii conspired against the Crown. It has been proven.
Ve do not bid for clemency."

There was a buzz around the hall; not everyone there
ad known who I was, had heard Cruithne from my lips.
Drustan ignored it, looking fixedly at Foclaidha.

"For your treachery," he said, "you will die. For the
lood ties between us, I grant it will be swift."

What I expected, I don't know, again. Somewhat else.
Truly, I'd not put thought to this day, to prepare myself
or it. Lyonette accepted poison, drinking it off at one
Iraught and laughing. Baudoin chose to fall on his
word. Is it more civilized, that way? No. In the end, it

is the same; death at the root. All the ritual in the world does not change that. And yet I was shocked when two of Drustan's Cruithne seized Foclaidha's arms and forced her to her knees, when Drustan himself rose from the throne, drawing his sword.

It flashed, once. He'd honed it keen for this day, and there is a great deal of strength in the folk of the Cullach Gorrym, for all that they are not as tall as those who came later. Clean through, he severed her neck.

Foclaidha's head rolled a little, eyes still open.

Her body fell heavily to the flagstones of the hall of Bryn Gorrydum, blood pooling at the neck.

I caught my breath in my teeth, repressing a squeak. Elua be thanked. Joscelin's hand closed on my elbow, bone-grindingly tight, and I was glad he was there. At the throne, Necthana and her daughters looked at the headless body of Foclaidha of the Brugantii, grim satisfaction on their dark, serene faces. To their right, the Twins grinned with fierce vindication.

"Let it end here," Drustan said softly, cleaning his sword and sheathing it. "Those who will swear fealty, may live. The lands of the Brugantii, I declare forfeit, and give unto the keeping of the Sigovae and Votadae, who alone among the Tarbh Cró kept faith with the Cullach Gorrym."

There was cheering at that, from those wild northern Picti who'd ridden to join Drustan's army. A wise choice, it transpired; a popular choice, on Drustan's part. It restored honor to the folk of the Red Bull.

The Black Boar reigned in Alba.

All exiles carry a map within them that points the way homeward. I looked to the east, the open windows of the hall of Bryn Gorrydum carrying the scent of rain, and a salt breeze from the sea, that mingled with the coppery odor of fresh-spilled blood. A warm breeze, summery. How many months had we been on the road, at sea? In Terre d'Ange, there would be flowers blooming, fruit trees bearing. I heard in my mind Thelesis de Mornay singing *The Exile's Lament*. *The bee is in the lavender; the honey fills the comb*. The Skaldi would be massing, moving, crossing the Camaelines, fording the Rhenus River.

While we waged a war, summer had come.

The affairs of state that remained would not be settled in a day. Days on end, it took, while Drustan heard petitions from tribal lords and commonfolk alike, dispossessed by Maelcon the Usurper, and restored to them their rights and lands. Nor was he idle on our behalf during this time, but it took some doing, to rally an army willing to dare the crossing, to convince them it was in the interest of Alba to defend D'Angeline soil. And of course, with the kingdom new-settled under its rightful leader, it was needful that sufficient numbers remain to enforce Drustan's rule, held in his absence by Necthana.

In the end, it was determined that some three thousand foot-soldiers and four hundred horse would make the crossing. To my surprise, Eamonn and Grainne and half the Dalriada would be among them. The others would return west to Innisclan, bearing word of victory, and bidding Rousse's waiting sailors to turn the ship homeward.

"I have come this far," Eamonn said stubbornly. "If the harpists in Tea Muir sing of our deeds, they will not sing of how Eamonn mac Conor of the Dalriada ran home rather than get his feet wet!"

Grainne his sister gave her lazy smile. "And I am minded to see the land that breeds such folk," she said, her grey-green eyes glancing at Quintilius Rousse, who coughed to hide his blush. She looked at me and winked, then; I repressed a smile. One could not help but like the Twins.

Elder Brother's blessing or no, the crossing would be difficult, especially with the horses. Poring over maps, Rousse and Drustan decided it would be best done if we marched south, to the point where the Straits were narrowest. It would take us through the lands of the Eidlach Òr, who had proved loyal; they would cheer Drustan's triumph. Elua willing, we would make landfall in northern Azzalle, in Trevalion, where we could make contact with Ghislain de Somerville, and perhaps the former Duc de Trevalion, if Marc's recall from exile had been successful.

If not for the fears that gnawed at me like a canker, it would have been a pleasant journey. Alba is a fair, green isle, and bountiful. It was an old Tiberian road along which we marched now, in a long, snaking train; along the eastern coast and to the south, those were the areas in which the armies of Tiberium had gained a solid foothold until Cinhil Ru united the tribes and pushed them back across the sea.

Blessed Elua was still wandering in Bhodistan and no Master of the Straits had ruled the waters, then. From whence, I wondered, had that enigma come? I remembered Alcuin in Delaunay's library, ancient scrolls and codices spread across the table, pondering, his quicksilver mind trying to tease out the heart of the riddle. If he'd learned aught before he died, he'd not had time to tell me. I wished he were here now, that I might ask him. Having once seen that terrible face moving on the waters, I'd no wish to see it again, and I misliked trusting to the promise of a mystery.

One of my fears, not the least of them; I feared for the Cruithne. Three thousand warriors on foot, four hundred mounted. It was not a great number, not set against the hordes of Skaldi. I had seen them fight, and they were fierce . . . fierce, and undisciplined. Cinhil Ru had ousted the Tiberians through sheer numbers, once the tribes all rallied to fight under the banner of the Cullach Gorrym; but the numbers favored Waldemar Selig. And Selig had studied the tactics of Tiberium.

Whether or not the Skaldi would follow orders, I doubted. Remembering the fractious tribal rivalries that pervaded the encampment at the Allthing, I could well imagine it would be hard to maintain the iron rank-and-file discipline that had made ancient Tiberium such a formidable foe. That was one point in our favor, albeit a small one.

Selig still had the numbers. And the Allies of Camlach.

So I brooded as we marched, each glorious day that dawned hastening my unease, the warm balm of sunlight serving to remind me of time's swift passage.

"Will you take it all upon your shoulders, Phèdre?" Joscelin asked me quietly one day, jogging his mount alongside mine. How he knew my thoughts, I don't know; I must have been wearing them on my face. "Can you slow time, or shorten the road we travel? I was reminded, not long ago, not to take upon myself that which is not mine to carry."

"I know," I said, sighing. "I can't help but worry. And the Skaldi . . . ah, Elua, you've seen them! If the Cruithne are riding toward death, they're doing it at my word, Joscelin."

He shook his head. "Not yours; Ysandre's. You but carried it for her. And 'twas their choice, made freely."

"It may have been the Queen's word, but I spoke it, and did all in my power to persuade their choice." I shivered. "The Dalriada wouldn't be here if I hadn't. None of them would."

"True." To his credit, Joscelin said it without his usual wry twist. "But Drustan rides for love, and a pledge. *Love as thou wilt.* You cannot gainsay it."

"I'm afraid of this war." I whispered it. "What we witnessed in Alba . . . Joscelin, I never want to see the like again, and it will be as nothing to what awaits us in Terre d'Ange. I don't have the strength to face that much death."

He didn't answer right away, gazing forward, his profile in clear relief against the green fields. "I know," he said finally. "It scares me, too. There'd be somewhat wrong with us if it didn't, Phèdre."

"Do you remember waking up in that cart, after Melisande betrayed us?" I asked him. He nodded. "I could have died, then. I wouldn't have cared. Hating her was the only reason I had to live, for a while." I touched the diamond at my throat. "I don't feel the same, now. I'm afraid of dying."

"You remember Gunter's kennels?" He gave me the wry look. "Hating you kept me alive, then, when I thought you'd betrayed me. If you'd asked me before, I'd have sworn I'd kill myself before I endured such humiliation. And Selig's steading? You shamed me into living."

I remembered shouting at him, shoving him where he knelt, wounded and chained, and flushed. "I was desperate. Are you going to do the same to me?"

"No," Joscelin said, though he grinned as if the prospect weren't entirely displeasing to him, which gave me a strange sensation, a fact I kept to myself. "They are," he said, twisting in the saddle and nodding to the rear. "That's what I came to tell you, actually."

I turned to look.

Rousse's men were marching behind us; there weren't enough horses to mount them, they'd fought on foot.

They marched in formation, four columns six deep. The Admiral, his leg still healing, rode alongside them. As I watched, the foremost row grinned, and one man—Remy, who'd taught Hyacinthe to fish—stepped out in front, carrying a tight-wound standard. The others in his row shifted, so they formed a wedge.

Phèdre's Boys, he'd called them. Atop a wide-barreled chestnut gelding, Quintilius Rousse chuckled.

Remy unfurled the standard and held it aloft with a clear D'Angeline shout, letting the banner snap in the breeze. They'd made it themselves; sailors are great tailors. Where they begged the cloth, I don't know; I heard later the gold thread cost them dear.

It was a sable banner, bearing a ragged circle of scarlet at its center; crossing the scarlet, a golden dart, barbed and fletched. It took me a moment before I realized.

Kushiel's Dart.

"Oh, Blessed Elua!" I stared, then remembered to close my mouth. Grinning like a monkey, Remy pounded the foot of the standard on the road, and began their marching-chant; all of them took it up, even Quintilius Rousse roaring along with the refrain, half-unintellible with laughter.

"Whip us till we're on the floor, we'll turn around and ask for more, we're Phèdre's Boys!"

"Oh, no!" I laughed helplessly, numb with shock and hilarity, and infinitely thankful that the Cruithne, who regarded the proceedings with good-natured bewilderment, didn't understand D'Angeline. "Elua! Joscelin, did you know about this?"

"I might have," he admitted, an amused glint in his blue eyes. "They need to believe, Phèdre, to fight for something. A name, a face they know. Rousse told me as much, and I've seen it, too, in the Brotherhood. We can't become Companions, not truly, until we're pledged to a ward. These men have never seen Ysandre de la Courcel. You, they know."

"We like to hurt, we like to bleed, daily floggings do we need, we're Phèdre's Boys!"

"But . . ." I asked, still laughing, ". . . like *that*?"

Joscelin shrugged, grinning. "You sang the seas calm, and you drove the Dalriada to war, whatever it took. They know that. That's why they adore you. But everyone needs to laugh in the face of death. They're following an *anguissette* into battle. Give them credit for seeing the absurdity of it. *You've* been dwelling on it long enough."

"I'll give them more than credit." Turning my horse, I cantered back a few paces and dismounted in front of Remy with his standard, bringing the line to a halt. He hid a mischievous smile; I reached up and grabbed his auburn sailor's queue, tugging his head down to kiss him. He came up from it wide-eyed and gasping. The D'Angelines cheered and shouted. "Any man who survives," I said to them, remounting, "I swear to you, I will throw open the doors of the Thirteen Houses of the Night Court!"

They cheered at that, long and loud, then took up their chant again as I rode back to rejoin Joscelin and the column began to move.

"And how," he asked me, "do you propose to do that?"

"I'll find a way," I said, light-hearted for the first time in many days. "If I have to take an assignation with the Khalif of Khebbel-im-Akkad, I swear, I'll find a way!"

So we marched through Alba, through the lands of the Trinovantii and the Canticae, as summer wore on, the grain turning from green to gold in the fields, and apples swelling on the bough, until we reached the old Tiberian settlement of Dobria, where the Straits were most narrow.

It was a clear day, when we arrived. We paused for a moment atop the cliffs, the high, white cliffs of Dobria, before riding onward to the beach-head, some miles away. The greensward goes right up to the edge, and then they drop away sheer, down to the Straits, only seabirds wheeling between with harsh cries.

"There," Drustan said, and pointed.

Faint and distant, across miles and miles of grey water, we could see it. Terre d'Ange.

Home.

$\mathscr{S}$EVENTY-FIVE

The folk of the Eidlach Òr had been busy.

Drustan had sent his fast-riders ahead, bearing word of our need. And Alba had responded, eager to obey the restored Cruarch. Boats, boats of every ilk, small one-masted ships, oar-boats, scows, fishing boats, rafts; they had them ready, in abundance. A vast and motley flotilla filled the harbor, awaiting our arrival.

"This is going to be ugly," Quintilius Rousse muttered, casting a practiced eye over the assembled vessels.

It took nearly two days, coordinating the arrangements. The Cruithne sailed, but only along the coast; precious few had ever crossed deep water. Phèdre's Boys were spread thin, sharing their precious expertise; the Dalriada were valued second, who had sailed fearless between Alba and Eire. We quartered the horses as best we could, though only a few of the ships had holds designed for it. Others would cross on rafts, blindfolded; if they panicked, Rousse warned, let them go, rather than capsize.

Somehow, amidst it all, an ancient Alban fisherman wound his way through the crowds, plucking at Drustan's cloak, peering at him with a wizened face.

"Lord Cruarch," he said tremulously. "You tell them, do not fish the deep waters! Three spear-casts off the coast, that's as far as they may go; aught else, is the Sea-Lord's hunting ground!"

"I'll tell them, grandfather," Drustan said politely. "But you needn't fear, we're not here to fish. And the Sea-Lord has sworn us safe passage."

"Tell them!" the old fisherman insisted. "Cullach Gorrym to the north and west, *you* don't know! The Eidlach Or, we fish these waters. *We* know."

"I will tell them," Drustan repeated.

He did, too, addressing the army as we stood massed on the shore, some third boarded with the horses, the rest awaiting his order. A short speech, the wind off the sea whipping his words away.

"We cross now to follow a dream, of two kingdoms united! We cross now to honor a pledge, that I made, long ago, to Ysandre de la Courcel, who is Queen of Terre d'Ange, that lies over the waters! Does any man or woman among you wish to turn back, do so now, and do it with my blessing; I ask no one to risk death for this dream, this pledge. But do you seek honor and glory beyond countless bards' telling, follow now, and find it!" They cheered him, for that; his face glowed. "This, I tell you. The Lord of the Waters has sworn us safe passage; we shall reach the other side. I have done it before, and I know! These waters are his territories; respect his sovereignty, and harm no creature. What do you say? Will you dare the crossing?"

They would, and said as much, shouting and waving

arms. The sound echoed across the harbor. A party of northern Picti, the loyal Tarbh Cró, raised their voices the loudest, attempting to blend in with the crowd and disguise the fact that they came late, racing from hurried farewells with some of the more eager women of the Eidlach Òr. Still glad enough to have allies among the Red Bull, Drustan overlooked their tardy arrival.

"Then let us go!" he cried, and the exodus began.

Quintilius Rousse was right; it was ugly. Even with the horses already boarded, it took nearly an hour before the last man was aboard, and our ungainly flotilla began moving out of the harbor. Rousse had commandeered one of the better ships, which would bear Drustan mab Necthana, as well as Hyacinthe, Joscelin and I, who were of no help at sailing. We would be safer, all of us, with the Admiral than anywhere else.

It would have been a comical sight, I imagine, in less serious circumstances; a small continent's worth of ill-matched vessels, moving awkwardly across the water. Leaning over the side, I watched one of Phèdre's Boys shout at a hapless group of Cruithne, attempting to drive a raft with oars, their uncoordinated efforts sending it spinning in slow circles.

"Azzalle has a fleet," Quintilius Rousse muttered, seeing the same thing. "Mayhap 'twould be better if we crossed alone, and sent the fleet back for them."

"Azzalle's fleet may be halfway up the Rhenus River, my lord Admiral," I reminded him. "As might your own. But if you think it best, give the order now, before anyone founders."

He looked dourly at the struggling raft. Under the D'Angeline sailor's frantically gestured orders, the Cruithne got the knack of it and began moving forward. "Let 'em try. I'm not minded to cross the Straits more than once, unless I need to."

I couldn't blame him for that, not after having seen the Master of the Straits; I'd no wish to risk seeing him again, either. And in truth, once we got underway, a strange thing happened. The winds held, light and steady, blowing off Alba's shore toward distant Terre d'Ange; the winds held, but the sea grew calm, scarce ruffled by the breeze. Our fleet strung out in a ragged line, lurching forward, slowly and surely. The shore fell away behind us, white cliffs looming, receding yard by yard, until the yards became a mile, and one mile two. The Albans didn't lack for courage nor hardihood; set to an unfamiliar task, they laid to with a will, hands calloused by sword-hilts wrapped around oars, backs bent to the task.

Here and there, across the water, D'Angeline voices arose in a rower's chant, marking the time, adapting the words of their chosen marching tune to an oarsman's beat.

"Man or woman, we don't care; give us twins, we'll take the pair! But just because we let you beat us; doesn't mean you can defeat us!"

Other voices took it up, Cruithne and Eiran alike, meaningless syllables mangled in foreign tongues. At the helm, tacking slowly to keep apace of the fleet, Quintilius Rousse shook his head and grinned. "Never been anything like it!" he shouted. "This crossing will go down in history, I promise! And Elder Brother bids fair to keep his word!" He jerked his chin at Hyacinthe. "What do you say now, Tsingano? Care to point our way to landfall, eh?"

Hyacinthe stood in the prow, gazing out at the smooth waters, wrapped in his saffron cloak, now salt-stained and travel-worn, and gave no answer.

With a frisson of alarm, I made my way to his side. "What is it? What do you see?"

He turned his face to me, black eyes blurred with the *dromonde*, wide and unseeing. "That's just it. I don't. I can't see our landing."

"What does it mean?"

Hyacinthe looked back at the sea. "It means," he said softly, "that somewhere between here and the far shore, lies a crossroads, and I cannot see beyond it."

I would have asked him somewhat else, but a great clamor arose at that moment off our port bow, shouts of laughter, scuffling and blows. Such was the noise of it that all of us who were idle on deck went to look, even Hyacinthe, forgetting his fears.

It was one of the small rafts, with some fourteen of the Tarbh Cró—Segovae tribesmen, they were—and a single D'Angeline. Without enough oars to go around, three of the northern warriors had disported themselves by lying at the edge of the raft and peering into the clear, still waters, thrusting their arms into the sea and wriggling their fingers, attempting to catch fish bare-handed.

A good trick in riverbeds, I am told; it shouldn't have worked at sea. Nor would it, save for one very large, very curious eel.

Which one of the Segovae had caught round the middle with both hands, and hauled onto the raft, thrashing like fury. It was that eel they were trying to subdue, with shouts and flailing blows of oar and fist, and Rousse's sailor yelling out helpful directions in incomprehensible D'Angeline, the raft rocking wildly.

I think we all laughed, for a moment. Until one of the Segovae caught the eel a good pounding blow on the head and it shuddered and became still, wet and gleaming on the raft, a full five feet or longer.

And the wind went dead.

And I remembered what the fisherman had said.

The Tarbh Cró came late, they hadn't heard Drustan's

warning. And the D'Angeline sailors wouldn't have understood. He'd spoken in Cruithne; I hadn't translated it. They had their orders from the Admiral, they knew what we were about.

Three spear-casts off the coast, aught else is the Sea-Lord's hunting ground.

We were three spear-casts and farther; we were miles at sea. In the sudden absence of wind, it was if the world had drawn a deep breath and held it.

I did the same.

Before, the Master of the Straits came with gathering darkness and lashing rains, driving toward us across the waves. This time, it was different. This time, the very sea itself erupted. In the midst of our motley fleet, the waters boiled, boats and rafts tilting on end, passengers crying out and scrabbling for a hold.

And from the maelstrom, the vast face arose.

Those vessels closest slid one way, plunging down the enormous slope of the form's streaming hair; those on the outer circle, as we were, tipped the other. For a moment, I swear, the ship nearly stood on her prow, awash in a sheet of water. Somewhere, Quintilius Rousse was roaring orders, inaudible over the rushing sea. I clung grimly to the railing, both hands locked in a death-grip, and vowed to Elua that I would light a candle for my old tumbling-master if I survived. A man's figure slid across the steep slant of the wooden deck, his desperate shout cut short, disappearing in the foaming sea.

Up and up, taller and vaster than I remembered, the face of the Master of the Straits arose, transparent and shining, with the flicker of living fish and bits of weed glimpsed in the water that shaped his features.

Then he held and rose no further, and the seas fell level with a thunderous clap, our ship crashing back on its keel. The impact jarred my grip loose; I was flung half over the side, the railing catching my midriff. All around the surging waters, our impromptu fleet bobbed like corks on a flood, holding a half-drowned army, horses screaming in panic, some already swimming, churning and terrified.

"Phèdre!" A strong hand entwined in my tangled cloak, hauling me back on deck; Joscelin, soaked to the bone and wide-eyed with shock. I looked for Hyacinthe, and saw him safe, some yards away, where he'd been swept. And then I had no time left to look for survivors, for the Master of the Straits spoke.

Towering as high as the cliffs, it seemed, glistening and huge, his face rose above us, and the terrible maw opened to loose the thunder's voice.

"WHO HUNTS MY SEASSS?"

I know what I know; what I saw, what I heard. I would swear it: The Master of the Straits spoke D'Angeline. I heard it, Hyacinthe, Joscelin, the Admiral; we all did. But the eel-catching Tarbh Cró on the raft below us cried out in terror, at the same moment that Drustan mab Necthana, the Cruarch of Alba, stepped forward on our now-steady deck, unfaltering despite his lurching gait.

"They are my men, Sea-Lord!" he cried in Cruithne, straining his neck to stare up at the Master of the Straits. "I failed to warn them! I am to blame!"

The face looked down, water streaming from on high. "YOU LEAD . . . ALBAN?"

Quintilius Rousse, swearing, abandoned the helm to come forward. " 'Tis my ship and I command it, you old bastard! If you've come to take a toll, take it from me!"

More than anything, I did not want to leave the safety of the railing, Joscelin's hands holding me anchored, secure, out of the notice of that awful water-wrought face looming above us. More than anything.

With a sinking feeling of despair, I murmured to Joscelin, "Let be." His grip tightened on my arms, and I turned to look at him. He bowed his head and let go, and I stepped away from the rail, raising my voice to the towering seas. "My lord, I am the emissary of Ysandre de la Courcel, Queen of Terre d'Ange!"

The face of the Master of the Straits turned my way. Water, cascading, shaping a fluid mockery of flesh and bone. Lightning flashed in the eyes; the dark mouth opened. "I WILL TAKE YOU ALLLLL!"

For what happened then, I lack words. The face flowed, dissolving, shaping the vast glassy hump of a wave; flowed, and flowed under our ship, lifting it. We rose on the crest of it like a toy boat, and the wave surged forward. It surged, and did not break. Like a charging bull, it rushed down the Straits, unending, unbreaking, and our ship born atop it, bearing us southward. There are those who doubt, but I swear it is true.

Mile upon mile we travelled, twice, thrice the length of our crossing, longer mayhap. How long it took, I cannot say. Terror gave way to wonder, then a slow mingling of despair. Were all behind us drowned? I could not help but fear so. Onward and onward we rushed, the great wave never breaking.

Until, at last, an island rose before us, thrusting bleak and lonely into the sea. Closer and closer the wave brought us, still riding its crest, and I saw no inlet, and thought we should be dashed to death against its tall, grey cliffs.

There, at the final moment, I saw it; a narrow harbor carved in the rock, ringed by high walls. It was toward that we sped. At the mouth of the harbor, the great wave sighed, and flowed *backward* beneath us, the deadly crest receding to a gentle slope. Our ship slid down it, easing between the high cliff walls, and whether Quintilius Rousse had aught to do with it, I cannot say, but that wave deposited us in the small, still harbor as neatly as a cat laying a mouse at its master's feet.

I was afraid it was an apt comparison.

Sodden in places, salt-stiff where clothing had dried, and lulled into near-paralysis by our fearful passage, we began to gather our wits, shaking off the awe and looking about. There were thirty-some of us on the ship, mostly Cruithne, with eight horses in the hold. It was one of Drustan's men who saw it first, pointing with a sharp cry.

A promontory of rock jutted into the harbor. Steps, terraced and smooth, led down to the water. Above were more broad steps, cut into the cliff-face, leading upward. Behind us, nothing but the harbor walls and open sea, empty. I glanced up to where, high above us, columns rose into the sky, distant and foreshortened, for all the world like a Hellene temple. The sky was grey, and the white marble of the columns blurred against it.

But that wasn't what had caused the Cruithne to point.

Standing on the promontory, two robed figures awaited us.

Seventy-six

"I will go." It was Drustan who spoke first, quick and firm, his dark eyes resolute in the blue masque of his face. I remembered how he had stepped forward, unhesitating, to take the blame for the Tarbh Cró.

One could not help but admire him.

And realize his worth to the folk of Alba.

"No, my lord." I shook my head, feeling the mass of my hair windblown and heavy with seawater. What would my loss cost Terre d'Ange? A nation at war had no need of one rather travel-worn *anguissette*. "We are near D'Angeline shores. It is my place to go."

While we argued in Cruithne, Quintilius Rousse peered over the edge of the ship, gauging the open water that lay between our vessel and the steps, mindful of the fact, which we ignored, that no one was going anywhere until it was bridged. The taller of the robed figures came to the edge of the promontory, pushing back his grey cowl to reveal himself a young man with dark hair and unassuming features.

"The waters are deep, sirrah," he said in a calm, carrying voice, speaking in archaic D'Angeline. "Bring your ship in close, and thou mayest lower a plank."

"Hear that?" Rousse turned around, snapping his fingers at the closest Cruithne, who stared uncomprehendingly at him. "Go on, to oars! We're bringing this ship ashore!" The Admiral turned his best glare on me. "Whatever's in your head, lass, no one's going in alone, Queen's emissary or no. So tell these wild blue lads to bend their backs, and we'll see what game Elder Brother's playing at."

I did, feeling a little foolish. Drustan gave Rousse a deep look, and went to the stern to survey the seas for any sign of our missing fleet. If he could buy the Albans' safety with his life, I thought, he would still do it. But Rousse was right, we didn't know why the Master of the Straits had brought us here.

"What do you see?" I asked Hyacinthe, as the oars dipped raggedly and the ship drifted close to the terrace.

He gazed at the cliff wall, the broad steps, smiling strangely. "I see an island," he murmured. "What do you see, Phèdre nó Delaunay?"

To that, I had no answer. And, in short order, the ship came alongside the promontory and Quintilius Rousse gave word to drop anchor. The gangplank was lowered, but none of us disembarked, standing instead on deck and awaiting word from our strange hosts.

The second figure drew back his cowl: an older man, white-haired. "Those among thee, the Master wishes to see," he said, in the same archaic D'Angeline dialect his companion had used. I spared a quick glance at Drustan, and saw him frowning. He did not understand the words. The old one pointed, unerring. "Thou, thou, and thou. Thou."

Drustan, Rousse, myself . . . and Hyacinthe.

Joscelin stepped forward, and his daggers crossed and flashed as he gave an armed Cassiline bow. "Where she goes," he said softly, "I go. I have sworn it, in Cassiel's name."

"Violence will not avail thee." It was the younger who spoke, smiling faintly. He nodded his dark head at the sea, and it rippled in response, our ship rocking. "Thy companions are safe, on First Sister's shores. Wilst jeopardize their safety?"

I translated quickly, and Drustan caught Joscelin's arm, understanding. "My folk, my people; he says they have them safe, brother. I beg you do nothing to bring them harm."

Joscelin did not release his daggers as I gave him Drustan's words, though his knuckles grew white with strain. "To damnation and beyond," he said; his voice was faint, his expression terrible. "I have sworn it, Phèdre."

The lives of three thousand and some innocent Albans, and near all of Rousse's men stood at risk. "Joscelin," I whispered, "I will kill you or myself before I let anyone else die for your vow, I swear it."

He looked at me; what he would have said, I don't know. The older of the robed men lifted his hand and spoke, forestalling him. "He is Companion-sworn," he said to the younger, who bowed his head, acceding. "Let him come."

Drustan watched the proceedings intently, dark gaze darting from face to face. I translated and he nodded, releasing his grip on Joscelin's arm.

"Gildas will take thee to the Master of the Straits," the younger man said. "I will see to the others. Thou art weary, and fearful. We offer rest and succor."

I repeated his words to Drustan, who nodded again and spoke reassuringly to his men. It was decided.

So, I thought, as we disembarked, crossing the gangplank, our footsteps sounding hollow above the water; the Master of the Straits has servants, and mortal ones. Do they wield his power, to ruffle the waves, or merely speak his command? The face of the waters spoke, and all understood; these men speak D'Angeline, the old tongue of courtly lays.

These things I thought as we mounted the steps, climbing upward into the skies. Gildas led, Rousse and Drustan behind, the young Cruarch's misshapen foot causing his pace to slow somewhat as he scrambled from step to step. I followed, Joscelin stuck to my side like a tall Cassiline burr while Hyacinthe trailed behind us. I would have spoken to him, but his shuttered expression forbade it. Behind us, we heard the reassuring clamor of the remainder of our party disembarking, the skittering hoofbeats of frightened horses on stone, the babble of voices trying to communicate in foreign tongues.

We climbed and climbed, mounting into the sky. It was a vast temple at the summit, and no mistake. A broad path branched to the right at the foot of it, but further stairs awaited us before, steep and narrow, wrought of white marble. My breath grew thin and came in gasps, and I'd been living hard, riding with the

Cruithne. I heard the men and horses turn off at the branching path, and envied them. Rousse was panting too, and I heard Hyacinthe's breath ragged in his throat; Drustan set his face with grim determination and showed no sign of fatigue, though he labored twice as hard as any of us.

Joscelin . . . Joscelin was Cassiline. He'd run miles behind Gunter's thane's horse, through deep snow, and come out of it glaring hatred. I shook off his hand when he sought to brace my elbow, aiding me up the steps.

And white-haired Gildas wasn't even winded.

So we gained the temple.

It is my fate, it seems, to fall privy to rare and splendid vistas in a state of exhaustion too profound to care. At the summit of this lonely isle, where columns of white marble rose into open air, like a prayer uttered to an unheeding god, I bent over and gasped for breath, fixing my gaze on the lone figure at the center of the temple.

He was tall and robed in grey, like the others, yet unlike, for the color of his robe shifted under the open skies, dark and pale with the changing light, hanging motionless in the breeze. His hair hung long and unbound, iron-grey, I thought; then it too shifted, changing color with the scudding clouds. He stood alone, his back to us, and a great bronze vessel, broad and shallow, stood beside him on a tripod, at the heart of the rectangular structure.

"Come," Gildas said, and began to walk.

We followed him across the white marble flagstones.

The tall figure turned as we drew near, regarding us with sea-green eyes, revealing a face at once ancient and elemental, mantled in iron-grey locks, a face as white as shell and older than bones, shifting and fluid, with a power in it that rose from the very depths of the ocean.

I had seen the face of the waters, terrible and powerful.

A sending, no more. A thought born of a sea-rooted mind, the reaching hand of power. This . . . *this* was the Master of the Straits.

"My lord," I whispered, and knelt.

Drustan mab Necthana took one lurching step forward, locking gazes with the Master of the Straits. The high breeze lifted his scarlet cloak. "Lord of the Waters," he said evenly. "You gave your pledge. When the Cullach Gorrym ruled in Alba, you would allow us the crossing. Why have you brought us here?"

The Master of the Straits smiled, and his eyes lightened to the color of sun-shot mist. "You were warned, young Cruarch," he said, and though his mouth moved, the words seemed to arise from the very wind, echoing around the open temple. "You were warned . . . Alban."

A gift of tongues, the Skaldi claimed I had; witchery. I had Delaunay for a teacher, no more and no less. The Master of the Straits had the gift of tongues, for I swear it, I heard the words in D'Angeline, but Drustan heard Cruithne, and replied in kind.

"Lord of the Waters," he said sharply. "You gave warning as a hunter lays bait. Why have you brought us here?"

On my knees, I thought, mind racing. Drustan was right, the honeyed promise of safe passage, a toothless warning, easy to discard. The Master of the Straits wanted something of us. What? Beside me, Joscelin's hands hovered over his hilts. Quintilius Rousse stood like a bull ready to charge, head lowered. Hyacinthe was swaying on his feet, barely upright.

"Why?" the Master of the Straits mused, and the seawinds sighed around us. He clasped his hands behind his back and gazed at the far oceans. "Why." He turned back to us, and his eyes were as dark as thunderheads. "Eight hundred years I have ruled, chained to this rock, claimed by neither earth nor sky!" He raised his voice, and the winds lashed us and the clouds roiled, the seas far below beating themselves in a frenzy against the cliffs. His hair rose on the wind, standing around his face like a dreadful corona. "Eight hundred years! And you ask me *why?*"

We braced ourselves, recoiling against the wind; through the fingers raised to shield my face, I saw Drustan mab Necthana leaning into it, eyes narrowed. *"Why?"* he asked, shouting the word. "Lord of the Waters, you hold my people hostage! *Why?*"

The winds died, the Master of the Straits smiled once more, his eyes softening back to sea-green. "Alban," he said, caressing the word. Reaching out one hand, he pointed to the gold signet ring, Rolande's ring, on Drustan's hand. "You have the courage, to live the dream that will free me. Your mother saw it, in the dark behind her eyes. The swan and the boar. Alban and D'Angeline, love defiant. But it is only half."

I understood. It was my gift, Delaunay's training, to hear the unspoken thing, to see the connections beneath the surface. I rose. "My lord," I said carefully. "This I understand to be true. You are bound here, to this isle, whether you will it or no. You wish to break this binding. Two things are needful. One is the union of Alban and D'Angeline, present in the betrothal of Drustan and Ysandre. What is the other?"

"Ahhh." He took a step toward me and caressed my face with one hand, as if he had the power to mold my flesh like water. I closed my eyes and shuddered profoundly. "One who hears, and listens, and thinks. That is well. You have named the riddle. Answer it in full, and you may leave." Drawing his hand back, he swept his arm across the shallow cauldron, sleeve trailing, taking on the hue of bronze.

The cauldron was filled with water that rippled and stilled, reflecting not sky, but the face of Ysandre de la Courcel, who sat in a makeshift throne, the accoutrements of a war-camp behind her, listening intently to someone unseen. Drustan gave a short cry, and Quintilius Rousse pressed his fist to his brow.

"Answer it in full," the Master of the Straits said, and smiled, and his eyes were as bleached as old bones, "and you shall have my aid in full. Fail, and the seas shall claim you." He pointed to the western skies, where the sun sank low and red over the waters. "One night, I give you. When the sun stands overhead tomorrow, you will answer, or die."

SEVENTY-SEVEN

Gildas led us to the tower, which spiraled skyward from its perch on a lower crag, down another series of broad marble steps at the far side of the temple, then along a wide, paved path.

We followed silently, all of us lost in our own thoughts, the setting sun throwing our shadows black and elongated before us. It lit the tower like flame, drenching the grey walls with gold, shining unexpected on oriel windows of colored glass, rare and wondrous. The uppermost chamber of the tower was ringed all around with them, and two other tiers, staggered with the plain.

A pretty sight; it would have surprised me, if my capacity for surprise wasn't flattened. We entered the reception hall, and found a neat company of servants turned out to await us, ordinary men and women—is-lefolk, I guessed them—clad in simple linens.

"Thy shipmates are well-tended, thy horses stabled," Gildas said to us, and the stilted formality of his courtesies seemed sincere. "No harm will come to thee in this place. By thy leave, we offer the Master's hospitality. Warm baths, dry clothes, wine and supper."

"And the rest of my folk?" Drustan asked when I had translated for him. "Does this . . . this priest stand surety for their safety?"

I asked in D'Angeline. Gildas bowed, grey robes swishing, remaining grey, unlike his Master's. "First Sister lies . . . thence," he said, pointing in a southerly direction. "Some three leagues. She is rich in kine and fowl and cider, and thy folk have been brought safe to her shore. Do thou no harm here, and they shall be well. On my head, I swear it."

With that, Drustan had to be content, and Quintilius Rousse as well, whose sailors were with the Cruithne host.

"Will the Master of the Straits dine with us?" I asked Gildas. He shook his head.

"Nay, my lady. Each other's company, will you share."

"You serve him." I eyed his robes, at odds with the simple clothing the patiently waiting servants wore. "Are you his priest?"

He hesitated at that. " 'Tis true we fill the bronze bowl with seawater, Tilian and I; once at sunrise, once at sundown. And betimes we may speak as his voice, when it is needful. Thus are we privileged to serve. But we cannot break the *geis* who are born to the Three Sisters."

I remembered the bronze bowl on its tripod, shallow, but vast. Twice a day, they must descend those interminable steps down to the sea, returning with it brimming; thrice, today, because of us. No wonder he'd not gotten winded. "The binding upon him, it may not be broken by one born to the isles?"

Another pause, then Gildas inclined his head a fraction. "As thou sayest. Wilt honor us by accepting our hospitality?"

"Yes," I said, since there seemed little point in declining; and, "Thank you," for he had handed me unwitting the key to the riddle; although he took it as thanks for the hospitality, as I meant him to do.

So, I thought. That is that.

How it fell out with the others, I cannot say, but I was led up the winding stair to a sumptuous chamber. Three house servants were my guides, a young woman, and two of middle age, quiet and demure. I do not suppose there was much gaiety involved in serving the Master of the Straits.

The rooms were gorgeously appointed, and I, raised in the Night Court, do not say such things idly. The bed itself was a marvel, ebony posts carved in fantastic forms, the coverlet of velvet, tasseled in gold. The bath was of solid marble, and the ewers in which they carried heated water were silver.

"From whence does this come?" I asked curiously, undoing my brooch and setting aside my salt-stained cloak. The youngest maid, undoing my stays, caught sight of my marque and suppressed a gasp.

"From the bounty of the sea's floor," one of the older women murmured, pouring steaming water into the bath.

Shipwrecks, I thought, shedding my clothes.

They whispered in awe.

I realized, then, what was different; peasant-stock, these islefolk, so one doesn't expect too much . . . D'Angeline, they spoke, but if the blood of Elua and his Companions flowed in their veins, it was nowhere evident in their features. No, they were purely mortal, earth-born and bred, with none of the odd outcroppings of gift or beauty that marked even the lowest-born of D'Angeline peasantry. Elua had loved shepherdesses and fishing-lads alike, he'd not scrupled at peerage, that was a human construct. But Elua and his Companions had set no trace on the bloodlines of these folk.

And then I climbed into the bath and forgot such concerns.

There is no situation so dire that a hot bath cannot improve one's outlook; so I have always found to be true. And I have never been ashamed to revel in luxury. Not since my contract with de Morhban had I been treated as I was accustomed; I gave myself up to it without a second thought. Soaps and perfumed oils, they brought, combs and scissors, until I was utterly and thoroughly pampered, cleansed of sea-crossing, hard riding, war and its labors.

I could live like this, I thought.

Then I thought of the Master of the Straits and shuddered.

They brought clothing when my bath was finished, old-fashioned and gorgeous. The bounty of the sea's floor. Whose trunk, I wondered, had held the gown I chose? It was a bronze satin, rich and shimmering, the neckline worked a handspan deep with seed pearls. There was a hairpin, too, with a spray of pearls, that fastened at the crown of the head and twined into my sable locks.

Yes, I admired it in the mirror, a weighty affair of dark glass, gilt-edged and massive. What would one expect?

A foot-servant came, then, bowing unobtrusively, to escort me to dine.

The dining hall was one of those set about with oriel

windows. A long table shone with polish, set with plates of silver and white linen cloths. The others had already been summoned. Quintilius Rousse caught his breath when I made my entrance.

"My lady Phèdre," he said, bowing and extending his arm.

We had all, it seemed, received the same treatment. The Admiral was positively resplendent, in a russet coat and a brocade vest, his white shirt spilling a froth of ruffles down his broad chest. Hyacinthe wore a doublet and breeches of midnight-blue, pewter slashes showing at his sleeves. I'd not seen him out of Tsingani gauderie; he looked every inch a young nobleman, albeit with a melancholy cast. Joscelin wore black, reminding me with a pang of Delaunay in his austerity, a chain of square-linked silver glittering on the placket of his doublet, his fair braid like a marque down the center of his back. His Cassiline arms made an odd addition, although he'd foregone his sword.

I daresay Drustan cut the strangest figure among us, in a black silk shirt with a ruffled cravat, moleskin breeches of charcoal-grey and a coat of deep-red velvet. His face, marked with the blue whorls of a Cruithne warrior, seemed an exotic affectation. And yet, in a peculiar way, it became him.

I curtsied; they bowed. Quintilius Rousse escorted me to my chair, and we dined. We dined very well in the castle of the Master of the Straits, with darkened windows around us, served by his staff with downcast eyes. We dined, and spoke little, until the plates were cleared, and a bowing servant set a tray with a decanter of cordial and five glasses upon the table. Rousse poured.

"So," he said, taking a drink and smacking his lips, setting his glass on the polished wood with a solid thud, glancing around with his keen blue gaze. "We've a riddle to solve. Shall we pool our wits, and put to it, then?"

No one answered. I took a sip of cordial; it burned, sweet and agreeable, in my throat. Glass in hand, I rose, going to one of the windows, gazing out at the dark night, the invisible sea below. What had Delaunay trained me for, if not for this? To tease out the thread of a riddle and unravel it. They spoke the tongue of ancient ballads on this isle. I leaned my brow against the window, feeling the glass cool and smooth against my skin.

"You know."

Soft-spoken words in Cruithne. I did not turn to look at Drustan mab Necthana, but nodded, moving my head against the glass. I had read a thousand ancient tales, in D'Angeline, in Caerdicci, in Skaldi, in Cruithne. Translations from the Hellene, which I had scarce begun to master. I knew. These things have a pattern, a structure, and I was trained to see such things. I knew.

Drustan drew a sharp breath. "There is a price."

I laid my hand on the window, seeing its shape stark against the darkness. "There is always a price, my lord Cruarch. This one happens to be worth it."

He rose, then, and bowed; I turned around to meet his eyes. "Know that I will pay it if I can."

There was naught else to say, so I nodded once more. Drustan twisted the signet ring around his finger, dark eyes holding mine, then left.

"What did he say?" Quintilius Rousse asked, bewildered. "By the ten thousand devils . . . I thought we were here to resolve a mystery!"

"Ask Phèdre," Hyacinthe said, his voice hollow, raising his haunted face. "She thinks she has solved it. Ask her, and see if she will speak." He slid his hands blindly over his face, and let them fall, helpless.

"If this riddle is mine to answer in full, then I will,"

I said softly; his pain tore at my heart. "Don't begrudge me that, Hyacinthe."

He gave a choked laugh, then stood unsteadily. "Would that Delaunay had left you where he found you! I rue the day he taught you to think."

I'd no answer to that, either. Hyacinthe made me a mocking bow in his best Prince of Travellers style, the slashes in his sleeves flaring eloquently. Quintilius Rousse scowled at his exit, shaking his head.

"I like this not at all," he growled, picking absently at a tray of sweets. "If you've an answer, lass, share it! Let us put our heads together, that all may benefit!"

"My lord Admiral," I said. "No. If Anafiel Delaunay found this answer, he would not share it. Nor can I. If you come to it on your own, so be it."

Quintilius Rousse muttered something about Delaunay's folly. Joscelin moved, restless, coming to stand next to me, hands clasped behind his back, gazing out upon darkness.

"I'm not going to like this, am I?" he said quietly.

I shook my head. "No."

He stared at the unseen sea until I laid my hand upon his arm. "Joscelin." He looked at me, then, reluctant. "Since the day you were assigned to ward me, I've been a trial to you. A thousand ways I've strained your vows, until your very Brotherhood declared you anathema. I swear to you, I'll only do it once more." I cleared my throat. "If we must . . . if we must part, you must abide it. You were trained to serve royalty, not the ill-conceived offspring of Night Court adepts. You swore your sword unto Ysandre's service. If you would serve her, protect Drustan. Promise me as much."

"I cannot promise it." His voice was low.

"Promise me!" My fingers bit into his arm.

"I do Cassiel's will! No more can I swear."

It would have to be enough; I could ask no more than I would give. I released him. "Even Cassiel bent his will to Elua," I murmured. "Remember it."

"Remember you are not Elua," Joscelin said wryly.

SEVENTY-EIGHT

I did not sleep well that night, in the Master of the Straits' fabulous four-posted ebony bed. My heart and mind alike were too full. Once I rose, opening the door of my chamber onto the tower landing, candle in hand, gazing at the closed doors of my companions' sleeping-quarters. I would have gone somewhere, to someone, then; but I knew not whom.

So I returned to my vast, lonely bed and dozed, tossing, waking in a tangle of linens.

I wished Delaunay were here.

Day broke, and whiled onward; I found the library, that housed a hundred books believed lost, pages thick and stiff with their drowning, ink blurred, but still readable. There was a whole volume of poems by a famous Hellene poetess that I had never read entire; Maestro Gonzago would have given his eyeteeth to see it. I read slowly, trying to translate the words into D'Angeline, wishing I had pen and paper. They were beautiful, so beautiful I wept, and forgot where I was, until Tilian came to fetch me.

Noon was nigh.

They led us back along the broad, winding path; strange, how familiar it seemed. The Master of the Straits awaited us in his temple, open on all sides to the breezes.

I never understood, before, how sacrificial victims

could go consenting. I thought of Elua, baring his palm to the blade. I thought of Yeshua, taking his place upon the wooden tree. No two sacrifices are the same, and yet all are, in the end. It is the commitment to belong, wholly, to that which claims one.

"Have you an answer?" the Master of the Straits asked, and his voice rose like the wind, all around us, his eyes the color of sunlight reflected on water. I shivered; enough of a coward, it seemed after all, to wait on another's response.

None came.

"Yes, my lord," I said, my voice sounding small and mortal. I raised my eyes to meet that sea-shifting gaze. "One of us must take your place."

I heard Hyacinthe laugh, despairingly.

The Master of the Straits looked at me with eyes full of thunderclouds. "Are you prepared to answer in full?"

Joscelin drew a long, hissing breath, his hands flexing above his daggers. Quintilius Rousse made a startled sound, and Drustan bowed his head, twisting the signet ring on his finger. He had guessed; Earth's oldest children. They are closer to the old tales, to the workings of fate.

"Yes," I whispered. "Yes, my lord."

"No."

I was not sure, for a second, who had spoken; it sounded so little like Hyacinthe. My Prince of Travellers, light-hearted and careless; no longer, not since Moiread's death. He gave a choked laugh and ran his fingers through his black ringlets. "You summoned me, my lord. I am here. I will stay."

The Master of the Straits was silent.

And I knew, then, that everything before had been but play.

"No," I whispered, turning to Hyacinthe. My hands

rose, shaping his face, almost as familiar as my own. "Hyacinthe, no!"

He held my wrists gently. "Breidaia dreamed me on an island, Phèdre, do you remember? I couldn't see the shore. The Long Road ends here, for me. You may have unraveled the riddle, but I am meant to stay."

"No," I said, then shouted it. "No!" I turned to the Master of the Straits, fearless in my despair. "You seek one to take your place; you posed this riddle, and I have answered! It is mine to answer in full!"

"It is not the only riddle on these shores." There was a sorrow in his voice, eight hundred years old. The sun stood overhead, casting the Master of the Straits' face into shadow as he bowed his head. "Who takes my shackles, inherits my power. Name its source, if you would be worthy to serve."

Joscelin turned aside with a sharp cry; I think, until then, he thought there was still a way he might answer. I raised my face to the sun, thinking, remembering. The library in the tower, the lost verses. Delaunay's library, where I had spent so many sullen hours, forced to study when I'd rather have entertained patrons; I'd have given anything, to have them back now. Alcuin, hair falling like foam to curtain his face, poring over ancient codices. Joscelin's voice, unwontedly light, a rare glimpse of the Siovalese scholar-lord's son he'd been born. *He's got everything in here but the Lost Book of Raziel. Can Delaunay actually read Yeshuite script?*

The pieces of the puzzle came together; I lowered my gaze, blinking.

"It is the Book of Raziel, my lord."

The Master of the Straits began to turn my way.

"Only pages." Hyacinthe's voice was like a hollow reed sounding. "Pages from the Lost Book of Raziel, that the One God gave to Edom, the First Man, to give him mastery over earth and sea and sky, and took away for his disobedience, casting it into the depths." The Master of the Straits stopped and considered him. Hyacinthe gave his desperate laugh, black eyes blurred with the *dromonde*, seeing at last. "A gift of your father, yes? The Admiral calls him the Lord of the Deep, and tosses him gold coins, for he is superstitious as sailors are. But the Yeshuites name him Prince of the Sea; the angel Rahab, they call him, Pride, and Insolence, who fell, and was cleaved and made whole, who fell, but never followed." The words came faster, tumbling from his lips, his blank gaze seeing down the tunnel of eight centuries. I remembered a blazing fire, the sound of fiddles skirling, Hyacinthe playing the timbales while an ancient woman cackled in my ear. *Don't you know the* dromonde *can look backward as well as forward?* "He begot you, my lord, upon a D'Angeline girl, who loved another. Who loved an Alban, son of the Cullach Gorrym, a mortal, one of Earth's eldest. Is it not so?"

"It is so," the Master of the Straits murmured.

Hyacinthe ran his hands over his face. "The Straits were still open then, free waters . . . he took her here, to this place, this isle, the Third Sister, still untouched by the Scions of Elua, and she bore you here . . . though she loved you, she sang in her sorrow and captivity like a bird in a cage, until her song carried across the waters, and the Alban who loved her sailed the Straits to free her . . ." He fell silent.

"They died." The words rose around us, filled with the sea's deep surge, ceaseless and sorrowing. "The waves rose, their boat overturned, and the deep water took them. I know where their bones lie." The Master of the Straits gazed across the sea from his vast, open temple, the fluid shifting of his features fixed in grief.

"And the One God punished Rahab's disobedience,

and bound him to His will," Hyacinthe whispered. "But for the heart of a woman he could not sway and his own lost freedom, Rahab took his vengeance, and laid a *geis* upon you, my lord. He brought up scattered pages, from the deep, to give you mastery over the seas, and he bound you here, that Alba and Terre d'Ange would ever be separated by the waters you ruled, until love daring enough to cross the breach was born once more, and one came willing to take your place."

The Master of the Straits spoke with the finality of a wave crashing to shore, and I knew, then, that I had lost. "It is so."

Hyacinthe straightened; his face cleared and he laughed, a raw gaiety to it this time. "Well, then, my lord, will I serve?"

"You will serve." The Master of the Straits inclined his head, his eyes gone a dark and compassionate blue. "A long and lonely apprenticeship, until you are ready to take on the chains of my *geis*, freeing me to leave this earth and follow Elua's path, where Heaven's bastard sons are welcome."

"You have used us harshly, Elder Brother," Quintilius Rousse muttered darkly. "What's to become of the lad, then?"

"I have used you less harshly than fate has used me." The Master of the Straits turned an implacable face to him. "The sea has loved you, friend sailor; count it a blessing. Half your folk would have died in the crossing had I not taken you in hand. My successor will be bound to this isle, as was I. That curse will not be broken until the One God repents of my father's punishment, and His memory is long."

"What of the Straits?" Drustan asked in Cruithne; his brow was furrowed with the effort of following the proceedings, for Hyacinthe's words had been in

D'Angeline. Enough, though, he understood. "Will the crossing remain forbidden?"

"You hold that key." The pale hand pointed once more at the gold signet on Drustan's finger. "Wed, and open the lock."

"Naught but twenty thousand howling Skaldi and the traitors of Camlach stand in the way," Quintilius Rousse said sardonically. "While we languish on a forsaken rock in the middle of the sea, with no army in sight."

"I promised my aid," the Master of the Straits said, unmoved. "And you shall have it." He swept his arm above the bronze vessel again, its waters rippling. "All that has passed in Terre d'Ange, I will show you. Your men and your horses and arms, I will bring safe to land. No more, can I do. Will you see it now?"

They looked at me; surprised, I looked back, and found I was trembling. Truly, there is a limit to what the mind can compass in one day. I'd risen prepared to chain my life to this lonely isle. It is a hard thing, to turn aside from so deep a path. "No," I said, shaking my head and struggling to keep my voice steady. "My lord, if it please you . . . I would ask a little time, an hour, mayhap. Might we have that long?"

"You may. I will send for you an hour before sundown." He bowed, then turned to Hyacinthe. "This day, I give you. Only know that your feet will never again leave this soil."

Hyacinthe nodded, sober-eyed.

He understood.

In the tower once more, in a sitting room with glassless windows, I called for wine, raising my voice sharply. The servants jumped, and hurried to obey; I was beyond caring, at that moment. I drank half a glass at a draught when it arrived, and looked hard at Hyacinthe. The others drew away, leaving us alone.

"Why?" I asked him. "Why did you do it?"

He smiled faintly, toying with the wineglass in his hands. There were dark smudges under his eyes, but now that the worst had come to pass, he seemed more himself. "I couldn't have, without you, you know. I didn't have the answer. It was so vast, I couldn't see it." He drank a little wine and stared past me out the window. "I knew it when I saw the isle, that my road ended here. I just couldn't see *why*. Last night, when I saw that you knew, I was afraid."

"Hyacinthe." My voice broke as I whispered his name, tears starting in my eyes. "A nation at war has no need of *anguissettes*. It should be me. Let me stay."

"And do what?" he asked gently. "Throw rocks at the Skaldi? Knife the dying? Tell their fortunes? A nation at war has no need of Tsingani half-breeds untrained to arms, either."

"You have the *dromonde*! It is more than I can offer!"

"It's the *dromonde* that brought me here, Phèdre." Hyacinthe took my hands in his and looked down at our interlaced fingers. "It's the *dromonde* that sets me apart from D'Angeline and Tsingani alike. If it has led me to a place where I belong, then let me stay." Releasing my hands, he touched the diamond at my throat. "Kushiel marked you as his own," he said softly. "Whatever target he had in mind when he cast his Dart, I think it was not the Master of the Straits."

I shuddered and looked away.

"Besides," Hyacinthe added wryly, "that damned Cassiline would only turn around the instant we reached dry land, swim the Straits, and damn the lot of us. Bad enough he's vow-blinded; being besotted with you makes him a positive menace."

"*Joscelin?*" Startled, I raised my voice. Joscelin

looked over, brows raised in inquiry. I shook my head at him, and he turned back to Rousse.

"Elua help him, if he ever comes to realize it." Hyacinthe traced the line of my brows, brushing my lashes with a fingertip; the red-moted eye. "And you."

"Hyacinthe," I pleaded with him, pulling away, glancing around the austere tower room. "Look at this . . . this place. You're the least-suited person in the world to end here! Without friends, laughter, music . . . you'll go mad!"

He looked around, shrugging. "I'll teach the Master of the Straits to play the timbales and the waves to dance. What would you have me say, Phèdre? If you could survive crossing the Camaeline Mountains in the dead of winter, I can survive one lonely island."

"Eight hundred years."

"Mayhap." Hyacinthe rested his chin on his hands. "The Prince of Travellers, chained to a rock. It's funny, isn't it?" I stared at him, until he shrugged again. "The rest of the Lost Book of Raziel is out there, somewhere. I've always been good at finding things. Who knows? Maybe there's somewhat in those drowned pages to free me. Or maybe someone good at riddles will find a way." He flashed his impossible grin. "It wouldn't be the least likely thing you've done."

"Don't," I begged, half-laughing through tears. "Hyacinthe, it's not funny."

"It is, a little." He looked more soberly at me. "Do me a favor, will you?" I nodded. "My house, the stable . . . it should go to my crew in Night's Doorstep. I'll write out a deed. Give it to Emile, I left him in charge. If there's aught left of the City of Elua when this is done, he'll know what to do."

"I promise."

"Good." He swallowed; it was a little harder, facing

the reality of what he'd chosen. "And make an offering to Blessed Elua in my mother's name."

I nodded again, my eyes blurred with tears. "Anasztaizia, daughter of Manoj." She had defied the Tsingani, and taught her son the *dromonde*. *What do you suppose she saw, eh? The* Lungo Drom *and the* kumpania, *or somewhat else, a reflection in a blood-pricked eye?* What Hyacinthe saw in mine, I knew; I could see it reflected in his, through my tears—a lonely tower on a lonely isle. "I will."

"Thank you." He stood up and walked to the window, looking out over the waves, surging golden beneath the late-afternoon sun. On the far side of the room, Rousse, Drustan and Joscelin watched us quietly. If they had not known it before, I was sure Joscelin had told them how deep-rooted the friendship between Hyacinthe and me was; Drustan understood Caerdicci better than he spoke it, he knew enough for that. Longer even than Delaunay, I'd known him, if only by a day. He had been my friend, when I had no one else to call the same; he had been my freedom, while I had been a bond-slave. He turned around to look gravely at me. "Phèdre, be wary of Melisande Shahrizai."

I touched her diamond. "Do you speak the *dromonde*?" I asked, fearful.

He shook his head. "No," he said, with a rueful smile. "Your life takes more odd turns than a Mendacant's tale. I doubt I could see past tomorrow sundown. It's easier to look backward, you know; it's all fixed, no matter how far back it reaches. I speak as one who knows you, no more. If you ever have a chance to confront her alone, don't take it."

"Do you truly think I don't hate her enough to trust myself?" I asked with a bitter laugh. "You weren't there in the wagon with me, when I awoke after her betrayal."

"I was there at the Hippochamp when I threw away my birthright to bring you out of the trance the mere sight of her sent you into," he said. "Whatever caused it, it's not all hatred. She should never have let go the leash when she set that collar on you. Don't give her the chance to lay a hand on it again."

It was fair; more than fair, it was likely true, in the darker corners of my soul, which I did not care to acknowledge. I bit my lip and nodded. "I won't. Blessed Elua grant I have a chance to heed your words."

"Good." He looked at all of us, then. "If you don't mind," he said quietly, "I'd like to be alone for a little while, I think. I may as well start getting used to it, before we say our farewells. And you've a campaign strategy to plan, once the Master of the Straits has shown you what he may. You'll need your wits about you."

SEVENTY-NINE

So it was that there were only four of us, and not five, who gathered once more atop the high temple of the Master of the Straits.

"You are ready?" he asked, in that voice that spoke many tongues at once. Numb with grief, it no longer seemed so strange to me.

"Show us what you will, my lord," I said for us all.

The Master of the Straits swept his arm through the air above the bronze vessel, the trailing sleeve of his robe shifting to amber in the low sunlight. "Behold," he said. "War."

The word held all the cold, benighted terror of the ocean deeps. We stood around the tripod and watched as pictures formed on the surface of the water.

Skaldi, tens of thousands of them, armed with spear and sword and axe, helms on their heads, bucklers on their arms; thousands of Skaldi, pouring over D'Angeline borders through the Northern Pass. Bands of Skaldi riding across the flatlands and ranging along the Rhenus, hurling spears at D'Angeline ships sailing on the river, whirling and retreating from the answering volley of arrows. Skaldi in the lower passes, holding ground, drawing D'Angeline soldiers eastward.

And in the mountains of Camlach, Isidore d'Aiglemort, glittering in armor, waited in command of some five thousand men, all answering to the flaming sword of the Allies of Camlach.

I pressed my fist against my mouth, watching. They had *known* Selig's invasion plan, I'd told them as much! I had thought Ysandre had believed. Was it too much to ask, that an entire army obey the Queen's command, on the say-so of a Servant of Naamah turned runaway Skaldi slave? And one convicted of murder, I remembered grimly. But surely Ysandre was clever enough to credit the intelligence elsewhere.

"Wait," said the Master of the Straits.

The pictures on the water changed.

The Skaldi horde swept down from the Northern Pass like locusts, killing as it came. I saw Waldemar Selig himself, massive atop his charger, commanding the left flank. Kolbjorn of the Manni, whom Selig trusted, led the right. The horde was strung out, the center falling behind; there were so many of them, it wouldn't have mattered if the D'Angelines hadn't known.

I saw the apple-tree banner of Percy de Somerville flying beneath the silver swan of House Courcel as a vast portion of the D'Angeline army withdrew from the lower passes, wheeling and turning, regrouping and surging north across Namarre to intercept the Skaldi.

And in the mountains of Camlach, I saw Isidore d'Aiglemort raise his hand and shout a command. Did he know, I wondered, that Selig had betrayed him? His force, arrayed in deadly efficiency, was poised to descend. Quintilius Rousse, his voice ragged with tears, called curses down on d'Aiglemort's head.

And then, inexplicably, confusion broke out among d'Aiglemort's ranks; the Allies of Camlach, turning, milling. I stared at the waters, trying to sort out what was happening.

When I saw, I wept.

The rearguard of d'Aiglemort's own force had fallen upon his men, slashing and killing. And here and there among them, in the pockets where the fighting was fiercest, I saw crude banners lashed onto spear-poles; the insignia of House Trevalion, three ships and the Navigator's Star. Young men, who went down fighting wildly; I could see the cry their lips shaped as they fought and slew. I'd heard it, long ago, chanted as they rode in triumph. Bau-doin! Bau-doin! It had been Gaspar Trevalion's plan to send Baudoin's Glory-Seekers into Camlach. Whatever part they may have played in the schemes of the Lioness of Azzalle, they paid their debt in full that day.

They didn't fall alone, the Glory-Seekers of Prince Baudoin de Trevalion. There had been others among the Allies of Camlach loyal to the Crown. They had to have known it was suicide. Even as I watched, horror-stricken, the Duc d'Aiglemort rallied his loyal forces, shouting soundlessly.

But it had been enough to shatter d'Aiglemort's attack. A handful of surviving rebels fell back and peeled away, retreating at speed down the mountains. The quickest among d'Aiglemort's men would have pursued, but the Duc held them back, gathering to assess his forces. He was too clever for haste in battle.

Those rebels captured alive, d'Aiglemort interrogated. One of them—one of the Glory-Seekers—laughed and spat at the Duc, while d'Aiglemort's men wrestled him to his knees and put a sword to his neck. D'Aiglemort asked him somewhat. Even without hearing, I could guess the answer by the terrible expression on Isidore d'Aiglemort's face.

He hadn't known Waldemar Selig had betrayed him.

He knew it now. He killed the messenger.

Would that the Master of the Straits' charmed basin hadn't shown what happened to the fleeing rebels . . . but it did. We watched as they gained the fields of Namarre, d'Aiglemort's force following in leisurely pursuit. Bent on escaping the Allies of Camlach, they ran straight into the forces of Waldemar Selig.

Joscelin made a strangled sound. I turned away.

"Watch," said the Master of the Straits, his voice remorseless.

It was a slaughter. It was swift, at least; the Skaldi are trained to kill efficiently, and Selig's warriors especially. I watched them sing as they killed, blades reddened. Doubtless I'd heard the songs before. In the vague distance, I could make out the shining hawk banners of d'Aiglemort's advance guard, beating a prudent retreat, unseen by the Skaldi invaders.

And then the bulk of the D'Angeline army swept onto the scene.

The fighting was too widespread to compass. We pieced it together, watching. Percy, Comte de Somerville rode at the head of the army, driving a wedge into the weak middle of the Skaldi masses. Ah, Elua, the bloodshed! It was dreadful to behold. I tried to number the banners in the D'Angeline army, and could not. Siovalese, Eisandine, L'Agnacites, Kusheline, Namarrane; no

Azzallese, for they were ranged along the northern border, holding the Rhenus.

And no Camaeline, for they were with d'Aiglemort or dead.

I saw the gold lion of the Royal House of Aragon flying above a company of foot-soldiers, some thousand strong, who wore flared steel helms and fought with well-trained efficiency, using long spears to force back the Skaldi foot.

I saw, to my surprise, the Duc Barquiel L'Envers at the head of two hundred Akkadian-taught cavalry, harassing the right flank of the Skaldi with short-bows. Drustan mab Necthana leaned forward, alert with interest; I couldn't blame him. The Duc grinned broadly as he rode, the ends of his burnouse trailing at the base of a conical steel helm, and his riders wheeled and turned like a flock of starlings, releasing a deadly shower of arrows. One took Kolbjorn of the Manni through the eye, and I wasn't sorry to see it. I'd had my doubts of Barquiel L'Envers, who had been my lord Delaunay's enemy for so long, but I was glad, now, he was on our side.

In the end, the Skaldi were simply too many. The Comte de Somerville's wedge broke the Skaldi center, driving a dreadful swathe of carnage; the right flank was in disarray, breaking up in a surge to meet L'Envers' fleeting attacks.

But on the left, to the east, was Waldemar Selig. I watched, unable to look away, as Selig gathered his forces, roaring soundlessly, and brought them to bear on the D'Angeline army, closing in from behind on the rearguard of the Comte de Somerville's driving wedge.

It was a rout. To de Somerville's credit, it was an orderly one. I never fully understood, until then, how he'd come to the title of Royal Commander. I understood that day. A line of L'Agnacite archers, protected by the cavalry, took their positions, kneeling with longbows in hand. Faces grim, they held their position, firing volley after volley, holding the Skaldi at bay while the D'Angeline army retreated. Most of them would die, although Barquiel L'Envers' men, riding like Rousse's ten thousand Akkadian devils, saved more than a few.

But the D'Angeline army's flight was secured.

They fell back on Troyes-le-Mont, in the foothills of northern Namarre. Later, I learned, de Somerville had known it was likely; Troyes-le-Mont had been made ready for their retreat, stocked and garrisoned, fortifications in place.

Ysandre de la Courcel, who would stand or die with Terre d'Ange, was there.

It was the first thing we'd seen, in the waters of the Master of the Straits' bronze basin, and it was the last. The face of Ysandre de la Source, the Queen of Terre d'Ange. Drustan drew a deep breath. Then the moving images faded from the surface of the water. In their place rose a map of Terre d'Ange.

"Do you understand?" the Master of the Straits asked, and pointed. "Here," he said, indicating the location of Troyes-le-Mont, "the D'Angeline army is beseiged." His finger moved in a small circle. "All around, the Skaldi threaten." He traced the northern border of Azzalle. "Here, too, in lesser numbers, but enough to harry. Here, and here," he pointed at the lower passes, "the fighting is at a standstill. The numbers were too few. And here," he indicated the eastern edge of Eisande, that bordered on Caerdicca Unitas, "a force of the allied Caerdicci city-states holds, lest the Skaldi break through."

"Cowards," Quintilius Rousse muttered, his voice full of loathing. "The best they would offer, no doubt. My lord, can you tell me where my fleet lies?"

"They fly the swan?" the Master of the Straits asked; it surprised me, a little, that he did not know for a surety, although the faces on the water gave no names. Rousse affirmed it. "Here." The bone-white finger moved along the course of the Rhenus. "They hold the northern border with the Azzallese."

"Good lads," Rousse said gruffly.

"Then the Duc de Morbhan let them go," I mused. "Where's de Morbhan, anyway? Did anyone see his banner?"

Heads shook. I pored over the basin, frowning. "Where is Isidore d'Aiglemort?" I asked the Master of the Straits, forgetting to be afraid of him. "He commands an army still, yes?"

"The silver-haired hawk of the north." The pointing finger hovered over an area along the upper border of Camlach and Namarre. "Here, today," the Master of the Straits said; his fingertip touched the surface of the water, and the map rippled and wavered. "Tomorrow, near. He has trapped himself in his folly."

"Good," I said bitterly, thinking of Baudoin's Glory-Seekers, the hundreds of loyal Camaelines who'd died to pin him there. I touched the diamond around my throat. "Where is Melisande Shahrizai?"

The Master of the Straits hesitated, then shook his head. The sun, setting in the west, filled his mutable eyes with bloodred fire. Gildas and Tilian waited some feet away, agitated; it was time to descend the steps and refill the bronze basin. "Great events, I see reflected," said the Master of the Straits. "Small, I cannot see, unless the face is known to me."

"History hinges on small events," Quintilius Rousse said direly. Joscelin shifted, the sun at his back throwing the cruciform shadow of his sword-hilt across the bronze waters.

"There," Drustan mab Necthana breathed in Cruithne, ignoring us all. Leaning forward, he tapped the site of Troyes-le-Mont with one finger as had the Master of the Straits, marking the spot where Ysandre's face had last been seen. Circular ripples spread outward, obliterating the map. When the waters stilled, it did not reform, but merely reflected sky and setting sun. "There is where we will go!"

He looked up at me, dark eyes gleaming in his blue masque. I glanced at Quintilius Rousse, the only one among us with military expertise, who looked to the Master of the Straits.

The tall, robed figure turned away, pacing to the far verge of the temple. "The Cruarch of Alba spoke truly when he said I did not play you fair. I will set your fleet where you will, where the shore touches sea. No more can I do. I have no mastery over land, to traverse it at will. First and Second Sisters I rule from the Third, though I may not leave her soil. No more can I do."

"My lord Admiral?" I held my gaze on Quintilius Rousse.

Rousse cleared his throat. "To the mouth of the Rhenus, then, Elder Brother, and as far up her shores as your wind may drive us." He scratched his chin and looked at the rest of us. "We'll rendezvous with my fleet and Ghislain de Somerville's forces and secure the northern border. Mayhap combined we can think of a way to break the siege on Troyes-le-Mont."

I translated this for Drustan, who nodded curtly. Young and lovesick he might be, but not such a fool as to throw away his people's lives in a desperate charge.

"Tomorrow at dawn," the Master of the Straits spoke, turning round to face us, his face terrible and pale against the darkening skies. "The seas will carry you where you wish. Be ready."

"We will be," I whispered, shivering.

We were dismissed. Gildas and Tilian hurried past us to take up the bronze vessel, lifting it gently from the tripod and carrying it with exquisite care to the verge of the steps. I watched them disappear, piece by piece, as they descended one step at a time. I did not envy their job.

Walking back toward the tower, I gazed up the length of it, oriel windows lit from within, blazing amber, cobalt, ruby and sea-green across the rocky terrain. The chamber at the very top of the tower was ringed all round with them.

Hyacinthe.

EIGHTY

We set sail at dawn.

Needless to say, much of the evening was spent in planning. At our request, the servants brought pen and ink and a clean-scraped parchment; there was no new paper to be had, on the Three Sisters. I sketched out a map of Terre d'Ange and the battle as we knew it, with Rousse, Joscelin and Drustan looking over my shoulder, adding and correcting.

Necessity had dictated by now that communication among us was accomplished in a polyglot babble, D'Angeline, Caerdicci and Cruithne mingled together. I could not be everywhere to translate. I daresay anyone listening would have found it nigh incomprehensible; nonetheless, everyone made themselves understood.

Hyacinthe listened with shadowed eyes.

We had told him, of course, what had transpired in the Master of the Straits' bronze mirror of seawater. He heard it without comment, sorrowing at the news.

It pained him to hear our plans, I could tell. After a time, when we had dined—absentmindedly from dishes brought into the library, where we worked—he bowed and took his leave.

"I'll see you off in the morning," he said softly.

I watched him go; and felt, unexpectedly, Joscelin's gaze upon me. He smiled wryly when I took notice, and shrugged, opening his hands. In the depths of a Skaldic winter, we hadn't needed words. I understood.

"My lord Admiral," I said. Quintilius Rousse looked up from pondering a drawing of a Caerdicci catapult scavenged from the library shelves. "You do not need me, I think, to plan a war."

"You trace a fair line . . ." He caught himself, shaking his head, and a compassionate expression crossed his scarred face. "No, my lady. We don't need you tonight."

Nodding my thanks, I returned to my chamber.

If the maidservants had labored to find fitting sea-treasures to adorn me last night, it was nothing to what I set them to now. I think, at least, that they enjoyed it; the young one giggled a great deal. Scavenging through trunks, piling high gorgeous garments cleansed and restored with loving care, they found another deemed acceptable; deep amber, like a low-burning flame, with gold brocade on the fitted bodice. A caul of gold mesh, to hold my hair; and, I swear it, tight-sealed vessels from some noblewoman's toilette, with cosmetics untainted by the sea.

I leaned close to the darkened glass of the old mirror, brushing a hint of carmine on my lips. Red, echoing the mote that blossomed on my left iris, startling against the dark bistre. My eyes, I touched with kohl; I have never used a great deal of color. I do not need it.

My attendants drew in a collective breath when I stood.

" 'Tis like somewhat from an old lay," the eldest said, hushed. I ruefully glanced in the mirror.

"It is," I said, thinking of Hyacinthe's fate. "Very like."

His door was unlocked. Candle in hand, he glanced up sharply when I turned the handle and opened it; I caught him readying for bed, coatless, in a white shirt and dark breeches. He took one look at me, then another, staring hard.

"I'm not Baudoin de Trevalion," he said harshly. "I've no need of a farewell gift, Phèdre."

I closed the door behind me. "If it's easier on you to be cruel," I said softly, "I understand. I will go. But if it's not . . . how do you want to remember it, Hyacinthe? On a battlefield outside Bryn Gorrydum, or here, like this?"

For another long moment he stood staring, then gave his best sweeping bow, high spirit rising, flashing his white grin. "To the Queen of Courtesans!"

In that moment, I loved him.

"And the Prince of Travellers," I said, inclining my head.

Of what passed between us that night, I will not speak. It had no bearing on aught that happened before or after, and was of no concern to anyone save Hyacinthe and myself. Seldom enough have I had the luxury of bestowing my gift, Naamah's art, where I chose. I chose that night, and I do not regret.

We were awake when the sky began to grey in the east.

"Go," Hyacinthe said, kissing my brow, his voice unwontedly tender. "Before my heart breaks. Go."

I went.

From my sea-buried finery, I changed into my travelling attire, Quincel de Morbhan's gift, cleaned with the same care as the gown I'd worn. I laid it back in the trunk, thanking the bleary-eyed servants, and went out to rejoin my companions.

On the wind-swept temple, we took our leave, the Master of the Straits standing silent as a statue, only his robes stirring. I would not relive that moment, for gold or jewels. How Hyacinthe endured it, I cannot say, but he had a word for each one of us, while our ship rocked on the water far below, and Tilian and Gildas oversaw the loading of our crew.

"My lord Cruarch," he said to Drustan, in the Cruithne taught him by Moiread and her sisters, "I will be watching." Hyacinthe grasped Drustan's hands, gold signet uppermost. "Blessed Elua keep you safe."

Drustan nodded. "The Cullach Gorrym will sing of your sacrifice," he said quietly. Their eyes met; there was no need of translating.

As the Cruarch made his lame progress to the steps, Quintilius Rousse stepped up to embrace Hyacinthe. "Ah, lad!" he said roughly. "You guided us through the mists to safe landing. I'll not forget." He wiped his eyes. "I'll curse the name of the Master of the Straits no more, Younger Brother. If there's aught you need sail for, send the wind to whisper in my ear."

"Bring them safe to shore," Hyacinthe said. "I ask no more than that, my lord Admiral."

Rousse left, and Joscelin took his place. "Tsingano," he murmured, gripping Hyacinthe's wrists. "I have no words."

Hyacinthe smiled wryly. "Funny. There's plenty I could say to you, Cassiline. You've come a long way since first I saw you, baited by Eglantine tumblers. You made the beginnings of a fair Mendacant, even."

"That I owe to you." Joscelin's hands tightened on Hyacinthe's wrists. "And a lesson in courage, too, Tsingano." He said the traditional Tsingani farewell, then; he must have learned it among the *kumpanias*. "I will speak your name and remember it."

"And yours." Hyacinthe leaned forward, and spoke in a low tone, so low I could not overhear. Awaiting my leavetaking, I turned to the Master of the Straits, who stood watching with eyes opaque as clouded crystal.

"Why did you let us cross for a song?" I asked abruptly, the question arising from wherever unanswered mysteries dwell. "And Thelesis de Mornay, and others. Why?"

The clouded eyes met mine. "My mother sang," the Master of the Straits said softly, his voice merging with the winds. "Sometimes, she sang to me. It is the only kindness I remember. After eight hundred years, I hunger for new songs."

I shivered and drew my cloak about myself. "I have no kindness to give you, my lord of the Straits, nor thanks. The price of your freedom is too high."

He did not answer, but only bowed. He knew, I think, the measure of that price.

Then Joscelin was gone and it was time to say goodbye.

Atop the lonely isle, Hyacinthe and I looked at one another.

"You're right," he said. "From Mont Nuit to the Palace, we would have ruled the City."

That was all he said and all there was to say. For a moment, I clung to him, then he pried my fingers gently from about his neck. "Elua keep you, Phèdre," he whispered. "Go. Get out of this place."

All the long way down, step by broad step, I didn't dare look back. Tear-blinded, I made the descent, helped over the gangplank by Elua knows who. Colors and faces blurred; I heard Quintilius Rousse shouting, and the clanking of the chain as the anchor was weighed. Our ship set her prow toward the open seas, and a breath of wind came at our back. Up went the sails, snapping as they bellied full. Grey cliff walls rushed by in a blur, and we were clear, free of the isle, setting a northward course.

I looked back, then, when we were on the open sea. I could see them still, the columns of the temple rising atop the promontory, two small figures; one robed, still as a statue, the other smaller, black ringlets wind-tossed.

A shout drew my attention. One of Drustan's Cruithne pointed.

There, in the rigging, Joscelin clung, one-handed, feet braced in the ropes. His free hand clutched his sword, torn free of its scabbard; he held it aloft, the rising sun sparking a steel gleam from its length, a wild and dangerous tribute. High atop the cliffs, Hyacinthe's figure raised one hand in farewell and held it.

I laughed until I cried, or cried until I laughed. I am not sure which. Not until the isle was out of sight did Joscelin sheathe his sword and climb down, dropping the last few yards.

"Are you all right?" he asked me, only a little breathless.

"Yes," I said, drawing in my breath in a gasp. "No. Ah, Elua, Josce-lin . . . what did he say to you, at the end?"

Leaning on the railing, he looked at the water surging past the ship as the Master of the Straits drove us back up the coast of Terre d'Ange. "He said not to tell you," Joscelin said. "He said not knowing would drive you mad."

I jerked my head, stung. "He did not!" I retorted in

outrage, although it sounded very like something Hyacinthe might have said. Joscelin glanced at me out of the corner of his eye.

"No," he admitted at last. "He said if I let harm befall you, he would raise the very seas to fall upon me and crush me."

That, too, sounded like Hyacinthe. I gazed at the empty waters falling away behind us, smiling through my tears. "My friend," I whispered, "I will miss you."

All day the eldritch wind blew, driving us northward. We rode upon its crest, surging forward, coast-hugging, heading for the northern tip of Azzalle. Quintilius Rousse held hard at the helm, shouting commands in D'Angeline and bastard Cruithne. We kept a lookout for the remainder of our fleet, but no other vessels were to be seen on these waters.

When we reached the point where the Rhenus opened onto the sea, we saw why.

They had been brought there before us, all of them. The sandy-beached mouth of the river was clogged with craft, ships and oar-boats and rafts, a vast encampment awaiting us on the southern shore of the river. They hailed us with great shouts, crowding the shore. Standing in the prow, I watched Drustan's eyes alight, rejoicing to see his people alive and hale.

Half would have died in the crossing, the Master of the Straits had told Quintilius Rousse. In truth, it was a dubious undertaking; who was to say it was not true? One life measured as naught against hundreds. And yet Hyacinthe was my friend, and I grieved for him.

We tossed lines ashore, and dozens of willing hands drew us landward; disembarking in triumph, nearly the whole of our company reunited on solid ground, hands clasped, backs thumped, tales were exchanged. Our arrival followed theirs by mere hours, it seemed; we heard the stories, unbelievable to any save us, of how the great waves had cradled their fleet, to the shores of First Sister and back, depositing them safe as mother's babes on the silted shores of the Rhenus.

There had been losses, it was true, when the Master of the Straits had first risen from the waves. Seventeen men, and four horses. I added their lives, in my mind, to the price of his freedom. Dear-bought, indeed.

But most were alive.

The Twins had taken command in our collective absence, and made a good job of it. None spoke of it at the time, but I heard later how the army despaired, cast upon the shores of First Sister, and how it was Grainne who rallied their spirits, sparking them with her own indomitable will; Eamonn, Eamonn had kept them organized, pasturing the horses, drying and cleaning their sea-damped arms, setting parties to forage, finding coast-dwellers of the Eidlach Or who spoke D'Angeline to communicate with the islefolk, a skill garnered from years of trading shouted news with Azzallese fishermen. Indeed, he found some who had known Thelesis de Mornay, and given her shelter in her exile.

And when the face of the waters returned, rising to tower above the bay and ordering them back to the fleet, it was the Twins who convinced the army to obey. I was not there, and cannot properly give voice to what transpired, but it gave grist to the bardic mills of the Dalriada for many a generation.

Quintilius Rousse lost no time in reuniting with his men. Not a one among them had been lost and, indeed, the discipline he had instilled in them may be credited for the low number of losses on shipboard. Assembling his decimated crew, he asked for volunteers among them, picking the five best riders to depart ere the sun's dying rays fled the west.

Eastward, they would ride, in search of Ghislain de Somerville, who had with him the army of Azzalle and Rousse's fleet. I stood at the Admiral's side as they set off, saluting us both, carrying the banner of House Courcel and the makeshift flag that bore the insignia of Kushiel's Dart.

Phèdre's Boys.

How Kings and Queens bear it, sending innocent folk to die in their name, I do not know. I had been through terror and grief in the past two days; all I wanted, swaying on my feet, was to lay my head in a quiet place and sleep. But Quintilius Rousse's sailors grinned in the saddle, saluting, and rode out in a thunder, horses trampling their own long shadows as they set their heads to the east.

"They will bring ships, my lord Cruarch, when they find my fleet," Rousse said to Drustan in slow Caerdicci. "Ships such as will bear the whole of your army up the Rhenus!"

His eyes gleamed at the prospect. Drustan nodded.

"Tonight we make camp," he said in Cruithne, looking to me to translate. "We celebrate the living and honor the dead. Tomorrow, we ride to war!"

EIGHTY-ONE

It took some time to get the whole of our camp in motion, but we set out ere the sun had risen too high.

We were short of horses and; to my surprise, Grainne sought me out and invited me to ride in her war-chariot, brought at great pains and carefully salvaged from our long and deadly crossing.

I made no protest, glad enough of her offer. It is the

first and last time I have ridden in such a conveyance, and I will say this much; there is no luxury to the ride. My teeth fair rattled out of my head as her chariot lurched and jarred across the uneven terrain.

Still, I could not but be impressed with the skill with which she guided her team, legs braced, reins wrapped round one arm, leaving the other hand free to wield spear or sword. We travelled along the shore of the Rhenus, most of us; there were only a handful of ships worth salvaging. Hard going, for their part, as the current was against us; still, their oars dipped and beat, and the wind lay at our backs.

So we made progress, on foot and on horse, in chariot and ship, cutting a broad swathe along the flatlands. Some few villages we passed, filled with Azzallese riverfolk; they looked askance at us, fearful of the Cruithne, though their pride demanded they show it little. With Quintilius Rousse and Joscelin, I labored to allay their fears, although I think it did but confuse them the worse, to hear courteous words from the lips of a Night Court-trained adept in the company of woad-stained barbarians.

Still, they knew of the war, and that was some news; no village but had its militia, sturdy men armed with homemade weapons, keeping a keen eye on the river, lest the Skaldi attempt to bridge it. When we asked after Azzalle's army, they pointed us ever eastward.

Two full days' march we put in, and half another, sleeping the sleep of exhaustion in between, before Rousse's riders returned, catching us at midday of our third march. They rode hell-for-leather, Phèdre's Boys, having accepted fresh mounts, but no changes of couriers.

I confess, my heart lifted to see them coming, the Courcel swan and my own ludicrous insignia, Kushiel's tattered Dart, defiant on the breeze. I clutched at

Grainne's arm and she drew up the chariot. Someone shouted for Quintilius Rousse, and he made his way to the forefront, even as the riders thundered upon us, reining in their mounts, hooves spattering dirt.

"My lord Admiral!" the first among them cried out, his voice ragged with exertion and pride. "The fleet comes!"

He pointed, and we saw them, rounding a bend of the Rhenus, rowing at full speed down the broad, rushing river: the Royal Fleet, decked out in full regalia, every mast flying the swan. Such was their speed, the riders had scarce beaten them.

I knew then how the Cruithne army had felt, seeing our modest ship; we cheered, all of us, and hurried to catch lines cast ashore.

Over thirty ships, all told; their masts made a forest on the river. Quintilius Rousse, his face beaming joy, roared orders, relayed in a babble of Cruithne and Eiran, getting Drustan's army on board. When it was done, the ships fair groaned, riding low in the river. The oarsmen were hard-put to turn us about, beating against the current; but somehow, fate favored us, a fair wind arising at our backs, filling the sails and making their task easier.

The Master of the Straits honored his debt still, I thought, standing in the prow and gazing upriver.

Having seen to her team and made certain her chariot was stowed with proper care, Grainne came to join me. We rode in the flagship, with Rousse; a second ship drew alongside, Eamonn hailing us. Grainne shouted back, laughing, blowing kisses to her twin. I smiled to see it.

"We cannot honor the Dalriada enough for what you have done," I said to her. Grainne gazed at Drustan, who stood listening attentively to Quintilius Rousse.

"You have given us a part in a story the bards will sing to our children's children," she said, laying one hand over her belly and giving her private smile. "Such is the dream of the Dalriada. Even Eamonn knows, in his heart." She put her arm about me, then. "We heard what befell your friend. I am sorry, for his loss. He had a bold spirit, and a merry one."

"Thank you," I said softly, tears stinging my eyes. Hyacinthe. It was a kindness in her, that I have never forgotten. There are those who are awkward in the face of sorrow, fearing to say the wrong thing; to them, I say, there is no wrong in comfort, ever. A kind word, a consoling arm . . . these things are ever welcome. Grainne knew it; such was her gift, a shrewd kindness, to know what was needful to the hearts of those around her.

We were another day on the river, our progress slow in the overladen ships, despite the fair winds. Still, there was no shortage of men to arm the oars, and no one of us grew overtired. The Segovae of the Tarbh Cró put in long hours in self-imposed atonement for what had befallen us during the crossing of the Straits, their hands raw and bleeding, until word of their efforts reached Drustan. He spoke to them, then, and made it clear that he didn't hold them to blame for it.

It was fairly done, and generous; I held myself as much to blame, for having failed to warn Rousse's sailors. But in truth, the Master of the Straits had rigged and baited the trap, and I think we'd have fallen into it no matter how it transpired.

Rousse's riders had found the fleet with Ghislain de Somerville and half the Azzallese forces; this was the word they had brought back to us. The other half was under the command of Marc de Trevalion, further southeast. Between the two of them, they covered a long stretch of border, and the half-destroyed remnants of four bridges that might be used to cross the Rhenus. We would sail as far as the first bridge; beyond that, Rousse's ships could not travel. Their value lay in securing the length of the river between bridge and sea; we'd only caught them massed at the bridge because a tenacious party of some fifteen hundred Skaldi was rumored to be gathering for an assault on the bridge.

I do not think a river-crossing ever played any part in Selig's invasion plan; surely, from what we had seen, the bulk of the Skaldi horde had flooded through the Northern Pass. But if he did gain control of Azzalle's border, he would have unlimited access to Terre d'Ange, and a strong foothold in the flatlands. And if he did not, with a mere handful of men—and a few thousand were little more than that, to Selig—he tied up the forces of an entire province and ensured that Azzalle's army wouldn't fall upon his back.

A leader who thinks. Gonzago de Escabares had spoken truly.

When the shouting clamor of battle, steel on steel, reached our ears, I knew we must be nigh.

We saw it first, in the flagship. The Skaldi had found an engineer or two among their number, and in the absence of Rousse's fleet, mounted a full-scale effort to restore the bridge. They'd adopted Tiberian tactics, digging fortifications along shore and constructing narrow rolling walls to shelter the builders.

Tiberian soldiers, however, wouldn't have broken ranks and disregarded order halfway through the process, forging forward under cover of a hail of spears, inching crude rafts along the half-drowned bridge supports. Only a few hundred had gained D'Angeline soil, but the rest were bidding fair to cross, keeping Ghislain's men a spearcast's length at bay. He'd only seven hundred under his command; and I learned, later, that his archers had spend their arsenal over the past two days, hoping to hold off the Skaldi until our arrival.

They'd succeeded, if only barely.

The Skaldi froze, as our thirty-odd ships drew upriver. I daresay they'd posted a lookout for the fleet's return two days ago, but that discipline too had crumbled in the blood-fever of launching a full attack. My heart filled with icy fear at the familiar sight of them, Skaldic warriors, iron-thewed and ferocious.

It's as well that D'Angeline women don't ride into battle. Quintilius Rousse never hesitated. Each ship had a full complement of his own sailors on board, trained to obey the Admiral's voice without thinking. He raised it now, roaring orders as if to shout down the ocean, incomprehensible commands that only sailors understand.

The Skaldi began to chant Waldemar Selig's name.

I daresay Drustan mab Necthana grasped Rousse's plan quickly enough; leaping onto the prow of the flagship, his misshapen limb no obstacle to his agility, he called out to the Cruithne. On each ship, a line of archers formed along the shoreward side, protecting the sailors who scrambled overboard like monkeys, catching cast lines and hauling the ships toward the shallow waters along the foreign bank.

At the bridge, the Skaldi broke ranks, the greater number surging back toward the flatlands. If nothing else, they are bold; those trapped on D'Angeline soil never looked back, but began composing their death-songs. I heard the sound of it rise, fierce and hard, chilling my spine. No doubt the Azzallese felt the same.

Our ships grounded in the shallows. Planks were lowered with a crash, some reaching the bank, some landing in water. Drustan, red cloak whipping around him, shouted orders. Ramps were dropped into the holds, horses brought up, wild-eyed and terrified, Cruithne and Dalriada scrambling to arms.

It was something to see, an entire army boiling over the fleet's edge, plunging down planks, churning water and soil into mud. I understood, for a brief moment, why poets sing of such things.

And then the fighting began.

It didn't last long. Fierce as the Skaldi are, they are men, and bleed and die like men; and nothing, in all Waldemar Selig's planning, had prepared them for Drustan's wild army, blue-whorled faces spilling out of ships, fighting with a ruthless ferocity that equalled their own.

What he had told them of D'Angelines, I can only guess, but if the Skaldi trapped between Ghislain's men and the river thought to find their opponents soft, they soon found otherwise. The Azzallese fought with dire efficiency under his command, any reluctance at serving under a L'Agnacite lord, it seemed, resolved by the return of Marc de Trevalion.

I saw it all, from shipboard, warded by Joscelin and a loyal handful of Phèdre's Boys; after what had happened outside Bryn Gorrydum, Quintilius Rousse wasn't minded to take any chances with my safety.

When it was done, Drustan's Cruithne returned, bloodstained and victorious. They'd taken few losses, although the Lords of the Dalriada were unhappy at the necessity of having to leave their war-chariots aboard the ships. The ships themselves, alas, were well and firmly grounded. It took fifty men or more to push the flagship free; Rousse left Jean Marchand in charge of the rest, and the oarsmen took us across to D'Angeline soil.

We found the Azzallese grimly attending to the aftermath of battle. It is a thing one need see only once to make it a familiar sight, etched forever in memory. We descended together, a small party; Rousse, Joscelin and I, with two of Phèdre's Boys, Drustan, Eamonn and

Grainne, and a small honor guard of Cruithne and Dalriada.

The blue-painted faces of the Cruithne no longer seemed strange to me, but the Azzallese stared as they pointed us toward Ghislain de Somerville. Drustan understood some of the whispers, I think; he was quick to learn, and had gained some D'Angeline during our journey. Nonetheless, he gave no sign of it. Eamonn, who understood none of it, scowled; while he bore no woad on his face, his lime-stiffened hair marked him well enough as a barbarian.

Grainne, surrounded by staring D'Angeline warriors, smiled and did not look in the least displeased.

We came upon Ghislain de Somerville in the midst of directing the disposal of the Skaldi dead. I had heard he was a sensible man, and indeed, if not for his standard-bearer standing near, I'd not have known him for a lord's son. Wide-framed and sturdy, he was attired in a well-worn cuirass, simple steel and oiled leather straps. He took off his helmet as we approached, running a gauntleted hand through damp golden hair.

"I didn't believe it when your men told me, lord Admiral," he said bluntly. His eyes were a pale blue, like his father's, and he had the broad features of a L'Agnacite farmer.

Quintilius Rousse bowed, as did Joscelin; I curtsied. Drustan and his folk remained upright, owing no obeisance to D'Angeline peerage.

"My lord de Somerville," Rousse said, "this is Drustan mab Necthana, the Cruarch of Alba. And Eamonn and Grainne mac Conor, Lords of the Dalriada."

I translated for them, and they did bow, then, or at least inclined their heads. Ghislain de Somerville looked at them with something like wonder.

"You really did it," he said in awe, and gave a startled bow back to them. "Your majesties."

"Not I," Rousse said gruffly. Putting a hand on my back, he shoved me forward. "Phèdre nó Delaunay, Ysandre's emissary."

"The Queen of Terre d'Ange," Ghislain said automatically. His eyes widened at me. "*You're* Delaunay's whore?"

I do not think he meant it ill; thus had I met his father, returning from my sojourn to Valerian House, the day the old Cruarch of Alba had met with Ganelon de la Courcel. I remembered well how Delaunay had sent Alcuin to the Royal Commander, Percy de Somerville, that night. It had sealed the compact between them, I think; if Delaunay did not take de Somerville into his confidence, still he was nothing loathe to trust his loyalty. But that was what Alcuin and I had been to Percy de Somerville. Delaunay's whores. No surprise that his son knew naught else.

What did surprise him was a pair of Cassiline daggers flashing out of their sheaths, Rousse's sailors hissing in disapproval, a curt order from the Cruarch of Alba, and half a dozen Cruithne and Dalriada blades pointed at his neck. I was right, Drustan did understand a fair bit of D'Angeline.

Ghislain de Somerville blinked.

"My lord," I said calmly. "I was born to an adept of the Night Court, trained by Cecilie Laveau-Perrin of Cereus House, and completed my marque in bond-service to Anafiel Delaunay de Montrève. Is my lineage in question, or the merit's of Naamah's Service?"

"Not at all." Ghislain blushed; a smell of apples arose, mark of the Scions of Anael. "But the Servants of Naamah do not generally serve the Palace in, in such a capacity."

Quintilius Rousse coughed. Drustan raised his eyebrows in inquiry. A rare glint in his eye, Joscelin translated the comment for him at some length in Caerdicci patois; Drustan relayed it to the rest in Cruithne.

Eamonn gave an unexpected grin, and Grainne laughed out loud, putting a friendly arm about Ghislain de Somerville's shoulders. "They should," she said to him in Eiran. "Why else do you think the Dalriada came to fight for you?"

Truly, a stranger crew never landed on the shores of Terre d'Ange.

I took pity on Ghislain. "My lord," I said. "We have a very long story to tell you, but the short truth of it is, we have brought Alba's army, in accordance with the wishes of the Queen of Terre d'Ange, and we are in grave need of your guidance. That the Royal Army is beseiged at Troyes-le-Mont, we know, and little more. Will you grant us your hospitality and share your news? We bear foodstuffs of our own; I give my word that we'll not strip your camp."

"Are you jesting?" Ghislain de Somerville gathered himself with a shake, carefully disengaging Grainne's arm. "You saved our hides, you're welcome to aught we have. Bring your folk ashore, we'll welcome them all!" He strode off shouting, and Azzallese scrambled to obey.

"He smells like apples," Grainne said thoughtfully.

"Yes," I agreed. "He does."

EIGHTY-TWO

Ghislain de Somerville had more to recommend him than a pleasant odor.

Once his initial astonishment had passed, he proved a shrewd and able commander. The worktable in his tent was covered with detailed maps. He showed us exactly where Marc de Trevalion's forces were aligned along the Rhenus, and where the Skaldi had made sorties, the latest of which had nearly succeeded. He pointed out the course of the invasion through the Northern Pass, laying out his father's plan for the retreat to Troyes-le-Mont, giving us a thorough briefing on events since our departure.

Everything, it seemed, had gone according to plan; the problem was, quite simply, that no matter how cunningly they planned, there were too many Skaldi.

"All they have to do is wait," he said, his face grave, circling the point that marked the fortress with one finger. "There's a good well, and deep, no chance of losing water, and Father saw to it that Troyes-le-Mont was well stocked. But still, their food can only last so long, and Selig's got the whole damned country at his disposal. As long as his discipline holds . . ." He shrugged and shook his head.

Drustan pointed to the map and asked something in Cruithne.

"How many Skaldi?" I asked.

"Thirty-odd thousand." Ghislain's face was heavy.

I translated it; Drustan went pale under his tattooing. "And in the fortress?" I asked.

"We can't be sure what losses we took." Ghislain slid another map out and laid it atop the other, a sketch of the fortress. "Eight thousand, before the battle; how many survived, I don't know. Most, I think. They have an outer wall here, and trenches and stake-pits here, and here, with a second wall of fortifications here." He pointed, indicating. "So far, they've held this belt of ground, but my news is no fresher than yours, if the Master of the Straits' sea-mirror told true. After that, they've naught but the fortress itself."

"And after that?" Quintilius Rousse asked.

Ghislain met his eyes. "Prince Benedicte is doing all he can to rally a force among the Caerdicci city-states. If we had sufficient numbers, we could pin the Skaldi between us like hot metal on an anvil and hammer them. But the Caerdicci look to their own. It doesn't sound as though any help's coming from that quarter."

"Then they fall," Joscelin said softly. "And Terre d'Ange falls with them."

As long as Selig's discipline holds . . .

I stared at the map. "We have one chance," I said, thinking aloud, unaware that I'd spoke until Ghislain de Somerville looked quizzically at me. "Selig's army, it's fractious, there must be, what, a hundred tribes, at least?" I glanced at Joscelin. "Remember the day we rode into the Allthing?" I asked. He nodded soberly. "Some of them are blood enemies. If we stir them up, break Selig's discipline . . . it's somewhat, at least."

"And how do we do that?" Rousse asked skeptically; but Ghislain was eyeing the map intently.

"The Cruithne scared them," he said thoughtfully, tapping the map. "All those blue faces . . . the Skaldi didn't know what to make of it. I could see that well enough, from the far shore. They're a superstitious lot, you know. If we could harry their flanks, small strikes, retreating fast . . . it would give them somewhat to think about, at any rate. We'd need a secure retreat, somewhere in the mountains here. Someplace hidden."

I looked at Drustan, Eamonn and Grainne, and did not yet translate. "How many of us would be like to survive?" I asked Ghislain. "Truly."

Glancing up from the map, he drew a deep breath. "None," he said quietly. "In the end? None. We'd live as long as we were lucky, and no longer. And it may be that we'd die for naught. You're right, it's our only chance; but it's a slim one at best."

"Thank you," I told him, and then repeated it all to Drustan in Cruithne.

He took it soberly, walking half-gaited away to gaze out the door of the tent, startling the Azzallese guard. Eamonn and Grainne glanced at each other.

"Tell him I'll see his folk returned to Alba's shores," Quintilius Rousse said gruffly to me. "Every last blue-stained, lime-crested one of 'em. We didn't ask 'em here to commit suicide."

I think Drustan understood, for he answered before the words were out of my mouth. "And what happens to your Hyacinthe?" he asked me, turning around, holding up one hand, light flashing on the gold signet. "If I do not wed Ysandre," his face was strained, "if I die, if Ysandre *dies*, and the curse remains unbroken, what happens to him? And how do we get home, if the Lord of the Seas remains chained to his rock, wroth with our failure? What song will sing us home, Phèdre nó Delaunay?"

My eyes burned with tears; I had brought him here. "I don't know," I whispered. "My lord, I am so sorry."

"The fault is not yours." His deep eyes dwelled on mine. "You followed your Queen's command; my destiny is my own, and you cannot change it. But I must give my people the choice. It is my destiny, but it is not their war. If they are to die, they must have the manner of choosing, to take their chance against wave or sword."

I nodded, scarce seeing him. Drustan called sharply to Eamonn and Grainne, and they left, taking their guard with them. I related his words to the others.

"It's fair," Ghislain said softly, tracing Troyes-le-Mont on the map, head low. "Whatever you told them, they couldn't have understood the odds. None of us did."

He looked up then, his face grim. "But if you go, I'm going with you. My father's in there." He gave Joscelin a hard look. "And if I'm not mistaken, so is yours, Cassiline."

We spoke of it that night.

The stars were clear and bright in the vast black sky, familiar D'Angeline stars. There is no quiet place in a war-camp, but I found Joscelin a little distance away from our tents, seated beneath an elm and gazing at the camp. There was no celebratory atmosphere, as there had been after the defeat of Maelcon's army; this had been a skirmish, no more, a small victory in a hopeless war. The Azzallese cleaned their arms and wondered grimly what was next. There were fires burning wherever Drustan's army was encamped, discussion going long into the night.

"Did you know?" I asked Joscelin, sitting beside him.

He shook his head. "I wasn't sure. I knew it was possible. I didn't see our banner, on the isle, but there were so many."

"I'm sorry," I said softly.

"Don't be." His voice was rough. "House Verreuil has always served. Did you know, my father fought in the Battle of Three Princes? That's when he won the title Chevalier." One corner of his mouth quirked. "You know, the one you bestowed on Rousse's men."

"I've no right to grant lands, though."

"No." He stared at the stars. "Verreuil's a small estate, but it's been in the family for six hundred years. Shemhazai's line, you know. We kept up the library, sent one son a generation to the Cassiline Brotherhood, and served the throne of Terre d'Ange as need required."

"Is it just your father?" I asked in a low voice.

Joscelin shook his head again. "No," he said quietly. "Luc would have gone with him."

"Luc?"

"My older brother." He sighed, resting his chin on his knees. "I've a younger, too, but they'd have made Mahieu stay. Mother's comfort, the youngest; Father's strength, the eldest. It's the one born in the middle goes to Cassiel. So they say, in Siovale. My sisters used to tease. Three of those, too, you know."

And eleven years since he'd seen any of them; I remembered that, well. It must be twelve by now. Better than half my life, and near as much for Joscelin. I'd come to think of him as nigh as rootless as myself, but it wasn't true.

I wanted to say something, but I'd no words. I took his arm instead, and he looked ruefully at me.

"I thought I'd have a chance to see them," he said. "Before . . . well, before the end. At twenty-five, they let us visit home, in the Brotherhood, if we've served well . . ." He shivered. "Or . . . they would have. I'm anathema, now. Does my family know, do you think? Or do they know only that I'm a condemned murderer, convicted of killing Anafiel Delaunay?"

"No one who knew you would believe it, Joscelin."

"What do they know?" There was a hard note in his tone. "I was ten years old, Phèdre! How do they know what I became?" He turned his forearms, starlight glinting on his steel vambraces. "I hardly even know myself, anymore," he whispered. "Ah, Elua! Did we come all this way for nothing more than this?"

"I don't know," I murmured, gazing past the campfires, across the darkened land. I had known the number of the Skaldi, had seen them, but even so . . . thirty thousand. Somewhere out there in the darkness, they camped around a fortress and made ready to rend the very fabric of all I held dear.

Joscelin drew a long breath, gathering himself. "Whatever may come in the morning, we'll make ready to ride to Trevalion. It's well-garrisoned and Ghislain's promised his hospitality. Rousse will spare a guard for you, too. His men wouldn't let him do aught else."

I looked at him and said nothing.

"No." His jaw set stubbornly; even by starlight, I could see the white lines forming alongside his nose. "Oh, no. Don't even think it."

"They came at my word."

"They came at the *Queen's* word! You did but carry it!"

"Ysandre de la Courcel did not play on the Twins' jealousy to spur the Dalriada to war," I said. "Or leave her oldest friend in the world bound to a lonely rock to win passage toward a doomed battle. I can't run from this, Joscelin."

"What in Rousse's seven hells do you think you can do?" he shouted at me. "It's a war!"

I shrugged. "Put a face on what they're fighting and dying for. That's what you told me, isn't it?"

He had no answer for that. "And if they vote to retreat?" he asked, looking away.

"I'll go to Caerdicca Unitas and offer my services to Prince Benedicte," I said. Joscelin glanced back at me, surprised. "What other course is there? Drustan will stay, no matter what. Mayhap if the Caerdicci hear of the Cruarch of Alba's sacrifice, it will sway some few of them."

"The Caerdicci won't fight for Terre d'Ange," Joscelin said softly. "The city-states are more fractious than the Skaldi, and more jealous than the Twins. Not even Naamah's wiles can bind them together, Phèdre."

"I know," I said. "But it's better than waiting to fall into Selig's hands." Rising, I stooped and kissed his cheek. "I'm sorry about your family. I'll pray for them, Joscelin."

"Pray for us all," he whispered.

I did, too. It had been a long time since I'd truly offered prayer to Blessed Elua, and not just the desperate pleas one gasps out in terror. I prayed to Elua and all his Companions, not only those who had marked me, for wisdom, for guidance, for some glimmer of hope to hold against our despair. I prayed for the safety of Joscelin's father and brother, for Ysandre de la Courcel and all immured in Troyes-le-Mont, for Drustan and the Twins and all of their folk, Rousse, Phèdre's Boys, Ghislain and Trevalion and all the Azzallese, and Hyacinthe, alone at sea. For the Night Court and all her Houses, for the poets and players of Night's Doorstep, for Thelesis de Mornay and Cecilie Laveau-Perrin, for the kind seneschal of Perrinwolde, and all his family.

In the end, I think I prayed for everyone I'd ever known, and everyone I'd never met, heart and soul of Terre d'Ange. Whether it did any good, I cannot say, but if my heart was no more at ease, it drove me at least to the sleep of exhaustion.

And in the morning, Drustan gave the answer of his people.

"We will stay and fight."

He gave it in Caerdicci, that all might understand. Ghislain de Somerville looked hard, not sure he'd heard him aright. "All of you?"

Drustan gave a short nod. "If you will swear us this," he said, switching to Cruithne; longer speeches were still difficult for him. "If we fall, someone must carry word to Alba. Our families and friends must know how we died. The poets must sing of our deeds."

I translated his words, and then said to him in Cruithne, "I promise it." He fixed his deep look on me.

"I swear it will be so, my lord Cruarch." To Ghislain, I said in D'Angeline, "I swear it. In the Queen's name."

Joscelin made a faint, despairing sound.

"Joscelin, think about it. If we fail . . . if I cannot cross the Straits," I said reasonably to him, "Who can?"

"She has a point, Cassiline," Quintilius Rousse observed.

"It was Caerdicca Unitas last night," Joscelin muttered sourly. "Tomorrow she'll want you to sail to Khebbel-im-Akkad. If you ask me, lord Admiral, we ought to lock her in a dungeon and throw away the key."

"Then it is decided. I've sent word to Marc de Trevalion, asking to meet," Ghislain said, interrupting us. Hauling out one of his maps, he pointed to a spot along the Rhenus. "We'll make our conference here. If Trevalion agrees, we'll combine our forces under his command. With yesterday's victory, we may even be able to spare a few hundred men. Lord Admiral, by your leave, I'd as lief have you stay with your fleet, and command the defense of the western banks." He looked up inquiringly.

It was something of a blow, I think; Rousse had been at the heart of our quest for so long. But Ghislain was right, it made more sense for him to remain in command of his fleet. Quintilius Rousse knew little of battle tactics on land; Ghislain de Somerville was the Royal Commander's son. Rousse nodded slowly. "As you bid, my lord."

"Good." Ghislain rolled up the map. "Strike camp. We're moving out."

EIGHTY-THREE

On the morrow, Joscelin and I—and Drustan and the Twins as well—said our farewells to Quintilius Rousse. I had come to be very fond of the bluff Admiral, and realized, in the face of leaving him, how we had all come to depend on his strength.

"Elua keep you, girl," he said roughly, folding me in his massive embrace. "You've enough courage for ten, in your own perverse way, and your lord's bedeviled sense of honor to boot. If you need to cross the Straits again, you know I'm the man to do it."

"Thank you," I whispered. "Would you carry another, if need be?"

"Anyone you name," he vowed.

Rousse would honor his word, I knew; he released Phèdre's Boys to ride with us, over my protests. Thirty-odd sailors would make no difference on the Rhenus, but it had become a point of honor with them. Catching the adamant look on Joscelin's face, I left off protesting and acceded with grace. They, too, had the right to choose.

We made good time on that day's march, and reached the meeting-place before nightfall.

If Marc de Trevalion was astonished by the sight of three thousand and more Albans, he hid it well, bowing to Drustan with grave courtesy. I knew him only from his trial, where he had shown the same demeanor. Ghislain de Somerville, he greeted as a son; indeed, de Somerville was betrothed now to his daughter Bernadette, recalled from exile along with her father.

Who among them actually held title to the duchy of

Trevalion was unclear. Later, I came to understand that it was to be held in trust for Ghislain and Bernadette's firstborn. They were both sensible men, and it was no point of animosity between them, neither seeing cause to quarrel over a parcel of land when the whole of Terre d'Ange stood at stake.

To me, he said kindly, "My cousin Gaspar spoke well of your lord Delaunay. He held him always in the highest regard, and indeed, I have never had aught but respect for him."

I nodded my thanks and swallowed; no matter how distant the grief was, it always brought it on fresh, to hear Delaunay's name spoken familiarly.

Ghislain de Somerville laid out our story, in blunt terms. De Trevalion listened without interrupting as he sketched our plan. When Ghislain was done, he rose to pace slowly, hands clasped behind his back. "You know the odds of your survival?" he asked somberly.

"I know. We all do."

Marc de Trevalion nodded. "Then you must try," he said quietly. "I'll coordinate with your captain-at-arms. Never fear, we'll hold the Rhenus, for as long as Troyes-le-Mont stands."

"Thank you, Marc," Ghislain said simply.

So are such things decided. I left them to the debate of maps and strategies, begging paper and ink of de Trevalion and setting to composing a letter.

"What are you doing?" Joscelin asked, straining to see over my shoulder. I sanded the wet ink and shook it off.

"Thelesis de Mornay," I said, showing him. "If . . . if neither of us live through these next weeks, she'll be able to carry word to Alba. The Master of the Straits has allowed her passage before, and Hyacinthe knows her." I smiled wryly at his expression. "Did you think I was counting on doing it myself? I know the risk my choice entails."

Joscelin shook his head. "I'm not sure whether to be glad or frightened that you grasp it," he said softly.

I blew on the still-damp ink. "Be glad," I said, "for the sake of Alba."

I was glad in turn, then, that Phèdre's Boys were with us. With Joscelin at my side, I found Remy and held up the scrolled letter, in a leather carrying-case.

"I've a mission," I said to him, calculating, "for the boldest and shrewdest among you. I've need of seeing this letter carried across hostile terrain to the City of Elua, and delivered into the hands of the Queen's Poet. Have you men who will serve, Chevalier?"

"Have I?" he exclaimed, holding out his hand and grinning. "Give it here, my lady, and they'll see it reaches safe berth, sure as any ship that ever sailed!"

I gave it to him with a good will, watching as four riders set out with alacrity, armed with de Trevalion's latest intelligence, on a course that would take them wide of battle. Better odds than we would have, at least, and it would ensure my promise to Drustan would be kept. I would have sent them all, if I could.

"You're not quite as foolhardy as you seem," Joscelin said thoughtfully, watching them go.

"Not quite," I agreed. "Only just almost. I wish you'd go with them, Joscelin."

He gave me his dryly amused look. "Will you never be done testing my vow?"

"No." I swallowed against an unexpected pain in my heart. "Not if I have my choice in the matter, Cassiline."

It was as close as either of us had ever come to a declaration of feeling; moreover, it was a flag of defiance waved in the face of despair. Joscelin did not smile, but bowed, with the deep-bred Cassiline reflex. "Elua grant you the chance," he murmured. "I'm willing to live with it, if it means your survival."

Another time, we might have spoken more, but this was war. I was soon called back, to serve as translator for Drustan mab Necthana and our D'Angeline commanders, as we plotted our dangerous course.

"Would that I could tell you aught of d'Aiglemort," Marc de Trevalion said, shaking his head. "But he's sealed his forces up within the foothills of the Camaelines, and no one knows where. As well beard a badger in his den as track him there." He pointed to the map. "There's your likeliest retreat. I've one piece of advice for you," he added, glancing at Ghislain. "Take out Selig. If their information is good," he continued, nodding at Joscelin and me, "and I've no reason to believe it isn't, Waldemar Selig is the key. If he falls, the Skaldi are leaderless."

The Skaldi believed Selig was proof against arms. I wished I could believe otherwise; but I remembered that night, when I would have killed him, and was unsure.

"We'll try," Ghislain de Somerville murmured. "You may be sure of that."

"My lord de Trevalion," I asked, "what befell Melisande Shahrizai?"

Marc de Trevalion's face hardened; he'd issues of his own with Melisande, whose machinations had brought his House down. But he shook his head again. "The last I knew, the Cassiline Brotherhood was looking for the Shahrizai, to bring them in for questioning. But I never heard they found them."

Nor likely to, I thought; Melisande would see a Cassiline coming at five hundred paces. Well, no mind. I touched the diamond at my throat. Wherever she was, it was not on the battlefield.

In the morning, we rode to war.

I will not detail the provisioning of the army, the considerable difficulties entailed in transmitting a plan of such scale to a vast force, with language ever a barrier. Suffice it to say that all was done in the end, though my voice was ragged from serving as translator.

It is much to Ghislain de Somerville's credit that we proceeded as smoothly as we did. Despite his initial discomfort, he dealt evenly with our unlikely force, and found a common bond with Drustan mab Necthana, who was not too proud to appreciate another's skill.

Much credit also goes to Eamonn of the Dalriada, who had an exacting mind for detail. If we were well provisioned and the dispersal of arms and mounts went without difficulty, much of it was Eamonn's doing. As much as the Twins baited each other, I saw, in that exodus, why Grainne stood by him. They were a formidable team.

We marched southward, swinging wide to the east, into Camlach, to avoid detection by Selig's forces. It is a dire thing, being part of an army on the move. I would not wish it on anyone. But we gained, in time, the rolling hills of river-wrought Namarre and a vantage point from which to spy on the siege.

Several Skaldi met their death in that effort. Waldemar Selig, no fool, had posted scouts along the perimeter of the land he held. But he had not reckoned on the Cruithne, whose woodcraft surpassed aught that I had seen. Drustan appointed an advance party, and they did their job excellently, emerging silent and deadly from the very landscape to dispatch the Skaldi watchers in our route.

Thus did we come to a place in the hills, overlooking the plain on which Selig's army was encamped.

"So many," Drustan breathed in Cruithne, lying on his belly like the rest of us to gaze down at the scene.

I had known; I had counted the numbers at the All-thing, I had seen them in the Master of the Straits' bronze mirror, and I had heard them from Ghislain de Somerville. Nothing had prepared me for the sight. From where we lay, the Skaldi army teemed around the fortified bulwarks surrounding Troyes-le-Mont like ants around an anthill. Swarms of tiny figures bustled over the plain, gathering here and there in strategic points to attack the bulwark. We could see how thin defenses were spread inside the wall, the weakening points vulnerable to attack.

It wouldn't be long before the Skaldi won through, forcing the defenders into the fortress itself. Percy de Somerville had chosen Troyes-le-Mont because it was defensible—and because it wasn't surrounded by a city filled with innocent, unarmed D'Angelines—but Selig had studied Tiberian tacticians.

They were building siege towers.

"That's the best place to strike," Ghislain said practically, jutting his chin at a tower under construction on the outer edge of the encampment. "They're well out of bow range, so they'll not be on the lookout for attack, and their attention's fixed on the tower. Do you agree?"

I translated for Drustan, who nodded in agreement.

"Good." Ghislain stared hard at the besieged fortress, thinking, no doubt, of his father, then drew back cautiously. "We'll plan our retreat in stages," he said, gazing at the hills behind us with all the thoughtfulness of a farmer plotting his orchard. "We need to be able to make a clean break of it."

If anyone had doubted that he'd inherited his father's gift for military tactics, they didn't after that day. The course of our retreat stretched for miles into the foothills, leading Skaldi pursuers through a deadly series of setbacks, and at last into a narrow gorge which could be blocked, forcing the Skaldi to retreat.

It took two days to plan the attack, Ghislain verging on overcautious before finally giving his approval. I was glad, though, when I learned that Drustan planned to lead the strike.

Fifty Cruithne, they had decided, including the best archers on the fastest mounts. It was the largest number able to get near undetected, and the smallest able to get the Skaldi's notice.

I was not there to see it, remaining at the furthest retreat point, a steep, wooded hill, with Joscelin, Phèdre's Boys, and the bulk of our army; it was part of Ghislain's plan to conceal our numbers from the Skaldi.

But I heard, later. We all did.

Drustan's Cruithne struck at the first glimmer of dawn, when they could barely pick out the shape of the siege tower against the darkling sky and the Skaldi were but indistinct forms, most still wrapped in their bedrolls.

No warning did they give, but rode out of the hills like something from a nightmare, streaming across the plain, blue-masqued and eerie, slamming into the edge of the Skaldi forces and dispatching steel death. A hundred or more Skaldi died in their sleep that dawn. It grieved me, to know this; but it had grieved me more, to hear how many the Skaldi had slain in their path.

Following Ghislain's plan, the Cruithne thrust pitch-soaked torches into the Skaldi campfires, wheeling to hurl them at the wooden siege tower, Drustan throwing the first himself. By the time the Skaldi camp came full awake, buzzing like a kicked hornet's nest, the Cruithne were already in retreat, horses wheeling, archers delaying pursuit with a rain of unerring arrows—Barquiel L'Envers' Akkadian tactics, that Drustan had admired.

It bought them time, but not much.

The Skaldi came after them.

They caught the rearguard, scrambling to gain the foothills. A dozen Cruithne died there, a desperate stand quickly overwhelmed by sheer numbers. Drustan never looked back, shouting his men onward. The Skaldi followed—and encountered the first setback.

On the high crags lining their retreat, Ghislain de Somerville had positioned L'Agnacite bowmen. Steady and unflappable, able to cover far greater distances than the Cruithne archers with their short-bows, Ghislain's men shot down the foremost ranks of the Skaldi, until the dead themselves posed a formidable obstacle.

No longer than that did they linger, climbing quickly out of danger, each with his own designated path of retreat. When the Skaldi won free, Drustan's men were in full flight.

How many Skaldi pursued, I cannot say; hundreds, at least. I think close to a thousand. At one point, the path divided in a triune fork; the Cruithne took the middle route. Those Skaldi who sought to flank them on either side met with Dalriada slings and spears, driving them back. Eirans are particularly fond of slings, which they use with deadly efficacy.

Even so, it was a near thing. I was there when Drustan brought his men pounding up the steep, narrow gorge, horses lathered and near exhaustion, the warriors little better; and the foremost Skaldi were close on their heels.

"Now!" Ghislain shouted.

Positioned on the cliffs on either side of the gorge, D'Angeline and Alban soldiers alike thrust the butt ends of their levers beneath the rocks, pushing hard.

Ghislain de Somerville had planned well; an avalanche of boulders and smaller rocks tore loose and rained down like thunder, blocking the passage. The Skaldi drew back, milling, and the archers went to work.

A great many Skaldi died. But they are not cowards, nor ever have been. A few hundred remained, drawing back out of arrow range and conferring. Presently, a contingent rode back.

The others stayed, and advanced, shields over heads, to begin clearing the passage.

Selig's doing, I thought. They'd never have conceived it on their own.

Ghislain watched grimly, then made his decision. "We retreat," he said sharply, calling it out aloud. "Retreat!"

So we fled eastward, further into the hills.

When we crossed back into Camlach, I could not say. As afternoon wore on to dusk, I was concentrating on nothing more than staying on my horse, and not posing a burden to anyone around me. Ghislain had been prepared for the possibility. He left a company of archers in place, to slow the Skaldi progress; by the time they won through, we would be long gone. We laid baffles and false trails, all the while retreating deeper into the mountains. Now and again, one of the Cruithne archers would catch up with us, gasping a report.

What we would have done without their woodcraft, I do not know. No great black boar loomed out of the twilight to guide us, but I felt the presence of the Cullach Gorrym nonetheless. And Drustan, his arms bloodstained to the elbows, worked tirelessly to coordinate with them, sending scouts to spy out safe passage.

Not until Ghislain de Somerville gauged from their reports that we were out of danger did we make camp for the night. I fairly fell out of the saddle, bone-weary and exhausted with terror. If I had not survived the flight through the Skaldic winter, I think I would have given up and died that night.

Even so, it was not given me to rest.

A last one of Drustan's scouts returned from the south,

eyes starting and wild in the blue masque of his face, breathing like a marathon runner and pointing from whence he'd come. Drustan gave an incredulous frown, and I dragged myself near to listen.

"What is it?" Ghislain de Somerville asked, catching my arm.

"He says there's an army, my lord." I wasn't sure I'd heard it aright either. "A D'Angeline army, encamped in a valley, not a mile south of here."

ÉIGHTY-FOUR

"Isidore d'Aiglemort."

Ghislain de Somerville said his name like a curse. I didn't blame him. None of us did, who were D'Angeline. I heard Joscelin's breath hiss between his teeth at the name.

I explained briefly to Drustan, who nodded, understanding, his dark eyes deepset. He had been betrayed by his cousin Maelcon; he understood such things. "We'll make camp nonetheless," I said, confirming it with Ghislain. We'd get no further that night, and d'Aiglemort's forces were unaware of our presence.

One would think the very heavens would storm their disapproval on such a night, but in truth, the skies held clear. My exhaustion forgotten, I wrapped myself in my cloak and sought out the Cruithne scout who'd spotted the army of Duc Isidore d'Aiglemort, questioning him at some length.

When I was done, I went looking for Ghislain de Somerville and found him overseeing the care of the horses, who were worth their weight in gold to us.

"My lord," I said to him, "you said if the Caerdicci

would rally sufficient forces, we could crush the Skaldi as if between hammer and anvil. How many would you need?"

"Ten thousand, perhaps, in sum. Maybe less, if we could coordinate with the defenders in Troyes-le-Mont." He looked sharply at me. "Why? The Caerdicci won't venture past their borders. We both know it is so."

I looked to the south, and shivered. "I have a thought."

I told him what it was.

Ghislain de Somerville gave me another long, hard look. "Come with me," he said. "We need to talk."

His fairly appointed commander's tent with the work-table had been left in Azzalle; this was a simple field-soldier's shelter, luxurious only in that most of our army had nothing but a bedroll. We had travelled light, but for the most necessary provisions. I sat on a folding camp-stool while he paced, lit by a solitary lamp.

"If you think it madness, my lord," I said finally, unable to bear it, "then say so."

"Of course it's madness," he said abruptly. "But so is what we did today, and will do again tomorrow, if we do not choose another course. And if it goes as it did today, we will die in slow degrees, until we grow too tired or too slow or too careless, and the Skaldi catch us. If they're not already scaling the fortress walls." Stopping his pacing, Ghislain de Somerville sat on his bedroll and covered his face with his hands. "Ah, An-ael!" he sighed. "I was born to rule apple orchards, to tend the land and love its folk. Why do you send me such terrible choices?"

"Because, my lord," I said softly, "you were born to tend the land and love its folk, and not to put them to the sword. No other among us could devise a plan that would make this work."

"It might be done." He lowered his hands on his knees

and looked gravely at me. "Even if it can . . . if we fail, we stand to lose everything, and I do not know if I can bear to see our people slain by D'Angeline hands. Phèdre nó Delaunay, are you certain of him?"

"No," I whispered, feeling cold despite the warmth of the night and the glow of lamplight. "There is one trump card, one thing he does not know, that might be enough . . . but I am certain of nothing, my lord."

"I wish you were," Ghislain de Somerville murmured, hands flexing on his knees. He smiled ruefully. "Did you know my father likes to wager? L'Agnacites have a weakness for it, I don't know why. But he always said the one man he'd never wager against was Anafiel Delaunay."

"My lord," I said, alarmed, "I am not him. Even if I had half his wisdom, I would fear to advise you in this."

"If you had half his wisdom, you might never have conceived this." He gazed at the flickering lamp-flame. "But you have, and I must wager on something. I'll speak with the Cruithne scout, and see what more we may learn. When I've a plan, I'll let you know."

I nodded and rose, according him a grave curtsy, one offered in the Night Court only to scions of the Royal House. I kept my composure leaving his tent; it was only outside, beneath the stars, that I staggered and had to catch myself, terrified by the enormity of the risk in what I had proposed.

Never had I judged a patron wrongly, not Childric d'Essoms, not Quincel de Morhban, not even Melisande Shahrizai, when all was said and done. But Isidore, Duc d'Aiglemort, was no patron of mine, and by his own deed, traitor to Terre d'Ange. If I was wrong, we would all pay. And the payment would be exacted in blood.

"Where were you?" Joscelin asked when I returned,

his sharp tone betraying his concern. He glanced at my pale face. "What is it? Is aught amiss?"

"No," I said, through chattering teeth. He flung a cloak around me; his Mendacant's cloak, stained and travel-worn, the splendid colors dulled by rain and sea. I huddled into its warmth. "Not yet."

"You'll be the death of us all," Joscelin muttered, and wondered why I laughed in despair.

By the time we surrounded the valley in which d'Aiglemort's army was encamped, he knew.

It was much simpler, in truth, than the elaborate plan of retreat that Ghislain de Somerville had devised. Secure in their valley, the Allies of Camlach had posted only a few sentries; indeed, we would never have found them, had the Skaldi not pressed us to flee as far as we did.

Gauging the change of posting, Drustan's deadly Cruithne dispatched the sentries with ease. Archers and slingers found hiding places along the narrow egresses. The battle of Bryn Gorrydum, the flight from the Skaldi; all, it seemed, had been a rehearsal for this endeavor.

The rest of our army scaled the heights, encircling the valley. Ghislain placed his scant number of L'Agnacite warriors to the fore, to give us the semblance of a D'Angeline force. By dawn—less than a day and a half later—we were in place.

This time, I was there. It was my idea.

We had glimpsed the Camaeline forces by then; well over three thousand, by my count. They looked hungry, and weary, I thought. It was hard to tell, at a distance.

When the sun struck gold into the valley, Ghislain de Somerville gave the signal. We'd two trumpets among us, but they sounded like a dozen, ringing brazen from the mountains as our troops rose and stepped into view, lifting their standards.

The silver swan of House Courcel, the apple tree of de Somerville, the ships and the Navigator's Star of House Trevalion; and too, the people of Alba, the Cullach Gorrym and the Tarbh Cró, the Eidlach Òr and the Fhalair Bàn, the white horse of Eire. They flew proud, blazing in the sun. And our heralds, three of them, grinning under their chosen standard as it flew beneath the white flag of treaty: A ragged splash of red, crossed by Kushiel's Dart.

Phèdre's Boys. Remy winked at me. That was an argument I'd lost.

It took the Allies of Camlach by surprise. Deep in the valley they turned, hands shading eyes, gazing up the steep mountains at the bright army surrounding them on all sides. One stood alone and fearless, and the sun glittered on his mail and his fair hair.

Kilberhaar, I thought.

Ghislain de Somerville stepped up to a precipice, cupping his hands about his mouth. "Isidore d'Aiglemort!" he shouted, his voice echoing from the crags. "We wish to parley! We send our heralds in good faith! Will you honor the concords of war?"

Easier to shout down than up; the shining figure gave an exaggerated bow.

"Go," I said to Remy and his two companions. "Elua keep you."

"You promised to throw open the doors of the Night Court," he reminded me.

"All that you desire, and more." I laughed, a sob catching in my voice. "Come back safe and claim it, Chevalier."

Spurring their mounts, they rode down a narrow mountain path, to be met by d'Aiglemort's men. We had no choice but to wait. If d'Aiglemort played us false, we could exact a terrible revenge, from this vantage, but their lives were forfeit. We watched as they were led to d'Aiglemort, relaying our request.

Those are surely the longest moments I have passed, atop that mountain, waiting to see if Isidore d'Aiglemort would honor the concords of war.

In the end, he did. A number of Camaelines surrounded Remy and his companions in clear warning. The white flag showed vivid against the valley floor. And Isidore d'Aiglemort and a handful of chosen warriors rode-slowly up the winding trail.

He came armed and mailed, but helmetless, pale hair bright in the sun, black eyes narrowed and glittering. Without the least sign of fear, he rode straight to Ghislain de Somerville, ignoring the L'Agnacite bowmen who fell in around him, arrows nocked and pointed at his head.

"I am here, *cousin,*" Isidore d'Aiglemort said with exaggerated courtesy; all the Great Houses are kin, in some manner. "You wished to speak with me?"

"The emissary of Ysandre de la Courcel, Queen of Terre d'Ange, wishes to speak with you," Ghislain replied, his broad, handsome features impassive. "Your grace."

D'Aiglemort turned, scanning the arrayed forces, gazing over my head. I saw him take in the blue-whorled faces of the Cruithne and check himself, startled. Drustan mab Necthana ground his teeth. But this was a D'Angeline affair. I stepped forward and raised my voice.

"My lord," I said.

"You." Isidore d'Aiglemort looked down at last, and frowned. "I know you."

"Yes, my lord." I inclined my head. "I gave *joie* to you at the Midwinter Masque, when Baudoin de Trevalion played the Sun Prince. You remembered, when last we met." I saw him remember, placing me. "You were fostered among the Shahrizai," I said softly. "They should have taught you to recognize the mark of Kushiel's Dart, my lord."

Thoughts flickered across his face, too quick to follow. His emotions, he concealed. "Delaunay's *anguissette*," he said dryly. "I remember. Melisande begged a favor, for a plan gone awry. I thought you gone, among the Skaldi. But your lord's death was not of my will, *anguissette*."

"So I am given to understand," I said, with a calm I did not feel.

He raised his pale brows. "You are not here for revenge? Then what?" D'Aiglemort glanced around at the Alban army, pressing close around us. "You bring the Picti? Why?" One could see the thoughts connect behind his eyes. "Delaunay. That's what he and Quintilius Rousse were about."

"My lord." It took all of my training to keep my voice level and my gaze upon his. "This is the army of the Cruarch of Alba and Ghislain de Somerville. And we are here to offer you the choosing of the manner of your death."

D'Aiglemort's men reacted, then, reaching for their swords despite the vast number arrayed against them. The Duc held up his hand, expressionless. "How do you say?"

"You are a dead man, Kilberhaar." I saw the blood leave his face at the Skaldi name, and was glad. "Waldemar Selig used you for a fool. He'll not let you live, if he defeats us; the D'Angelines know you for a traitor, and will not abide it. Selig's smart enough to clean up after himself, and wise enough to leave no blade aimed at his back. I know, I spent considerable time in his bed, thanks to you. You're dead, no matter who wins. We can offer you a chance to die with honor."

Isidore d'Aiglemort threw his head back, eyes blazing. "What possible reason would I have to take it, *anguissette*?"

"I am Phèdre nó Delaunay," I said softly, "and I can give you a reason, my lord. Because if you do not, and Selig prevails, Melisande Shahrizai will dance upon your grave."

I have seen men take their death-wounds, and their faces looked much like d'Aiglemort's, contorted in a terrible rictus, as if hearing some dreadful jest. His eyes, blazing horribly in his stricken face, never left mine. I had gambled, and guessed aright. He'd not known of Melisande's betrayal.

"Melisande was in league with Selig?" he asked harshly.

"Yes, my lord. I saw a letter, in her own hand. I know it well. I ought to." I dared not take my eyes from his. "You would be well-advised to do her no more favors."

He turned away then with a curse, staring out over the valley, where his army was arrayed. Leather and steel creaked as the Alban forces shifted, waiting. Ghislain de Somerville stood as stolid as an oak, and with as much expression. Drustan watched, dark eyes thoughtful. Joscelin hovered at my elbow in Cassiline attentiveness, and I was glad of his presence.

What Isidore d'Aiglemort thought, I cannot guess.

"I am the sword you would plunge into Selig's heart," he said presently, not turning around.

"Yes, your grace." It was Ghislain who answered. "Camael's sword."

D'Aiglemort laughed humorlessly. "The betrayer of the nation turned its savior." He stood motionless, looking down at his army. A knot of men surrounded our three heralds, not to ward, but to listen, starved for news.

They were D'Angelines alike, after all, and no one tells tales like a sailor, except perhaps for Tsingani and Mendacants. Faint snatches of sound and laughter rose from the valley, as Phèdre's Boys sounded their marching-chant. *Whip us till we're on the floor* . . . "Will you feed them?" d'Aiglemort asked abruptly. "Ysandre cut off our supply-train, and sealed the doors of Camlach against us."

"We will," Ghislain said quietly.

D'Aiglemort turned around then and met his eyes. "What do you propose?"

"I propose that we unite our forces and mount an attack on Selig's army." Ghislain gave a faint, wry smile. "And strike as hard as we can for Waldemar Selig. No one's asking you to die alone, cousin."

"Selig is mine." The tone was calm, but the black eyes glittered. "Swear it, and I will grant what you ask."

"I swear," Ghislain de Somerville said, and his face grew stern. "Do you pledge your fealty to Ysandre de la Courcel, on Camael's honor, and in the name of Blessed Elua?"

"I'll pledge my loyalty to the destruction of Melisande Shahrizai," d'Aiglemort said in his harsh voice. Ghislain glanced at me. I touched the diamond at my throat and nodded.

It would do.

EIGHTY-FIVE

Descending into the valley to join d'Aiglemort's army was tense. I did not think he intended to betray his word—he couldn't break the Skaldi siege without our aid, any more than we could without his—but if he did, that would be the time to do it, when our forces were strung out in long winding lines, bringing down not only the men, but provisions, pack-mules, and the unwieldy war-chariots the Dalriada would not abandon.

I know Ghislain de Somerville and Drustan mab Nec-thana were both alert and wary to the possibility, re-maining mounted and full-armed throughout the journey. Isidore d'Aiglemort, who had ridden bare-headed to meet us, watched with a hint of contempt. Guiding his mount effortlessly down the steep trail, he came along-side us.

"You were the Cassiline, weren't you?" he asked Jos-celin. "I remember. Melisande's favor."

"Yes, my lord." Joscelin's tone was edged with bit-terness. "I was the Cassiline. Joscelin Verreuil, formerly of the Cassiline Brotherhood."

"You're better off," d'Aiglemort said dryly. "Steel and faith are an unnatural mix. I'm impressed, though. I'd have thought slavery would kill a Cassiline. I'll want to hear, later, all you know of Waldemar Selig." Nudging his horse, he left us. Joscelin stared after him.

"If we didn't need him," he said savagely, "I swear, I'd put a knife in his heart! How can you possibly trust him?"

"He was a hero, once," I murmured. "Whatever else he may have been, he was that. If we succeed, or even if we die trying, he'll be remembered as a hero in the end. Without this, his name will ring through D'Angeline history—whatever remains of us to tell it— as Waldemar Selig's dupe. And he dies knowing Meli-sande used him to do it."

Joscelin was silent for a moment. "She could have gained the nation with him," he said presently. "Why?"

I shook my head. "The Skaldi would still have invaded. Selig was using him too. Who knows what he promised her? At his side . . . she stands to gain two nations. Ten thousand Camaelines know Isidore d'Aiglemort betrayed the Crown, he had an army at his back. Melisande plays a deep game. If Selig wins, you can count the survivors who know her role on one hand. He'll have an empire. And he'll take a Queen to consolidate it."

"Is that what you think?" Joscelin threw his head back, shocked. I gave him a rueful smile.

"What else? Melisande plays for high stakes. I can't think of any higher. Unless," I added thoughtfully, "it would be to eliminate Selig once he'd gained the throne and mastered his realm."

"How could she bear so much blood on her hands?" Joscelin asked softly, gazing at the Camaeline army sprawled in the valley before us. "How could anyone?"

"I don't know." I shook my head again. "Except that it's the game that compels her. I don't think she ever reckoned the cost in human lives, not truly." Delaunay, I thought, had been the same, a little bit, though his reasons were nobler. They had their pride alike, in the playing out of their deep-laid schemes. I remembered how he had showed me to her, when all the City was buzzing to know about his second protégé. And I remembered how she had let him know, through me, that she was the architect behind the fall of House Trevalion.

"Either way," Joscelin said soberly, "it's monstrous."

I did not disagree.

We reached the valley floor without incident, crowded together in a throng of D'Angelines and Albans alike. The Allies of Camlach stared at our forces, the blue-painted Cruithne, in wonder. They were gaunt and feverish, with a fierce, fugitive air; we wasted no time in setting up an encampment and beginning the process of sharing out our foodstuffs.

It was a strange mood that prevailed, and my own mood was no less peculiar. Gaiety and despair commingled as word spread of the planned assault. I thought that my mood would lighten, with the success of our endeavor; whatever happened, at least, I would not be responsible for leading anyone to die at d'Aiglemort's hands. Instead, it deepened. Everything seemed very clear and sharp to me, and yet it was as if I stood outside myself, watching.

They made conference long into the night, tallying the numbers, arranging our joined forces into the most effective array of legions. D'Aiglemort and his captain of infantry; Ghislain; Drustan and the Twins; and I, on hand to translate, with Joscelin as my ever-present protector. The Cruithne and the Dalriada had little notion of battle formation, but they grasped it quickly enough.

Still, it was agreed that the Camaeline infantry would form the front line of our attack. Isidore d'Aiglemort's reputation was no fluke; he was an extremely skilled soldier, and every man who served under him was trained and disciplined. Once the Skaldi had begun to rally, we would loose the Alban army, cavalry and chariots sweeping around the outer flanks, followed by the hordes of foot soldiers.

And when chaos ensued, the Camaeline infantry would part, and d'Aiglemort's cavalry would penetrate into the heart of the Skaldi forces, driving toward Waldemar Selig. He would be at the forefront of the attack on Troyes-le-Mont, I could well guess; Selig was not one to lead from behind. They would have to pierce deep to reach him.

"How good is he?" Isidore d'Aiglemort asked abruptly,

looking up from our hastily sketched battle plan to meet Joscelin's eyes. "Do you know, Cassiline?"

Joscelin returned the gaze unblinking. "He disarmed me," he said flatly. "In the heat of battle. He is that good, my lord."

I expected some comment from the Duc d'Aiglemort, but he somehow took Joscelin's measure in the long stare that they exchanged, and only nodded, lamplight gleaming on his silver-pale hair. "Then I shall have to be better," he said quietly, touching the hilt of his sword.

Joscelin hesitated, then spoke. "Don't wait to engage him. He'll move inside your guard if you do. He fights without thinking, the way you or I breathe. And don't be fooled by his size. He's faster than you think."

"Thank you." D'Aiglemort nodded again, gravely.

We spent the whole of the next day making ready to march, while scouting parties rode ahead, searching out our Skaldi pursuers, and reporting back on the state of the siege. We had word before we set out the following morning: The fortifications had fallen, and the Skaldi were at the gates of Troyes-le-Mont.

It had been the right decision, to seek Isidore d'Aiglemort's aid. Even if our plan of harrying the Skaldi had worked, we'd not have had the time to divide their forces. I'd no head for warfare and strategy, there was no more I could do, save translate when needed, and stay out of the way when not. I had played my last card. What happened next was out of my hands.

Why, then, did I feel this strange unease, this nagging feeling of something undone?

All through the long march back toward Namarre, it persisted. I gazed at the people who surrounded me, seeking an answer in their faces. Now that our course was set and we were in motion, the strangeness in them had passed, giving way to grim resolution. Here and there, I saw the inward-looking gaze of those facing death; and here and there, too, I saw the hope and defiance. Drustan mab Necthana had it, riding with his head high, dark eyes shining. No matter what else, he was riding toward Ysandre, whom he loved. Grainne and Eamonn had it, too, sharing grins; I saw how alike they looked, then, in the face of battle.

I looked at Ghislain de Somerville, and his expression was set and hard. He had planned as best he could, the Royal Commander's son. His father could have done no better. Isidore d'Aiglemort glittered in his armor, his gaze fixed on the distance like an archer's upon a faraway target, a faint smile upon his face as he rode toward his fate.

And Joscelin, who rode at my side, quiet and worried. It gave me a pain in my heart to look at him.

Blessed Elua, I prayed, what would you have me do? Nothing but silence answered. I prayed to Naamah, then, whose servant I was. Whatever it was, it was not in her service. All I could do, and more, I had done in Naamah's name.

And I was Kushiel's chosen.

I prayed to him.

My blood surged like the tide, whispering in answer. All my life, I had honored Elua; since I was a child, I had served Naamah. But it was Kushiel who had marked me, and Kushiel who claimed me now. I felt his presence, enfolding me like a mighty hand. My lord Kushiel, I prayed, what must I do?

You will know . . .

How long had we been on the road? I could not count the number of weeks, months. It seemed a long time, a very long time, since that dreadful day when Joscelin and I had failed to outrace death to Delaunay's door. And yet, now, it would come to an end, and it seemed too fast. We made our camp in the foothills, a prudent distance from the battle.

Come morning, we would attack.

I went with Ghislain and the others to survey the siege. With the sun settling low over the plain, we could see the embattled fortress, still flying the Courcel swan, an island in a sea of Skaldi forces. Beyond the breached bulwarks, the half-burned skeleton of a siege tower leaned against one wall; and there, on the plain, was the charred wreckage of the tower Drustan's Cruithne had ignited.

But there were two towers yet, moved nearly into position, and the Skaldi were making ready a great battering ram to try the gates. Only the archers and the trebuchet in the fortress were keeping them at bay. If the Skaldi got one of their towers in place and swarmed the parapet, it would soon be done. They were withdrawing out of range, now, with the setting sun, to renew efforts with the dawn.

"We'll wait for daybreak," Ghislain murmured, "and pray they know us for allies, in the fortress. The sooner they counterattack the Skaldi rear, the better our chances."

"You think they'll flock to aid the d'Aiglemort eagle?" Isidore d'Aiglemort asked wryly. "Don't count on their being quick, cousin."

"My father is no fool." Ghislain stared through the gloaming at the distant fortress. "Drustan's men are flying the Cullach Gorrym. He'll know."

"If he can even see the Black Pig, over thirty thousand howling Skaldi." D'Aiglemort drew back from the vantage, and shrugged matter-of-factly. "We'll do as much damage as we can, and pray it's enough to break the siege. But for every minute your father hesitates, and for every minute it takes for them to marshal a counterattack, we'll die by the hundreds."

One of Phèdre's Boys—Eugène, whom Quintilius Rousse had prized for his long vision—gazed out over the battlefield and made a choked sound, pointing.

It was hard to make out events at such a distance, the figures tiny, but not so hard that we couldn't see the line of prisoners being led among the camps of the Skaldi, shoved and stumbling. Their gowns made bright spots of color against the dust and steely turmoil of a warcamp.

Women, all of them; D'Angeline women.

Selig's army had cut a swathe through northern Namarre before Percy de Somerville's force had intercepted them. We'd not seen it before. They had taken slaves.

We watched it silently, too far away to hear if they cried out. I doubt it. They would have been some weeks among the Skaldi. One grows numb to almost anything, after a while. Still, I could not look away, until Joscelin took my shoulders and pulled me gently back. I pressed my face to his chest and shuddered. When I lifted my head, Isidore d'Aiglemort was watching us both, his expression somber.

"I am sorry," he said quietly. "For what was done to you both. For what it's worth, I am sorry."

Joscelin, holding me, nodded.

"Daybreak," Ghislain de Somerville said grimly.

EIGHTY-SIX

I awoke a little past moonrise.

It was the rustling tide in my blood that awoke me, Kushiel's presence around me like great bronze wings, setting my blood to beating in my ears. Lifting my head from my bedroll, I gazed across our sleeping camp and saw everything washed in a red haze of blood, staining armor, faces, horses drowsing with heads low and a rear leg cocked.

For every minute that passed, they would die by the hundreds.

Kushiel's voice whispered in my ear.

Now . . .

I covered my face with my hands and knew.

It was not such a difficult thing, to arise without waking anyone near me. Our sentries were posted outward, they'd no orders to restrain movement within the camp. And I know how to be quiet. It is the first thing they teach, in the Night Court. Before anything else, we learn it; to be unobtrusive, invisible, to attend unseen and unnoticed.

Delaunay taught us too.

Leaving Joscelin was the hardest, because I knew he'd never forgive me for it. I stooped over him as he slept, lying silvered in the moonlight, like Endymion in the old Hellene tale. I pressed my lips to his brow, light enough that he only murmured in his sleep. "Good-bye, my Cassiel," I whispered, smoothing his hair.

Then I rose, and pinned about me my travelling cloak, a deep brown velvet, Quincel de Morbhan's gift. It was dark enough to serve. I picked my way through our darkened camp—no fires had been allowed, lest the Skaldi spot them—and sought out Isidore d'Aiglemort.

He came awake in an instant when I knelt by his side, inborn Camaeline reflexes sending him reaching for his sword. Its point was at my throat before I could speak.

"You," he said, eyes narrowing in the moonlight. "What is it?"

"My lord." I spoke in a low voice that would not carry. "The fortress will be ready for your attack."

Sheathing his sword, d'Aiglemort stared at me. "You'll be captured."

"Not before I gain the wall." I wrapped my arms around myself and shivered. "The Skaldi camp is full of D'Angeline women. I can get close enough. And I can give a warning Ysandre will understand."

D'Aiglemort shook his head slowly. "Do you not understand? Selig will make you talk. You'll give us all up for dead."

"No." A dreadful laugh caught in my throat. "No, my lord. I am the one person who will not."

It was too dark for him to make out the scarlet mote in my left eye, but I saw him look anyway, and remember. Isidore d'Aiglemort pushed his shining hair back from his face. "Why are you telling me?" he asked in a hard voice.

"Because you, my lord, are the one person who won't try to stop me," I said softly. "Help me get past our sentries. A hundred lives for every minute, you said. I can save a thousand, at least; mayhap three times that many. I gave you the choice of your death. The least you can do is honor mine."

I thought he might refuse, but in the end, he gave a curt nod. I had chosen well, in Isidore d'Aiglemort. We walked together to the outskirts of our encampment, where one of his men was posted. D'Aiglemort called him aside for a word, and the soldier obeyed with alacrity. It is no discredit to him that he did not see as I slipped past in the shadows. He was not looking to be deceived.

So I left the camp.

When all was said and done, I have made harder journeys. It could not even compare to Joscelin's and my flight through the frigid depths of a Skaldic winter, and it was fraught with none of the unnatural terrors of crossing the Straits. But there are ways and ways for a thing to be difficult, and in some of them, this was the hardest journey of all.

Once I left d'Aiglemort behind, I was alone.

It took a great deal of care, climbing soundlessly down the foothills. I'd have taken a horse, if I dared, but Ghislain's L'Agnacite archers were posted with orders to shoot at anything that stirred on the approaches. I would not test their skill, even shooting blind. They can shoot a crow in a cornfield by the rustle of the grasses, and a horse makes a good deal of noise, and a sizeable target by moonlight.

I made a small target and very little noise.

It took me an hour and better to make my descent, moving quickly after I cleared the outermost perimeter of our guards. I clambered downward using hands and feet alike, and my hands were torn by the rocks. But I gained the plain.

Two hours, I gauged, to cross it and make my way to the fortress walls. It was little more than a mile to reach the outer skirts of the sprawling Skaldi army, but making my way through the encampment would be a slow process.

It was enough. I had at least four hours until dawn.

The plain lay still and silent beneath the high, bright moon, and I crossed it in an agony of terror, starting at every sound. It is a wonder to me, that the small creatures of the field—mice, rabbits, a night-hunting snake—do not flee the advent of war for miles all around. Once an owl's cry made me jump, tangling one foot in the hem of my gown, sending me sprawling to earth. With both hands planted in the rich soil of Terre d'Ange, I tried to slow the terrified beating of my heart. I found a smooth rock beneath one hand, and carried it with me.

I went onward.

A child's ploy, to distract the Skaldi sentry dosing on his spear; nothing more. I threw the rock, hurling it with all my might. It fell to earth with a dull thud, and he looked that way. I passed the other way, drawing my hood about my face. Never despise a trick because it is simple, Delaunay said; the old ploys endure because they work.

That would be the most dangerous part, I thought.

Until I reached the Skaldi camp.

The fortified earthworks that surrounded Troyes-le-Mont had been breached in a dozen places, undermined by sappers, burst with rams. It would have gone even quicker, had Selig had catapults but, mercifully, it seemed, that was one element of Tiberian technology that had proved too difficult for his Skaldi engineers to replicate with any accuracy.

Bad enough they had learned to build siege towers.

Mindful of the Alban attack some days before, Selig had posted sentries at the largest breaches; but they were looking for an army, not a lone intruder. Circling the bulwarks at a distance, I spotted a gap scarce large enough to admit a child, where the sappers had broken through and abandoned the place when their cohorts had succeeded elsewhere.

The earth-and-timber walls cast a deep shadow. Crouching in it, I worked feverishly with both hands, widening the hole until it was large enough to get my head and shoulders into it.

Halfway through, I got stuck. It was a tight fit and something, I don't know what—the clasp of my girdle, mayhap—caught on the rough timbers that formed the framework of the bulwark. I wriggled frantically, struggling not to panic, striving to remain silent. I was stuck fast. Kushiel, I thought, you did not send me to die here. I gave one last convulsive push, and something gave way, allowing me to spill out on the far side of the wall.

Collecting myself, I knelt in the darkness and glanced around.

I was behind enemy lines once more.

Far ahead of me stood the embattled fortress, looming against the night sky. The outer windows were darkened, but I could see lights moving deep within, and torches on the battlements, where patrols went to-and-fro, keeping a watch on the quiet Skaldi camp.

Between us lay the Skaldi.

Taking a deep breath, I left the wall and began to make my way through the encampment.

The outermost ranks were the easiest. Trusting to Selig and the sentries, they slept deeply, rolled in their cloaks, letting the embers of their watch-fires burn low. The Skaldi had no fear of being seen; all the world knew where they were.

Picking my torturous way among them, I could see where the divisions lay, tribal and deeply ingrained. I had seen it at the Allthing; I knew. Here and there, among the slumbering camps, lay lines of division. Manni and Marsi, Gambrivii, Suevi and Vandalii . . . I picked my way among them, following the invisible faultlines, avoiding an outstretched hand here, an iron-thewed leg there.

It is not to say that there were none awake and watching, and none who saw me. Some Skaldi were, and did, much as I sought to avoid it. But they saw—what? A lone D'Angeline woman, young and disheveled, shivering with fear. I kept my head bowed, and angled toward the direction from which they'd brought the prisoners, praying it would suffice.

Elua was merciful; it did.

So many Skaldi! It was unreal to me, the numbers of them. And they looked so harmless, sleeping, fierce mustaches and braided beards like adornments on their sleep-softened faces, shields and weapons set aside like children's toys. Would that they were no more than they seemed in slumber.

It grew more difficult the closer I got to Troyes-le-Mont. I held my line toward the prisoners' camp as long as I dared, but at last I must cut inward, heading for the fortress, toward where the burned skeleton of a siege tower reared up above the moon-glimmering water of the moat. Selig had patrols posted here, roaming along the perimeter, keeping an eye on the defenders.

All my wiles I used to avoid their detection; even so, it scarce sufficed. I ducked back hard to evade an approaching patrol, huddling in the shadow of a firm-planted shield.

The corner of my cloak caught the edge of a stack of spears, sending them clattering to earth.

The nearest Skaldi, his arm thrown carelessly over a young D'Angeline woman, stirred and lifted his head. He blinked at me, bleary-eyed, then smiled slowly.

"Where do you run to, little dove?" he asked in Skaldi, raising himself on one arm. "Come, I'll show you your new home!"

One looks for aid where one can, in times of fear; my terrified gaze slid to the woman beside him. Her eyes were wide and clear. She had been awake. We stared at each other in the moonlight, D'Angelines alike, and I realized that she wore the rent and dirt-stained robes of a priestess of Naamah.

Of course; we were in Namarre, Naamah's country.

But I had not thought the Skaldi would raid her temples.

"Where are you going, messire?" she asked in D'Angeline, catching his arm and drawing him back to her. "Would you leave me to the cold?"

If he did not understand her words, he understood her intent, laughing and nuzzling her neck. Crouched in the shadows, I held her gaze as it watched me over the warrior's shoulder, bleak and resolute. I mouthed the words silently—thank you—and fled into the darkness, offering a blessing to Naamah, who had protected her Servant.

So I gained the ruined siege tower.

How often had I cursed Anafiel Delaunay for forcing me to endure the endless drill of our tumbling-master? I have repented of it since; I repented of it now, grasping the scorched timbers and hauling myself upward.

Up, up into the night I climbed, facing the grey stone walls of Troyes-le-Mont, from which I was separated only by the width of the narrow moat. The tower had gotten close; if they'd bridged the moat, it was high enough to clear the battlements.

But they hadn't, and the distance of their failure was the distance of my fate. I climbed as high as I dared, charcoal from the burned framework smudging my torn hands and rent clothing. Still, a kind of exhilaration overcame me, as it had on the rafters of Selig's Great Hall.

On the sloping underside of the nearest tower was a *muertriere*, an opening from which the defenders could shoot at the attackers below. Surely, I thought, it must be manned in such times. I broke off bits of burned timber from the framework of the siege tower, tossing them at the narrow window.

Lights moved within, torches bobbing. I saw the blur of a D'Angeline face, removed quickly and replaced with the point of a crossbow's quarrel, aimed in my direction.

My blood beat in my ears.

"Hold!" I cried aloud, letting my voice ring clear in

the night. "In the name of Ysandre de la Courcel, hold!"

The archer held; and shouts arose from the Skaldi patrol. Figures raced in the darkness below me, swarming the base of the tower. The crossbow withdrew, replaced by the same face, perplexed eyes meeting my own.

I clung to the framework, leaning out as far as I dared, letting the faint torchlight from the battlements above illumine my face. "Tell the Queen," I shouted, "that Delaunay's other pupil has done her bidding!"

That much, and no more, I got out, before hands grasped me from below, dragging at me. My fingers lost their grip, splinters wedged beneath my nails; then I was loose and falling, my head striking hard against a timber before I was caught ungently by Skaldi arms.

They forced me down the burned tower, pushing me harshly, but not letting me fall when my trembling arms gave way or my feet slipped from the supports. I could hear the uproar arising in the camp, watchfires fanned to a blaze as I was brought to earth.

One of the Skaldi shoved me as my feet touched ground and I stumbled, falling to my knees before the captain of the watch on patrol. He cuffed me once, then glowered.

"What were you doing, eh?" he asked in Skaldic, cursing me. "Did you think to gain the castle? Your place lies that way, slave!" He pointed toward the prison camp. "Do you know the punishment for flight?"

"She can't understand you, Egil," one of my captors laughed, twisting a hand in my hair. I would have laughed too, if I hadn't feared hysteria. They thought I was a runaway slave. Steel and flame and Skaldi faces streaked across my vision, and the rank smell of a battlefield filled my senses. Somewhere, a rider approached.

"Oh, I think she understands." It was a different voice, deep and commanding, and rich with irony. I knew it. I knew it well, better than I cared to remember. My Skaldi captor wrenched at my hair, tilting my head back, forcing me to meet the speaker's eyes. He was tall, taller even than I recalled, the breadth of his shoulders looming against the fortress behind him. His hazel eyes, meeting mine, narrowed, and his lips curved in a smile. "Don't you, Faydra?" Waldemar Selig asked softly.

Eighty-seven

"Yes, my lord Selig." I forced the words out.

Dismounting and handing his reins to a waiting thane, Waldemar Selig stepped forward and struck me twice across the face. My head reeled. "That," he said calmly, "I owed you." Grabbing my forelock in his fist, he yanked my head up and stared at me. "What were you doing on the tower?"

I stared back at him and kept silent.

Twice more he struck me, hard and fast. "What were you doing?"

Touching my tongue to my lower lip, I tasted blood.

"She shouted somewhat," one of my captors said helpfully.

"What was it?" Selig asked, not relinquishing his grip.

They argued over it, puzzling out the words in phonetic D'Angeline. Swaying on my knees, I watched Selig's lips move silently as he tried to put the words together. He spoke passable D'Angeline. I knew. I'd helped teach him. "Tell the . . . tell the Queen that Delaunay's other . . . other . . . something . . . has done her . . . ." The words were too badly mangled for his ear. Frustration seized him, and he shook my head like a rattle. "Send for one of the prisoners," he ordered.

It was the priestess of Naamah; she was closest. Summoning a measure of dignity, she wrapped her stained red robes around her as they herded her across the plain. Her gaze slid across my face as if without recognition as she stood listening to the garbled phrase the patrol captain repeated.

"Tell the Queen that Delaunay's other pupil has done her bidding," she said coolly in D'Angeline.

I do not think she reckoned on Selig's comprehension; it unnerved her, a little, when he smiled. I watched his smile fade, though, and knew bitter triumph. The words meant nothing to him. "Thank you," he said to Naamah's priestess in curt D'Angeline, adding in Skaldic. "Take her back among the prisoners." She glanced back once over her shoulder, then I saw her no more. Selig considered me, still holding my head up-tilted. "It will go better for you if you tell me," he said, almost gently. "I don't owe you a quick death, but I'm willing to give it you, if you'll speak."

He was handsome, for a Skaldi; I have said as much. The torchlight born by warriors pressing round glinted from the gold fillet that bound his hair, the gold wire that twisted his beard into twin forks. My face ached, and tears stood in my eyes. I did laugh, then. I'd nothing left to lose. "No, my lord," I said simply. "I will take the other choice."

Cursing, he released his grip on my hair, thrusting me away. He turned to look thoughtfully at the fortress. "You claim to find pleasure in pain," he said. "Then let Ysandre de la Courcel see how well Waldemar Selig pleases her spies."

I have said, too, that Selig was a clever man. He knew well the merits of controlling the minds of one's enemies. He had a vast space cleared in front of the fortress, just beyond the range of the archers, and had it ringed round with torch-bearers. The barbican over the gate of Troyes-le-Mont was full-lit by then, and no doubt the defenders were watching; I knew it; Selig knew it too. Two of his thanes walked me out into the middle of the space, forcing me to my knees. White Brethren, their pelts tied loosely around their necks in the warmth of summer, woolens exchanged for steel and leather.

Selig wore white wolf-hide too, snowy by moonlight, trimming the tunic beneath his armor. He stepped into the circle of torchlight and wrenched at the neck of my gown, tearing it open. I felt the night air moving upon the bare skin of my back.

"Ysandre de la Courcel!" he shouted, his voice carrying. "See what becomes of spies and traitors!"

I heard the sound of his belt-dagger rasping clear of its sheath, felt the point of it placed against the skin of my left shoulder blade. The White Brethren held my arms as he began to cut.

Waldemar Selig was known to be a mighty hunter. Unlike D'Angeline nobles, Skaldic lords do not have servants to perform distasteful chores. They skin and gut their own kills. When Selig scored a strip of flesh from my back and began slowly to pull it down, I knew what he intended.

He was going to skin me alive.

I have known pain; Elua knows, I have known it. But nothing had ever prepared me for this. I gasped aloud as he cut, and when he took the strip of flesh, slippery with blood, in a pincerlike grip and began to draw it down, I screamed.

And it would go on for a long time.

Pain burst red across my vision, staggering me. I knew where I was, and did not. Kushiel, I thought, and my blood roared in my ears, beating like wings. I have done all I could. It was a relief, to surrender at last, at long last. I could hear my voice still, whimpering, ragged with pain, and Selig's whisper in my ear, tell me, tell me. These things happened, I know. And yet it all seemed distant and far beyond me, minor tempests on the outskirts of the maelstrom of agony I inhabited. The world lurched sideways through a bloodred haze, and hands dragged me upright. Pain blossomed all through me, finding a home at the base of my spine, radiating outward. Pain obliterates everything else. In pain, there is only the eternal present. I fell into it as if into a dark, bottomless well, seeing the bronze mask of Kushiel hanging before me, stern and compassionate, bronze lips moving, speaking words I felt in my bones. Pain redeems all. It is the awareness of life, a reminder of death. I saw faces, other faces, mortal and beloved: Delaunay, Alcuin, Cecilie, Thelesis, Hyacinthe, Joscelin . . . and more, flickering too fast to number, Ysandre, Quintilius Rousse, Drustan, the Twins, Phèdre's Boys, Master Tielhard, Guy . . . some I didn't expect, Hedwig, Knud, Childric d'Essoms, the old Dowayne, Lodur One-Eye . . . even, at the end, my mother and father, dimly remembered, and the Skaldi mercenary who had tossed me in the air and laughed through his mustaches . . .

Melisande.

Ah, Elua! I did love her once . . .

It was the cessation of pain that brought me back. Selig's knife had halted in the course of parting my skin from my flesh, paused in an incredulous moment. A voice was speaking, one I knew, clear words ringing on the night air in heavily accented Skaldic.

"Waldemar Selig, I challenge you to the holmgang!"

They let me go, then, and I fell over, my cheek cradled on the dusty, trampled field. I bled into the dirt and blinked unbelieving at the figure that had parted the Skaldi ranks.

Stolen armor and a stolen horse for disguise—he had done it before—and Cassiline arms, summer-blue eyes behind the wild, desperate dare.

"Elua, no," I murmured against D'Angeline soil.

Waldemar Selig stood staring, then laughed; laughed and laughed. "It would have been too much to ask!" he declared joyfully, spreading his arms. "Ah, All-Father Odhinn, you are generous! Yes, Josslin Verai, let us dance upon the hides, and then . . ." He turned, roaring his words toward Troyes-le-Mont. "Then let Terre d'Ange see how Waldemar Selig deals with her champions!"

These are the things the Skaldi love, the stuff of legend. Twenty spears pointed at Joscelin as he dismounted and his stolen mount was seized. They stripped away his stolen armor, too, while a ripple ran through camp as they searched for a suitable hide to stake out for the holmgang. Hauled to my knees and held in place by the two White Brethren, I saw it all. Selig's hazel eyes gleamed keen and bright as he tested the heft of his shield.

No one would lend one to Joscelin. He stood at ease in the Cassiline manner, only the steel vambraces on his forearms to protect him. I knelt bleeding, rife with pain, and cursed him in my soul. Whether Selig defeated him or no, it didn't matter. He wasn't fool enough to throw victory away on a game of honor. He would break Joscelin; or worse, use me to do it.

Joscelin, Joscelin, I thought, tears running unheeded down my face, You've done it, you've truly done it, and killed us all with your damnable vow.

They took their places at opposite ends of the hide. Joscelin crossed his arms and bowed. Waldemar Selig thrust his sword into the air, and the Skaldi shouted; one voice, thirty thousand throats. They began to pound their weapons upon their shields, a measured beat. Selig turned to the dark watching fortress and swept a mocking bow. I knelt, awash in pain.

And the holmgang began.

I would like to tell it in poets' words, this deadly dance they enacted on a few square feet of hide, before the whole of the Skaldi army and the silent defenders of Troyes-le-Mont. I would that I could. But they were fast, so fast, and I had come back a long way from Kushiel's realm. I saw swords flickering in the torchlight, streaks of steel awash in ruddy light, the sound of clashing metal lost in the beating surge of spear-butts against Skaldic shields. I saw Joscelin's hair, wheat-gold against the darkness, fan out in a tangle of Skaldi braids as he spun, evading Selig's biting blade. Fast; not fast enough. I saw his sleeve darken with spreading blood as the edge of Selig's sword slashed his arm above the vambrace.

The beating rhythm hesitated, waiting to see if blood would spatter the hide. Selig tossed aside his cracked shield and reached for another, knowing without looking that a loyal thane was at hand. Joscelin loosed the buckles of his vambrace one-handed, sliding it up and tightening it in place over the wound, using his teeth.

Laughing, Waldemar Selig attacked, and the beat resumed.

And I saw Joscelin deflect his blow with one sweeping gesture, ready for the attack, his other hand coming up to resume the two-handed grip on his sword-hilt, and his sword slid high across the darkness as Selig raised his shield to parry, the point scoring a line across Selig's jaw.

It bled red rivulets into his tawny-brown beard with its gold-wrapped fork; bled red rivulets, that dropped fat red drops of blood onto the hide.

The Skaldi ceased their pounding.

In silence, Joscelin bowed and sheathed his sword.

Waldemar Selig wiped one palm along his jaw and shook it contemptuously, spattering blood. "For that," he said softly, raising his sword to point it at Joscelin's heart, "I will let you live long enough to see what is left of her when I am done, and have given what remains to my men."

I knew the whiteness of perfect despair.

Joscelin lifted his gaze to Selig's, and stood motionless, his blue eyes tranquil. "In Cassiel's name," he said, in a voice calm beyond calm, "I protect and serve."

And he moved, flowing like water.

All the Cassiline forms have names: poets' names, lovely and serene, drawn from nature . . . birds on the wing, mountain streams, trees bending in the wind. It is how they name what they do.

Except for the one they call *terminus*.

There is a play, a famous play—its name was lost in white light of despair—in which a Cassiline Brother performs the *terminus*. I saw a player act it out, once, in the Cockerel. I knew it, then, swaying on my knees, held upright by my Skaldi guards. When Joscelin, spinning in my direction, tossed his right-hand dagger in the air and caught it by the blade, I knew. When he brought his left-hand dagger to his throat and set its point, I knew.

It is the last act the Perfect Companion may perform.

I met his eyes, the dagger in his right hand balanced to throw at my heart, the dagger in his left poised to cut his throat. I had judged him wrong. Truly, he had come to save us both, in the only way left to us. I had not known, until that moment, how very deeply I had feared my fate.

"Do it," I whispered.

Joscelin looked over my shoulder and froze.

And then moved like lightning, his right hand whip-

ping forward to throw the dagger. It caught the White
Brethren guard on my left in the throat and he fell backward with scarcely a gurgle, his hand leaving my arm.
I swayed, unbalanced. Joscelin was coming toward me
at a dead run, scarce pausing to snatch the hilt out of
the Skaldi's throat. My other guard released me, fumbling for his sword. Too late; the crossed daggers took
him high too, opening gaping wounds on either side of
his neck. Heedless of the pain it caused, Joscelin grabbed
my arm unhesitatingly, hauling me to my feet and plunging toward the fortress.

Half-dragged, staggering in his wake and in agony, I
saw it. The portcullis was being raised. The Skaldi army
roared behind us as the drawbridge crashed down across
the moat. We raced desperately across the ruined earth,
my lungs burning for air, each step an agony of blos-
soming pain.

That was when the night skies lit on fire.

From atop the battlements, the trebuchet were loosed,
and gouts of flame seared the night; *feu d'Hellas*, liquid
pitch, ignited and burning. It soared in an arc over our
heads, splattering into the front line of our Skaldi pursuers, sending them rolling and screaming to earth. I
heard Selig's voice, rising above it all. "Advance!" he
roared. "Advance, and get ahead of it, you fools!"

How many listened, I don't know; enough, I daresay.
But then the earth shook, and from the dark mouth of
the gate a mounted sortie emerged.

Four Siovalese cataphracts, riders and horses alike
covered head to hoof with armor, gleaming silver and
gold by firelight. They pounded past us on either side,
slamming into the wall of the approaching Skaldi. And
on their heels, twenty-odd light-armed riders, turbaned
and helmed, uttering a fierce Akkadian ululation. One
swooped by me like a mounted hawk, a deft hand pluck-

ing me up to sling me across the pommel of his saddle. Jouncing in pain, I dimly saw Joscelin take the hand of another, swinging up behind him in the saddle.

We wheeled, and turned. The cataphracts split off and surged back toward the drawbridge, heavy hooves pounding; the other riders roiled in a semicircle against the Skaldi, fingers plucking at horsemen's bows. The trebuchet atop the fortress thudded dully, and more *feu d'Hellas* lit the air, glittering bright above the furious mien of Waldemar Selig, who stared unbelieving as his prize escaped.

Hoofbeats echoed as we fled across the drawbridge, the defenders of the gatehouse already working frantically at the winches. The last members of the sortie made it with desperate leaps, horses stumbling on the slanted planks.

The drawbridge shuddered into place, and they cut the ropes raising the portcullis, dropping it with a resounding crash. We had gained the inner ward. Slung across the saddle, limp and bleeding, I scarce heeded the commotion as the gatehouse guards rallied against the Skaldi who threw themselves in waves at the moat, driving them back coolly with a rain of crossbow-fire.

Safe within the stone walls of the fortress courtyard, the riders of the sortie dismounted, jesting with disbelief to find themselves still alive. My rescuer was among them, removing his conical steel helm and running a hand through his short-cropped, pale hair.

"Who would have thought," Barquiel L'Envers said ironically, "I'd risk my life for a member of Delaunay's household?"

I met his wry violet gaze as he helped me down from my awkward position, but then my feet touched the flagstones, and my strength gave way. I kept going, crumpling to a heap in the courtyard of Troyes-le-Mont.

ÉIGHTY-ÉIGHT

"Let her be!"

There was a crowd around me, that much I knew; and then Joscelin was there, mercifully, making them stand back and give me space to breathe. I clung to his hand as he knelt beside me, desperately grateful for his presence.

Then the cry, "Make way for the Queen!"

No fool, Ysandre; she had come with an Eisandine chirurgeon, who felt at me with cool hands, turning me on my stomach and examining Selig's damage, cleaning away the blood.

"It is not so bad as it looks," she said, reassuring, sending her assistant scrambling for a needle and thread. "He was aiming for pain and not death."

I gritted my teeth as she set the flap of skin back in place, anchoring it with deft stitches. But I did not cry out; they had heard enough of that, I reckoned. I could hear Ysandre murmur something to Joscelin, and his quiet reply. When it was done, the chirurgeon applied a salve and bound it tight with clean bandages, and I rose to my feet, my blood-soaked gown hanging loose from my shoulders.

By this time the courtyard stood full and waiting with the greater part of the D'Angeline Royal Army, amassed behind its lords and commanders, who stood aligned with Ysandre de la Courcel, the Queen of Terre d'Ange, flanked by two Cassiline Brothers. All of them, waiting on my words.

It was a little overwhelming.

Stiff with pain, I made my curtsy to Ysandre. I think

she might have stopped me, if we had been alone; I saw her catch her breath. I managed. "Your majesty," I said, forcing my voice to steadiness.

"Phèdre nó Delaunay." She inclined her head. "Have we read your message aright?"

I took a deep breath and gazed at the sea of waiting faces. "An army of seven thousand stands ready to attack Selig's rearguard at daybreak," I said aloud, hearing a murmurous echo as my words were passed backward through the ranks.

Percy de Somerville, looking gaunt and tired, kindled to life. "Elua!" he exclaimed. "Seven thousand Albans!"

"No, my lord." I shook my head. "Half the force is Alban. The other half is Isidore d'Aiglemort's army."

This time, the murmur rose nearly to a roar, surging in waves through the courtyard. I wavered on my feet, and Joscelin caught my arm, steadying me. Disheveled and unwashed, hair in a half-braided tangle, one sleeve dark and stiff with blood, he looked nothing like his Cassiline brethren, and about ten times as dangerous.

"D'Aiglemort!" Barquiel L'Envers said in disgust. "Whose fool idea was that?"

"Mine, my lord," I said evenly. "Implemented by my lord de Somerville's son."

"Ghislain?" The light in Percy de Somerville's eyes grew brighter. "Ghislain is with them?"

I nodded, fighting exhaustion. "Ghislain and a few hundred of his men. He left Marc de Trevalion in command in Azzalle, with Admiral Rousse. They planned the attack together; Ghislain, I mean, and d'Aiglemort and Drustan. And the Twins." I saw his face go blank. "The Lords of the Dalriada."

"Then Rousse is alive, and Marc, too." It was Gaspar Trevalion, his salt-and-pepper hair gone greyer in the months since I'd seen him. I learned later that he had-lingered too long aiding Ysandre and de Somerville in organizing the defense of Troyes-le-Mont, and been cut off from returning to Azzalle to fight with his kinsman.

"Yes, my lord," I said. "When we left them."

"Thanks to Elua," he murmured, grey eyes resting kindly on me, "for their safety, and yours."

"Why would Isidore d'Aiglemort aid us?" asked a quiet voice. I recognized Tibault, the Siovalese Comte de Toluard, more soldier than scholar now.

"Because," I shifted, and winced. My back throbbed and burned like fire. D'Aiglemort had been right, they were loathe to trust him. I hadn't reckoned on this difficulty; I'd not reckoned on being alive. "He is D'Angeline, my lord, and he is dead no matter what happens. I gave him the choice of a hero's death."

Barquiel L'Envers looked hard at me. "Are you that sure of him, Delaunay's pupil, that you'd risk our lives on it?"

"Yes, my lord." I held his gaze. "Why did you come for me, when you despised my lord Delaunay?"

"Because." L'Envers' eyes glinted, acknowledging my point. "Because we are D'Angeline, Phèdre nó Delaunay. And young Verreuil afforded Selig's men with a distraction." He clapped his hand on Joscelin's shoulder. "Good thing we came before you played out your Cassiline end-game, yes?" He laughed at Joscelin's level stare. "But d'Aiglemort is a traitor. Whatever Delaunay may have thought of me, I never let the Skaldi in the door. What does d'Aiglemort care who sits the throne, if he's dead either way? We set him up, with Baudoin's men. Do you think he wouldn't take the chance to serve us the same?"

Ysandre watched us, giving nothing away; the lords and the army were waiting on her decision.

"Oh, Isidore d'Aiglemort cares," I said softly. "And

he wants revenge." I touched the diamond at my throat. "He is not playing for you, my lady," I said to Ysandre. "He is playing against Melisande Shahrizai."

There was a silence.

"That would do it," L'Envers admitted slowly.

"My lord de Somerville," Ysandre said crisply, turning to Percy. "We will support our allies and mount a counterattack on the Skaldi army. Will you so command it?"

Percy de Somerville bowed, his face firm with resolve. "Your majesty, I will." Willingness, and relief, in his voice; his son was leading those allies.

There was a muffled sound from the gatehouse. One of the defenders ran panting into our midst, saluting de Somerville. "They're breaking up the siege tower to lay timbers across the moat, my lord," he said, wiping his forearm across his brow. "Selig's out there, madder than a pricked bull."

"Use everything we have!" I didn't know the lord who spoke; a Kusheline, by his accent. Excitement was beginning to spread in the wake of Ysandre's pronouncement. "Set an archer at every arrow-slit, and rain down fire upon them! We've only to hold out till dawn!"

Cheering arose, setting my ears to ringing.

"No!" Percy de Somerville's voice quelled it. He glared at the lord who'd spoken. "Listen well," he said grimly into the subdued quiet that followed. "The *last* thing we want to do is make Waldemar Selig think we can afford to waste our armaments in fending him off. The moment he thinks we're confident, he'll start to ask himself why. We need to dig in, and let him think we've overextended ourselves. He's angry; good. Keep him mad and hungry, and above all, *keep his attention on the fortress*! Let him get as close as you dare, before you drive him back!" With a quick glance at Ysandre for permission, he began issuing orders, sketching out a plan of defense, and calling for the muster of the whole of the army.

I knew, then, that my role was done, truly done, and could have wept with relief to see the amassed forces in the courtyard surge into action, following de Somerville's commands, sure and orderly. Ysandre looked at me with compassion.

"Come," she said, gesturing toward the inner gate. "You shouldn't be standing, let alone walking and talking. I've a few attendants, inside. Let us at least make you comfortable. Messire Verreuil, will you assist?"

"A moment, your majesty," Joscelin murmured, turning aside to catch Tibault de Toluard's sleeve. "My lord, can you tell me if my father is here? He is the Chevalier Millard Verreuil, of Siovale. My brother Luc would be with him, and four or five men-at-arms, perhaps."

De Toluard hesitated, and shook his head regretfully. "I'm sorry, messire Verreuil. There are some sixteen hundred Siovalese, and I do not know them all. You might ask the Duc de Perigeux, who commands for Siovale."

"His grace de Perigeux is on the battlements," a passing soldier commented. "Or was, at last count. One of the trebuchet's not firing. South wall, I think."

"No, it was the west," came a dissenting voice.

Other voices offered comments; the Siovalese commander, it seemed, was to be found wherever mechanical difficulties arose—they are clever with such things, Shemhazai's line—and no one knew of Joscelin's father or brother.

"Go find him," I said, seeing Ysandre arch an impatient brow. "I'm fine."

Joscelin looked incredulously at me. "You're a long way from fine," he muttered, picking me up unceremoniously, careful of my injuries, though heedless of my dignity. "Your majesty," he said, nodding to Ysandre.

Inside, it was quieter. Thick stone walls surrounded us, and one might almost forget that a siege was being waged outside. Only three ladies-in-waiting attended the Queen; they would have been legion, in the Palace, but Ysandre was enough Rolande's daughter that she would not permit her household staff to follow her to war. Those who had come had done so of their own choice. The Eisandine chirurgeon—whose name was Lelahiah Valais—checked my bandages once, then tended to the gash on Joscelin's arm and departed, bowing.

After a change of clothes—a gown borrowed from one of Ysandre's ladies-in-waiting—I felt a little more myself. Ysandre had bread and cheese and wine brought in for us. I was not hungry, but I ate a bit, as it does not do to disdain a Queen's hospitality, and indeed, it settled my frayed nerves, and a glass of wine helped to dull the throbbing pain to a more bearable level.

"We don't have much time," Ysandre announced, sitting upright in a chair and looking at Joscelin and me with a direct gaze. "Whatever happens this day, I want you both to know that I issued a pardon before we left the City, proclaiming your innocence in the death of Anafiel Delaunay. And all who are here know as much."

Tears stung my eyes. "Thank you, my lady," I murmured, overwhelmed with gratitude that she should remember such a thing, in the midst of war. Joscelin bowed, echoing my thanks with heartfelt fervor.

Ysandre waved them away. "I'm sorry I didn't dare it earlier," she said bluntly. "But if word reached d'Aiglemort or Melisande Shahrizai, it would have alerted them. And even to the end, we were not entirely sure who could be trusted."

"You didn't find Melisande," I said, hoping to hear

otherwise. Ysandre shook her head grimly.

"The Cassiline Brotherhood kept eyes and ears open as they bore messages, but we didn't dare search openly, for the same reason I couldn't pardon you publicly. If she had means of contacting Waldemar Selig, she might have told him we were prepared, and he would have changed his plans. Our chances were slim enough as they stood," she added, nodding soberly at the fortress walls.

"Of course," I said politely, though I wished it were not so. Ysandre stood and paced, shooting restless glances at the doorway. Her own Cassiline guards stood back, watching attentively, and occasionally stealing furtive looks at Joscelin, who ignored them.

At last she halted, and asked in a tentative voice, quite unlike her usual cool tone, "It is true, then, that Drustan mab Necthana rules as Cruarch in Alba? Did he send any word for me?"

So that was it. I had forgotten, in all that had happened, that a young woman's heart was at stake in the matter. I nearly smiled, then; to my surprise, Joscelin did, ducking his head to hide it, eyes crinkling at the corners. "Your majesty, I saw him crowned before we left Alba's shore," I said firmly, and added honestly, "If he sent no word, it is because he did not know what I intended. And I did not tell him because I did not expect to survive this last journey, and his honor is too great to have allowed me to make it. I have seen it, again and again, that he would put himself at risk in his people's stead. But this, I can tell you. Alone among our allies, Drustan mab Necthana rides toward Troyes-le-Mont with his head held high and a joyful heart, because he rides toward you. The dream that you shared together, of two mighty nations ruled side by side, lives on in him. If his people had not risen up to follow him, he would have set out to retake his throne alone, and had he fallen in the attempt, his last thought would have been of you."

Ysandre kept her restraint, but color glowed in her pale cheeks. "Thank you," she murmured.

"Your majesty," Joscelin said soberly, "one of the great honors of my life is Drustan mab Necthana calling me brother. He is a courageous and good leader, and I think in his quiet Cruithne way, he is very madly in love with you."

Her blush deepened. "I didn't think Cassilines were supposed to notice such things," Ysandre said tartly, masking her reaction. Her own Cassiline guards held their expressions impassive.

"No," Joscelin said wryly, glancing at me. "They're not."

"Your majesty!" A soldier in a mail shirt, his helmet under his arm, appeared at the door. "The sky is beginning to lighten. My lord de Somerville would have conference with you."

Ysandre left, then, taking her guards and attendants with her, leaving Joscelin and me alone.

It was hard to speak of it, after what had happened.

"How did you know?" I asked softly.

He shook his head. "I don't know. I awoke, and knew somewhat was amiss. When I saw you had gone, I just knew. And I knew what Selig would do, if he caught you."

"I thought you'd betrayed us all, for your vow. Before the end." I had to say it. "I'm sorry."

"I don't blame you." He gave me his wry look. "You know, it is something every Cassiline learns, the *terminus*. But no one's ever used it in living memory." He studied his hands. "I nearly killed us both."

"Joscelin." I touched his face. "I know. And until the

day I die, I will be grateful for it." There was more, so much more I wanted to say to him, but I could not find the words, and there was no time for it. Joscelin caught my hand and held it hard.

"It would have saved Hyacinthe the trouble of drowning me, if I'd let Selig have you," he said with a lightness neither of us felt. We could hear shouting outside the door, and the sound of running feet. "Can you walk? We might find out what's happening."

"I would have walked here, if you'd have let me," I said, struggling to stand. "You should go find your father."

Joscelin cocked his head, listening, then shook it. "It's too late. I'd only be in the way, and take his mind off the battle." He gave a rueful smile. "At least he knew I was no murderer, before the end."

It was small consolation, but it would have to do. I squeezed his hand once more, in lieu of things unsaid. "Come on."

Eighty-nine

We made our way through the fortress, sidling along the walls to avoid the lines of rushing soldiers. The ascent up the southeast tower was the worst, climbing the narrow spiral of stairs. Joscelin did his best to shield me, but the passage was too small; once or twice I nearly cried out as my back brushed against a rough outcropping of stone.

Still, we made our way upward, and gained the battlements of the eastern wall, guessing aright that the command watch would be stationed there.

In the leaden light of predawn, it was like a scene

straight out of hell. I had been amid the Skaldi camp, but I'd not understood, until then, what life had been like for those besieged in the fortress.

An ocean of Skaldi surged on the plain below, breaking like waves at the edge of the moat, spears and arrows arching upward toward the parapet. Pots of *feu d'Hellas* smoked and stank on the battlement, the east-pointing trebuchet cranked and waiting. Archers crouched at the arrow-slits with crossbows, their seconds standing by with a replacement strung and ready. A longbow can fire six arrows to the single bolt of a crossbow on the field, but there is no weapon better in defending stone.

Amid this chaos, cool and composed behind one of the high merlons of the crenelated wall, stood Ysandre de la Courcel, Queen of Terre d'Ange, in discussion with Percy de Somerville, Gaspar Trevalion and Barquiel L'Envers. Spotting Joscelin and me in the tower, de Somerville sent a detachment of soldiers to escort us, shields braced outward against Skaldi weapons.

"Good," de Somerville said calmly. "I'm glad you're here. Selig's got his temper under control. He's still focused on the assault, but he just sent out scouting parties in six directions, and I think he's increased the guard on the perimeter. What's Ghislain's angle of approach?"

"Due east," I said, pointing toward the foothills.

De Somerville put his eye to the arrow-slit and squinted through it. "How long until they arrive, if they began to move at first light?"

"Two hours?" I guessed.

Joscelin shook his head. "They'll be moving in a hurry, and Selig's sentries will give warning, long before they get there. I wouldn't worry about scouting parties— they're no match for the Cruithne—but once they're on flat ground, they'll be seen. The Skaldi won't wait, they'll take the battle to them. An hour, no more, I think."

"If Selig divides his forces, we're in trouble." Barquiel L'Envers tucked the trailing end of his burnouse more securely beneath his helm. "He could leave ten thousand men here to keep us penned in, and still outnumber the Albans two to one."

I rose on tiptoes to peer through the arrow-slit. Below, out of arrow-range, Waldemar Selig rode a tall horse, a mighty figure, ranging back and forth along the line, shouting exhortations at the Skaldi.

"They'll follow Selig," I said, drawing back. "If he turns, they'll all go. And Isidore d'Aiglemort is aiming for him."

I could see how little they liked it still, mistrusting d'Aiglemort's loyalty. I didn't blame them.

"So be it," Percy de Somerville said at length. "Cousin." He nodded at Gaspar Trevalion. "With your folk in Azzalle, we can spare you from the field the most, and you're the only one I trust to make the choice. With the army mustered below, we need a signal we can see from the gatehouse. Use the trebuchet, and *feu d'Hellas*. If Selig breaks east and his army follows, fire east, and we fall on their rear. If he divides his forces, fire west, and we'll sweep to the left and engage their weak side."

"It will be done," Gaspar Trevalion murmured. "Elua be with us all."

They took their farewells, then, the men clasping each other's hands. Percy de Somerville bowed to Ysandre.

"Your majesty," he said soberly. "I served under your grandfather for many years. But if I die today, I die proud to have served under you."

She stood very tall and straight on the grey walls of the battlements. "And I to have been served by you, Comte de Somerville. Elua's blessing upon you."

To my surprise, Barquiel L'Envers grinned, and kissed his niece on the brow. "Take care of yourself, Ysandre, you make a damned good Queen. We'll do our best to see you stay one." He nodded at Joscelin and me. "Keep these two with you, will you? They seem to be damnably hard to kill."

I did not always like the Duc L'Envers, but I could not help loving him then.

When they were gone, Ysandre shivered, and wrapped her deep-blue cloak with the Courcel swan embroidered in silver at the collar tight around her.

"I must speak to Farrens de Marchet, who commands the trebuchet crew on the western wall," Gaspar Trevalion said apologetically. "Will you not go below to safety, your majesty?"

"No." Ysandre shook her fair head. "I will stay here, my lord. Terre d'Ange stands or falls with us this day, and so do I."

"We'll stay," I said to Gaspar. It made no earthly difference, save for L'Envers' flippant comment, but it was enough. He nodded and set off quickly, a company of shields with him.

We stood there and watched the skies lighten as dawn broke full in the east, and the sun slowly began to clear the horizon. Joscelin kept a watchful eye to the arrowslit, looking for our army. A handful of Ysandre's House Courcel guard, as well as her ever-present Cassilines, surrounded us; still, I think there was no one else to whom she dared speak her mind.

"I have your book, still, your majesty," I said presently, casting about for something to say. "Your father's diary. It is with my things, in our camp. I kept it with me, all this time."

"Did you read it?" She smiled sadly. "It was very beautiful, I thought."

"It was. He loved wisely, too. Delaunay lived for the memory of that love." I didn't mention Alcuin, though I was glad, now, that Delaunay had known a second happiness.

"I know." Ysandre glanced down into the courtyard far below and to the fore of us, filled with a tight mass of men. "I'm glad he made his peace with my uncle before he died. My mother caused a great deal of pain, I think."

"Yes." I couldn't gainsay her. "People do, for love, or for power."

"Or honor." She looked sympathetically at me. "I'm sorry you were drawn into this Phèdre. Please know that whatever happens, you have my gratitude for the role you played. And for . . . for what you told me of Drustan." She smiled at Joscelin. "Both of you. What became of your friend?" she asked then, remembering. "The Tsingano? Is he with Ghislain's army?"

It hurt to think of Hyacinthe; I caught my breath, and met Joscelin's eye, glancing round from the arrow-slit. "No, your majesty," I said. "It is a long story, our journey, and Hyacinthe's may be the longest."

"A Mendacant's tale," murmured Joscelin.

We told her, then, there on the battlements of besieged Troyes-le-Mont, while arrows clattered against the merlon and her guards kept watch. I began it, but Joscelin told it better, with all the skill he'd gained in his Mendacant guise. It was his tribute to Hyacinthe, and I let him have it, as he had let me have mine, the last night on that lonely isle.

Hyacinthe would have liked it, I think.

Gaspar Trevalion came back to find his Queen round-eyed with awe, uncertain whether or not to credit our tale.

"De Marchet is ready," he said brusquely, returning

us to the dire reality of our situation. "He'll fire on my command. Any sign of d'Aiglemort or the Albans?"

"No, my lord." I had been watching, while Joscelin told the story of Hyacinthe and the Master of the Straits. "Not yet."

Gaspar glanced up at the sky, turning a pale blue as the sun rose steadily. "Pray they don't fail us," he said grimly. "They've near filled the moat with rubble at the barbican, and Selig's sappers are digging under the northwest tower. Farrens said they felt the stone tremble underfoot. They're moving one of the siege towers toward the north wall, too. We've let him get deadly close, if help doesn't come."

"It will come," I said, with a confidence I didn't feel. It was harder to believe, here.

"It is coming." Joscelin, back at the arrow-slit, pressed his eye to the aperture. His hands, flat against the wall, clenched, fingertips digging into stone. "It *is* coming. My lord! Look!" Heedless of station, he grabbed Gaspar's arm and drew him to the wall.

Gaspar Trevalion looked silently, then drew back. "Your majesty," he said, gesturing for her to look. Ysandre took a turn for a long moment, then stepped away and drew a shuddering breath.

"Phèdre," she whispered. "You brought them. You should see."

I stepped up to the arrow-slit, standing once more on my toes and ignoring the pain of my injuries, and looked.

In the distance, at the base of the foothills, a shining line of silver advanced toward the fortress.

High on the battlements of Troyes-le-Mont, we had the advantage of sight, despite the greater distance; still, it was not long before Selig's sentries spotted their advance. None of his scouting parties had returned alive, and it was a mercy that Ghislain had found a path where they could descend undetected, but there was no hiding an entire army, once they were on level ground.

I gave way to Ysandre at the arrow-slit—she was Queen, I could do no less—but it was agony, not to see. I bore it as long as I could, then stepped out from behind the merlon, to stand at the low crenelation. Joscelin was a mere step behind me, and I thought for an instant that he would drag me back to safety, but he merely gave me a quick glance and set himself at my side, vambraces crossed before him.

We didn't have much to fear, as the attention of the Skaldi began to shift direction.

Nothing I have ever seen can compare to it, unless it be the seas roiling under the duress of the Master of the Straits. It was so vast, the Skaldi army, spread like an ocean across the plain. Word came from the eastern rearguard, the tiny figures of Selig's sentries pelting across the torn ground, and the mighty army began to surge.

It hit the outskirts of his forces with a ripple, and built to a swell, moving toward us. By the time it crested and broke against the fortress, throwing our attackers into chaos, the silver line of advancing soldiers had drawn nearer.

The outermost ranks of Skaldi broke, racing on foot and on horse across the plain to engage the oncoming enemy. The silver line halted and shrank, kneeling, and Ghislain de Somerville's L'Agnacite archers fired over their heads, a rain of black arrows arching down on the Skaldi. Then the line rose, shields raised to form a bar of silver, and advanced.

These were Camaeline soldiers, born to the sword and drilled within an inch of their lives. Undisciplined and fierce with battle, the Skaldi broke against them like a wave against a wall, crashing, falling, dashed back. And the wall advanced.

At the base of the fortress, milling confusion ensued, Skaldi sappers and engineers abandoning their posts. Fearless in the melee, Waldemar Selig rode back and forth, shouting at them, ordering them to hold their places.

Disorderly and milling, they held, enough to hold our forces pinned within Troyes-le-Mont.

Far across the plain, the silver line of d'Aiglemort's infantry pushed forward, moving relentlessly into the Skaldi horde, which overran them on both sides, threatening to overwhelm them with sheer numbers.

That was when the Alban forces struck.

Cavalry to the right flank, and war-chariots to the left, foot soldiers swarming after both, streaming from behind the Camaeline infantry, wild and terrifying, they threw the entire battle into chaos.

But the numbers were against them.

Even at this distance, I could see the blood run in rivers of red, see our allies cut down. I turned without realizing it, found my hands clutching at Gaspar Trevalion's arm.

"Give the signal!" I begged him, desperate. "They're dying out there!"

At the foot of the fortress, beyond the moat, Selig's discipline held, ten thousand strong. Gaspar shook his head, ignoring my grip.

"We have to make it out the gate," he said, his voice heavy with grief. "We're no good to them if Selig's men can pick us off one by one."

I whirled away from him with a sharp cry, staring across the battlefield.

Near drowning in a sea of Skaldi, still, somehow, the Camaeline infantry held its line. Now they dug in, shields raised, fending off the dreadful numbers, and parted.

Slowly, like a massive gate opening, the line broke and opened. A single horn sounded, clear and defiant, its sound rising above the shouting.

Into the breach, the Camaeline cavalry charged; the Allies of Camlach, all who remained, with Isidore d'Aiglemort at their head.

He betrayed our nation, and all we hold dear. I make no excuse for that. But if the poets sing of the last charge of Isidore d'Aiglemort, they do so with reason. I know. I was there. I saw the mounted Allies of Camlach drive into tens of thousands of Skaldi like a wedge, faces bright with Camael's battle-fire, swords singing.

The shock of it went clear through the Skaldic army.

I heard the cry that arose, too, as the Skaldi gave way before them, some dying, some swirling away. "Kilberhaar!" they cried, falling and fleeing. "Kilberhaar!"

On his tall horse, Waldemar Selig turned, sensing himself the target of that fierce-driving wedge. All around the sides of battle, Skaldi and Alban fought, desperate and bloody, the Skaldi numbers prevailing.

But the center was coming for him.

Selig rode back and forth. Selig drew his sword, and held it aloft in one massive fist, while the White Brethren flanked him, and his forces roiled.

Isidore d'Aiglemort drove toward his heart.

"Kilberhaar!" Selig roared, pumping his sword-arm skyward. Wheeling his horse, he plunged toward the center of the battle, scattering his own forces. "Kilberhaar!"

Howling, the Skaldi followed.

"Now!" Gaspar Trevalion shouted. His standard-bearer waved the Courcel swan with wild urgency, and the trebuchet crew set torches to the *feu d'Hellas* and loosed the counterweights. The bucket sprang forward, casting an arching mass of liquid flame over the eastern front of the Skaldi army.

In the courtyard, Percy de Somerville gave a single command.

Up came the porcullis, dented by the battering ram; down came the drawbridge, and the keepers of the barbican loosed a cover of crossbow-fire. Four by four, the defenders of Troyes-le-Mont came streaming forth, reforming in neat lines and falling on the rearguard of Selig's men.

Truly, the Skaldi were caught between hammer and anvil.

We were all standing clear on the battlements now, forgotten targets, as the slaughter below ensued. Percy de Somerville's army fell on the Skaldi like lions, a siege's worth of pent rage in their blood, felling everything in their path.

And at the center, Waldemar Selig drove to meet Isidore d'Aiglemort.

I do not need to tell it; all the world knows that story. How they came together at the heart of the battle, two titans, natural-born warriors both of them. We saw, from the battlements, how the shining wedge of d'Aiglemort's cavalry thinned, growing narrower, driving still, ever inward. How the silver eagle of death, d'Aiglemort's standard, faltered at last, dipping and falling, overwhelmed beneath a sea of Skaldi.

And Isidore d'Aiglemort, atop his black horse, fought onward, alone.

They met, at the end; d'Aiglemort went down, the black horse slain. We thought him lost, buried under Skaldi. Then he arose, silver hair streaming beneath his helmet, a Skaldi axe in one hand. He threw it left-handed, as Selig rode up on his tall horse.

He killed the horse.

Always, it is the innocent who suffer, the beasts of the field, the Servants of Naamah. So it is, always, in times of war. Selig's steed went down with a crash; Selig arose cursing. And they fought, there on the plain, on foot and alone. They fought, the two of them, like lovers staging a Showing in Cereus House. There are those who think it wrong, to make such a comparison. But I was there.

I saw.

How many wounds Isidore d'Aiglemort had taken to get there, I cannot say. They counted, on his body, when the armor was stripped from him: Seventeen, no less, they counted. Some of those were Selig's. Not all.

Waldemar Selig, proof against weapons. So the Skaldi believed. But while battle raged around them, he fought Isidore d'Aiglemort, the traitor Duc of Terre d'Ange.

Fought him, and died.

I do not scruple to say it. When d'Aiglemort's sword found a gap in Selig's armor and pierced it to the hilt, I cried out my relief. Waldemar Selig sank to his knees, disbelieving. D'Aiglemort, dying, sank with him, both hands on his sword-hilt, thrusting it home.

So they met their end.

✑NINETY

After that, it was nearly a rout, despite the numbers.

Those tribal fault-lines I had so carefully traversed through the Skaldi encampment turned into gaping chasms as bands of warriors broke away; some by the thousand, others by the hundreds, and some even fracturing steading by steading, in the scores and dozens.

Percy de Somerville's troops pursued them with merciless efficiency. And at the center of the battlefield . . .

"Your majesty!" I pointed toward the northeast, where a band of mounted Cruithne was cutting a swath toward the site of d'Aiglemort and Selig's battle. The standard of the black boar, the Cullach Gorrym, flew proud overhead, and at the forefront, sword swinging tirelessly, rode a familiar figure, scarlet cloak swirling from his shoulders.

"Drustan." Ysandre touched her fingers to her lips, eyes wide with wonder. "Is it really?"

"Oh, it is," Joscelin assured her. "That's Drustan mab Necthana!"

His riders won through as we watched, forging a ring around the fallen figure of Isidore d'Aiglemort. To the southeast, the war-chariots of the Dalriada raced in mad circles, sowing chaos and terror in the hearts of the Skaldi, and their foot-soldiers carried the Fhalair Bàn, the White Horse of Eire.

A clamor arose closer to home, coming from the courtyard.

Later, I learned what had happened; a desperate party of Skaldi, abandoned by Selig and caught by the unexpected emergence of the entire garrison of Troyes-le-Mont, stormed the gate ere it could be closed. They came close enough on the heels of the emerging army that the defenders of the barbican dared not shoot.

That was how, then, they gained the courtyard.

We could see it well enough, atop the battlements. A handful of de Somerville's D'Angeline infantry had doubled back to engage them. If the field was in chaos, not so the courtyard; a fierce battle was being waged before the inner gate, with a small knot of D'Angelines fending off thrice as many Skaldi.

Gaspar Trevalion called sharply to our archers, and

half of them peeled off, clattering down the tower stairs to align themselves along the parapet of the inner wall overlooking the courtyard, but they faced the same problem as the gatekeepers. There was nowhere to shoot without striking the defenders.

The mass of warriors surged, all helms and flailing steel, seen from above. One figure among the D'Angelines stood out, tall as the tallest Skaldi, making a space around him. It was a pity he was so outnumbered.

From beneath his helmet, a long braid of wheat-blond hair swung like a whip as he fought.

Joscelin made a sharp sound; I thought for a second that he'd been struck, "Luc!" he cried, the bright morning air snatching the word from his lips. "Luc!"

"Your brother?"

He gave me an agonized nod, hands clenching and unclenching in fists as he crossed his vambraces unthinking.

I grasped his arms and shook him, ignoring the pain it cost me. "Can you get to him?" I didn't bother to wait for an answer, seeing in his eyes that he had already gauged the feat. "Then go! Name of Elua, Joscelin, go!"

White lines formed at either side of his nose and mouth. "If ever there was a time when I dared not—"

I dug my fists into his hair and dragged his face down to mine, kissing him hard. "I love you," I said fiercely, "and if you ever want to hear those words from my lips again, you will *not* choose this idiotic vow over your brother's life!"

Joscelin's blue eyes went wide and startled, so close to my own. I let him go and he took one step backward, pressing the back of one hand to his mouth. We stared at one another; and then he whirled, dashing for the tower. I swear, I could hear every step of his headlong descent. His figure emerged on the inner wall, diminished by distance, but I could hear the clarion battlecry.

"Verreuil! Verreuil!"

Gaspar's bowmen gave way, but he scarce hesitated at the parapet, launching himself over its edge, twin daggers drawn.

I measured the drop later for myself; it was thrice a grown man's height, at least. Joscelin's leap, arching, carried him into the thick of the Skaldi attackers; they scattered, I think, as much out of awe as anything. His plunge was like a meteor, but he landed on his feet, and came out of his crouch spinning. A pause of breathing-space, and his daggers flashed into their sheaths. Out came his sword in a two-handed grip, and he lit into the Skaldi like lightning unchained.

A steady roar arose and grew from the D'Angeline defenders, centering on the tall form of Luc Verreuil, whose mighty efforts suddenly doubled in strength.

They won, of course. They had to win.

"Joscelin Verreuil has sworn his sword to my service," Ysandre said in my ear, bending down low and amused despite it all. "I remand it to you, in perpetuity. And that is my gift, for your service, Phèdre nó Delaunay."

I nodded, accepting her gift. What else was I to do?

Thus was the day won.

In the end, those Skaldi remaining fled the field or surrendered, those who'd gained some measure of Waldemar Selig's wisdom. Below the battlements, Percy de Somerville's standard-bearer dipped his pennant, giving the signal, and Gaspar Trevalion ordered the horns sounded. The sun was well beyond its apex, and the horns sounded lonely and sad across the ruined plain.

The courtyard was won, the fortress of Troyes-le-Mont stood undefeated. Her armies and allies came limping home.

I had not forgotten the lessons of Bryn Gorrydum. Over the protests of my Queen, who could not find Joscelin to halt me, I went out to give water to the wounded and dying.

So many lost, on both sides. If my back burned like fire, so be it. I had won the right, through my own blood and sweat and tears, to minister to the dying. That is the secret that none dares tell who fights for a cause. Dying, we are all alike. I was Kushiel's chosen; I knew. Pain levels us all. Little enough comfort I had to give. But what I had, I gave.

I do not dare voice it, to anyone save Joscelin, but the Skaldi were the worst. Every time I saw fair hair bright with blood beneath a helmet, I thought it might be Gunter Arnlaugson. He had treated me fair, as best as was in him, and I had repaid him with ruin. I feared to face him, for that.

I never did find Gunter, nor any of the folk of his steading. I can only pray they were among those who had the sense to flee early, having gained some sense of the true depth of our fierce D'Angeline pride, having dwelt so long on our borders.

Waldemar Selig, I found; and d'Aiglemort.

They lay close together, those fallen, and Drustan's Cruithne surrounded them. Their horses nodded, heads low and weary. Drustan mab Necthana saluted me, staggering as he slid from the saddle and his lame foot gave way beneath him.

"Tell Ysandre . . ." he said, and caught at his pommel.

"Tell her yourself," I replied, catching him, gesturing frantically for Lelahiah Valais and her apprentices. They came, quick and compassionate; Eisheth's folk have a gift for healing, among other things.

As I had gifts.

Waldemar Selig, who had taken them unasked, lay

upon the field, his body broken and twisted, forked beard pointing skyward and asking unanswered questions of the heavens. I could have answered them, if he'd asked, if he'd ever asked. But he had not asked me, reckoning the soul of Terre d'Ange lay within its warriors, and not its whores. I laid my hand upon his cold face, closing those asking hazel eyes.

"We are alike, my lord," I murmured. "We are all alike, in the end, and none of us to be had merely for the taking."

I heard laughter, then, faint and bitter.

Seventeen wounds, I have said. It was true. But Isidore d'Aiglemort was not quite dead of them when I found him.

"Phèdre nó Delaunay," he whispered, clutching at my hand. "I am afraid of your lord's revenge."

At first I thought he meant Delaunay; then I knew, through his clutching fingers, who he meant. Bronze wings of fear beat at my eardrums. I gave water to the dying, lifting the skin to his lips. "You have paid, my lord, and paid in full," I said compassionately. "And Kushiel sends no punishment that we are not fit to bear."

Isidore d'Aiglemort drank, and sighed; sighed, and died.

That, I kept to myself. It was no one's concern but our own; his, mine and Kushiel's.

Then I heard the wailing of the Dalriada.

It is an unearthly sound, high and keening, raising the hair at the back of my neck. I did not need to be told what it signified, that so many mourned at once. Releasing my grasp on d'Aiglemort's lifeless hand, I rose and turned. Some distance from me, Drustan shook off the healers' ministrations, standing awkwardly, his eyes dark with concern in the blue masque of his face.

We saw the Dalriada, clustered around one of the

chariots, whose team stood steaming in the traces, heavy-headed. I could see the grief on Grainne's face, as she looked our way.

"Ah, no," I said. "No."

It was a long walk across the torn field, with the dead lying twisted in my path, blood seeping slow and dark into the dry soil and shredded rootlets. Drustan made it with me, his gait halt and painful; I daresay it cost him as much as it did me, pain flooding my body.

"Eamonn," I whispered.

They had taken him from the chariot and arranged his limbs so that he lay proud and straight on the blood-soaked earth of Terre d'Ange, and tugged at his armor so it concealed the terrible rent a Skaldi spearhead had made in his side. His hair, never as bright as his sister's, was stiffened to a white crest with lime, spiky against the dark soil.

Drustan seized his belt-knife and raised it unhesitating, sawing at a thick lock of his black hair. It gave way and he knelt reverently, placing the lock beneath Eamonn's cold hands.

"He was braver than lions and more stalwart than an oak," he said somberly to Grainne. "His name will live forever among the Cullach Gorrym."

She nodded, her grey eyes bright with tears.

I had brought him here. I did not have the right to mourn. "I'm sorry," I murmured to Grainne, to Drustan, to the Dalriada; to all of them, my voice choking. "I'm so sorry."

"My brother chose his fate." Even clad in bloodstained armor, Grainne had her dignity, her kindness. "You made him choose to be more than he would have, otherwise. Do not deny him that honor."

And I had scorned Joscelin, for his Cassiline pride. It is true, we are the same, in the end. Bowing my head, I borrowed Drustan's belt-knife, and cut a lock from my own hair, laying it thick and shining beside the Cruarch's. "Elua keep you, Eamonn mac Conor." I remembered how he had kept the army organized, when the Master of the Straits had parted us; how his sensible manner had aided Ghislain de Somerville when we struck out on D'Angeline soil. "We would have failed without you."

Kneeling, I wept, and wept for all of us.

"Phèdre." A familiar voice, exhausted. I looked up to see Joscelin, mounted, scratched but unharmed. There were dark circles beneath his eyes. "You're in no shape to do this."

It was true; I knew it well enough to rise, obedient. All the length and breadth of the battlefield, D'Angeline troops were about the grim business of gathering the dead and tending to the dying, aided by chirurgeons and healers. "Your brother?" I asked him. "And your father?"

"They are well enough." Joscelin's voice was hollow. "They survived." He bowed to Grainne from the saddle, a Cassiline bow. "I grieve for your loss, my lady."

I turned to her and translated unthinking. Grainne smiled sadly. "Give him our thanks, and go with him, Phèdre nó Delaunay. We will tend to our own."

Drustan's nod echoed her words, and Joscelin extended his hand to me, leaning down from the saddle. I took it, and mounted behind him, and we began the long, slow ride back to Troyes-le-Mont.

Ninety-one

D'Aiglemort's surviving forces decided to a man to pursue the fleeing Skaldi.

The aftermath of war is a dreadful thing. If ever I had envied Ysandre de la Courcel her crown—and I had not—that would have cured me of it. To her fell the terrible choices of apportioning blame and punishment, upon the living and the dead.

In the end she chose wisely, I think, granting amnesty to those Allies of Camlach who chose their own dire fate, vowing their lives to hunting down the remainders of Selig's vast army. No one gainsaid it, the memory of Isidore d'Aiglemort's last, sacrificial battle too fresh in mind. As for those Skaldi who had surrendered; it was my counsel, among that of others, to accept ransom for them. I knew well how much D'Angeline treasure had found its way across the border, thanks to d'Aiglemort's sanctioned raids. In truth, I'd no heart for further bloodshed. But neither, I think, had Ysandre, nor many of her supporters.

So the Skaldi were ransomed, and sent home, and the borders were sealed against them.

Enough had died.

As for the reunion of Ysandre and Drustan, I was there to witness it. So were some thousands of D'Angelines and Albans. He came riding, with the Alban army at his back, while she threw open the gates of Troyes-le-Mont to welcome him.

They greeted each other as equals, then clasped hands, and he drew her hands to his lips and kissed them. Our conjoined armies shouted approval, though I did not see it reflected in all the eyes of the D'Angeline nobility.

Wars come and go; politics endure.

For those seeking a higher degree of romance, I can only say that Ysandre and Drustan knew too well who and what they were: The Queen of Terre d'Ange and the Cruarch of Alba. With the armed forces of two nations watching, they dared be no less, and no more. I have come to know Ysandre passing well, since then, and I believe what fell between them behind closed doors was another matter. I know Drustan, too, and I know how he loved her. But they were monarchs alike, and had ever understood it would be so, and that is the face they showed to the nation.

One thing was sure; no one, publicly, would dare speak against their union. We owed our lives and our sovereignty to Alba, and their allegiance was unquestioned. Amid the mourning and burying, the ransoming and the celebrating, a date was set, a wedding to be held in the City of Elua.

Joscelin and I were another matter.

I met his father and his brother, and two men-at-arms who had survived the terrible battle.

What I had expected . . . I don't know. Nothing, truly; I was numb for days afterward, too tired to think. I spent days and nights at Ysandre's call, translating at will, for Cruithne and Skaldi alike. There were some others as skilled, it is true, in all that mass of folk, but none she trusted as she did me, Delaunay's other pupil. And there were the hospital wards too, with many Albans in them; and some of Phèdre's Boys; as well, of whom no more than a dozen had survived. Wracked with anguish, I spent time at each of their bedsides.

Still, I found the time, when Joscelin informed me that House Verreuil would be leaving.

With d'Aiglemort's forces committed to the pursuit of

the Skaldi, it freed Percy de Somerville to release the most far-flung vestiges of the Royal Army. The standing army, of course, would remain intact, mobilizing to reinforce the Skaldi border, but those who had abandoned home and hearth to serve were dismissed with thanks and honor; especially the wounded. There was a special ceremony, too, for the valiant spear-company of the Royal House of Aragon, whose commander made pledges of friendship on behalf of his King with not only Ysandre, but the young Cruarch of Alba as well.

Percy de Somerville's reunion with Ghislain had brought tears to my eyes, father and son embracing, pounding one another's backs with L'Agnacite disregard for onlookers.

The Chevalier Millard Verreuil, the stump of his missing left hand bound in a sling, was cooler with his son; but it was only his way, I think. He was a tall, lean man, with greying hair in an austere Siovalese braid and the same old-fashioned beauty as his middle son. I had learned, since the battle, that he had been the first in the courtyard to reach the inner gate, had lost shield and hand alike defending it.

"I understand you are somewhat of a scholar," he said gravely when Joscelin had made the introductions.

I opened my mouth, and closed it. It was not entirely untrue, but I had never been thus introduced. "I do but sample from the feast-table of my forefathers," I said in Caerdicci, quoting the Tiberian orator Nunnius Balbo. Joscelin's father smiled unexpectedly, the corners of his eyes crinkling.

"Naamah's Servants are seldom so learned in Siovale," he said, laying his sound hand on my shoulder. "A rebellion against the teachings of Shemhazai, mayhap."

"Shemhazai had his passions, my lord," I replied, smiling back at him, "and Naamah her store of wisdom."

The Chevalier Verreuil laughed, patting my shoulder. "I have heard what you did," he said, growing serious once more. "Terre d'Ange owes you a great debt for your service."

I inclined my head, uncomfortable with praise. "If not for your son, I would be dead many times over, my lord."

"I know." He shifted his sling and rested his gaze on Joscelin with quiet pride. "Whether or not I agree with the path you have chosen, I cannot say, but you have acquitted yourself upon it with honor."

Joscelin bowed and said nothing. His brother Luc, half a head taller than both of them, grinned.

"Can't disagree, seeing the cause!" he remarked, beaming at me. Luc had the same fair hair and blue eyes as his brother, but an open, merry cast to his features that must surely be their mother's legacy. "Elua! Will you come visit us, at least, Phèdre? You ought to give me a fair chance before you decide on Joscelin!"

I wasn't sure how Joscelin would take his brother's teasing; we'd scarce had a private moment to speak since I'd kissed him on the battlements. I didn't even know what it meant myself. But glancing sidelong at him, I saw the corner of his mouth twitch with the shadow of a smile. "Neither of us have decided anything, my lord," I replied to Luc, "but I would be honored to see Verreuil."

He grinned again, clapping Joscelin on the shoulder. "You can come too, I suppose. Did you know you're an uncle five times over? Jehane's been wed six years, and Honore almost four."

"I will, someday," Joscelin murmured.

"You would be welcome," his father said firmly. "Any day. Your mother longs to see you." He looked gently upon me. "And you will always be welcome in our home, Phèdre nó Delaunay. I knew the Comte de Montrève, you know. I think, in the end, he would have been very proud of his son Anafiel, and what he has wrought in you."

"Thank you, my lord." It meant more than I would have guessed. Tears stung my eyes, and I hoped that, somewhere in the true Terre d'Ange that lies beyond, Delaunay had won his father's pride.

I stood back and let them make their final farewells alone, then. There was a small party of Siovalese departing all together that morning. Luc Verreuil turned in the saddle as they rode away, the sunlight bright on his wheat-blond hair. "They sing some interesting songs about you in the hospital ward, Phèdre nó Delaunay!" he shouted, laughing.

"Blessed Elua." I could feel the flush rising. Wounded or no, Rousse's damned sailors, Phèdre's Boys, would teach that damned song to anyone who would listen.

"They adore you," Joscelin said dryly. "They've earned the right."

I shuddered. "But in front of your *father*?"

"I know." He watched them ride away, joining the train of Siovalese. "He wanted to speak to the Prefect about rescinding his edict against me."

My heart, unexpectedly, leapt into my throat. "What did you say?" I asked, striving to keep my voice calm. Joscelin glanced at me.

"I said no." Another faint smile twitched at the corner of his lips, glinted in his blue eyes. "After all, I have my vow to think of."

How long had it been since I had laughed, truly laughed? I couldn't remember. I laughed then, and felt it like a clean wind in my spirit, while Joscelin regarded me with amusement.

"We do need to talk, though," I said, when I had

caught my breath. He nodded, sobering. But just then one of Ysandre's pages came at a run across the drawbridge, searching for me; I was needed, and our conversation must be put off that day.

As it was the next, and the day after. So it is with common folk, when the affairs of the mighty command their attention. And whatever part Joscelin and I had played in the tapestry of war, we were but bit players once more, in the arena of politics.

Ysandre kept her court at Troyes-le-Mont, while the nation restabilized. D'Angeline nobles came daily to the fortress, renewing pledges of loyalty in some cases; in others, divulging the disloyalty of their peers. She gauged them all with an astuteness beyond her years, aided by the counsel of Gaspar Trevalion and Barquiel L'Envers—and too of Drustan mab Necthana, who understood a great deal more than most people reckoned. They betrayed themselves, sometimes, those who had plotted against her, gazing in startlement at his face, blue-whorled and strange. It was not strange to me, not any longer. I met privately with him each day to tutor him in D'Angeline, and was ever more impressed with his quiet, intuitive wisdom.

A constant watch was kept on the battlements, and every day the horns sounded, announcing some new arrival. I grew inured to it, scarce wondering any more who approached, merely marking the banners and insignia, checking them against the catalogue Delaunay had required Alcuin and me to memorize. I knew a great many of them, although Alcuin had known them all.

I was at the smithy, settling an argument for two of the minor lords of the Dalriada regarding repairs to their war-chariots—a new linch pin and wheel-rims—and took no notice of the horns that morning, until Joscelin appeared and caught at my arm.

"What is it?" I asked.

His face was unreadable. "Come and see."

"The work is done, let them have the chariots," I said to the smith. "The Cruarch will see you paid for your labor." I do not like to admit it, but some of the D'Angeline craftsmen who had flocked to Troyes-le-Mont were inclined to take advantage of the Albans. I hurried into the keep after Joscelin, mounting the spiral stairs of the tower, ignoring the faint twinges of pain from my still-healing back.

On the battlements, he pointed to the west, where a party was advancing toward the fortress. "There."

They rode in a square formation, arranged around a single figure at their center, with two outriders on either side. Standards flew at the corners of the square. I knew the device; a raven and the sea.

Quincel de Morhban.

I caught my breath, wondering, and then felt Joscelin's fingers at my elbow, a grip almost hard enough to hurt. I knew the figure de Morhban's men surrounded, too. There was no mistaking it, even at a distance; proud and straight in the saddle, head held high, rippling curtain of blue-black hair.

The world rippled in my vision, crenellated walls of the battlements tilting sideways. Only Joscelin's grip held me upright. At my throat, Melisande's diamond sparkled like the sun and hung heavy as a millstone.

"Melisande," I whispered. "Ah, Elua!"

Ninety-two·

İ do not think the Duc de Morhban could have brought her in without aid. It was her own kin who had betrayed her, the two outriders proving to be Shahrizai, riding hooded even in the heat of summer, shadowing their features. Younger members of the House, they were: Marmion and Persia, who sold their cousin's whereabouts to Quincel de Morhban in return for his favor.

After we had departed the shores of Terre d'Ange in Rousse's flagship, de Morhban had kept his word, interrogating the Admiral's men. Rousse hadn't told them everything, but enough, and they gave away enough for de Morhban to put events together. And too, rumors reached his ears, as surely they had Melisande's, that members of the Cassiline Brotherhood, serving as couriers for Ysandre's loyal allies, asked about Melisande Shahrizai where they rode. De Morhban was no fool, and had held sovereignty in Kusheth long enough to know how to deal with House Shahrizai. He kept his knowledge to himself and waited for matters to unfold.

While the nation went to war, Quincel de Morhban bided his time. When mighty waves roiled the Straits and word reached him of an Alban fleet landing on D'Angeline soil, he cast the die and went a-hunting Melisande Shahrizai.

He found her, in an isolated hold in southern Kusheth, preparing to journey, as Marmion and Persia had said he would.

That much, they knew, having aided her; not enough to convict her. Word spread like wildfire through

Troyes-le-Mont as Melisande was brought into the keep. Everyone knew something, it seemed. And no one knew enough. Melisande played a deep game. The edifice of proof of her guilt had crumbled on the battlefield.

"I'm sorry," Ysandre said compassionately to me. "I would have spared you this, if I could."

I drew a deep breath and shivered. "I know, my lady."

The hearing was held in the throne room, cool and dim behind thick stone walls, lit by lamps and torches even in the heart of summer. I stood behind Ysandre's throne, behind her two Cassilines and the rank of her Courcel guard. Even Joscelin was no comfort in this, although he stood close at my side.

Quincel de Morhban came forward to bend his knee before Ysandre, pledging his loyalty. What he said, I cannot remember; all my senses were fixed on one point in that room. He stood aside, then, and Melisande Shahrizai came forward, flanked by his men, though they dared not touch her.

"Lady Melisande Shahrizai." Ysandre's voice, cool as a blade, cut through the flame-streaked air. "You stand before us accused of treason. How do you plead?"

"Your majesty." Melisande curtsied, smooth and graceful, her face calm and lovely, "I am your loyal servant, and innocent of the charge."

I could see Ysandre lean forward. "You are charged with conspiring with Isidore d'Aiglemort to betray the nation and seize the throne. Do you deny this?"

Melisande smiled; I knew that smile well. I have seen it a thousand times, waking and sleeping. Torchlight glimmered on her hair and her ivory features, making twin stars of her deep blue eyes. "For a thousand years, House Shahrizai has served the throne," she said, and her voice was like honey, rich and sweet. We who are D'Angeline, we are vulnerable to beauty, always. I could hear the assembled crowd murmur. "His grace de Morhban makes charges, but he offers no proof, and has much to gain, if his loyalty and my estates alike are at stake." Melisande turned out her hands in an eloquent gesture, lifting her gaze to Ysandre's. Such surety, such confidence; her guilt lay buried beneath the battlefield, in the long sleep of death. "Where was he, when battle was waged for D'Angeline sovereignty? Yes, your majesty, I refute the charge. If he has proof, let him offer it."

How much, in truth, de Morhban had guessed, I was not sure; but I knew then how much he had told her: nothing. The isolation that had protected Melisande had made her vulnerable, and Quincel de Morhban had disarmed her in the only way possible. He had kept her shrouded in ignorance.

"You are charged too," Ysandre said, watching her closely, "with conspiring with Waldemar Selig of the Skaldi."

It took Melisande by surprise. I could see her eyelids flicker. Then she laughed, easily and gracefully. "Does the Duc claim as much? Well might I say it of him, or anyone, your majesty. It is an easy charge to make, that may not be gainsaid by the dead."

"No," Ysandre said. "Not de Morhban."

Melisande grew still, her gaze sharpening as she regarded Ysandre. "Do I not have the right, your majesty, to know who accuses me?" she asked, her voice low and dangerous.

Ysandre did not waver, but made a slight gesture with one hand. The rank of her guard parted in front of me, and I stepped forth trembling.

"I do," I said softly, meeting Melisande's eyes. I raised one hand and grasped the diamond at my throat, tearing it loose with one sharp jerk. The velvet lead broke, and I held the diamond in my hand, cords trailing. I tossed it on the flagstones between us. "That is yours, my lady," I said, taking a shuddering breath. "I am not."

In the profound silence of the throne room, Melisande Shahrizai went a deadly white.

To her credit, she gave no other sign, but stood unmoving as the two of us looked at one another. Then, impossibly, she gave a short laugh and looked away. "My lord Delaunay," she murmured, gazing into the distance. "You play a considerable end-game." No one spoke as her sapphire-blue gaze returned to rest thoughtfully on me. "That was the one thing I couldn't fathom. Percy de Somerville was prepared for Selig's invasion. You?"

"I saw a letter you wrote to Selig, in your own hand." My voice was shaking. "You should have killed me when you had the chance."

Melisande stooped and picked up the diamond lead that lay between us, dangling it from one hand. "Leaving you the Cassiline was a bit excessive," she agreed, glancing at Joscelin, who stood impassive, eyes blazing. "Although it seems to have agreed with him."

"Do you dispute this charge?" Ysandre raised her voice, cool and implacable, severing the tension between us. Melisande looked at the diamond in her hand, closing her fist around it, arching her brows.

"You have proof, I assume, of their story?"

"I have Palace Guards who will swear they saw them with you the night of Anafiel Delaunay's murder." Ysandre's expression was calm and merciless. "And I believe, my lady Shahrizai, that thirty thousand invading Skaldi attest to the truth of their tale."

Melisande shrugged. "Then I have no more to say."

"So be it." Ysandre summoned her guard. "You will be executed at dawn."

No one, not Trevalion nor L'Envers, not de Morhban nor the assembled peers, and not her Shahrizai kin, heads downcast, spoke in her defense. I watched, trembling, as the Courcel guard surrounded Melisande, escorting her out of the throne room.

"It's over," Joscelin murmured at my ear. "It's over, Phèdre."

"I know." I touched my throat, where no diamond lay, and wondered why I felt so empty.

I spent a long time in the hospital wards that day and evening, finding solace in tending to the injured. I'd no medical skills to speak of, although Lelahiah Valais had a shy young student who was kind enough to instruct me in simple matters, changing bandages, and washing fevered wounds with herbal infusions. Mostly, it helped the wounded to see a kind face, to have a listening ear. I had scavenged parchment and ink from the tiny library, some days ago. I took letters for some of them, who had come to realize that they would never see home again.

A small kindness, but it meant a great deal to the dying. I spent much of my time with the Cruithne and Dalriada, who could not even communicate with the healers who tended them. Drustan had a veritable sheaf of letters already, that he had promised would reach Alban soil, and bards and brehons to read them, if their recipients could not.

Wise enough in his own way, Joscelin left me be. I do not think he ever understood, truly, what lay between Melisande and I. How could he, when I scarce understood it myself? It would have been simpler, before I dared the crossing of Selig's camp, before the torture. I despised her for what she had done, both to me, and to Terre d'Ange.

And yet . . .

Elua knew, I had loved her once.

It was well into the small hours of the night when the messenger found me. Unsure of his errand, he looked uncomfortable, whispering in the quiet air of the sickroom. "My lady Phèdre, I am bid to summon you. The Lady Melisande Shahrizai would speak with you, if you are willing."

If you ever have a chance to confront her alone, don't take it.

I did not forget Hyacinthe's words. But I went anyway.

There were two guards at her door; Ysandre's, and loyal. Even though they knew me, they checked me carefully for weapons before admitting me. It was an irony, that Melisande had a chamber to herself. No one else did, save Ysandre, with the fortress full to overflowing. But she was a peer of the realm, and a scion of Kushiel; she deserved as much, her last night on earth. I wondered who had been displaced, that she might spend it in comfort.

It was a small chamber, two chairs, a writing table and a bed only. I entered, and heard the door closed behind me, the bolt shot fast.

Melisande, seated in one of the chairs, glanced up as I entered. "I wasn't sure you'd come," she remarked in greeting, arching her perfect brows. "And without your warder, too."

"What do you want?" I remained standing.

She only laughed, that rich laugh that turned my very bones to water; even now, even still. "To see you," she said, then. "Before I die. Is that so much to ask?"

"From you," I said, "yes."

"Phèdre." Her lips shaped my name, her voice gave it meaning. I caught at the back of the second chair to steady myself, and her eyes watched me, amused. "Do you hate me that much?"

"Yes," I whispered, willing it to be true. "Why don't you?"

"Ah, well." Melisande shrugged. "I was careless, and you played the hand I dealt you. Shall I blame you for that? I knew you were Delaunay's creature when I dealt it. It might have been different, if I had claimed you for my own, and not given you leave to choose."

"No," I said.

"Who can say?" She smiled wryly. "But I will admit, I underestimated you gravely. You and that half-mad Cassiline of yours. I've heard tales, you know, from the guards. You went to Alba, they say."

I clutched the chair-back. "What did Selig promise you?" I asked, making my voice hard.

"Half an empire." Melisande leaned back casually. "I heard his name when he offered marriage to the daughter of the Duke of Milazza. I was curious. He thought I offered him Terre d'Ange. But I would have taken Skaldia in the end, you know. Or our children would have, if I'd not lived to see it."

"I know." I did not doubt it; I had guessed as much, the deep workings of her plot. A wave of hysterical laughter bubbled up within me, caught in my throat and left me choking. "You might have been happy with him, my lady," I said wildly. "He'd worked half his way through the *Trois Milles Joies* with me."

"Did he?" she murmured. "Hmm."

I closed my eyes to shut out the sight of her. "Why did you flee the City, when Ganelon died? I thought you knew."

By the sweeping sound of her skirt, I could tell Melisande had risen. "No. I knew Ganelon was dying, that's true. And I knew that Thelesis de Mornay had an audience with Ysandre, and the next day, her guards were asking questions about the night Delaunay was killed."

A silken rustle of a shrug. "I thought the King's Poet had persuaded Ysandre to open a new investigation into his death. It was enough to render my absence prudent."

Her plans were already in motion, then. It wouldn't have mattered, if Joscelin and I hadn't staggered out of the white depths of Skaldic winter with a wild tale on our lips.

I opened my eyes to see Melisande gazing out the narrow window of her chamber at the dark night. "Why?" I whispered, knowing the question was futile, needing to ask it anyway.

She turned around, serene and beautiful. "Because I could."

There would never be any other answer. As much as I might wish for a reason I could understand, in my heart, and not only in the dark, intuitive part of me that shuddered away from such comprehension, it would never come.

"It would never have been different," I said harshly, willing the words to hurt her, willing her to flinch under their impact. Never, before, had I known what it was to desire another's pain. I knew it then. "No matter what you did, no matter what claim you put on me, I would never have aided you in this."

"No?" Melisande smiled, amused. "Are you so sure of that, Phèdre nó Delaunay?" Her voice, low and hon-eyed, sent shivers across my skin, and I stood rooted as she crossed the room. Almost idle, one hand traced the line of my marque, hidden beneath my gown; it awak-ened the wound Selig had dealt me, and pain flared out-ward, suffusing my body. I could feel the heat of her presence, her scent. Nothing had changed. My will bent before hers as she cupped my cheek with one hand, face rising obediently to hers, my world tilted around her axis. "That which yields," she murmured, lowering her lips toward mine, "is not always weak."

A kiss; almost. Her lips brushed mine and withdrew, hands leaving my skin, and I staggered in the abyss of her sudden absence, in a shock of yearning.

"So your Tsingano said." Melisande looked at me, eyes gone cold. "I remembered as much. But I should have paid closer attention when he told me to choose my victories wisely." She sat down in the facing chair and nodded at the door. "You may go now, and leave me to consider my death."

I went.

I knocked blindly at the door of her chamber, stumbling through it when Ysandre's guards shot the bolt and opened it, finding the stone wall of the hallway with fumbling hands.

"Are you all right, my lady?" one of them asked, anxious. I heard the door close hard behind me and nodded.

"Yes," I whispered, knowing I was not, not at all, but that there was nothing they could do to help, nor anyone. We should both, I thought, have listened to Hyacinthe. The dreadful laughter threatened to rise, and I bowed my head, sliding my hands across my face.

Melisande.

ℰNINETY-THREE

I spent the night alone atop the battlements.

The drowsing guards let me be, disturbing me only to offer a sip of cordial from their flasks, leaving me alone with my turmoil. I have always found there to be solace in the vastness of open spaces, beneath the vault of the heavens. It is a comfort, in anguish, to be reminded of the scale of one's own troubles against the mighty breadth of the world.

What would I have done, truly, if Melisande had bought my marque instead of paying it, if she had never loosed the lead she set upon me? I was sure, very nearly entirely sure, that I had spoken the truth.

Very nearly. But she had accomplished her intent; I would never be entirely sure of it, not entirely.

In the end, of course, it didn't matter. What had happened was done, and my choices made. At dawn, Melisande Shahrizai would be no more, condemned to death by accusation. And no one, ever, would be troubled by her again.

Except for me.

Such were the thoughts that ran through my mind as I passed the long night's vigil, listening to the quiet stirrings of the sleeping fortress, the murmur of guards, the rattle and stamp of horses in the stable, the occasional creak of a door. These things I heard, and no more.

Joscelin found me as the skies were turning a dull grey, and I was thinking how I had seen far too many bloody dawns. I was a Servant of Naamah, my daybreaks should be stained with the red blood of the grape, and not mortal flesh.

"You went to see her," he said in a low voice behind me. I nodded without looking. "Why?"

"I don't know. I owed her that much, I suppose." I turned around, then, seeing his familiar face sober in the grey light. "Joscelin, there are things I will never be able to forget. And there will be times I need to try."

"I know," he said gently, coming to stand beside me. "You know that I could never hurt you, even if you asked it of me?"

"I know." I drew a deep breath and took his arm. An *anguissette* and a Cassiline; Elua help us. "We've survived thirty thousand Skaldi and the wrath of the Master of the Straits. We ought to be able to survive each other."

Joscelin laughed softly, and I buried my face in his chest. There was so much between us, and so much that would ever *be* between us. And yet, I knew, I did not want to be without him.

We stood like that for a long while, and I felt the long night's dread leave me. The grey skies were paling, the rays of the new sun stealing long and low across the battlements. Soon, it would be done, and over.

So I was thinking, as the sound of shouting and the rattle of guards running in armor arose.

Time and enough for the night watch to be relieved; yet I did not remember it happening like this, new guards taking over stern-faced, a harried commander interrogating the members of the night watch, who were all shaking heads and urgent denial.

"What is it?" Joscelin caught at the captain as he passed.

"They were to execute the Lady Melisande Shahrizai at dawn," he said, his face grim. "She's gone. Two guards dead at her door, and the keeper of the postern gate." Shaking off Joscelin's hand, he added, "Excuse me," and hurried onward.

Atop the battlements, we stared at one another, and a last desperate laugh caught in my throat worked its way loose. "Melisande," I gasped. "Ah, Elua, no!"

Ysandre turned the fortress upside down, sent riders in all directions, and had everyone at liberty that night questioned; everyone. She found no trace of Melisande, who had vanished like an apparition. Not even Joscelin was exempted from her interrogation; nor was I. Surely, not I. Ysandre summoned me to the throne room, and I knew what it was like, to stand before her where Melisande had stood.

"She sent for you that night," Ysandre said, her voice cold and hard as steel. "And you went. Do not deny it, Phèdre, we know as much from the hospital wards. Why?"

I answered her as I had Joscelin, except that I clasped my hands together to hide their shaking. "Your majesty, I owed her that much."

"Whatever you owed her, the coin she paid was treason." Ysandre's face was implacable. "We do not reckon debts thusly, in Terre d'Ange."

"She spared my life, once," I whispered. *I'd no more kill you than I'd destroy a priceless fresco or a vase.* "And I did not. That much, I owed her."

"And what else?" Ysandre's fair brows raised.

"Nothing." I raked my hands through my hair and choked on the terrible laughter that still welled inside me. "Your majesty, the only proof of her treason rests on my word. What need had I to save her but remain silent?"

Ysandre's face changed, turning compassionate; she knew, well enough, the truth of my words. "You're right, of course. I'm sorry, Phèdre. But you must understand, while she is free, with allies to aid her, I will never rest easy on my throne."

"Nor should you." I murmured the words, escorted from the royal presence with considerably more courtesy than I'd been brought with. The Queen of Terre d'Ange had apologized to me; it was something to note.

In the first flush of victory, I had regarded everyone who had fought at Troyes-le-Mont as friend and ally. When the politicking set in later, I regained a measure of perspective. But after Melisande's flight, it changed, and I could look at no one in the same light.

One of us was a traitor.

The mystery went unresolved in the end. Wherever

Melisande Shahrizai had gone, and whoever had aided her, their complicity was buried deep enough that it was never uncovered. And there was a realm to be governed, and a wedding planned. Riders continued to issue forth from Troyes-le-Mont, canvassing the breadth of the nation. Melisande would find no welcome on D'Angeline soil.

It was enough. It would have to be enough.

In a formal ceremony of thanks, Ysandre de la Courcel restored the sovereignty of the fortress to the Duchese de Troyes-le-Mont, who had evacuated her holdings to spend the battle safe under the hospitality of Roxanne de Mereliot, the Lady of Marsilikos. A considerable portion of the Skaldi ransom would go to restoring the estate and compensating the folk of Troyes-le-Mont for their losses; some would go to paying the army's retainers, and the remainder to making good against the swath of devastation the Skaldi had cut through Namarre, including the restoration of Naamah's temples.

I was glad to hear it, having not forgotten the priestess of Naamah who had saved me in the Skaldi encampment. These things, Ysandre faced with a pragmatic fortitude, setting herself resolutely to dealing with them.

Grapes were beginning to hang heavy on the vine when we shifted our encampment, beginning the long triumphal journey south to Terre d'Ange.

Of all the journeys I have made, though this was one of the shortest, surely it was the most glorious. Encumbered by a goodly number of D'Angeline troops and the whole of the Alban army, our progress was slow, for the folk of Terre d'Ange turned out the whole length of the way, throwing blossoms in Ysandre's path and cheering her as their Queen. They cheered Drustan, too, who rode beside her, coming to stare at his blue features, and staying to shout and throw petals.

Among the Cruithne and the Dalriada—the quick, dark folk of the Cullach Gorrym, the fair Eidlach Òr, the brawny Tarbh Cró and the tall Fhalair Bàn—not a one had departed for Alba's shores, waiting on the promised wedding that would bond our two peoples and open the Straits for good. I rode often alongside Grainne's chariot on that journey, to let her know that Eammon's loss was not forgotten; not by me, at least.

I said nothing of the bloodstained sack that swung from her chariot. The Dalriada have their own superstitions. Eamonn's body lay buried in the fields of Troyes-le-Mont; if his sister wished to ensure that his head would watch forevermore over the seat of the Dalriada in Innisclan, it was not my place to gainsay it. Drustan knew, I think; all the Cruithne did. I never told Ysandre, though.

So we came at last to the City of Elua, which had been long weeks preparing for our arrival, and rode in triumph through her streets, while the whole of the City turned out to greet us.

It was a strangeness to me, to ride in that procession. Only once before had I witnessed a military triumph in the City of Elua. It had been the day of Alcuin's debut, and I remembered it well. How I had watched, from the terrace of Cecilie Laveau-Perrin's townhouse, those who had passed; so many of them dead. The Lioness of Azzalle and Baudoin de Trevalion, at whose side Melisande had ridden. Ysandre with her grandfather, Ganelon de la Courcel. And oh, the Allies of Camlach, with Isidore d'Aiglemort at their head. It had seemed so clear and orderly, seeing it from above.

Nothing is as it appears from beyond.

And Anafiel Delaunay had been alive that day, winning at *kottabos*. And Alcuin, Alcuin who had borne the auction of his virginity with such dignity.

I could not explain the tears that pricked my eyes as we rode in triumph through the City of Elua. Most took them for tears of joy for a safe homecoming, and I let it stand, the feeling running too deep in me for words.

Decimated by sickness and war, the City had room enough to hold us all; common soldiers in the barracks, and Alban nobles housed within the Palace. I had no home, but Ysandre retained me in her service, giving me a suite of rooms within the Palace itself, for she had need still of my skills as a linguist.

Then, there were joyful reunions.

Chiefest among them was Cecilie Laveau-Perrin, who came with Thelesis de Mornay to pay a visit. I was glad enough to see the Queen's Poet, but I had not reckoned on how my heart would swell to see Cecilie, her beautiful face so gracefully aging, the gentle affection in her pale blue eyes. I fell on her neck and wept unabashedly.

"There, there," she murmured, patting my back. "There, there." When I had regained my composure, she took my face in her hands. "Phèdre, child, few of Naamah's Servants ever know truly what it is to walk in her footsteps. I have prayed every day for your safe return."

Joscelin hovered awkwardly in the background, unsure how to respond to this unexpected display of emotion on my part. But Cecilie had lost none of the niceties of Cereus House, and put him at ease instantly, taking his hands and giving him the kiss of greeting.

"Such a beautiful young man, Joscelin Verreuil," she said lightly, turning his hands in hers and studying the Cassiline vambraces he wore, coupled now with midnight-blue Courcel livery. "And a true hero, as well." Cecilie's eyes twinkled as she tapped his vambraces. "Never let it be said Naamah lacks a sense of humor."

He blushed to the roots of his hair, and bowed. "From the Queen of the Night-Blooming Flowers, I will accept such a compliment."

Thelesis de Mornay regarded us all fondly with her dark, glowing gaze. "Truly," she said in her musical voice, "Elua's blessing is on this day. For all that is lost, yet so much is won."

Her words struck a chord in me, granting sanction to grief and joy alike. It was true, there had been so many losses, so many that I felt their absence like a stone in my heart. And yet, indeed, we had won so much: victory and freedom for the earth and soul of Terre d'Ange, love, liberty and our very lives. It was fitting and meet that we should celebrate these things. So say the tenets of Blessed Elua, who shed his blood for the land, for humanity, and smiled. Through war and death and betrayal . . . the bee is in the lavender, the honey fills the comb.

We were home.

ꞈNINETY-FOUR

In defiance of death, D'Angelines celebrate life.

It is for this reason, I think, above all, that Ysandre and Drustan's wedding became the grand affair that it did. And for anyone tempted to think that she kept me in her service out of kindness in those weeks of preparation, let me say: I earned my keep.

Somewhere amid the chaos, I found time to tend to those promises of my own I had to fulfill. Thelesis de Mornay was a great boon, setting the deeds of our quest and the great battle to verse, and translating them as well into Cruithne; for I had promised Drustan that his folk would know of their deeds. How many people she interviewed for this tale, I cannot say, but a great many of them. Though her health was never so good as it had been before the fever struck her, she spent herself tirelessly on her craft.

It became in the end a mighty epic, and she worked all the days of her life on the Ysandrine Cycle, so-named because it charted the tumultuous ascension of Ysandre de la Courcel to the throne of Terre d'Ange—though it is, in truth, many folks' stories, mine own included. But she had been Ganelon's favorite poet for many years, and knew well enough how to turn out verse for an occasion, so we had the beginnings of it in time for the wedding. As it happened, she had begun work on it from the day four couriers styling themselves Phèdre's Boys stormed into the City with a letter in hand, and news of great doings.

A party of riders hand-picked by Drustan set forth for Azzalle to meet Rousse's fleet and be carried to Alba, carrying the tale locked in memory to Cruithne and Dalriada alike, bearing assurance of a victory won and an alliance made, and the return of the Cruarch to come. Quintilius Rousse himself guaranteed their crossing, having left Jean Marchand in command of the fleet and Marc de Trevalion to hold the border, that he might come to the Palace in person, roaring and bluff as ever, gathering me in an embrace that nearly cracked my ribs.

On behalf of those couriers who had brought my plea to Thelesis de Mornay, and the rest of Phèdre's Boys, I kept my vow made on the ancient Tiberian roads of Alba, and met with Jareth Moran, Dowayne of Cereus House, First among the Thirteen Houses of the Night Court. The token he had given me the night of Baudoin's natal festivities was long gone, seized along with all of Delaunay's holdings, but Cecilie Laveau-Perrin came at my side, and made a bargain with him that would have made an adept of Bryony House weep with envy.

Fifteen tokens, one for each of Phèdre's surviving Boys, to grant free passage to any of the Thirteen Houses on the eve of Ysandre's wedding. But he was no fool, Jareth Moran. My name and my tale were known, in some part, an odd scarlet thread in the tapestry of D'Angeline victory; Delaunay's *anguissette*, who had survived slavery in Skaldia, who had ridden to Alba. I was born and bred to the Night Court, raised in Cereus House. The Dowayne opened his doors to Phèdre's Boys, and traded on my name to restore a measure of luster to the mythos of the Night Court.

No matter that I'd had naught to do with him since I was ten years old and Delaunay came to claim me. I'd been born to it, which was true. And I kept my promise, which was what mattered to me.

For the last of it, I brought the deed to Hyacinthe's house and his holdings to his crew in Night's Doorstep, finding Emile as he had bid me, and giving into his keeping the deed that Hyacinthe had written on scraped parchment in the lonely tower of the Master of the Straits. Emile wept and kissed my hands, blessing me profusely; out of joy, in part, and out of sorrow for Hyacinthe's fate, in larger part. It touched me, to see how much, truly, they had cared for him.

Prince of Travellers.

I made an offering, then, in his mother's name, at the temple of Elua where we had gone together after Baudoin's death. Clutching the scarlet anemones, damp with dew, I laid them at the base of the statue, kneeling to kiss Elua's cool marble feet. "For Anasztaizia, daughter of Manoj," I murmured, smelling all around me the moist soil and green things growing, the deep shade of the mighty oaks. Far above me, Elua's vast features bent an enigmatic smile through the gloaming twilight.

I knelt there a long while.

This time, it was Joscelin's hands that bid me rise; but the priest of Elua was there, the same, I swear it, though all priests and priestesses resemble each other in some way, for they are all part of an unbroken line of service. He smiled at us, barefooted in the damp mast, hands in the sleeves of his robe.

"Cassiel's child," he said gently, remonstrating Joscelin, "do not rush. You have stood at the crossroads and chosen, and like Cassiel, you will ever stand at the crossroads and choose, choose again and again, the path of the Companion. The choice lies ever within you, the crossroads and the way, and Elua's commandment to point you on it."

Joscelin gave him a startled look, but the priest was already reaching out one hand, laying it upon my cheek.

"Kushiel's Dart and Naamah's Servant." He smiled, leaf-shadowed in the twilight; a smile of blessing, of remembrance, I thought. Who could say? I believed him the same priest. "Love as thou wilt, and Elua will ever guide your steps."

He left us to linger there.

When he had gone, I laughed. "It seems my turn for dire prophecy has passed."

"You can have mine," Joscelin said wryly. "It seems *I'm* doomed to make the same choice a thousand times over."

"Are you sorry?" I searched his face in the faint light.

"No." Joscelin shook his head. "No," he whispered, and took my face in his hands, lowering his head to kiss me, unbound hair the color of summer wheat falling forward to curtain us.

It was sweet, very sweet, and I felt the rightness of it

in our shared breath, the steady beat of his heart matching time with my own.

When he lifted his head, the shadow of a smile curved his lips. "But there will likely be times when I am."

"Likely there will," I murmured. "As long as it's not now."

"No," he said, and smiled in full. "Not now."

Above our heads, Elua's marble hands remained spread in blessing.

Thus did I keep the promises I had made on that long and terrible journey; and afterward, you may be sure, Ysandre de la Courcel had me dancing attendance upon her to make up for time lost on my own business. While she bid fair to make a wise and compassionate ruler, she was also a D'Angeline noblewoman approaching her wedding-day, and indulged her foibles accordingly. Never in her life had she been allowed the luxury of being girlish; if she seized it now, I, who had been raised to fripperies, could not blame her.

One such which demanded my attention was the be-decking of Alban royalty in D'Angeline finery: to wit, the splendid gown Ysandre commissioned for Grainne.

The Queen of Terre d'Ange was more than a little fascinated with the Warrior Queen of the Dalriada. There must have been threescore women fighting among the Albans, but Grainne was the only one whose status was, in its own way, comparable to Ysandre's.

Eamonn's death had not diminished her. If her bright spirit was banked with sorrow, it was deepened as well. She stood patiently beneath the Royal Tailor's prodding as he fitted her, showing a glimmer of her old amusement as she caught my eye.

The gown, a glory of scarlet silk and gold brocade, was too narrow through the waist, though she had been measured no more than a week prior. I listened to the tailor's muttering and laughed.

"How long?" I asked Grainne in Eiran.

"Three months." She laid her hand on the faint swell of her belly and smiled complacently. "If it is a boy, I will name him Eamonn."

"Is it Rousse's?"

She smiled again. "It may be so."

Ysandre raised impatient brows. She spoke some bit of Cruithne, but the Eiran dialect took time to master, or great necessity. I'd had the advantage of both. I explained to her what Grainne had said.

"She fought," Ysandre said in astonishment, "with *child*?"

"It was too soon to be sure, then," I said diplomatically. There is a dreadful Eiran tale about an ancient Queen running a footrace great with child; I spared her that, and was glad I'd not told her about Eamonn's head, preserved in quicklime.

"Will Quintilius Rousse wed her?" Ysandre inquired.

I translated for Grainne, who laughed.

"I do not think it matters to her, my lady," I replied.

"That's fine," Ysandre said to the Royal Tailor, waving one hand dismissively. "Make the adjustments." She looked consideringly at me. "What of you, near-cousin? Will you wed your Cassiline?"

One does not refuse to answer a direct question from one's sovereign, but glancing at her face, I saw that she was genuinely interested. "No, my lady," I said simply. "Anathema or no, Cassiline vows bind for a lifetime. Joscelin betrays them every day he is with me, and that is his choice. To wed would be a mockery, and that he cannot do, nor I ask."

Ysandre, I think, understood; her ever-present Cassiline guards stared straight ahead, and what they thought, I cannot guess, nor did I care.

"Will you return to Naamah's Service?" she asked then.

"I don't know." I busied myself with assisting Grainne as she divested herself and dressed in her own garb, handing her kirtle over the tailor's folding modesty-screen. It was one of those questions that lay between Joscelin and I, and one we had avoided. I faced it now, in part, meeting Ysandre's gaze. "You have been kind, your majesty, and I have assurances of hospitality from good friends." It was true; Gaspar Trevalion had promised I should never want for aught, and Cecilie and The-lesis as well. "But if I am rich in friends, I am penniless in pocket."

This, too, was true; and a considerable fortune awaited me as a Servant of Naamah. There were other reasons, too, but those were harder to voice. Poverty, everyone understood.

"Oh, *that*!" Ysandre laughed, beckoning to a page. "Summon the Chancellor of the Exchequer. Tell him it's regarding Lord Delaunay's estate."

He came with alacrity, a lean and grizzled man, clutching sheaves of paper. Ysandre had dismissed the Royal Tailor by then, and given Grainne leave to go, which she took, bending one last look of quiet amuse-ment my way.

"Go on," Ysandre bid the Chancellor, reclining on a couch and sipping at a glass of wine. I sat in a chair and gazed with perplexity as he cleared his throat and shuf-fled through his papers.

"Yes, your majesty . . . regarding Anafiel Delaunay's estate, the townhouse in the City, and all its holdings . . . it seems these were purchased from the judiciary by one . . ." he peered at a parchment, ". . . Lord Sandriel

Voscagne, who deeded it to . . . well, it doesn't matter, we can begin proceedings for its reclamation at your insistence, my lady Phèdre, or the Exchequer will recompense you the full amount of the sale . . ."

"Why?" I interrupted out of pure bewilderment.

The Chancellor of the Exchequer looked at me over his papers, startled. "Oh, you didn't . . . your majesty . . . well, of course, my lady, his lordship Anafiel Delaunay filed the papers some time ago, naming you his heir, you and one . . ." he consulted a sheet, ". . . Alcuin nó Delaunay, deceased. By her majesty's proclamation of your innocence, our seizure is now unlawful, and we must by rights recompense you."

I opened my mouth and closed it, in my shock picturing the house as I'd last seen it, a dreadful abattoir, Delaunay dead and Alcuin dying. "I don't want it," I said, shuddering. "Not the house. Let Lord Sandriel or whomever keep it. If I am owed . . ." It was hard to credit. "If I am owed, well, then, fine."

"Yes, of course, quite," the Chancellor said absently, shuffling through his papers. "Recompense in full." Ysandre sipped her wine and smiled. "And then there is Montrève, of course," he added.

"Montrève?" I echoed the word like a simpleton.

"Montrève, in Siovale, yes." His gaze came into focus as he found the document for which he was searching, tapping it smartly. "With his disinheritance, upon his father's death, it passed to his mother, and thence to Lord Delaunay's cousin, Rufaille, who is, sadly, listed among the dead of Troyes-le-Mont." The Chancellor cleared his throat again. "A codicil in the will of the Comtesse de Montrève specifies that if he should die without issue, the estate would revert to her son Anafiel Delaunay or his heirs. And that, it seems, is the case, my lady."

Although his words clearly formed sentences, I could

make no sense of them. He might as well have been speaking Akkadian, for all I understood.

"What he is saying, Phèdre," Ysandre said succinctly, "is that you have inherited the title and estate of Comtesse de Montrève."

I stared blankly at her. "My lady will have her jest."

"Her majesty does not jest," the Chancellor of the Exchequer said reproachfully to me, and rattled his sheaf of papers. "It's all very clear, and documented in the archives of the Royal Treasury."

"Thank you, my lord Brenois," Ysandre said graciously to the Chancellor. "Will you draw up the papers of investiture?"

"Your majesty." He bowed deeply, hugging his sheaves to him, and hurried out of the royal presence.

"You knew," I said to Ysandre, my voice sounding strange to my ears. She took a sip of wine and shook her head.

"Not about Montrève, no. That only came to light after the lists were published, and Lord Brenois determined that Rufaille de Montrève had designated no heir. You may refuse, of course. But it was Delaunay's mother's wish that the estate return to her son, or his line. And he chose you, you and the boy Alcuin."

"Delaunay," I whispered. He had never told me. I wondered if Alcuin had known. "No. I'll . . . I accept."

"Good," Ysandre said simply.

Afterward the matter was concluded in her mind, and Ysandre consulted with me on some small choices of jewelry and hairstyle for her wedding-day; what I said, I have no idea. My mind was reeling, dumbstruck. She was Queen of Terre d'Ange, Montrève was naught to her. A tiny, mountainous Siovalese holding with nothing to offer but a score of men-at-arms and a decent library, it was interesting only in that it had begotten Anafiel Delaunay, whom her father had loved.

So it was, to her. To me, named by the ancient Dowayne of Cereus House for what I was, a whore's unwanted get, it was somewhat else indeed.

When she was done with me, I went in search of Joscelin.

"What's wrong?" he asked in alarm, looking at my flushed face, my eyes bright as with fever. "Are you all right?"

"No." I swallowed. "I'm a peer of the realm."

Ninety-five

Thus did it come to pass that I attended the wedding of Ysandre de la Courcel and Drustan mab Necthana, Queen of Terre d'Ange and Cruarch of Alba, as the Comtesse Phèdre nó Delaunay de Montrève.

I kept Delaunay's name, out of pride. What I had, he had given me; much of what I was, he had made me, under the name he had chosen, and not that to which he was born. I never forgot, never, that it had been he who, with two words, turned my deadliest flaw to a treasure beyond price.

Ysandre rescinded her grandfather's old edict against Delaunay's poetry and, after twenty-odd years, his verses were once again spoken openly, charged with all the passion and brilliance of his youth.

At the wedding-feast Thelesis de Mornay would debut her epic verses, in praise of bride and groom alike. But at the ceremony itself, she recited one of Delaunay's poems.

I daresay the whole world knows it now; it was a rage

of fashion for months afterward in the City, for lovers to quote the verse of Anafiel Delaunay to one another. Then, no one had heard it, and I wept at the final words.

I, and thou; our hands meet and a world engendered.

It was fitting, for the two of them, truly rulers of two worlds, conjoined into one. The ceremony was held in the Palace gardens, with gay pavilions erected on the lawn and a fragrant bower under which they stood. Elua's temple is everywhere in Terre d'Ange where earth meets sky. It was an old priestess who performed the ritual, silver-haired, her face lined and lovely with age.

Ysandre looked as beautiful as a summer's day, in a gown of periwinkle silk, her pale hair done up in a crown, laced with gold filigree, in which blue forget-me-nots were twined. I had counseled her well, if I had so advised her. As for Drustan, he was truly a vision to D'Angeline eyes, all his Pictish barbarism recreated in our luxuriant textiles, the red cloak of the Cruarch hanging in velvet folds from his blue-whorled shoulders, gold torque against his bare brown throat.

This, too, set quite a fashion.

As King and Queen, they had greeted each other, but when the words were spoken and they shared a kiss to seal it, it was as man and woman, husband and wife. I saw Ysandre's eyes sparkle as they parted, and Drustan's white smile, and I cheered them, with a whole heart. I knew, better than anyone, at what cost this union came.

We dined, then, on the greensward, and there were many tables laid, shining with white linen and settings of silver and gold; and I was seated, with Joscelin, at their own table, albeit far from the center where they reigned. For each of us, a nuptial goblet, silver chased in gold, depicting the siege of Troyes-le-Mont and the victorious alliance that followed. I have mine still, and it is among the chiefest of my treasures.

Suckling pigs were roasted whole, and pheasants, and oysters rushed packed in ice from the Eisandine coast, mutton and venison and tender rabbit, cheeses and apples soaked in brandy, pears and a spicy currant sauce; there were crisp green sallets with shredded violet-petals and comfits and glaces. And through it all washed a river of wine, soft oaken whites, crisp rosé and hearty red, while musicians strolled and servants bustled.

When the sun sank low, the torches were kindled, a thousand candles set in glass globes about the garden, a beacon summoning to moths. Then did Thelesis de Mornay recite her fledgling verse, that would grow one day into the Ysandrine Cycle. Strange, to hear one's name spoken in passing poem; although the focus of these verses was Ysandre and Drustan, my tale was woven in it. Not a little drunk, I leaned my head in my hand and listened.

After that, came the toasts, which I will not recount. I had to rise when Grainne, resplendent in the crimson-and-gold gown of Ysandre's choosing, gave hers in a thick Eiran accent. It was something to do with the Fhalair Bàn and the honor of the Dalriada, and a wish for fruitful joy; I cannot remember, now. I must have rendered it well enough, for everyone cheered. When I had done, Grainne gave me thanks and named me her sister, with an embrace and a deep glimmer of amusement that was not entirely sisterly.

I'd not told Ysandre that, either; only that the Lords of the Dalriada had been persuaded. Later I learned that Quintilius Rousse had related the tale of how I had brought the Twins into accord, and Ysandre laughed until she wept.

It was her fault, for making me her ambassador. Still

I grieved that never again would Eamonn balance his sister.

Drustan made a toast, then, and to my great pride, he gave it first in Cruithne, then in near-flawless D'Angeline. His dark eyes shone with wine, and the flickering light of a thousand candles turned the intricate blue whorls of woad into a subtle, shifting pattern on his skin.

"We have won this day's joy at great price," he said solemnly. "Let us treasure it all the more, and pledge, together, that as Ysandre and I have joined our lives, so will our nations be joined, in strength and harmony, that we may never be any less than what we are today."

It was well-said, and they cheered him wildly; he gave a courtier's bow and sat down.

Then Ysandre stood. So young, to have borne what she had, but there was steel in Ysandre de la Courcel, forged between the bitter triangle of Rolande, Isabel and Delaunay, hammered on the anvil of her grandfather's rule, mettle tested in the dreadful siege of Troyes-le-Mont.

Tempered, by love.

"D'Angeline and Alban alike," she said. "We give praise this day to Blessed Elua, and celebrate his words! Why are we here, if not for that? Nation, home and hearth, land, sea and sky, kith and kin, friend and lover, mistress and consort—" A rippling laugh answered, and she smiled. "—and husband and wife, we honor Elua's sacred precept. Join me, then, on this day and ever after, and love as thou wilt."

No other sovereign would have given such a toast, I think; but this was Terre d'Ange, and Ysandre was our Queen.

We drank, and drank deep, servants filling our nuptial

goblets with *joie,* that clear, bright cordial that made the torches burn brighter.

Afterward, the musicians struck up in earnest, and we danced on the green lawn, while the soft candlelit twilight faded unnoticed and the stars kindled in the black sky, a scent of flowers heady in the summer night. I danced first with Joscelin, and then Gaspar Trevalion bowed and extended his hand, and after that I lost count, until Drustan mab Necthana claimed a dance.

There were whispers, at that; some of the nobles knew who I was, and some did not, but now my name was known, and Kushiel's Dart gave me away. Always, at court, there runs the murmuring river of politics, beneath the surface at any occasion.

Drustan ignored it and so did I; he danced well for an Alban, despite his lameness. I remembered the first time I'd heard his name. *Ysandre de la Courcel shall teach a clubfoot barbarian Prince to dance the gavotte.* So she had, and I danced with him now, while we smiled at one another. Cullach Gorrym, Earth's eldest children. It meant nothing to the D'Angelines, but they had not been there when the black boar burst from its copse outside Bryn Gorrydum. I had.

We always did understand one another, Drustan and I.

I had patrons there, too. I'd chosen my assignations from among the highest-ranked in the realm, that last year or so. I gave none of them away. It was not the place to acknowledge such things. Some, like Quincel de Morhban, would not have cared; others depended on the discretion of Naamah's Servants. It did not matter. I knew, and they knew, whose patron-gifts were etched indelibly onto my skin, link by link, forming the chain of my marque that rendered me free.

In the small hours of the morning, Ysandre and Drustan took their leave, and we followed them as far as the bedchamber, a great crowd of mixed folk, shouting out good wishes—and some bawdy ones—and pelting them with a hailstorm of petals, until they, laughing, closed the bed-chamber door and barred it, petals clinging to their hair, and Ysandre's grim Cassilines turned us away, with an especially dour look for Joscelin.

No end to the revelry, though; the Queen had bid it carry on until dawn, and I saw it through to the end, having a deep need in my soul for a joyous daybreak to cleanse away the memories of too many others.

Joscelin, too; he understood. We had had the first dance together, and we had the last. Later I would laugh to hear the forays he had endured in between, staged by D'Angeline lords and ladies curious to test the virtue of a Cassiline apostate. Then I merely rested safe in the circle of his arms, glad to be there, where neither of us ever thought to find ourselves.

And we watched the sun rise over Terre d'Ange.

The days that followed were full of activity, for there remained a great deal to be done; but my role in it, for the most part, had come to an end. When the Chancellor of the Exchequer bestowed upon me the balance of the proceeds from the sale of Delaunay's estate, I begged of him the name of a reliable agent, and made arrangements for the care and investment of my unexpected wealth.

With some portion of these funds, Joscelin spent his days making preparations for our journey to Montrève. We would not ride alone, it seemed, for three of Phèdre's Boys, among those survivors of the wounded at Troyes-le-Mont, begged leave to be dismissed from Rousse's service and enter mine.

Quintilius Rousse acceded and Ysandre agreed to the increase in Montrève's allotment of men-at-arms, and that is how I came to acquire three Chevaliers; Remy,

Ti-Philippe and Fortun. Why they persisted in their extravagant loyalty, I never understood—although Joscelin laughed and said he did—but I was glad of their presence, for I had no few trepidations regarding the welcome I would find in Montrève.

The folk there had been loyal to Delaunay's father, the old Comte de Montrève and, so far as I knew, to his cousin as well; Delaunay, they'd not known since his youth, and me they knew not at all. Born and bred to the Night Court, I was no blood kin of theirs. I was not even Siovalese.

On the day before our departure, I received one last surprise. A royal page came to fetch me, claiming strangers at the Palace gates were asking for me.

Joscelin came with me as I hurried through the Palace, fearful of who awaited. His face was set and grim, hands hovering over his dagger-hilts; he had leave to wear his Cassiline arms even in the presence of the Queen. It was a kindness of Ysandre's, who had seen how he felt stripped without them—and a cleverness, too, for he would ever have guarded her life as his own, or mine.

What I expected, I could not say, but we found awaiting us a young couple in simple, well-made country attire.

"My Lady de Montrève," the young man said and bowed; his wife curtsied. His face, as he straightened, was familiar, but I was too disconcerted by the greeting to place it. "I am Purnell Friote, of Perrinwolde. This is my wife, Richeline." She bobbed another curtsy. He gave me an open grin, eyes friendly beneath a shock of brown hair. "My nephew taught you to ride a horse, do you remember? The Lady Cecilie said you might have need of a seneschal."

I did remember, with such delight that I kissed them both, to their blushing surprise. It was only then that

Cecilie showed herself, smiling at the success of her venture.

"Gavin swears Purnell can do aught that he can, and twice as swiftly," she said as I took her hands in gratitude. "My Perrinwolde's grown too small to hold the expansion of the Friote clan, and you'll have need of your own folk about you. Let them work with Montrève's folk, and it will ease your way, for you'll find no kinder hearts in Terre d'Ange."

Better advice I never had, and if Montrève made me welcome, it was due in no small part to the efforts of Purnell and Richeline Friote, who came willing to learn the ways of the estate, and in such an open and friendly manner that it won the hearts of the Siovalese as easily as Perrinwolde had won mine.

So it was that we were a party of seven when we departed, amid too many farewells to count, striking out once more on the open road and bound for Montrève.

"When we are settled," I said to Joscelin, as the City of Elua dwindled behind us, "there is somewhat that I want to do." He looked inquiringly at me. "I want to visit L'Arène, to find Taavi and Danele."

Joscelin smiled, remembering. "I'd like that, actually. You think mayhap they might accept a gift of thanks, now that you're a peer of the realm?" he added, amused.

"They might," I said. "And they might know someone willing to tutor me in Yeshuite." I glanced over to see his fair brows rise. "If Delaunay knew it, he never taught me. And the Master of the Straits was fathered and cursed by Rahab, who serves the One God of the Yeshuites. If there's aught to be found that might break his binding, it's in Yeshuite lore."

"Hyacinthe," Joscelin said softly.

I nodded.

"Well, then, we'll go to L'Arène." He laughed. "And, Elua help us, you can pit yourself against the gods."

I loved him for that.

Onward we rode to Montrève.

Ninety-six

It is one thing to visit a country estate, it is another to inherit one. Even with the very capable aid Cecilie had bequeathed me, it took the better part of a year to settle into the rhythms of Montrève, to gain the trust and good-will of its folk, who were understandably perplexed at how a Siovalese holding had passed into the possession of a City-bred Servant of Naamah.

Montrève itself was beautiful, a green jewel set in the low mountains. To Joscelin, born in Siovale, it was nearly a homecoming. We rode the length and breadth of it together, and fell in love with its simple charm, its rugged hills and green valleys, the unexpected pleasure of a meadow. It is sheep country, there, and it transpired that I was rich in flocks.

The manor-house itself was all quaint elegance, with touches of Eisandine luxury; Delaunay's mother, I guessed. It had small, brilliant gardens, rambling with colorful flowers for three-quarters of the year, grown wild for lack of tending. Richeline Friote made these her especial care.

And there was a library, where Anafiel Delaunay had spent his boyhood study, immersed in the Siovalese love of learning. I found his name one day, scratched with a knife-point into the wooden surface of a reading table, and had to fight back tears.

Joscelin's love of the land, my love for Delaunay;

these things, I think, along with the good nature of the Friotes and the bold, cheerful manner of my three Chevaliers, won over the folk of Montrève. Once we were at last ensconced, I began to write letters, and Phèdre's Boys leapt at the chance to play courier, crossing the realm with correspondence. I wrote to Ysandre, with gratitude, to Cecilie Laveau-Perrin and Thelesis de Mornay, with small tales of our doings, to Quintilius Rousse and Gaspar Trevalion, with greetings; and always, with a plea for news. I wrote even to Maestro Gonzago de Escabares, in care of the University of Tiberium, and Remy was gone months on that adventure.

And I bought books, and in L'Arène, Ti-Philippe found Taavi and Danele, owners of a prosperous tailor's shop in the Yeshuite quarter.

That spring Joscelin and I rode to visit them, and held a happy reunion. Impossible to believe that scarcely a year ago we had met on the road, where they had saved our lives. The girls had grown taller, and our Skaldi pony, still with them, had grown fatter. If they would still accept no reward, I repaid them as best I was able, with a sizeable commission for livery. The insignia of Montrève was a four-quartered shield, with a crescent moon upper right and a mountain crag lower left. That was ever the standard we flew at the manor, but for Phèdre's Boys, I added my own devices: Delaunay's sheaf of grain, and the sign of Kushiel's Dart.

We returned from L'Arène the richer in renewed friendships, and with one addition: Seth ben Yavin, a young Yeshuite scholar who stammered and turned red in my presence, but was nonetheless doggedly persistent in his teaching.

All that spring and well into summer I studied with him, and the days slid by like water. Sometimes Joscelin joined us, but not always; the lure of the mountains was stronger, and he would rather, he declared, learn it from me. As I gained some small proficiency, Seth began to forget I was an *anguissette* and sometime Servant of Naamah, and grew more at ease in my company, arguing and debating happily.

It was good to have my mind challenged and occupied, for it kept me from restlessness. We had not spoken of that, of what would happen when Kushiel's Dart began to prick. I was an *anguissette*; it would. But for now, even I had had a sufficiency of pain.

When deep summer began to give way to early fall, Seth begged leave to depart, having family duties to resume. He left with Fortun to accompany him, a generous purse of his own, and another to accompany a list of books and codices he felt I might need, and for which he promised to search. I had a long way to go in my studies, but I knew enough to begin my quest.

The leaves were beginning to turn gold when Gonzago de Escabares arrived.

He came unannounced, with a lone apprentice tending him, two horses and a well-laden mule between them; a little greyer and stouter, but otherwise unchanged. I threw myself on him with a cry of joy, and he laughed.

"Ah, little one! You'll give an old man the fits. Come, I'm near starved to the bone. Didn't my Antinous teach you aught about hospitality?"

I led him into the manor, talking all the while, I am sure, while Joscelin looked on with polite bewilderment and ordered their horses stabled, and the mule unpacked.

Seth ben Yavin had been a paid tutor; Maestro Gonzago de Escabares was my first genuine guest. In an unexpected state of nervousness, I nearly drove the household staff mad with half-brained requests, until Richeline calmly and firmly ordered me to attend to my guest and leave the arrangements to her.

Over wine, which the Maestro quaffed heartily, and an array of cheeses and sweetmeats, which also met a quick end, I learned that he had been travelling in the northern city-states of Caerdicca Unitas, learning of the upheaval along the Skaldic border. An old colleague of his in Tiberium had received my letter, and he decided to pay a visit, bringing an apprentice who wished to learn of de Escabares' method of studying the world.

It had been his plan to return home to Aragonia and begin drafting his memoirs, but upon receiving my letter, he had determined to come first to Montrève, which lay nearly on his way.

"I would have sent word, my dear, but I would have outpaced it," he said, eyes twinkling. "We travelled like the wind, did we not, Camilo?"

His apprentice coughed and hid a smile, murmuring something about a rather slow breeze.

I laughed and patted Gonzago's hand. "I'm just glad you're here, Maestro."

After they had retired and rested for a time, we dined, a meal of sufficient rustic splendor that even the Maestro was content. For my part, I ate little, overwhelmed with grateful pride that such hospitality was mine to offer. I knew full well all credit was due to the household of Montrève, and not me; but they had done it on my behalf, investing their pride in mine, and I was grateful.

While we dined, I spun the long story of our journeys, beginning with the death of Alcuin and Delaunay. Much of it, Gonzago knew, but he wanted to hear it firsthand. Tears filled his eyes at the start; he had, in deep truth, been very fond of Delaunay. To the rest of it, told in turns by Joscelin and me, he listened with a historian's tireless fascination. Afterward, he told us of his travels, and the knowledge he had gleaned. The Caerdicci city-states were falling over themselves to establish trade with the no-longer-isolated nation of Alba, jealous of the status enjoyed by Terre d'Ange and her ally, Aragonia.

By the time our meal was cleared and we were lingering over brandy, the apprentice Camilo's head was nodding, and Gonzago sent him to bed.

"A good lad," he said absently. "He'll make a fine scholar someday, if he can stay awake long enough." He rose, ponderously. "I've some gifts here for you, if he's not misplaced them," he added. "I brought a beautiful Caerdicci translation of Delaunay's verse . . . pity, I'd have looked up some Yeshuite texts for you if I'd known . . . and somewhat odd, beside."

"I'll fetch your bags for you, Maestro," Joscelin offered, heading for his guest-room. Gonzago sank back down with a grateful sigh.

"A long trip on horseback, for an old man," he remarked.

"And I thank you again for making it." I smiled at him. "What do you mean, somewhat odd?"

"Well." He picked up his empty goblet and peered at it; I refilled it with alacrity. "As you know, I was in La Serenissima for some time, which is where my friend Lucretius sought me. I have an acquaintance there, who charts the stars for the family of the Doge. Lucretius inquired for him there, explaining his business. He even had to show the letter, with your seal. They're all suspicious in La Serenissima." He swirled the brandy in his goblet and drank. "At any rate, my stargazing acquaintance eventually told him that I had gone on to Varro, and gave him the name of a reputable inn. Ah, there you are!" He seized upon the pack that Joscelin brought. "Here," he said reverently, passing me a twine-bound package.

I opened it with care, and found it to be the Caerdicci translation. It was beautiful indeed, bearing a tooled-leather cover with a copy of the head of Antinous, lover of the Tiberian Imperator Hadrian, worked upon it.

Joscelin laughed. "A Mendacant's trick, if ever there was one!"

"Truly, Maestro, it's lovely, and I thank you," I said, leaning to kiss his cheek. "Now will you keep me in suspense all night?"

Gonzago de Escabares gave a rueful smile. "You may wish I had, child. Having heard your tale, I have my guess; hear mine, and make your own. Lucretius and his apprentice bedded down at the inn, and in the morning, he found he had a guest. Now, he is an eloquent man, my friend Lucretius; he is an orator after the old style, and I have never known him to be caught short of words. But when I asked him to describe his guest, he fell silent, and at last said only that she was the most beautiful woman he had ever seen."

The nights were still warm, but I felt a chill all the length of my spine.

"Melisande," I whispered.

"Ask Camilo," Gonzago said bluntly. "I did, and he said that she had hair the color of night and eyes the color of larkspur, and her voice made his knees go weak. And that lad doesn't have a poetic bone in his body." Reaching into his pack, he drew out a large bundle in a silk drawstring bag. "She said since he was carrying a letter from the Comtesse de Montrève to me, would he carry this to me, for the Comtesse de Montrève."

He handed me the bundle, and I took it with trembling hands, feeling it at once soft and heavy.

"Don't open it!" White lines of fury were etched on Joscelin's face. "Phèdre, listen to me. She has no hold on you, and you owe her nothing. You don't need to know. Throw it away unopened."

"I can't," I said helplessly.

I wasn't lying, either. I couldn't. Nor could I open it.

With a sharp sound, Joscelin tore the parcel from my hands and wrenched open the silken drawstring cords, reaching inside to yank out its contents.

My *sangoire* cloak unfolded in a slither of velvet drapery to hang from his grip, rich and luxuriant, a red so deep it was almost black.

We all stared at it, saying nothing. Gonzago de Escabares' eyes were round with perplexity; I don't think he knew what it was. I did. Joscelin did. I had been wearing it that last day, the day Delaunay was killed. The day Melisande had betrayed us.

"What in the seventh hell is this supposed to mean?" Joscelin demanded, throwing it down on the couch beside me. He gave a bewildered laugh, running his hands through his hair. "Your *cloak?* Do you have the faintest idea?" He looked at me, then looked again. "Phèdre?"

I did know.

Someone had aided Melisande, had helped her escape from Troyes-le-Mont. Whoever it was, they had never been found. Ysandre's suspicion, in the end, had fallen most heavily on Quincel de Morhban and the two Shahrizai kin, Marmion and Persia. If they were exonerated, it was only because there was no proof and it was too ludicrously obvious, all of them too canny to stage such a blatant ploy. But there was another reason, I knew. I spent that night atop the battlements, and never heard a sound. The guard at the postern gate was killed by a knife to the heart. He'd seen his killer; it was someone he trusted, face-to-face. And the guardsmen of Troyes-le-Mont didn't trust anyone who hadn't fought at their side. Certainly he would have challenged any one of the Kusheline nobles, approaching him in the dark of night.

Someone he trusted. Someone we all trusted.

And now Melisande was in La Serenissima, close

enough to the family of the Doge to learn in a day that their soothsayer had received a visitor. Prince Benedicte's eldest daughter, Marie-Celeste, was wed to the Doge's son . . . a near-incestuous knot of the deadly Stregazza, who had poisoned Isabel L'Envers de la Courcel.

Ysandre's nearest kin who were of the Blood.

Oh, I knew. My hands closed on a fold of the *sangoire* cloak, feeling the rich velvet beneath my fingertips. I could smell, faintly, Melisande's scent. Why had she kept it? I couldn't answer it, my mind shying away from the question. But what she meant it for now, I knew well enough.

A challenge, an opening gambit.

I touched my throat, bare of her diamond.

Somewhere in that deadly coil of La Serenissima, a plot was hatching. It was a long way, a very long way, from Ysandre's throne in the City of Elua. But intrigue has a long reach, when thrones are at stake. Someone, at Ysandre's right hand, concealed poison at their heart.

And I could find them out.

That was what the cloak meant, of course. Melisande knew full well how I had served Delaunay, Alcuin and I. He'd let her know as much. Like her, he was a master, and could not bear to be entirely without an audience . . . one solitary witness, who could appreciate his artistry, the tremendous scope and complexity of his undertaking. Whoremaster of Spies, his detractors called him, when the halcyon days of Ysandre's wedding and D'Angeline victory had passed.

Witness and opponent, Melisande had chosen me as her equal.

I was an *anguissette* and a sometime Servant of Naamah, that much, the world knew; trained to observe, to remember, to analyze. Not many knew that. Even those who did put little stock in it. I had been at the wrong place at the right time, nothing more. I nearly believed it myself, and sometimes, I think, it was true.

Others would find it easy to believe.

Who would the gatekeeper have trusted?

I could count them on my fingers. Gaspar Trevalion, Percy de Somerville, Barquiel L'Envers; a half a dozen others. No more.

I could find out, as I had found out that Childric d'Essoms served L'Envers, as I had found out that Solaine Belfours was Lyonette de Trevalion's puppet. People will speak before an *anguissette*, careless as with no other, not even the pillow-talk of the Night Court. I stroked the velvet pile of the *sangoire* cloak. Delaunay had sent all the way to Firezia to find dye-makers who could recreate it. We'd lost the art, in Terre d'Ange. That didn't happen often. *Such a beautiful color,* Melisande had said, once. *It suits you.*

It would be easy, so easy, to begin again; I was born to it, I thought, blinking away the red wash that hazed my vision. Joscelin began every morning with the smooth execution of the Cassiline forms drilled into him since he was ten, that deadly, private dance he now performed in the gardens of Montrève, while members of the household watched with covert admiration.

And I, I channeled my gifts and their awful yearnings into my studies, which I was loathe to abandon. No reason to do so, truly. What texts I had, I could easily forward to the City; aught else, I carried in my own skull. And there were Yeshuites aplenty in the City, to carry on Seth ben Yavin's teaching, and the Royal Library, and booksellers, too. And the bequest of Delaunay's house, largely unspent, enough to buy a home in the City, a modest home.

Montrève.

There was Montrève, but it would continue; I was

fooling myself, if I thought it needed my hand. It had its own staff and holdings, and I need never doubt the loyalty of Purnell and Richeline, happily installed, making of it a home such as his parents had at Perrinwolde, in the absence of the Chevalier and his Lady, Cecilie.

I could always come back. I would, too. I loved it here.

Almost as much as I had loved being Delaunay's *anguissette*, bright star in Naamah's crown.

Joscelin.

Ah, Joscelin, I thought, and could have wept. My beautiful boy, if not so chaste; truly, I had an ill-luck name. How many times had I proved a trial nigh beyond bearing, how many times had I promised; this is the last? The old priest—he was the same, I was sure of it—had said it. *You have stood at the crossroads and chosen, and like Cassiel, you will ever stand at the crossroads and choose, choose again and again, the path of the Companion.* My fault, my doing. I sank my hands into the deep, heavy fabric of my *sangoire* cloak. So many times I had worn it; so many assignations, always blind to Delaunay's purpose, obedient nonetheless.

It would be different, to do it knowing. It would be different, carrying the secret of my own purpose locked within the vault of my heart, playing counter to Melisande's deadly game.

It would be harder.

My heart beat faster at the prospect, and the tide of desire surged within my blood, relentless and unending. How close need I get, before someone's careless lips spilled the secret, revealing their lord or lady to be the traitor of Troyes-le-Mont? For there were Ysandre's ladies-in-waiting, too, those three who had dared to follow her into the teeth of war. I knew their names and faces, locked in memory. Who knew, but that one of them was Melisande's last line of defense?

She always rewarded generously those who had served her. I touched my throat, still bare. No matter; her generosity too was emblazoned on my skin, the finial at the nape of my neck that completed my marque, forever etched by Master Tielhard's exquitely painful tapper, hers, her doing. A gown of sheerest gauze, studded with diamonds. They had bitten deep into my flesh, when I knelt for her.

They had bought me my freedom.

Melisande.

They might cost her freedom yet.

If I had lost my mentor, still, I was not without resources. I had the friendship of the sovereigns of two nations, the Lady of the Dalriada, the Royal Admiral. I had the kindness of a revered scholar of the University of Tiberium to aid me, the goodwill of the Yeshuite community, and a standing claim with one of the *kumpanias* of the Tsingani. I had friends high and low, and the enduring love of the successor to the Master of the Straits, my dearest friend.

And I had the Perfect Companion.

"Phèdre?" Joscelin repeated my name, the question still in his voice, echoed in Gonzago de Escabares' perplexed gaze. So much thought, to have passed in the blink of an eye. I drew a deep breath and looked at Joscelin's face, familiar and concerned; against all odds, beloved.

No more dire prophesies, I had laughed, not reckoning with what I was, with what the priest had named me, sure and true. Kushiel's Dart and Naamah's Servant.

Love as thou wilt, and Elua will ever guide your steps.

"I'll tell you," I said, "Tomorrow."

If you enjoyed Kushiel's Dart,
you won't want to miss . . .

KUSHIEL'S
CHOSEN

(0-7653-4504-8)

Here is an excerpt of this provocative
and erotic sequel, available now
in paperback from Tor Books

ONE

No one would deny that I have known hardship in my time, brief though it has been for all that I have done in it. This, I think, I may say without boastfulness. If I answer now to the title of Comtesse de Montrève and my name is listed in the peerage of Terre d'Ange, still I have known what it is to have all that I possess torn from me; once, when I was but four years of age and my birth-mother sold me into servitude to the Court of Night-Blooming Flowers, and twice, when my lord and mentor Anafiel Delaunay was slain, and Melisande Shahrizai betrayed me into the hands of the Skaldi.

I have crossed the wilds of Skaldia in the dead of winter, and faced the wrath of the Master of the Straits on the teeming waters. I have been the plaything of a barbarian warlord, and I have lost my dearest friend to an eternity of lonely isolation. I have seen the horrors of war and the deaths of my companions. I have walked, alone and by night, into the vast darkness of an enemy encampment, knowing that I gave myself up to torture and nigh-certain death.

None of it was as difficult as telling Joscelin I was returning to the Service of Naamah.

It was the *sangoire* cloak that decided me; Melisande's challenge and the badge of my calling that marked me as an *anguissette*, Kushiel's Chosen, as clearly as the mote of scarlet emblazoned since birth in the iris of my left eye. A rose petal floating upon dark waters, some admirer once called it. *Sangoire* is a deeper color, a red so dark it borders upon black. I have seen spilled blood by starlight; it is a fitting color for one such as I, destined to find pleasure in pain. Indeed, the wearing of it is proscribed for any who is not an *anguissette*. D'Angelines appreciate such poetic niceties.

I am Phèdre nó Delaunay de Montrève, and I am the only one. Kushiel's Dart strikes seldom, if to good effect.

When Maestro Gonzago de Escabares brought the cloak from La Serenissima, and the tale by which he had gained it, I made my choice. I knew that night. By night, my course seemed clear and obvious. There is a traitor in the heart of Terre d'Ange, one who stands close enough to the throne to touch it; that much, I knew. Melisande's sending the cloak made it plain: I had the means of discovering the traitor's identity, should I choose to engage in the game. That it was true, I had no doubt. By the Night Court and by Delaunay, I have been exquisitely trained as courtesan and spy alike. Melisande knew this—and Melisande required an audience, or at least a worthy opponent. It was clear, or so I thought.

In the light of day, before Joscelin's earnest blue gaze, I knew the extent of the misery it would cause. And for that, I delayed, temporizing, sure in my reasoning but aching at heart. Maestro Gonzago stayed some days, enjoying the hospitality I was at such pains to provide. He suspected somewhat of my torment, I do not doubt. I saw it reflected in his kind, homely face. At length he left without pressing me, his apprentice Camilo in tow, bound for Aragonia.

I was left alone with Joscelin and my decision.

We had been happy in Montrève, he and I; especially he, raised in the mountains of Siovale. I know what it cost Joscelin to bind his life to mine, in defiance of his Cassiline vow of obedience. Let the courtiers laugh, if they will, but he took his vows seriously, and celibacy not the least of them. D'Angelines follow the precept of

Blessed Elua, who was born of the commingled blood of Yeshua ben Yosef and the tears of the Magdelene in the womb of Earth: *Love as thou wilt*. Alone among the Companions, only Cassiel abjured Elua's command; Cassiel, who accepted damnation to remain celibate and steadfast at Elua's side, the Perfect Companion, reminding the One God of the sacred duty even He had forgotten.

These, then, were the vows Joscelin had broken for me. Montrève had done much to heal the wounds that breaking had dealt him. My return to the Service of Naamah, who had gone freely to Elua's side, who had lain down with kings and peasants alike for his sake, would open those wounds anew.

I told him.

And I watched the white lines of tension, so long absent, engrave themselves on the sides of his beautiful face. I laid out my reasoning, point by point, much as Delaunay would have done. Joscelin knew the history of it nearly as well as I did myself. He had been assigned as my companion when Delaunay still owned my marque; he knew the role I had played in my lord's service. He had been with me when Delaunay was slain, and Melisande betrayed us both—and he had been there that fateful night at Troyes-le-Mont, when Melisande Shahrizai had escaped the Queen's justice.

"You are sure?" That was all he said, when I had finished.

"Yes." I whispered the word, my hands clenching on the rich *sangoire* folds of my cloak, which I held bundled in my arms. "Joscelin . . ."

"I need to think." He turned away, his face shuttered like a stranger's. In anguish, I watched him go, knowing there was nothing more I could say. Joscelin had known,

from the beginning, what I was. But he had never reckoned on loving me, nor I him.

There was a small altar to Elua in the garden, which
Richeline Friote, my seneschal's wife, tended with great
care. Flowers and herbs grew in abundance behind the
manor house, where a statue of Elua, no more than a
meter tall, smiled benignly upon our bounty, petals
strewn at his marble feet. I knew the garden well, for I
had spent many hours seated upon a bench therein, considering my decision. It was there, too, that Joscelin
chose to think, kneeling before Elua in the Cassiline
style, head bowed and arms crossed.

He stayed there a long time.

By early evening, a light rain had begun to fall and
still Joscelin knelt, a silent figure in the grey twilight.
The autumn flowers grew heavy with water and hung
their bright heads, basil and rosemary released pungent
fragrance on the moist air, and still he knelt. His wheat-
gold braid hung motionless down his back, runnels of
rain coursing its length. Light dwindled, and still he
knelt.

"My lady Phèdre." Richeline's concerned voice gave
me a start; I hadn't heard her approach, which, for me,
was notable. "How long will he stay there, do you
think?"

I turned away from the window that looked out at the
garden loggia. "I don't know. You'd best serve dinner
without him. It could be a good while." Joscelin had
once held a vigil, snow-bound, throughout an entire
Skaldic night on some obscure point of Cassiline honor.
This cut deeper. I glanced up at Richeline, her open,
earnest face. "I told him I am planning to return to the
City of Elua. To the Service of Naamah."

Richeline took a deep breath, but her expression didn't
change. "I wondered if you would." Her voice took on

a compassionate tone. "He's not the sort to bear it easily, my lady."

"I know." I sounded steadier than I felt. "I don't chose it lightly, Richeline."

"No." She shook her head. "You wouldn't."

Her support was more heartening than I reckoned. I looked back out the window at the dim, kneeling figure of Joscelin, tears stinging my eyes. "Purnell will stay on as seneschal, of course, and you with him. Montrève needs your hand, and the folk have come to trust you. I'd not have it otherwise."

"Yes, my lady." Her kind gaze was almost too much to bear, for I did not like myself overmuch at this moment. Richeline placed her fist to her heart in the ancient gesture of fealty. "We will hold Montrève for you, Purnell and I. You may be sure of it."

"Thank you." I swallowed hard, repressing my sorrow. "Will you summon the boys to dinner, Richeline? They should be told, and I have need of their aid. If I am to do this thing before winter, we must begin at once."

"Of course."

"The boys" were my three chevaliers; Phèdre's Boys, they called themselves, Remy, Fortun and Ti-Philippe. Fighting sailors under the command of Royal Admiral Quintilius Rousse, they had attached themselves to my service after our quest to Alba and the battle of Troyes-le-Mont. In truth, I think it amused the Queen to grant them to me.

I told them over dinner, served in the manor hall with white linens on the table, and an abundance of candles. At first there was silence, then Remy let out an irrepressible whoop of joy, his green eyes sparkling.

"To the City, my lady? You promise it?"

"I promise," I told him. Ti-Philippe, small and blond,

grinned, while solid, dark Fortun looked thoughtfully at me. "It will need two of you to ride ahead and make arrangements. I've need of a modest house, near enough to the Palace. I'll give you letters of intent to take to my factor in the City."

Remy and Ti-Philippe began to squabble over the adventure. Fortun continued to look at me with his dark gaze. "Do you go a-hunting, my lady?" he asked softly.

I toyed with a baked pear, covered in crumbling cheese, to hide my lack of appetite. "What do you know of it, Fortun?"

His gaze never wavered. "I was at Troyes-le-Mont. I know someone conspired to free the Lady Melisande Shahrizai. And I know you are an *anguissette* trained by Anafiel Delaunay, who, outside the boundaries of Montrève, some call the Whoremaster of Spies."

"Yes." I whispered it, and felt a thrill run through my veins, compelling and undeniable. I lifted my head, feeling the weight of my hair caught in a velvet net, and downed a measure of fine brandy from the orchards of L'Agnace. "It is time for Kushiel's Dart to be cast anew, Fortun."

"My lord Cassiline will not like it, my lady," Remy cautioned, having left off his quarrel with Ti-Philippe. "Seven hours he has knelt in the garden. I think now I know why."

"Joscelin Verreuil is my concern." I pushed my plate away from me, abandoning any pretense of eating. "Now I need your aid, chevaliers. Who will ride to the City, and find me a home?"

In the end, it was decided that Remy and Ti-Philippe both would go in advance, securing our lodgings and serving notice of my return. How Ysandre would receive word of it, I was uncertain. I had not told her of Melisande's gift, nor my concerns regarding her escape. I did not doubt that I had the Queen's support, but the scions of Elua and his Companions can be a capricious lot, and I judged it best to operate in secrecy for the moment. Let them suppose that it was the pricking of Kushiel's Dart that had driven me back; the less they knew, the more I might learn.

So Delaunay taught me, and it is sound advice. One must gauge one's trust carefully.

I trusted my three chevaliers a great deal, or I would never have let them know what we were about. Delaunay sought to protect me—me, and Alcuin, who paid the ultimate price for it—by keeping us in ignorance. I would not make his mistake; for so I reckon it now, a mistake.

But still, there was only one person I trusted with the whole of my heart and soul, and he knelt without speaking in the rain-drenched garden of Montrève. I stayed awake long that night, reading a Yeshuite treatise brought to me by Gonzago de Escabares. I had not given up my dream of finding a way to free Hyacinthe from his eternal indenture to the Master of the Straits. Hyacinthe, my oldest friend, the companion of my childhood, had accepted a fate meant for me: condemned to immortality on a lonely isle, unless I could find a way to free him, to break the *geis* that bound him. I read until my eyes glazed and my mind wandered. At length, I dozed before the fire, stoked on the hour by two whispering servant-lads.

The sense of a presence woke me, and I opened my eyes.

Joscelin stood before me, dripping rainwater onto the carpeted flagstones. Even as I looked, he crossed his forearms and bowed.

"In Cassiel's name," he said, his voice rusty from hours of disuse, "I protect and serve."

We knew each other too well, we two, to dissemble. "No more than that?"

"No more," he said steadily, "and no less."

I sat in my chair gazing up at his beautiful face, his blue eyes weary from his long vigil. "Can there be no middle ground between us, Joscelin?"

"No." He shook his head gravely. "Phèdre . . . Elua knows, I love you. But I am sworn to Cassiel. I cannot be two things, not even for you. I will honor my vow, to protect and serve you. To the death, if need be. You cannot ask for more. Yet you do."

"I am Kushiel's chosen, and sworn to Naamah," I whispered. "I honor your vow. Can you not honor mine?"

"Only in my own way." He whispered it too; I knew how much it cost him, and closed my eyes. "Phèdre, do not ask for more."

"So be it," I said with closed eyes.

When I opened them, he was gone.